select
editions

Reader's
Digest

The condensations in this volume
are published with the consent of the authors
and the publishers © 2009 Reader's Digest.

www.readersdigest.co.uk

The Reader's Digest Association Limited
11 Westferry Circus Canary Wharf London E14 4HE

Printed in Germany
ISBN 978 0 276 44438 8

THE READER'S DIGEST ASSOCIATION LIMITED, LONDON

contents

in the spotlight

Whales, jellyfish, futuristic underwater
dirigibles, and secret installations on atolls in
Micronesia . . . Welcome to the world of Clive
Cussler! For more than thirty years, the so-called
Grand Master of Adventure has been creating
larger-than-life, imaginative stories that combine
thrilling oceanic derring-do with horrible villainy on
an awesome scale. *Medusa* delivers that recipe in
spades, pitting NUMA heroes Kurt Austin and Joe
Zavala against the might of the Chinese government *and* a deadly virus. We hope you'll enjoy it, and
be as spellbound as we were by its intriguing mix of
whaling-ship history and modern-day threat.

author in focus

While Clive Cussler devotes his non-writing time to
conserving underwater archaeology for the real-life
NUMA®, **Lawrence Anthony's** cause is the preservation
of Africa's wildlife. As founder of The Earth Organization,
which aims 'to protect the environment and enhance the
survival potential of all life forms, through education,
action and example', he has won many awards for his
conservation work. He also campaigns on behalf of the
Zulu people of South Africa, to ensure they uphold their
rights and traditions during the transition to a multiracial
society. Lawrence Anthony's knowledge and love of the
country and the animals he writes about is profound. His
passion for elephants is evident on every page.

Medusa

Clive Cussler with Paul Kemprecos

Kurt Austin of NUMA is working off the coast of Bermuda, exploring the ocean's depths, when a bathysphere, steered by his best friend Joe Zavala, is attacked. Meanwhile, far away in Micronesia, a top-secret undersea lab, in which scientists have been researching the medical properties of a rare jellyfish, known as the Blue Medusa, disappears. Even as he works desperately to save Joe, Kurt begins to wonder if the two events are linked—and, if so, who is behind them.

Prologue
The Pacific Ocean, 1848

In all his years sailing the world's oceans, Captain Horatio Dobbs had never known the sea to be so barren. The captain paced the quarter-deck of the New Bedford whaling ship *Princess*, grey eyes darting like twin lighthouse beams to every point of the compass. The Pacific was a disc-shaped blue desert. No spouts feathered the horizon. No grinning porpoises danced off the bow. It was as if life in the sea had ceased to exist.

Dobbs was considered a prince in the New Bedford whaling hierarchy. In the waterfront bars where hard-eyed harpooners gathered, or in the parlours of the rich Quaker shipowners on Johnny Cake Hill, it was said that he could sniff out a sperm whale at fifty miles. But only the rank smell of a simmering mutiny had filled the captain's nostrils of late.

The entry he had penned in the ship's logbook the night before summed up the troubles he faced. He had written:

March 27, 1848. Fresh breeze, SW. Not a whale in sight. Hard luck hangs over voyage like a stinking fog. Trouble brewing in the fo'c's'le.

Dobbs had a clear view of the length of the ship from the elevated quarter-deck, and he would have had to be blind not to see the furtive glances of his crewmen. No hand had yet been lifted in mutiny, but his officers had reported that the usual grumbling among the crew had become more vehement.

Dobbs was six foot four and had a profile like a cliff. He was confident he could put down a mutiny, but that was the least of his worries. A captain who returned to port without a profitable cargo of oil had committed the unpardonable sin of costing the ship's owners their investment. No crew worth its salt would ever ship out with him.

The whaling expedition had gone downhill since the crisp autumn day when the gleaming new ship had pulled away from the bustling wharf to a roaring send-off. Dobbs was bewildered by the change in the ship's fortunes. No ship could have been better prepared for its maiden voyage. The *Princess* was built of sturdy oak that could withstand the toughest seas. A beam of nearly thirty feet gave her room to store 3,000 casks of oil in her hold. Four whaleboats rested in wooden davits that overhung the deck rails. Other mariners scorned the wide-bodied and square-ended New England whaling ships, but the rugged 100-foot craft could sail for years through nasty conditions that would have had their sleeker counterparts leaking at the seams.

As the *Princess* left the dock, a spanking breeze had filled the great square sails that hung from the three masts, and the helmsman had steered a course east out of the Acushnet River and into the Atlantic Ocean. Pushed by steady winds, she had made a fast crossing to the Azores. After a brief stop in Fayal to load up with fruit, the vessel had pointed its bow towards the southern tip of Africa, rounding the Cape of Good Hope with no mishaps.

But in the weeks that followed, the *Princess* had zigzagged across the Pacific without seeing a single whale. Dobbs knew that finding whales had more to do with a solid knowledge of weather and migratory patterns than luck, but as he scanned the distant skyline, he began to wonder if his ship was cursed. He pushed the dangerous thought from his mind, strode over to the ship's cook, and said, 'Play us a song.'

Hoping to lift morale, the captain had urged the cook to play his weather-beaten fiddle every day, but the cook knew that the crew thought his fiddling scared the whales away. On top of that, he was down to two strings, so he played the same limited repertoire the crew had heard a dozen times before.

As the cook sawed away, the captain ordered the first mate to take charge of the quarter-deck. He climbed down the narrow companionway to his cabin and sat at his desk. He scanned his charts, but he had tried all the usual whaling grounds with nothing to show for his efforts. He sat back in his chair, closed his eyes and let his chin drop to his chest. He had only dozed off for a few minutes before the wonderful words he hadn't heard in months penetrated his veil of sleep.

'She *blows*!' a voice repeated. 'Thar she blows.'

The captain's eyes snapped wide open, and he vaulted up the ladder to the deck. He squinted against the bright sunlight at the main masthead a hundred feet above. The mastheads were manned in two-hour shifts, with the lookouts standing inside iron hoops on small platforms.

'Where away?' the captain shouted to the mainmast lookout.

'Starboard quarter, sir.' The lookout pointed off the bow. 'There.'

A huge hammer-shaped head rose from the sea a quarter of a mile away and splashed down in an explosion of spray. *Sperm whale*. Dobbs barked at the helmsman to steer for it. Deck hands scrambled into the rigging with the agility of monkeys and unfurled every inch of canvas.

As the ship came slowly around, a second lookout shouted down. '*Another*, Captain!' His voice was hoarse with excitement.

Dobbs peered through his spyglass and let forth a deep whooping laugh. A whole pod of whales. He was looking at a potential fortune in oil.

The cook had stopped playing. He stood on the deck dumbfounded, his fiddle hanging limply at his side.

'You did it, cook!' the captain shouted. 'You fiddled up enough sperma-ceti to fill our hold. Keep on playing, damn it.'

The cook gave the captain a gap-toothed grin and played a jaunty sea shanty as the helmsman brought the ship up into the wind. The sails were trimmed. The ship ploughed to a stop.

'Clear away the larboard boats!' the captain roared. 'Move smartly, men.'

Dobbs ordered three boats launched. The slender whaleboats splashed into the sea. The boat crews clambered down the side of the ship, took their places on the benches and dug their oars in. As soon as each whaleboat cleared the ship, its crew hoisted a sail to gain another few knots of speed.

Dobbs watched the boats fly like a flight of arrows towards their targets.

'Easy does it, boys,' he murmured. 'Steady as she goes.'

'How many, Captain?' the cook called out.

'More than enough for you to burn a ten-pound steak for every man on board. You can heave the salt pork over the side,' Dobbs yelled.

The captain's laughter roared across the deck like a full gale.

CALEB NYE ROWED for all he was worth in the lead boat. His palms were raw and bleeding and his shoulders ached. Sweat poured down his forehead, but he didn't dare lift his hand off his oar to wipe his eyes.

Caleb was eighteen, a wiry farm youth from Massachusetts, on his first voyage. His 1/210 share, or 'lay', put him at the bottom of the pay scale, but he'd signed on anyhow, drawn by the prospect of adventure. The eager lad reminded the captain of his own first whaling voyage. His willingness to bend to every task had gained him the respect of the whalemen, who treated him as a mascot.

The rowers were under the command of the first mate, a scarred veteran of many whaling voyages. As the ship's green hand, Caleb bore the brunt of the officer's nonstop patter.

'Come be lively, Caleb me boy,' the mate cajoled. 'Put your back into it, lad. And keep your eyes on my pretty face—I'll look out for mermaids.'

The mate, who was the only one allowed to face forwards, was watching a big bull whale swimming on a collision course with the boat.

'Stand and face,' he ordered the harpooner.

Two seven-foot-long harpoons rested in bow cradles. Their razor-sharp barbs made it almost impossible for a harpoon to come free once it had been embedded in the whale's flesh.

The bowman shipped his oar and unsheathed the two harpoons.

Eighteen hundred feet of line ran from each harpoon through a groove in the bow to a box where the rope had been coiled with exquisite care. From there the line ran down the length of the boat to the stern, where it was given a turn or two round a post, then run forwards to a tub.

The mate swung the tiller and pointed the bow at the whale's left side, placing the harpooner in position to make the throw. When the whale was twenty feet away, the mate yelled at the harpooner, 'Give it to him!'

Bracing his knee against the boat, the harpooner pitched the spear like a javelin and the barb sank into the whale's side behind its eye. Then he snatched up the second harpoon and planted it a foot behind the first.

'Stern away!' the mate shouted.

The oars dug into the water, and the boat shot back several yards.

The whale huffed steam through its blowhole, raised its great flukes high in the air, and brought them down with a thunderous clap, slapping the water where the boat had been seconds before. The whale lifted its tail in the air a second time, buried its head in the sea, and dived. A diving sperm whale can descend to 1,000 feet at a speed of twenty-five knots. The line flew out of its tub in a blur.

The boat skimmed over the wave tops in a mad dash that whalers called a Nantucket sleigh ride. A cheer burst from the oarsmen, but they tensed when the boat stopped moving; the whale was on its way back up. Then the huge mammal surfaced in an explosion of foam and thrashed around like a trout caught on a lure, only to plunge once more to the depths. The routine was repeated over and over. With each cycle, more line was hauled in, until only a hundred feet or so separated the whale and boat.

The whale's great blunt head swung round towards its tormentor. The mate saw the aggressive behaviour and knew it was the prelude to an attack. He yelled at the harpooner to move aft. The two men exchanged places in the rocking boat, tripping over oars, oarsmen and lines in a scramble that would have been comical if not for the potentially fatal consequences.

The mate grabbed the lance, a long wooden shaft with a sharp, spoon-shaped point, and stood in the bow like a matador ready to dispatch a fighting bull. The mate expected the creature to roll on its side, to allow it to use the sharp teeth lining its lower jaw to best advantage.

The harpooner swung the tiller over. Whale and boat passed each other only yards apart. The whale began its roll, exposing its vulnerable side. The mate plunged the lance into the whale with all his strength. He churned the shaft until the point was six feet into the animal's flesh, penetrating its heart. He yelled at the crew to reverse direction. *Too late*. The whale had clamped the midsection of the slow-moving boat between its jaws.

The panicked rowers fell over each other trying to escape the sharp teeth. The whale shook the boat like a dog with a bone. Then the jaws opened, the mammal pulled away, and the great tail thrashed the water. A geyser of blood-tinged steam issued from the spout.

'Fire in the hole!' an oarsman shouted.

The lance had done its deadly work. The whale thrashed for a minute before it disappeared below the surface, leaving behind a pool of blood.

The rowers lashed their oars across the gunwales to stabilise the sinking craft and plugged the holes with their shirts. Despite their efforts, the boat was barely afloat by the time the dead whale surfaced and rolled onto its side.

'Good work, boys!' the mate roared. 'One more fish like this and we'll be heading for New Bedford to buy candy for our sweethearts.' He pointed to the approaching *Princess*. 'See, boys, the old man's coming to pick us up. Everyone's all right, I see.'

'Not *everyone*,' the harpooner called out. 'Caleb's gone.'

THE *PRINCESS* LAUNCHED the reserve boat, but after a fruitless search in the bloodstained water, the damaged whaleboat was towed back to the ship.

'Where's the green hand?' the captain asked as the bedraggled crew climbed back on board the *Princess*.

The first mate shook his head. 'The lad went over when the whale struck.'

The captain's eyes were shadowed in sadness, but death and whaling were no strangers. He turned his attention to the task at hand. He ordered his men to manoeuvre the whale's body until it was under a staging on the ship's starboard side. Using hooks, they rolled the carcass over and hoisted it to a vertical position. Before starting to strip off the blubber, they used an iron hook to extract the whale's innards and haul them onto the deck to examine them for ambergris, the valuable perfume base that can form in the stomach of a sick whale.

Something was moving inside the big stomach pouch. A deck hand assumed it was a giant squid, a favourite meal of sperm whales. Using his sharp spade he cut into the pouch, but, instead of tentacles, a human leg flopped out. He peeled back the stomach walls to reveal a man, curled up. The deck hand grabbed the man's ankles and pulled the limp form out onto the deck. An opaque, slimy substance enveloped the man's head.

'It's Caleb!' the mate shouted. 'It's the green hand.'

Caleb's lips moved, but they made no sound.

Dobbs strode over and stared at Caleb for a moment before ordering the mates to carry the green hand to his cabin. They stretched the youth out on the captain's bunk and stripped off his slime-coated clothes.

'Lord, I've never seen anything like it,' the first mate muttered.

The handsome farm boy of eighteen had been transformed into a wizened old man of eighty. His skin was bleached ghostly white. A lacework of wrinkles puckered the skin of his hands and face as if they had been soaked in water for days. Dobbs laid a hand on Caleb's arm, expecting him to be as icy cold as the corpse he resembled. 'He's on fire,' he murmured.

Assuming his role as the ship's doctor, Dobbs placed wet towels over Caleb's body to bring down the fever. From a black leather medicine case he produced a vial of opiate and got a few drops down Caleb's throat. The youth rambled for a few minutes before slipping into a deep sleep. He slept for more than twenty-four hours.

When his eyelids finally fluttered open, he saw the captain sitting at his desk. 'Where am I?' he mumbled through dry, crusted lips.

'In my bunk,' Dobbs growled. 'And I'm getting damned sick of it.'

'Sorry, sir.' Caleb furrowed his brow. 'I dreamed I died and went to hell.'

'No such luck, lad. Seems the spermaceti had a taste for farm boys. We pulled you out of his belly.'

Caleb remembered the whale's round eye, then being tossed into the air, arms and legs spinning like a pinwheel, and the shock of hitting the water. He recalled moving along a dark passage, gagging for breath in the heavy, moist air. The heat had been unbearable. He had quickly passed out.

A horrified look came to his pale, wrinkled face. 'The whale ate me!'

The captain nodded. 'I'll get cook to fetch you some soup. Then it's back to the fo'c's'le with you.'

The captain relented and let Caleb stay in his cabin until all the blubber had been rendered into oil and stored in barrels. Then he summoned the hands on deck. He praised them for their hard work, and said: 'You all know that a whale ate the green hand like Jonah in the Bible. I'm happy to say that young Caleb will soon be back at his work. I'm cutting his pay for time lost. The only one on this ship who's allowed to shirk his job is a dead man.'

The comment brought a few grins from the assembled hands.

Dobbs continued. 'Now, men, I must tell you that young Caleb looks different to how you remember him. The foul juices of the whale's innards have bleached him whiter than a boiled turnip.' He cast a stern eye on the crew. 'I'll allow no one on this ship to make light of another man's misfortune. He's no different from the rest of us under that white skin. Now, let's get us some whales.'

The captain had purposely called Caleb a Jonah, a seaman's name for a sailor who attracted bad luck. Maybe if he made light of it he'd suck the wind out of the sails of unfavourable comparisons to the biblical character who'd been swallowed by a great fish.

A few hands quietly suggested heaving Caleb over the side. Fortunately, everyone was too busy for mischief. The sea that had been so barren now teemed with whales. It was as if the *Princess* had become a magnet for every whale in the ocean.

Every day, the boats were launched after cries from the lookout. The cast-iron try-pots bubbled like witches' cauldrons. An oily pall of black smoke hid the stars and sun and turned the sails a dark grey. Within months of Caleb's encounter with the whale, the ship's hold was filled to capacity.

Before the long voyage home, the ship had to be resupplied and the weary crew given shore leave. Dobbs put into Pohnpei, a lush island known for its handsome men, beautiful women, and their willingness to provide services and goods to visiting whalemen.

Caleb stayed on board and watched the drunken comings and goings of his fellow hands with a benign smile. The captain was relieved that Caleb showed no interest in shore leave. The young man's bleached hair and skin might cause problems with the superstitious islanders.

Dobbs paid a courtesy visit to the American consul. During the visit the consul was notified that a tropical sickness had struck the island. In his log Dobbs wrote:

Last day of shore leave. Captain visits US Consul A. Markham, who conducted tour of ancient city named Nan Madol. Upon return, Consul advised of sickness on island. Ended liberty and left island in a hurry.

The remnants of the crew stumbled back onto the ship and promptly fell into a rum-soaked snooze. The captain ordered the sobered-up hands to raise the anchor and set sail. With a steady breeze, Dobbs and his men would be sleeping in their own beds in a few months' time.

Less than twenty-four hours after the *Princess* left the port, a fo'c's'le hand named Stokes awakened around two in the morning and raced to the rail to purge his stomach. Several hours later, he developed a fever and a rash over much of his body. Brownish-red spots appeared on his face and grew until his features looked as if they were carved in mahogany.

The captain treated Stokes with wet towels and had him placed under a makeshift tent on the foredeck. Fresh air and sunlight might help the man, and isolation could possibly prevent the spread of his illness.

But the disease spread through the hands like a wind-blown brush fire. An impromptu infirmary was set up on the foredeck. The captain emptied his medicine kit. He feared that it would only be a matter of hours before he and the officers fell ill.

The captain checked his chart. The nearest landfall was called Trouble Island. Whalers normally shunned the place. A whaling crew had burned a village and killed some natives there after an argument over a stolen cask of nails, and the inhabitants had attacked several whalers since the incident. There was no choice. Dobbs put the ship on a course for the island.

The *Princess* soon limped into a cove lined with white sand beaches, and the ship's anchor splashed into the clear green water. The island was dominated by a volcanic peak, wisps of smoke playing around its summit. Dobbs and the first mate took a small boat ashore to replenish fresh water. They found a spring and were on their way back to the ship when they came across a ruined temple.

The captain gazed at the temple's walls, overgrown with vines. 'This place reminds me of Nan Madol,' he said.

'Pardon me, sir?' the first mate said.

The captain shook his head. 'Never mind. We'd best get back to the ship while we can still walk.'

Not long after dusk, the mates fell sick, and Dobbs, too, succumbed to the disease. With Caleb's help, the captain dragged his mattress onto the quarter-deck. He told the green hand to carry on as best he could.

Caleb somehow remained untouched by the plague. He carried buckets of water to the foredeck to cure the terrible thirst of his crewmates and kept an eye on Dobbs and the officers. Dobbs lost consciousness, and, when he awoke, he saw torches moving about the deck. One torch came closer, and its flickering flame illuminated the garishly tattooed face of a man, one of a dozen or so natives armed with spears.

'Hello?' said the islander, who had high cheekbones and long black hair.

'You speak English?' Dobbs managed.

The man lifted his spear. 'Good harpoon man.'

Dobbs saw a ray of hope. In spite of his savage appearance, the native was a fellow whaler. 'My men are sick. Can you help?'

'*Sure*. We got good medicine. Fix you up. You from New Bedford?'

Dobbs nodded.

'Too bad,' the native said. 'New Bedford men take me. I jump ship. Come home.' He smiled. 'We watch you burn up from fire sickness.'

A quiet voice said, 'Are you all right, Captain?'

Caleb had emerged from the shadows and now stood in the torchlight.

The native leader's eyes widened and he spat out a single word. '*'Atua!*'

The captain had picked up a smattering of Oceanic and knew that *'atua* was the islanders' word for 'a bad ghost'. Rising onto his elbows, Dobbs said, 'Yes. This is my *'atua*. Do what he says or he will curse you and every-one on your island.'

Caleb had sized up the situation and went along with the captain's bluff. Lifting his arms wide above his head for dramatic effect, he said, 'Put your weapons down or I will use my power.'

The native leader said something in his language and the other men dropped their killing tools to the deck.

'You said you could do something about the fire sickness,' the captain said. 'You have medicine. Help my men or the *'atua* will be angry.'

The islander seemed unsure of what to do, but his doubts vanished when Caleb removed his hat and his silky white hair caught the tropical breeze. The islander issued a curt order to the others.

The captain blacked out again. His slumber was filled with weird dreams, including one in which he felt a cold, wet sensation and a sting on his chest. When he blinked his eyes open, it was daytime, and the ship was rigged with full sail against a clear blue sky.

The first mate saw Dobbs struggling to sit up and came over with a jug of water. 'Feeling better, Captain?'

'Aye,' the captain croaked between sips of water. The fever had gone, and his stomach felt normal except for a gnawing hunger. 'Help me to my feet.'

The captain stood on wobbly legs, with the mate holding an arm to steady him. The ship was on the open sea with no island in view.

'How long have we been under way?'

'Five hours,' the mate said. 'It's a miracle. The men came out of their fever. Rashes disappeared. Cook made soup, and they got the ship moving.'

The captain felt an itch on his chest and lifted his shirt. The rash was gone, replaced by a small red spot and a circle of irritation.

'What about the natives?' Dobbs said.

'*Natives?* We saw no natives.'

Dobbs shook his head. Did he dream it all in his delirium? He told the mate to fetch Caleb. The green hand made his way to the quarter-deck. A smile crossed his pale face when he saw the captain had recovered.

'What happened last night?' Dobbs said.

Caleb told the captain that after Dobbs had passed out, the natives had left the ship and returned carrying wooden buckets that emitted a pale blue luminescence. They went from man to man. He couldn't see what they were doing. Then the natives left. Soon after, the crew started waking.

The captain asked Caleb to help him down to his cabin. He eased into his chair and opened the ship's log. He wrote down every detail, as he remembered it. Then he gazed with longing at a miniature portrait of his pretty young wife, and finished his entry with a declaration: *Going home!*

Fairhaven, Massachusetts, 1878

The French mansard-roofed mansion known to the townspeople as the Ghost House stood back from a secluded street behind a screen of beech trees. Guarding the driveway were the bleached jawbones of a sperm whale, placed upright in the ground so their tips met in a Gothic arch.

A shiny black horse-drawn carriage clattered through the whalebone gate. The driver, a heavyset man whose expensive russet suit and matching derby hat failed to cloak his rough-hewn features, tied up in front of the big house. He climbed the porch steps and announced his arrival using the brass door knocker shaped like a whale's tail.

A man opened the door, and a smile crossed his pallid face.

'Strater, what a pleasant surprise,' Caleb Nye said. 'Come in, come in.' Caleb's skin had grown even whiter over the years. Age had added wrinkles to skin that looked like parchment to begin with, but he still retained his boyish smile. He led the way to a spacious library lined with floor-to-ceiling bookcases. The wall sections not devoted to books on whaling were decorated with large, colourful posters that had the same motif: a man caught in the jaws of a sperm whale.

Strater went up to one particularly lurid poster. The artist had made liberal use of crimson paint to depict blood flowing from the harpoon shafts into the water. 'We made a bundle of money out of that Philadelphia show.'

Caleb nodded. 'Thanks to your skills as a showman.'

'I'd be nothing without my star attraction,' Strater said. 'The minute I laid eyes on you, I saw the potential for fame and fortune.'

Their partnership had begun a few nights after the *Princess* docked in New Bedford. The oil barrels had been off-loaded, and the owners tallied the take and calculated the lays. Crewmen went off in a raucous mob to celebrate in the waterfront bars that were more than willing to relieve the whalers of their hard-won earnings.

Caleb had stayed on the ship. When the captain had come back onto the *Princess* with Caleb's pay, he asked if he was going home to his family farm.

'Not like this,' Caleb had replied with a sad smile.

The captain handed him the pitifully small amount of money he had earned. 'You have my permission to stay on board until the ship sails again.'

About the same time, Strater had been in a seedy bar a few blocks from the ship. The former prize fighter and carnival pitchman was down on his luck and almost broke. He was nursing a mug of ale when the crewmen from the *Princess* burst into the bar and proceeded to get drunk. Strater perked up his ears and listened with interest to the story of Caleb Nye, the green hand who was swallowed by a whale. The bar patrons greeted the tale with loud scepticism.

'Where's your Jonah now?' a barfly shouted above the din.

'Back at the ship, sittin' in the dark,' he was told. 'See for yourself.'

'The only thing I want to see is another ale,' the barfly said.

Strater had slipped out of the bar and made his way to the waterfront. He climbed the ramp to the lantern-lit deck of the *Princess*. Caleb was standing by the rail, staring at the sparkling lights of New Bedford. His features were indistinct, but they seemed to glow with a pale luminosity. Strater's showman juices had started flowing.

'I have a proposition for you,' Strater told the young man. 'If you accept it, I can make you a rich man.'

Caleb had listened to Strater's proposal and seen the possibilities.

Within weeks, he was telling his story, standing with harpoon in hand, in front of a moving diorama. Strater had hired an artist who had painted reasonably accurate pictures on a long strip of canvas several feet high. The canvas was slowly unrolled to reveal pictures of Caleb in the whaleboat, the attack by the whale, and a fanciful depiction of his legs sticking out from between the mammal's jaws. The show played to enthralled audiences in cities and towns along the eastern seaboard. After a few years, Strater and Caleb retired from public life as rich as the wealthiest whaling captains.

Strater bought a mansion in New Bedford, and Caleb built a house in the village of Fairhaven across the harbour. He rarely went out in daylight. When he did leave his mansion, he covered his head and shaded his face with a hood. Known to his neighbours as the Ghost, he became a generous benefactor who used his fortune to build schools and libraries for the community. In return, the townspeople protected the privacy of their homegrown Jonah.

Looking at the poster, Strater shook his head. 'It almost makes me want to go on the road with the show again.'

'Let's talk about it over a glass of wine,' Caleb said.

'I'm afraid we don't have time,' Strater said. 'I carry a message to you from Nathan Dobbs.'

'The captain's oldest son?'

'That's right. His father is dying and would like to see you.'

'*Dying!* That's not possible! You have told me yourself that the captain looks as hale and hearty as a young bull.'

'There was an accident at one of his mills. A loom fell over and crushed his ribs. We must go now. His time is short.'

THE ROAD TO THE DOBBS MANSION wound round New Bedford Harbour and climbed to County Street. Nathan Dobbs greeted Strater and Caleb at the door and thanked them profusely for coming. He was tall and lanky, the younger image of his father.

'I'm sorry to hear about your father,' Caleb said. 'How is he?'

'Not long for this world, I'm afraid. I'll take you to him.'

The spacious parlour overflowed with the captain's ten children and countless grandchildren. Nathan asked Strater to make himself comfortable and escorted Caleb to the captain's room.

Captain Dobbs lay in his bed, tended by his wife and doctor. Although his leonine mane had gone silver-grey, his craggy features were more youthful than would have been expected for a man in his sixties. But his eyes had a far-off look, as if he could see death creeping closer. The captain's wife and doctor withdrew, and Nathan lingered by the door.

Dobbs saw Caleb and managed to crack a smile. 'Thank you for coming, Caleb,' he said in a hoarse whisper.

'You told me never to question the captain's orders.'

'Aye,' Dobbs wheezed. 'And I'll give you more good advice, green hand. Don't stick your nose where it doesn't belong. Tried to fix a baulky loom. Didn't move fast enough when it keeled over.'

'I'm sorry for your misfortune, Captain.'

'*Don't* be. I have a faithful wife, handsome children, and grandchildren who will carry on my name.'

'I wish I could say the same,' Caleb said in a wounded voice.

'You've done well, Caleb. I know all about your generosity.'

'Generosity is easy when there's no one to share your fortune with.'

'You have shared it with your neighbours. And I have heard of your wonderful library of books on the old trade.'

'Whaling gave me the life I have. I collect every volume I can on it.'

The captain closed his eyes and seemed to drift away, but after a moment his eyelids fluttered open. 'I have something I want to share with you.'

The captain's son stepped forward and presented Caleb with a mahogany box. Caleb opened the lid. Inside the box was a book. Caleb recognised the worn blue binding.

'The log of the *Princess*, Captain?'

'Aye, and it's yours,' the captain said. 'For your great library.'

Caleb drew back. 'I can't take this from you, sir.'

'You'll do as your captain says,' Dobbs growled. 'My family agrees that you should have it. Isn't that right, Nathan?'

Nathan nodded. 'We can think of no person more worthy, Mr Nye.'

Unexpectedly, the captain raised his hand and placed it on the log. 'A strange business,' he said. 'Something happened on that island of wild men. To this day, I don't know if it was God's work or the Devil's.'

The captain closed his eyes. His breathing became laboured, and a rattling sound came from his throat. He called his wife's name.

Nathan gently escorted Caleb from the room and thanked him again for coming.

As Strater and Caleb left in Strater's carriage, Caleb's mind went back to the island and its inhabitants, the sickness and the strange blue lights.

Dobbs was right. It had been a strange business indeed.

Chapter 1

Anhui Province, People's Republic of China, Present Day

The helicopter circled above the village like a noisy dragonfly. Dr Song Lee looked up from the bandage she was applying to a cut on a young boy's arm and watched as the helicopter hovered and then started its vertical descent to a field at the edge of the settlement.

The doctor gave the boy a pat on the head and accepted her payment of half a dozen fresh eggs from his grateful parents. She had treated the wound with a herbal poultice, and it was healing nicely. With little in the way of medicine, the young doctor did the best she could with what she had.

Dr Lee joined the noisy throng rushing to the field. Excited villagers surrounded the helicopter. Lee saw the government markings on the fuselage and wondered who from the Ministry of Health would be coming to her remote village.

The helicopter door opened and a short, portly man wearing a suit stepped out. He took one look at the crowd and an expression of terror crossed his broad face. Lee eased her way through the mob to greet him.

'Good afternoon, Dr Huang,' she called out in a voice strong enough to be heard above the babble. 'This is quite the surprise.'

The man cast a wary eye over the crowd. 'I hadn't expected such a large reception.'

Dr Lee laughed. 'Don't worry, Doctor. These people are quite harmless.'

She took Dr Huang by the hand and led him through the swarm of onlookers. The villagers started to follow, but she waved them off and gently explained that she wished to speak to the gentleman alone.

Back at her hut, she offered Dr Huang the folding chair she sat in to treat patients, then boiled water for tea on a camp stove. She poured a cup for her visitor, who took a tentative sip, as if he were unsure it was sanitary.

'This is a far cry from Harvard Medical School,' Huang said, gazing in fascination at the hut, with its walls of mud and thatched roof.

'This is a far cry from *anywhere*,' Lee said. 'There are some advantages. My patients pay me in vegetables and eggs, so I never go hungry, but it's next to impossible to find a good caramel caffè latte.'

Huang and Lee had met years before at a mixer for Asian students and faculty at Harvard University. He was a visiting professor from China's

National Laboratory of Medical Molecular Biology. She was finishing her graduate studies in virology. The young woman's quick wit and intelligence had impressed Huang, and they had continued their friendship after returning to China, where he had risen to a high position in the ministry.

'You must be wondering why I'm here,' Huang said.

Dr Lee liked and respected Huang, but he had been among a number of highly placed colleagues who were conspicuously absent when she needed someone to speak out on her behalf.

'Not at all,' Lee said with a note of haughtiness. 'I expect you are carrying the authorities' apology for their heavy-handed treatment of me.'

'The state will never admit that it is wrong, Dr Lee, but you have no idea how I have regretted not standing up in your defence,' he said. 'I can only offer my most humble apologies. At the same time, I did work behind the scenes to keep you out of jail.'

Dr Lee decided that it would be unfair to pick on Huang. Nothing he could have done would have changed the outcome. She forced a smile. 'Your apology is accepted, Dr Huang. Since you do not bear the thanks of a grateful nation for my service, what *are* you doing here?'

'I come as the bearer of bad news, I'm afraid.' Although they were alone, he lowered his voice. 'It has returned,' he said in a near whisper.

Lee felt an icy coldness in the pit of her stomach. '*Where?*' she asked.

'To the north of here.' He rattled off the name of a remote province.

'When was it first detected? And have you found its source?'

'About three weeks ago. No source yet. The government immediately isolated the victims and quarantined the villages to prevent its spread. They are taking no chances. We are working with the World Health Organisation and the US Centers for Disease Control.'

'That's quite different from the last response.'

'Our government's secrecy regarding the SARS epidemic damaged China's reputation as a world power,' Huang said. 'Our leaders know that secrecy is not an option this time.'

The Chinese government had come under international fire because it kept the first SARS epidemic secret from the world, causing delay and slowing treatment that could have prevented deaths. Song Lee was working as a teaching physician in a Beijing hospital when the epidemic broke out. She had urged her superiors to take action, but they warned her to stay silent.

The had virus spread to more than two dozen countries, infecting more than 8,000 people. Almost a thousand died, and a pandemic of worldwide proportions was narrowly averted. The Chinese government imprisoned the doctor who had told the world that the cases were being under-reported and that patients were being driven around in ambulances to keep them away from the World Health Organisation's notice. Others who had tried to expose the cover-up also became targets. One of them was Dr Lee.

'You still haven't told me what this has to do with me,' she said, making no attempt to keep the heat out of her voice.

'We are assembling a research team and want you to be on it.'

Lee's anger spilled out. 'What can *I* do?' she asked. 'I am simply a country doctor who treats life-threatening diseases with herbs.'

'I implore you to put your personal feelings aside,' Huang said. 'We need you in Beijing. Your combined expertise in virology and epidemiology will be invaluable in developing a response.' Huang folded his hands together as if in prayer. 'I will get down on my knees to beg, if you wish.'

She gazed at his anguished face. Softening her voice, she said, 'It won't be necessary to beg, Dr Huang. I'll do what I can. How soon do you need me?'

Huang's face lit up. 'Now,' he said. 'The helicopter is waiting for you.'

Her belongings could fit into a small valise. She would only have to inform the village elders and bid her patients goodbye.

Standing, she extended her hand to seal the bargain. 'Done.'

THREE DAYS LATER, Dr Lee sat in an auditorium at the Ministry of Health, listening to experts from around the world. Bearing no resemblance to the country doctor who had delivered babies by candlelight, she wore a pinstripe suit over a blouse of Chinese-flag red, and a touch of make-up had lightened the amber complexion that had been darkened by outdoor life.

Soon after she had arrived in Beijing, Lee had gone on a shopping spree, courtesy of the People's Republic of China. At the first shop, she tossed her cotton jacket and slacks in the trash. With each subsequent purchase she redeemed a bit of her lost self-respect.

In her mid-thirties, Song Lee was slender, with small hips and breasts, and long legs. While her figure was adequate but unremarkable, it was her face that turned heads. Long dark lashes shaded alert, questing eyes, and full lips alternated between a friendly smile and a slight, more serious pucker when she was deep in thought.

Since arriving in Beijing, she had attended a dizzying schedule of briefings and had been impressed at the swift reaction to the outbreak, as staff were mobilised around the world. China was taking the leading role in the fight against the SARS outbreak and everyone she talked to seemed confident that basic health practices could contain the situation, while researchers continued to look for the source and develop an appropriate vaccine.

At the end of the presentation Dr Lee left the auditorium with Huang, who led her away to a quiet corner.

'It is reassuring to hear that a pandemic is unlikely,' she commented.

'On the contrary, Dr Lee, a pandemic is a *certainty*. And it will kill millions before it runs out of victims.'

Song Lee glanced at the door to the auditorium. 'That's not what I heard in there. Everyone seemed optimistic that this epidemic can be contained.'

'That's because the speakers don't know all the facts.'

'What *are* the facts, Dr Huang?'

'There is something I must tell you . . . This business about SARS . . . well, it's a fraud.'

Lee glared at Huang. 'What are you saying?'

'The epidemic we are concerned about is caused by *another* pathogen, a variation of the influenza virus that is more dangerous than SARS. It spreads faster, and the mortality rate is much higher. We have been feeding the experts misleading information. When they have asked for specimens of the strain to help with their research, we have given them the old SARS virus. We are trying to prevent a panic.'

Dr Lee stared in disbelief. 'Hasn't this country learned its lesson about secrecy?'

'We have learned it very well,' Dr Huang said. 'China is working with the United States. We and the Americans have agreed to keep the existence of this new pathogen a secret for now.'

'We saw before that delay in releasing information costs lives,' Lee said.

'We also saw forced quarantine,' Huang said. 'Hospitals shuttered, travel and commerce interrupted. We can't tell the truth now. There's no way to stop this pathogen until we've developed a vaccine.'

'You're sure of this?'

'The Americans have sophisticated computers. They have created models suggesting we can temporarily contain the disease, but it will eventually break out and we *will* have a worldwide pandemic.'

'Why didn't you tell me all this back in the province?' Lee asked.

'I was afraid you might think I had betrayed you before and wouldn't believe me,' Huang said.

'Why should I believe you now?'

'Because I am telling the truth . . . I swear it.'

Dr Lee was confused and angry, but there was no doubt in her mind that Dr Huang was being forthright. 'You mentioned a vaccine,' she said.

'A number of labs are working on it,' he said. 'The most promising drug is being developed in the US at the Bonefish Key lab in Florida. They believe a substance derived from ocean biomedicine will produce a vaccine that will stop this pathogen.'

'You are saying that *one* lab has the only viable preventative?' Lee almost laughed at the absurdity despite the direness of the situation.

'It's still in development,' he said, 'but, yes, our hopes are high. It might go even faster if you were there as the representative from China.'

'I'm willing to do anything I can. But what if the vaccine doesn't work?'

A haunted look came to Huang's eyes, and his voice dropped to a whisper. 'Then only divine intervention can help us.'

THE INFLUENZA EPIDEMIC of 1918 appeared suddenly, striking the world as it was trying to stitch itself back together after the devastating war that had ripped it apart. The epidemic raged through Spain, killing 8,000,000 people, and for that accomplishment was dubbed the Spanish flu, though it hit many other countries as well. There was no known cure. Victims would sicken in the morning, break out in the telltale mahogany-coloured rash within hours, and die before nightfall. Millions died; a billion were infected. Before it petered out in 1919, influenza had killed more people than five years of brutal war had. It was worse than the Black Death.

The grim statistics raced through Dr Song Lee's mind as she covered the last leg before setting foot on Bonefish Key. She had flown into Fort Myers and caught a limo to the Pine Island Marina, where she met a colourful local character named Dooley Greene. He had taken her on his boat through the mangroves to the island. A man was waiting on the dock.

'Hi, Dr Lee,' the man said, extending his hand. 'My name is Max Kane. Welcome to Fantasy Island. I'm the director of this little speck of paradise.'

In his faded Hawaiian shirt and denim shorts, Kane looked more like a beach bum than a respected ocean microbiologist. A Chinese scientist of his stature would not have been caught dead without his white lab coat.

'I'm pleased to meet you, Dr Kane,' Lee said, glancing round at the rippling palm trees and a whitewashed building perched on a low, grassy rise a few hundred feet back from the dock. 'I've never seen a research lab in such a picturesque setting.'

Kane gave her a grin. 'Not half as picturesque as the island's current inhabitants.' He grabbed her suitcase. 'C'mon, I'll show you to your quarters.'

They followed a crushed-shell pathway to a row of neat cabins painted flamingo pink. Kane opened the door of one cabin and ushered Lee inside. A bed, chair, dresser and desk had been tucked into the snug space.

'It's not the Ritz, but it has everything you need,' Kane said.

Lee thought about her one-room shack in the Chinese countryside. 'I'm sure I'll be very comfortable here.'

Kane placed the suitcase on the bed. 'Let's get you something cold to drink,' he said, 'and I'll show you around, if you're up to it.'

They walked back to the patio in front of the resort-style building. While Song rested in an Adirondack chair, Kane went into the building and brought out two glasses of mango and orange juice on ice. Sipping the delicious drink, she let her eyes wander along the tranquil shoreline.

'It's hard to imagine that there is a lab doing vital work here,' she said.

'People would wonder if we put up barbed wire and guard towers. We've worked hard to project the image of a sleepy little research centre whose work is so boring that no one would want to visit.'

'Where are the lab buildings?'

'We had to get a little sneakier when it came to the research space. There are three labs farther inland. The labs are pretty well camouflaged. Google Earth would see only trees.'

'What about security? I didn't see any guards.'

'Oh, they're there,' Kane said with a tight smile. 'The kitchen and maintenance staff are all security people. There's an electronic-surveillance centre that keeps track of anyone coming too close to the island twenty-four/seven. They've got cameras all over the place.'

'What about the water-taxi man, Mr Greene? Is he in on the deception?'

Kane smiled. 'Dooley worked for the old resort before Hurricane Charlie drove it into bankruptcy. He transports people and supplies between the island and the mainland. He's never been further inland than the dock. He's a bit of a windbag, so if he does spout off about something he's seen out here the people who know him will figure that he's making it up.'

'He was curious about me. I put him off as best I could.'

'I'm sure everyone on Pine Island will know within hours about your visit, but I doubt anyone will care.'

'That's good. I must confess that I'm nervous enough at the enormity of the task confronting us and the consequences if we fail.'

He considered her answer and then said, 'I'm optimistic from what we have done so far that we will *not* fail.'

'I don't mean to be disrespectful, but I would feel more at ease if I knew the scientific basis for your optimism.'

'Scepticism is the lifeblood of scientific inquiry,' Kane said. 'I'll do my best. Are you up for a leisurely walk? I think better on my feet.'

They struck off along one of the shell paths that laced the island, a holdover from the nature trails cut for guests at the old resort.

'How did you end up at Bonefish Key?' Lee asked.

'I worked at Harbor Branch marine lab for several years,' Kane said. 'They were among the first to recognise the potential for pharmaceuticals from marine organisms. But I wanted to concentrate on antiviral agents, so I left and, with foundation money, established a new lab here. We were doing well scientifically, but last year the lab's funding dried up. The heirs of our prime benefactor challenged the legality of the foundation in court and won their case. Sorry to say it, but the developments in China saved our butts.'

'No need to apologise,' Lee said. 'We Chinese invented yin and yang. Opposing forces can create a favourable balance. Tell me, how did Bonefish Key become the centre of research on the newest epidemic?'

'Pretty much by chance,' he said. 'I'm chairman of a board that advises the Feds about scientific discoveries that have defence or political implications. I had routinely passed along news of a possible breakthrough in antiviral research to the Centers for Disease Control. When the new virus strain was discovered in China, we were recruited to find a way to fight it. The funds put us on the fast track in our research.'

'You said you were optimistic about your progress,' Lee said.

'Guardedly so. You know the hurdles in developing an antiviral agent.'

Lee nodded. 'How can I be of help during my time here?'

'We're homing in on a single antiviral chemical. We could use your expertise in virology as we put the stuff through the tests. At the same time,' he added, 'I'd like you to develop an epidemiological plan on how best to use the vaccine once we have synthesised it.'

'How close are you to synthesis?' she asked.

'I wish we were closer, but we're almost there,' he answered.

Kane turned down a well-worn path that branched off from the main walking trail. After about a hundred feet, the path ended at a cinder-block building. A man was standing in front of a door of reinforced steel. He wore tan shorts and a blue T-shirt and could have passed for a maintenance man, but instead of tools a side arm hung from his wide leather belt. He didn't look surprised to see them, and Lee recalled what Kane had said about camera surveillance.

The man opened the door and stepped aside to allow his visitors in. The interior of the building was cool and dark except for the light coming from dozens of glass tanks that held various types of sea life.

Kane led the way to a side door and punched some numbers in the combination lock. The door opened into a smaller chamber that was completely dark except for the cold blue light coming from a vertical, tube-shaped water tank. The glow emanated from a number of undulating circular forms that rose and fell in the tank in a slow-motion dance.

Song Lee was mesmerised by the ghostly figures. 'They're beautiful.'

'Meet the Blue Medusa, Dr Lee,' Kane said. 'Our research efforts have been concentrated on this lovely creature. Its venom is one of the most complex chemical compounds I've ever come across.'

'This jellyfish is the source of the compound you're trying to synthesise?'

'Uh-huh. The tiniest amount of the medusa's venom is fatal to humans, but the entire fate of millions of people could rest on the lowly creature in that tank. I can fill you in after you've had a chance to rest.'

Dr Lee's scientific mind was hungry for details. 'I don't *need* any rest,' she insisted. 'I want to start now.'

Song Lee's roselike delicateness hid thorns that had been sharpened by her dealings with a stonehearted Chinese bureaucracy. Kane couldn't prevent the faint smile that came to his lips.

'I'll introduce you to the staff,' he said.

Kane guided Lee through the labs, introducing her to the other scientists who were working on the Blue Medusa project. She was particularly impressed with Lois Mitchell, Kane's first assistant and project manager. But jet lag eventually caught up with Lee, and she caught a good night's sleep in her comfortable cabin.

In the days that followed, Dr Lee threw herself into her work. She rose early and worked late. Her daily kayak paddle through the mangroves was the only recreational break in her ferocious schedule. She knew that it was only a matter of time before the virus got loose.

Then, one day, she and the rest of the scientific staff were asked to attend a meeting. To applause, Dr Kane announced that the compound they had been looking for had been identified. He and a handpicked team would go into seclusion to put the final touches on the synthesis at a new lab. He could not say where the lab was located, only that it was nearer to the resource. Lee agreed to stay on at Bonefish Key with a skeleton crew so she could finish her epidemiological analysis and lay out an immunisation plan.

Dr Huang had asked to be kept informed of Dr Lee's progress. The only place on the island where cellphone service was available was at the top of an old water tower. Every day after her work, Lee climbed the tower and summarised the progress of the project for her old friend and mentor.

There was no way she could have known that her every word was being relayed to unfriendly ears.

Chapter 2
Bermuda, Three Months Later

The taxi driver warily eyeballed the man standing on the kerb outside the arrival gate at Bermuda's L. F. Wade Airport. His potential fare had an unruly ginger beard and hair pulled back in a pigtail. He wore faded jeans, high-top red sneakers, Elton John sunglasses with white frames and a linen jacket over a T-shirt with a picture on it of Jerry Garcia from the Grateful Dead.

'Please take me to the harbour,' Max Kane said. He opened the door, threw his duffle bag in the back seat, and then slid in beside it. The driver shrugged and put the taxi in gear. A fare was a fare.

Kane sat back and closed his eyes. His impatience had ballooned with each mile travelled over the past twenty-four hours. The long flight from the Pacific Ocean to New York and the two-hour trip here were nothing compared to the dragging minutes it took for the taxi to get to the waterfront.

Kane directed the driver to stop near the gangway of a turquoise-hulled ship. The distinctive colour and the letters NUMA emblazoned on the hull below the ship's name, *William Beebe*, identified the vessel as belonging to the National Underwater and Marine Agency, the largest ocean-study organisation in the world.

Kane shoved a wad of bills at the driver and then briskly climbed up the gangway. A pleasant-faced young woman wearing the uniform of a ship's officer greeted Kane with a warm smile.

'Welcome to the *Beebe*, Dr Kane. My name is Marla Hayes. I'm the third mate. I'll show you to your cabin and give you a tour of the ship.'

'If you don't mind, I've come a long way and I'm anxious to see the B3.'

'No problem,' Marla said, leading Kane towards the ship's fantail.

The 250-foot-long search-and-survey ship was the marine equivalent of a professional weightlifter. With its stern-ramp A-frame crane and wide deck, the fantail was the business end of the ship. It bristled with the winches and derricks that scientists used to launch underwater vehicles and devices that probed the depths. Kane's eyes went to a large tangerine-coloured globe resting in a steel cradle beneath a tall crane. Three portholes protruded from the sphere's surface.

'There it is,' Marla said. 'I'll come by in a while to see how you're doing.'

Kane thanked the young woman and walked cautiously round to the other side of the sphere. He saw a man in a Hawaiian shirt and cargo shorts standing in front of a circular opening slightly more than a foot in diameter. The man's head was inside the globe, his right shoulder angled through the hatch as if he were being devoured by a bug-eyed monster. A string of salty curses echoed from inside the globe.

Kane set his duffle bag down and asked, 'Tight quarters?'

The man bumped his head as he backed out of the opening, prompting a few more colourful oaths, and brushed away a shock of steel-grey hair from eyes that were the blue of coral. He had a broad-shouldered frame that was over six feet, and he must have weighed 200 pounds. He grinned, showing perfect white teeth against his bronzed features.

'Very tight. I'd need a shoehorn and a can of grease to get me into this antiquated refugee from a marine-salvage dump,' he said.

A dark-complexioned face poked from the hatch, and its owner said, 'Give it up, Kurt. They'd have to baste you with WD-40 and pound you in with a sledgehammer.'

The broad-shouldered man made a face at the unpleasant image. He extended his hand in introduction. 'I'm Kurt Austin, project director for the Bathysphere 3 expedition.'

The man in the sphere wriggled out feetfirst and introduced himself. 'Joe Zavala,' he said. 'I'm the engineer for the B3 project.'

'Nice to meet you both. My name is Max Kane.' He jerked his thumb at the sphere. 'And I'm scheduled to dive a half-mile into the ocean in this antiquated refugee from a marine-salvage dump.'

Austin exchanged a bemused glance with Zavala. 'Pleased to meet you, Dr Kane. Sorry to cast doubt on your sanity.'

'You wouldn't be the first. You get used to it when you're doing pure research.' Kane removed his sunglasses, revealing blue eyes. 'And please call me Doc.'

Austin gestured towards the orange globe. 'Don't pay any attention to my earlier comment, Doc. I'd make the dive in a heartbeat if the bathysphere came in a bigger size. Joe is the best deep-sea guy in the business. He's made the diving bell as safe as any NUMA submersible.'

Zavala cast an appraising eye on the sphere. 'I used technology that wasn't available back in the thirties, but otherwise it's the original Beebe-Barton design that set the record by diving three thousand and twenty-eight feet in 1934. The globe shape was beautiful in its simplicity. Beebe realised that a sphere was the only way to deal with the pressure at great depth. It would distribute the pressure evenly around its entire surface.' He squatted next to the globe and ran his hand over the thick skids that the legs rested upon. 'I've added emergency flotation bags in the runners. There's more than a little self-preservation involved, Doc. I'll be making the dive with you.'

Kane rubbed his palms together like a hungry man savouring a juicy steak. 'This is a dream come true,' he said. 'I pulled every string I could to get on the dive list. William Beebe is responsible for my career in marine microbiology. When I was a kid, I read about the glowing deep-ocean fish that he found. I wanted to share Beebe's adventures.'

'My biggest adventure so far has been trying to stuff myself through that fourteen-inch door,' Austin said. 'Try it on for size, Doc.'

Kane, who was about five foot eight, hung his jacket on the bathysphere's frame, then poured himself headfirst into the sphere, doubled his body with the skill of a contortionist, and poked his head out of the circular opening. 'It's roomier in here than it appears from the outside.'

'The original bathysphere was four feet nine inches in diameter, and had walls one and a half inches thick made of fine-grade, open-hearth steel,' Zavala said. 'We've cheated a little. The portholes are polymer instead of fused quartz. The tether is Kevlar rather than steel, and we've replaced the copper communications link with photo-optic fibre.'

Kane exited the sphere and stared at it with near reverence. 'You've done an amazing job, Joe. No way would I have missed this opportunity.'

Austin said, 'I understand you were in the Pacific Ocean.'

'Yeah. Contract work for Uncle Sam. Pretty routine stuff. We're about to wrap it up.'

The third mate was making her way across the deck, accompanied by two men and a woman carrying video cameras, lights and sound equipment.

'That's the NUMA film crew,' Austin said to Kane. 'They'll want to interview the intrepid divers on camera.'

A look of horror came over Max Kane's face. 'Can they wait until I hop into the shower and trim the porcupine quills on my chin?'

'Joe will fill them in while you clean up. I'll see you in the bridge after the interview,' Austin said. 'We'll go over the plans for tomorrow.'

As he headed for the bridge, Austin reflected on how Beebe's books had stirred his imagination when he was a boy.

Born and raised in Seattle, Austin had followed his boyhood dreams, studying systems management at the University of Washington. He also attended a prestigious deepwater diving school, specialising in salvage. He worked a few years on North Sea oil rigs and put in a stint with his father's ocean-salvage company, but his spirit of adventure needed freer rein. He joined a clandestine underwater-surveillance unit of the CIA that he led until it was disbanded at the end of the Cold War. Then he moved over to NUMA to head up the Special Assignments Team that investigated out-of-the-ordinary events above and below the world's oceans.

When Austin had heard that the National Geographic Society and the New York Zoological Society were sponsoring a docudrama on Beebe's historic half-mile bathysphere dive of 1934, Austin persuaded the NUMA brass to let Zavala design a state-of-the-art bathysphere. The diving bell would be launched from the agency's research vessel, *William Beebe*. Like all government agencies, NUMA had to fight for its share of the federal funding pie, and favourable publicity never hurt.

Trailed by a cameraman and sound technician, Zavala and a freshly scrubbed Kane climbed to the bridge after being interviewed in front of the bathysphere. Austin introduced Kane to the captain, an experienced NUMA hand named Mike Gannon, who spread a chart out on a table and pointed to Nonsuch Island off the northeast tip of Bermuda.

'We'll anchor as close as possible to Beebe's original position,' the captain said. 'We'll be about eight miles from land with just over a half-mile of water under the ship's keel.'

'We decided on a shallower location than the original so we could film the sea bottom,' Austin explained. He turned to Kane. 'We've been doing all the talking so far, Doc. What do you hope to get out of this expedition?'

Kane gave the question a moment's thought. 'Miracles,' he said with a mysterious smile.

'How so?'

'When Beebe reported hauling phosphorescent fish in his trawl nets, his fellow scientists didn't believe him. Beebe hoped the bathysphere would vindicate his research. Like Beebe, my hope is to dramatise the miracles that lie beneath the surface of the ocean.'

'Biomedicine miracles?' Austin asked.

Kane's dreamy expression vanished, and he seemed to catch himself. 'What do you mean, biomeds?' His voice had an unexpected edge to it. He glanced at the video camera.

'I Googled Bonefish Key. Your website mentioned a morphine substitute your lab developed from snail venom. I simply wondered if you had come across anything similar in the Pacific Ocean.'

Kane broke into a smile. 'I was speaking as an ocean microbiologist . . . *metaphorically.*'

Austin nodded. 'Let's talk miracles and metaphors over dinner, Doc.'

Kane opened his mouth in a yawn. 'I'm about to hit the sack,' he said. 'Sorry to be a bother, Captain, but I wonder if I could have a sandwich sent to my cabin. I'd better get some sleep so I can be fresh for tomorrow's dive.'

Austin said he would see Kane in the morning. He watched Kane thoughtfully as he left the bridge, wondering at his edgy response.

THE NEXT MORNING, the NUMA ship headed out to sea. Ploughing through low-mounding water, it travelled for another hour before dropping anchor.

'Ready to take the plunge, Doc?' Austin asked.

'I've been ready for nearly forty years,' Kane replied.

Zavala tossed two inflatable cushions and a couple of blankets through the door of the B3. 'Beebe and Barton sat on cold, hard steel,' he announced. 'I've decided a minimum of comfort will be necessary.'

In turn, Kane produced two skullcaps from a bag and handed one to Zavala. 'Barton refused to dive unless he wore his lucky hat.'

Zavala pulled the cap down on his head. Then he crawled through the bathysphere's hatch. He curled up next to a control panel. Kane got in next and sat on the window side. Zavala turned the air supply on and called out to Austin, 'Close the door, Kurt, it's draughty in here.'

'See you for margaritas in a few hours.' Austin gave the order to seal the bathysphere.

A crane lifted the 400-pound hatchcover into place. Using a wrench, the launch crew screwed ten large nuts over the bolts. Kane shook hands with Austin through an opening in the centre of the door that allowed instruments to be passed in and out without having to move the cumbersome cover. Then the crew screwed a nut into the hole to seal it.

Austin picked up a microphone connected to the bathysphere's communications system and warned the divers they were about to become airborne. The winch growled and the crane hoisted the B3 off the deck, swung it over the side, and kept it suspended twenty feet above the heaving ocean surface. Austin called the bathysphere on the radio and got Zavala's go-ahead to launch. The B3 splashed into the crystal-clear waters and the crane lowered it until it was just under the surface.

Zavala's metallic-sounding voice came over a speaker mounted on a deck stand. 'Thanks for the soft landing,' he said.

'This crew could dunk this doughnut in a cup of coffee,' Austin said.

The winch let out fifty feet of cable, and the bathysphere stopped for the final safety inspection. Zavala made a quick run-through of the B3's air-supply, circulation and communications systems. He called up to the support ship.

'Tight as a tick, Kurt,' he called. 'All systems go. Ready, Doc?'

'Lower away!' Kane said.

The sea's foamy arms embraced the bathysphere like a long-lost denizen, and with only a mound of bubbles to mark its descent the hollow sphere and its two passengers began the half-mile trip to King Neptune's realm.

THOUSANDS OF MILES from Bermuda, in a dimly lit room 300 feet below the surface of the Pacific Ocean, a row of television screens displayed green-hued pictures showing schools of fish darting past the B3's cameras like wind-blown confetti. A dozen or so men and women were gathered round the only screen that did not display the sea bottom. All had their eyes glued to a blue-and-black depiction of the globe and the letters NUMA. While they watched, the logo vanished to be replaced by a shot of the B3's cramped interior. A pair of cameras mounted on the interior wall were transmitting pictures of the bathysphere cabin to laboratories around the world.

'*Ya-hoo!*' Lois Mitchell yelled, pumping her arm in the air. 'Doc's on his way. And he's wearing his lucky hat.'

The others joined in her applause, then the room went silent as Max Kane began to talk, his words and mouth slightly out of synchronisation.

'Hello, everyone. My name is Dr Max Kane, and I'm broadcasting from a replica of the Beebe-Barton bathysphere. We're about to re-create the half-mile Beebe-Barton dive made in 1934. The bathysphere's pilot is Joe

Zavala, a submersible pilot and marine engineer with the National Underwater and Marine Agency. Joe is responsible for designing the bathysphere replica.'

Zavala had rigged voice-activated controls that allowed the divers to switch camera views. His face replaced Kane's on the screen, and he began to describe the B3's technical innovations. Lois was only half listening, more interested in the NUMA engineer's dark good looks than his shoptalk.

'I envy Doc,' she said without removing her gaze from Zavala's face.

'Me, too,' said a grey-haired man seated to Lois's right, a marine biologist named Frank Logan. 'What a great scientific opportunity!'

Lois smiled slightly; her desire to spend time in the bathysphere with the handsome Zavala had nothing to do with science. Well, maybe *biology*.

The camera went back to Kane.

'Great job, Joe,' Kane said. 'I'd like to offer personal thanks to everyone who has helped make this project possible. National Geographic, the New York Zoological Society and NUMA.' He put his face closer to the camera. 'I'd also like to give my best to all the denizens at Davy Jones's Locker.'

The room echoed with loud whoops and applause.

Logan, a soft-spoken Midwesterner, slapped his thigh in his excitement. 'Wow!' he exclaimed. 'Nice of Doc to recognise us denizens slaving secretly away down here in the Locker.'

A soft gong echoed throughout the room, and a green light blinked over a television monitor that showed what looked like a diamond diadem against dark velvet.

Logan said with a wry grin, 'Looks like your company has arrived.'

Lois wrinkled her nose. '*Damn*. I wanted to watch the rest of Doc's dive.'

'Bring your guest back here to watch the show,' Logan suggested.

'Oh, *no*! I'm getting rid of him as quickly as I can,' Lois said, bustling from the room.

Lois Mitchell was nearly six feet tall, and in her late forties she had packed a few more pounds on her frame than she would have preferred. The voluptuous figure didn't live up to contemporary ideals of beauty, but artists of a bygone day would have drooled over her curves and creamy skin, and the way her thick raven hair fell to her shoulders.

She descended a spiral staircase to a brightly lit passageway. The tube-like corridor connected to a small chamber occupied by two men who stood at an instrument panel facing a heavy-duty double door.

One man said, 'Hi, Lois. Touchdown is in forty-five seconds.'

The cluster of sparkling lights displayed on the monitor set into the instrument panel had materialised into a submersible vehicle slowly descending through the murk. It resembled a large utility helicopter that had been stripped of its main rotor and was powered by variable-thrust turbines on the fuselage. Two figures were silhouetted in the bubble cockpit.

The room reverberated with the hum of motors. A diagram of the lab on the control panel began to blink, indicating that the air-lock doors were open. After a few moments, the display stopped blinking, signifying that the doors had closed. The floor vibrated with the thrash of powerful pumps. When the water had been expelled from the air lock, the pumps went silent, and a green light flashed over the doors. At the push of a button on the control panel, the doors opened, and a briny smell rushed out. The submersible rested in a circular domed chamber. Curtains of seawater rolled off the fuselage and swirled down gurgling drains.

Lois strode over and greeted the man emerging from the passenger's side of the cockpit. He was a couple of inches taller than she was and wore blue jeans, sneakers, and a windbreaker and baseball cap both emblazoned with the logo of the company that provided security for the lab.

She extended her hand. 'Welcome to Davy Jones's Locker. I'm Dr Lois Mitchell, assistant director of the lab while Dr Kane is away.'

'Pleased to meet you, ma'am,' the man said in a deep-voiced Southern drawl. 'My name is Gordon Phelps.'

Lois had expected to see a quasi-military type like the tough-looking guards she had glimpsed on trips to the surface support ship, but Phelps looked as if he had been assembled from spare parts. His arms were too long for his body, his hands too big for his arms. With his sad-looking eyes and large mouth accented by a drooping moustache, he had a hound-dog quality about him. He wore his dark brown hair in unfashionably long sideburns.

'Did you have a pleasant shuttle ride, Mr Phelps?'

'Couldn't have been better. The best part was seeing the lights on the ocean bottom. Kept thinking this must be Atlantis.'

Lois cringed inwardly at the overblown comparison to the lost city. 'Glad to hear that,' she said. 'Come to my office.'

She led the way along another tubular passageway, then up a spiral staircase to a low-lit, circular room with a transparent domed ceiling.

Phelps swivelled his head in wonder. 'Talk about a water view! This is unbelievable.'

'This is Dr Kane's office. I'm using it while he's away. Have a seat.'

Phelps pulled up a chair. 'I'd like to thank you for your valuable time, Dr Mitchell. You must have lots better things to do besides talking to a boring old security guy.'

If you only knew, Lois thought. She gave her visitor a polite smile. 'How can I help you, Mr Phelps?'

'My company sent me to probe for weaknesses in the sea-lab security.'

Lois wondered what kind of an idiot had sent Phelps to waste her time. She pointed towards the transparent ceiling. 'We've got three hundred feet of ocean separating us from the surface. There's a patrol ship up there with armed guards from your company. How could we be any more secure?'

Phelps furrowed his brow. 'With all due respect, Dr Mitchell, there is *no* security system in the world that can't be breached.'

Lois ignored the condescending tone. 'Very well, then, let's start with a virtual tour of the facility,' she said.

She swivelled her chair and tapped a computer keyboard. A three-dimensional diagram that looked like a series of globes and connecting tubes appeared on the monitor.

'The lab consists of four large spheres, arranged in a diamond shape and connected by tubular corridors,' Lois began. 'We're at the top of the administrative pod . . . here. Below us is the crew's quarters and mess hall.' She manipulated the cursor to highlight another globe. 'There's a control room and some labs in this pod. This pod contains the small nuclear plant. Air is supplied through a water-to-oxygen set-up. The complex was not meant to be permanent, so it has compressed-air capabilities that allow it to attain negative buoyancy. It could be moved to another location.'

'This is one hell of an engineering job.' Phelps pointed to a hemispheric shape in the centre of the rectangle. 'Is this where the shuttle came in?'

'That's right,' Lois said. 'The minisubs attached to the underside of the transit module are used for specimen collection, but they can also be used to evacuate the lab.'

'What about the fourth module?' Phelps said.

'Sorry, top secret.'

'That's OK,' Phelps said. 'If it's not too much trouble, I'd like to see the nonrestricted areas.'

Lois Mitchell frowned. She picked up the intercom phone and called the control room. 'Hello, Frank,' she said. 'This is going to take longer than I expected. Anything new with Doc? No? OK, I'll keep in touch.' She replaced the phone and stood. 'C'mon, Mr Phelps. This is going to be fast and furious.'

FIFTY MILES FROM Davy Jones's Locker, the rolling surface of the dark sea erupted in an explosion of foam and spray. A twenty-foot-long aluminium tube burst from the centre of the churning geyser, sped skywards at a sharp angle, and quickly dived back towards the waves in a curving trajectory.

Within seconds, the cruise missile had levelled out, until it was travelling twenty-five feet above the wave tops, so low that its passing left a wake in the water. Powered by its solid-fuel rocket booster, the missile quickly accelerated, and by the time it had shed its rocket and the fan-jet engines had kicked in it was cruising at 500 miles per hour.

The missile's unsuspecting target was a large, grey-hulled ship anchored near the red-and-white buoy that marked the location of the undersea lab. Assigned to protect the lab, the *Proud Mary* carried two dozen guards proficient in the use of every type of small arms as well as an array of electronic sensing gear that could pick up vessels or planes approaching.

In its leap from the ocean, the missile had blipped on the ship's radar screen for only a few seconds. Inactivity had dulled the operator's edge, and he was engrossed in a motorcycle magazine when the missile made its brief appearance, before dropping from surveillance's view. The ship had infrared sensors, but even if the missile had been flying at altitude they would have failed to pick up the low-temperature heat from its engines.

Undetected, the missile streaked towards the *Proud Mary*, carrying a half-ton of high explosives in its warhead.

LOIS MITCHELL AND GORDON PHELPS were making their way along the passageway to the control room when they heard a loud *whump* that seemed to come from far over their heads. Lois stopped in her tracks.

'I've never heard anything like *that* before,' she said. 'I'd better check to make sure all the lab systems are operating as they should be.'

'Good idea,' Phelps said amiably.

They started walking towards the door at the end of the passageway. A few steps from the control-room module, the door hissed open, and Frank Logan burst through, his pale face flushed with excitement.

'Lois! I was coming to get you. Did you hear that weird noise—'

Logan stopped short. Lois turned to see what he was staring at.

Phelps was holding a pistol in his hand, dangling it next to his thigh.

'What's going on?' she said. 'We don't allow weapons in the lab.'

Phelps gave her a hangdog look. 'Like I said, no security system is totally foolproof. Lab's under new management, Dr Mitchell.'

His voice now had an edge that hadn't been there before. Phelps told Logan to stand next to Lois so he could keep an eye on him. As Logan complied, the control-room door hissed open again, and a lab technician stepped through. Phelps instinctively brought his gun round to deal with the interruption. Logan, seeing Phelps's distraction, tried to grab his gun.

They struggled, but Phelps was younger and stronger and would have got the upper hand even if the gun had not gone off. A red stain blossomed on the front of Logan's white lab coat and he crumpled to the floor.

The lab tech bolted back into the control room. Lois ran over and knelt by Logan's motionless body. 'You killed him!' she said.

'Aw, hell,' Phelps said. 'Didn't mean to do that.'

Lois stood up and confronted Phelps. 'What *did* you mean to do? Are you going to shoot me too?'

'Not unless I have to, Dr Mitchell. We'd hate to lose you.'

Lois Mitchell stared defiantly at Phelps for a few seconds before she wilted under his unrelenting gaze. 'What do you want?'

'For now, I want you to round up all the lab folks,' he said. 'Then we're going for a little ride.'

Chapter 3

In the early stages of the dive, pilot fish, silver eels, motelike clouds of copepods and strings of lacelike siphonophores drifted past the portholes like tiny ghosts, along with shrimp, translucent squid, and snails so tiny that they resembled brown bubbles.

At 700 feet, Zavala switched the B3's searchlight off. He looked out of the window and murmured an appreciative exclamation in Spanish. Zavala had grown up in Santa Fe, and the view through the porthole looked like a New Mexico sky on a clear winter's night. The darkness sparkled with stars, some continuously flashing, others just once. There were floating threads of luminescence, and glowing smudges that could have been novae or nebulae in a celestial setting.

The cabin was as hushed as a cathedral, so when Kane saw an undulating form float by the porthole his response was like a gunshot.

'*Wow!*' he exclaimed. 'An Aurelia jellyfish.'

Zavala smiled at Kane's excitement. 'You had me for a second there, Doc. Thought you'd seen the Loch Ness monster,' he said.

'This is so much better. The medusas are among the most fascinating animals under the sea . . . Hey,' Kane said, 'what was that?'

'You see a mermaid, Doc?' Zavala asked.

Kane pressed his face against the porthole. 'I'm not sure *what* I saw,' he said, 'but I know it was *big*.'

Zavala flicked on the searchlight and peered through the porthole. 'Gone,' he said, 'whatever it was.'

Kane turned to the camera. 'Until the bathysphere's dive, Beebe's fellow scientists never believed that he had seen fish with glowing teeth and neon skin. He got the last laugh when he proved the abyss abounded with such strange creatures.'

'They're getting stranger all the time,' Zavala said, pointing at himself. 'The locals swimming around out there must think that you and I are pretty unsavoury-looking additions to their neighbourhood.'

Kane's loud guffaw echoed off the bathysphere's curving walls. 'Joe is right: humans have no right being where we are at this moment . . . Hey, there's some lantern fish. Man, they're beautiful. Look, there's—*Whoops!*'

Suddenly a strong vibration passed through the sphere. The B3 first lifted up, then dropped, in slow motion. Wide-eyed, Kane glanced around, as if expecting the sea to come pouring in through the sphere's shell.

Zavala called the support vessel. 'Please stop yo-yoing the B3, Kurt.'

'Sorry for the rough ride,' Austin said. 'The cable went slack in the cross swell, and we moved too fast when we tried to adjust.'

'Not surprising, with the length of cable you're handling.'

'Now that you bring up the subject, you might want to check your depth.'

Zavala glanced at the display screen and tapped Kane on the shoulder. Kane turned away from the window and saw Zavala's finger pointing at the gauge. Three thousand and thirty feet. They had exceeded the original bathysphere's historic dive by two feet.

Max Kane's chin dropped down practically to his Adam's apple. 'We're *here*,' he announced, 'more than half a mile down!'

'And almost out of cable,' Kurt Austin said. 'The sea bottom is around fifty feet below you.'

Kane slapped Joe Zavala's palm a high five. 'I can't believe it,' he said. His face was flushed with excitement. 'I'd like to take this moment to thank the intrepid William Beebe and Otis Barton,' he continued, 'for blazing the trail for all who have followed. What we have done today is a tribute to their courage . . . We're going to be busy for a while shooting pictures of the sea bottom, so we're signing off for a few minutes. We'll get back to you when we're riding to the surface.'

They cut television transmission, positioned themselves next to the portholes with still cameras, and shot dozens of pictures of the strange glowing creatures that the bathysphere's lights had attracted.

Eventually, it was time to head back up. Zavala called Austin on the radio and told him they were ready to ascend.

The B3 swayed slightly, vibrated, then jerked from side to side.

Zavala pulled himself into a sitting position. 'Getting bounced around down here, Kurt. Sea picking up?' he enquired.

'It's like a mirror up here.'

'Joe,' Kane shouted, 'there it is again . . . the monster fish!' He jabbed his index finger at the window.

A shadow passed near the edge of the searchlight beam and turned towards the bathysphere.

As Zavala pressed his face against a porthole, every hair on his scalp stood up and saluted. He was looking into three glowing eyes, one of them over the other two. The sphere jerked again.

'We're seeing cable oscillations near the surface,' Kurt's voice came over the speaker. 'What's going on?'

There was another jerking movement.

'There's something out there,' Zavala said.

'What are you talking about?' Austin asked.

Zavala wasn't sure himself, so he simply said, 'Haul us up.'

'Hang tight,' Austin said. 'We're starting the winch.'

The bathysphere seemed to stabilise. The numbers on the Fathometer blinked, showing that the sphere was moving up towards the surface. Kane broke into a relieved grin, but the expression on his face froze as the bathysphere jerked once more. A second later, the men in the B3 were levitating as if plunging on a runaway elevator.

The bathysphere had gone into free fall.

KURT AUSTIN LEANED AGAINST the ship's railing and saw the B3's tether cable oscillating like a plucked violin string. He spoke into the headset microphone that connected him with the bathysphere.

'What's going on, Joe? The cable is going crazy.'

Austin heard garbled voices, the words inaudible against a background of metallic clanging. Then the line went dead.

Austin strained his ears. *Nothing.* Not even a whisper of static. He removed the headset and examined the connections. Everything was in place. He unclipped his belt radio and called the captain in the ship's bridge. 'I've lost voice communication with the B3. Is the video transmission coming through?'

'Not since it was cut off,' Captain Gannon reported. 'All systems are out.'

A frown crossed Austin's tanned face. It made no sense. If one system failed, another should have taken over.

Austin replaced his headset and instructed the crane operator to reel the cable in. As it slithered out of the water, the operator's voice came over Austin's headset. 'Hey, Kurt, something's wrong. There's no weight resistance at the other end.'

The NUMA film crew, sensing the tension in the air, stopped filming.

When the cable came out of the water, it snapped like a bullwhip, the bathysphere no longer attached. The operator swung the dangling cable over the ship and Austin went over and picked up the end. The strands were as even edged as the bristles of a paintbrush. 'Damned thing snapped!'

Watching from the bridge, the captain had seen Austin examining the cable. He hustled down to the deck. 'What the hell happened?'

Austin shook his head. 'I wish I knew.'

'The press boats have been calling in,' the captain said. 'They want to know what happened to the video transmission.'

Austin scanned the cordon of encircling boats. 'Tell them that there was a problem with the fibre-optic cable. We need time to figure this thing out.'

The captain called the bridge and relayed Austin's suggestion.

'It's going to be all right, isn't it, Kurt?' Gannon asked with worry in his eyes. 'The B3's flotation bags will bring them to the surface, right?'

Austin squinted against the glare coming off the water. 'The bathysphere is a long way down; let's give it a while. But we should ready an ROV.'

The remotely operated vehicle, or ROV, has become the workhorse of undersea exploration. Controlled by means of a tether, an ROV can dive deep, manoeuvre into the tightest spaces, and transmit television images, allowing the operator to travel to the depths without leaving the dry comfort of the ship. The vehicle was equipped with two manipulators for collecting samples, and several cameras, including high-resolution colour video.

A telescoping boom swung the ROV off its cradle and lowered it into the sea. Then Austin stepped into the remote-sensing control centre on the main deck. The remote's movement was controlled by a pilot with a joystick. Images from the video feed were transmitted to a screen above the console.

Moving in a descending spiral, the ROV travelled in minutes the same distance it had taken the bathysphere hours. The remote blasted through schools of fish, scattering them like leaves. Its twin searchlights picked out brownish-green bottom vegetation undulating in the current. There was no sign of the Bathysphere 3.

Austin said, 'Start searching, in parallel passes, a hundred feet long.'

The ROV cruised about twenty feet over the vegetation at five knots. It finished its first hundred-foot pass, then travelled back with fifteen feet separating it from the first pass.

Austin clenched and unclenched his fists, impatient with the glacially slow pace. Other crew members now gathered round the screen, but no one spoke except for Austin and the ROV pilot.

Five minutes passed. The picture transmitted by the ROV's electronic eye was the same unchanging monotonous carpet of brownish green.

'*Wait*,' Austin said. He had seen something. 'Go to the left.'

With a jiggle of the joystick, the pilot pivoted the vehicle. The twin searchlights picked up mud splatter around the rim of a crater. A mud-covered, domelike shape protruded from the centre of the crater. Now Austin saw why the B3 hadn't surfaced: its flotation bags were buried deep in mud.

The pilot pointed the ROV's searchlights at the sphere. Austin stared at the image. He was pondering the technical challenge involved in freeing the B3 from the clutches of the sea when a shadow appeared on the right-hand side of the monitor. It was there for an instant, then gone.

'What was that?' the pilot asked.

Before Austin could venture a guess, the screen went blank.

ZAVALA LAY ON HIS SIDE, his right arm pinned under his hipbone, his left curled up to his chest. His legs were immobilised by a soft weight. Ignoring the shards of pain stabbing under his ear, he lifted his head and saw Kane stretched belly down across his knees.

In the dim, battery-powered light, Zavala saw that the cabin was littered with papers, clothing, bottles of water, seat cushions and other loose items. Zavala reached for his headset and held it to his ear. *Silence*. He tested Kane's headset. Not even a hint of static.

The loss of communication was ominous, but Zavala's optimistic nature would not let him dwell on such bad luck. He wiggled one leg, freed his foot, and used it to shove Kane's body off the other leg. Kane rolled onto his back, and a low groan escaped his lips.

The painful exertion triggered waves of nausea in Zavala. He unclipped the first-aid kit from the wall and broke open an ampoule, waving it under his nostrils. The acrid odour snapped him to alertness.

He removed the good-luck cap. Gingerly probing his scalp with his fingertips, he found a lump that felt as big as an egg. He poured water from a canteen on a compress bandage and held it lightly against his head. Even the slight pressure was painful, but the throbbing eased.

Zavala removed Kane's skullcap and applied the compress. Kane winced, and his eyes blinked wide open.

'Ow!' he said. A good sign.

'Sorry, Doc, Florence Nightingale couldn't make it, so you're stuck with me,' Zavala said. 'Try moving your toes and fingers.'

Kane flexed his hand and foot joints. 'Nothing seems broken.'

Zavala helped Kane sit up, then said, 'What do you remember, Doc?'

Kane pursed his lips in thought. 'I was looking out of the window, recording my observations.' He glanced at his headset.

'Don't bother,' Zavala said. 'The headsets don't work.'

'We're not connected to the surface?'

'Temporarily . . . Keep talking.'

Kane took a deep breath. 'We saw some kind of weird big fish. Next, I remember heading for the moon. Then blotto. I don't get it. Why haven't they winched us up by now?' He noticed that the B3 was perfectly still, and he seemed to catch his breath. 'We're not moving, Joe. What's happened?'

Zavala wanted to avoid panic, but there was no sugar-coating their situation. 'We seem to be sitting on the bottom, Doc.'

Kane looked at the instrument panel and saw that the systems were operating on batteries. 'Oh, hell! The cable must have snapped.'

'That's almost impossible. And there could be other reasons for the breakdown. But even if we were no longer connected to the surface, we've got other options.'

Kane brightened. 'Duh, of *course*! Your flotation system.'

Zavala managed a smile. 'What do you say we pop up to the *Beebe* lounge and mix a pitcher of margaritas?'

'What are we waiting for?' Kane was as ebullient as a condemned man given an eleventh-hour reprieve.

'The compressed-air tanks are in the centre of the platform, and they feed into flotation bags that are stuffed into the skids,' Zavala explained. 'When the GO switch is activated, doors open in the sides of the skids, compressed air fills the bags instantly, and they lift us to the surface, where the ship can snag us.'

Kane rubbed his palms together in anticipation. 'Margaritaville, here we come.'

Zavala slid over to the instrument panel and a plastic box attached to the wall next to it. He unsnapped the box's cover to reveal a red button emblazoned with an arrow pointing up.

'This is a two-step process,' he explained. 'This button arms the system, and that identical button on the control panel activates it. When I say go, you hit the switch, and I'll do the same with mine. Then hold on. There's a ten-second delay.'

Kane put his finger to the button Zavala had indicated. 'Ready.'

'*Go*,' Zavala said.

Zavala prepared himself for a muted bang and a whoosh, but at the end of ten seconds nothing happened. He told Kane to try again. Again, nothing happened. Zavala checked a troubleshooting display that would have indicated a system malfunction but saw nothing amiss.

'Something must have got banged around when we hit the bottom,' Zavala said. 'Don't worry, I programmed in a manual back-up system.'

Zavala opened another panel and looped his fingers through a handle attached to a cable. Pulling the cable, he explained, would produce a small electrical current that would trigger the flotation mechanism.

He clenched his teeth and yanked. Nothing happened. He tried several more times, but it was no use. The manual trigger failed to activate.

Kane watched with growing apprehension. 'What's wrong?' he asked.

Zavala stared into space, letting his mind's eye travel through the workings of the flotation system. His gaze wandered to the window.

He flicked the searchlight on and was puzzled when he didn't see a glimmer. Sliding a flashlight from its wall rack, he pointed the light out of the window. The light failed to penetrate the darkness.

He passed the flashlight to Kane. 'Take a look.'

Kane peered through the porthole. 'Hell, there's black mud against the windows.'

'We came down hard. There's nothing wrong with the system. The mud is blocking the flotation doors.'

Kane was silent for a time. When he did speak, it was almost in a whisper. 'We're screwed, aren't we?'

Zavala reached out and gripped one of Kane's wrists tightly. 'Calm down, Doc,' he said evenly. 'We're in a tough spot, yes, but it's far from hopeless. The folks on the *Beebe* must know something has happened. Kurt will figure out a way to haul us up somehow.'

Kane snorted. 'Austin's an impressive guy, but he's not a miracle man.'

Zavala thought about the countless times Austin's courage and resourcefulness had snatched them back from the edge of disaster.

'I've worked with Kurt for years, and if anyone can get us out of here, he can. We've got more than three hours of air and enough power to give us light and heat. Our biggest problem will be boredom. Since we've been thrown together by the fates, maybe we should know more about each other. Tell me about your work,' Zavala said.

Kane's face lit up, and he seemed to forget his claustrophobic surroundings. 'My speciality is the phylum Cnidaria, which includes the class commonly known as jellyfish. The focus of my lab's research is ocean biomedicine. We think the ocean will be the most important future source of pharmaceutical compounds.'

'Like the Amazon rain forest?'

'There are similarities. Take curare, for instance. The Amazon Indians used it as a paralysing poison on their arrow tips, but its muscle-relaxant properties make it useful as a medicine.'

'And you see similar potential for jellyfish?'

'That and *more*. Jellyfish, squid, octopuses, snails. We think the ocean will far surpass anything that's been found in the jungle.'

'What sort of work were you doing in the Pacific Ocean?' Zavala asked.

'I was working on a project that could affect every man, woman and child on this planet.'

'Now you've *really* got my attention. Tell me more.'

'*Can't*,' Kane said, 'top secret. I've already said too much. If I told you more, I'd have to kill you.'

He realised the absurdity of his threat, given their dire circumstances, and began to giggle uncontrollably. Zavala choked back his laughter. 'Laughing uses up too much oxygen.'

Kane became serious again. 'Do you really think Austin is going to come to our rescue?'

'He's never failed before.'

Kane pretended he was zipping his mouth shut. 'Then the nature of our work will have to remain classified in case there is a slim chance that we'll get out of this damned hollow steel ball.' He managed a smile. 'Your turn, Joe. Tell me how you came to NUMA.'

'NUMA hired me right out of college. They needed a good mechanic.'

Zavala was being typically modest. The son of Mexican immigrants, he had graduated from New York Maritime College with a degree in marine engineering. He had a brilliant mechanical mind and expertise in every known kind of propulsion engine. He was NUMA's top submersible designer of manned and unmanned vehicles, and a skilled aircraft pilot as well.

'You make it sound like NUMA hired you to change tyres in the agency's motor pool,' Kane said. 'We wouldn't be alive if it hadn't been for the modifications you installed in the B3.'

Zavala shrugged. Despite his reassurances, he knew that their rescue was problematic. He glanced at the display panel: slightly more than two hours of air left. Sleepy from the effects of stale atmosphere, he closed his eyes and tried not to think about the air supply ebbing away.

ONCE AGAIN, Austin watched, tightlipped, as the dripping tether snaked from the ocean without its payload. He swore a sailor's oath at the loss of the ROV, and called the captain in the bridge.

'The ROV cable's been sheared off just like the bathysphere's,' Austin said. 'Looks like someone worked it over with a pair of hedge clippers.'

'This is *crazy*!' Gannon said. 'Should I send down another ROV?'

'Hold off for now,' Austin said. 'I need to think this through.'

Austin stared at the sapphire surface of the sea. He pushed aside thoughts of the two men locked in a steel ball half a mile below the ship's hull and focused on the retrieval of the bathysphere as a salvage problem. His nimble mind began to formulate a rescue plan and assemble the equipment he would need to carry it out.

Ten minutes later, Austin and Gannon were standing in the ship's garage, where all the submersibles were housed, in front of Bubbles, a puffy-limbed, anthropomorphic metal figure that resembled the Michelin man. The transparent dome capping the figure could have come from a bubblegum dispenser.

Bubbles's technical name was 'atmospheric diving suit', or ADS. A diver using the ADS could go to great depths for eight hours without having to worry about the killing water pressure or the need to decompress.

Bubbles was an experimental ADS owned by the US Navy, a successor to the Hardsuit 2000, which had been developed for submarine rescue. The *Beebe* was transporting it as a courtesy to a rendezvous with a Navy ship near Bermuda after the B3 expedition.

Gannon stood with his hands on his hips, vigorously shaking his head. 'I can't let you do this, Kurt,' he said. 'Bubbles is a *prototype*. She hasn't been field-tested yet. Last I heard, she's got a for-sure depth limit of only twenty-five hundred feet.'

'Joe would tell you that any engineer worth his salt builds in a huge safety factor.' Austin pinioned the captain with his coral-blue eyes. 'Joe and Kane will die from lack of air if we don't do something about it.'

'I know that, Kurt! I just don't want someone else dying senselessly.'

Austin realised he had come down too hard and backed off. 'Neither do I. So here's my offer: you get Bubbles gussied up for a dive, I'll get an opinion on dive limits from the Navy and abide by whatever they tell me.'

Gannon had learned a long time ago that Austin was a primal force, as unstoppable as the east wind. 'What the hell,' he said with a lopsided grin. 'I'll get Bubbles ready to go.'

Austin gave him a thumbs up, and hurried to the bridge. A satellite phone connected him with an officer in the Diving Systems Support Detachment in California. He quickly laid out his predicament.

The officer let out a low whistle. 'I sympathise with your problem, sir, but I can't give you permission to use the Hardsuit. That has to come from higher up. I'll connect you.'

'I'll deal with the Navy brass,' Austin said with thinly veiled annoyance. 'I just want to know if the new Hardsuit can dive a half-mile.'

'That's what the tests were supposed to determine,' the officer said. 'The weak spots in an ADS have always been the joints. With the new joint design, theoretically it's possible to go deeper, maybe to five thousand feet. But if there is one tiny flaw, you could have a massive failure.'

Austin thanked the officer and said he would clear the dive with the officer's superiors, although he didn't say *when*.

While Austin had been discussing the Hardsuit with the officer, a nagging thought had been buzzing around in his head like a mosquito. Heading back down to the ROV control centre, he found the young woman who had tracked the ROV still sitting at her station. He asked her to rerun the last sixty seconds of its video. She clicked her mouse and Austin watched the ROV soar over the undulating vegetation covering the sea floor. Its camera soon picked up the bathysphere's dome protruding from the crater.

'Freeze the image right there,' Austin said. He pointed to a dark area in the upper-left-hand corner of the screen. 'Now, run it in slow motion.'

The shadow moved off the screen.

The ROV operator stared at the screen. 'I don't remember seeing that.'

'It was easy to miss,' Austin said. 'We were focused on finding the B3.'

He asked her to enlarge the image. It broke apart as it was blown up, but Austin nonetheless detected a vague manta ray shape to the shadow. He asked her to print the image, and to play back the final transmission from the bathysphere.

The screen displayed a picture of Kane, who was rattling off an excited description of the luminescent fish swimming round the bathysphere when suddenly he stopped short and pressed his face against the window.

'Hey, what was that?' Kane said.

The camera switched to Zavala. *'You see a mermaid, Doc?'*

Back to Kane. *'I'm not sure* what *I saw, but I know it was big.'*

Austin snatched up the print-out and headed for the aft deck. The big double doors on the garage were wide open, and the Hardsuit had been wheeled out under the crane that would lift it off the deck.

'Did you contact the Navy?' Gannon said.

'A Navy engineer told me that, theoretically, Bubbles could dive to five thousand feet.'

'Wow! Did you get an OK to use it?'

'I'll work on it later,' Austin said with a quick smile.

'Why did I even ask?' the captain said.

Austin inspected the machine and then asked the crew to hook the severed end of the bathysphere's cable to the ADS frame. While they tended to his request, Austin hurried to his cabin and exchanged his shorts and T-shirt for thermal underwear, a wool sweater and wool socks. He zipped himself into a crew coverall and pulled a knitted cap down over his thick mane of hair. Although the Hardsuit had a heating system, the temperature inside could drop to forty degrees at depth.

Back up on deck, Austin quickly explained the rescue plan. Making a silent plea to the gods of dumb luck to look approvingly on this venture, he climbed up a stepladder and eased his muscular body into the lower half of the Hardsuit, which separated into two parts at the waist. Once the top half of the suit was on, he tested the power, communications link and air supply. Then he gave the order to launch.

The frame and Hardsuit were lowered into the water. Austin called for a halt at thirty feet down to retest the systems. Everything was in working order. He reached out with his hand-pod clamp and detached the hook from the frame. First making sure the hook was clamped tightly, he gave the order to send him to the bottom of the sea.

After passing 2,000 feet, Austin was aware that the suit now had entered uncharted territory, but his mind was too busy with other things to contemplate the possibility that it might have been pushed beyond its limits. The quick descent kicked up bubbles that obscured his view of his surroundings through the Plexiglas dome that encased his head. At 2,800 feet, he felt a change in the speed of his descent, and Gannon's voice came on the intercom. 'We're slowing you down so you don't drill a hole through the bottom, Kurt.'

'Appreciate that. Hold at three thousand.'

The winch soon slowed to a stop. The curtain of bubbles cleared around the dome and Austin switched on lights.

'You're on your own from here on,' the captain said. 'We'll let out cable as you move.'

Scattered groupings and pinpoints of phosphorescence could be seen beyond the range of the searchlights, and odd-looking luminescent fish nosed up to the faceplate of Austin's helmet.

Austin pressed down with his left foot and two vertical thrusters whirred, raising him up a yard or so. Next he used his right foot to activate the horizontal thrusters, moving him forwards several feet. He activated the suit's camera zoom and focused on an anglerfish attracted by the light.

'Picture's coming through,' the captain reported. 'Good definition.'

'I'll see if I can find something for the family album. Moving out.'

Skilfully handling the thruster controls, Austin piloted the Hardsuit horizontally, tilting forwards slightly, cable trailing behind. The 700-pound ADS moved through the water as if on wings. Austin focused on a small sonar screen glowing yellow. Employing a range of fifty feet to either side of the suit, it cut a swath a hundred feet wide. It tracked his position, heading, speed and depth as it read the bottom.

A dark object appeared on the screen, approximately twenty-five feet to his right and down.

Austin manoeuvred the Hardsuit into a sharp right turn and descended until the searchlights reflected off the gleaming plastic-and-metal surface of the ROV, lying on its back like a dead beetle.

Gannon also saw it. 'B3 should be within spitting distance.'

Austin extended the range of his search 100 feet, then spun round slowly. The sonar picked up another object close by. Austin hovered some twenty feet over the B3. The temperature inside the Hardsuit had dropped, yet sweat beaded his forehead. The difficulty of the task in this hostile environment having dawned on him, he knew that a mistake made in haste could be fatal. He took a deep breath, pressed the vertical-control pedal, and began his descent to the bathysphere entombed in mud below.

THE B3 WAS QUICKLY BECOMING a globe-shaped freezer as its battery-operated heating system fought a losing battle against the deep-ocean chill. Joe Zavala and Max Kane had wrapped blankets round themselves like Navaho Indians and sat back-to-back to conserve heat. Their lungs laboured to extract oxygen from the rapidly thinning air.

The bathysphere had an auxiliary air tank, but Zavala wondered if it was worth prolonging the misery. At the same time, he stubbornly fought the urge to give up. Closing his eyes, he imagined he was resting after a hike in the mountains around Sante Fe, not trapped at the bottom of the cold sea.

Clunk!

Something had thumped against the bathysphere. Zavala pressed his head against the wall. He could hear a gritty, scraping sound, then another clunk, followed by several more.

Morse code for *k*, he realised.

Then, after an agonising pause, he heard *a*.

Kurt Austin.

Kane had been sitting with his head down and hunched over his knees. Raising his chin, he glanced towards Zavala with unfocused eyes. 'Wha'sat?' he said, his words drunkenly slurred from lack of oxygen.

Zavala's lips widened in a ghost of a smile. 'The *cavalry* has arrived.'

AUSTIN CROUCHED on top of the bathysphere like a spider, a current threatening to push him off his perch. He hooked the cable to the top of the sphere, clamped a manipulator onto the cable to keep himself from floating off, and manoeuvred the suit's thrusters so that they were facing down into the mud surrounding the sphere.

He depressed a foot pedal and was immediately enveloped in a blinding cloud of stirred-up silt that settled after a moment. He turned the Hardsuit's searchlights off. The faint glow coming through the B3's previously buried windows indicated that systems were still operating.

Austin unclamped his manipulator and began to tap out a new message on the bathysphere's skin. He got out only a few letters before the current suddenly caught his suit and pushed him several feet away from the sphere. Regaining control, he returned to finish tapping out his message.

'Haul away!' he shouted into the suit's microphone.

ZAVALA HAD LISTENED carefully to the measured tapping coming through the skin of the B3. He'd caught the first few letters. After a pause, he'd caught the rest: *Float.*

Hell, Kurt, if I could float, I would float.

The bathysphere was still stuck in the mud, and Zavala vacillated between anger and despair. Maybe this was all a dream brought on by lack of oxygen. Maybe he was playing out a rescue that existed only in his mind.

A buzzer yanked him back to reality.

A red light blinked madly on the control panel. He realised that the light had been going on and off for some time, but his slow-moving mind had not realised it was warning that the air supply was about to end.

He reached for the spare tank, and turned on the valve. Air hissed into the cabin and blew the fog from his brain. He pulled the cable, then hit the manual switch for the flotation system and waited for something to happen.

AUSTIN HOVERED ABOVE the bottom of the ocean with the Hardsuit's lights trained on the top of the B3. The cable went taut as, a half-mile above his head, the winch began to turn, but the bathysphere didn't budge. Dire scenarios marched through Austin's head: the hook would break and the sphere would remain trapped in the suction created by the mud; the flotation system wouldn't work; worst of all, both men were unconscious.

'Anything happening at your end?' Gannon called down.

Austin saw that the cable splice was unravelling. 'Just keep hauling.'

He gritted his teeth as if he could lift the B3 through sheer will-power. The bathysphere remained where it was. The cable unravelled some more.

'*Move*, damn it!' he yelled.

Plumes of mud billowed around the bathysphere. Then the sphere pulled free, popping from the mud like a cork from a bottle. Austin's triumphant yell blasted through the ship's public-address system.

The B3 was ten feet from the bottom, then twenty, and still there was no sign of air-bag deployment. What was Joe waiting for? Maybe the flotation doors were clogged with mud. Austin kept pace, rising slowly with the bathysphere, his eyes glued to the cable. As the last strand of cable splice gave way, doors along the sides of the sphere suddenly blew open and six air bags blossomed and rapidly filled. The bathysphere rocked back and forth, stabilised, then began to ascend.

'They're on their way,' he notified Gannon.

'You're next,' the captain said. 'How are you?'

'I'll be a lot better topside.'

Austin steadied the thrusters so that he was in a vertical position, and was ready when the Hardsuit jerked at the end of the cable. As the suit began its long trip, Austin turned off his lights and saw that he was not alone.

He was surrounded by luminescent sea creatures that hung in the blackness like stars. Occasionally, he saw something moving like airplane lights across the night sky. Then his eye caught movement to the left. Turning his head, he saw what looked like a trio of amber eyes moving closer.

An alarm went off in Austin's brain. He'd been focusing on the rescue and forgotten about the sinister shadow loitering nearby when the cables were cut on the B3 and the ROV.

When Austin switched on the Hardsuit's searchlights, they reflected off the smooth, dark surface of something shaped like a flattened teardrop. It was a submersible of some kind, most likely an automated underwater vehicle, or AUV, because he couldn't see a tether. The glowing eyes on the leading edge were apparently sensors, but Austin was more interested in the sharp-edged metal mandibles protruding from the front of the vehicle.

The vehicle moved fast, gliding at a depth where the mandibles would intersect the cable pulling him to the surface. Austin stomped on his vertical-thrust pedal and he shot up several feet, his attacker passing below.

Gannon was watching the encounter on the ship's monitor. 'What the hell was *that*?' he yelled.

'Something that wants me for dinner!' Austin yelled back. 'Haul faster!'

The nimble AUV was quick to adjust its strategy and speed. Coming in for a second attack, it slowed to a walking pace, stalking its target.

Austin waited until the thing was just yards away and then tapped his foot pedal. The Hardsuit rose a few feet, but not fast enough to escape the attacker. He raised his arms defensively. The AUV's extended manipulators crashed into him, slamming his head against the inside of the helmet. The impact knocked him sideways, and he swung at the end of his cable like soap on a rope. Pain shot up his left arm from the wrist.

The AUV went for another pass, but rather than coming straight for

Austin, it feinted a frontal attack, then angled upwards towards the cable. As Austin was dazed, he was slow to give the vertical thrusters juice. The AUV's pincers caught his right arm at the elbow and closed around it.

With his left manipulator, Austin grabbed onto a mandible and powered himself down, then up, operating like a yo-yo. The mandibles were designed for horizontal rather than vertical movement, and the weight of the vehicle worked against it, bending the mandible so that it was useless. Then the blade snapped at the base. The AUV thrashed wildly, peeled off, and disappeared into the darkness.

'Kurt, are you OK?' the captain's voice rang in Austin's earphones.

'Fine, Cap,' Austin managed to croak. 'Haul me up.'

THOUSANDS OF MILES AWAY, Lois Mitchell was trying to quell a riot in the mess hall, where Gordon Phelps had herded the staff at gunpoint. Someone had noticed that Dr Logan was missing, and when Lois said that he had been shot dead the news had prompted a chorus of anger and fear.

Lois tried to shout down the cacophony. When that didn't work, she lined up several mugs on the counter and filled them from a coffeepot. The simple ritual had a calming effect. After the uproar had quieted and she could be heard, Lois flashed a sweet smile.

'Sorry this isn't a Starbucks Grande, but it will have to do for now.'

Her attempt at humour triggered an outburst from a female lab tech whose pale face and tearful eyes indicated that she was on the verge of hysteria. 'How can you be so calm knowing Dr Logan was murdered?'

Stubbornly refusing the urge to break into tears herself, Lois said, 'Dr Logan is lying outside the control room with a bullet in his heart. He was killed by the man who locked us in here. If you want to avoid the same fate, I suggest you take several deep breaths and calm down. We are dealing with ruthless people who have the resources to gain entry into a heavily guarded facility three hundred feet below the ocean's surface. I don't know who they are or how many are involved, but we are completely at their mercy.'

'What do you think they want, Lois?' asked one of the biologists.

'I'm sure they'll let us know,' she replied. 'In the meantime, let's have something to eat. It's important we keep our strength up. *My God!*' she said with her rollicking laugh. 'I sound like an actor in a disaster movie telling everyone to remain calm after the plane crashes in the jungle.'

The comment produced nervous smiles. A couple of people headed for the kitchen and, in short order, returned with a tray stacked with sandwiches.

Fear must have sharpened the scientists' hunger because they devoured the sandwiches like victims of a famine.

They were cleaning up when the mess hall reverberated with loud humming. Everyone stopped working and listened. After a few moments, the humming stopped, and the floor jolted as if jarred by an earthquake. There was a second jolt, and the room shuddered and swayed.

Those still standing fought to keep their balance, and there was an outcry of alarm, but the room went silent when the door burst open and two men armed with short-barrelled machine pistols cleared the way for Phelps.

Phelps grinned and said, 'Looks like we arrived too late for lunch.'

'What's happening to the lab?' Lois asked.

'Don't you remember what I said about going for a little ride? The lab's being moved to a new neighbourhood.'

Lois thought she must be going mad. 'That's *impossible.*'

'Not really. All we had to do was hitch the lab to a tow truck, so to speak.'

'What happened to our support ship?'

'It's out of action,' Phelps said. He issued an order to the gunmen: 'Take these folks to their quarters.'

The gunmen stepped aside to allow the scientists to pass.

Lois went to follow her colleagues through the door, but Phelps reached out and held her arm. He shut the door, pulled up a chair, and asked Lois to sit down. Then he sat in another chair and leaned on the backrest.

'I've been looking at your bio, Dr Mitchell. Pretty impressive.'

'Is this a job interview?' Lois said in an icy voice.

'I guess you could call it that,' Phelps said. 'You've been doing some work that my bosses are interested in.'

'Who are your bosses?'

'They're kinda shy. Just think of them as the folks that sign my pay cheque.'

'Did they pay you to kill Dr Logan?'

He frowned. 'That was an accident, pure and simple.'

'An accident like hijacking the lab, I suppose.'

'Look, Dr Mitchell, you may not like me, but it's best for you and your staff if we try to get along because we're going to be working together.'

'What do you mean?'

'When we get to the new location, you'll continue your research. You'll have free run of the lab except for the control room. You'll report your results to me and I'll pass them on to my bosses.'

'And if we refuse to work for you?'

'We'll just leave you down here on your own and withhold food and oxygen until you feel like working again. The rules are simple: If you go on strike, you will die. Not my idea, but that's the way it is.'

'What happens after we complete our research? Are you going to kill us?'

Phelps was a hard man and seasoned mercenary. But he had his own peculiar sense of honour that would not allow him to harm a woman, especially one as attractive as Lois Mitchell. There was no room in his business for personal attachments, but he vowed to keep a close eye on Lois.

'They hired me to hijack this nifty hideaway and to make sure you keep on working. My contract doesn't say anything about killing you or your friends. When the work is done, I plan to take you from the lab and drop you somewhere close to civilisation. We'll probably run into each other in a bar in Paris or Rome someday and have a big laugh over this.'

Lois had no desire to see Phelps ever again. More importantly, she had no idea whether Phelps was telling the truth or not. The strength seemed to flow out of her body. She felt as if she were being smothered, even though her lungs were hyperventilating. She concentrated on her breathing, and after a moment the hammering of her heart began to subside.

Lois rose from her chair. 'I'd like to go to my quarters now.'

Phelps nodded. 'I'll be in the control room if you need me.'

Lois made her way to her room. She crawled into her bunk and pulled the covers over her head, as if she could shut out the world she found herself in, but to no effect. Thankfully, after a few minutes, she fell into a fitful slumber.

THE B3'S PASSENGERS had been rushed into the *Beebe*'s sickbay, treated for bumps and bruises, and given a rubdown to get their circulation going. Then the medic buried them under piles of blankets and let them sleep.

When Joe Zavala awoke, the first thing he saw was Kurt Austin's face. 'Guess I'm not in heaven,' he croaked.

Austin held up a round, brown glass bottle with a wooden screw cap. *Tequila!* 'Maybe you are,' he said.

Zavala's lips parted in a cracked smile. 'A sight for sore eyes,' he said. 'When did you get back on board?'

'They peeled me out of my suit around half an hour ago,' Austin replied. 'Feel like telling me what happened?'

Zavala nodded. 'Let me warm my outside first, then I'll warm my inside.' It took fifteen minutes under the hottest shower he could stand before warmth finally seeped into Zavala's bones. Austin handed him a plastic cup of tequila through the shower-stall door, then went to his cabin, showered, and changed.

By the time Austin returned, Zavala was sitting in a chair sipping tequila. Austin helped him walk to the mess hall and ordered two pastramis on rye. They devoured their sandwiches, then Zavala sat back in his chair and described the harrowing plunge to the bottom of the ocean.

'I still can't figure out how that cable snapped,' Zavala said.

'It *didn't* snap,' Austin said. He opened the case he'd brought with him and extracted a laptop, which he set on the table. He showed Zavala the video the Hardsuit camera had filmed of his encounter with the AUV.

Zavala uttered an appreciative *Olé!* as Austin dodged the deadly pincers. 'Nice work, Kurt, but don't quit your day job to become a matador.'

'I don't intend to,' Austin said. 'Bullfighting technique aside, how hard would it be to programme an AUV to cut the bathysphere's cable?'

'Not hard at all. But it would take some sophistication to build the AUV in the first place. It's a slick piece of engineering. Very agile. Learns from its mistakes and is quick to adjust. Why do you think it attacked you after scuttling the B3?'

'Nothing personal. I think I was what the military calls collateral damage.' He pointed at the screen. 'Someone sicked Fido there on the bathysphere. It went for me because I happened to be in the neighbourhood.'

'Who would want to torpedo the B3 project?' Zavala said.

'I've been wondering the same thing. Let's see if Doc is awake.'

KANE WAS NOT only awake but quite chipper. He had showered and wrapped his body in a terry-cloth robe, and was sitting chatting with the medic.

'Now I know what it feels like to be a canned sardine,' he said. 'Thanks for the rescue, Kurt. I can't believe the cable broke.'

'It didn't break,' Zavala said. 'Kurt says that it was cut.'

'*Cut?*' Kane's lower jaw dropped open. 'I don't understand.'

Austin showed Kane the video of the AUV, and said, 'Can you think of anyone who would want to put the bathysphere on the bottom?'

Kane shook his head. 'Nope. What about you?'

'Joe and I are as much in the dark as you are,' Austin said.

Gannon's voice came over the ship's intercom. 'Call coming in for Dr Kane,' the captain said. 'Can he take it?'

Austin took the intercom's receiver from the wall and handed it to Kane.

Kane listened to someone on the line, and said, 'That's impossible! . . . Yes, of course . . . I'll be ready.'

When Kane had clicked off, Austin asked, 'Is everything all right?'

'Not really,' Kane said. His face had turned the colour of cold ashes. 'If you'll excuse me, I've got to talk to the captain.'

After he had left, Austin stared at the door for a moment, then shrugged and said to Zavala. 'You spent quality time with Doc . . . Did he say anything that might shed some light on this mystery?'

'He talked about jellyfish a lot.' Zavala dug into his memory. 'One other thing stood out. He said he was working on some research that could affect every man, woman and child on the planet.'

'Did he elaborate?'

Zavala shook his head. 'He said that if he told me what he'd been working on he would have to kill me.'

Austin's mouth turned up in a lopsided grin. 'He actually *said* that? Seems ironic, considering that you were minutes away from a grisly death.'

'We had a good laugh about it, but I think he was sincere.'

Austin pondered Zavala's reply. 'What do you make of that call Doc got?'

'He was upset, no doubt about that.'

Austin suggested that they talk to Kane again. As they stepped out onto the deck, they saw Kane and the captain walking in their direction. Kane was carrying his duffle bag.

'We were on our way to see you folks,' said the captain, pointing to the lights of an approaching vessel. 'That's a US Coast Guard cutter coming in for Dr Kane.'

The cutter stopped around a hundred yards from the ship. Austin helped Kane put his flotation vest on and walked him to the ramp at the stern, where a Zodiac inflatable boat was waiting. Kane thanked Austin, Joe and the captain for all their help.

'Sorry you have to leave, Doc,' Austin said.

'Not as sorry as I am to go.' He smiled, and added, 'Beebe's adventures pale by comparison to our dive.'

'Going back to Bonefish Key?'

'No, not for a while . . . I'll be in touch.'

Kane got into the Zodiac. The inflatable pushed off into the chop and bounced over to the Coast Guard vessel.

'We don't really know very much about Doc,' Zavala said. 'It's time we remedy that. I'll ask Paul and Gamay Trout to check into Bonefish Key.'

AT WASHINGTON'S REAGAN National Airport Kane's plane taxied to a section reserved for VIPs. A strapping young man sporting a military brush cut greeted Kane as he stepped onto the tarmac. Aviator sunglasses shaded the man's eyes, even though it was night-time, and his black suit would have sent a conspiracy theorist into a swoon.

The man led the way to a black Humvee, opened the rear door for Kane, then got in front next to the driver, who was also dressed like an undertaker. After leaving the airport, they raced along the George Washington Memorial Parkway as if there was no speed limit, skirted the city, and headed towards Rockville, Maryland.

Before long, the Humvee was pulling up outside a large office building. The sign out front identified the building as the Food and Drug Administration's headquarters.

Kane was escorted to a side entrance and then to a nondescript conference room where a dozen or so people sat round a long oak table. He went round the table shaking hands and was greeted with hellos or smiles from everyone except a stranger who identified himself as William Coombs, representing the White House.

Kane sat down next to a firm-jawed man wearing the uniform of a lieutenant in the US Navy. His name was Charley Casey.

'Hello, Max,' he said. 'How was your trip from Bermuda?'

'*Fast*,' Kane said. 'Hard for me to believe that a few hours ago I was a half-mile under the ocean.'

'I watched the dive on TV,' Casey said. 'Too bad you lost contact with the surface just when things started to get really interesting.'

'*Interesting* isn't the word for it,' Kane said. 'But it's nothing compared to the craziness about the lab. Any news?'

The lieutenant shook his head. 'We're still trying to make contact with the Locker, but there has been no response.'

'You might want to bring Dr Kane up to date on the details as we know them, Lieutenant Casey,' Coombs said.

The lieutenant nodded, opened a folder, and pulled out several sheets of paper. 'We've pieced together a scenario based on witness statements. Reports are still coming in, but here's what we have so far. Yesterday, at approximately fourteen hundred hours our time, a cruise missile was launched against the *Proud Mary*, the lab's support ship.'

Kane shook his head in disbelief. 'A *missile*? That can't be true!'

'I'm afraid it is. No one was killed, but a dozen were injured. The *Mary* got off a mayday and the Navy cruiser *Concord* rescued the survivors. Our guess is that what happened to the lab was sudden and catastrophic.'

Kane slumped in his chair as he tried to digest the implications of Casey's statement. He rallied after a moment, reminding himself that he was a scientist who dealt with facts, not suppositions.

'How long before we can check out the lab itself?' he asked.

'The *Concord* is sending down a remotely-operated vehicle,' Casey said. 'All we can do at this point is to wait for them to report in.'

'I hope the Navy is doing more than sitting on its hands,' Coombs said. 'Have you tracked the source of the missile?'

The lieutenant raised an eyebrow. During his naval career, Casey had frequently encountered clones of the White House man, with their inflated sense of power, and had learned to cloak his disdain under a polite veneer.

He prefaced his answer with a pleasant smile. 'The Navy can walk and chew gum at the same time, Mr Coombs,' he said. 'We've reconstructed the probable trajectory of the missile, and we've got planes and ships vectoring in on the launch position.'

'The White House isn't interested in trajectories or vectors, Lieutenant. Has the source of the launch been tracked? If it was launched by a foreign power, this could have serious international repercussions.'

'The missile could have come from a ship, a sub or a plane, sir, that's all we know at this time. But I can tell you one thing: this has all the earmarks of a well-organised and well-financed plan.'

'You won't get any argument from me on that score,' Kane said. 'About the same time the *Proud Mary* was being attacked, an attempt was made to sabotage the bathysphere dive.'

Kane waited for the noisy reaction to subside and then laid out the details of the attack on the sphere and Austin's rescue dive.

'This thing with the lab is starting to make sense now,' Coombs said. 'Someone wants to destroy our project.'

'That's my take on it, too,' Kane said. 'The people behind the attack must have figured that I'd be ripe for the picking in the bathysphere.'

Dr Sophie Pappas, the sole female member of the scientific board, asked, 'Why didn't these people wait until you were back on the lab? Instead of two simultaneous attacks, they only would have had to mount one.'

'Good question.' Coombs turned to Kane. 'Could the work of the lab go on without you?'

Kane nodded. '*Sure*. As director, my job is to ride herd on the project.

Lois Mitchell, my assistant, knows more about the actual nuts and bolts. She could easily wrap up this project in days without me. On the other hand, I know enough to reconstitute the work with the scientists remaining at Bonefish Key. It would take time, but I could get things moving again.'

'Not if you're dead,' Coombs said. 'But the lab's work could continue without you, which means that it may *not* have been destroyed.'

'Your theory makes sense in a nutty sort of way,' Kane said.

'Thank you. Have we informed the Chinese government of the attacks?'

'After the meeting, I'll contact Colonel Ming, my Chinese counterpart on this project,' Casey said. 'Perhaps he knows something that can help.'

'I hope so. This incident couldn't have come at a worse time,' Coombs said. He snapped his fingers, and his assistant went over to a large-screen computer at the end of the table and brought up a map of China.

'This red spot shows the village where the original outbreak occurred. These other three dots show that the epidemic has broken the quarantine and is spreading, possibly through the water table. The bug is leaping from village to village. Once it gets into the big cities, there will be no stopping it from spreading to the rest of the world.'

There was silence around the table for a moment, then Casey said, 'How long before it strikes an urban area?'

'The computers say seventy-two hours from midnight.'

'That still gives us time to stop it with the vaccine,' Casey said.

'Not without the lab.' Coombs leaned back in his chair and tented his fingers. 'Let's back up. Who would benefit from scuttling the work of the lab?'

'I'll pass on that one until we know more,' Kane said.

'OK, then,' Coombs said with a shrug. 'Maybe somebody can answer the question about how the attackers knew about the existence *and* location of a top-secret facility. The research was removed from Bonefish Key to the Locker so we could keep a tight lid on it and be closer to the resource.' He frowned. 'What about that woman at your lab? The scientist the Chinese sent over as a liaison?'

'Dr Lee?' Kane said. 'I'll vouch for her. She was a whistle-blower during the SARS epidemic. Her contributions to the project have been vital.'

'So were Oppenheimer's during the original Manhattan Project,' Coombs said. 'That didn't keep his loyalty from being compromised.'

'Before you indict Dr Lee, I'd like to point out that I was the only one at Bonefish Key who knew the location of the lab. That information could have come from an outside source. What about the security company?'

Lieutenant Casey said, 'The ocean-going cowboys might not have been as tightlipped as government operatives.' The lieutenant had made no secret of his opposition to outsourcing the security arrangements for the lab to a civilian company.

'You're out of line, Lieutenant.' Coombs's face flushed with anger.

The lieutenant's phone trilled, heading off an argument over the use of private warriors. He had a brief conversation with the caller and hung up.

'The ROV is on the lab site,' he announced. 'There is no trace of the lab, no wreckage to suggest that the Locker has been destroyed.'

'What's this all mean?' Coombs demanded.

Casey gave him a bleak smile. 'Taking a wild guess, Mr Coombs, I'd say this means that Davy Jones's Locker has been *hijacked*.'

'How could anything that big simply disappear?' Kane asked.

'You fellows figure out how this facility was hijacked under the nose of the US Navy,' Coombs said. 'I'm going to see that Dr Kane does a similar vanishing act.' He turned to Kane. 'You're going to a safe house, Dr Kane.' Coombs raised his hand to cut off Kane's protest. 'Sorry for the inconvenience, but someone wants you out of the picture.' The White House aide turned to the others. 'I'm going to recommend to the President that he prepare the country for a state of emergency,' he said. 'We'll contact the Centers for Disease Control and tell them this is the big one.'

'I'll inform Vice-President Sandecker directly,' Casey said. 'He maintains contacts at NUMA and will enlist them in the search for the lab.'

'Good idea,' Coombs said and, unable to resist the gibe, he added, 'Maybe their guy Austin can give the Navy some help doing its job.'

Chapter 4

A few minutes after one o'clock in the morning, an inflatable boat softly bumped against the hull of the *William Beebe* and four figures dressed in camouflage suits clambered up the side of the ship on rope ladders suspended from padded grapnel hooks. They vaulted over the rail one by one and dashed across the deck as silently as the shadows they resembled.

Except for the night watch on the bridge, the crew were sound asleep in their cabins. Austin was awake, however, and after staring at the ceiling, his mind churning, he got up and made his way to the bridge. He knew the night watch always kept a coffeepot brewing. He climbed the exterior stairs to the starboard bridge wing. A man's voice came through the partially open door. The words were growled rather than spoken, and had an accent Austin couldn't place, but one word stood out from the others. *Kane.*

Austin's well-honed instincts came into play. He moved away from the door and edged up to a window. He saw Third Mate Marla Hayes, a male crewman and Captain Gannon standing together in the pilothouse. The captain must have been rousted from his bunk because he had a jacket on over his pyjamas and slippers on his feet.

Four figures wearing commando outfits were gathered round the seamen. Hoods covered the faces of three of the commandos, the fourth having removed his to reveal an Asian face with jade-green eyes and a clean-shaven head. All four cradled short-barrelled automatic weapons, carried side arms, and had knives hanging at their waists.

'I'll tell you again: Dr Kane is no longer on this ship,' Gannon was saying. 'He left hours ago.'

The unhooded commando reacted with a short, stabbing blow to the captain's solar plexus. 'Do not lie to me!' he snapped.

The captain doubled over, but he managed to gasp out a reply. 'Kane is not here. Search the whole damned ship, if you don't believe me.'

'No, Captain,' his assailant said. '*You* will search the ship. Tell everyone to come up to the deck.'

Gannon reluctantly gave the order over the *Beebe*'s public-address system for all officers and crew to assemble on the fantail.

Gannon's assailant and two of his accomplices herded their prisoners towards the door leading out onto the wing. Austin saw the move and climbed up a ladder that provided access to the radio tower on the pilothouse roof. From his perch, he watched the group descend to the main deck. He climbed back down and peered in a window. One attacker had been left to guard the ship's control centre.

Austin descended the stairs to a lower deck, quietly opened the door to Zavala's cabin and stepped inside. 'Didn't you hear the captain tell the crew to gather on deck?' he asked.

Zavala rubbed the sleep out of his eyes, and sat up. 'I heard him,' he said, 'but I'm not crew, so I stayed in the sack.'

'Your skill at splitting hairs may have saved your butt,' Austin said.

Zavala suddenly came to life. 'What's going on, Kurt?'

'Uninvited company. A bunch of heavily armed gentlemen looking for Kane. Gannon told them he's not on the ship, but they didn't believe him.'

Zavala muttered something in Spanish, then bounded out of bed and pulled on a pair of jeans and a windbreaker. 'What sort of firepower are we dealing with?' he asked.

Austin told him about the machine guns and pistols. Zavala frowned. Neither man had weapons.

'We'll have to improvise,' Austin said.

Austin checked the passageway. Seeing it was clear, he led the way to the bridge, with Zavala behind. The commando was still inside. Austin pointed to his own chest, then to the roof ladder. Zavala nodded. As soon as Austin was on the roof, Zavala tapped on the window and waved at the commando, who burst onto the wing with his machine gun at waist level.

'*Buenas noches*,' Zavala said, brandishing his friendliest smile.

Zavala's Latin charm fell on deaf ears. The man pointed his gun at Zavala's midsection. Zavala raised his hands. The man was reaching for a radio at his belt when Austin called down from the roof.

'Yoo-hoo,' Austin said, 'I'm up here.'

The man looked up and saw a steel-haired gargoyle grinning down at him. He brought his gun up, but Austin leapt off the roof and landed with his full weight on the man's shoulders. The man folded like a rag doll under the impact and the machine gun flew from his hand. Zavala dived for the weapon and deftly snatched it up.

Austin prodded the man with his toe and when there was no response, he rolled him over onto his back and pulled the mask back to reveal broad-faced Asian features. Blood drooled from the man's mouth.

'He's going to need a good orthodontist when he wakes up,' Zavala said.

Austin felt for a pulse. 'He'd be better off seeing the undertaker.'

They dragged the body inside the bridge, and Austin radioed a quick mayday. Then they descended to the deck. Crouching low and taking advantage of the shadows, they made their way to the fantail. The powerful floodlights used to illuminate night operations bathed the deck in bright light. The crew and officers were huddled in a tight knot, guarded by two of the commandos. The clean-shaven man had his machine gun in one hand while with the other he was brandishing a photo of Kane.

'Tell me where this man is hiding,' he said, 'and we will let you go.'

When no one took him up on the offer, he strode over and grabbed an arm that belonged to Marla. He forced her to her knees, and said, 'If Kane does not appear in five minutes, I will kill this woman. Then we will kill one of your crew every minute until Kane comes out of hiding.'

Austin lay belly-down on the deck next to Zavala, trying to train his sights on the commando. 'I can't nail Bullethead,' Austin whispered. 'Even if I could, his pals might go on a shooting spree.'

'What we need is a *tank*,' Zavala agreed.

Austin stared at his friend. 'You're a *genius*, Joe.'

'I am? Oh, hell,' he said as if something had occurred to him. 'The Humongous? That's an ROV, Kurt, not an army tank.'

'It's better than nothing, which is what we've got,' Austin said.

He quickly outlined a plan.

Zavala saluted to show that he understood, then sprinted off to the remote-control centre. Austin slipped through a door to the ship's garage.

Built with treads that allowed it to crawl along the sea bottom, the Humongous was about the size of a Land Rover. It carried a battery of cameras, magnetometers, sonar, water samplers and other instruments.

Austin stood in front of the ROV, waiting, as precious seconds went by. Then the vehicle's searchlights snapped on, the electric motors began to hum, and the mechanical manipulator arms waggled to signal that Zavala was at the controls.

Austin went behind the ROV and climbed on top. Inside the control room Zavala gave the vehicle power. The Humongous lurched forwards and crashed into the double doors, pushing them wide open. As it emerged onto the deck, Zavala waved the manipulators round and worked the claws, adding to the dramatic effect.

Marla's would-be executioner whirled around to see what looked like a giant crustacean heading directly for him. Marla took advantage of the distraction and ran for safety. One of the other commandos saw the third mate trying to escape and aimed his weapon at her fleeing figure.

Austin snapped off a stuttering fusillade that stitched a row of holes across the man's midsection. The clean-shaven man and the other commando took cover behind a crane and peppered the oncoming Humongous with hundreds of rounds. Fragments of plastic, foam and metal filled the air until, finally, the hail of bullets triggered an electrical fire.

Austin gagged on the acrid smoke filling his nostrils. He could feel the Humongous veering drunkenly and disintegrating beneath him. He dropped off the back and dived behind a tall air vent, hit the deck, and rolled several feet. He stopped and fired a blast directly above the stroboscopic muzzle flashes in front of him. It was a lucky hit. One of the guns went silent. Austin kept on shooting until he had emptied his gun of bullets.

A moment later, the clean-shaven man took advantage of the lull and ran for the side of the ship, away from the glaring lights on the fantail.

Austin stepped out into the open, pointed his empty gun at the fleeing man, and yelled, 'Hey, Bullethead! Don't leave so soon. Fun's just starting.'

The man stopped and turned to face Austin. The Humongous was now ablaze, and the man's face and strange green eyes were visible in the light of the flickering flames. A smile came to his evil features.

'You're bluffing,' he said. 'You would have shot me if you had the chance.'

'*Try* me,' Austin said, squinting with one eye as if taking aim.

Either the man didn't buy Austin's bluff or he didn't care. He let out a snarl and dashed towards the railing, firing from the hip as he ran. Austin ducked for cover, and when he dared look again, the man had disappeared. He heard the sound of an outboard motor starting and ran to the railing. Within seconds the boat had disappeared into the darkness.

He was listening to the motor fading into the night when there was a new sound on the deck behind him.

Footfalls.

Austin pivoted into a crouch, only to relax when he saw why the man had decided to bolt. Zavala had emerged from the control centre and was trotting towards him. They both grabbed fire extinguishers from a bulkhead and sprayed the Humongous with foam until the blaze was under control.

Austin went over to the bodies lying on deck and removed the masks, revealing cruel faces with Asian features.

'Now we know why the B3 was attacked. Doc Kane . . . We've got to talk to him.'

'Doc made it pretty clear that his work was none of our business.'

Austin's lips tightened in the smile that, in Zavala's experience, had always presaged trouble. 'That's too bad,' he said. 'Because I'm *making* it our business.'

Shanghai, China

The licence plate on the silver Mercedes S65 AMG sedan that emerged from the garage under Pyramid Trading Company's fifty-storey building displayed only the number 2, suggesting that the car's owner enjoyed extreme wealth. Vanity plates were auctioned off for millions of dollars to affluent and superstitious bidders who believed that the low numbers would bring good luck.

To reinforce that good luck, the car's skin was fashioned from rocket-proof armour plate, its tinted-glass windows were bulletproof, and an armed guard sat in the front seat next to the driver. For added security, it was sandwiched between two Mercedes G55 AMG SUVs, each carrying a driver and five guards armed with lightweight Type 79 submachine guns.

The motorcade sped along the banks of the Yangtze River, then turned off the highway and headed towards the destitute neighbourhoods that are the embarrassing underside of the largest and wealthiest city in the People's Republic of China. The procession plunged deep into the warren of slums, entering a hellish landscape that was so burnt-out and devoid of human life even the most desperate slum-dwellers avoided it. The vehicles pulled up next to an abandoned brick warehouse. Weathered plywood covered the windows, broken glass littered the oil-soaked parking lot, but the razor wire topping the electrified chain-link fence that gleamed in the headlights was brand new.

The man riding shotgun in the sedan's front seat got out and opened the rear door. The lone passenger emerged and walked briskly towards a loading platform, accompanied by his bodyguard. As the men climbed the platform stairs, a door on well-greased rollers slid silently open. They entered the warehouse and the door slid shut.

The passenger from the Mercedes was a small man dressed in a blue hand-tailored suit and a neatly knotted silk tie. Silver hair, neatly parted, and black-plastic-framed glasses gave Wen Lo an avuncular air of bland respectability more befitting a desk clerk in a three-star hotel than the head of a giant real-estate and financial consortium that was the cover for global prostitution, gambling and drug operations.

Waiting inside the warehouse were three men in blue-green hospital gowns and a pair of heavily armed guards carrying tasers, side arms and clubs that hung from their wide leather belts.

A weasel-faced man dressed for the operating room stepped forward. 'An honour to have you visit us, sir,' he said, giving a quick bow of the head.

Wen Lo responded with a barely perceptible nod. 'Tell me how your work is coming, Dr Wu,' he said.

'We are making progress,' Wu said with cheerful optimism.

Although the lower part of Wen Lo's face smiled, his jade-green eyes didn't mirror the expression. 'Please show me your progress, Dr Wu.'

'I'd be glad to, sir.'

Wu led Wen Lo and his bodyguard through two sets of airtight chambers and along a corridor that ended in a thick glass door. Wu pressed an electrical switch that unlocked the door and the three men stepped into a cellblock.

As they walked between the dozen cells a few inmates pushed their faces close to the barred openings and called out to Wu and his guests to help them.

Wen Lo, his face devoid of pity, turned to Wu. 'What is the source of these lab rats?' he asked.

Dr Wu, who was rewarded handsomely for his work, had convinced himself that his research was for the good of mankind. Although his work required that he suppress his humanity under a thin veneer of medical non-involvement, the coldness of Wen Lo's question stunned him.

'As medical professionals, we prefer to call them *subjects*. This lab is surrounded by a no-man's-land that even the most desperate slum-dwellers avoid but it's easy to lure them in with promises of food and money. People in the slums rarely report the missing, and the police never follow up.'

Wen Lo said, 'Show me the next phase.'

Wu escorted the two men out of the cellblock to a black-walled room. One wall was half glass, like the viewing area for a maternity ward. Visible through the glass were a number of beds, each occupied and enclosed in a transparent cylinder. Figures in white protective suits moved like ghosts among the beds, checking electronic monitors and IV tubes.

'The subjects have been injected with the new pathogen and are proceeding through the stages of the virus,' Wu said.

'If the subjects were left on their own, they would die?' Wen Lo asked.

'Within twenty-four hours. The disease is always fatal.'

Wen Lo asked to see the next phase.

They set off down another corridor and entered a second observation area similar to the first. The room on the other side of the glass held eight gurneys enclosed by cylinders. On the gurneys were four men and four women. Their faces looked as if they had been carved from mahogany, and it was difficult to tell if they were alive or dead.

'This is phase three,' Wu said. 'These subjects show the dark rash that is typical of the virus, but they are still alive.'

'You call these ripe vegetables in your little garden *alive*, Dr Wu?'

'They are still breathing, and their vitals are sound. The experimental cure is helping.'

'Would you like to be infected and helped by your cure, Dr Wu?'

Wu couldn't miss the implied threat. Sweat trickled down his back. 'No, I would not, sir. The cure is imperfect at this time. The virus's ability to adapt to any treatment we try has made our task difficult.'

'In other words, you have failed.'

'Success is possible,' Wu said. 'But it will take time.'

'Time is the thing we have in little supply, Wu. But don't worry, we are near to developing a highly promising cure at our offshore facility. You will go there to make sure the work is satisfactory.' Wen Lo turned back to stare at the forms on the gurneys. 'Dispose of this material. The subjects in the cellblock too. We will find our way out.'

AN HOUR LATER, Wen Lo got off the elevator on the top floor of the Pyramid Trading Company building, where he had a penthouse office suite. He made his way across an enormous room decorated in French Empire style.

Floor-to-ceiling windows lined one long wall, but he paid no attention to Shanghai's tapestry of lights. He stood in front of a tall wall cabinet and barked a password at a hidden voice-identification device. The cabinet rolled aside to reveal a metal door.

Wen Lo pressed his hand against a panel that examined the whorls of his fingertips and the lines of his palm, and the door opened with a click, admitting him into a circular room. The only furniture was a plastic-and-aluminium table and three chairs. The blandness of the room obscured its function as a communications centre, its walls and ceiling containing a sophisticated system of microphones, projectors, transmitters and receivers.

Wen Lo settled into a cushioned chair, looked across the table at the other two chairs, and uttered a single word. 'Begin.'

The LED lighting in the ceiling dimmed except for a cone-shaped shaft of light that illuminated each chair. The air in one shaft seemed to shimmer as if superheated, becoming wavy, then darkening with tiny swirling motes, until a fuzzy silhouette formed, amorphous at first, then more solid, outlining first shoulders and then a head. Details filled in: eyes and nose, flesh and clothing. In short order, Wen Lo was looking at a three-dimensional laser projection of a man so real that he could almost touch it.

The man's face was the mirror image of Wen Lo's, which was not surprising, because they were two of a set of triplets. They both had the same high forehead, beetled brow and unfathomable eyes, but the projected man's scalp was clean-shaven. Where the menace in Wen Lo's face was understated, the projected face had an unvarnished, street-thug toughness around the mouth and chin that suggested barely restrained violence.

'Good evening, Brother Chang,' Wen Lo said.

'Good evening to you, Brother Wen Lo. Number One is about to join us.'

The air under the third light went through the same wavy sequence. The hologram that appeared in the chair was of a man dressed in a red silk robe and wearing a round, high-brimmed hat. The face was long and lean, with arched brows over a prominent forehead, cunning cat-green eyes and a long, thin moustache that draped down below his chin.

Wen Lo clapped his hands upon recognising the apparition. *'Bravo!'* he said. 'Dr Fu Manchu, if I am not mistaken.'

The hologram responded with a knife-edged chuckle. 'Congratulations, Wen Lo,' Fu Manchu said. 'You are looking at the master criminal who is preparing to unleash the Yellow Peril against the world.'

This silken embodiment of evil was a clever illusion carved in light by the latest in computer and laser technology. The system that brought the triplets together for their meetings could be manipulated, using data on figures real or imagined, to create any image desired. But although Fu Manchu was an illusion, the voice behind the leering archfiend belonged to a flesh-and-blood person who ran a criminal empire that the fictional villain could only have dreamed of.

In the tradition of the age-old crime cults known as the Triads, the triplets who ran the organisation were ranked by numbers rather than names, given them according to their order of birth. Wen Lo was *Two*, and he directed the Triad's criminal enterprises behind a thin screen of respectability. Chang was *Three*, and he was in charge of the global network's security, including the gangs that infested Chinatowns in every major city. The triplet behind the Fu Manchu mask served as CEO, overseeing criminal and legitimate operations, a responsibility that went with the name *One*.

'I understand that your expedition to Bermuda was less than successful, Chang. Dr Kane escaped from the bottom of the ocean.'

'Our machine cut the bathysphere's cable. There was no way anyone could have saved it at that depth.'

'Apparently, *someone* did. His name is Kurt Austin. The television reports say he is an engineer with NUMA. Also, how do you explain your botched attack on the NUMA ship?'

Chang scowled. 'We met unexpected resistance,' he said.

'We cannot afford any more slip-ups. We would not be dealing with this situation if you had kept a closer eye on things at your lab, Wen Lo.'

The third triplet had been enjoying the discomfiture of his brother, but now it was his turn to squirm under the cold gaze of the archvillain. 'I accept full responsibility. The laboratory guard who brought the virus to his home province did not follow the proper decontamination safeguards.'

'Has the virus spread further?' Fu Manchu asked.

'It has broken past the quarantine. The government is trying to contain it.'

'Not good,' Fu Manchu said. 'Our plan was to release the virus selectively when we had a vaccine to control it. We are trying to destabilise the government and profit from the spread of the disease. Wiping out the human race would be rather counterproductive, don't you think? Is there any word of Dr Kane?'

'He never returned to Bonefish Key. He seems to have disappeared.'

'His disappearance doesn't concern me as much as the possibility that he now is aware that he is a target. Fortunately, he is no longer vital to the completion of the project. But the work cannot be allowed to regerminate at Bonefish Key.'

'The only one who can reconstitute the project, other than Kane, is Dr Song Lee, the representative the People's Republic sent to Bonefish Key to work with US scientists,' Chang said. 'She is about to be disposed of.'

'See that it is accomplished quickly and cleanly,' Fu Manchu said. 'And you, Brother Wen Lo, what is the status of the vaccine?'

'The vaccine will soon be a reality, and we can proceed with the next phase. I have ordered our land lab closed and its contents liquidated.'

'Very good. That's all for now.'

Fu Manchu bowed his head. His evil face began to disintegrate, and then vanished. Moments later, the second hologram vanished too.

Wen Lo rose from his seat and left the room. There was much to do.

Chapter 5

The Bermuda Coast Guard cutter had responded quickly to Austin's mayday. After a quick look at the bodies littering the aft deck, the guardsmen hurriedly called in the Marine Police Service. Within hours, a six-man crime-scene investigation team arrived at the NUMA ship, and began interviewing the crew.

'Is there any chance the men were pirates?' Detective-Superintendent Colin Randolph asked.

'These guys weren't interested in the scientific equipment that pirates normally go after when they hit a research vessel,' Austin replied. 'They knew Dr Kane had been aboard and they were looking for him.'

'I'll put this down as an isolated attack, then. I suspect that the assailants' boat is long gone. I'd like full statements from you gentlemen and every crew member on board.'

As Zavala took the first interview, Austin walked a short distance from the activity on the aft deck, and punched in a number from his phone list.

A low, cool female voice answered his call. 'Hi, Kurt,' said Gamay Morgan-Trout, 'congratulations. Paul and I watched the bathysphere dive on TV until the transmission got cut off. How was the briny deep?'

'Briny and deep and memorable. I'll tell you about it later. Sorry to interrupt your sabbatical, but I need a favour. I'd like you or Paul to wangle an invitation to the Bonefish Key marine lab in Florida. They discourage visitors, but if anyone can get in it's you.'

'Didn't the director of Bonefish Key make the B3 dive with Joe?'

'Yes. His name is Max Kane. But don't expect any help from him.'

'I'll give it a try, Kurt. What exactly should I be looking for?'

'I don't know. Anything that strikes you as funny.'

Gamay responded with a soft chuckle. 'I love the crisp specificity of your directive, Kurt.'

'It's a management course they teach called Cover Your Ass 101. The first lesson in CYA is that if anything goes wrong, it's not your fault. Call me when you or Paul get to Bonefish Key.'

Austin clicked off, burning with impatience. Until he and Zavala managed to extricate themselves from the police investigation, Paul and Gamay Trout would have to be the team's eyes and ears.

PAUL TROUT WAS NEAR the end of the seminar he was leading on global warming when his cellphone began to vibrate. Without missing a beat, he reached into his jacket pocket, shut off the phone, and threw the next graph up on the projection screen, only to hear a soft ripple of laughter behind his back. He turned, curious at what could be so humorous about an ocean-salinity pie chart.

No one was looking at the chart. Every eye in the room was staring out of the window at an attractive red-haired woman who was on the lawn doing jumping jacks and waving a cellphone in the air at the same time.

A seminar participant sniggered. 'Who *is* that crazy woman?'

A faint smile came to Trout's lips. 'I'm afraid that crazy woman is my wife. Please excuse me.'

A quiet gasp of disbelief followed Trout's exit from the room, but he was used to such reactions. He was a good-looking young man with large hazel-coloured eyes and light brown hair neatly parted down the middle and combed back at the temples, Gatsby style. In a tailored suit that draped his six-foot-eight physique perfectly, he was impeccably dressed as usual. But while he displayed a sly sense of humour, people often found his serious demeanour at odds with that of his more vivacious wife.

Trout stepped out into the hall and phoned his wife. 'Quite the show you put on for my seminar on climate change,' he said in his dry New England tone. 'The body temperature of every male in the room rose twenty degrees. Your little striptease may have set off a new round of global warming.'

'Sorry,' Gamay said lightly, 'but Kurt called and you weren't answering your phone. Kurt needs somebody to go to Florida to look into the Bonefish Key Marine Center. He'd like us to snoop around and let him know if anything there strikes us as *funny* . . . As in *peculiar*.'

'It's going to be awkward trying to get out of my schedule,' Paul said.

'I've finished my research dives,' Gamay said. 'While you wrap up, I'll head off to Florida. You can follow when you're done.'

Paul glanced at his watch. 'Let's discuss it over lunch,' he said. 'I'll meet you in the cafeteria after I cool down my seminar group.'

He had been amused but not surprised at his wife's attention-getting technique. Her open personality was the opposite of Trout's New England reserve, but they had been immediately attracted to each other from the time they first met at the Scripps Institution of Oceanography in La Jolla, California. Paul was studying for his PhD in ocean science, while Gamay had changed her field of interest from marine archaeology to marine biology and was working towards her doctorate also.

NUMA's former director, James Sandecker, had recognised their unique talents and when they graduated he asked them to join the Special Assignments Team under Austin's leadership. After their last assignment, they had been invited to come back to Scripps and had jumped at the chance.

Trout ran through the rest of his presentation. Gamay was waiting for him in the cafeteria when he was done.

'It's a good thing I'm leaving this place,' she complained, dipping a

French fry into a puddle of ketchup. 'I must have put on twenty pounds since we got here. I'm blowing up like a tick.'

Paul rolled his eyes. Gamay was up at six every day for her five-mile run that burned off any possible trace of culinary excess. Although she was only two inches short of six feet tall, she carried no more than 130 pounds on her small-hipped frame.

Paul eyed a tall glass that contained a frothy strawberry concoction. 'Maybe you shouldn't have the frappé,' he said.

Gamay brushed a strand of dark red hair out of her eyes and flashed a dazzling smile. 'Last one . . . promise.'

'Easy promise to keep, now that you're leaving town. What do you know about Bonefish Key?'

Gamay took a long sip and dabbed the pink moustache off her upper lip with a napkin. 'Only what I've read in scientific journals. It's on the west coast of Florida. They've made some discoveries that have led to patents in the field of biomedicine.'

Furrowing his brow, Paul said, 'Why not go through Kane?'

'I asked Kurt the same question. He said not to expect help from Kane. He'll explain later.'

'You could try using your NUMA bona fides to leverage a tour of the place.'

'I thought of that. The NUMA connection might get me in the front door, but I don't know if I'd get the kind of access that would do us any good.'

Paul nodded in agreement. 'You'd get the VIP treatment and a quick tour by a PR flack. Kurt apparently wants us to take a look behind the scenes.'

'That's OK, I think I can wangle an overnight stay.'

'While you work on that, I'll see if I can get you on a flight to Florida first thing tomorrow.'

The next morning, Paul drove Gamay to the airport, gave her a goodbye kiss, and said he would see her in a couple of days.

THE FLIGHT WAS SMOOTH, and Gamay used some of the time to read up about Bonefish Key. When the plane landed at Fort Myers Airport late in the afternoon, the efficient NUMA travel bureau had arranged for a van to deliver her to the Pine Island ferry landing.

A twin-hulled powerboat was tied up at the dock. The grizzled man at the wheel had a nut-brown tan that only partly hid the creases in his genial face.

'I guess you're going out to Bonefish,' he said. 'I'm Dooley Greene.

I make runs for the marine centre, which kinda makes me the official greeter.'

Gamay tossed her duffle bag in the double-hull and stepped on board with the sureness of someone who spent a lot of time on boats.

'I'm Dr Morgan-Trout,' she said, shaking his hand. 'Please call me Gamay.'

'Thanks, Dr Gamay,' he said, unable to avoid the honorific. Emboldened by her friendliness, he added, 'Pretty name. Unusual too.'

'My father was a wine nut. He named me after his favourite grape.'

Dooley uncleated the line and pushed the boat away from the dock. They headed out into the bay.

'How long have you worked for the centre?' Gamay asked.

'I was the dockmaster for the Bonefish Key Inn back when every fisherman and boater on the waterway used to hang out at the bar. After the hotel got beat up by Hurricane Charlie, the owner went bankrupt. When the marine centre bought the property, Dr Kane asked me to run the water taxi and carry supplies.' He reached into his shirt pocket and pulled out a business card. 'I don't live on the island,' he said. 'Call me if you want to get off it. Phones don't work there unless you climb up the water tower.'

She took the card. 'Dr Mayhew called me from the island.'

'They got a radiotelephone set-up for the mucky-mucks to use.'

The boat left the open water and wound its way through a green maze of mangroves. Eventually, they rounded a turn and headed to an island that appeared more solid than its surroundings. The pointed top of the white water tower Dooley had mentioned rose above the trees like a coolie hat. He tied the boat to the small dock and turned off the motor.

A grassy slope rose up to a patio and the verandah of a white-stucco building. It was practically hidden in the sunbaked palmettos, the light breeze carrying their damp perfume to Gamay's nostrils. A snowy egret waded along the shore. It was a picture-postcard perfect Florida scene, but the unearthly stillness gave her an uneasy feeling.

'It's so quiet,' she said, speaking in a whisper. 'Almost spooky.'

Dooley chuckled. 'The lodge is built on an Indian mound. The island belonged to the Calusa before the white man killed them off. People still pick up on the bad stuff.'

'Are you saying the island is haunted, Dooley?'

'No Indian ghosts, if that's what you mean. But everything that's been built here seems to have come to a bad end.'

Gamay picked up her duffle bag and climbed up on the dock. 'Let's hope that doesn't include *my* short visit, Dooley.'

She had tried to leaven the gloomy mood with her joke, but Dooley wasn't smiling when he followed her up on the dock.

'Welcome to paradise, Dr Gamay.'

AS DOOLEY ESCORTED GAMAY down the dock to the island, they encountered a young Asian woman coming their way.

''Afternoon, Dr Song Lee,' Dooley said. 'I got your kayak all ready for you before I made my run to Pine Island.'

''Thank you, Dooley.'

Lee's eyes darted to Gamay, who assessed her expression as neither friendly nor unfriendly. Neutral, maybe.

'This is Dr Morgan-Trout,' Dooley said. 'She's visiting the island for a couple of days. Maybe you two could go kayaking together.'

'Yes, of course,' Lee answered without enthusiasm. 'Pleased to meet you, Doctor. Enjoy your stay.' She brushed Gamay's extended hand with hers, and continued along the dock.

Dooley stopped at the end of the dock. 'This is as far as I'm allowed to go,' he said. 'Give me a call if you need me.'

Gamay thanked Dooley and climbed the stairs to the patio. The front door of the lodge burst open just then, and a man in a white lab coat came springing down the stairs from the verandah to the patio.

'Dr Morgan-Trout, I presume,' he said, flashing a quick smile. The handshake he gave Gamay was as limp and damp as a dead fish. 'I'm Dr Charles Mayhew, acting keeper of this madhouse while Dr Kane is away.'

Gamay smiled. 'Thank you for having me as a guest on the island.'

'Our pleasure,' Mayhew oozed. 'You have no idea how thrilled we were to learn that NUMA had invited Dr Kane to dive in the bathysphere.'

'Will I get a chance to meet Dr Kane?' Gamay asked.

'He's on a field project,' Mayhew said. 'I'll show you your room.'

They climbed to the verandah and passed through double doors to a lobby. Beyond the lobby was a large, sunny dining room furnished with rattan chairs and tables of dark wood. Screened-in windows wrapped around the room on three sides. A smaller room off the dining room was called the Dollar Bar, harking back to the days when guests signed dollar bills and stuck them on the wall, Mayhew explained.

Gamay's simple room was off a hallway a few steps from the bar. It had natural wood walls, an old metal-frame bed and a dresser, and it projected a look of seedy comfort. Gamay put her duffle on the bed.

'Happy hour starts in the Dollar Bar at five,' Mayhew said. 'Make yourself at home. If you'd like to take a stroll, there are nature trails all over the island.' He bounded off with his bouncy stride.

After a refreshing cat nap, Gamay took a shower, slipped into white shorts and a pale green cotton blouse that complemented her dark red hair, and made her way to the Dollar Bar. About a dozen people in lab coats were sitting round tables.

Dr Mayhew got up from a corner table, came over to the bar, and greeted Gamay with his quick smile. 'What can I get you to drink, Dr Trout?'

'A Gibson would be fine,' she replied. 'Straight up, please.'

Mayhew relayed the order to the bartender, who shook the gin, poured, and put three onions on a stick, making it a Gibson martini instead of a martini with olives.

Mayhew guided Gamay and her drink back to the corner table. Pulling out a chair, he introduced her to the four people seated round the table, explaining that they were all part of the centre's development team.

'What brings you to the Island of Dr Moreau?' asked the lone female at the table, who introduced herself as Dory Bennett, a toxicologist.

'I heard about this wonderful bar.' Gamay glanced around at the practically bare walls, and with a straight face added, 'It seems that a dollar doesn't go as far as it used to.'

There was a ripple of laughter around the table.

'A woman scientist with a sense of humour,' said Isaac Klein, a chemist.

'Dr Klein, are you saying I don't have a sense of humour?' Dr Bennett asked. 'I find your scientific papers *very* funny.'

The good-natured ribbing drew another round of laughter.

Dr Mayhew said, 'Dr Bennett forgot to mention that the centre's assistant director is a woman as well: Lois Mitchell. When she's here, the island is not as male dominated as might appear at first glance.'

'Will I get to meet her?' Gamay asked.

'Not until she gets back from—' Dr Bennett caught herself midsentence. 'She's away . . . in the field.'

Gamay pretended she hadn't seen Mayhew gently nudge Bennett's arm and looked around the room. 'Is this the lab's entire staff?' she asked.

'This is a skeleton crew,' Mayhew said. 'Most of our colleagues are working in the field.'

'It must be a very large field,' she said in a lame attempt at humour.

There was deafening silence.

Finally, Mayhew said, 'Yes, I suppose it is.' He glanced around at the others, who took his comment as a signal to force grins on their faces.

'I met another woman on the dock,' Gamay said. 'Dr Lee.'

'Oh, yes, Dr Song Lee,' Mayhew said. 'I didn't count her because she's a visiting scientist and not regular staff. She's extremely shy, and even dines in her cabin by herself.'

Chuck Hallum, who headed the immunology section, said, 'Speaking of off-islanders, what *really* brings you to Bonefish Key?'

'My interest in marine biology,' Gamay said. 'I've read about the groundbreaking work you've been doing in biomedicine. I was planning to visit friends in Tampa and couldn't pass up the opportunity to take a look.'

A bell rang to announce dinner, and they moved into the dining room. The chef had prepared fresh-caught redfish, with a pecan crust and seared to perfection, washed down with a French Sauvignon Blanc. Conversation around the table was on the light side, with little talk about work.

After dinner, the scientists moved out onto the verandah. There was more chatter, almost none of it having to do with the lab. As darkness deepened, most drifted off to their cabins.

'We hit the sack early here,' Mayhew explained, 'and we're up with the sun.'

He asked Gamay a few more polite questions about her work at NUMA, then excused himself and said he would see her at breakfast.

Gamay decided to call Paul to let him know she had arrived and, remembering what Dooley had said, she followed a path to the foot of the water tower. She started up the tower, only to stop in midstep. A female voice was coming from the platform, speaking in what sounded like Chinese.

The conversation ended after a minute or two, and Gamay heard footfalls descending. She backed down the ladder and hid behind a palmetto. She watched Dr Lee descend the ladder, then hurry off down the path.

Gamay followed the path to the cabins. All were dark except for one, and, as she watched, the light in its window went out. She stood there looking at the darkened cabin, wondering what to do.

She decided to go back to the water tower. There, she left a voicemail on Paul's phone, saying she had arrived. Then she headed back to her room.

She sat on her screened-in porch and tallied up the impressions of the few short hours she had spent on the island. Mayhew and his people were laughingly clumsy in their attempts to be evasive whenever talk touched on Dr Kane, the centre's mysterious field project, or the whereabouts of the rest of the staff. She was intrigued, too, by the young Asian scientist who had given her the cold shoulder at the dock.

As she sat in the darkness listening to the sounds of the night, Gamay was beginning to understand why Dooley hadn't smiled when he welcomed her to paradise.

DETECTIVE-SUPERINTENDENT RANDOLPH seemed to be everywhere at once. He hovered over the forensic experts who were collecting evidence, listened to the witness interviews for discrepancies, and went over the *Beebe* with a fine-tooth comb. He and his team worked late into the night before they took advantage of the temporary sleeping quarters that Gannon had arranged for them.

The next day, the bodies were transported to the mainland for autopsies. Austin and Zavala cleaned up the bathysphere then supervised the removal of the wreckage of the Humongous by crane from the deck of the *Beebe* to a carrier boat, then to a garage on the mainland.

Satisfied that this last piece of major physical evidence was in police hands, Randolph thanked Gannon and his crew for their cooperation and said the ship was free to leave.

He gave Austin and Zavala a ride in his car to the airport, and by late afternoon Zavala, an experienced pilot, was taxiing a small NUMA jet up to a hangar at Reagan National Airport in Washington. Austin and Zavala then went their separate ways, agreeing to touch base the following day.

AUSTIN LIVED IN A CONVERTED Victorian boathouse, part of an estate that he had bought when he was commuting to CIA headquarters in nearby Langley. At the time, it had reeked of mildew and old age, but its location on the banks of the Potomac River persuaded him to open his wallet and spend countless hours of his own fixing it up.

Following his usual ritual, Austin dropped his bag in the hall, went in the kitchen and grabbed a bottle of beer from the refrigerator, then walked out on the deck to fill his lungs with the damp-mud fragrance of the Potomac.

He tossed back the beer, and then went into his study. He plucked a Miles Davis record from his extensive jazz collection and put it on the turntable. Then he plunked himself down in front of his computer. While the details were still fresh in his mind, he wanted to pound out a first draft of his report on the attack on the B3.

Shortly before midnight, he crawled into his bed high in the boathouse turret. He awoke refreshed around seven the next morning. He made a pot of Jamaican coffee and toasted a frozen bagel he found in his pitifully empty refrigerator. Thus fortified, he returned to his report.

After a quick review, he sent his words off on electronic wings to NUMA director Dirk Pitt. Then he showered, shaved and called Paul Trout, who told him that he had received a voicemail from Gamay confirming her arrival at Bonefish Key but had yet to talk to her.

Austin then gave Trout a condensed version of his report.

'Now I know why you told Gamay that the dive was *memorable*,' Trout said. 'Where do we go from here?'

'I'm hopeful Gamay will turn up something on Kane. He's our major lead right now. Joe and I will compare notes and figure out our next move.'

Austin said he would keep Trout posted, and was about to thaw out another bagel to make a tuna sandwich when the phone trilled.

He checked the caller ID. Then he pushed the SPEAKER button, and said, 'Hello, Joe, I was just about to call you.'

Zavala got right to the point. 'Can you come over right away?' he asked. 'I've got something I want to show you.'

Austin couldn't miss the unmistakable note of excitement in Zavala's soft-spoken voice. 'I'll be over in an hour,' he said.

Slightly less than an hour after Joe's call he pulled up in his turquoise-coloured Jeep Cherokee in front of a small building in Arlington. At the front door, he punched the entry code into a keypad and stepped into the main living level. The space looked like the interior of an adobe building in Santa Fe. The floors were dark red Mexican tile, the doorways arched, and niches in the whitewashed walls displayed colourful folk art that Zavala had collected on trips to his ancestral home in Morales.

Austin called out Zavala's name.

'I'm down in Frankenstein's lab,' Zavala yelled up from his basement.

Austin descended the stairs to a brightly lit workshop. Zavala had utilised every square inch for his collection of lathes, drills and milling machines. Odd-shaped metal parts whose functions were known only to Zavala hung from the walls, and mounted in glass cases were scale models of the cutting-edge underwater vehicles Zavala had designed for NUMA. A Stuart model steam engine he was restoring sat on a table. Zavala never hesitated to get his hands greasy when it came to tinkering with mechanical contrivances, but today he was facing a computer screen.

He wheeled his chair aside to give Austin a clear view of the monitor.

Floating in a slow rotation against a black background was a three-dimensional neon-blue image of the manta-ray AUV that had cut the bathysphere cable and attacked Austin.

Austin let out a low whistle. 'That's it. Where did you find this thing?'

'I went back to the video from the Hardsuit camera, slowed the action and culled details here and there. I used those to create a rough outline of the AUV.' He called up an article from a magazine. 'Then I compared it with the AUVs in my database. At first I couldn't find a match anywhere. After I'd breezed through military models and scientific applications, I looked to industry. But oil, gas and communications didn't pan out, so I tried commercial fishing.'

Austin looked at the photos with the article. 'Jackpot,' he said.

'The vehicle in the magazine piece is used to film experimental fishnet designs,' Zavala said.

'That accounts for the manta shape,' Austin noted. 'You'd need something flat to get under the nets, with no projecting fins that might catch.'

'The pincers allow the AUV to cut its way through tangled nets,' Zavala said. 'It's used by a Chinese company, Pyramid Seafood Exports, headquartered in Shanghai.'

'*Chinese?* That's significant. The men who attacked the ship were Asian. The weapons they carried were Chinese. But why would a legitimate fishing company be involved in the attacks on the *Beebe* and the bathysphere?'

'I may be able to answer that question after seeing my friend Caitlin Lyons at the FBI's Asian Crime Unit later today,' Zavala said.

Austin had to admit that Zavala's wide network of women friends sometimes came in handy. 'Have you figured out how the attack on the B3 may have been set up?' he said.

'The vehicle could have been launched from any of the press boats watching the bathysphere dive,' Zavala said. 'But my guess is that it went into the water hours before the dive, and was put into sleep mode and programmed to wake up after a certain time to begin the hunt.'

'How would it have picked its target?'

'Sonar combined with the optical sensors would look for a vertical line. The AUV homes in on the B3's tether. Snip-snip. There goes the B3.'

'And there goes Doc Kane and the mysterious research project that was going to affect everybody on the planet.'

'Any word from Kane since he took off into the wide blue yonder?' Zavala asked.

'I've tried a number of official and unofficial channels,' Austin answered. 'Bonefish Key may be our only lead.'

'Doubt he's there. Somebody wanted him to die a horrible death at the bottom. Bonefish Key would be the first place to look after the *Beebe*.'

A look of alarm crossed Austin's tanned face. He dug his cellphone out of a pocket and called Paul Trout.

'Paul, I may have been too casual when I asked you to poke around Kane's lab. Gamay should be alerted to possible danger from the people who wanted to take down Kane.'

Trout said, 'Don't worry, Kurt, Gamay can take care of herself.'

'I know she can,' Austin said. 'Just tell her not to take any chances.'

HAVING WARNED THE TROUTS, Austin put in a call to NUMA and asked for a dossier on the Pyramid Trading Company. The agency's computer centre was one of the greatest repositories of specialised information in the world. Austin said he would talk to Zavala after he'd studied the results of the search. He got back in his Jeep and drove to the thirty-storey glass tower, overlooking the Potomac, that housed NUMA's headquarters.

A thick file was sitting on his desk. He opened the file, but had only made it to the first page when his telephone buzzed. Caller ID couldn't identify the number. He realised why after he picked up the receiver and heard the crisp voice of James Sandecker, the founder and long-time director of NUMA before he was appointed Vice-President of the United States.

As usual, Sandecker got right to the point. 'Pitt forwarded your report on the B3 incident to me. What in blazes is going on, Kurt?'

'I wish I knew, Admiral,' Austin said, using Sandecker's hard-earned Navy title over his more recent political one.

'It was a miracle no one was hurt. Are you making any progress?'

'We think there's a Chinese connection,' Austin said. 'The AUV that went after me and the B3 is the same model as that used by a Chinese fishing company that's part of a multinational called Pyramid Trading. The men who attacked the ship carried Chinese weapons and were Asian. Joe will chase down any possible criminal connection. I'll check with the Bermuda police to see if their forensics turned up anything. We think Doc Kane's research may hold the key. Gamay is on Bonefish Key checking out the lab.'

Sandecker chuckled. 'Gamay's not likely to learn a thing. The work they're doing is highly classified.'

'Sounds like you know what the lab is up to.'

'This is part of something very big, Kurt, and we'll have to move quickly. The situation is reaching critical mass. I'm setting up a meeting that will explain things. I'll call you in about an hour, so stand by. In the meantime, pack your bags for a trip.' Sandecker hung up without another word.

Austin stared at the phone in his hand. He pushed speculative thoughts aside and soon was engrossed in the file on his desk. It didn't take him long to learn that Pyramid was no ordinary corporation.

Chapter 6

Mayhew drained his coffee mug. Then he reached under his chair and handed Gamay a plastic bag with a clean lab coat in it. 'Ready for the tour, Dr Trout?'

Gamay rose from the breakfast table and buttoned herself into the coat. 'Anytime you are, Dr Mayhew.'

He replied with the inevitable switched-on smile. 'Follow me.'

They took an unmarked shell path and came upon a one-storey cinder-block building painted a light mossy green. The air vibrated with the hum of unseen electric motors.

'Resource cultivation is done in this building,' Mayhew said. 'It may look like a garage, but this lab is on the leading edge of biomedical research.'

The dimly lit building housed dozens of large, lighted fish tanks. The air was heavy with a wet, fishy smell.

'These seawater tanks are precisely maintained to replicate exactly the habitat of the marine organisms they contain,' Mayhew explained.

'How many different organisms are you researching?' Gamay asked.

'Dozens of species and subspecies. Let me show you the star of the show.'

Mayhew went over to a tank that housed several vibrantly coloured red blobs, each about the size of a grapefruit. Short, pointed tentacles surrounded their mouths. They festooned the rocks inside the tanks.

'This must be the sea flower that I read about,' Gamay said.

'The staff like to give common names to the creatures,' Mayhew said. 'There's the sea star and the sea blossom, and so on. Ironic, when you realise that these exquisite creatures are efficient killing machines superbly engineered to attract small fish close enough to sting and devour.'

'There's another irony,' Gamay said. 'Despite being poisonous, they may be able to cure disease.'

'Killing and curing aren't mutually exclusive. Curare is a good poison that's used in medicine. Botox too.'

'Tell me about the sea star, Dr Mayhew.'

'Gladly. That little beauty is related to another sponge discovered in 1984, when Harbor Branch Oceanographic was diving off Bermuda, and found to contain a chemical that in lab tests killed cancer cells. We found fragments of an unknown specimen not far from the Harbor Branch dives, dived deeper to find the sponge's true habitat and found whole sponges that also contained the cancer-killing chemical.'

'Does the star's potential live up to its beauty?' she asked.

'The Harbor Branch specimen produced a chemical dozens of times more potent than the most powerful drug. The star is twice that strong.'

'An exciting discovery. Do I detect a note of smugness in your voice, Dr Mayhew?'

The scientist widened his mouth in a smile that for once did not look pasted on his face. 'We've got a long slog ahead of us before we can license the chemical to a pharmaceutical company. We have to find a way to produce it in quantity, but the potential rewards are mind-boggling.'

Gamay cast her eyes around the lab. 'What's in the other tanks?'

'More sponges, different varieties. Each specimen has its own chemical characteristics. We're looking at cures for a host of human ailments. The possibilities are endless.' Mayhew attempted to move the tour along.

'I'm a bit puzzled,' Gamay said, subtly resisting the push of his guiding hand. 'I'm sure I read on your website that you were doing research on other invertebrates. I haven't seen any species of Cnidaria.'

The question seemed to catch Mayhew by surprise. He glanced reflexively at the door to a walled-off section of the lab. 'Jellyfish? Well . . .'

Mayhew may have been an accomplished scientist, but he was an amateur at cloak-and-dagger. Gamay's eyes followed the direction of his revealing glance, and she gave him her most charming smile.

'I'll bet you forgot,' she said, taking him by the arm.

'It's not that,' he said. 'It's . . . We don't like to disturb them.' He was folding under her unrelenting gaze. 'Well, I suppose it won't do any harm.'

He opened the door and ushered Gamay into a room that was dark except for the light emanating from a tall, cylindrical transparent plastic tank four feet across and eight feet high. The light came from a dozen or so jellyfish, each about the size of a cabbage, that glowed with pulsating blue lights.

A figure on a ladder was bending over the top of the tank. Dr Bennett, the toxicologist, opened her mouth in surprise. 'Dr Mayhew, I didn't expect—'

'I leaned on Dr Mayhew to show me this part of the lab,' Gamay explained. 'I hope I'm not disturbing you.'

'Not at all,' Bennett said with a halfhearted smile. She brandished a long-handled dip net in her hands. 'This procedure can be a little tricky at times.'

Gamay shifted her gaze back to the undulating, vaguely cube-shaped forms and their strange acrobatic ballet. Threadlike tentacles were attached to a lacy fringe that rimmed each diaphanous creature.

'In all my years of diving,' she said, 'I don't think I have ever seen anything this beautiful.'

'Or as deadly,' added Mayhew. 'The medusas in this tank produce a toxin that would put a cobra to shame.'

Gamay dug into her memory. 'This is a box jellyfish, isn't it?' she asked.

'That's right. *Chironex fleckeri*, the sea wasp. Its sting can kill a human being in under three minutes.'

Dr Bennett pulled a mask over her face and dipped the net in the tank. To Gamay's surprise, the jellyfish didn't shy away from the net but clustered closer to it, making it easy to snag one and transfer it to a beaker. In the process, the colour of the jellyfish deepened and the pulsating became more frequent, as if they were agitated.

'I've never seen jellyfish act in that fashion before,' she said. 'They'll usually try to avoid any threat they perceive.'

'Jellyfish are predators,' Mayhew said, 'but most species simply drift around, encountering their meals by chance. The eye in jellyfish is more acutely developed, so combined with its jet-propulsion capabilities, a jellyfish actually can chase down its intended meal.'

Slowly shaking her head, Gamay said, 'I'm not sure I understand. You said "most species". Didn't you say these were box jellyfish?'

Dr Mayhew realised that he had said more than he had intended. 'I misspoke a moment ago,' he said. 'Actually, it's closely related to the sea wasp, but more highly developed and aggressive.'

'What is its potential pharmaceutically?'

'We're in the early stages of study, but the chemical it produces is far more complex than anything we've encountered. Experimenting with this delicate creature is like riding an untamed stallion.'

'Fascinating,' Gamay said.

Mayhew glanced at his watch. 'Thank you, Dr Bennett,' he said. 'We'll leave you alone now with your poisonous friends.'

Mayhew guided Gamay out of the room and back into the main lab. He showed her some other species under study, then they left the resource-cultivation building. It was nearly midday.

'I'm as hungry as a horse,' Mayhew said. 'Let's break for lunch.'

After a long break, the tour continued to another cinder-block building, which contained almost all computers and no tanks. Mayhew said the computers were matching chemicals to diseases. Gamay glimpsed Dr Song Lee. Her eyes were glued to a computer. Mayhew chatted nonstop about nothing in particular, and Gamay figured he was just stretching things out.

The tour was over by midafternoon. Mayhew seemed relaxed for the first time since Gamay had met him. He excused himself, and asked if Gamay would mind if he didn't accompany her back to the lodge.

'Not at all,' she said. 'See you at happy hour.'

As she left the lab building area, Gamay felt as if she had been given the bum's rush. Since setting foot on the island, she had been wined, dined, zipped through a packaged tour, and prepped to be sent on her way.

Mayhew had been correct to fear a trained observer. Gamay had easily seen through his smoke screen. There was no doubt that he had tried a verbal bait and switch concerning the jellyfish tank's occupants. The collegial little research group was a façade. No amount of barroom cheer could hide the fact that the island was a secretive, pressurised environment.

GAMAY MADE HER WAY to the dock. Dooley Greene was painting a skiff. He saw her approaching and removed the cigar stub from his mouth.

''Afternoon, Dr Gamay,' he said with his jack-o'-lantern grin.

'Could I borrow one of the kayaks, Dooley? I've got a few hours, and thought it might be nice to explore the mangroves.'

Dooley plunked his paintbrush into a can of turpentine. 'I'd be glad to show you around in my boat, Dr Gamay. You'll see a lot more and save yourself some paddling.'

Having nothing else to occupy her time, Gamay got into Dooley's boat. He headed away from the dock, and, once clear of the island, goosed the throttle. The double hulls cut through the flat water like scissors through silk. Within minutes, they entered a small bay enclosed by mangroves.

Dooley kept the boat pointed towards an old wooden cabin cruiser that lay off the tip of a mangrove island, with its stern in the water.

'Hurricane pushed that wreck up onto an oyster bar,' Dooley said. 'Makes a good navigation point when you're cruising around the mangroves. It can get confusing out here at times, even with a GPS.'

The boat had gone past the tip of Bonefish Key, a long, tapering point. The dock was no longer visible, and palmettos obscured the water tower.

'You must know these waters like the back of your hand,' Gamay said.

Dooley squinted at the sun-dappled water. 'It all looks the same, but you get so you can pick out little details that most people wouldn't see.' He opened a storage box and pointed to a pair of goggles. 'I cheat when I go out fishing at night,' he said with a smirk. 'Got these night-vision gogs over the internet. Got some spare ones back at the boathouse.'

'Where does Dr Lee go kayaking?'

'She paddles down the back side of the barrier beach. Lots of birds there. I'll show you.'

Dooley headed between two mangroves. The passage narrowed, funnelling them to a dead end. Dooley brought the boat to a halt and handed Gamay a pair of binoculars. She raised them to her eyes and saw dozens of snowy egrets and great blue herons wading in the shallows.

Dooley pointed to a wooden stake that stuck out of the water a few feet from the shore. 'That marks a path that leads across the island. Only a few hundred yards, and there's good surf fishing on the other side.'

Dooley powered up the outboard motor, and they sped out of the V-shaped cove and towards the wrecked boat. He made a sharp turn and headed back towards Bonefish Key. Minutes later he was expertly bringing them alongside the dock.

JOE ZAVALA SAT BEHIND the wheel of his 1961 Chevrolet Corvette, cruising along Interstate 95 to Quantico, Virginia. The convertible top was down, the powerful V-8 engine under the hood purred like a contented tiger, and he was about to meet a beautiful woman. Life was sweet.

Around forty miles southwest of Washington, he turned off the highway onto a tree-shaded road that led to a checkpoint. He showed the guard his NUMA credentials, had his name matched against a visitors' list, and followed the signs to the main building of the FBI Academy.

Surrounded by 385 acres of woods, the campus-style complex consisted of twenty-one buildings of a soothing honey colour connected by a network of glass-enclosed corridors.

Zavala went through the front entrance of the main building and checked in at the reception desk, saying he had an appointment with Agent Caitlin Lyons. He was given a security badge with his name on it to wear. A woman was assigned to guide him through the maze of buildings and corridors.

When he heard a commotion that sounded like a gunfight at the OK Corral he knew that he was near the shooting range.

The guide ushered him in and pointed to a row of booths. 'Number ten,' she said. 'I'll wait outside. Gets a little noisy in here. Take your time.'

Zavala nodded his thanks, and took some ear protectors from an attendant. Then he went over to a booth and stood behind a woman who was firing at a silhouette of a man. She stood with her pistol in both hands, slowly and methodically pumping bullets into the target.

Zavala had no desire to startle a trained FBI agent while she had a gun in her hand. He stood behind her patiently until she turned and saw him. She beckoned for him to step into the booth. She replaced the spent magazine with a full one, handed him the pistol, and pointed towards the target.

The Walther PPK was a favourite of Zavala's. He raised it to eye level, flicked the safety off, and released six shots in rapid succession. Every squeeze of the trigger found the centre circle of the bull's-eye over the heart. He flicked the safety back on and handed the gun back to the woman.

She said something he couldn't hear. He removed his ear protectors and she said it again. '*Show-off.*'

She put the pistol in a hip holster and they made their way to the door, first dropping off their ear protectors. The guide was waiting in the hallway, but Caitlin said she would show Zavala to the lobby when their meeting was over.

'Let's go for a walk,' she said.

They strolled along a shady path that was a world away from the sound of gunfire and the smell of cordite in the shooting range.

Caitlin Lyons was an attractive woman in her thirties with a peaches-and-cream complexion, and dark blonde hair that was tucked under a black baseball cap.

'Not bad shooting, Joe. Ever think of joining the FBI?'

'As soon as they have a navy,' Zavala said.

Caitlin laughed. 'You were very brave to come up to me when I had a gun in my hand. You know what they say about a woman scorned . . .'

Zavala winced. His dark good looks and unassuming manner made him popular with many women around Washington. He had gone out with Caitlin, but their budding romance was interrupted by a mission for the Special Assignments Team. He had not got back to her until now.

'*Scorned* is an ugly word, Cate. I was planning to get in touch with you after my last job.'

'Don't worry, Joe,' she said with a smile, 'I'm not angry at you for leaving me to run off on another NUMA mission. I'm a cop, I might have done the same. And I wasn't looking for anything permanent, anyhow. Besides, if I need you, all I have to do is turn on the TV and I'll see those Latin good looks. I watched the bathysphere dive. Very exciting.'

'The most exciting part was what you *didn't* see.'

Caitlin gave him a quizzical look, and he pointed to a park bench. They sat down, and Zavala told her about the attack on the bathysphere, Austin's close call, and the connection to the Pyramid Trading Company.

She let out a low whistle. '*Pyramid*. You couldn't have chosen a worse bunch to tangle with. You and Kurt are damned lucky to be alive.'

'What do you know about Pyramid?'

'Let me give you some perspective,' Caitlin said. 'My job is to keep Asian crime as far from US shores as possible and to solve crimes when they do occur. It's a losing battle. We've had Asian criminal enterprises in this country since the early 1900s, starting with the Chinese tongs. The tongs started as social clubs but then became gangs. They are still thriving today as part of an international network that's dominated by the big criminal organisations known as the Triads. Pyramid is one of these. Some of its enterprises are legitimate. But it's also involved with extortion, murder, prostitution, drugs, loan-sharking and money laundering.'

'The tried and true,' Zavala said.

'It's also got a network of gangs in every city. The names all start with *Ghost*: the Ghost Devils, the Ghost Shadows, the Ghost Dragons. You get the picture. They do the dirty work: intimidation, enforcement, murder.'

'What about the legal side?'

'The criminal stuff is the bedrock, but it has evolved into an organisation with legitimate businesses: manufacturing, real estate, movies. And, as you discovered, commercial fishing.'

'Does the Pyramid leadership have a human face?'

'As a matter of fact, it has *three*. The company is run by a set of triplets.'

'That's an unusual arrangement.'

'Not when you consider the extent of their empire. Pyramid is like a country unto itself. It has a huge treasury, an army of thugs at its command, and a diplomatic corps that interacts with the Chinese government. Traditionally the government has supported the Triads, because the Triads produce money, keep order and are patriotic. Now it's trying to put Pyramid out of business.'

'Why the sudden change of heart?'

'The Chinese military has been in business with the Triads for years. Pyramid is particularly tight with the Army, giving it political muscle to defend its criminal interests, but the government is worried this cosy arrangement has given Pyramid too much power. They've put thousands of corrupt officials in jail, but they really began to push after the safety scandals. China lives on its exports. And anything that threatens them threatens the stability of the country, and therefore its rulers.'

'Tell me about the triplets,' Zavala said.

'Not much *to* tell. Pyramid's front man is an immensely rich guy named Wen Lo. No one has ever seen the other two triplets.' She paused. 'Now it's my turn, Joe. Why would a Triad want to sabotage the bathysphere?'

'Kurt thinks they were after Dr Kane because of a secret research project he was involved in. Does that sound plausible?'

'Anything is possible with this gang. Tell you what, Joe, if Pyramid is involved in *anything*, it's part of something very big. Pyramid doesn't do things in half measures.'

'Would the government crackdown have anything to do with what we've talked about?'

'Possibly. Pyramid has reacted like a wounded snake since the purge began, killing cops, judges and top officials as a warning to the government to keep its hands off. But I don't see the connection with Dr Kane.'

'Neither do I. Can you help?'

'I'll put you in touch with Charlie Yoo. He's an agent that the Chinese security agency sent over to work with the FBI. He's a specialist in gangs. But a few words of advice, Joe, because if I know Pyramid, you and Kurt are in their sights. And they won't miss a second time.'

PYRAMID TRADING was also on the lips of Colonel Ming. The slender, soft-spoken man with a thick head of silver hair stood outside a dilapidated building in the slums of Shanghai. There had apparently been an attempt to burn the building, but the fire-fighters had nipped the fire in the bud.

Ming turned to the Ministry of Health official, who had called him. 'I'm not sure why you asked me to come here,' he said. 'It appears that the city has the situation well in hand.'

'This was no ordinary building and this was no ordinary fire,' said the official, whose name was Fong. 'We found a number of people locked in cells. They had been left there to burn, but, fortunately, even though they were in poor condition, they were able to talk. They said they had been kidnapped, and that many people had been taken from their cells, never to return. We believe they were moved to labs, and, from the equipment we found, it seems they were the subjects of experiments.'

'What kind of experiments, Fong?'

'We don't know. But we did find traces of a virus strain that is of some concern to our ministry. It is the same virus that caused an outbreak in a village to the north, brought there by a person from Shanghai.'

'Quite the coincidence,' said Ming.

'Even more, the person was employed in a security capacity by Pyramid Trading based here in the city. And Pyramid owns this building.'

'I think I know where you are going with this, Fong. It's well known that the Army operates a string of brothels in partnership with Pyramid. But there's no connection to this,' he said with a wave of his hand.

'I understand that, Colonel, but perhaps you might want to re-examine your partnership when I tell you that we found in the building the remains of dozens of human beings, discovered in a crematory. We think they had been used in the experiments.'

Ming's reaction was one of combined fear and revulsion: fear that his name had been linked to Pyramid, revulsion over the experiments.

'Thank you,' he said. 'I shall look into it and take appropriate steps.'

'I hope so,' Fong said. 'This is not good for China. Whoever is responsible must be brought to account, but it must be done quietly.'

'I am in complete agreement,' Colonel Ming said.

DOOLEY GREEN LOOKED UP from the outboard motor he'd been repairing and his mouth widened in a gap-toothed grin when he saw the young Asian woman coming his way.

''Afternoon, Doctor,' he said. 'Going to take another crack at that bird?'

Dr Lee tapped the zoom lens of the digital camera hanging from a strap round her neck. 'Yes, Dooley. You know how determined I am to get a photo of that beautiful roseate spoonbill.'

'Kayak's waiting for you,' he said. 'I'll fetch your gear.'

Dooley got a paddle and flotation vest from the boat shed. Then he and Lee walked along the beach to where a light blue fibreglass touring kayak sat on the sand with its bow partway in the water. Lee slipped her arms through the vest and eased her slender body into the cockpit. Dooley handed her the paddle and pushed the craft into the water.

'Good luck with that spoonbill,' Dooley called out.

Lee headed along the shore of the island and emerged from the mangroves into a small bay. She pointed the kayak's prow towards the stranded cabin cruiser, then left the bay and headed into the funnel-shaped cove that Dooley had entered earlier that day with Gamay.

As she paddled further into the cove a blue heron took off with a mighty flap of its long wings. Lee watched the bird until it was out of sight, then spotted a pair of snowy egrets in the shallows. Her heart skipped a beat at the flash of pink behind one of them.

The egrets moved, and she brought the camera up to her eye. Through the viewfinder, she saw a bird that looked like a flamingo with a duck bill, the roseate spoonbill. She snapped off several pictures, then reviewed them. They were perfect. Lee was smiling when she took up her paddle again.

With a few strokes, she sent the kayak towards a weathered grey wooden post that marked a narrow break in the otherwise impenetrable tangle of mangrove roots. The kayak's hull came to rest on shore.

Lee stepped into knee-deep water and hauled the kayak onto the narrow beach. She grabbed her rucksack and walked through a tunnel of trees for a hundred feet or so before she broke into an open area. A sandy path wound through the shrub for a few hundred yards to the other side of the island, ending at a beach. She strolled along the beach for a short distance and plunked down on the sand with her back against a driftwood log.

A blue-hulled fishing boat was anchored offshore just beyond the line of breakers. She had seen the boat several times in the past week or so, but it had stayed a respectful distance away. She examined it through the zoom lens of her camera but saw no one on deck.

Giving in to her weariness, she fell asleep. When she awoke, she noticed that the blue-hulled boat had vanished. She frowned. She had regained her privacy, but it was time to go back to work. She got up, brushed the sand from her shorts, and headed across the island to her kayak.

When Lee broke through the tree canopy, she saw that the kayak was no longer where she had left it on the beach. Turning back to the island, she saw blue plastic gleaming in the grass. The kayak had been pulled up into the tall grass on one side of the beach. Wondering why anyone would do such a thing, she stepped into the grass to retrieve it. It was a remote spot, and she felt uncomfortable knowing there was someone else on the island.

She was pulling the kayak back towards the water when she felt a prick-ling sensation that had nothing to do with the sun on the back of her neck. She turned and saw a man, his eyes hidden behind dark sunglasses.

He had soundlessly materialised from the scrub and now blocked Lee's way. His hardened Asian features seemed to have been hammered on an anvil, and his thin-lipped mouth looked as if it could not be prised into a smile with a crowbar. Making him even more formidable was the automatic weapon cradled in his arms, the muzzle pointed at her heart.

Despite her fears, Song Lee managed to croak, 'Who are you?'

'I am the ghost who watches,' he said with no change of expression.

What nonsense, Lee thought. The man was obviously deranged. She tried to assert control over the situation. 'Did you move my kayak?' she asked.

She thought she saw a slight nod of the chin.

'Then I'd appreciate your help in pulling it back to the water.'

He smiled for the first time and lowered the gun. Thinking that maybe her bluff had worked, she turned to grab the kayak.

'Dr Lee?'

Hearing her name, she knew this was no random encounter. She saw a movement out of the corner of her eye and felt an explosion at the back of her skull. She was unconscious before she crashed face down into the mud.

THE FBI'S J. EDGAR HOOVER Building headquarters on Pennsylvania Avenue is the antithesis of the bucolic, tree-shaded campus at Quantico. The hulking, seven-storey structure was made of poured concrete, in the Brutalist architectural style popular in the 1960s.

Caitlin Lyons had called ahead, easing Zavala's entry into the FBI's inner sanctum. There was the visitor's badge, and the guide, a serious young man this time, who miraculously managed to navigate the labyrinth of corridors without having to resort to map or GPS. He led Zavala to an office.

A man sat behind a desk talking on the phone in Chinese. He waved Zavala to a chair, continued chatting a minute, then ended the conversation and set the receiver back in its cradle. Popping up like a jack-in-the-box, he shook Zavala's hand as if trying to coax water from a reluctant pump.

He flashed a friendly smile. 'Sorry to keep you waiting,' he said with a New York accent. 'I'm Charlie Yoo.'

Yoo was a pencil-thin man in his mid-thirties. He wore a stylishly cut shiny grey suit with a cobalt-blue shirt and blue-and-red-striped tie, a sarto-rial style more in keeping with a cocktail hour at the Willard Hotel than the bowels of the FBI, where conservative navy-blue suits were the norm.

'Nice to meet you, Agent Yoo. I'm Caitlin's friend, Joe Zavala.'

'The man from NUMA . . . great organisation, Joe. Please call me Charlie. Caitlin said you were looking into the Pyramid Triad.'

'That's right. She thought you might be able to help. Someone tried to sabotage a NUMA operation, and we have circumstantial evidence that the seafood subsidiary of Pyramid Trading may have been involved.'

Yoo hiked his eyebrows like Groucho Marx. 'Excuse me for being sceptical, Joe, but that doesn't seem like Pyramid's MO. What's your evidence?'

'Let me fill in the background. A few days ago, NUMA launched the Bathysphere 3, a replica of a historical diving bell, in waters off Bermuda. The dive was broadcast all over the world. An underwater robot cut the bathysphere's cable.'

'Whoa!' Yoo said, a wide grin on his boyish face. 'An underwater *robot*. That's pretty wild stuff, Joe.'

'I thought so at the time. When the cable was cut, the sphere was buried a half-mile down in muck. I was inside.'

Yoo leaned forward across the desk. His grin had disappeared. 'You're not kidding, are you? How'd you get out of a situation like that?'

'Kurt Austin, my partner at NUMA, made a rescue dive, and we were able to activate our flotation system. While we were on our way to the surface, the robot went after Austin. The robot is identical to one that Pyramid's seafood division uses to inspect nets,' Zavala reached in his pocket and extracted the magazine article about the Pyramid seafood division's AUV. He put photos from Austin's Hardsuit camera next to it. Yoo read the article and studied the photos.

'Wow!' Yoo said. 'OK, Pyramid tried to sabotage your dive. But why?'

'Haven't a clue. Which is why I went to see Caitlin. She said Pyramid Trading was the baddest of the bad when it came to Chinese Triads, and that you were a specialist in Chinese gangs around the world.'

'I'm *more* than a specialist, I'm a former gang member. I'm from Hong Kong originally. My parents moved my family to New York, where I joined the Ghost Shadows, one of the biggest gangs in the country.'

'Caitlin said the Ghost Shadows is a Pyramid gang.'

'That's right. My family saw what was going on and moved back to China to keep me out of the gangs. Pop had a bicycle-repair shop, and he kept me so busy I was too tired to get into trouble. I kept my nose clean, went to college. Now I'm part of a special unit from the Ministry of

Security. I'm over here for a few months to share intel with the FBI.'

'Caitlin said that Pyramid was consolidating its power, and that's one of the reasons it's in hot water with the Chinese government.'

'Caitlin's the expert on the Triads. I'll go along with what she says.'

'She also said that the front man for Pyramid is a guy named Wen Lo.'

There was a slight tick, a second, as Yoo paused before answering.

'As I said, Caitlin knows more about the Triads. I'm familiar with the organisation at street level, but others can tell you about the leaders.'

Yoo talked about gang ritual for another five minutes before glancing at his watch. 'Sorry to cut you short, Joe, I've got an appointment to keep.'

'No problem,' Zavala said. He rose from his chair. 'Thanks very much for your time, Charlie.'

Yoo flashed a smile and said, 'You've stirred up my curiosity about this robot. Let me poke around and see if I can come up with anything else.'

Yoo jotted down Zavala's cellphone number and wished him good luck. Once a guide had collected Zavala, Yoo locked the door. Stone-faced, he punched in a number on his cell. The signal flashed around the world several times, passing through a series of filters, until it was untraceable.

'Report, number thirty-nine,' a gruff voice said.

'He just left,' Yoo said. 'He knows far too much for comfort.'

Yoo relayed the gist of his conversation with Zavala.

'This is a fortunate happenstance,' the voice said. 'Zavala is small fish. Use him as bait. I want you to take Austin alive and bring him to me.'

'I'll get on it immediately,' Yoo said.

ZAVALA WAS IN HIS Corvette on the way back to NUMA headquarters when his cellphone buzzed. It was Charlie Yoo.

'Hi, Joe, I've got something for you on the Pyramid Triad.'

'That was fast,' Zavala said with genuine surprise.

'We lucked out. There's an ongoing surveillance of a gang-connected alien-smuggling operation. After I told the guys at the Bureau about our little chat, they invited us to sit in. Might give you a chance to talk to some of the other Asian crime specialists.'

'When and where?' Zavala asked.

'Tonight, on the other side of the river. Your partner Austin is invited too.'

Zavala hung up and called Austin to tell him about Yoo's invitation.

'I'm expecting a call from Sandecker in a few minutes,' Austin said. 'I have no idea what the old sea fox wants. I'll catch up with you later.'

'Call me when you shake loose. And don't let him keep you too long.'

'Not a chance, pal,' Austin said, and, in words that would come back to haunt him later, added, 'Hell, Joe, I wouldn't want you to have *all* the fun.'

THE SECOND HAPPY HOUR in the Dollar Bar was a repeat of the first gabfest. The vacuous chitchat around the table ground on Gamay's nerves, but she had to admit that the dinner that followed was superb, featuring freshly caught shrimp in a savoury jambalaya.

By nine o'clock, all the lab staff had gone to their cabins, leaving Gamay alone. She waited another half-hour until everyone had settled in, then followed the shell path to Song Lee's cabin. The windows were dark.

Gamay climbed onto the small porch and knocked softly at first, then harder. There was no answer. Gamay hurried along the path to the waterfront. Lee's kayak was not in the boat shed. Impulsively, Gamay lifted the second kayak from its rack and set it on the beach.

Then she had another thought, and dashed back to the boathouse to grab Dooley's night-vision goggles. She slipped them over her head, shoved the kayak in the water, got in, and paddled furiously.

She headed out into the bay. The stranded cabin cruiser was greenish and grainy through the goggles. She paddled directly to it to get her bearings, then turned in to the funnel-shaped cove Dooley had shown her earlier that day. When she found the post that marked the break in the mangroves, she paddled to shore, got out of the kayak, and was pulling it up onto the beach when she stumbled over Song Lee's rucksack, which was lying in the sand.

Gamay struck off inland, following the path through the thicket of trees, carrying her wooden kayak paddle in one hand. The path emerged into the open, meandering through the scrub. The whisper of the waves washing the beach provided a backdrop to the insect chorus.

With the aid of the night-vision goggles, Gamay moved quickly along the path. She paused where it broke out onto the beach and looked round. Two sets of footprints led off down the beach. Like a hound on a scent, she followed the prints around a bend, slowing only when she saw a yellow glow in the distance. There was a house up ahead, partially hidden by trees, and light was spilling through a window.

She crept up to the house and put her back to the wall a few feet from the window. She could hear a man and a woman speaking excitedly in Chinese: the man sounded angry, the woman hysterical.

Gamay edged up to the window, pushed the goggles up on her forehead, and peered through the glass at a sparsely furnished room illuminated with gas camp lanterns. Song Lee was sitting at a kitchen table across from a brutish-looking Asian man. An automatic weapon lay on the counter next to the stove. The man had apparently just run through his reserve of patience. He brought his hand back and slapped Lee across the face. The blow knocked her to the floor.

The man turned away from Lee to get his weapon—a big mistake. Lee got to her knees and plucked a steak knife from a rack that was within arm's reach. She plunged it into the man's thigh, then pulled it free. Letting out a scream of pain, he dropped the gun and grabbed his bleeding leg.

Lee stood up and dashed for the door. Bellowing with rage, the man lunged after her, but she was too quick for him. She burst through the screen door and ran down the beach.

The man picked his gun up and limped to the door. Standing in the doorway, he shouted in Chinese, and raised the gun to shoulder level.

Gamay stepped from the shadows just then, raised the kayak paddle high, and brought it down on the man's head with all her strength. The handle snapped like a dry twig, and the man crashed to the ground.

Gamay hoped the blow had knocked him out, but he soon groaned and began to stir. She pulled the goggles down and sprinted along the beach, calling out Song Lee's name. The scientist stopped and wheeled round to face her pursuer. She clutched the steak knife defensively in her hand.

Gamay ripped the goggles from her head. 'It's me . . . Dr Trout!'

'Doctor . . . What are you doing here?'

Gamay glanced back towards the house. 'No time to talk,' she said. 'I slowed your friend down only for a second.'

Gamay tossed away the paddle, and she and Lee ran along the beach. In their haste, they missed the path and had to go back. But within minutes they were on the other side of the island.

There was a soft footfall on the path, and seconds later a figure burst from the bushes. The man who had held Song Lee prisoner flicked on a flashlight and snarled in triumph. He was surprised to see Gamay, but only for an instant, and quickly brought his gun to bear on her midsection.

Gamay put her head down and charged like a bull, butting the man in the stomach. He had abdominal muscles like a stone wall. He brought down the gun's stock on her head in a blow that knocked her to the ground. Through a grey haze she punched his wounded leg and heard him scream in pain.

Lee leapt onto the man's back, clinging to him, but he shook her off and she fell to the ground. He stood there unmoving, staring at her; then the gun dropped from his hand and he crumpled to his knees. The beam from his flashlight fell on the handle of the steak knife protruding from his chest.

'Who is he?' Gamay asked, as she helped Lee to her feet,

'I don't know. He came up while I was getting my kayak and struck me with his gun. He said others were coming in a boat to take me away.'

Gamay suddenly put her hand on Lee's arm. '*Listen,*' she said.

Excited voices talking in Chinese could be heard coming along the path.

Lee's kayak had been hidden in the grass. They dragged it to the water. Lee produced a spare paddle for Gamay to use. They shoved their kayaks off the beach and paddled madly. They were about a hundred feet from the mangroves when flashlight beams probed the water around them.

The shafts of light reflected off the shiny fibreglass hulls. They tensed, expecting gunfire, but the lights blinked out.

'They are going back to their boat,' Lee said. 'They'll come round the other end of the island and intercept us. What should we do?'

'Paddle as if our lives depended on it . . . because they *do*.'

They put their backs into each stroke and made it out of the cove, but the sound of a boat engine soon shattered the quiet of the night.

A silhouette loomed ahead. They were coming up on the grounded cruiser. Gamay paddled towards it with Lee right behind. They climbed aboard, pulling their kayaks up behind them, and lay face down on the rotting deck.

Through cracks in the hull, they saw a spotlight slowly pass along the cruiser. For a second, Gamay entertained a flash of optimism, but that faded as the search boat changed direction, circled the wreck, and came closer. The spotlight filtered through the cracks and fell on their faces.

The women's pursuers peppered the cruiser with gunfire, pumping round after round into the pilothouse. Splinters showered the two women. Gamay covered her head with her hands and cursed her stupidity. The only thing they had accomplished by climbing onto the boat was to give these bozos some target practice. It would be a matter of seconds before the bullets found them.

Then the firing stopped.

Gamay expected the attackers to swarm aboard, but instead a bottle filled with flaming gasoline arced through the air and landed on the deck. Crackling fire spread in a blazing puddle that lapped at their feet. The heat became unbearable. The two women stood up, preferring to be shot rather than be burned to death. But the boat carrying their assailants was moving away from them and picking up speed.

'*Jump!*' Gamay yelled.

They dived into the water and swam away from the burning wreck. They had only gone a short distance before they heard a boat engine again.

Gamay's hopes were dashed. They were coming back to finish them off.

The boat slowed and its spotlight played over the water, finally finding the pair of swimmers. Gamay expected that the rattle of gunfire would be the last thing she would ever hear, but instead a familiar voice rang out.

'*Gamay*,' Paul Trout called, '*is that you?*'

She stopped swimming and began to tread water. She stuck a hand in the air. The boat edged closer, looming over them, and she looked up to see Paul Trout's long arms reaching down to pull her to safety.

ZAVALA SWUNG his Corvette into the parking lot of the Eden Center shopping mall in Falls Church, Virginia, as Charlie Yoo had instructed. The agent was waiting for Zavala in a black government-issue Ford Crown Victoria.

He rolled down the window. 'Where's your friend Austin?'

'Delayed,' Zavala said. 'He'll catch up with us later. Or we can wait.'

Yoo frowned. 'You can call him later and tell him where you are. Hop in.'

Zavala slid into the Crown Victoria and Yoo drove off. After a short drive, they came to a dark and deserted industrial park.

Zavala expected Yoo to pull over and park so that they could walk the rest of the way to the stakeout. Yoo slowed the car to a crawl, then, without stopping, hooked the steering wheel over to the right and accelerated through an open gate. He kept his foot on the pedal, swerved behind the building in a g-force turn, then pointed the car at a garage door. Zavala braced himself for the impact, but then the headlights showed that the door was open. Yoo finally hit the brakes inside the warehouse, sending the car in a fishtail skid into a wall of cardboard cartons. The boxes split open, spilling dozens of plastic-wrapped fortune cookies over the hood. The car's air bags exploded, cushioning the impact further.

Zavala caught his breath, then reached down and unclasped his seat belt. He was slow to anger, but as he pushed the air bag aside and got out he wanted to rip Yoo's head off.

The overhead lights snapped on. Charlie Yoo was nowhere to be seen, but Zavala was surrounded by several Asian men, all dressed in black running suits and carrying automatic weapons that were pointed at him.

The closest man poked Zavala in the gut with the barrel of his gun. '*Move*,' he ordered.

Austin FLIPPED OVER the last page of the voluminous file on Pyramid Trading Company and leaned back in his chair. The picture that the file painted was of a vast corporation with no regard for human life. It had exported tainted fish, killer pet food and unsafe tyres. Under international pressure, the Chinese government had admitted that there was a problem with Pyramid and promised to remedy the situation. But there was nothing to explain why Pyramid would go after Kane and his research project.

As questions whirled around in his mind, the phone buzzed. He picked it up to hear the unmistakable voice of Admiral Sandecker.

'Kurt. Please be out front in five minutes.' Sandecker hung up without further explanation.

Austin put the Pyramid file in a desk drawer, then turned out the lights and headed for the elevator. Five minutes later to the second, he walked out of the front door of NUMA headquarters as a dark blue SUV pulled up.

A young man in a naval officer's uniform got out of the back of the SUV and greeted Austin, who recognised Lieutenant Casey, an up and-coming officer Sandecker had introduced him to at a White House reception.

'Hello, Kurt,' Casey said. 'Climb aboard.'

Austin got in the back seat with Casey, and the SUV swung out into the traffic. 'Nice to see you again, Lieutenant. Where are we headed?'

'Not *us*. It's where *you're* going.' Casey pointed. 'Right there.'

The SUV had only gone a couple of blocks before pulling over again. Austin thanked Casey for the ride, got out of the SUV, and walked up to the entrance of a restaurant. A neon sign spelled out the name AEGEAN GROTTO.

The restaurant's owner, an ebullient native of Naxos named Stavros, ambushed Austin as he stepped over the threshold.

'Good evening, Mr Austin. How are things at the Fish House?' Many of his patrons worked as scientists or technicians at the NUMA headquarters.

'As fishy as ever,' Austin said with a slight smile.

'Your friend arrived a few minutes ago,' Stavros said. He led Austin to an alcove at the rear of the dining room.

The man seated at the table gave Austin a quick wave of recognition.

Austin pulled out a chair and sat down opposite Max Kane. 'Hello, Doc,' he said. 'This is a pleasant surprise.'

'I'm shocked that you were able to see through my masquerade.'

'You almost had me, then I noticed your hairline was listing to starboard.'

Kane snatched the black wig from his head. With a flick of his wrist, he sent it gliding like a Frisbee towards a nearby table where two men were seated. The wig almost landed in a bowl of soup. They glared at Kane. One man stuffed the hairpiece under his jacket, then went back to his dinner.

Kane burst into laughter. 'Don't look so worried, Kurt. Those guys are my baby sitters. They're the ones who insisted that I wear the rug.'

Austin gave Kane a tight smile, but he was in no mood for idle talk. In the short time he had known the colourful microbiologist, Austin had almost lost one of his team, seen the B3 project scuttled, and fought an undersea robot a half-mile down in the ocean. He wanted answers.

He skewered Kane with his coral-hued eyes. 'What the hell is going on, Doc?' he asked.

Kane sagged in his chair, as if the wind had gone right out of him. 'Sorry, Kurt. I've spent the last few days with those creeps in a safe house subsisting on pizza and fast food. I'm starting to get a little loopy.'

Austin handed Kane a menu. 'Here's my antidote for fast food. I recommend the psari plaki, fish Athenian-style. Tsatziki for appetiser.'

When Stavros arrived with glasses of ouzo, Austin raised his glass. Looking Kane straight in the eye, he said, 'Here's to a discovery that is going to affect every man, woman and child on the planet.'

'I guess I owe you an explanation,' Kane said.

'I guess you do,' Austin replied.

Kane took a blissful sip of ouzo and put his glass down. 'About a year after I had moved the lab to Bonefish Key, we acquired a rare species of jellyfish related to the sea wasp. We named it the Blue Medusa because it had an amazingly bright luminescence, but what really blew our minds was the toxin that the thing produced.'

'How so, Doc?'

'It doesn't kill. It immobilises the prey so that it can dine on food that is still alive. That's not unknown in nature. Spiders and wasps like to keep a fresh snack handy. The Blue Medusa toxin is the most complex naturally produced chemical I've ever seen. It puts up a wall that keeps pathogens at arm's length. The doomed prey enjoys the best of health while it waits to be devoured.' Kane leaned across the table and dropped his voice. 'Suppose we could put those same protective qualities in a drug for humans.'

Austin pondered Kane's words. 'You'd have an all-purpose pill,' he said. 'What the snake oil salesmen used to call a cure-all.'

'*Bingo!* Only this was no snake oil. We had found a medical miracle that just might neutralise some of the greatest scourges of mankind, the ailments caused by viruses, from the common cold to cancer.'

'So why all the hush-hush?' Austin asked. 'If people knew you had discovered a cure-all, the world would build statues in your honour.'

'Hell, Kurt, at first we were nominating ourselves for the Nobel Prize in Medicine. But then we realised that we were about to open Pandora's box. Say we give this boon to the world. The average life span increases stratospherically. Instead of six billion souls on the planet, we'd have twelve billion. Picture the pressure that would put on land, water, food.'

'You could have riots, wars, governments toppled and starvation.'

Kane spread his hands apart as if to say *Voilà!* 'Now imagine what would happen if we kept the discovery secret.'

'Nothing is secret for ever. Word would leak out. People with life-threatening diseases would be pounding down the doors of City Hall. Chaos.'

'The scientific board that advises the government on promising scientific discoveries reached the same conclusion,' Kane said. 'We were in a quandary. So we compiled a report, which we transmitted to the government. Then fate intervened. An epidemic broke out in China, an influenza-type virus with the potential to set off a worldwide pandemic. And guess what? Our crazy little lab held the key to the cure.'

'Is that what you meant when you said your research could impact everyone on the planet?'

Kane nodded. 'The government took over the lab, locked the doors, and worked with the Chinese government to keep the research under wraps until we could come up with a synthesised form of the chemical. They put out a cover story suggesting that the new virus was simply an outbreak of SARS and thus controllable. Which it isn't. It's a mutated strain that's even more virulent than the virus that killed millions in the 1918 flu pandemic.'

Austin let out a low whistle. 'With the ability people have to globe-hop now,' he said, 'that 1918 figure would be a drop in the bucket.'

'This time it's the *whole* bucket, Kurt. The Feds classified our findings and made all the lab people government employees, so that anyone talking out of turn could be prosecuted for treason. Then they moved most of the research to a secret undersea lab.'

'Why not stay at Bonefish Key?' Austin asked.

'Too public, for one thing. But there were practical reasons too. We wanted to be near the resource. The Blue Medusa is found primarily in and around a specific deepwater canyon. And we wanted to quarantine our work. We were developing an enhanced version of the medusa, a sort of superjellyfish, more aggressive than the original.'

'Are you saying you were working with malignant mutant life-forms?'

'Essentially, yes. Don't worry, we took great care during the genetic engineering to prevent the possibility of proliferation: they can't reproduce and would eventually die out in the open.'

'That's still playing with dynamite, Doc.'

'I know, I know,' Kane said, his voice tightening. 'But we were under intense pressure from the government. The virus is spreading. We had to have greater quantities of the toxin to conduct our synthesis experiments. I was working at the lab when I heard I'd been nominated for the B3 dive, so I left my assistant, Lois Mitchell, in charge and took a leave of absence. You know the rest.'

'Only up to the point when the Coast Guard snatched you.'

'The call I got on the *Beebe* was to tell me that the secret lab had vanished. The security ship guarding the lab was heavily damaged by a missile, and the whole undersea complex of labs had disappeared.'

Stavros arrived then from the kitchen with their appetisers. When he'd gone Kurt said, 'How far had the research gone when the lab disappeared?'

'We were on the verge of being able to produce the synthesised version of the chemical in quantity. We were going to skip over the clinical trials. There wasn't time. We had to have the medicine manufactured and in place if and when the virus spread to other countries.'

'Have you thought of who might be behind the lab's disappearance?' Austin asked.

'I've been turning the question over in my mind for days. All I've got in return has been a headache.'

'Only a government or a big organisation would have the resources to attack the bathysphere, launch a missile and move the lab,' Austin said.

'My thoughts exactly. It follows that only a government would have the resources to untangle this mess. Without that lab, we have no defence against the pandemic.'

'The Navy must have ships searching,' Austin said.

'They're combing the area. But the people who did this would have expected a Navy search and done something to forestall it. A White House guy at my board meeting said he had heard Vice-President Sandecker sing your praises, and I saw what you did when the bathysphere was all but lost. So I put out the word that I wanted to see you. And here we are.'

'I'll do what I can, but you will have to be totally up front with me, Doc. No holding back.'

'You'll have my full cooperation, Kurt.' Kane looked over at his body-guards. 'My baby sitters are giving me the eye. I have to leave. They think that there's a whole army of assassins waiting out there to do me in.'

'They're only trying to keep you alive. I'll pick up the tab.'

Kane jotted down a number where he could be reached. Then he left the restaurant, trailed by the two men.

LIEUTENANT CASEY was waiting outside the restaurant in the SUV. As Austin got in, he handed him a phone. Sandecker's voice crackled on the line.

'Dr Kane fill you in on the situation, Kurt?'

'He told me about the Blue Medusa research and the missing lab.'

'Good. This thing is ready to blow up if we don't find the lab and get hold of that vaccine. I'll put the whole damn US Navy at your disposal.'

'How long do we have, Admiral?'

'The CDC computers say the virus will hit the major Chinese cities in seventy-two hours. Once the virus goes beyond China's borders, it will become unstoppable. The President is gearing up the National Guard so he can declare a state of emergency.' His voice softened. 'Good luck, Kurt.'

Austin handed the phone back. 'When do we leave, Lieutenant?'

'We have to be at the airport at three a.m.'

Austin said he would see Casey in a few hours and got out of the SUV in front of the NUMA tower. He called Zavala's number on his way to his office to retrieve the Pyramid file but got no response. He wasn't surprised. His friend might have joined the surveillance team and be unable to talk. Austin left him a message to call back as soon as he was clear.

Austin picked up the file, then got on the elevator and headed to the fifteenth floor. He followed a corridor to a door marked NUMASAT and stepped into a large, dimly lit space lined with television screens. The screens displayed information from NUMA's satellite system, a complex network that collected information about oceans from around the world for scientists.

Presiding over the network was an eccentric genius named Jack Wilmut, who supervised the system from a console in the centre of the room.

'What a surprise to find you here at headquarters, Kurt.'

Austin pulled a chair up to the console. 'Don't kid me, Jack. You could figure out exactly where I am in a second. I've got a favour. I've lost contact with Joe. Can you find him?'

'I'll do my best,' Wilmut said. 'What's he got?'

'Try finding his phone.'

Wilmut traced Zavala's cell through its GPS chip. He tapped the keyboard in front of him, and seconds later the screen displayed a blinking red star on a map of the city. Wilmut enlarged the map and switched to a satellite picture. The star was on one of a couple of dozen rectangles, apparently the roofs of large buildings. He zoomed in.

'Looks like an industrial complex,' Wilmut said.

'I need an address,' Austin said.

Wilmut punched a button and GOOD LUCK FORTUNE COOKIE COMPANY appeared on the screen. 'Guess he likes Chinese food,' he said.

Austin thanked Wilmut, and rode the elevator down to the garage to pick up his Jeep Cherokee. As he drove along the Potomac, he found Caitlin's number in his directory. She immediately recognised his voice.

'This must be my lucky week,' she said. 'The two handsomest men at NUMA calling me. How are you, Kurt?'

'I'm a little worried about Joe. Do you know anything about an FBI Asian gang stakeout involving Charlie Yoo?'

'No such thing, Kurt. Charlie is a guest of the Bureau. He is notified of field ops only at our discretion, and we don't have anything like that going.'

'That's what I thought,' Austin said. 'Thanks for your help, Caitlin.'

Austin clicked off and, driving with one hand, reached for a rack under his seat, pulled out the holster containing his Bowen revolver, then stomped on the gas.

Chapter 7

Relying on his knowledge of local waters, Dooley had kept his boat's running lights turned off until he coasted in to the dock and killed the motor. Only then did Gamay confront Paul.

'Before I burst from curiosity, please tell me how you happened to dash from one coast to the other and arrive just in time to rescue the fair maidens in distress. You weren't scheduled to arrive for a couple of days.'

'Kurt called and said he might have unknowingly sent you into danger. I couldn't reach you by phone, so I put the seminar on hold and flew out. I was at the Pine Island Marina looking for a ride to Bonefish Key when Dooley saw me and asked what I was doing. When I mentioned your name, he offered to take me to Bonefish. He then noticed that two kayaks were missing, and figured out where you might have gone.'

'Thanks, Dooley,' Gamay said. She gave him a peck on the cheek. 'You're probably wondering what all this is about.'

'You learn that it's healthier to mind your own business around here, Dr Gamay, but I'll admit to being a little curious about what's going on,' he said.

'You're not the *only* one.' Gamay glanced at Song Lee, who had been huddled on a seat during the trip to the mainland.

Dooley tied up the boat and led the way to his trailer. He extracted a six-pack of Diet Coke from the refrigerator, passed three cans around along with a bag of Goldfish crackers. Without saying a word, he took his shotgun out of a locked cabinet. With the 16-gauge slung over one arm, he ambled out to the dock with the rest of the six-pack.

Song Lee and the Trouts sat round a kitchen table. She sipped her Coke like an automaton and stared into space.

Gamay sensed that Lee was in shock. 'You're safe now, Dr Lee,' she said.

Lee turned her head, and Gamay saw tears glistening in her eyes. 'I'm a doctor,' Lee said. 'I'm supposed to *save* lives, not *take* them.'

'You saved our lives,' Gamay said. 'That man and his friends would have killed us both.'

'Do you have any idea who they were?' Paul asked.

Lee wiped the tears away. 'He was waiting for me where I had left the kayak and forced me to go to the house. We were waiting for people coming to take me away. I pleaded with him. We argued. That's when I grabbed the knife and ran.'

Gamay put her hand on Lee's arm. 'You'd better start at the beginning.'

Lee took a deep breath, then began to tell her story. She had been born in a rural part of China, excelled in science as a college student, and went to study at Harvard Medical School on a grant from the Chinese government. Having seen the ravages of disease among the poor of China, she wanted to do something about it. Returning to China, she found a job with a government programme targeting the health of slum-dwellers. The work centred on immunisation and eliminating the sources of disease. Her success led to a position in a hospital.

Finally, Lee told Gamay how she had been exiled to the countryside after questioning the government's response to the SARS epidemic, and about her redemption and assignment to Bonefish Key, to work on a vaccine, based on an ocean organism, for a new virus strain.

'The Blue Medusa Dr Mayhew showed me?'

'That's right.' She seemed surprised. 'I'm amazed that he allowed you to see it,' Lee said. She stared at Gamay as if she were seeing her for the first time. 'I just realised that I really don't know who you are.'

'I'm a marine biologist with NUMA. I came to Bonefish Key because I was interested in ocean biomedicine. Dr Mayhew said the Blue Medusa was a new species.'

'That's right. Bigger and more aggressive than the sea wasp. After the work moved to the new lab, they were going to use genetic engineering to produce a more powerful toxin.'

'I wasn't aware there *was* another lab,' Gamay said.

'It was secret. They called it Davy Jones's Locker. Dr Kane and Lois Mitchell, his assistant, left Bonefish Key and took a number of scientists and technicians with them. I stayed on to chart the probable spread of the virus and how best to contain it.'

Song Lee's eyelids had been drooping as she talked, and Gamay suggested she lie down on the sofa. Then she and Paul stepped out of the trailer into the warm Florida night.

'Thanks for coming to our rescue, Galahad,' Gamay said.

'Sorry if Sir Dooley and I cut it too close,' Paul said.

Trout's cellphone buzzed. Austin was calling to check on Gamay.

'I'm in Florida now,' Trout said. 'Gamay is all right. But she was attacked along with a Bonefish Key scientist named Dr Song Lee, who was working on something called the Blue Medusa.'

'I want to talk to Dr Lee in person,' Austin said. 'Call NUMA and have them send a plane down to pick you up. Meet me at Washington airport.'

'I'll get right on it.'

'Thanks. I've got another favour.' He gave Trout a phone number. 'Call Cate Lyons, Joe's friend at the FBI. Tell her I'm heading for the Good Luck Fortune Cookie factory in Falls Church. Got to go.'

THE GPS UNIT indicated that Austin was a block from his goal. Reasoning that a turquoise Cherokee might attract unwanted attention, he parked it in an alley between two industrial buildings and made his way on foot to the front gate of the Good Luck Fortune Cookie Company.

The gate was locked. Austin walked the perimeter of the chain-link fence to the rear gate. He pushed the gate open and made his way to a loading dock lit by a single bulb, keeping to the shadows as much as possible.

He wondered if he had the right address. Those doubts vanished when a figure stepped out from behind a Dumpster and blinded Austin with a powerful flashlight.

A deep voice said, 'Hold it right there, soldier. Put your hands in the air.'

Austin stopped in his tracks and did as he was told. He sensed someone creeping up behind him and felt his pistol slip from its holster.

'That's better,' said the voice. 'Turn round . . . *real* slow. I'm giving you a friendly warning. These guys call themselves Ghost Devils, and they mean it. I wouldn't screw with them.'

At least a half-dozen other figures had materialised from the shadows.

'Are you a ghost or a devil?' Austin asked.

The man stepped closer. 'Just a guy doing his job. The name is Phelps.' A tall man in his late forties, he wore jeans, Doc Martens, a black T-shirt that displayed his muscled arms and a US Navy Seals baseball cap on his head.

'Where's Joe?' Austin asked.

Phelps pointed his flashlight at the loading-dock door. 'That way.'

The door slid up. Phelps led the way up the stairs to the dock and herded Austin through the door into the dark warehouse. Phelps hit a switch, and the interior was flooded with light. The big space was empty except for two chairs side by side facing a screen.

'Fortune cookie business must not be very good,' Austin said.

'You don't want to know *your* fortune. The folks I work for aren't too happy with you.'

Austin would have agreed that his prospects for a long and happy life were slim. In addition to Phelps, he was guarded by the tough-faced Asians, all men in their twenties, dressed in black running suits and shoes. They looked dangerously unpredictable.

Phelps called to a couple of Ghost Devils. They went through a door and came back after a minute with Zavala. They shoved the two NUMA men into the chairs and handcuffed them to the armrests.

Zavala's face was caked with dried blood, but he managed to smile when he saw Austin. 'Hi, Kurt, nice of you to crash the party. Time to leave?'

'You'll have to ask Mr Phelps. Are you OK?'

'Charlie Yoo set me up, and some of these guys used my face for a punching bag, but nothing broken that I know of.'

'We'll have to remember to pay them back for their hospitality.'

The warehouse went dark just then, and the two men were enveloped in almost total blackness. After a moment, a spotlight directly overhead blinked on, and they found themselves at the centre of a circle of white light. A second spot came on about twenty-five feet in front of them.

The screen was gone, revealing a table covered in green baize. Behind the table sat a woman. She was dressed in a purple two-piece outfit, and a cloak the same colour was draped round her shoulders. Her dark hair was parted down the middle, and high, arched brows framed a Eurasian face.

Austin stared at the woman in disbelief. 'This is crazy,' he whispered, 'but I *know* her. She's the Dragon Lady.'

Zavala looked at Austin. 'I've seen worse-looking dragons. Why don't you introduce me?'

'Not sure I can, Joe. The Dragon Lady wasn't a real person. She was a character in a comic strip, a stereotypical femme fatale who was always causing trouble. Damn. What was her name?'

The woman's lips parted in a smile. 'My name is Lai Choi San,' she said in a voice that would have been seductive if it hadn't been drained of emotion. 'Bravo, Mr Austin. Few people know I have another name. I have been looking forward to this meeting.'

'I wish I could say the same,' Austin said. He could hardly believe he was talking to a comic-strip character. 'Why did you invite us here?'

'For a start, I want you to tell me the whereabouts of Dr Kane,' she said.

Austin shrugged. 'Kane is under protective custody. Apparently, someone is trying to kill him.'

'*Really?*' she purred. 'Who would want to do that to the brilliant doctor?'

'The same people who hijacked the lab that was developing a vaccine from the medusa toxin.'

The woman gave him a slow-burn stare, and her face actually seemed to glow with anger. 'What you don't know,' she said, 'is that Pyramid *created* the new virus. Our pharmaceutical company was experimenting with an influenza vaccine and inadvertently produced the more virulent strain. They wanted to destroy it, but wiser heads prevailed.'

'Why didn't wiser heads prevent the virus from breaking out?'

'That was an accident, something we would have avoided until we had developed the antidote, which would have gone to members of my organisation first. You see, the virus fitted in with our larger plan of destabilising the government. The SARS outbreak almost toppled China's leaders. Just think how the public would react to their impotence in dealing with an even more lethal virus. They would see Pyramid step in and cure the masses. In return, we would acquire power and fortune. We would replace the government.'

Austin stared at the apparition. 'You're willing to wipe out scores of your countrymen to stir up trouble with your government?' he asked.

'What if we killed a few hundred, or even a few million, Chinese?' she said. 'We have a billion people.'

'You're insane. You'll never be able to keep that virus contained. It's going to hit your big cities in a couple of days. It will be in every country in a week or so.'

'It's our government that is insane. Pyramid has been in our family for generations. Past governments that have tried to destroy our organisation have paid the price. We were here long before those so-called leaders were even born. We won't be thrown into history's dustbin.' The figure at the table seemed to glow incandescently as she launched into a diatribe against the Chinese government for having the audacity to take on the organisation.

Zavala had been staring spellbound at the woman. 'Kurt,' he whispered, 'I can see through her. Look at her right arm, the one she's waving around.'

Austin focused on the moving right arm. Through the material of her silk sleeve, he caught faint glimpses of the brick wall behind her.

'You're right,' he said. 'She's nothing but a holographic projection generated by a computer.'

The Dragon Lady noticed Austin's grin and stopped her tirade. 'You are a strange man, Mr Austin. Don't you fear death?'

'Not from someone who's no more real than a comic strip.'

'Enough!' she snarled. 'I will show you how real I am. My brother Chang awaits you. He will make sure your death is long and painful.'

She issued an order in Chinese, and the guards moved in.

'*Wait* a minute,' Austin called out. 'What if I can produce Dr Kane?'

She barked a second order, and the guards froze in their tracks.

'You said that Kane was in protective custody,' she said.

'I was lying . . . Let me make a phone call and I'll set him up.'

'A futile effort, Mr Austin,' she said. 'I no longer care whether Kane lives or dies. His project is near completion and his services are not needed . . . Goodbye.'

Austin expected the Ghost Devils to move in again, but they were staring towards the rear of the warehouse.

The hologram shimmered. 'What is that?' she asked.

In answer, an amplified voice came from outside. 'This is the FBI. Throw your weapons aside and come out with your hands up.' It was a woman's voice, speaking through a bullhorn.

Phelps had been off to the side, watching the exchange between Austin and the hologram. He stepped out of the shadows and yelled a command in Chinese to the Ghost Devils, who ran back towards the loading-dock door.

Phelps remained under the spotlight, pointing Kurt's Bowen in their direction. Beside him the Dragon Lady's face fuzzed at the edges and broke up into a cloud of swirling and sparkling motes.

'What were you saying about the lab vaccine?' Phelps asked.

'The American and Chinese governments have been secretly working to develop the vaccine to head off a deadly virus, but your outfit stole the lab.'

'I know all about the lab,' Phelps said. 'I'm the one who hijacked it.'

'If that's true,' Austin said, 'then you know where the lab is. Work with us to take it back from these clowns.'

'You weren't kidding about the bug spreading to the States, were you?' Phelps said. 'I've got family in the States.'

Austin looked him straight in the eye. 'There's nothing to prevent them from getting sick. You can't let that happen.'

There was a pause. 'I won't. But I've got to do it my own way.'

Phelps turned his head at the sound of shots and shouting in the distance. He reached into his shirt pocket and pulled out the key to the handcuffs, which he set on the floor. Then he unclipped Austin's holster from his belt, slipped the Bowen back in it, and sent it skittering across the floor and out of sight. A second later, he disappeared into the shadows.

When the warehouse lights snapped on a moment later, he was gone. Cate Lyons had one hand on the light switch, the other on a pistol.

When she saw Austin and Zavala, she came running over to them.

'Are you guys OK? God, Joe, you look like hell. Sorry I'm late. I was waiting for back-up. They're searching the building, but I think everybody got away. Will one of you tell me what's going on?'

She picked the key off the floor, unlocked Austin's handcuffs, and did the same for Zavala. Austin stood up and retrieved his Bowen.

'We'll tell you on the way back to Washington,' he said.

AT 3 A.M. the navy-blue SUV pulled up to a hangar at Reagan National Airport and parked next to a sleek Cessna Citation X jet that had NUMA emblazoned in black on its turquoise fuselage. Austin and Casey emerged from the SUV's back seat, and the lieutenant handed over a plastic pouch.

'This packet contains the nuts-and-bolts details of the mission we talked about on the drive here,' Casey said. 'Good luck, Kurt.'

'Thank you, Lieutenant,' Austin said as they shook hands. He retrieved his duffle bag from the SUV and handed it to a baggage handler, who loaded it into the jet's cargo hold. Tucking the pouch under his arm, he stepped up to the open door and paused there. Headlights were bearing down on the Citation from a red Corvette racing across the tarmac.

The car slammed to a stop next to the hangar. Zavala emerged, grabbed his duffle, tossed it to the handler, and bolted aboard.

The cabin seating was an arrangement of beige leather chairs and a sofa that could all be made into beds. Zavala stretched out in one of the chairs, yawned, and said, 'Any idea where we're going?'

Austin plunked himself down on the sofa and held the pouch up so Zavala could read the top-secret label affixed to the outside.

'Our marching orders,' he announced.

He broke the seal with his thumbnail and extracted the thick wad of paper from inside. He unfolded the first page, which was covered with diagrams, and then passed it over to Zavala. Zavala glanced at the diagrams.

'These are the blueprints for the underwater lab they call Davy Jones's Locker,' he said, his dark eyes sparkling with excitement. With loving care, he spread the diagrams out on a table. He studied every detail of the spheres and connecting passageways.

'*Brilliant*,' he said with unabashed admiration after a few minutes. He crinkled his brow. 'It's hard to believe anything this size could vanish.'

'The designers built in flotation capability, and a stabilisation system to keep it level during movement. The hijackers only had to hook onto the lab, get it pumped up to neutral buoyancy, and tow it away,' Austin said.

'If this was such a big secret,' Zavala said, 'how did the hijackers know where Davy Jones's Locker was located?'

'The lab's security was outsourced to a private contractor,' Austin said, 'and that may have been the weak point. The Navy talked to the support-ship survivors. They said the crew got a request from their security company to shuttle a representative down to the lab a short while before the attack. They said he was a friendly guy with a Southern accent. Phelps, of course. He admitted he hijacked the lab.'

'What was the lab's last position?'

Austin dug a map out of the pouch and spread it on the table. An area in the Pacific Ocean had been circled near the island of Pohnpei in Micronesia.

Zavala sat back and laced his hands behind his head. 'Gee, *that* narrows it down,' he said sourly. 'It could take months to find the lab.'

'Sandecker says we have to wrap it up in less than seventy-two hours.'

'I'm surprised the old sea dog didn't ask us to solve the problem of global hunger and the energy crisis in our spare time.'

'Don't give him any ideas,' Austin said.

The sound of approaching jet engines broke the morning stillness. Austin got up and went to the door. A NUMA jet was taxiing up to the hangar. Three figures emerged and walked across the tarmac towards the Citation.

Austin greeted the Trouts, and welcomed the Asian woman with a friendly smile. 'You must be Dr Song Lee,' he said, offering his hand. 'I'm Kurt Austin. This is Joe Zavala. Thank you for coming to Washington.'

'And thank you for sending Paul and Gamay to Bonefish Key, Mr Austin,' Lee said. 'I'd be dead if they hadn't arrived when they did.'

Kurt's eyes drank in Song's flowerlike beauty. 'That would have been a shame, Dr Lee,' he said. 'Please have a seat. We don't have much time.'

Song Lee settled into the sofa and looked around in wonderment. This grey-haired man, with his broad shoulders and sculpted bronze profile, was intriguing. And his dark-complexioned friend Zavala had the swashbuckling air of a pirate prince.

'The Trouts told me about the attack on the bathysphere,' Lee said. 'Do you know where Dr Kane is?'

'Safe in protective custody. But he has filled me in on the work at Bonefish Key and the undersea lab they called Davy Jones's Locker.'

Lee's jaw dropped. 'I was aware of the secret facility, of course,' she said, 'but I had no idea it was under the sea!'

'The lab's work and location were tightly held secrets, but somehow it was hijacked along with the staff. Joe and I think that the lab's disappearance, the bathysphere attack, and the attempt to kidnap you are all connected. Dr Kane told me about the medusa project. What was the exact nature of your work at the Florida lab?'

'I'm a virologist trained in epidemiology,' Lee said. 'I stayed on Bonefish Key to concentrate on the probable path an epidemic would take and how best to position our resources and the vaccine-production facilities.'

'What would have happened to the project if you had been kidnapped?'

'Not much,' she said with a shrug of the shoulders. 'The plans are almost all in place, waiting for the cure to be synthesised into a viable vaccine. With the lab gone, there isn't much chance of that happening.'

'Don't give up hope, Dr Lee. The lab is the object of a massive search. In fact, Joe and I are on our way to Micronesia to see if we can help.'

Lee dropped her gaze to the map. 'You're going to Pohnpei?' she asked. 'The island was the epicentre of the deadly epidemic that struck the Pacific whaling fleet in the mid-1800s. This is extremely significant.'

'In what way, Dr Lee?'

'At Harvard, I did a paper for a Professor Codman that was based on an article I came across in an old medical journal. The doctor who wrote the article had compiled statistics about a group of New Bedford whaling men who had been virtually disease-free for much of their long lives.'

Austin tried to glance at his watch without being obvious. He had little interest in oddball medical phenomena.

'It has been a great pleasure meeting you,' he said. 'We're going to be taking off soon . . .' The Citation's engines were warming up.

'Hear me out, Mr Austin,' Lee said with unexpected firmness. 'The men in the study group had all crewed aboard the whaling ship *Princess*. They became ill after the ship stopped in Pohnpei. The symptoms of the disease were almost identical to those of this latest epidemic.'

'I still don't see the connection to the lab . . .'

It was Song Lee's turn to be impatient. 'It's right there in front of you, Mr Austin. The crew all survived! They should have died, but instead they enjoyed robust health for the rest of their lives. Somehow, they were cured.'

'Are you saying that what cured the whalers might work for the new virus?' Austin asked.

'Precisely.'

Austin's mental machinery kicked into gear. A bunch of whalers lived disease-free to a ripe old age after a trip to Micronesia, the same neighbourhood where the Blue Medusa lived. He connected that to what Kane had told him about the toxin keeping its prey healthy until the medusa made a meal of it. He glanced around at his colleagues.

'The log of the *Princess* for that expedition would make interesting reading,' Paul Trout commented.

'I tried to track the 1848 logbook down,' Lee said. 'My research led me to New Bedford. A dealer in antique books named Brimmer said he might be able to locate it, but I was about to leave for home and had to put the whole thing aside.'

The pilot's voice called back from the cockpit. 'We've been cleared for early takeoff. Anytime you're ready . . .'

'Thank you, Dr Lee,' Austin said. 'I apologise for cutting you short, but we're really about to leave.'

'I want to come with you,' she said without thinking.

'That's not possible,' Austin said. 'We'll be on the move, and things could get rough. Joe has uncovered information that suggests a Chinese Triad named Pyramid is involved in all this.'

'A *Triad*?' She got over her surprise quickly. 'Why would a Triad be interested in the search for an antiviral vaccine?'

Zavala answered. 'The Triad developed the virus to destabilise the Chinese government. Your vaccine would have spoiled their plans.'

'All the more reason to take me with you. I'm intimately acquainted with the research programme, and there may be something relevant on Pohnpei.'

Austin sat back and folded his arms. Despite his body language, he was enjoying Song Lee's display of pluckiness.

'Go ahead, Dr Lee. You've got thirty seconds to make your case.'

She nodded. 'I believe that the Blue Medusa the lab was using in its research was part of native medicine used to cure the crew of the *Princess*. And if we can find the place where it happened, it might lead us to the lab.'

'That's a pretty slim premise, Dr Lee.'

'I know that, Mr Austin. But it's *something*. Right now, we have nothing.'

Zavala chuckled softly. 'Lady's got a point,' he said.

Austin threw his hands in the air. 'Looks like I'm outgunned, Dr Lee.' He turned to the Trouts. 'Get in touch with Lieutenant Casey and tell him that Dr Lee has joined us.' He paused in thought, then said, 'And while we're away, see what you can do about tracking down the *Princess*'s logbook.'

'We'll start with Perlmutter and let you know,' Paul said.

Chapter 8

St Julien Perlmutter customarily worked into the wee hours and slept until long after the sun had risen. So when the telephone beside his king-size bed gonged like a ship's bell and awoke the renowned naval historian from a sound slumber, his usually sunny greeting had an edge to it.

'St Julien Perlmutter here. State your damned business in a brief manner. And you'd better have a good excuse for calling at this ungodly hour!'

'Good morning, Julien,' said a female voice. 'Hope I didn't wake you.'

The ruddy features that were almost hidden under a thick grey beard underwent a miraculous Hyde-to-Jekyll transformation. The scowl disappeared, and the sky-blue eyes suddenly sparkled with good humour.

'Good morning, my dear Gamay,' Perlmutter purred. 'Of *course* you didn't wake me up. I was in that delightful state between sleep and waking, dreaming of breakfast.'

Gamay chuckled. It was rare when the 400-pound Perlmutter *wasn't* thinking about food. 'I'm glad to hear that, Julien, because Paul and I would like to come over and see you. We'll bring you a treat.'

Perlmutter smacked his lips at the prospect. 'I'll get the coffee brewing.'

He replaced the receiver and swung his feet out of the bed, which was set into an alcove off a huge combination living room and study. Perlmutter made his home in an N Street carriage house a few blocks from the Trouts' town house. The shelves that lined every wall sagged under the weight of thousands of books. More books were stacked on tables and chairs, and piled on the floor. Experts acknowledged his vast collection to be the finest accumulation of historical ship literature ever assembled.

Slipping a red-and-gold paisley robe over his purple silk pyjamas, Perlmutter went to the kitchen to put on a pot of Papua New Guinea coffee. He felt almost human by the time the doorbell rang.

'Smoked Scottish salmon, blini and caviar, and fresh-baked croissants,' Gamay said, holding out a flat cardboard box.

Smiling, Perlmutter took the box and led the way to his kitchen. He poured the coffee and doled out the early brunch on three plates. They all sat round a polished wooden kitchen table, one of the few flat surfaces in the carriage house not piled high with books.

'Sorry for the early-morning call,' Paul began, 'but there is some urgency to our search. We're trying to track down the 1848 logbook of a whaling vessel named the *Princess*. Could you tell us where to start?'

Perlmutter's bushy brows bobbed up and down. 'Caleb Nye's ship!' he exclaimed.

Gamay tossed her head back and laughed in surprise. 'You never cease to amaze, Julien,' she said. 'We mention a whaling ship, one of hundreds, and you have the name of the captain on the tip of your tongue.'

'Only because the young man had a memorable experience. Caleb was not the captain. He was the ship's green hand, the newest crew member. He claimed to have been swallowed by a sperm whale.'

Paul turned to Gamay. 'You're the marine biologist in the family. Would it be possible for a sperm whale to swallow a man?'

'Sperm whales have been found with giant squids in their stomachs, so, physiologically, it might be possible.'

Perlmutter rose from the table. He opened a tall metal storage container, and pulled out a poster. It announced, in huge circus typeface, that *Caleb Nye, a living Jonah*, would be giving an ILLUSTRATED PRESENTATION at the FIRST PARISH METHODIST CHURCH IN WORCESTER, MASS. The engraving, coloured by hand, showed a sperm whale attacking a whaleboat.

'Caleb Nye produced affidavits from the master of the ship, Captain Horatio Dobbs, and fellow crew members saying that the story was true. You said you were looking for the 1848 log of the *Princess*?' asked Perlmutter.

'That's right,' Paul said. 'We're hoping you can help us find it.'

'A wise decision. I suggest that you start with Rachael Dobbs, a great-great-great-granddaughter of the good captain. She lives in New Bedford, and is the curator of the Dobbs Museum.'

Paul said, 'We could be there in a couple of hours.'

'Splendid. I'll give her a call.'

Perlmutter consulted a Rolodex and dialled the number. He chatted amiably with someone, then hung up and said, 'She'll see you at three o'clock, but she had some good news and some bad news. The good news is that the logbook of the 1848 voyage was given to Caleb Nye. The bad news is that a fire destroyed Nye's library.'

'Without the log, we don't know where the *Princess* stopped,' Paul said.

'True,' Gamay said. 'But Caleb Nye was an eyewitness to the voyage. He told hundreds of people about his experience. We might find something somewhere with the details of his trip.'

'It's worth a talk with Ms Dobbs,' Perlmutter said. 'By the way, you never said why you were interested in the log.'

'It's a long story,' Paul said. 'We can tell you over dinner when we get back. Your choice. Our treat.'

AS THE CITATION X streaked west over North America all was quiet in the cabin, where the passengers slept soundly.

Song Lee had been the first to turn in, followed by Joe Zavala, who was stretched out on a thickly padded chair. Kurt Austin had read for a short while, then he had set Casey's file aside and glanced at Song, who was sleeping on the sofa. Austin went up to the cockpit and radioed the ground-crew manager at Los Angeles Airport. He came back, settled into another chair, and within minutes had slipped into a deep slumber.

When the passengers got off at LAX to stretch their legs, the ground-crew manager was waiting to hand Lee a plastic bag. At Austin's request, the manager's wife had put together a change of clothes to replace the T-shirt and shorts Lee had been wearing since Bonefish Key.

When Lee opened the bag, she let out a cry of delight, and dashed into the hangar. She squeezed in a quick shower before dressing, and a brief phone call, and then the jet leapt into the sky again and set a course for Honolulu. With the California coastline fading behind in the distance, Lee came over and sat next to Austin. She was wearing black cotton slacks and a white cotton blouse that looked stylish on her slim figure.

'I understand you arranged for the delivery of my new wardrobe,' she said. 'Thank you very much, Kurt. The clothes fit me perfectly.'

'Sailors are good at taking measurements with their eyes,' Austin said.

He saw Zavala mouthing the word *Smooth*, and realised that he had compared Song Lee's lithe body to a boat keel. Quickly changing the subject, he said, 'Dr Kane mentioned the development of a larger and more poisonous genetically modified version of the medusa.'

Lee nodded. 'He wanted to produce more toxin. The goal was to produce the vaccine in volume. We transferred the genes that produced the essential compounds to a bacterium that could be quickly cultivated for the vaccine.'

'Dr Kane said that the medusa toxin doesn't kill outright but paralyses the prey and keeps it healthy and fresh.'

'An antiviral has to kill the pathogens without hurting the host. The medusa toxin went beyond that, actually *protecting* its host organism's health . . . for a while, anyway. The process is called hormesis. In small doses, a toxin can trigger repair mechanisms in the body, maybe even retard ageing. It works in the same way exercise does, by stressing the body so that it changes the metabolism for the better.'

'Could hormesis have anything to do with the New Bedford anomaly?'

'It could have *everything* to do with it. Administered in the proper amount, the medusa toxin could have improved subjects' health and prolonged their lives.'

'Let's talk about the new flu virus. How bad would it be if the epidemic goes beyond China's borders?' Austin asked.

'*Very* bad. If this virus hits your country, it would kill a minimum of two hundred thousand people, maximum possibly millions. But even in the hundreds of thousands, the epidemic would overwhelm the health system. The medical community has worried about a mutant flu virus for years.'

'How does the new virus spread?'

'The old virus spread by contact. The mutant strain may spread that way, but, even more disturbing, it may spread through the water.'

'Which means that the virus could be introduced into drinking water.'

'That would make its spread even more difficult to control. Everyone drinks water, while personal contact is a hit-or-miss thing. It's possible that the whole human race could become infected.'

Song Lee felt emotionally drained by the implications of her dry recitation and expected Austin to share her pessimism. But, to her surprise, he said, 'Thank you for your analysis, Dr Lee, but we can't let that happen.'

'What do you mean to do?'

'Once we find the lab, we'll make sure that the staff is safe. Then we'll retrieve the research and allow vaccine production to move ahead. And then we'll proceed to sink the Triad. How's that sound to you, Joe?'

'Sounds like we'll need some chow to keep us going. I'll see what I can rustle up in the galley.'

Austin had summed up his strategy as casually as if he were talking about making a soccer play. Zavala was throwing breakfast together. Lee saw no sign of madness or misplaced humour in the face of either man, only steely resolve.

For the first time since she had learned that Davy Jones's Locker had vanished, she began to hope.

THE TROUTS HAD TO WAIT until the afternoon for an available NUMA jet, but New Bedford was only about an hour's flight from Washington. With Gamay navigating, Paul drove their rented SUV directly to the Greek Revival mansion that housed the Captain Horatio Dobbs Museum.

The Trouts climbed to the porch, passing between tall Doric columns, and rang the bell. A middle-aged woman opened the door.

'Oh,' she said, her smile vanishing. 'I thought you were the electrician.'

Gamay said, 'I'm afraid not. We're from the National Underwater and Marine Agency. We called you earlier today from Washington.'

The smile returned. 'Oh, yes, Mr Perlmutter's friends. Come in. I'm Rachael Dobbs. Excuse me for being a bit flustered. The Dobbs Foundation rented a patio tent for a jazz concert tonight, and there's a problem with the sound system.'

The Trouts stepped into a high-ceilinged vestibule and Rachael Dobbs gave the Trouts a tour of the mansion. Then they went out onto a broad deck overlooking a formal garden bordered with rosebushes. She seated the Trouts at an umbrellaed table and brought out glasses of iced tea.

'Thank you for the tour,' Gamay said. 'It's a beautiful house.'

'The captain and his wife moved up here from Johnny Cake Hill. The whaling merchants wanted bigger homes that reflected their status in the community. Now, how may I help you? St Julien said on the phone that you were interested in one of the captain's logbooks.'

'We received a query from a virologist who asked us about an epidemic that struck the Pacific whaling fleet in 1848,' Gamay said. 'We want to see if we can find any mention of the event. But I believe you told St Julien that the logbook for the 1848 voyage was destroyed,' Gamay said.

'Unfortunately, yes,' Rachael said with a sigh. 'Caleb Nye's whaling library went up in flames when his house burned to the ground.'

'Isn't it curious that the captain would have given his log to a former crewman?' Gamay said.

'Not really. The captain would have known about Caleb's collection. Also, there was a peculiar bond between the two men. It was said that the captain felt personally responsible for what happened to the young man. He wrote an affidavit saying that the Jonah story was true. It was read at Caleb's travelling show and helped make Caleb a rich man.'

Rachael excused herself to answer the doorbell and came back a moment later. 'The electrician is here. We could talk later, if you don't mind waiting.'

'We're on a tight schedule,' Gamay said. 'Do you have any suggestions on how we might find out more about Caleb Nye?'

'You could start in our basement. We have a section of the diorama Nye used in his presentations. Perhaps I can show it to you when I'm not so busy. In the meantime, there is the New Bedford Whaling Museum. And there is one other avenue, although I hesitate to suggest it.'

'We're grasping at straws,' Paul said.

'Well, then,' she said with a shrug, 'you might talk to Harvey Brimmer. He deals in antique documents from a shop on Johnny Cake Hill.'

'Why do you hesitate to recommend Mr Brimmer?' Paul asked.

'There have been rumours of forgeries, but either the rumours are false or he's too slick to get caught. I believe the latter.'

'Thank you for the warning,' Paul said.

The Trouts gave Rachael a donation to the museum on their way out.

'Good luck with your research,' she said in parting, then scurried off to meet the electrician.

'Wasn't Brimmer the guy Song Lee contacted when she was looking for the logbook?' Paul asked.

'I'm sure that was his name,' Gamay said. 'Maybe we'll have more success than she did.'

BRIMMER'S SHOP was on the ground floor of a three-storey clapboard building. The black wooden sign over the door was so faded it was almost impossible to make out H. BRIMMER ANTIQUE BOOKS, MAPS AND DOCUMENTS.

The Trouts stepped into the shop and adjusted their eyes to the dim light. Several filing cabinets lined walls that were covered with paintings showing various aspects of the whaling trade. At the centre of the room was a large wooden table covered with dozens of maps of all sizes.

A door at the back of the shop opened in response to the jingling of the doorbell and a thinly built man stepped out.

'Good afternoon,' the man said with a smile. 'I'm Harvey Brimmer. May I be of some assistance?'

'I'm Paul Trout, and this is my wife, Gamay. We're looking for any material you might have on Caleb Nye.'

Brimmer's watery blue eyes widened behind his wire-rimmed bifocals. 'Caleb Nye! Now, that's a name you don't hear very often. How did you come to know about our local Jonah?'

'My wife and I are whaling-history buffs. We came across Caleb's name in connection with Captain Horatio Dobbs. We were on our way to the Whaling Museum and saw your sign.'

'Well, you are in luck. I can put my hands on some brochures from his travelling show. They're in storage at my workshop.'

'We wondered if there were any logbooks available for the *Princess* that may have survived the Nye mansion fire,' Gamay said.

Brimmer frowned. 'The fire was a tragedy. But I believe I may be able to help you. There's a little-known story about Caleb Nye. He married a Fairhaven girl, but the family was not pleased at her betrothal to someone considered a freak, rich as he was, and they kept the matter quiet. The Nyes had a daughter who was given some of the books from the library as a dowry. I may be able to get my hands on a *Princess* logbook. I'd need a finder's fee up front.'

'Of course,' Gamay said. 'Would you be able to find the logbook for 1848, the year of Captain Dobbs's last whaling voyage? We'd be prepared to pay whatever it takes.'

Brimmer pinched his chin between his forefinger and thumb. 'I have contacts I can check with, but I'd need a few hours. Can I call you?'

Paul handed Brimmer a business card with his cellphone number on it. 'Please let us know as soon as you hear something,' he said. He wrote a cheque for the large finder's fee and they shook hands all round.

BRIMMER WATCHED through the window of his shop until the Trouts were out of sight, then he went to his office behind the showroom. He picked up the phone and dialled a number from his Rolodex.

'Harvey Brimmer,' he said to the person at the other end of the line. 'I've got more buyers interested in the book we talked about a few days ago. The price may go up. Yes, I can wait for your call. Don't be too long.'

He hung up and sat back in his chair, a smug expression on his face. Years before, a young woman at Harvard had asked about the *Princess* logbook of 1848. He told her he would put out the word, but she said she would have to wait because she was going home to China. He hadn't thought about the enquiry again until a few weeks ago when an Asian man dropped by the shop looking for the same item.

Brimmer didn't know what was going on, but there was nothing a dealer liked better than to have collectors bidding against one another. This promised to be a profitable day.

THE TROUTS STEPPED from the dim shop into the afternoon sunshine and walked up Johnny Cake Hill.

'What did you think of Brimmer?' Paul asked.

'I think he's a slippery old eel,' she said. 'Did you see his expression change when we mentioned Dobbs's 1848 logbook? He'll dig out the first logbook he can get his hands on, forge a date, and try to sell it to us.'

'I'd love to read the paper that Song wrote at Harvard,' Paul said.

Gamay slipped her BlackBerry out of her handbag. 'Do you remember the name of Lee's professor?'

'How could I forget?' Paul said with a smile. 'His name was Codman.'

'Trout . . . Cod . . . Why are all you New Englanders named after fish?'

'Because we didn't have wine connoisseurs for fathers.'

'Touché,' she said.

She called up the Harvard Medical School on her BlackBerry, typed Codman's name into a person finder, and called the number shown on the screen. Lysander Codman answered the call.

'Hello, Professor Codman? My name is Dr Gamay Morgan-Trout. I'm a friend of Dr Song Lee. I'm hoping that you remember her.'

'Dr Lee? How could I forget that brilliant young woman? How is she?'

'We saw her yesterday, and she's fine. She's working with some NUMA colleagues of mine, but she mentioned a paper she had done at Harvard and submitted to you. It has something to do with a medical phenomenon called the New Bedford anomaly.'

'Oh, yes,' Codman said, chuckling. 'It was an unusual subject.'

'We told Song Lee we'd be in the neighbourhood, and she asked if my husband and I could swing by and pick up a copy for her. She's lost the original.'

'Normally, I wouldn't hold on to a student's paper, but the subject was so bizarre I kept it. I'm sure I can put my hands on it.'

Gamay gave Paul a thumbs up. 'Thank you very much, Professor. We'll be there in a little over an hour, if that's convenient.'

She jotted down directions to Codman's office. Minutes later, she and Paul were heading north out of the city.

THE VOICE OF THE PILOT crackled over the Citation X's cabin intercom.

'Sorry to wake you folks up, but we're making our approach to Pohnpei. Please make sure your seat belts are buckled.'

Austin yawned and looked over at Song Lee, who was rubbing the sleep from her eyes. She pressed her nose against the Plexiglas window. The island below was roughly circular, surrounded by a thin barrier reef enclosing a vast lagoon of intense blue. Luxuriant green forests laced with waterfalls covered the soaring peak towering over the island.

'It's *beautiful*,' she said.

'I stopped here on a NUMA research ship a couple of years ago,' Austin said. 'The tall volcanic peak is Mount Nahna Laud. It inspired European explorers to call the place Ascension Island. It seemed to them to rise right up to heaven,' said Austin. 'Look, you can see the ruins of the old city at Nan Madol on the southeast coast. They call it the Venice of the Pacific. Maybe we can explore it after we're through with our other business. Tell you what, I'll take you out to dinner with a water view and introduce you to *sakau*. It's the firewater that the locals make from pepper plants.'

Song gazed with curiosity at Kurt. He was as excited as a schoolboy at the prospect of returning to Nan Madol. The fact that he faced a herculean task and held the lives of hundreds of thousands of people in his hands didn't seem to faze him. His self-assurance must be catching, she thought, because she said, 'Yes, I'd like that. Perhaps we should visit Nan Madol sooner than later. It might have a bearing on this other "business", as you called it.'

'In what way, Dr Lee?'

'It's a strange story from the first mate of the *Princess*. The island the ship sailed to when the crew became sick was known to be unfriendly to whalers. So, after dropping anchor, he and the captain went ashore to see if there were any natives there. They didn't see anybody, but they did come across some ruins. The captain remarked on the strange carvings similar to those he'd seen at Nan Madol.'

'So if we can find an island that has ruins like Nan Madol,' Austin said, 'then there's a chance the *Princess* stopped there.'

'That's what I was thinking,' Lee said.

'How does that help us find the lab?'

'When I was at Bonefish Key, I heard that the field lab was running short of blue medusas. There was no assurance that the mutant would be the answer, in which case other avenues would have to be explored. There was a plan to collect medusae from a newfound source. If the lab is still working on the vaccine, it would need medusas. Which means that if we find that source, the lab may be nearby.'

Austin thought for a moment, then said, 'I know a guide named Jeremiah Whittles who lives in Kolonia, which is the biggest town on Pohnpei. He took me out to the ruins the last time I was here. It might be worth talking to him to see if he knows anything that might help.'

The Citation X circled one last time, then glided in for a perfect landing. As they stepped out of the plane, their lungs filled with warm air laden with the heavy scent of tropical flowers. It was like stepping into a steam room, but nobody complained about the heat or humidity after being cooped up for so many hours in the temperature-controlled cabin.

The pleasant-mannered customs officer stamped their passports and welcomed them to Micronesia. Lee had left her passport back on Bonefish Key, but a State Department call ahead to Honolulu had produced temporary paperwork that would get her in and out of the islands.

The lobby was deserted except for a man in baseball cap, T-shirt and shorts holding a square of cardboard with NUMA printed on it.

Austin introduced himself and the others in the party.

'Nice to meet you,' the man said. 'I'm Ensign Frank Daley. Pardon my disguise, but we're trying to keep this operation low-key. We've got a chopper waiting to take you to my ship, the cruiser *Concord*.'

As they walked out to the grey Sikorsky Seahawk that had been awaiting their arrival, Austin asked Daley the status of the search.

'We've covered hundreds of square miles using surface and air. We've got six Navy ships working the waters around the lab site. A NUMA research vessel has come in to help out. My ship is the command centre,' the ensign said. 'Nothing so far.'

Austin had been thinking about his conversation with Lee. 'Dr Lee has a lead we'd like to pursue on the island. Could you give Joe a lift out to the ship and pick us up in a few hours?'

'The Navy is at your beck and call, Mr Austin,' Daley said.

While the sixty-five-foot chopper carried Joe off to join the search flotilla, Austin and Lee exited the airport terminal to look for the taxi stand. A young man in his twenties was leaning against a faded maroon Pontiac station wagon, with KOLONIA TAXI CO. painted on the door. Austin approached the man and asked him if he knew a tour guide named Jeremiah Whittles.

'Old Jerry? For sure,' the man said with a bright smile. 'Hop in.'

As the Pontiac pulled away from the kerb, a black Chevrolet Silverado pick-up that had been parked several car lengths behind the station wagon followed it into Kolonia, a town of about 6,000 whose ramshackle Main Street had a frontier air about it. The Pontiac turned off Main into a residential neighbourhood and stopped in front of a neat yellow house.

The Silverado passed the Pontiac wagon and pulled up a short distance ahead where the driver could watch in his rearview mirror as Austin and Lee went up to the front door. Austin rang the bell and heard someone inside say hello. A moment later, a slightly built man who looked to be in his eighties answered the door.

Jeremiah Whittles's eyes widened in surprise. 'Is that Kurt Austin? My God, I don't believe it! How long has it been?'

'Too long, Whit. How are you?'

'Older, but not necessarily wiser. What brings you here, Kurt?'

'Some routine NUMA stuff for the Navy. I'm showing Dr Lee here around. She's interested in Nan Madol, and I couldn't think of anyone more knowledgeable on the subject than Pohnpei's best-known guide.'

'Make that best-known *former* guide,' Whittles said. 'I'm retired now. C'mon in.'

With his pink-skinned pate, thin aquiline nose, kindly yet inquisitive blue eyes behind wire-rimmed bifocals, and slightly stooped shoulders, Whittles resembled a friendly buzzard.

He led the way through rooms filled with Micronesian folk art and settled his visitors on a screened-in porch.

Whittles asked Lee what she knew about Nan Madol.

'Not a lot, I must confess,' she said. 'Only that it has been called the Venice of the Pacific.'

'Nan Madol is a far cry from the city on the Adriatic,' he said, 'but it is impressive nonetheless. It consists of ninety-two artificial islets dating back to AD 1100. The builders rafted hexagonal basalt pillars to the tidal flats and reef off Tenwen, and stacked them horizontally to make artificial, flat-topped islets. A grid of shallow canals connects the islets to one another.'

'Do you know of any ruins engraved with unusual carvings similar to those of Nan Madol on another island?' Lee asked.

'Only one instance,' Whittles said. 'I've heard reports of a temple similar to the temple known as the Cult of the Healing Priests, but I've never been able to verify it.'

'What exactly was this cult?' Austin asked.

'It originated on an island near Pohnpei. The priests travelled round the islands tending the sick and became known for their miraculous healing.'

Austin exchanged glances with Lee.

'As a doctor,' she said, 'I'm very interested in the healing part.'

'Wish I could tell you more,' Whittles said, 'but the civilisation degenerated from the effects of internecine warfare and there is no written record.'

'What do the carvings at Nan Madol represent?' Lee asked.

'I can show you better than I can tell you,' Whittles said.

He went into his study and dug through his filing cabinets, returning with a brown envelope. He opened the envelope and pulled out a stack of five-by-seven photos. He picked out one and handed it to Lee.

'This is the façade of the temple as seen from a canal,' he explained. 'There's a hollow space under the temple's floor that seems to have been some sort of pool. This picture shows the carvings on the interior.'

Lee stared at the photo for a moment, then passed it over to Austin, who studied the bell shapes in it and then looked up.

'Jellyfish?' he asked.

'It appears to be,' Whittles said. 'Not sure why.'

'I'd like to see this place in person,' Austin said, his eyes sparkling with excitement. 'Can you tell us where it is?'

'I can show you exactly, but I hope you brought your bathing suit. The platform the temple rested on got knocked around in an earthquake years ago and sank into the canal. Not too deep. Maybe twelve feet or so.'

Austin looked at Lee. 'What's your pleasure, ma'am? Head off to our ship or check it out?'

'I think the answer to that question is obvious,' she said.

Austin asked to borrow a telephone book and within minutes had arranged to rent a boat and some scuba equipment. Whittles marked the temple's location on a tourist map of the ruined city. They thanked him and then went back out to the waiting Pontiac. As the taxi headed towards the harbour, the Chevy Silverado followed a few lengths behind.

DR CODMAN GREETED the Trouts in the lobby of a Harvard Medical School building. The professor was a tall, loose-boned man who had the type of long, big-toothed face that seemed to raise the possibility that some of the old Yankee families had bred with horses.

Codman led the Trouts to his spacious office and asked them to make themselves comfortable while he poured cups of Earl Grey from a pot. He then plunked himself behind his desk and held up a bound report so the Trouts could read the title on its cover: THE NEW BEDFORD ANOMALY: A STUDY OF IMMUNE RESPONSE AMONG CREW FROM THE WHALING SHIP *PRINCESS*.

'I've had a chance to browse through Dr Lee's paper,' Codman said. 'It's even more curious than I remember.'

'Curious in what way, Professor Codman?' Paul asked.

'You'll understand when you get into it. Dr Lee's treatise is based mostly on the work of a doctor in immunology here. A newspaper reporter had interviewed retired whaling men, looking to chronicle their exploits, and noticed that a group in their seventies and eighties had been almost completely disease-free for a good part of their lives. The story caught the doctor's eye and he organised a team of physicians to investigate. They talked to the men and the physicians who had treated them. They found that the men had all served on the whaling ship *Princess* during a single voyage in 1848 and been infected on that voyage with a tropical illness. They were compared to men from other ships, and the statistical differences healthwise were startling. The doctors backed up their findings with tables and graphs and so on.'

'Yet you expressed some doubt over Dr Lee's findings,' Gamay said.

Professor Codman sat back in his chair, tenting his fingers. 'The preliminary stating of facts didn't bother me as much as her conclusions,' he said after a moment. 'The basis for Dr Lee's paper was built on empirical evidence that I found hard to swallow: primarily, her observations on the anecdotes told by the men involved, recollected decades after the event.'

'What was the nature of those recollections?' Paul asked.

'They all had the same story: they fell ill after leaving port, became unconscious, and woke up the next day in good health.'

'Was spontaneous remission a possibility?' Gamay asked.

'Judging by the ferocity of a flulike plague that rampaged through the fleet then, as well as its high mortality rate, I'd say spontaneous remission was not likely.'

'You said the crewmen all told the same story,' Gamay said. 'Wouldn't that strengthen the account of what happened?'

'A whaling vessel was a community unto itself. I think they developed a shared story line.' He paused. 'Only the first mate had a different version.'

'Did he contradict the crew's version?' Gamay asked.

'No. In fact, he supplemented it. He recalled the ship dropping anchor at an island, even going ashore with the captain. He also remembered the captain mentioning seeing glowing blue lights and feeling a stinging sensation in his chest. He woke up feeling as if he had never been sick.'

'That's interesting about the stinging sensation,' Gamay said. 'Do you think the captain was talking about a primitive version of inoculation?'

'He seemed to have been going in that direction. He said all the surviving crew and officers had a reddish mark on their chests. The lights could have been hallucinations or the electrical phenomenon known as Saint Elmo's fire and the marks insect bites. In any case, inoculation can prevent disease but isn't known to cure it.' He handed the report to Gamay. 'I'm sure you will find this fascinating reading.'

The Trouts were walking back to their car when Paul's cellphone trilled.

He listened for a moment, then said, 'OK.' He clicked the phone shut, and said, 'Guess we owe our friend Brimmer an apology. He's got the 1848 logbook from the *Princess*. He'll meet us at his workshop to turn it over.'

HARVEY BRIMMER PUT the phone down and eyed the four Asian men in his office. They were in their twenties, dressed identically in black leather jackets and jeans. They had arrived in New Bedford not long after Brimmer had made the call about the logbook. Their leader, a thin-faced youth with a scar running down his right cheek, was the one who had visited the bookshop before. He had told Brimmer to call the Trouts.

'They're on their way,' Brimmer said. 'Why do you want to see them?'

The leader pulled a gun out of his shirt. 'We don't want to *see* them, old man,' he said, smiling. 'We want to *kill* them.'

He ripped the phone line from the wall, then ordered Brimmer to hand over his cellphone, which he pocketed.

Brimmer's blood ran cold. He was smart enough to figure out that, as witness to a double murder, he would not be allowed to live. As he sat behind his desk, he thought about the spare cellphone he kept locked in one of its drawers. When he saw his chance, he would make his move.

THE BATTERED SKIFF Austin had rented on the Kolonia waterfront was powered by an outboard that belonged in a museum of nautical artefacts. He was glad to see that the scuba gear he'd rented was in better shape than the boat. As an afterthought, he purchased a throwaway underwater camera encased in plastic. Then, after stowing the dive-gear bag, he helped Song Lee into the boat and they set off at a slow but steady pace along the coast.

Nan Madol was about forty-five minutes by boat from Kolonia. As they caught their first glimpse of the enigmatic islets, Austin reached back into his memory to recall what Whittles had told him about the ruins.

Built mostly in the twelfth century, the city served as a residence for nobility and mortuary priests, and its population never went beyond a thousand. The mortuary spread over fifty-eight islands in the northeast part of the city, while the administrative sector, where the nobles lived and the warriors were quartered, was located on the southwestern part of Nan Madol.

The rectangular islets were all basically the same. Retaining walls, built by stacking heavy, prismatic basalt columns, surrounded cores of coral rubble. Once the walls reached several feet above sea level, platforms were built on top as foundations for living areas, or temples, or even crypts.

In the drawing Whittles had sketched for Austin, the temple of the Cult of the Healing Priests was in the mortuary sector. The temple was entered through a portal in the outer wall, which enclosed a courtyard, then through another portal in a second wall.

Austin steered the boat into the city, cruising past crumbling walls. They waved at the passengers in a couple of open boats carrying tourists, and went past a guide leading several kayaks like a row of ducklings.

Consulting Whittles's map, Austin turned onto a dead-end canal lined by basalt walls and palm trees. In bygone days, the temple would have presided over the terminus of the canal, but the only sign it had ever existed was a jumbled pile of columns that stuck a foot or so above the surface.

Austin killed the engine and dropped anchor within yards of the debris.

He tucked his wallet and phone in the waterproof bag and slipped into the dive gear. He rolled over the gunwale into the tepid water, came back up and gave Song Lee a quick wave, then bit on the regulator mouthpiece and dived down several feet into the slow-moving brownish-green water.

He switched on a waterproof flashlight he had bought at the shop. Visibility was limited in the murky water, but the light picked out the broken basalt that had once been the islet's foundation. Austin swam round the perimeter, then again at a different depth. He saw an opening where basalt slabs had fallen at an angle and poked his flashlight into the cavity. The light petered out, suggesting that there was open space behind. Austin twisted through the tight space, banging his air tank against the basalt.

Once he was through the passage, Austin swept the flashlight around and saw that he was in a cavelike chamber created when the inner and outer walls collapsed against one another. There was something peculiar about the way the shadows fell on the debris to his right. He swam closer, and saw that a slab had fallen and was blocking some columns, thus creating a breach.

Austin slithered through the breach, and, after swimming a few yards, came upon an almost perfectly rectangular entryway. He made a quick visual check to assure himself that the entryway wouldn't collapse, then swam through it and into the temple itself.

Austin's flashlight immediately fell on the pool that Whittles had described. It was rectangular, about twenty feet long and fifteen feet wide. Debris had fallen in it, but Austin estimated it was around twelve feet deep. Playing his light against one of the walls, he saw that he was not alone.

Carved on the wall were six male figures dressed in loincloths. They were standing in profile, each holding a basin over his head. Three figures faced one another on either side of a huge bell-shaped jellyfish, whose tentacles dropped down to a waist-high stone dais built against the wall. There were identical carvings and daises on each wall. Austin moved in closer, tracing the contours of one of the jellyfish with his fingers, as if doing so would connect him with the ancient cult of healers. Then he dug out the camera, clicked off a dozen shots, and tucked it away.

Eager to tell Lee what he had found, Austin swam out of the temple, wriggled through the outer walls and looked up to see the boat silhouetted against the shimmering surface. As he ascended, his ears picked up the high-revving buzz of a boat engine. He wondered why anyone would be speeding through the peaceful canal. Then an alarm went off in his brain.

He followed the anchor line up. His head broke the surface a few feet from the boat. Pushing his mask up on his forehead, he saw an inflatable pontoon boat entering the canal and speeding in his direction. It was too far away for him to see the passengers' faces clearly, but the sunlight glinted off the shiny bald pate of Chang, the Triad's gang leader who had attacked the *Beebe*. The needle on Austin's danger meter swung into the red zone.

Song Lee was sitting in the rental boat, oblivious to the looming threat. Austin yelled, pointing at the inflatable. The smile Lee had greeted his reappearance with became a puzzled frown. Austin was close enough to see the grin on Chang's face as he knelt in the bow with a weapon up to his shoulder. He would have been on them in seconds, but the kayaks seen earlier entered and blocked the way. The inflatable swerved to miss the kayaks, but its wash capsized two of them.

Austin took advantage of the seconds lost in performing the tricky manoeuvre. '*Jump!*' he yelled to Lee.

She put her hands on the boat's gunwale and tumbled over into the canal just seconds before Chang's bullets ripped into the boat.

Austin put one arm round her waist, as if leading her through a waltz step, and with his free hand pointed the flashlight at his face. She had reflexively taken a gulp of air before hitting the water but now had used up her supply and was flailing in panic. Austin released her, took a deep breath, then removed the regulator from his mouth and pointed to the bubbles streaming from the mouthpiece.

Lee's eyes were wide with fright, but she understood what Austin was trying to convey. She took the mouthpiece and clamped it between her teeth. As she filled her lungs, the panic in her eyes subsided. She then passed the mouthpiece back to Austin.

Buddy-breathing would keep them alive, but there was still Chang and his men to deal with. Chang could easily have waited until Austin and Lee used up their air supply. But he was impatient. This became clear when Austin saw a foamy splash in the water, then another. Chang's men were diving off the boat.

Austin drew air into his lungs, passed the mouthpiece back to Lee, and pointed with his index finger. *This way.*

Taking Lee by the hand, he swam deeper, towards the entrance of the temple enclosure. At a disadvantage without air, Chang's men were quickly outdistanced. By the time their prey vanished through the temple wall, the men were swimming back to the surface. Chang's boat moved back and forth, searching for telltale bubbles. Not seeing any, Chang ordered that the inflatable move farther out into the canal.

Inside the temple Lee was buddy-breathing like a pro, but she almost gulped down a mouthful of water when Austin showed her the wall carvings. She shook her head in frustration at not being able to talk. Austin pointed to the camera clipped to his vest and signalled *OK* with his thumb and index finger.

They perched on the edge of the temple pool, taking in the marvellous carvings, until Austin checked the air supply, tapped his wristwatch and pointed towards the temple entrance. Buddy-breathing was using up the air in the tank twice as fast. Lee nodded in understanding. They swam side by side until they came to the outer wall. Austin signalled Lee to wait.

He slipped out of his vest and swam out into the canal. Looking up to the surface, he saw no sign of Chang or the rental boat. He heard the sound of an engine, but to his practised ear it sounded different from the inflatable's high-revving one. Moving closer to the foundation of the islet, he surfaced and peered out from behind an outcropping where the basalt base had collapsed.

A tour boat was moving along the canal towards the rental boat, which was submerged except for the bow. Chang and his men had vanished.

Austin waved until someone in the tour boat saw him. When the boat turned in his direction, he took a deep breath and went back for Song Lee. He gave her a thumbs up, and together they slowly rose to the surface.

THE SEAHAWK quickly covered the distance to the *Concord*, hovered over the stern for an instant, then dropped slowly onto the large circle painted on the deck. Zavala climbed out of the helicopter and was greeted by a grey-haired man in a khaki uniform.

'I'm Hank Dixon, Mr Zavala,' the man said, extending his hand. 'I'm commander of the guided-missile cruiser *Concord*. Welcome aboard.'

'Thanks, Captain. You can call me Joe. My boss, Kurt Austin, is busy in Pohnpei, but he'll be coming along in a couple of hours. Ensign Daley told me that the *Concord* is acting as central control for the search flotilla.'

'That's right. C'mon, I'll show you what we've been doing.'

The captain led the way to the midship's search-and-rescue centre, just off the main deck. A dozen men and women, sitting in front of computer monitors, were processing information that was streaming in from the ships and aircraft involved in the search.

'How close are we to the lab site?' Zavala asked.

'It's approximately three hundred feet directly under the ship's hull.' Dixon stepped over to a computer screen. 'Those circular depressions you see in the ocean bottom match the feet of the legs supporting the Locker.'

'There are no drag marks,' Zavala observed. 'That indicates the lab was lifted off the site. Can you show me the site on the satellite map?'

Dixon asked a technician to bring up a map-and-satellite image.

'We've been using orbiting spy satellites to look for infrared emissions,' Dixon said. 'The lab was west of Pohnpei, between Nukuoro Island to the north and Oroluk Island to the south. We've drawn lines from all three islands and dubbed our main search area the Pohnpei Triangle.'

'Those red squares must be areas that have been searched,' Zavala said.

'That's right. We've also got fixed-wing aircraft and helicopters making visual checks. The squares designate the territory that's been scoured with sonar. We've put choppers down on a few of the islands and talked to the inhabitants, but nobody's reported anything suspicious. And we've got acoustical sensors down. There are three antisub submarines equipped with electronic ears so sensitive they can hear a fish sneeze out patrolling the perimeters of the triangle.'

'You might want to tell your subs to use their acoustical detectors to listen for the sound signature of a Russian Typhoon-class submarine.'

Dixon gave Zavala an odd look. 'You think the *Russians* are involved?'

'No,' Zavala said, 'but one of their old subs might be. Looks like you've got all bases covered. I'll contact the NUMA ship to see if I can borrow a submersible so I can get a look first hand at the site.'

'I'll give them a call,' Captain Dixon said, then added, 'I'm running out of ideas. You got any suggestions?'

Zavala stared at the vast area represented by the satellite image. The Federated States of Micronesia consisted of more than 600 islands scattered across a million and a half square miles of the Pacific.

'The good news is, your search plan is terrific, Captain. Given enough time, I don't doubt you would find the lab.'

'Thanks.' The captain narrowed his eyes. 'What's the bad news?'

Zavala gave him a sad smile. 'We don't *have* time.'

PAUL TROUT DROVE the rented SUV into the deserted back lot of a four-storey mill that had been abandoned decades before when New Bedford's textile business pulled out of the city. A security light over the front door illuminated a small wooden plaque: BRIMMER'S ANTIQUITIES, 4TH FLOOR.

The mill was otherwise dark, except for the nightlights in a discount-furniture showroom and a yellow glow in a fourth-floor window.

Paul reached for his cellphone and called Brimmer's number.

'Strange,' Paul said. 'Light's on but Brimmer's not answering. Are your antennae picking up the same vibes that I'm getting?'

Gamay wrinkled her nose. 'More like a bad smell,' she said. 'What do you want to do?'

'I don't know if the information in the logbook will help Kurt and Joe find the missing lab,' Paul said. 'But, with lives involved, I say we go for it.'

He parked the SUV in the shadows, and they cautiously approached the main entrance.

'Unlocked,' Paul said. 'Brimmer's expecting us.'

'But he didn't answer the phone,' Gamay said. 'If he isn't in his office, he wouldn't leave the door unlocked.'

They walked the length of the 500-foot-long building, eventually coming to another door. This one was locked. Continuing on round a corner of the building, they came upon the fire escape that zigzagged up to the top floor. They climbed it and tried the door at each landing, but all were locked.

Paul jabbed the doorjamb on the top floor with his car key. The wood was soft with rot. He took a step back and threw his shoulder against the door. The latch ripped out of the jamb. Gamay produced a small halogen flashlight from her handbag, and they stepped inside.

Their footfalls echoed as they walked across the dust-layered floor. The vast space where workers once tended hundreds of looms was as still as a tomb. They headed towards the far end of the room, where light was seeping under a door, and came to a drywall partition. Cartons were stacked against it. BRIMMER was written in ink on the boxes.

Paul picked up a two-by-four from a pile of debris, hefting it like a baseball bat, and whispered to Gamay to knock on the door. She did, softly. When there was no answer, she stepped aside, and he did his battering-ram imitation again. The door popped open at first nudge.

The floor was littered with books and papers. The light visible outside through the window came from a desk lamp on a table that also supported a computer and Brimmer's body. The antiquities dealer was sprawled face down, his hand stretched out towards a cellphone several inches from his fingertips. The back of his suit was perforated with a single bullet hole.

'Judging from the mess, I'd say someone was looking for something,' Gamay said.

'The 1848 logbook? Doesn't that seem far-fetched?' Paul asked. He flipped Brimmer's cell over so the display screen showed. 'He was calling the police,' he said. 'He got as far as 91 . . .'

'We'd better be on our toes,' Gamay said. 'The murderer knew we were coming to see Brimmer.'

Paul picked up Brimmer's cellphone, punched in the second 1 to complete the emergency call. When the police dispatcher answered, Paul said his name was Brimmer, gave the address, and said somebody was prowling around in the building. He suspected they were armed and dangerous.

Paul hung up and put the phone back in Brimmer's lifeless fingers.

He and Gamay slipped out of Brimmer's office and quickly made their way across the wide loom floor. Paul set the two-by-four against the wall, and they stepped out onto the fire escape, only to stop short.

The rickety old fire escape was trembling, and there was the *tunk-tunk* of ascending footfalls on the cast-iron steps. The Trouts ducked back inside, and Paul picked up the two-by-four he'd just left behind. They plastered themselves flat against a wall on either side of the door. He tightened his grip on the length of wood.

Low male voices could be heard, then a quick exclamation of surprise. The men had found the smashed latch. Then the voices ceased.

The door opened slowly. A figure stepped inside, followed by another. There was a spark, as the lead man flicked on a cigarette lighter. Paul calculated that he would have a second to act and brought the two-by-four down on the head of the second figure. The man with the cigarette lighter turned at the *thwack* of wood smacking skull. He was holding a revolver in his other hand. Paul jammed him in the midsection with the end of the two-by-four, and followed up with a blow to the head as the man doubled over.

The Trouts dashed through the door, then flew down the steps and raced to their vehicle. As they drove away from the mill, they passed two police cruisers speeding towards it, lights blinking but sirens silent.

Gamay caught her breath, and said, 'Well, that was a neat double play.'

'Thanks. I guess we've reached a dead end on the logbook . . .'

Gamay pursed her lips in thought for a moment. 'Captain Dobbs wasn't the *only* one who wrote down his memoirs,' she said.

'Caleb Nye?' he said. 'All his records went up in flames.'

'Rachael Dobbs mentioned the diorama. Isn't that a record of sorts?'

Suddenly energised, Paul said, 'It's worth a try.'

He pumped the SUV's accelerator and headed across town to the Dobbs mansion. Rachael Dobbs was saying good night to the cleaning crew that had cleared up after the jazz concert and was about to close down the building. She looked less frazzled than when they had seen her earlier.

'You found Mr Brimmer's shop, I trust?' she said.

'Yes, thank you,' Gamay said. 'He couldn't help us. But then Paul and I remembered the Nye diorama that you mentioned. I know it's late but do you think it might be possible to see it?'

'Well . . . your generous contribution made you members of the Dobbs Society in good standing,' Rachael said. 'Let's go down to the basement.'

The basement of the Dobbs mansion was big and musty. They wove their way through antique odds and ends to a floor-to-ceiling cabinet that Rachael explained was an airtight, temperature-controlled walk-in safe. She opened the safe's double doors to reveal metal shelves stacked with plastic boxes, each labelled. A cylinder-shaped object around six feet long, wrapped in plastic, filled the lowest shelf.

'This is the Nye diorama,' Rachael said. 'I'm afraid that it's a bit heavy, which is probably why no one has dragged it out to have a look at it.'

Working together, the Trouts hefted the package and carried it upstairs. At Rachael's suggestion, they took it out to the tent, where there was space to unwrap it. They removed the plastic carefully and unrolled the diorama.

The first panel was an oil painting around five feet high and six feet wide, depicting a whaling ship tied up at a dock. There was a caption under the picture: JOURNEY'S END.

'We must be looking at the last section of the diorama,' Rachael said. 'This shows a ship unloading in New Bedford.'

The colours of sea and sky were still bright, but the other colours were garish, in the style of a circus poster. The brushstrokes were bold, as if the paint had been applied in a hurry.

'The technique is rough,' Gamay said, 'but the artist had a good eye for detail. You can even see the name of the ship on the hull: *Princess*.'

'As I understand it,' Rachael Dobbs said, 'Nye stood in front of the diorama as it was unrolled from panel to panel and fleshed out the details with his story. The lighting would have been dramatic, and maybe there were sound effects. You know, someone behind shouting "Thar she blows!"'

The next panel showed the *Princess* rounding a point of land that the caption identified as the tip of Africa. In another panel, the ship was at anchor against the backdrop of a lush volcanic island. The caption read: TROUBLE ISLAND—LAST PACIFIC LANDFALL.

Paul continued unrolling the diorama. A particularly interesting panel showed what appeared to be a white-haired man lying on the deck over the caption: MODERN-DAY JONAH.

'It's the *Ghost*,' Rachael said. 'This is marvellous! This shows Caleb Nye as he must have looked after he'd been cut out of the whale's stomach.'

Rachael could hardly contain her excitement, and started talking about a fundraiser to restore the diorama. Paul and Gamay found the diorama fascinating but of little help. Yet they kept going until they came to the last panel, SETTING SAIL, almost a mirror image of the first panel, only there was a crowd of people on the dock, and the ship's sails were unfurled.

Paul stood up to stretch his legs, but Gamay noticed that there were a few more feet of canvas. She asked him to keep unrolling, expecting to see a title panel. Instead, they were looking at a map of the South Pacific.

'It's a map of the 1848 voyage of the *Princess*,' Rachael said. 'Those position notations show where the whales were caught. The map would have shown Caleb's audience where his adventures had occurred.'

Gamay got down on her hands and knees and followed a line with her index finger from Pohnpei to a speck called Trouble Island. The island's position had been noted next to it.

The Trouts jotted down the coordinates and rolled the diorama back up. While Rachael Dobbs went to close up the museum, the Trouts went out into the garden.

Paul said, 'I think it's all linked somehow: the present and the past, the Blue Medusa, the miraculous cure of the men aboard the *Princess*.'

'Don't forget that somebody thought the log was important enough to kill Brimmer over,' Gamay said. 'We should let Kurt know what we found.'

LIKE ANY GOOD DETECTIVE, Joe Zavala decided to begin his search for Davy Jones's Locker at the crime scene. He was readying a one-person submersible borrowed from the NUMA ship when a call came through the NUMA net for him.

After a moment or two, a female voice came over Zavala's earphones. 'How's the search going, Joe?'

'Hi, Gamay, nice to hear from you. Nothing so far here. How about you?'

'We may have something,' she said. 'We tried to contact Kurt but the call wouldn't go through, so we tracked you down. We came across the coordinates for a place called Trouble Island, about a hundred miles from the lab site. It may be where the crew of the *Princess* underwent their miraculous cure. Not sure how it relates to the missing lab, but maybe it will help.'

'Give me the info,' he said, 'and I'll check it out.'

Zavala took the coordinates, thanked Gamay, then made his way to the bridge and gave the coordinates to Captain Campbell.

'This atoll is closest to the position your friends gave you,' Campbell said after poring over the chart table for a minute or two. 'Doesn't look like much, and it's within a red rectangle, which means it was searched visually. What do you think?'

'An American whaling ship was supposed to have stopped at an island on that spot in 1848,' Zavala said.

'But islands can disappear. Your island might have sunk into the sea after a volcanic eruption, an earthquake, or a flood. It could be a reef or rock below the surface now, and even a satellite wouldn't pick it up. You'd have to get in for a close look.'

Zavala made his way to the ship's communications centre and borrowed a computer. He linked the computer to a surveillance satellite and zeroed in on the atoll. Was it possible this unnamed atoll had once been an island?

He zoomed the satellite camera in on the tiny speck. Typical Pacific atoll: a minuscule island with a few palm trees encircled by a lagoon and ringed with a coral reef that was mostly solid and with no opening big enough for a vessel of any size to pass through with the lab in tow. Nothing could be seen in the clear waters of the lagoon.

Zavala tried Austin's phone number, but there was no reply. He stared into space and contemplated his course of action. Well aware that he was probably wasting time and fuel, he picked up an intercom phone, called the bridge, and asked the captain if he could borrow his helicopter to take a closer look at the atoll.

Crew members helped Zavala load an emergency raft onto the helicopter. He got into the cockpit and started to work the controls. Moments later, the chopper lifted off the ship, and shot off on a northerly course.

Seen from an altitude of 500 feet, the ocean was a sun-sparkled blue-green blur. Zavala passed a couple of ships from the search flotilla, looking in other areas. The blinding sheen off the water prevented him from seeing the atoll until he was almost on top of it.

He banked the helicopter and looked down at a handkerchief-sized patch of sand with its few palm trees. The atoll looked exactly as he had seen it on the satellite image. He headed down for a closer look, and brought the helicopter onto a soft pontoon landing 100 feet from the atoll's island, which was oddly located at one end of the lagoon rather than at its centre.

As the rotors whirled to a stop, Zavala stepped out onto one of the chopper's pontoons. He muscled the raft out of the cockpit, set it in the water and yanked an inflation cord. There was a hiss from the carbon dioxide capsule as the raft inflated. Zavala climbed in and paddled to shore.

He pulled the raft up on the blinding white sand and walked round the perimeter of the island. He felt like a shipwreck victim on one of the miniature desert islands that cartoonists like to draw.

The tropical sun beat down like a blowtorch on his head. He sought shelter in the shade of the few pitiful palm trees and surveyed his surroundings. He frowned. This insignificant speck of sand could never have been Trouble Island. It was just a rinky-dink atoll. He walked back to his raft and turned for a last look. A glint of light came from near the top of a palm tree.

Zavala went back and stood under the tree. He craned his neck but couldn't determine the source of the reflection. He clambered onto the palm's trunk, which grew at an angle, and climbed up to where the broad fronds branched out. He found the source of the reflection immediately. Sunlight was glancing off the lens of a miniature video camera attached to the trunk.

Zavala realised, as he looked at the lens, that it was possible the camera was looking back at him. He backed down the palm's trunk, only to stop halfway. The tree had a slick, unnatural feel to it. He unsheathed the knife at his belt and dug its point into the trunk, but it went in only so far. He peeled back a section of the trunk and got another shock: it seemed to be made of woven plastic fabric covering a hard metal core.

He sheathed his knife and shimmied down the trunk to the sand. He walked several paces to the right, then to the left. The camera swivelled to follow him. *Oh, hell.*

Zavala sprinted across the atoll, shoved his raft off the beach, and dug into the water with his paddle. He had to get back to the radio in the helicopter. He looked over his shoulder, expecting all the demons of hell to be after him, but was encouraged that no attempt was being made to stop him.

Then the oddest thing happened. The bottom of the lagoon rose up to meet him, bursting from the water in a long, shiny mound directly in front of him. Then the mound parted, and a huge black fin ripped through the bottom of the lagoon, rising until it towered more than forty feet above Zavala's head. He was looking at the conning tower of a giant submarine. Seconds later, the submarine deck lifted the raft into the air. The helicopter headed skywards at the same time and teetered for a moment before both raft and helicopter slid off the rounded deck and hit the foaming water.

Water poured into the raft. Zavala tried to climb back on the sub's deck, but his fingers slid off the slick, wet metal and the fast-flowing torrents pushed him back into the lagoon.

He choked on seawater, gasping for breath like a beached fish. Then something like a baseball bat slammed into the side of his head. He saw a brief explosion of brightness before his eyes and then felt a numbing pain. Then someone pulled the shades down, and Zavala was in darkness.

Chapter 9

The tour boat captain wasn't sure what to make of the people he had pulled out of the Nan Madol Canal. 'What happened, man?' he asked.

Austin pointed to the rental boat, which was sinking at a sharp angle, with only a foot or so of the bullet-riddled bow sticking out of the water.

'Leaky boat,' he said.

'I heard a lot of noise,' the captain said. 'Sounded like guns.'

Austin clamped his hand on the captain's shoulder and turned him round. 'See that bag floating over there?' Austin said. 'Can we pick it up?'

The doubtful look in the captain's face suggested he was starting to regret his decision to pluck his new passengers from the water, but he moved the boat closer so Austin could retrieve the dive-gear bag. Austin unzipped the bag and pulled out his wallet. He peeled off a fifty.

'This is to cover the tickets for the boat ride.' He gave the captain another fifty-dollar bill, and said, 'This is for asking no more questions.' Holding out a third fifty, he wrapped his arm round the captain's shoulders and, speaking low, said, 'How much longer is left in the tour?'

'I dunno . . . half an hour, maybe,' the captain said.

'This is yours if you cut that time in half.'

The captain grinned, and the three bills disappeared into his pocket.

'You just bought the boat, man,' he said. 'You and the lady, have a seat.'

Fifteen minutes later the boat was pulling up to the dock at Kolonia.

While Lee went off to the rest room to freshen up, Austin made his way to the dive shop. He returned the scuba gear but produced a NUMA credit card and asked the crestfallen owner to charge the cost of replacing the boat.

As the boat owner was writing out the purchase order, he said, 'Your friend catch up with you?'

'What friend?' Austin asked.

'Asian guy driving a pick-up truck. Didn't leave his name. Showed up a few minutes after you took off. I told him you were going out to the ruins.'

Austin did a good job hiding his surprise. He thanked the owner and went into the men's room to change into dry clothes. Then he dug his cellphone from the bag. He noticed that the Trouts and, most recently, the captain of the *Concord* had called him. He returned Dixon's call first.

'Glad to hear from you, Kurt. I've got some bad news. Joe has disappeared. He borrowed a NUMA helicopter from the agency's ship and flew to the north of here to take a closer look at an atoll. We lost him on radar.'

'Did he send off a mayday?' Austin asked.

'Not a whisper,' Dixon answered. 'Whatever happened must have happened fast.'

'How soon can you have the chopper pick me up?' Austin asked.

'It's on its way.'

Austin clicked off and was about to call the Trouts. But Lee was coming his way, and he put his cell away to hail a taxi.

Austin was only slightly worried about Zavala. The charming young Mexican-American had an amazing talent for survival. He was more worried about the fact that Chang had known that Austin was on the island. He couldn't figure it. Only a few trusted people knew that they were in Pohnpei.

The taxi dropped them off at the airport, and they went out to the tarmac to await the return of the Seahawk. Austin started to tell Lee about Zavala's disappearance, but she couldn't contain her excitement.

'Do you know what we discovered in that place?' she said. 'It was a *hospital* or clinic, where the medusa toxin was administered to cure people! I can't wait to tell Dr Huang about this. He'll be *thrilled*.'

'Who is Dr Huang?' Austin asked.

'He's with the Ministry of Health, and was the one who brought me into the medusa project. He asked me to keep him informed.'

'When was the last time you talked to him?'

'I called him when we stopped at Los Angeles to tell him that we were coming to Pohnpei.'

'That explains how Chang and his buddies knew we were here.'

'Oh, no, you don't think . . .'

Austin shrugged. 'Our mission is top secret,' he said. 'Very few people knew we were coming here. But Chang must have had someone on our tail from the second we landed. How well do you know Dr Huang?' he asked. 'Could he be an informant?'

She thought about Huang's failure to fight her exile and his deceptive manner in bringing her into the medusa research. 'Dr Huang is a brilliant but fearful man. It would not take much to bend him to someone's will.'

'I'd suggest that you keep Dr Huang in the dark from now on.'

The distant *whup-whup* of rotor blades announced the imminent arrival of the helicopter from the *Concord*. In less than an hour the Seahawk was landing on the aft deck of the Navy ship.

Captain Dixon helped Song Lee off the helicopter, and said, 'Welcome to the *Concord*, Dr Lee. Your government has been trying to get in touch with you. We've got a teleconferencing set-up you can use. My communications officer will take you there.'

Lee turned to Austin. 'You'll have to excuse me, Kurt. Thank you for an interesting day.'

'My pleasure,' he said. 'Perhaps on our next tour of Nan Madol we can spend more time above water.'

An officer arrived and led Lee to her teleconference. Dixon said he would show Austin on a chart where Zavala had disappeared. On the way to the bridge, the captain said aircraft in the vicinity had made several sweeps around the atoll, but there was no sign of Zavala or the helicopter.

Austin studied the atoll's location, wondering what had attracted Zavala to the tiny speck of land, and then punched in Gamay's number on his cell.

'Kurt! We've been worried. What's going on?'

'We had a run-in with one of the Triad leaders in Nan Madol. The Triad had an informant. We're back on the *Concord*, but now Joe is missing. He borrowed a helicopter and went off to check out an atoll.'

'We gave him the atoll's coordinates,' Gamay said. 'It's located approximately where Trouble Island was, the place Captain Dobbs stopped at with his whale ship.'

'You found the logbook?' Austin asked.

'No,' she said. Gamay told Austin about the visits to the Dobbs mansion and Brimmer's store, and finding Brimmer's body in the mill. Austin fumed as he listened. The vast criminal organisation seemed to have eyes and ears everywhere. He asked for the coordinates from Nye's diorama and said he would check them out.

'In the meantime call Sandecker and bring him up to speed,' Austin said. 'I'll get back to you when I know more.'

After signing off, Austin sat down in front of a computer and called up a satellite image using Nye's coordinates. The atoll Austin saw didn't match the position on the map, but a radar reading of Joe's trajectory showed that he seemed to be heading directly for it.

Austin zoomed in on the tiny speck. The monitor showed a palm-studded patch of sand encircled by a coral reef. Nothing unusual, except for a dark streak near one side of the lagoon. He ran through the possibilities: school of fish, coral, undersea vegetation, shadows . . . Nothing seemed to fit. He looked up earlier images of the island: the streak was larger then. As he dug back into the satellite photos, hour-by-hour, he saw that the streak had disappeared. He went further back, and stopped in his tracks. A cigar-shaped object had taken the place of the streak. The conning tower protruding from the object identified it as a submarine.

With growing excitement, Austin backed up in the photo file even further. There was no submarine in the lagoon now, but he saw a dark spot which, upon enlargement, showed the unmistakable outline of a helicopter.

'Thank you, Caleb Nye,' Austin said loud enough to be heard by Dixon, who leaned over his shoulder to study the computer monitor.

'Who?' the captain asked.

'He was a nineteenth-century whaler, and he just helped me find Joe.'

Austin ran through the series of satellite photos.

'Damn,' the captain said. 'I think you've got something, Kurt. We need to get in for a closer look. We'll have to assume that the atoll is protected by a sensor system. Night-vision devices and radar are a worry, of course, but I'm most concerned about thermal sensors.'

'Any way we can get round those security measures?' Austin asked.

'A low-flying helicopter might be able to blend into the sea clutter on a radar screen,' Dixon said. 'If the insertion was quick, there is a chance you could pull it off. We could position some ships within hailing distance so we can come to the rescue if you get in a jam.'

Austin needed no further encouragement. 'That's settled,' he said.

Song Lee was in another part of the ship, sitting behind a table and staring at a blank screen. The communications officer made a call to inform the other participants in the teleconference that all was ready, then he left Lee alone in the room.

The screen fuzzed for a second and then an image appeared of six people sitting at a table in a dark-panelled room. She recognised two people as being from the Ministry of Health, but the others were strangers to her.

A silver-haired man wearing the uniform of the People's Liberation Army said, 'Thank you for this meeting, Dr Lee. My name is Colonel Ming. Since time is short, I'll spare the introductions and get down to business. This committee is the counterpart of a similar group that we are working with in the United States. I have been asked to be the spokesman because the Army is at the forefront of the effort to contain the epidemic.'

'I have been out of touch,' Lee said. 'I know only that the virus has managed to spread despite the quarantine that has been imposed.'

'That's correct,' Ming said. 'The Army was able to contain the epidemic for a time, but this is an enemy we are not equipped to fight. The virus is winning. It is dangerously close to Beijing, Shanghai, Hong Kong and Chongqing. The Ministry of Health projects that the spread is accelerating. It will hit Beijing first and then the other cities less than two weeks later. You understand better than I what that means.'

'Yes, I do, Colonel,' she said. 'In military terms, it would be like lighting a fuse leading to many different ammunition dumps. The embers thrown out by those explosions will ignite other fuses around the world.'

Ming pressed his lips together in a tight smile. 'I understand you were involved in planning for the worst-case scenario, as this appears to be.'

'That's correct, Colonel Ming. I drew up the plans to establish vaccine-production centres in locations where it could be best distributed. But the last I knew the problem was how to produce millions of doses of vaccine quickly enough. If the virus mutated you might have to tailor a vaccine instantly. Tech-based vaccines grown in an animal or human cell could produce three hundred million vaccines in a year.'

'The whole population of the planet could be wiped out in less time than that,' Ming said.

'That's true,' Lee said, 'which is why the lab was looking into the genetic engineering of vaccines. You don't manufacture the vaccine but instead produce the molecule that makes it work.'

'And what were the results of this research?'

'I don't know. The lab had moved to its new location by then. I didn't have clearance for the final phase.'

'So even if we find the lab and produce the vaccine, it may be too late?'

'To put it bluntly, yes.'

Colonel Ming turned to the others. 'Any questions? No? Well, thank you very much for your time, Dr Lee. We will be in contact with you again.'

The screen went blank. Song Lee went out onto the deck, where she looked around for Kurt Austin's reassuring face. She climbed to the bridge, and asked Dixon if he had seen Austin.

'Oh, hello, Dr Lee,' the captain said. 'Kurt said to tell you that he had left the ship.'

'*Left? Where?*'

Dixon looked at a chart and jabbed his index finger down on the wide expanse of ocean. 'Right now, I'd say that Kurt is just about here.'

'WAKE UP, TOVARICH!'

Joe Zavala floated in a nether world just below consciousness, but he was awake enough to know that the cold liquid being poured on his lips tasted like antifreeze. He spat the liquid out. The roar of laughter that followed jerked him into full consciousness.

Hovering over Zavala was a bearded face with a fourteen-carat grin. Zavala saw a bottle again being tilted towards his lips. His hand shot up, and he clamped his fingers round the man's thick wrist.

A startled expression came to the blue eyes at Zavala's lightning-quick move, but the gold-toothed grin quickly returned. 'You don't like our vodka?' the man said. 'I forget. Americans drink whiskey.'

Zavala unclenched his fingers. The bearded man pulled the bottle away and Zavala looked around at the cramped quarters. 'Where am I?' he asked.

'Where *are* you?' the man said. He turned, and, in a language Zavala recognised as Russian, translated the question for the benefit of three other bearded men. There was laughter and the vigorous nodding of heads.

'What's so funny?' Zavala asked.

'I told them what you said, and my answer, that you are in *hell*!'

Zavala managed a slight smile, reaching out his hand. 'In that case,' he said, 'I'll take that vodka you offered me.'

The man handed the bottle over, and Zavala took a tentative sip. As the fiery liquor trickled down his throat, he put his hand to his throbbing head and felt a bandage wrapped round it like a turban.

'Your head was bleeding,' the man said. 'It was the best we could do.'

'Thanks for the first aid. Who are you guys?' Zavala asked.

'I am Captain Mehdev and these are my officers. You are on a nuclear-powered Akula missile submarine, what you Americans call the Typhoon.'

'Nice to meet you,' Zavala said, shaking the captain's hand. 'My name is Joe Zavala. I'm with the American National Underwater and Marine Agency. You've probably heard of it.'

'Anyone who goes to sea is familiar with the work of NUMA,' Mehdev said. 'Your beautiful ships are known around the world.'

Zavala took another sip from the bottle and handed it back. 'No offence, Captain, but you should pay more attention to your driving. Your submarine surfaced right under me and my helicopter.'

Mehdev did another translation that his officers found hilarious, but when he turned back to Zavala he had a sombre expression on his face.

'My apologies,' the captain said. 'I was ordered to take the vessel to the surface and bring you aboard. I am sorry for the loss of your helicopter.'

'Who told you to take me prisoner?'

A frown came to Mehdev's genial face. 'The same criminals who hijacked my submarine and have held me and my crew prisoners,' he said.

Mehdev launched into his story. He was a Navy veteran of the Typhoon service who had gone into civilian work. The designers of the submarine had come up with the idea to use decommissioned Typhoons to carry freight under the Arctic Ocean. A corporate buyer purchased the sub, and it was Mehdev's job to deliver the vessel to its new owner.

The captain's instructions were to surface for an at-sea rendezvous. But a Chinese freighter carrying armed men met them and took over the ship. They were told to sail to the Pacific. Using a torpedo tube, the kidnappers launched a missile, targeting a surface ship. Then the Typhoon was involved in an operation to move the underwater lab off the ocean floor.

'Where is the lab now?' Zavala asked.

Mehdev pointed downwards with his index finger. 'About three hundred feet beneath our hull, at the bottom of a submerged caldera,' he said. 'A volcano eruption many years ago left the caldera in place of the island that was once here. Coral grew on the rim, establishing the reef you came across.'

'How did your vessel break through the reef?' Zavala asked.

'We didn't. We passed *under* it. The Japanese blasted a tunnel through the caldera, planning to use this place as a submarine base in World War Two, but the war ended before the plan was implemented.' Then Mehdev asked, 'What do you know of this lab? It must be important.'

'Very important,' Zavala said. 'The US Navy has planes and ships out searching. I flew over the lagoon. The water is as clear as crystal. Why didn't I see you?'

'We're below a camouflage net stretched across the lagoon. It's what you Americans call low-tech.'

'What about the island I landed on in the lagoon?'

'That is high-tech. An artificial platform on floats, kept in place through a propulsion system geared to a self-correcting navigational system. It provides an observation post to detect intruders. My understanding is, the people behind this scheme intended to use the atoll for transpacific smuggling.'

A pounding on the door interrupted their conversation. Then the door flew open, and an Asian man holding a machine pistol stepped into the cabin. Right behind him was Phelps. Phelps gave Zavala a lopsided grin.

'Hello, soldier,' he said. 'You're a long way from home.'

'I could say the same thing about you, Phelps.'

'Yes, you could. I see you've made friends with the captain and his crew. Too bad the party's over. These boys have work to do.'

Phelps ordered his guard to escort the captain and his crew back to their posts, then pulled up a chair and put his boots up on a small writing table.

'How did you find this little hidey-hole?' Phelps asked.

Zavala yawned. 'Dumb luck,' he said.

'I don't think so. Next question. Anyone else know about this place?'

'Only the US Navy. You and your pals can expect a visit from an aircraft carrier any minute.'

'Nice try,' Phelps said with a snort. 'The atoll would be swarming with ships and planes by now if the Navy knew about us. You've got yourself in a hell of a mess, Joe.'

Zavala's lips turned up in a slight smile. 'It only *looks* that way,' he said.

Phelps shook his head in disbelief. 'What do they give you NUMA guys to drink?' he asked. 'Bull's blood?'

'Something like that,' Zavala said. 'Now, I've got a question for you: why did you give us the key to the handcuffs and return Kurt's gun after our skirmish with your boss lady?'

Phelps slid his feet off the desk and leaned in closer. 'Actually, I've got *three* bosses,' he said. 'Triplets. Chang is in charge of the rough stuff. He's got a brother named Wen Lo who takes care of business. But the hologram you met in Virginia is the top dog. Don't know whether it's a he or she.'

'What do you mean?'

'Sometimes it's a man image, sometimes it's a woman. You never know.'

'What's with the holograms?'

'They don't trust anyone, not even one another.'

'How'd you get hooked up with this bunch of maniacs, Phelps?'

'I'm an ex-SEAL. Crazy or not, they pay better than the Navy. I was going to retire after this gig.' Lowering his voice, he added, 'Like I said, I've got family back home. You really think the virus will hit the US?'

'It's only a matter of a very short time.'

'Damn it, Joe, we've got to stop this thing.'

'*We?*' Zavala scoffed. 'I'm in no position to do *anything* right now.'

'I'm going to change that. I've been thinking how to work this out.'

Phelps's cellphone buzzed. He answered the call, listened for a moment, said, 'OK,' then hung up. He told Zavala to stay put and left the cabin.

Zavala got off the bunk and walked round the cabin, pondering. Phelps was a hired gun and killer, not the type he normally would choose as an ally, but their goals coincided. He went over to the sink and splashed water on his face. He was almost feeling normal when Phelps returned.

Phelps was wearing a black neoprene wet suit and carrying a big duffle bag. There was worry in his hound-dog eyes.

'We're going to have to postpone our talk,' he said 'That was Chang calling. Things just got more complicated. Feel like going for a swim?'

'I just had one,' Zavala said. 'Do I have a choice?'

'Nope,' Phelps said, handing the duffle bag to Zavala.

He told Zavala to suit up and left him in the cabin. Zavala opened the duffle and found a wet suit. He stripped out of his damp clothes and pulled on the neoprene top and bottom, then opened the door and stepped out.

Phelps was waiting with two men, also suited up for a dive. He motioned for Zavala to follow and led the way through the labyrinthine innards of the giant submarine. At one point, the guards split off, and Phelps stepped into a compartment at midship.

'Escape chamber,' Phelps said, pointing to a hatch over their heads. 'There's one on the other side of the conning tower that our guards will be using.'

He opened a bulkhead locker and pulled out two sets of scuba gear with wireless-communications capability. When they were ready, Phelps climbed up a ladder into a cylindrical chamber. Zavala followed.

The escape chamber was a tight fit for two men in full scuba gear. Phelps hit a switch that closed the floor, and water poured in. Once the chamber was flooded, he opened the hatch over their heads.

Phelps let air into his buoyancy regulator and swam up the escape shaft. Zavala followed close behind. They emerged from the submarine at the base of the lofty conning tower. The two guards were waiting for them. Each held a gas-powered speargun with a nasty-looking barb on the business end. Zavala ignored them and slipped his feet into his fins.

The greenish light that filtered through the camouflage net bathed the black hull of the submarine in a spectral glow. Zavala had once seen a Typhoon at dock, when the hull was mostly submerged, and had been impressed by its size, but that was nothing compared with seeing the gigantic sub and its massive conning tower in full.

A ducklike voice quacked in his headset, and Phelps waved to get his attention. 'Follow me. This is a technical dive. Three hundred feet plus, but you've got Trimix in your tank, so you'll be OK.'

Phelps switched on a waterproof dive light. With a fluttering kick of his legs, he propelled himself through the water, angling downwards. Zavala came next, with the two guards following his bubble trail.

They headed towards an amber cluster of sparkling lights. As they descended, Zavala saw that the lights were on the outside of four large globes attached to each other with tubelike connectors. He immediately recognised the lab from the diagrams he had studied.

'Davy Jones's Locker!' Zavala said.

'Quite the sight, isn't it?' Phelps said.

Zavala noticed something else. Ghostly blue forms were moving slowly in the shadows just beyond the reach of the lab's searchlights.

'Are those Blue Medusas I see?' he asked.

'Yeah,' Phelps said. 'You want to stay away from those puppies. They're hot-wired. We can do a nature tour later. We've only got a few minutes to talk. We're the only ones wearing communications gear, so don't worry about those guys on your tail. I was gonna keep you on the sub so we could work out a plan, but Chang said he wants you in the lab. Didn't say what he's got planned, but, one thing's for sure, he won't be throwing you a welcome party.'

'I didn't expect one,' Zavala said. 'How about *you* throwing me a lifeline?'

'I'll do my best. Meantime, be a good boy and don't give those guys with the spearguns an excuse to use you for target practice.'

They were directly above the hemispherical-shaped transit module at the hub of the lab complex. Phelps swam under the module, past four minisubmersibles attached to the underside, then up into a shaft that opened into a round pool.

Phelps removed his mask and communications unit, and Zavala followed his lead. The guards surfaced seconds later. All four men climbed out of the pool and hung their gear on wall hooks. The guards put the spearguns aside and produced machine pistols from their waterproof backpacks.

Phelps pressed a switch and a door slid open. He led the way along a corridor to another door that opened into a small room. Phelps told the guards to wait in the passageway, and then he and Zavala stepped inside.

Half of one wall was made of glass, allowing a view of a laboratory containing several workers dressed in white biohazard suits. The workers looked up when Phelps rapped his knuckles on the glass. All went back to work except one, who waved in acknowledgment and disappeared behind a door labelled DECONTAMINATION.

Minutes later, Lois Mitchell stepped into the room. She was wearing a lab coat and slacks, her raven hair damp from the decontamination shower.

'I know you,' she said, with a slight smile.

Zavala did a fast mental check of the women he had dated through the years and drew a blank. 'Have we met?' he asked cautiously.

Lois laughed. 'I saw you on TV,' she said. 'You were the engineer from NUMA who made the dive with Dr Kane in the bathysphere.' She furrowed her brow. 'What on earth are you doing *here*?'

'I could ask you the same thing,' Zavala said.

Phelps said, 'Dr Mitchell, this is Joe Zavala from NUMA.'

'*Lois*,' the scientist amended, extending her hand.

'Hate to break up this party,' Phelps said, 'but my boss is on his way to the lab. My guess is that he wants to check on your project.'

'Actually,' she said, 'he's coming to get the vaccine.'

Phelps narrowed his eyes. 'What do you mean?' he asked.

'While you were away, I told one of those people you have following me around that we've synthesised the toxin. Your boss will be able to take the vaccine culture with him and go into production immediately.'

Scowling, Phelps said, 'That's not good.'

'Wasn't that the purpose of this whole project, to produce a vaccine that can be given to the world?'

'You tell her,' Phelps said with a shake of his head.

'Once they have the vaccine,' Zavala said, 'they'll let the epidemic run until they bring down their government. Then they'll offer the cure to the rest of the world. Pay or die. You and your lab have become expendable.'

The colour drained out of Lois Mitchell's already pale features. 'What have I done?' she wailed.

'It's what you're *going* to do that counts,' Phelps said. 'And whatever we do, it had better be fast.'

Zavala was suspicious of Phelps's abrupt change from foe to friend. But he didn't have many options. He grabbed Phelps by the arm, and said, 'We need to talk.'

Chapter 10

'Five-minute warning, Kurt.'

Austin unbuckled his seat belt and stood by the Seahawk's open door. The helicopter slowed, then hovered over the predetermined point of insertion, a quarter of a mile from the atoll.

'Showtime, Kurt!' the pilot said.

'Thanks for the ride,' Austin said, while the chopper's copilot helped him push a six-foot-long inflatable boat out of the door. They lowered the boat into the sea using a motorised winch. Austin grabbed a two-inch line rigged to the helicopter's hoist bracket and slid down the rope, his hands protected by thick gloves. He then lowered himself into the sea and let go.

The Seahawk moved away and Austin breaststroked over to the inflatable and climbed aboard. It was stabilised by the weight of the gear pack secured to its makeshift wooden platform between its pontoons. He undid the tie-downs holding the supply pack and pulled out a paddle. He found a waterproof pouch that contained a handheld GPS and pushed the POWER button.

The tiny green screen blinked on, and it showed his position in relation to the island. He tucked the GPS back in its pouch and began to paddle towards the break in the reef.

It was a gorgeous night. The stars glittered like diamond splinters against the black velvet of the tropical sky, and the sea was on fire, glowing with silvery-green phosphorescence. There was little current and no wind, and he covered the distance in good time. But as he approached the narrow opening in the coral, the water surged in and out to create a barrier of turbulence that tossed the lightweight boat around like a rubber duck in a bathtub.

Paddling vigorously, Austin brought the bow around and charged into the opening, but failed to overcome the crosscurrents. He made another try.

The inflatable bounced, fishtailed and yawed. For a second, Austin thought he was going to be thrown sideways into the jagged coral. Then the inflatable squeezed through the opening and glided into the lagoon.

Austin killed the motor and waited. Five minutes passed, and there was nothing to indicate he had been detected. No blinding searchlights, no hail of bullets. He took the lack of a warm reception as an invitation to stay.

Austin dug his scuba gear out of the pack, buckling on his air tank and buoyancy compensator. He checked his GPS and began to paddle, until the black triangle on the GPS's screen merged with the circle marking where the satellite had shown the dark streak in the lagoon. The inexplicable disappearance of the Typhoon suggested that there was more to the lagoon than met the eye, and Austin had borrowed a tank containing a Trimix mixture in the event that he had to make a deeper dive than expected.

Austin pulled on his face mask and fins, chomped on his regulator mouthpiece, and rolled off the inflatable's right pontoon into the lagoon. He dived under the surface and descended about twenty feet.

As he neared the floor of the lagoon, he reached out with his gloved right hand. Instead of touching sand, his fingers pushed against a soft, yielding surface. He removed the glove, and discovered that what he thought was sand overgrown with marine life was a loosely woven net.

Austin slid his knife from its sheath on his thigh, pressed the point into the fabric, and sawed a cut in the net several inches long. He returned the blade to its sheath, and glided over the fake ocean bottom until he came to where he had seen the streak in the satellite picture. He saw that the streak was in fact a partially mended tear in the fake bottom.

Austin unhooked a dive light from his vest and, holding the light in front of him, squirmed through the opening. He brought his body straight up, paddling with his fins, and spun round. About a hundred feet away, faintly illuminated by starlight filtering through the net, was an enormous submarine.

Austin instinctively switched the light off, even though it seemed unlikely that anybody aboard the sub was aware of his presence. He swam away from the submarine, and saw pinpoints sparkling in the darkness below. He dived down, only to stop after a few moments to stare at a line of glowing blue objects.

Blue Medusas!

About six of them floated across his path of descent. He waited until the deadly jellyfish were out of range, then dived again towards the bottom. As he went down, he saw that the lights that had first caught his attention were beacons on the tops of four large spheres built round a hemispheric hub.

Each rested on four spindly legs with disc-shaped footings that resembled the legs of a spider.

One sphere had a transparent dome. Austin swam closer and saw two people under the dome: a dark-haired woman and Zavala. The two were sitting in chairs, apparently deep in conversation. Zavala didn't seem to be in any trouble, and, from the look on his face, he was enjoying himself. Only Joe Zavala could find an attractive woman at the bottom of the sea.

While Austin was trying to make sense of the scene, the woman looked straight up at him and stared. He peeled off like a fighter plane, swam down under the sphere, then towards the hemispheric hub. He remembered from the diagram that the hub was the transportation module. It had an air lock at the top of it for the cargo shuttle.

He swam under the module and found the hatch that allowed divers access to the module. He inflated the buoyancy compensator. Air from the tank flowed into the vest and he began a slow rise. His head broke the surface of the air-lock pool inside the hemisphere. He pushed his mask up on his forehead and saw that the circular room was deserted.

He swam over to a ladder and put the waterproof pouch holding his Bowen on the edge of the pool. Then he slipped out of his weight belt, fins and tank and set them next to the pouch. He climbed out, retrieved the Bowen from its pouch, and hung his scuba gear on a hook next to four other sets of dry gear. Then he listened for a minute at the only door.

All was quiet. Austin's Bowen filled one hand, and his other pressed the wall switch. The door slid quietly open. He set off along a corridor, determined to stir up some trouble.

It didn't take long.

He came to a door marked RESOURCE CULTIVATION SECTION. He opened it and stepped into a twilit chamber that was circular in shape, the walls lined with fish tanks that contained various jellyfish. But it was the larger, chest-high, circular tank at the centre of the room that caught his attention.

It contained at least a dozen giant jellyfish. Their bell-shaped bodies were a yard across; their tentacles were short, thick and ropy rather than the delicate streaming filaments seen on most jellyfish. They glowed with a pulsating neon blue that provided the sole illumination in the room.

He saw a movement that didn't come from inside the tank. A distorted face was reflected in the curving glass surface. Absorbed by the strange forms in the central tank, Austin had let himself get sloppy.

He whirled round and raised the Bowen, but the powerfully built guard who had been quietly stalking Austin brought the metal stock of his machine pistol down and it hit Austin's wrist. The gun flew from his fingers and clattered on the floor, and a fiery pain shot up to his shoulder.

Austin's right arm was momentarily useless, but with his left hand he reached up and grabbed the machine pistol. As he tried to wrench the weapon from the man's grasp, his assailant pushed him back against the tank. He slammed against the glass wall, but Austin, kept a tight grip on the gun, pushed it up and away from his body, and managed to twist the machine pistol away. His fingers lacked the strength to hold on to the weapon, and it splashed into the tank. Giant jellyfish scattered in every direction.

Both men stared at the lost weapon, but Austin was the first to rally. He lowered his head and butted the man in the chest, driving him back towards the wall. They both slammed against the row of tanks, dislodging a couple that crashed to the floor and broke open.

The gelatinous creatures in the tanks spilled across the floor. Austin lost his footing in the slippery mess and went down on one knee. He struggled to stand again, and the man kicked him in the side of the face.

But the man slipped in the slimy glop in his second attempt to kick Austin's head. The blow glanced off Austin's cheek, rattling his teeth, and knocked him over on his right side. The man, regaining his balance, produced a knife from a sheath on his belt and let out a yell. He dived on Austin with knife raised high.

Austin brought his left arm up in what he knew was a futile attempt to block the blade, but at the last second his groping gloved hand snatched up a shard of glass eight inches long and he plunged it into the man's neck. He heard a shriek of pain and felt a shower of warm blood from the severed jugular. The knife dropped from the man's fingers. He tried to get to his feet, only to crumple on rubbery legs as the life drained from his body.

Austin rolled out of the way before the man crashed down on him, and got unsteadily to his feet. His right wrist was on fire, and he had to use his left hand to retrieve his Bowen. As he stepped carefully round the spreading pool of blood and dozens of dying jellyfish, he took a quick glance at the big tank. The giant mutant jellyfish glowed even brighter. It was as if they had enjoyed the blood sport.

Austin wasted no time putting the nightmarish scene behind him. He set off down a corridor to search for Zavala, wondering what other delightful surprises Davy Jones's Locker would have to offer.

Chapter 11

It was Lois Mitchell who had suggested a place to formalise the just-formed alliance with Phelps. 'I've been using Dr Kane's office,' she said. 'The guards have been ordered not to bother me while I work. We'll be all right there for a while.'

'That OK with you, Phelps?' Zavala asked.

'Fine,' Phelps said, 'but we're going to have to do it my way. The lab is still controlled by Chang's goons, so we can't just take a stroll.'

Despite the direness of the situation, Zavala couldn't help but grin with appreciation when he saw the colourful schools of fish nosing around the clear Plexiglas dome that were the ceiling and walls of Kane's office.

'This is fantastic!' he said.

Mitchell smiled, and she said, 'I agree. I would spend a lot of time here even if it weren't a refuge from the guards. Please have a seat.'

'How much time do we have before your boss arrives?' Zavala asked Phelps, as they settled into chairs.

'He's probably just about landing on that freighter he uses as a base,' Phelps said. 'He'll use the shuttle to get down into the crater.'

'How can we get the staff away from the lab?' Zavala asked.

'I've been thinking about that,' Phelps said. 'We can use the minisubs under the transit hub. They'll each take four people. We've got fifteen scientists down here plus the cargo-shuttle pilot.'

Zavala forgot his throbbing head in his eagerness to go on the offensive. 'You and I can go out the way we came in,' he said. 'We've got to neutralise those guys on the Typhoon. How many will we have to deal with?'

'There are seven left on board, all armed and meaner than rattlesnakes.'

'They've had it easy up until now, so they've lost their edge and won't be expecting anything,' said Zavala, his mind racing ahead. 'OK, we get the people on the minisubs and they leave the lab . . . Where do they go?'

'Through the big tunnel in the side of the crater,' Phelps said. 'They've got enough power to get well beyond the reef, past Chang's freighter, to where they can surface and send out a mayday.' He glanced at his watch. 'I've got to get things ready for Chang's arrival. Why don't you two get to know each other better?'

'Ladies first,' Zavala said after Phelps had closed the door behind him.

Mitchell gave Zavala a brief overview of her work with Dr Kane and the medusa project, going back to Bonefish Key.

'I never dreamed it would come to this,' she said. 'And you, Mr Zavala, how did you come to be in this awful place?'

'I'm an engineer with NUMA. My boss, Kurt Austin, and I were asked by the Navy to help search for the lab. So here I am.'

Lois Mitchell didn't question him further. She seemed distracted. Then she blinked and focused behind Zavala. 'What was that?' she asked.

He turned and saw only the schools of curious fish caught in the light from the office interior. 'Did you see something?' he asked.

'I thought I saw somebody swimming.' She smiled 'Sorry, I've been down here too long. Probably a big fish.'

The incident seemed to bring her back to reality. Joe's charm and soft-spoken manner penetrated Lois's shell, and she began to relax. She was actually smiling until Phelps returned with the news that his boss was bringing along someone named Dr Wu.

'He's no doctor,' she said, 'he's a monster!'

'Maybe it's time you showed Joe the disk,' Phelps suggested.

Mitchell was stone-faced as she took a key on a chain hung from around her neck and unlocked a drawer in her desk. She pulled out a box holding a number of disks. She picked one out and slipped it into her computer.

'Wu is Chang's creature,' Mitchell said. 'His job is to check on our progress. When he's here, he kicks me out of my office. I found this disk in my computer after his last visit. I made a copy, then left the disk in the computer. He eventually realised he had left the disk behind and sent one of his thugs to retrieve it.'

A picture had come up on the screen. The camera showed Wu talking to a man in a suit, then switched to a view of some people lying in beds encased in transparent cylinders. Figures in protective suits moved among the cylinders. The camera zoomed in to show close-ups of the people in them. Some appeared to be asleep or possibly dead. Others had faces mottled with mahogany splotches and contorted in agony.

'From what I can determine,' Mitchell said in a tense voice, 'the film was shot at a lab in China where they were experimenting with vaccines the Triad created. They used human subjects, and, of course, they had to infect their subjects with the virus. He's worse than that Nazi Mengele, the concentration-camp doctor.'

A rage began to build in Zavala's chest, and when the film had ended he said, 'Someone is going to pay for this.'

'Funny to hear you say that,' a familiar voice said. 'I was thinking the same thing.'

Three heads turned simultaneously. And three pairs of eyes widened at the sight of Austin, who stood in the doorway, his Bowen in his left hand.

Zavala stared at his friend. He wasn't totally surprised to see him: Austin had a way of popping up when you least expected him. But his wet suit was covered with blood and jellyfish slime.

'Are you OK?' Zavala said.

'My right arm is feeling a little useless right now, but the blood isn't mine. On the way here, I stopped in a room with a big round tank. A guy jumped me, and we were waltzing around when some of the smaller tanks in the room broke and spilled their insides all over the floor.'

'The small tanks contained organisms in various stages of mutation,' Mitchell said. 'You're lucky the big tank didn't break. Those creatures were the final mutant phase, the one used to make the vaccine. Each tentacle contains thousands of nematocysts, tiny harpoons that inject the toxin into prey.'

'My apologies for the damage, but it couldn't be helped,' Austin said. He introduced himself to Lois Mitchell. 'When I saw you from outside the dome, I thought that only Joe Zavala could find a lovely woman at the bottom of the ocean.'

Her eyes widened. 'That was *you* I saw?'

Austin nodded. He turned to Phelps. 'From the conversation I overheard a few moments ago, it sounds like you've come over from the Dark Side.'

'That film nailed it for me,' Phelps said.

Austin glanced at Zavala, who gave him a nod, then came back to Phelps. 'Welcome aboard, soldier,' Austin said. 'What's our status?'

'Chang is on his way to the lab to pick up the vaccine,' Phelps said. 'Now that the vaccine's a fact, they won't need the staff or the lab. Joe and I have come up with a plan to get everyone off the Locker.'

Austin was squinting through the dome where he had seen a flicker of light. Recalling the visibility of the globe's interior to outside eyes, he hit the light switch, throwing the office into darkness.

'Your plan had better be a good one,' he said. '*Look.*'

All eyes turned to see the shuttle carrying Chang and Dr Wu as it descended towards the lab like a star falling in slow motion.

MINUTES LATER, the shuttle settled on the landing pad and the open roof over it closed again like two halves of a clamshell. Powerful pumps rapidly cleared the air-lock of water, but Chang nonetheless was seething with impatience. He finally burst from the shuttle like a moray eel springing from its den and slogged towards the exit door. The weasel-faced Dr Wu followed behind.

When the door to the air-lock hissed open, Phelps was standing in the adjacent chamber. He stepped up to Chang and greeted him with a lopsided grin. 'You got here fast, boss. Musta put the pedal to the metal.'

Chang stared at Phelps with barely concealed contempt. American jargon was lost on him, and it annoyed him when Phelps used it. He had never fully trusted Phelps and suspected his loyalty extended only to the next pay cheque.

'Enough talk!' Chang snarled. 'Where is the vaccine?'

'Dr Mitchell has it,' Phelps said. 'She's been waiting in the mess hall for you to arrive. The NUMA guy is with her.'

'And the laboratory staff? Where are they?'

'They're all tucked away in their quarters.'

'Make sure they *stay* there. You've disabled the minisubs, as I ordered?'

Phelps dug out four flat, rectangular boxes tucked in his belt. 'These circuits control the subs' power supplies,' he said.

Chang snatched the circuit boards from Phelps, dropped them on the metal floor, and ground them to pieces with his heel. He barked an order to his men, who had emerged from the shuttle carrying wooden boxes. Printed on the boxes in big bold red letters was HANDLE WITH CARE. EXPLOSIVES.

Phelps rapped the top of a box with his knuckles. 'What's going on with the firecrackers, Chang?'

'It's fairly obvious,' Chang said. 'You're going to use your expertise with explosives to blow up the lab. It has fulfilled its function.'

Phelps poked at the smashed electrical circuits with the toe of his boot. 'One problem,' he said. 'How are the scientists going to get off the lab?'

'The scientists have fulfilled their function. They'll stay with the lab.'

Phelps stepped in front of Chang and faced off. 'You hired me to hijack the lab,' he said. 'Killing a bunch of innocent people wasn't in my job description. You can count me out of this deal.'

Chang stretched his liverish lips in a death's-head grin. 'Very well then, Mr Phelps. You're *fired*.'

Chang's hand reached down to his holster and, in a lightning move, drew his pistol and shot Phelps point-blank in the chest. The impact threw Phelps backwards, and he crashed to the floor. Chang gazed at Phelps's twitching body with the expression of a craftsman who considered his job well done. Chang ordered one of his men to prepare the explosives, and then he charged off. Dr Wu followed a few paces behind.

Chang burst into the mess hall, and his jade-green gaze fell on Joe Zavala and Lois Mitchell, who were tied to their chairs and sat back-to-back under the watchful eye of the guards who had come down with Phelps.

Chang leaned close to Zavala. 'Who are you?' he demanded.

'You've got a short memory. We met on the *Beebe*. You left with your tail between your legs while Kurt Austin and I entertained your friends.'

'Of course. You're the NUMA engineer. How did you find us?'

'One of our planes flew over the atoll and saw something suspicious.'

'You're lying!' Chang grabbed the front of Zavala's shirt. 'I don't like being taken for a fool. If that were the case, planes and ships would be swarming around the atoll. Tell me how you found us.'

'OK, I confess. A little bird told me.'

Chang backhanded Zavala across the jaw. 'What *else* did your little bird tell you?' he asked.

'He told me that you are going to die,' Zavala burbled through bloody lips.

'No, my friend, it is *you* who are going to die.'

Chang let go of Zavala's shirt and turned to Lois Mitchell, who was staring in horror at Joe's bloodied face.

'Where is my vaccine?' Chang demanded.

She glared at Chang. 'In a safe place. Untie me and I'll get it for you.'

At a nod from Chang, his men untied her. She stood and rubbed her wrists, then went over to the walk-in refrigerator used to store food for the mess. Stepping inside, she came out carrying a large plastic cooler, which she placed on the floor. Dr Wu opened the cooler.

Packed in foam were a number of shallow, wide Petri dishes. Wu smiled. 'This is a miracle,' he said.

'Actually,' she said, 'it's nothing more than very innovative genetic engineering. The Petri dishes contain the microbial cultures that will allow you to synthesise the vaccine in quantity. Underneath are the three vials of the vaccine that you requested. Our job here is done. Mr Phelps said that we would be free to go once we completed the project.'

'Phelps is no longer in our employ,' Chang said.

Her face went ashen. 'What do you mean?' she asked.

He ignored the question, and ordered his men to tie her up again.

'Your friend Austin escaped me again,' Chang said to Zavala, 'but it will only be a matter of time before we meet. And when we do, I will take great pleasure in describing your last moments to him.'

Chang took the cooler from Wu's hand and ordered the doctor and the guards to return with him to the shuttle.

Austin stepped out of the walk-in refrigerator seconds after they left, holding the Bowen in his left hand. 'Good thing old Bullethead left when he did,' Austin said. 'I was starting to feel like a side of beef in there.'

He tucked the revolver under his right arm. Using a kitchen knife, he sliced the bindings holding Zavala, who reached for a napkin to staunch his bleeding lips. Despite the cuts and bruises, he was in good humour.

'Chang isn't going to be happy when he finds out that the vaccine cultures you gave him are bogus,' he said to Lois Mitchell.

She gave Zavala a knowing smile, and went back into the freezer. She came out with another cooler, almost identical to the first.

'Wait until he learns that we've got the *real* thing,' she said.

CHANG UTTERED an angry curse as he entered the air-lock chamber and saw that Phelps's body was gone. A trail of blood led off towards a corridor. Phelps must have survived the gunshot.

No matter. Phelps would die when the lab blew into a million pieces. Chang inspected his sapper's handiwork and ordered him to set the timer. Then he herded his men into the shuttle, and the pilot used a remote control to activate the pumps. The air-lock quickly filled with water.

As the shuttle rose through the opening halves of the clamshell roof, Austin stood in the air-lock control room watching the ascent on the instrument console's television monitor. He spun round at the sound of a footfall, only to lower the Bowen a second later.

Phelps stood at the entrance to the passageway with his lips contorted into a strained grin. He was stripped to the waist, and a makeshift bandage covered the left part of his chest. His face was pale, but his eyes were defiant.

'You look like crap,' Austin said. 'What happened to you?'

'I figured Chang was going to be on hair trigger, thanks to you NUMA boys, so on my trip back to Kane's office I grabbed a soft body-armour vest,' Phelps said. 'It only covered my vitals, and I didn't account for Chang's bad aim. Bastard nicked me in the shoulder. He got testy when I told him I wouldn't rig the explosives he and his boys brought down in the shuttle.'

'He planned to destroy the lab with people in it?'

'Oh, hell, they put down enough explosives to wreck the Great Wall of China. Sloppy work, though. Lucky they didn't blow themselves up.'

Phelps tossed a bundle of coloured wires on the floor in an expert's gesture of disdain for amateurish work.

'We've got to get everyone off the lab in the minisubs before Chang discovers that his explosives didn't go off,' Austin said.

Phelps pointed at the black discs that had been pulverised under Chang's heel. 'These are circuits for the subs' controls. Chang stomped them.'

'Damn!' Austin said. 'The subs were our only hope.'

'Still are,' Phelps said. 'I gave Chang some other discs for his temper tantrum. The originals are still in the subs.'

Austin grinned at Phelps. 'What say you get the subs ready while I round up the scientists?'

Phelps gave a quick salute and headed for the transit hub while Austin hurried to the mess hall. Zavala had already rounded up the staff, who looked weary and frightened.

Austin introduced himself, asked everyone to be quiet for a minute, then announced: 'We're abandoning the Locker.' He shushed the group again and warned them to move quickly. Questions would be allowed later.

The scientists climbed down to the minisub hatches. A few hesitated when they saw Phelps, but Austin told them to get into the subs. With some grumbling, they did as they were told.

'Are the subs likely to encounter Chang on their way out of the crater?' he asked Phelps.

'Not if they move fast. Chang will have gone back to his freighter to wait for the big boom. If the subs stay submerged as long as they can, they'll be well past Chang's ship, and can put out a mayday.'

Austin passed Phelps's advice along to the pilot of each sub. He delegated the shuttle pilot to take the lead vehicle. Mitchell got in one of them and held the cooler with the real vaccine cultures in it tightly on her lap. Then, one by one, the subs detached from the underside of the hub and followed the leader across the bottom of the crater and through the tunnel.

With the staff on its way, Austin turned to the next order of business: the Typhoon. As they got back in their wet suits, Zavala filled Austin in on the situation aboard the Russian submarine. Austin's view was not optimistic. Feeling was returning to his right arm, but he wouldn't be able to fire the Bowen. Phelps, with his wounded shoulder, would be of limited help.

Phelps noticed that two sets of scuba gear were missing and surmised that the pair of guards who had escorted Zavala from the sub had gone back with their comrades.

Zavala helped Austin lower Phelps into the pool and guide him down the shaft to open water. With Austin on one side of Phelps and Zavala on the other, all three slowly rose from the bottom up towards the Typhoon, whose gigantic shadow loomed near the surface.

By prearrangement, Austin and Phelps entered the hatch on the starboard deck of the giant fin and Zavala used the port hatch. Once inside the escape chambers they closed the hatch, pumped out the water, then opened the lower watertight door and descended the ladder. They whipped their masks off to see Captain Mehdev standing there with a curious look on his face.

The captain had been in the control room when an alarm went off signifying the air-locks were in use. He wasn't surprised to see Phelps and Zavala, but he raised a bushy eyebrow when he saw the stranger.

Zavala said, 'Kurt, this is Captain Mehdev, the commander of this incredible boat and keeper of the vodka cabinet.'

Austin extended his uninjured left arm for a handshake.

'Kurt Austin. I'm Joe's friend and colleague at NUMA.' Noticing the hostile glance Mehdev shot in Phelps's direction, he added, 'Mr Phelps is no longer working for the hijackers. He is helping us now.'

'I'm going to help you guys take your sub back,' Phelps said.

Mehdev shrugged. 'What can we do? We are sailors, not Marines.'

'Start by telling us where the guards are,' Austin said.

'Three are asleep in the officers' quarters,' Mehdev said, 'and the others are gambling in the wardroom. They like to be close to the gym and the sauna.'

'I think it's time we end their little sojourn at Club Med,' Austin said. 'Let's take care of the snoozers first.'

The four men filed through the control room, where Mehdev, who had been in the lead, whispered in Russian to the crewmen, who passed the word on to others, that it would be a good idea to stay out of sight. The captain then picked up some rolls of duct tape from the machine shop and continued through the labyrinth of pressurised compartments until they came to the first of the officers' staterooms.

Three off-duty guards awoke in the first room to find themselves looking down the barrel of Austin's revolver. They were trussed up by Zavala, had their mouths taped, and were tucked back in their bunks.

With Mehdev again in the lead, Austin and Zavala kept moving through the sub until they came to the wardroom. The captain poked his face through the doorway and asked with a smile if anyone needed anything. One guard looked up from his cards and answered with a growl that needed no translation. Still smiling, the captain withdrew.

'Four places but only three players,' Mehdev whispered to Austin and Zavala. 'Half a bottle of vodka gone.'

Austin didn't like having a stray guard wandering round the submarine, but he wanted to press his advantage. He nodded to Zavala, and they stepped into the wardroom with guns levelled. The slightly drunk guards were slow to react. Minutes later, they were face down on the floor bound with duct tape. Then the hunt was on for the missing guard.

They found him a few minutes after that. Or, rather, he found them. As the men entered the compartment that housed the sauna, the door opened and the guard stepped out wearing only a bathing suit. This time, it was Austin and Zavala who were slow to react. The guard was young and fast, and he reached into a nearby locker, grabbed a holster with a handgun in it, and bolted through the hatch into the next compartment. Austin gave chase into the innards of the submarine, Zavala right behind him until he came to a closed door. He and Zavala were pondering their next move when Mehdev caught up with them.

'What's on the other side of that door?' Austin asked Mehdev.

Huffing and puffing, the portly captain said, 'A cargo hold. A freight elevator goes up to a loading hatch on the deck. A catwalk from the elevator crosses over the bays to another elevator on the forward side of the hold, which is filled with empty cargo containers.'

After a quick conference, Austin plucked a flashlight off the bulkhead wall, turned the compartment lights off, and slowly opened the door. Zavala climbed the stairs to the catwalk to drive the guard towards Austin, who then would cut him off at the other end of the hold.

The vast interior hold, which took up almost a third of the sub's length, had been partitioned to separate one cargo from another. Austin stepped into the first bay and found a light switch. Floodlights hanging from the catwalk turned night into day. He made his way along a corridor between the metal containers until he came to a partition. He stepped through an opening into the next bay and repeated his search.

As Austin made his way through the hold, Zavala kept pace on the catwalk. They crossed the hold without incident until the last bay.

Austin assumed that the guard was still ahead of him, caught in the pincers of their manoeuvre. But the prey had hidden in a narrow space between container stacks. He waited for Austin to pass and then emerged. Moving quietly on bare feet, he lifted his gun and carefully took aim between Austin's shoulder blades.

'*Kurt!*'

The shout came from Zavala, who was peering over the rail of the cat-walk. Austin glanced up and saw his friend's pointing finger. Without a backward glance, he ducked round a big metal container as a bullet twanged off its corner. Then another gunshot rang out, this one from above. A moment later, Zavala called down.

'You can come out, Kurt. I think I got him.'

Austin peered round the corner of the container, then he waved up at Zavala. The guard lay dead in his bathing suit on the floor.

CHANG WAS A CLASSIC psychopath. He didn't have a drop of human empathy or remorse in his body, and for him killing was as easy as crossing the street. The other Triad triplets had channelled his murderous impulses to their own ends, giving him responsibility for the gangs. The job slaked his blood thirst by allowing him to participate in assassinations for commercial advantage, retribution or just plain punishment. But now he was far from the familial reins that had kept his barely restrained violence in check. He had delivered the vaccine cultures to the freighter, and then waited for a report from the submarine. The failure of the explosives to detonate, to destroy the lab and staff, had finally pushed him over the edge.

Chang got back in the shuttle with his most cold-blooded killers, and ordered the pilot to head back into the crater.

Carrying its cargo of murderers, the shuttle descended to the transit hub. The pilot activated the air-lock. Minutes later, Chang and his men burst out of the air-lock and almost stumbled over a box of C-4. A length of coloured wires had been tied in a bow and placed on top of the carton.

Chang stormed off to the control room, only to pause at the door. Suspecting that the room had been booby-trapped, he sent his men in first. They scoured the room and reported back that it was deserted and nothing was amiss. He stepped in to see for himself.

A metallic voice issued from the wall speakers. 'You're right, Chang. You and your pals are the only ones on the lab.'

Chang wheeled round, the stock of the machine pistol tight against his chest. 'Who's that?'

'SpongeBob SquarePants,' the voice said.

'*Austin!*'

'OK, I confess, Chang. You got me. It's Kurt Austin.'

Chang's eyes narrowed to slits. 'What happened to the scientists?'

'They are no longer on the lab, Chang. They left in the minisubs.'

'Don't toy with me, Austin. I destroyed the subs' power circuits.' A different voice came on the speaker: Phelps. 'Those were back-up circuits you stomped on,' he said. 'The subs were fully operable, boss.'

'*Phelps?*' Chang exclaimed. 'I thought you were dead.'

'Sorry to disappoint you, Chang. Austin ain't jerking you around. Dr Mitchell and all the other scientists are long gone.'

'I'll find them,' Chang shouted. 'I'll find you and Austin and kill you!'

'That's not very likely,' Austin said. 'By the way, the vaccine cultures they gave you are useless. The real ones are with the staff.'

A WHITE HATE FLOWED through Chang's bull-like body like a power surge. As the shuttle rose from the lab, he radioed the freighter, giving orders to start scouring the depths with sonar. A minute later, he got a reply. Sonar had picked up four shapes moving away from the atoll. Chang ordered the freighter to be on hand when the minisubs surfaced.

The shuttle went full speed towards the tunnel. Chang allowed a smile to cross his face, anticipating the looks on the scientists' faces when they saw the freighter bearing down on them. He was savouring the scene, imagining how they would react when he rose from the deep like Neptune, when he heard the pilot call out. Chang leaned forwards in his seat and stared out of the cockpit window.

A huge black shadow was bearing down on the shuttle.

The pilot recognised the massive blunt bow of the Typhoon hurtling right at them and he yelped like a frightened puppy. Chang yelled at him to turn, but the pilot's hands were frozen on the controls. Uttering a feral snarl, Chang grabbed the pilot by the shoulders, pulled him out of his chair, and took his place. He yanked the wheel hard to starboard.

The shuttle's turbines continued to drive it forwards, but after a few seconds the front came round to the right, narrowly edging the shuttle out of the way of a head-on collision with the 600-foot torpedo hurtling its way. But the Typhoon was moving at twenty-five knots, and it clipped the tail end of the shuttle, demolishing its rudder and sending the shuttle into a wild spin. The violent impact caused the cargo door to fly open, and water began flowing in.

The weight of the inrushing sea dragged the shuttle's tail down, and the front of the shuttle angled upwards like a dying fish. Chang's men grabbed onto the seats and pulled themselves up the slanting deck towards the cockpit.

Dr Wu struggled to join the pack, but the stronger guards pushed him under the water and his flailing arms soon grew still. Chang was not about to share the pocket of air with anyone. He turned round, pistol in hand, and shot any man who tried to encroach on his space. Within seconds, he had killed all his guards and was alone in the cabin.

By then the weight of the water in the shuttle had shifted forwards. Its nose levelled out, and the shuttle began to sink to the bottom of the crater. Chang fought to keep his head up in the diminishing pocket of air, but the bodies swashing around in the bloodstained water made it difficult.

More water came in, diminishing the pocket of air even more. Chang pressed against the ceiling of the shuttle with only a few inches left. As water filled his mouth and nostrils, he looked up, saw the monstrous shadow of the Typhoon gliding overhead, and with his last gasp uttered: '*Austin!*'

The owner of that name sat next to the Russian helmsman in the Typhoon's control room. The captain stood by Austin's side, relaying orders in Russian to the helmsman. Austin watched with pitiless eyes as the shuttle plunged to the bottom. He felt no sense of triumph. Not yet. He was all too well aware that the Triad was a *three*-headed monster.

Chapter 12

When the *Concord* failed to hear from Austin, Captain Dixon had moved the Navy ships under his command closer to the atoll.

The captain stood on the foredeck watching the atoll through binoculars in the dawn light, unaware of the drama that had transpired under the lagoon. He was pondering what his next course of action should be when Song Lee, standing beside him, pointed towards a patch of water.

'Captain Dixon, look!'

The massive conning tower of the Typhoon was breaking the surface several hundred yards east of the atoll. After a few minutes, two figures appeared in the lofty tower and waved their arms.

Dixon brought his binoculars to his eyes. 'I'll be damned,' he said.

He handed the binoculars to Lee.

She raised them to her eyes, and blurted, 'It's Kurt! And Joe!'

After another wave, the two men disappeared from the tower and emerged moments later from a hatch in the deck with an inflatable boat. Soon they were skimming over the waves towards the cruiser.

Song Lee was waiting on deck to throw her arms round Austin, then Zavala. Then Austin again. She gave him a kiss full on the lips.

Austin would have liked to prolong the pleasant experience, but he gently disentangled himself from her arms and turned to Captain Dixon.

'Have you seen any sign of the lab's staff?' he asked. 'They should have surfaced in the minisubs by now.'

Dixon shook his head. He called his first officer on the bridge and asked him to ask the other ships in the vicinity to be on the lookout for the surfacing minisubs. Moments later, a call came in from the NUMA ship. The first minisub had surfaced. Dixon issued an order to get the *Concord* under way. It rounded the atoll just in time to see a second sub popping out of the water, then the other two.

Austin let out the breath he had been holding.

A rescue crew pulled Lois Mitchell and the other scientists out of their minisubs and brought them back to the cruiser. As the boat came close, Lois saw Austin leaning over the railing. She waved, then pointed to the cooler in her lap. When she climbed aboard, she handed the cooler to Lee.

'Here's our vaccine,' Mitchell said, 'safe and sound.'

The joyful smile on Lee's face dissolved. She looked crestfallen as she held the cooler, as though someone had just told her it was radioactive.

'It's too late, Lois,' she said. 'The epidemic will explode throughout China within twenty-four hours and spread to the rest of the world within days. There is no time to produce the vaccine in the quantities we need.'

Mitchell took the cooler back, set it on the deck, and pushed the top back to expose a rack with dozens of aluminium cylinders in it.

'You weren't in on the last phase of the research,' Mitchell said, 'so you don't know how far we have gone.'

'I was aware that you had integrated the antiviral molecule into microbes in an attempt to speed up the synthesis process,' Lee said.

'We decided that was too slow,' Mitchell said. 'So we incorporated the toxin's curative protein in fast-growing saltwater algae.'

Lee's expression of dismay turned to laughter. She picked up a cylinder and said, 'This is wonderful.' Seeing the puzzled expressions on the faces of the three men, she explained. 'Algae grow at an incredible speed. Once we get these cultures to the production facilities, they can extract enough vaccine for hundreds of thousands of people within a few days.' She carefully placed the cylinder back in the cooler. 'This has to get to China as soon as possible.'

The captain picked the cooler off the deck. 'It's on its way,' he said.

Ten minutes later, the Seahawk carrying the cooler lifted off the deck and headed towards its rendezvous with a fast jet waiting at Pohnpei Airport.

Austin stood on the deck, watching the helicopter shrink to a speck. Song Lee had volunteered to escort the vaccine back to China. Austin was sad to see her go, but the evil smile of the Dragon Lady was already starting to overshadow his thoughts of Song's lovely face.

THE GIANT RUSSIAN submarine led the way into Pohnpei's harbour like a proud leviathan. Next was Chang's freighter, now manned by a Navy crew that had taken over after a destroyer had chased her down. Without orders from Chang, his crew had surrendered without a shot.

Phelps had come over from the submarine and was giving Austin and Zavala a tour of the vessel, showing them the state-of-the-art communications centre and the hologram-projection booth that Chang used to communicate with his other two triplets.

The last stop was the ship's salon. Austin made himself at home. He passed out three Havana-wrapped cigars from a humidor and lit them with a silver-plated lighter. He, Zavala and Phelps sat in plush red-velvet chairs and puffed on their cigars.

'Chang had a good nose for smokes,' Zavala said, looking around at the purple drapes and wood panelling. 'But his taste in decorating stinks.'

'Kinda reminds me of a Nevada whorehouse,' said Phelps. 'I stopped there one time to ask for directions.'

Austin smiled and took a few more puffs, then snuffed out his cigar. 'We've got to talk,' he said to Phelps.

'Talk away,' Phelps said.

'Joe and I are grateful for your help,' Austin said, 'but we've got that issue about the scientist you killed on board the lab.'

'It was an accident,' Phelps said. 'Lois will vouch for that.'

'I thought she didn't like you,' Zavala said.

'We've got to know each other better. She's a beautiful woman. I like them big-boned.'

Austin stared at Phelps, thinking he still had a lot to learn about human nature. 'Well, here's the problem,' he said with a heavy smile. 'You killed that man in the commission of a crime: the hijacking of US property and the missile attack on the support ship.'

'The missile attack was meant to distract the guards long enough to steal the lab,' Phelps said. 'I'll admit someone could have been killed, but I'm glad that didn't happen. I had no part in the security man's death . . . But I see what you mean.'

'Glad to hear that you understand the situation,' Austin said. 'I'm going to have to turn you over to the authorities when we land. I'll tell them the whole story, and that's sure to mitigate your punishment.'

'Ten years in the brig instead of twenty?' Phelps grinned. 'Well, sometimes you gotta do what you gotta do. Mind if I go tell Lois what's happening?'

Austin couldn't help admiring the man's calm. He nodded, then rose from his chair. They left the salon, and a few minutes later were in a pontoon boat headed back to the *Concord*.

Lois Mitchell was waiting there for them. Phelps peeled Lois away from the others, and they went off to talk while Austin and Zavala went to the wardroom to meet the captain and the scientists from the lab.

Dixon brought everyone up to date on the progress of the jet flying to China. It would be close, but the vaccine would make it there in time.

Austin glanced at his watch. He excused himself and went out on the deck. He asked several crewmen if they had seen Phelps and Mitchell, and he finally got an answer when one of them pointed towards shore.

'They took the inflatable into port,' the crewman informed Austin. 'They said they would be back in a couple of hours. Guy said to give this to you.'

Austin read the short, scrawled message: *Gotta do what you gotta do. P.*

An annoyed smile came to Austin's lips. Phelps had outfoxed him.

Austin looked towards Pohnpei. Phelps would be far away by the time local police mobilised. Nevertheless Austin asked a crewman to call the police, report a stolen launch and give them a description of Phelps.

Austin was pondering his next course of action when his cellphone rang. It was Lieutenant Casey.

'Congratulations, Kurt,' Casey said, 'the admiral gave me the good news.'

'Thanks, Lieutenant, but our work isn't done as long as the other Triad triplets are on the loose.'

'We're well aware of that, Kurt. I have someone who would like to talk to you.' A few seconds later, a man's voice came on the line.

'Good day, Mr Austin,' he said in a silken tone. 'Let me introduce myself. I am Colonel Ming of the People's Liberation Army.'

'Good day, Colonel Ming. How can I help you?'

'That's not why I called, Mr Austin. The question is, how can I help *you*?'

WEN LO EMERGED from his favourite nightclub with a gorgeous prostitute clinging to each arm. His walk was unsteady, but the Triad triplet wasn't too drunk to see that something was very wrong. His guards were gone. The two SUVs that escorted his armour-plated Mercedes everywhere were gone. A black Roewe sedan had taken the Mercedes's place at the kerb.

Standing next to the car was a granite-faced man in a dark suit. He opened the Roewe's rear door and motioned for Wen Lo to get in.

Wen Lo looked up and down the street. No pedestrians or traffic moved in either direction. The street obviously had been cordoned off.

Wen Lo dispensed the prostitutes with a shove and got in the Roewe. The granite-faced man shut the door and slid in front next to the driver.

As the car pulled away, a man in army uniform sitting in the back seat, said, 'Good evening, Wen Lo. My apologies for spoiling your night out.'

'Good evening, Colonel Ming. No apologies necessary. It is always a pleasure to see you, my friend.'

In this case, it was more of a relief than a pleasure. Colonel Ming was the liaison between the Army and the Triad, and both organisations profited handsomely from the hundreds of brothels that they jointly operated.

'The feeling is mutual, of course,' said the colonel.

'I must say that I was concerned when I saw my men were not at their posts and my car was gone,' Wen Lo said.

'Rest assured, they are safe,' Ming said. 'I thought it best not to have any distractions while we talked over a serious problem that has arisen.'

'Of course,' Wen Lo said. 'What sort of problem? Are you looking for a more luxurious apartment . . . or car?'

'This is not personal,' Ming said. 'This is business. The problem is in Pyramid's pharmaceutical division.' He stretched his hand out to a DVD player built into the back of the driver's seat and pushed the ON button.

Wen Lo's face appeared on the screen. He watched himself taking a tour of the secret lab with Dr Wu, whose voice was narrating, and close-ups of the subjects and their disease-ravaged faces.

'I am puzzled as to the nature of this facility your organisation is operating,' Ming said, as the DVD came to an end.

Wen Lo glanced at the men in the front seat. Speaking in a conspiratorial whisper, he said, 'I am taking you into my confidence, Colonel. The secret I am about to reveal is held by me and a few of the most powerful people in the government. The laboratory has been working on a revolutionary new vaccine that will not only contain a new outbreak of SARS but will cure dozens of other diseases caused by viruses.'

Colonel Ming lightly clapped his hands. 'That is *wonderful* news, Wen Lo! Congratulations.'

'Thank you, Colonel. It has been a long, hard road, but our work will put China in the medical history books. It will be a boon to mankind.'

'Excellent!' Ming paused for a moment, then said, 'I am not a medical person, but I wondered if it is customary to use human beings as lab animals.'

'Pardon me, sir, but they would be upset to be described in that fashion. They are all volunteers from the slums who faced miserable lives.'

The colonel nodded. 'Yes, I see your logic. Your lab served to shorten their misery. I applaud your humanity. But this disc raises some concerns. It is easily copied. I fear that it will surface in quarters where people will not be as enlightened as you and me. You see the potential for disorder?'

Wen Lo was well aware of the government's aversion to disorder. Through intimidation and assassination, he and his thugs often had stifled dissent when the government chose to pursue a hands-off policy.

'Yes, of course,' Wen Lo said. 'But the government controls the media and the internet. We can claim that the DVD is a fake. My organisation can deal with those who choose to make an issue of this matter.'

'All true,' Ming said. 'But we cannot control the foreign media, and the government has no wish to be associated even by implication with what the DVD shows. Since you are the public face of Pyramid, we feel it best if you disappear.'

'*Disappear?*' Wen Lo croaked.

Ming patted Wen Lo's knee. 'Don't be alarmed,' he said. 'We are old friends. We have arranged for you to quietly leave China. The government is prepared to work with Pyramid while you are out of the country.'

'I suppose that may work,' Wen Lo said with reluctance.

'We will need to know where and how to reach the number one person in your company,' Ming said.

'Impossible! We never meet face to face. We communicate electronically through holograms.'

A sad look came to the colonel's face. 'That is a shame,' Ming said. 'I'm afraid you will be brought to trial, and the outcome is a foregone conclusion. An example will be made of you.'

Wen Lo was well aware of the consequences of being made an example of in China. He knew men who had been executed for corrupt business practices.

'Very well,' Wen Lo said with a deep sigh. 'We use a simple telephone number to set up our hologram meetings.'

The colonel reached into his pocket and pulled out a pen and a small notepad, which he gave to Wen Lo. After a few seconds of hesitation, Wen Lo jotted down a number and handed back the pad and pen.

'Thank you,' Ming said, inspecting the number to make sure it was legible. He tucked the pad and pen back in his pocket. 'Now we can deal with your future. How does London sound, for a start? We can move you around as needs be. And, when it's safe, we can bring you home again.'

Wen Lo's mood brightened. 'London is fine. I have a house in Soho.'

Ming tapped on the window separating the back seat from the driver. The car pulled over to the kerb, and Ming said to Wen Lo, 'See you in London.'

The granite-faced man got out of the front, opened the door, and escorted Ming to a second Roewe sedan that had pulled up behind the first one. As Ming got into the second car, he said to the man, 'Make sure it's neat.'

As the colonel's car pulled away from the kerb, he tapped out a number on his cellphone. After a few rings, a man's voice answered.

'Mr Austin?' Ming said. 'I have the information you are looking for.'

While the colonel was talking, the granite-faced man walked back to the first car and got in next to the driver. He tapped on the glass partition and slid it open. Wen Lo looked right at him. This gave the man a perfect target when he shot Wen Lo in the right eye with a .22 calibre pistol.

WHEN JOE ZAVALA wasn't dating half the female population of Washington or tinkering with his Corvette's engine, he loved figuring out how things worked. To Zavala, Chang's hologram-projection room on the freighter was nothing but an elaborate engine whose purpose was to send and receive lifelike images.

With Austin standing by, Zavala prowled through the intricate arrangement of microphones, lenses, lasers, projectors and computers that surrounded the circular table and three chairs under hanging cones. After an hour, he stepped back and brushed his palms together.

'She's all set and ready to go, Kurt. You can project yourself with a push of that button.'

Austin peered up into one of the cones overhead. 'This isn't going to reassemble my molecules so that I end up with the head of a fly, is it?'

'Nothing to worry about. It's all high-tech illusion, smoke and mirrors.'

'Keep a fly-swatter handy, just in case,' Austin said, settling into a padded, contoured chair.

He studied the control panel for a moment, and then punched in the code number Wen Lo had given Colonel Ming.

Lights blinked and machinery hummed as a complex set of optics scanned every square inch of Austin's body and transmitted the information via electronic pulses to a computer that digested the information and sent it to another computer to be reassembled in a 3-D projector. Austin tensed his shoulders, expecting to feel an electrical tingle that never came.

Instead, the air under a cone across from Austin shimmered as if heated. A cloud of whirling motes began to form into the image of a human head and shoulders, transparent at first, becoming translucent, then solid, as the features filled in. Austin knew from his encounter with the Dragon Lady that the hologram was mutable and could be changed at a whim. But the face across the table was stranger than anything he could have imagined.

The eyes below the gracefully arched brows were the same jade-green as Chang's and the fleshy lips were feminine, but the soft-featured face was at odds with stubble on the chin and the professional wrestler's body. The third Triad triplet seemed to be neither man nor woman but a freakish combination of both, a hermaphrodite.

The hologram remained as still as a marble statue. The features were frozen, eyes staring straight ahead. Then the lips moved, and a mellow voice, neither male nor female, came through the surrounding speakers.

'We meet again, Mr Austin,' the hologram said.

'Should I call you Dragon Lady or Lai Choi San?' Austin asked.

'I am known as One to my followers. I was the first of my siblings to come into this world, by a few minutes. We Chinese are superstitious when it comes to numbers and believe a low number denotes good fortune.'

'From the way your luck has been going lately,' Austin said, 'you'd better look for a new number. Your holographic image is all out of whack too. Nothing is moving except for your mouth.'

'That's because I can't move my limbs.'

'What happened?'

'I was hoping you could tell me that, Mr Austin. The vaccine serum was transported directly to me. Upon the assurance of my brother Chang,

I orally vaccinated myself. I knew that the virus would spread to my city in a matter of hours and I wanted to be the first to be made immune.' The thin lips spread in a grotesque parody of a smile. 'It seems that the chemical was flawed. I became paralysed as I sat here trying to contact my brothers.'

'The cylinder Chang sent you contained a transitional vaccine that was going to be discarded. It could kill the virus, but it paralysed the host.'

'Then the research was a failure?'

'Not at all. The real vaccine is being produced throughout China and around the world in quantities that will stop the epidemic you started.'

The lips snapped back to a thin line. 'The fact that you are on Chang's ship tells me that my brother is no longer in the picture. He would never allow you to live if he were alive.'

'I'm afraid Chang became a victim of his own violent impulses.'

'Too bad,' the hologram said without sadness. 'Chang was brilliant in many ways but too often impetuous.'

Austin's jaw hardened. 'The murder of scores of innocent people,' he said, 'is not what most people would describe as impetuous.'

'That's because our family looks at the world in a different way from others. We have not survived all this time by being sentimental when it comes to the deaths of others, or even deaths in our own family.'

'Glad to hear that,' Austin said, 'because you won't shed any tears over the loss of your brother Wen Lo.'

'Wen Lo is dead too?'

'He ran afoul of the Chinese Army . . . another casualty of your insane scheme.'

'There was nothing insane about it. Our country's leadership is extremely fragile. The government would have reacted violently to protests in the streets. We would have encouraged the mob rule that would have followed and then stepped in to end the epidemic, and take over the reins of government. The plan was well thought out. We didn't anticipate the interference from you and your NUMA friends.'

'NUMA doesn't deserve all the credit,' Austin said. 'You planted the seeds of your own destruction when you decided to play at being a three-headed god.'

A flash of anger came to the staring holographic eyes. 'I could squash you like an ant, Austin.'

'You could, if you could lift a finger. The best you can look forward to is being hired as a hat rack. So long, One. The toxin will keep you alive for a long time. Have a good life.' Austin's finger was poised over the button that would end the transmission.

'*Wait!* Where are you going? You can't leave me all alone like this.'

The plea made no difference to Austin. He felt only revulsion towards the freakish figure. 'Then I'll make a deal with you,' he said. 'Tell me where you are and I'll relay the information to the Chinese government. You can take your chances with them.'

After a moment, the triplet reeled off an address in Hong Kong.

'Thanks, One. Now I'll give you some good advice. Forget any thoughts about bribing your way out of this. The government is appropriating all your assets. You have nothing to offer them.'

'I will kill you, Austin. Somehow, I will find a way.'

'Goodbye, Dragon Lady.' Austin pushed the button to halt the projection. '*Wait!*' The words came out of a formless cloud of dancing motes.

Zavala, who was standing off to the side, muttered something in Spanish.

Austin realised that he was soaked with sweat. Even though he was separated from it by thousands of miles, he felt he had never been so close to pure evil. As if awakening from a dream, he said, 'Did you jot down the address that thing gave me?'

Zavala nodded. 'What do you want to do with it?' he asked.

'When we get back to the *Concord*, call Colonel Ming and give him the information. It's his party from now on. Then go pour yourself a stiff shot of tequila, followed by another one, saving some cactus juice for me.'

Chapter 13
Bonefish Key, Five Weeks Later

Song Lee was sitting on the sunlit patio in front of the lodge going over some notes when she heard the drone of an outboard motor echoing through the mangroves. Recognising the sound of Dooley's boat, she looked up and smiled at his impending arrival.

Dooley had been her main contact with the outside world since she had returned to the island to work on her medical text on ocean biomedicine. Bonefish Key was practically deserted now. A small cadre stayed behind to tend to the specimen tanks, but with the project at an end, Dr Mayhew and his team had scattered to the four winds.

Dr Kane had visited once. He had breezed in with a camera crew to film the lab buildings before sweeping out again as if carried on the wind.

Although the Chinese and United States governments were still nervous about telling the whole story of their collaboration in stopping the near pandemic, the herculean effort to stop the virus was big news around the world. Kane basked in his celebrity, flying from interview to interview. He was using his status as pandemic guru to prise money from Congress to support the type of ocean biomedicine research that had saved the world.

Song Lee had been content to labour in anonymity, but the remoteness of the island had started to get to her. She often thought of the NUMA people who had swooped in to save her and the world. Most of all she missed Kurt Austin. A few weeks after she had arrived on the island, he had called her on one of the lab's radiophones. He was still on Pohnpei, helping with the recovery of Davy Jones's Locker.

The drone of the marine motor grew louder, and seconds later Dooley's double-hulled boat rounded the corner of a mangrove island. There were two people in the boat: Dooley, at the wheel, and, beside him, a broad-shouldered man wearing a Hawaiian shirt. As they approached the dock, the broad-shouldered man removed the baseball hat from his head, revealing a thick mane of steel-grey hair. Song was already up and running down to the dock by the time the boat bumped up against a piling.

'Brought you some company, Dr Lee,' Dooley said.

Song barely heard him. Her eyes were fixed on Kurt, who had a wide grin on his bronzed face. The grin grew even wider when he climbed out of the boat and Song threw her arms round him. He returned her embrace with enthusiasm. She planted a kiss on his lips that was warm and long, and might have gone on for ever if Dooley hadn't cleared his throat.

'Pardon me, folks, but I've got to get back to the mainland.' He extended his hand. 'Nice to meet you, Kurt. Call when you want to go back.'

'Thanks for the ride, Dooley,' Austin said. He asked Dooley to toss him his small rucksack.

As the boat disappeared into the mangroves, Austin said, 'I got back to Washington a few days ago and thought I'd hop down here to say hello.'

Lee hooked her arm in Austin's and led the way towards the lodge. 'I'm glad you did,' she said. 'How are Joe and the Trouts?'

'They're all fine. The Trouts just got back from New Bedford. The city's whaling museum was dedicating a room for Caleb Nye's diorama. It's part of a special exhibition on the strange voyage of the *Princess*.'

'And a very strange voyage it was,' Lee said. 'I start off my book with their experience on Trouble Island.'

'How is the book coming?'

'I've finished the outline and I'm doing supplemental research. I think the findings will revolutionise our understanding of viral immunology, particularly inoculation. But we have just scratched the surface of wonder drugs that will come from the ocean. It's ironic that the vaccine might never have been developed without the threat of the Triad's epidemic.'

'A classic case of yin and yang?' he asked.

'I hate to think that the opposing forces of good and evil were bound together in this case,' she said, 'but without one, the other would not have produced a benefit to the world.'

'More than one,' he said. 'China and US relations have never been warmer. And the Triad is no longer with us. Yin and yang on hormones.'

They had climbed the hill to the patio and settled into a couple of chairs that faced the waterfront.

Austin zipped open his rucksack and pulled out a bottle and two shot glasses. He poured each glass half full and offered one to Song.

'This is the Micronesian *sakau* I promised you. It's slightly narcotic, so it is best taken in small doses.'

They raised their glasses, and, after a moment of thought, Song said, 'Here's to warm relations between China and America.'

They clinked glasses. She sipped, made a sour face and put her glass down.

'It's an acquired taste, which is probably a good thing,' Austin said with a smile. 'As I recall, I also promised you a dinner with a water view.' He swept his hand in the air. 'Here's the water view. Dinner may have to wait until your work here is done.'

'Maybe not,' Song said. 'One of the lab techs caught some fresh redfish this morning and will be grilling them for dinner. Please join us.'

Austin accepted the invitation, and they sat on the patio talking until the dinner bell clanged. They ate in the dining room with a half-dozen staffers, then retired to the patio to enjoy an after-dinner drink.

'How's your research going on the New Bedford anomaly?' asked Austin.

'I've been going over what material I have. But so much is missing,' replied Song.

Austin reached into his rucksack again and pulled out a package wrapped in plain paper. He handed it to Lee.

'You might find this of interest,' he said.

Lee took the wrapping off and stared at the book in her hand. The blue leather cover was crinkled with age and weathered from the time it had spent at sea. She turned to the first page and read aloud:

'*November 20, 1847. Wind northwest at ten knots. Good ship* Princess *departs New Bedford on maiden voyage. Adventure and prosperity beckon. H. Dobbs.*'

'It's the missing logbook!' she said. 'Where did you find it?'

'The Trouts picked it up when they went to New Bedford for the dedication. Seems Harvey Brimmer's story about Caleb Nye's secret marriage was true. The book was part of a dowry he gave his daughter. It's been in her family since then. They'd like it back after you're done with it.'

Kurt and Song talked for hours, with the sensuous sounds and smells of the semitropic night in the background, and it was late when they realised that the rest of the staff had drifted off and they were all alone.

Austin glanced at his watch, and said, 'I had better call Dooley to have him pick me up. I have a meeting in Washington tomorrow.'

'Do you really have to go so soon?' she asked.

'Unfortunately, yes. I'm sorry to rush off.'

'Maybe you can rush back just as quickly.'

'I have the feeling we'll be seeing each other sooner than we think.'

'TOO BAD YOU GOT to leave Dr Lee so soon,' Dooley said as the boat headed towards the mangroves.

'That's OK,' Austin said. 'She's got a young guy to keep her company.'

'Sorry to hear that,' Dooley said with real concern. 'Anybody I know?'

'Probably not. His name is Caleb Nye.'

'Women,' Dooley muttered with a sad shake of his head.

Minutes later, they broke out of the mangroves into open water. Dooley goosed the throttle, and the boat raced across the moonlit waters of the bay to the distant mainland.

clive **cussler**

RD: Is it hard to keep coming up with so many great original ideas for books?

CC: It's not easy, but something usually crops up and I expand on it until it leads to interesting paths for fun plots.

RD: What was the starting point for *Medusa*—the historical whaling angle, perhaps, or advances in bio-med?

CC: A combination. The idea of the whaler, connected to a weird jellyfish with medicinal powers, seemed a natural storyline.

RD: The Blue Medusa in the novel is quite a jellyfish. Is it based on a real species, or is it just an imaginary creature?

CC: It's not based on a particular jellyfish. There are many species that are extremely dangerous and some can cause death within minutes after stinging.

RD: Could we derive more biomed remedies than we do from the oceans?

CC: Yes, I believe so. Bioscientists are working all over the world in an effort to find new remedies.

RD: What is Paul Kemprecos's background and have you worked with him often?

CC: Paul is a journalist who wrote a series about a detective who solved mysteries under the waters around Cape Cod. We've worked together on at least five books.

RD: Have you been down in a bathyscope and, if so, what was it like?

CC: I've had several invitations to do so but I'm sorry to say that something always came up to divert me. I did spend six days in an underwater habitat in St Croix.

RD: Which fascinates you most: new, underwater archaeological projects or exploring the diversity of life forms to be found in the ocean?

CC: Searching for shipwrecks of historic significance is my biggest fascination.

RD: **Your son, Dirk, has co-written books with you and explored the oceans alongside you. In what ways are you alike or unalike?**

CC: Dirk is really a chip off the old block. We both dive and we're both interested in searching for shipwrecks. He is president of the real-life NUMA, the National Underwater and Marine Agency.

RD: **Did you enjoy your time in the air force during the Korean War? Did it teach you anything long-lasting?**

CC: I wasn't particularly fond of my time in the air force. I'm just not a follower—too independent. Some of it I enjoyed, eg the men I met and worked with. It probably taught me a bit of humility.

RD: **You own 100 classic cars—an incredible number. Is the collection now complete, or are there models you still hanker after?**

CC: I think the number of cars in the museum is now up to about 108. There are many models I still hanker after. The one I love to drive is a 1929 Bentley Blower.

RD: **What's the most extraordinary item in your study?**

CC: There are so many: the paintings of ships we've searched for and found; thirteen models of shipwrecks we've discovered. Then there is my library of over 1,000 books about ships and the sea, with many individual copies signed by authors I'm proud to have known.

RD: **If you had to live on a boat, perpetually sailing, which ocean—or part of the world's oceans—would you choose, and why?**

CC: The South Pacific, because of its beauty and its leisurely lifestyle.

RD: **Have you sailed round Micronesia, and is it as gorgeous as you make out?**

CC: Yes, I've been to many islands in the South Seas and they're more beautiful than I can describe.

RD: **How would you like to be remembered by your family?**

CC: As a humorous, loving, and fun father.

RD: **If you could rule the world for a day, what would you change first?**

CC: Rule the world! What a thought . . . obviously, legislation to end all wars. But, the human race being what it is, I fear that is only a fantasy.

RD: **And if you could live your life all over again, would you change anything?**

CC: I wouldn't want to live my life over again. Can you imagine having to write forty books a second time.

The
Elephant
Whisperer

LAWRENCE ANTHONY
WITH GRAHAM SPENCE

'Under the microscope, living organisms are just a soup of chemicals and minerals. But what about what the microscope doesn't see? That life force, the vital ingredient of existence, can it be quantified?

'My elephant herd showed me that it can, and that understanding and generosity of spirit are alive and well in the pachyderm kingdom; that elephants are emotional, caring and extremely intelligent; and that they value good relations with humans.

This is their story.'

Lawrence Anthony

CHAPTER ONE

In the distance, the percussive shot of a rifle sounded like a giant stick of firewood cracking.

I jumped out of my chair, listening. It was a sound wired into a game ranger's psyche. Then came a burst . . . *crack-crack-crack.* Flocks of squawking birds scrambled, silhouetted in the crimson sunset.

Poachers. On the west boundary.

David, my ranger, was already sprinting for the trusty old Land Rover. I grabbed a shotgun and followed, leaping into the driver's seat. Max, my brindle Staffordshire bull terrier, scrambled onto the seat between us. With all the excitement buzzing he was not going to be left behind.

As I twisted the ignition key and floored the accelerator, David grabbed the two-way radio.

'Ndonga!' he bellowed. 'Ndonga, are you receiving? Over!'

Ndonga was the head of my Ovambo guards and a good man to have on your side in a gunfight, having served in the military. I would have felt better knowing that he and his team were on their way, but only static greeted David's attempts to contact him. We powered on alone.

Poachers had been the scourge of our lives since Françoise and I had bought Thula Thula, a magnificent game reserve of 5,000 acres in central Zululand. They had been targeting us for almost a year. I couldn't work out who they were or where they were coming from. I had talked often with the *izinduna*—headmen—of the surrounding Zulu tribes and they were adamant that their people were not involved. I believed them. Our employees were mainly local and exceptionally loyal. These thugs had to be from somewhere else.

Twilight was darkening fast. I slowed as we approached the western fence and killed the headlights, pulling over behind a large ant hill. David was first out as we eased through a cluster of acacia trees, nerves on edge, trigger fingers tense, watching and listening. Tightly choked pump-action scatterguns with heavy pellets were our weapons of choice against poachers, for, in the dark, in the bush, things are about as close and personal as you can get. As any game ranger in Africa knows, professional poachers will shoot first and shoot to kill.

The fence was just fifty yards away. Poachers like to keep their escape route open, and I made a circling motion with my arm to David. He nodded, knowing exactly what I meant. He would keep watch while I crawled to the fence to cut off the retreat if a firefight erupted.

An acrid whiff of cordite spiced the evening air. It hung like a shroud in the silence. In Africa the bush is never willingly mute; the cicadas never cease. Except after gunshots.

After a few minutes of absolute stillness, I knew we had been set up. I switched on my halogen torch, sweeping its beam up and down the fence. There were no gaps revealing where a poacher could have cut his way in. David flicked on his torch as well, searching for tracks or blood spoor indicating if an animal had been killed and dragged off.

Nothing. Just an eerie silence.

With no tracks inside the reserve I realised the shots must have been fired from just outside the fence.

'Damn, it's a decoy.'

As I said that, we heard more shots—muffled but distinctive 'crumps' on the far side of the reserve, at least forty-five minutes' drive on dirt tracks that are often little more than quagmires in the spring rains.

We jumped back into the Land Rover and sped off, but I knew it was hopeless. It was pitch-dark when we arrived at the eastern perimeter of the reserve, and we traced the scene with our torches. The tracks told the story. Two nyalas—among Africa's most beautiful antelopes—had been taken with high-velocity rifles. We could see the flattened, bloodstained grass where their carcasses were dragged to a hole in the fence, which had been crudely hacked with bolt cutters. About ten yards outside the fence were the studded tracks of a 4x4 bush vehicle that by now would be several miles away.

The light of my torch picked up a bloody tuft of charcoal-grey fur fluttering on the cut fence wire. At least one of the dead bucks was a male—the female nyala is light brown with thin white stripes on her back.

I shivered, feeling old and weary. Thula Thula had been a hunting ranch before I bought it and I had vowed that would end. No animal would be needlessly killed again on my watch. I didn't realise how difficult that vow would be to keep. Despondently we drove back to the lodge. Françoise greeted us with mugs of dark, rich coffee. Just what I needed.

I glanced at her and smiled my thanks. Tall, graceful and very French, she was just as beautiful as the day I had first met her catching a taxi on a freezing London morning twelve years ago.

'What happened?' she asked.

'A set-up. There were two groups. One fired some shots on the far boundary, then watched our Land Rover lights. As soon as we got there, the others bagged two buck on the eastern side.' I took a gulp of coffee and sat down. 'These guys are organised; someone's going to get killed if we're not careful.'

Ndonga was furious the next morning when I told him that more animals had been shot. He admonished me for not calling him. I said we had tried but failed to get a response.

'Oh . . . sorry, Mr Anthony I went out for a few drinks last night. Not feeling too good today,' he said, grinning sheepishly.

I didn't feel like discussing his hangover. 'Can you make this a priority?' I asked.

He nodded. 'We'll catch these bastards.'

I HAD BARELY got back to the house when the phone rang. A woman introduced herself: Marion Garaï from the Elephant Management and Owners Association (EMOA), a private organisation comprising several elephant owners in South Africa, which took an interest in elephant welfare. Her warm voice instantly inspired empathy.

She got straight to the point. She had heard about Thula Thula and the variety of magnificent indigenous Zululand wildlife we had. She said she had also heard how we were working closely with the local population in fostering conservation awareness and wondered . . . would I be interested in adopting a herd of elephants? The good news, she continued before I could answer, was that I would get them for free, barring capture and transportation costs.

You could have knocked me over with a blade of grass. Elephant? The world's largest mammal? And they wanted to give me a whole herd? For a moment I thought it was a hoax. I mean, how often do you get phoned out of the blue asking if you want a herd of tuskers?

OK, I asked, what was the bad news?

Well, said Marion, the elephants were considered 'troublesome'. They had a tendency to break out of reserves and the owners wanted to get rid of them fast. If we didn't take them, they would be put down—shot. All of them.

'What do you mean by troublesome?'

'The matriarch is an amazing escape artist and has worked out how to break through electric fences. She just twists the wire round her tusks until it snaps or takes the pain and smashes through. It's unbelievable. The owners have had enough.'

'Why me?'

'I've heard you have a way with animals,' she continued. 'I reckon Thula Thula's right for them. You're right for them. Or maybe they're right for you.'

That floored me. If anything, we were exactly 'not right' for a herd of elephant. I was only just getting the reserve operational and, as the previous day had proved, having problems with highly organised poachers.

I was about to say 'no' when something held me back. I have always loved elephants. Not only are they the largest and noblest land creatures on this planet, but they symbolise all that is majestic about Africa. And here, unexpectedly, I was being offered my own herd and a chance to help. Would I ever get an opportunity like this again? I asked how many.

'Nine—three adult females, three youngsters, of which one is male, an adolescent bull and two babies. It's a beautiful family. The matriarch has a gorgeous baby daughter. The young bull, her son, is fifteen years old and an absolutely superb specimen.'

'They must be a big problem. Nobody just gives away elephants.'

'As I said, the matriarch keeps breaking out. Not only does she snap electric wires, she's also learned how to unlatch gates with her tusks, and the owners aren't too keen about jumbos wandering into the guest camps. If you don't take them, they will be shot. Certainly the adults will be.'

I went quiet, trying to unravel all this in my head. The opportunity was great, but so was the risk. 'Hell yes,' I replied. 'I'll take them.'

I was still reeling from the shock of becoming an instant elephant owner, when I got another: the current owners wanted the herd off their property within two weeks. Or else the deal was off and the elephants would be shot.

I GREW UP in 'old' Africa, before the days of mass urbanisation, running barefoot under big skies in Zimbabwe, Zambia and Malawi. My friends were rural African kids, and together we ranged the wild world that was our back yard.

During the early 1960s my family moved to the sugar cane-growing coastal belt of Zululand, South Africa. The hub of the area at the time was a place out in the boondocks called Empangeni. It was a tough town with character. Stories are still told of leathery farmers partying all night and skidding their tractors through the main street swigging 'spook'n'diesel' (cane spirit mixed with a smidgen of Coca-Cola). For us teenagers, you had to hold your own and play a hard game of rugby to earn respect.

My shooting skills, honed in the deep African bush, also stood me in good stead, and farmers sent me out on their lands to bag guinea fowl and grouse for the pot. After school I left for the city, but my youthful memories of wild Africa followed me. I knew one day I would return.

That happened in the 1990s. I was poring over a map of the area west of Empangeni and was struck by the profusion of unutilised tribal land, far too feral for even the hardiest cattle. These trust lands gallop right up to the borders of the famous Umfolozi-Hluhluwe reserve, the first game sanctuary established anywhere in Africa and where the southern white rhino was saved from extinction.

The trust land, a massive tract of gloriously pristine bush, belonged to six different Zulu clans. An idea light-bulbed in my head: if I could persuade them to join in conserving wildlife instead of hunting or grazing, we could create one of the finest reserves imaginable. But to do this I would have to convince each tribal leader to agree individually to lease the land to a single trust. It would be called the Royal Zulu, and benefits such as job creation would go straight back into the struggling local communities.

Thula Thula, reputed to have once formed part of the exclusive hunting grounds of King Shaka, the near-deified warrior who founded the Zulu nation in the early nineteenth century, was the key to the project. It was a natural wedge abutting the tribal lands and forming a crucial eastern gateway to the reserves. And for the first time in fifty years it was on the market. Destiny? Well . . . who knows?

I took a deep breath, spoke nicely—very nicely—to my bank manager, and Françoise and I ended up as the new owners.

I FELL IN LOVE with it from the moment I went walkabout. It's something I still do, jump in the Land Rover and drive out onto the open savannahs or into the thickest, most thorn-scrubbed veld I can find, and go for a walk. There is nothing more energising than inhaling the tang of wilderness, loamy after rain, pungent with the richness of earth shuddering with life, or taking in the brisk, dry cleanness of winter. In the outback, life is lived for the instant. The land thrums with exuberance when everything is green and lush and is stoically resilient when it isn't. In the bush, simple acts give intense pleasures, such as sliding a sprig of grass into the tiny slot of a scorpion hole and feeling a tug that pound for pound would rival a game fish. Even today that triggers memories of my born-free adolescence as vividly as a lovelorn youth recalling his first heart-thudding kiss.

So too does the chime of songbirds, where even a panicked warning call is perfectly in pitch. Or watching life's endlessly fascinating passing show, the brutal poetry of the food chain where life is so precarious yet pulses so powerfully in every shape, colour and form.

Those solitary hikes in Thula Thula evoked the path I first walked as a child in untamed places. Now decades later I was bringing a herd of elephants, to me the definitive symbol of wild Africa, back to an ancient Zululand home. Thula Thula's landscape is an elephant's paradise: woodlands leading to sweet savannah, river banks choked with nutritious grasses, and water holes that never run dry, even in the bleakest of winters.

But we had to get cracking, with just two weeks to electrify the fences and build a sturdy boma. The word 'boma' means stockade, and with antelope it's a simple matter of erecting barriers high enough to stop them from leaping over. However, with five-ton elephants, stronger than a truck, it's a different ball game altogether. You have to spike the fences with enough megavolts to hold a juggernaut.

The electrical force is designed not to injure the animals; it's there only to warn them off. Thus it's vital that the boma is a replica of the reserve's outer border so that once they have learned that bumping into it is not much fun, they will later steer clear of the boundary.

There was no way we were going to be able to do all that in just two weeks, but we would certainly give it a damn good try.

I radioed David and Ndonga to come to the office.

'Guys, you're looking at the owner of a herd of elephants.'

Both stared for a moment as if I had gone loopy. David spoke first. 'What do you mean?'

'I've been given nine elephants.' I scratched my head, still hardly believing it myself. 'It's a one-off deal—if I don't take them they'll be shot. But the bad news is that they're a bit of a problem. They've broken through fences before—electric ones.'

David's face lifted in a massive grin.

'Elephants! Fantastic!' He paused for a moment, and I could see he was mulling over the same concerns that I had. 'But how are we gonna hold them here? Thula's fences won't stop ellies.'

'Well, we've got two weeks to fix them. And to build a boma.'

'Two weeks? For twenty miles of fence?' Ndonga spoke for the first time, giving me a doubtful look.

'We've got no choice. The current owners have given me a deadline.'

David's unfettered enthusiasm was gratifying and I instinctively knew he would be my right-hand man on this project.

Tall and well built with handsome Mediterranean features, David was a natural leader with a sense of purpose about him that belied his nineteen years. Our families have ties stretching back decades, and it was, I believe, fate that brought him to Thula Thula during this pivotal period. A fourth-generation Zululander, he had no formal game-ranger credentials, but that didn't worry me. He could do a hard day's work and was in tune with the natural world, which I have found to be one of the best recommendations for anyone, regardless of vocation. He had also been a top rugby player, a flank forward with a reputation for almost kamikaze tackles.

I called in the Zulu staff and asked them to put the word out among the local community that we needed labourers. To keep the *amakhosi*—local chieftains—on our side, I made appointments to explain what we were doing. Incredibly, most Zulus have never set eyes on an elephant, as nowadays the giants of South Africa are all in fenced sanctuaries. The last free-roaming jumbos in our part of Zululand were actually killed almost a century ago. So the main aim of visiting the chiefs was to explain that we were bringing these magnificent creatures 'home' again, as well as providing assurances that the fences were electrified on the inside and thus wouldn't harm any passers-by.

Then, just as we started to see progress, we ran up against a wall.

David came sprinting into the office. 'Bad news, boss. Workers on the western boundary have downed tools. They say they're being shot at. Everyone's too scared to work.'

I stared at him uncomprehendingly. 'What do you mean? Why would anyone shoot at a gang of labourers?'

David shrugged. 'I dunno, boss. Sounds like it has to be a cover for something else, perhaps a strike for more money . . .'

I doubted that, as the workers were paid a decent rate already. 'Let's try and find out what's going on. In the meantime we don't have much choice. Pay off those too spooked to work and let's get replacements. We've got to keep moving.'

I also gave instructions for a group of security guards to be placed on standby to protect the remaining labourers.

The next morning David once more came running into the office.

'Man, we've got real problems,' he said, catching his breath. 'They're shooting again and one of the workers is down.'

I grabbed my old Lee-Enfield .303 rifle and the two of us sped to the fence in the Land Rover. Most of the labourers were crouching behind trees while a couple tended to their bleeding colleague. He had been hit in the face by heavy shotgun pellets.

After checking that the injury was not life-threatening, we started criss-crossing the bush until we picked up the tracks—or spoor. It belonged to a single gunman—not a group, as we had initially feared. I called Bheki and my security *induna* Ngwenya, whose name means 'crocodile' in Zulu, two of our best and toughest Zulu rangers. Bheki is the hardest man I have ever met, slim with quiet eyes and a disarmingly innocent face, while Ngwenya, thickset and muscular, had an aura of quiet authority about him that influenced the rest of the rangers in his team.

'You two go ahead and track the gunman. David and I will stay here to protect the rest of the workers.'

They nodded and inched their way through the thorn veld until they believed they were behind the shooter. They slowly cut back and waited . . . and waited.

Then Ngwenya saw a brief glint of sunlight flash off metal. He signalled to Bheki, pointing to the sniper's position. Lying low in the long grass, they rattled off a volley of warning shots. The sniper dived behind an ant hill, fired two blasts from his shotgun, then disappeared into the thick bush.

But the guards had seen him—and, to their surprise, they knew him. He was a 'hunter' from another Zulu village some miles away.

We drove the labourer to hospital and called the police. The guards identified the gunman and the cops raided his thatched hut, seizing a dilapidated shotgun. Amazingly, he confessed without any hint of shame that he was a 'professional poacher'—and then heaped the blame on us, saying that erecting an electric fence would deprive him of his livelihood. He could no longer break into Thula Thula so easily. He denied trying to kill anyone, he just wanted to scare the workers off and stop the fence being built.

I asked to see the shotgun and the cops obliged. It was a battered double-barrelled twelve-bore, as ancient as its owner. The stock, held together with vinyl electrical tape, was scratched and chipped from thousands of scrapes in the bush. The barrel was rusted and pitted. There was no way this was the person responsible for our major poaching problem.

So who was?

THE CONSTRUCTION CONTINUED from dawn to dusk, seven days a week. It was back-breaking work, sweaty and dirty with temperatures soaring to 110 degrees Fahrenheit. But mile by torturous mile, the electric fence started to take shape, inching northwards, then cutting east and gathering momentum as the workers' competency levels increased.

Building a boma was equally gruelling, albeit on a far smaller scale. We measured out 110 square yards of virgin bush and cemented nine-foot-tall heavy-duty eucalyptus poles into concrete foundations every twelve yards. Then coils of tempered mesh and a trio of cables as thick as a man's thumb were strung onto the poles, tensioned by the simple expedient of attaching the ends to the Land Rover bumper and revving it taut.

But no matter how thick the cables, no bush fence will hold a determined elephant. So the trump card is the 'hot wires'. The electrification process is deceptively simple. All it consists of is four live wires bracketed onto the poles so they run inside the structure, while two energisers that run off car batteries generate the 'juice'.

Simple or not, the energisers pack an 8,000-volt punch. This may sound massive, which it is, but the shock is not fatal as the amperage is extremely low. But believe me, it is excruciating, even to an elephant with an inch-thick hide. I can vouch first-hand, having accidentally touched the wires several times during repairs, or while carelessly waving my arms in animated conversation, much to the mirth of my rangers. Your body shudders and unless you let go quickly you sit down involuntarily as your legs collapse. The only good thing is that you recover quickly enough to laugh about it.

Once the fence was up, the final task was to chop down any trees that could be shoved onto it, as this is an elephant's favourite way of snapping the current.

The deadline passed in an eye-blink and of course we were nowhere near finished. Then came the call I dreaded.

The herd had broken out again and this time damaged three of the reserve's lodges. We were bluntly told that unless we took the elephants immediately, the owners would have to make a 'decision'.

Françoise fielded the call and, crossing her fingers, said that we needed only to get our elephant proofing approved by KwaZulu-Natal Wildlife—the province's official authority—and all problems would be over.

Somehow the owners bought that and reluctantly agreed to an extension. But just a few more days, they warned, or else there would be a 'decision'.

That word again.

CHAPTER TWO

Exhausted teams were still hammering in the final fence nails when the Mpumalanga reserve manager phoned to say he could wait no longer and was sending them, ready or not. The elephants were being loaded and would arrive at Thula Thula within eighteen hours.

I hurriedly called our parks authority, KZN Wildlife, to come and inspect the boma, stressing that the animals were already on their way. Fortunately they were able to respond instantly and said an inspector would be at Thula Thula within a couple of hours.

David and I sped down for a final look-see, as I wanted everything to be perfect. But while we were double-checking that all vulnerable trees were beyond toppling distance from the fence, something suddenly struck me as odd. Something didn't look right.

And then I saw the problem. Damnit! While the electric wires were bracketed on the inside, the fence itself, including the heavy-duty cables, had been strung up on the outside of the poles. This was a fatal flaw, because if an elephant braved the power and leaned on the mesh it would rip off like paper. The poles thus provided at best flimsy inner-lateral support, literally just holding the fence up. Once the inspector saw this he would instantly condemn it. That meant the truck would be turned round and the herd sent back to certain death.

I clenched my fists in exasperation. How could we have made such an elementary error? It was too late to do anything, as the dust mushrooming above the savannah signalled the arrival of the inspector. I prayed we could bluff our way through, but inwardly I despaired.

The inspector was a decent guy and knew his business, making particular note of a large tambotie tree with gnarled bark knotted like biceps that was close to the fence. Tambotie is an exceptionally hard wood that blunts the sharpest chain saw, and the inspector remarked wryly that not even an elephant could snap this particularly 'muscular' one. He deemed it safe.

Then he went to check the meshing and my mouth went dry. Surely he'd notice the wire was on wrong side.

The gods were with us that day and, to my gut-churning relief, he—like us—didn't spot the obvious mistake. The boma was given the green light. I now had my crucial authorisation and summoned every available hand to secure the fence correctly.

The 600-mile drive south from their current home on the Mpumalanga reserve would take all day and much of the night, as the eighteen-wheeler needed plenty of pit stops to feed and water the jumbos. I wasn't concerned about the journey, as one of Africa's top elephant hands, Kobus Raadt, was in charge.

Then I got the news from Françoise—she had heard that the herd's matriarch and her baby had been shot during the capture. The justification was that she was 'bad news' and would lead break-outs at Thula Thula as well. While I understood the conventional reasoning behind the choice to kill the matriarch, I felt that the decision should have been mine. As elephants are so big and dangerous, if they create problems and pose a risk to lodges and tourists it is quite usual for them to be shot out of hand. However, I was convinced that I would be able to settle the herd in their new home.

The Zulus who live close to the land have a saying that if it rains on an inaugural occasion, that event will be blessed. That day it didn't just rain, it bucketed. The bruised skies sprayed down torrents, and I wasn't too sure the Zulus had this 'blessed' story right. When the truck arrived outside Thula Thula in thick darkness the deluge had turned the dirt tracks into mud.

Barely had we opened the gates to the reserve when a tyre burst, the reinforced rubber cracking loud as a rifle shot. This panicked the elephants, who had just seen their leader gunned down, and they started thumping the inside of the trailer like a gigantic drum, while the crews worked feverishly to change the wheel.

'It's *Jurassic Park*!' Françoise cried. We laughed, not necessarily with a great deal of mirth.

FRANÇOISE AND I first met in 1987 back in London at the Cumberland Hotel. It was freezing cold and I urgently needed to get to Earl's Court for a meeting. There was a long queue snaking up to the taxi rank outside the hotel, and the doorman, who knew I was in a hurry, said he would see if anyone would share a cab. As it happened, a gorgeous woman right at the front was also going to Earl's Court. The doorman asked if she would mind sharing and pointed at me. She leaned forward to get a better look, and then shook her head. It was the most emphatic 'No' I had seen.

Well, that's life. Rather than hang around I decided to take the underground, and, to my surprise, the same woman miraculously appeared next to me at the tube station.

''Ello,' she said in a thick French accent. 'I am Françoise.'

She said she felt guilty about not agreeing to share a cab and to make amends offered to show me which train to take. To say I was smitten would be putting it blandly.

She knew London well and asked if I was interested in jazz. I wasn't, but I also wasn't stupid enough to say so. In fact, I professed undying love for the genre. Thank the stars she didn't ask for proof—such as my favourite musician—and instead suggested that as jazz lovers we go to Ronnie Scott's Jazz Club that night. I pondered this for a fraction of a nanosecond before answering 'Yes' with more enthusiasm than absolutely necessary.

Apart from wondering why I had never appreciated jazz before, I spent much of that evening telling her of the magic of Africa—not hard in the middle of an English winter. Was there plenty of sun in Africa, she asked? I scoffed . . . was there sun? We invented the word.

Well, here we were twelve years later drenched to the marrow in the bush, wrestling with a gigantic wheel on a muddy rig loaded with elephants. I don't recall mentioning this could happen while piling on the charm during our first date.

THE SPARE WHEEL had scarcely been bolted on when to the surprise of no one the truck slid just a few yards before it sank into the glutinous mud, its tyres spinning impotently and spewing muck all over the place. No amount of cajoling, swearing, kicking or packing branches underneath worked. And, even worse, the elephants were becoming more and more agitated.

'We've got to sort this out quickly or we're going to have to release them right here,' said Kobus, his brow creased with worry. 'They cannot stay in the truck any longer. Let's just pray like hell the outer fence holds them.'

Fortunately, the driver, sick of all the pontificating, took matters into his own hands. Without a word he slammed the truck into reverse, and somehow skidded the huge rig out of the bog and veered off the greasy road into the savannah that had marginally more grip. Dodging tyre-shredding thorn bush and slithering past huge termite mounds he somehow kept momentum until he reached the boma.

Coaxing the animals from the truck was the next problem. However, as it had been an extremely stressful few hours, Kobus decided first to inject the herd with a mild sedative, using a pole-sized syringe. He climbed onto the roof of the trailer, which had a large ventilation gap, and David jumped up to give him a hand.

As David landed on the roof, a trunk whipped through the slats as fast as a mamba and lashed at his ankle. David leaped back, dodging the grasping trunk with a heartbeat to spare. If the elephant had caught him he would have been yanked inside to a gruesome death. As simple as that. Kobus told me he had heard of it happening before: a person pulled into a confined space with seven angry elephants would soon be meat.

Thankfully all went smoothly after this, and as soon as the injections had been administered and they had calmed down, the door slid open and the new matriarch emerged. She tentatively stepped onto Thula Thula soil, the first wild elephant in the area for almost a century.

The six others followed: the new matriarch's baby bull, three females—of which one was an adult—and an eleven-year-old bull. The last out was the fifteen-year-old three-and-half-ton teenage son of the previous matriarch. He walked a few yards and even in his groggy state realised there were humans behind. He swivelled his head and stared at us, then flared his ears and with a high-pitched trumpet of rage turned and charged, pulling up just short of the fence in front of us. He instinctively knew, even at his tender age, that he must protect the herd.

I smiled in admiration. His mother and baby sister had been shot before his eyes; he had been darted and confined in a trailer for eighteen hours; and here he was, a teenager, defending his family. David named him 'Mnumzane' (pronounced nom-zahn), which in Zulu means 'Sir'.

The new matriarch we christened 'Nana', which is what all Anthony grandchildren call my mum, Regina Anthony, a respected matriarch in her own right.

The second female in command, the most feisty, we called 'Frankie' after Françoise. For equally obvious reasons. The other names would come later.

Nana gathered her clan, loped up to the fence and stretched out her trunk, touching the electric wires. The 8,000-volt wires sent a jolt shuddering through her hulk. Whoa . . . she hurriedly backed off. Then, with her family in tow, she strode the entire perimeter of the boma, her trunk curled fractionally below the wire to sense the current's pulse, checking for the weakest link as she must have seen her sister, the previous matriarch, do often before.

I watched, barely breathing. She completed the check and, smelling the water hole, led her herd off to drink.

The crucial aspect of an electrified boma is fine-tuning how long you keep the animals inside. Too short, and they don't learn enough to respect the megavolt punch the fence packs. But if it's too long, they somehow figure out that it's possible to endure the convulsions for the few agonising seconds it takes to snap the strand—like the previous matriarch did. Once that happens they will never fear electricity again.

Unfortunately, no one knows exactly what that 'perfect period' is. Opinions vary from a few days for more docile elephants to three months for wilder ones. My new herd was anything but docile, so how long I should pen them was anybody's guess. However, what the experts had told me was that during the quarantine period the animals should have no contact with humans. So once the gates were bolted I instructed everyone to move off except for two game guards who would watch from a distance.

As we were leaving I noticed the elephants lining up at a corner of the fence. They were facing due north, the exact direction of their former home, as if their inner compasses were telling them something.

It looked ominous.

Soaked and freezing, with my personal magnetic needle pointing unwaveringly towards a warm bed, I left with a deep sense of foreboding.

HAMMERING ECHOED like a drumroll in my head. I wondered hazily where it was coming from. My eyes flickered open. The banging stemmed from a shuddering door. *Rat-a-tat. Rat-a-tat-a-tat.*

Then I heard yelling. It was Ndonga. 'The elephants have gone! They've broken out of the boma! They've gone!'

I leaped out of bed, yanking on my trousers and stumbling like a pogo dancer on one leg. 'I'm coming. Hang on!' I shouted and shoved open the top half of the bedroom's stable door that led directly to the farmhouse's lush gardens.

An agitated Ndonga was standing outside, shivering in the predawn chill. 'The two big ones started shoving a tree,' he said. 'They worked as a team, pushing it until it just crashed down on the fence. The wires shorted and the elephants smashed through. Just like that.'

Dread slithered in my belly. 'What tree?'

'You know, that tambotie. The one that KZN Wildlife *oke* said was too big to pull down.'

It took me a few moments to digest this. That tree must have weighed several tons and was thirty feet tall. Yet Nana and Frankie had figured out that by working in tandem they could topple it. Despite my dismay, I felt a flicker of pride: these were some animals, all right.

The last foggy vestiges of sleep vaporised like steam. We had to get moving fast. One didn't have to be a genius to grasp that we had a massive crisis on our hands as the herd was now stampeding towards the border fence. If they broke through that last barrier they would head straight into the patchwork of rural homesteads scattered outside Thula Thula. And as any game ranger will attest, a herd of wild elephants on the run in a populated area would be the conservation equivalent of the Chernobyl disaster.

Within minutes I had scrambled to raise a search party, and we gathered at the boma, astounded at the damage. The large tambotie tree was history, its toppled upper section tenuously connected to the splintered stump by a strip of its bark oozing poisonous sap. The fence looked as though a division of tanks had thundered through it.

Standing next to the shattered tree was the astounded Ovambo guard who had witnessed the break-out. He pointed us in the direction he had last seen the elephants heading.

Almost at running speed, we followed the spoor to the boundary. We were too late. The border fence was down and the animals had broken out.

Their tracks pointed north. There was no doubt that they were heading home to Mpumalanga, 600 miles away. To the only home they knew, even though it was a home that no longer wanted them— and where in all probability they would be shot. That's assuming game rangers or hunters didn't get them along the way first.

As daybreak filled the eastern sky, a motorist three miles away spotted the herd loping up the road towards him. At first he thought he was seeing things. Elephants? There aren't meant to be any elephants here . . . Half a mile or so later he saw the flattened fence and put two and two together. He had the presence of mind to call, giving us valuable updated information.

The chase was on. I gunned my Land Rover into gear as the trackers leaped into the back. Another mile up the road the herd's tracks veered into the bush, exactly as the motorist had told us. Thula Thula is flanked by vast forests of acacia trees and *ugagane* bush, which grows thickly with interwoven thorn-studded branches that are as supple and vicious as whips. It's a riotous tangle of hostile thickets, lovely and wild to view, but torturous to track in. The wickedly sharp thorns scarcely scratch an elephant's hide, of course, but to us soft-skinned species it was the equivalent of running through a maze of fish-hooks. The forest spread north as far as the eye could see. Could we find the animals in this almost impenetrable wilderness?

I looked up to the heavens, squinting against the harsh yellow-white glare that indicated we were in for a savage scorcher of a day, and found my answer—air support. For us to have a fighting chance of catching the elephants before some gunman did, we had to have a helicopter tracking above. There was one man I knew who could track from the sky—and, fortuitously, he was a family friend. Peter Bell was not only a technical genius at Bell Equipment, an international heavy-duty vehicle manufacturer, but also an expert game-capture pilot and a good man to have on your side in an emergency. I quickly drove back to Thula Thula and phoned him.

Peter didn't have to be told how serious the problem was, and unhesitatingly agreed to help. While he got his chopper ready, we continued the chase on foot. But we had barely infiltrated the acacia jungle when our Ovambo game guards, staring at what appeared to me to be a flinty patch of dirt, shook their heads. After some deliberation, they proclaimed the elephants had turned back.

I had inherited the Ovambos from the previous owner of Thula Thula, who thought highly of them. There are thousands of Ovambos in Zululand today, many of whom had fought in the South African Army during the apartheid wars. They're mostly employed in the security industry and are valued for their courage and weapon skills. They seldom socialised with my Zulu staff.

Ndonga had told me his team were expert trackers, which was why we were using them now.

'Are you sure?' I asked the head tracker.

He nodded and pointed towards Thula Thula. 'They have turned. They are going that way.'

This was news I was desperate to hear. Perhaps they would voluntarily return to the reserve. I grinned and slapped David on the back as we headed back through the bush towards home.

However, after twenty minutes of some of the toughest going I have ever experienced, I began to have doubts. Sweat was cascading down my face as I called over the chief tracker.

'The elephants are not here. There is no spoor, no dung and no broken branches. No signs at all.'

He shook his head, as if patiently consulting with a child, and pointed ahead. 'They are there.'

Against my better judgment we carried on a bit farther, and then I had had enough. There was something wrong here. It was obvious there were no elephants around. An elephant, due to its massive size and strength, does not need to be furtive. It leaves very clear tracks, piles of dung and snapped branches. It has no enemies apart from man, thus stealth is not in its nature.

Also, every indication was that they were heading towards their previous home. Why would they suddenly backtrack now?

I called David, Ngwenya and Bheki and told the Ovambos they were wrong; we were returning to the original tracks. The Ovambos shrugged but made no move to join us. I was too wrapped up in the intensity of the chase to think much about that at the time.

An hour later we picked up the spoor again—fresh and heading in completely the opposite direction. Why had the Ovambos chosen the wrong route? I could only surmise that they were scared of stumbling without warning upon the elephants in the wild terrain. There was no denying this was dangerous work.

In fact, a few years back in Zimbabwe, an experienced elephant hunter had been killed on a safari doing exactly what we were doing—tracking elephant in thick bush. Following what he thought to be a lone bull, he suddenly discovered that he had walked slap into the middle of a herd spread out in the heavy undergrowth. The first sign of this comes when one realises in horror that there are elephants behind, that you walked right past them without noticing. They had turned the tables and the enraged animals came at the hunter and his trackers. Completely surrounded, he and his men had no chance. They died grisly deaths.

We kept in radio contact with Peter, who flew tight search grids over the bush ahead. I was banking on the animals stopping at a watering hole to rest, allowing us to catch up precious miles. A factor in our favour was that they had Nana's two-year-old son in tow. We named him Mandla, the Zulu word for 'power', in honour of his incredible stamina in staying with the herd during the long chase. He would slow them down significantly, I hoped.

Eventually, after a long, hot, thirsty and frustratingly empty day, the sun dipped below the horizon, and we stopped. Tracking the animals in the thick stuff during daylight is bad enough; in the dark it's suicide. Reluctantly I called off the search and Peter agreed to fly again the next day.

We arrived home bedraggled and despondent, and flopped onto the lawn in front of the house. Françoise came out and took over, issuing instructions for food and handing out ice-cold beers.

We were exhausted. But a hearty meal followed by a soaking hot bath does wonders for morale, and an hour later I wandered out onto the open verandah and sat beneath the stars, trying to make sense of it all.

My Staffordshire bull terrier Max followed me. He was a magnificent specimen of the breed, forty pounds of brawn and muscle. I had got him as a just-weaned puppy and from that first moment he had tottered after me with unconditional devotion. His pedigree name was Boehringer of Alfa Laval, but Max suited him just fine. He would have been a trophy winner at shows except for one physical flaw: he had only one testicle. Which I thought was ironic—Max had more *cojones* than any creature I knew, man or beast. He was absolutely fearless.

And yet he was a pushover with children, who could pull his ears and poke his eyes and get nothing but a sloppy lick in return.

Max flopped at my feet, tail thumping on the floor. He seemed to sense my dismay, nudging me with his wet nose.

Stroking his broad head, I mulled over the day. What had possessed the herd to smash through two electrified fences? Why had the Ovambos made such a careless mistake with their tracking? Why had they then abandoned the search? There was something that didn't gel, some piece missing from the jigsaw.

Max's low growl jerked me out of my thoughts. I looked down. He was fully alert, head up, ears half cocked, staring into the dark.

Then a soft voice called out, 'Mkhulu.'

Mkhulu was my Zulu name. It literally means 'grandfather', but not in the limited Western sense. Zulus venerate maturity, and to refer to someone as a *Mkhulu* was a compliment.

I glanced up and recognised the shadowy figure squatting on his haunches a few yards away. It was Bheki.

'*Sawubona*,' I said, giving the traditional greeting. I see you.

'Mkhulu, there is a mystery here. People are making trouble,' he said, his tone conspiratorial. 'They are making big trouble.'

'*Kanjane?*' How so?

'A gun spoke next to the boma last night,' he continued, aware that he now had my full attention, 'and the elephants were shouting and calling.'

He stood up briefly and raised his arms, mimicking an elephant's trunk. 'They were crazy, maybe one was even shot.'

'*Hau!*' I used the Zulu exclamation for surprise. 'But how do you know such important things?'

'I was there,' he replied. 'I know the elephants are valuable, so I stayed near to the boma last night, watching. I don't trust the *amagweragwer.*' The word meant 'foreigners', but I knew he meant the Ovambo guards.

'Then the big females came together and pushed a tree onto the fence. There was much force and it fell hard and broke the fence and they went out. They were running. I was afraid because they came close past me.'

'Thank you very much,' I replied. 'You have done well.'

Satisfied that his message had been delivered, he stood up and stepped back into the darkness.

I exhaled loudly. Now that would explain a lot, I thought, my mind racing. A poacher shooting next to the boma, unaware of the elephants' presence, would certainly have put the jitters into the herd. But much as I liked Bheki, I had to treat his suspicions about the Ovambo guards with caution. Tribal animosity in Africa often runs deep, and I knew there was little love lost between the Zulus and the Namibians.

However, Bheki had certainly provided food for thought.

CHAPTER THREE

As dawn glimmered we drove to where we had left off yesterday and saw Peter's helicopter coming in low, circling like a hawk to select the best landing spot on the ribbon of potholed road. Seeing the chopper landing in billowing dust, a group of Zulu children came running up from the nearby village, gathering round the thudding machine and chattering excitedly.

The tracking team plunged back into the thorny bush to pick up the spoor on the ground, while I assisted Peter in tracking from the air. We flew north along the Nseleni River, scanning the spear-leafed reed beds for jumbo tracks and barely skimming the towering sycamore figs whose twisted roots clasped the steep banks like pythons. Then at last some news.

KZN Wildlife radioed in saying they had a report of a sighting: the herd had chased a group of herd boys and their cows off a water hole the previous afternoon. Fortunately there had been no casualties.

This underscored the urgency of the situation, but at least we now had a confirmed position. Peter dropped me near the team, lifted off and dipped the chopper as he altered course while I jumped into the Land Rover.

Then we got another call from KZN Wildlife. The elephants had changed direction and were heading towards the Umfolozi game reserve, KZN Wildlife's flagship sanctuary about twenty miles from Thula Thula. They gave us an estimated bearing, which we radioed to the chopper.

Peter found them in the early afternoon, just a few miles from the Umfolozi reserve's fence and some distance from our position on the ground. They were moving along steadily, and Peter knew it was now or never; he had to force them round before they broke into Umfolozi.

There is only one way to herd elephants from the air, and it's not pretty. You have to fly straight at the animals until they turn and move in the opposite direction—in this case back towards Thula Thula. Peter banked and then whirred down, blades clattering and coming straight at Nana, skimming just above her head and executing a tight U-turn, then coming back from the same angle again, hovering in front of the animals to block them going forward.

This is stomach-churning stuff, requiring top-level flying skills, rocksteady hands and even steadier nerves. If you fly too high, the elephants will slip through underneath and be gone; too low and you risk hitting trees.

At this stage the elephants had been on the run for more than twenty-four hours and were exhausted. They should have turned wearily away from the giant bird furiously buzzing them from above. That is what ninety-nine per cent of animals—even a creature as mighty as an elephant—would have done.

The herd stood firm.

Again and again the chopper came at them, the rotor clapping with rhythmic thunder as it virtually kissed the tree tops. Yet still Nana and her family refused to retreat, trunks curled in defiance whenever Peter came in low, judging his distance by inches. But they didn't budge. He radioed to us what was happening, and I realised that my herd was something else. Maybe I was biased, but they were special.

Eventually, through superb flying, Peter inexorably wore them down. Inch by inch he edged them round until they were finally facing Thula

Thula. Then he got them moving, herding them from above, deftly manoeu-vring his machine like a flying sheepdog.

I started to breathe easier, daring to believe everything was going to be all right. Back at Thula Thula, workers had spent the day mending the ruined fences, both at the boma and the border, and they radioed me to say everything was ready. We would still have to cut open a section of fence to drive them through, but we wouldn't know where to cut until they arrived.

Finally, after hours of tense aerial herding, we saw the helicopter hover-ing low on the far horizon. They were going to make it. Then I caught sight of Nana, pushing slowly through the bush just below the thundering heli-copter. All I could make out was the very tips of her ears and the hump on her back, but it was the most welcome thing I have ever seen.

Soon they all came into view, plodding on until they were at the road. Just a tantalising fifteen yards from the lowered fence, Nana tested the air with her trunk and halted.

The mood suddenly changed. Nana trumpeted her belligerence and drew her family up in the classical defensive position, bottoms together facing outwards like the spokes of a wheel, and they held their ground with grim determination. Peter continuously buzzed them . . . goading them to make that last little sprint into the reserve. But to no avail.

Nothing would move them, not even shots fired into the ground behind them. This was where they were going to make their stand. They were saying no more. It was something I understood with absolute clarity, a line in the sand.

Dusk fell, and in the glow of the strengthening stars I could see the murky shapes of the elephants still holding firm with iron defiance. I felt sick with despair. We had been so close to pulling it off. Peter banked and flew off. Realising their 'persecutor' had left, Nana turned her bone-tired family round and they melted into the thick bush.

I groaned. Now we would have to do it all again the next day.

ONCE AGAIN I was up before my 4 a.m. alarm rang, gulping down coffee strong enough to float a bullet, desperate to get going. David and the trackers were standing by, and as the first shards of pink dawn pierced the darkness we picked up the spoor from where Nana and her family had made their determined stand against the helicopter last night. The tracks again pointed north towards the Umfolozi game reserve, and we followed their new path through the thorny thickets, going as fast as we dared.

By now it was obvious we had some very agitated, unpredictable wild elephants on our hands, and I couldn't rid myself of the vision of them trampling through a village. The words 'conservation's Chernobyl' were etched on my mind as we picked our way through the dense bush.

Peter was unable to fly that day, so the chase was pared down to the bones—an elemental race on foot between the herd and us. But with their ten-hour lead, the odds were definitely uneven.

Meanwhile Françoise, tired of pacing round the house in anticipation, decided to do some sleuthing of her own. As the elephants had been in the area last night, she jumped into her car with Penny, our almost pure-white bull terrier, who was a couple of years younger than Max, and scoured the dirt tracks surrounding the reserve, asking anyone in sight, 'Haf you zeen my elefans?'

Few rural Zulus can understand English, let alone navigate the intricacies of a rich Gallic accent. Even fewer have clapped eyes on an elephant in their lives. Yet here, way out in the sticks, was a beautiful blonde stranger with an almost albino-white dog asking if there happened to be any strolling round. No doubt they thought the sun was frying foreign heads.

However, Françoise's search became quite famous as a local news agency picked it up and, by the time the report reached the boulevards of Paris, it had been rehashed so extensively that Françoise was portrayed as single-handedly pursuing elephants down a multilane highway.

In fact, the story of the elephants' escape and our chase was now being carried in local papers. People were following our progress and, fortunately for us, the media coverage focused on the plight of the elephants and the fact that there was a baby with the herd.

Later that morning, with some relief, I heard from KZN Wildlife that the elephants had broken into the Umfolozi reserve during the night at two different points several miles apart, crashing through the electric fence with ease as it was live-wired from the inside only. There in the reserve they would be safe, at least from the macho hunting brigade.

The herd had split into two groups during the night, with Nana, her two calves and Mnumzane in the one and Frankie and her son and daughter in the other. Only once they were deep in the sanctuary did they meet up again. How they did that defies human comprehension. It seems impossible to navigate in the dark so precisely without compasses or radios—yet the two groups had travelled up to seven miles apart and then came together in dense bush at a given point.

AT DAWN, Umfolozi's vastly experienced conservation manager, Peter Hartley, decided to assess the situation first-hand. While driving off-road he spotted the animals in the distance and got out to approach on foot without disturbing them. He knew from the number and descriptions that this was the Thula Thula herd. Cautiously advancing, he was still some distance away when suddenly Frankie swivelled. She had nosed his scent.

Elephants seldom charge humans unless they get too close, but, with a bellow of rage, Frankie came thundering at him. Hartley, caught by surprise, turned and ran for his life through the thorn veld, cutting himself as he scrambled through the barbed foliage. He leaped into his 4x4 and fortunately the vehicle started instantly as he sped off with five tons of storming juggernaut just yards behind.

Charging the conservation manager—of all people—seriously blotted the herd's already spotty reputation. Grim-faced, Hartley arrived back at the reserve's headquarters and told of his close escape. The senior rangers were now extremely worried. This was getting out of hand, and Hartley suggested they contact the former owners in Mpumalanga to get a more comprehensive background report. And what they heard they didn't like at all.

I was still in the bush when I got the radio call to come to Umfolozi to 'chat' about the situation. Urgently.

There was a funereal mood as I walked into the office. I knew most of these honest men of the bush, and they didn't look happy.

After a few pleasantries they got to the point. They spoke the words I was dreading. If they had known about the elephants' troubled background, they said they would never have granted the Thula Thula permit. The fact the animals had broken through two electric fences, chased cattle, refused to be cowed by a buzzing helicopter and had charged the conservation manager clearly indicated that this was a dangerous, unsettled herd. The risk of letting them remain in an area with rural settlements was too high.

That meant only one thing. The rangers were going to destroy the herd.

I interrupted. 'Guys, you have to remember that there's been a ton of publicity surrounding this break-out. The matriarch's baby especially has attracted a lot of attention and people all over the country are following the chase and rooting for them. If you shoot them now, all hell will break loose in the media.'

I then stressed that it was just bad luck that the herd had escaped. We had done everything by the book. Even KZN Wildlife's expert had pronounced the boma safe. Even he had not believed the herd would have been able to muscle down that single tree in the boma that initiated the break-out.

Once free, it was only natural that they would attempt to return to their original home. That's wired into their psyche. But as soon as I could acclimatise them at Thula Thula, they would be OK. I also pointed out that they hadn't hurt any humans, despite being on the run for three days.

I paused, acutely aware that I was arguing for the animals' lives. 'Please, gentlemen, can you give them one more chance? This won't happen again.'

After what seemed like an eternity, they said they would think about it.

I returned to Thula Thula, exhausted and forlorn, where I explained to David what had happened.

The experiences of the past days had illustrated for me that despite fashionable ecotourism, elephants didn't really count for much in the real world. This was a group of desperate and bewildered animals who had been on the run. But in Africa today elephants are simply competitors in the race for the land. In the West they are mere curiosities, while the East values only their ivory.

Our desperate three-day chase had hammered home to me the reality that these immensely powerful giants were actually as vulnerable as babies, at risk without someone fighting their corner. Once I grasped that, an almost irrational link was established, which would rechart my life. Like it or not, I felt part of the herd. Life had dealt them a cruel hand and I was determined to rectify what I could. I owed them that at least.

Finally some good news: KZN Wildlife agreed to a stay of execution. The elephants would be captured and returned to the boma at Thula Thula. But if they escaped again, the entire herd would be shot on sight.

This was to be both their and my last chance.

I WAS COMFORTED by the fact that my good friend Dave Cooper, Umfolozi's internationally respected wildlife vet and probably the top rhino expert in the world, would be in charge of the welfare of the elephants.

Capture always takes place early in the day to avoid heat stress. At six o'clock a helicopter carrying an experienced marksman in the shooter's seat thudded off to where the herd was last sighted. Dave remained on the ground so that any problems could be confronted as quickly as possible. After a few false alarms, the elephants were spotted and the pilot swooped down, coming in just above the tree tops in a tight bank and then dropping until he was hovering almost on the ground to turn the now-running animals, herding them towards a dirt track he could see scarring the plains several hundred yards ahead. That rudimentary road was pivotal, as the ground crew needed to get the heavy transport truck as close as possible to where the animals went down.

The marksman loaded the dart gun and readied himself as the pilot radioed his position to the ground crews. The herd was now in full flight, crashing through the bush with the clattering chopper blades egging them on. Suddenly Nana, family in tow, broke through the tree cover and into open ground at the area chosen for darting.

The pilot deftly shifted to just behind the stampeding animals, offering a clear view of their broad backs.

Crack! The .22 shell fired a hefty aluminium dart filled with M99, a powerful anaesthetic customised for elephants and other large herbivores, into Nana's rump. The matriarch is always darted first, followed by the other larger animals. The calves are darted last to prevent them from being trampled or smothered by the larger family members. Nana's calf was in fact too small to dart safely from the air and Dave was warned to make up a dart and immobilise the calf on the ground.

As soon as one dart hit, another was rapidly loaded and fired. The fluffy bright red feathers of the dart stuck out of the rumps of the running animals like beacons. The shooter must work quickly. Any delay between shots would have comatose elephants spread out all over the bush, complicating matters immeasurably.

Once the last dart struck true the marksman gave a thumbs up and the pilot gained altitude and hovered as first Nana, then the others, started to stagger and sink to their knees before collapsing in slow motion. It is surreal when these galloping giants suddenly lose momentum and their tree-trunk legs turn to jelly as they buckle in the dust.

The ground team's speeding trucks were now less than a mile away. The timing was spot on, and the helicopter bumped gently down in a whirlwind of red dust.

Dave hurried to where Nana lay in the dirt. The baby, Mandla, was standing nervously next to her fallen body. He flapped his ears and reared his tiny trunk, instinctively trying to protect his prostrate mother. Dave got into position and fired a light plastic dart loaded with the smallest effective dose into the baby's shoulder.

As Mandla's knees folded, the vet broke a twig off a nearby *guarri* tree and placed it inside the end of Nana's trunk to keep the airways open. He did the same to the other elephants, then went back to Nana, squeezing ointment into her exposed pupil, pulling her huge ear over her eye to protect it from the blossoming sun.

The other slumbering beasts got the same treatment, and he methodically checked each one for injuries. Fortunately, none had fallen awkwardly, breaking bones or tearing ligaments.

The ground team arrived and immediately reversed up to Nana. As the matriarch, they wanted her loaded first. This was done by unceremoniously winching the animal up into the air feet first and depositing the body at the rear entrance of the huge purpose-built truck. Then she was pulled and pushed into the truck by teams of men where she was revived by Dave with an injection of M5050. Once all of the elephants were aboard and awake, the trucks revved off to Thula Thula. The animals recovered during the ninety-minute journey and, although a little wobbly, Nana again led her family into the boma, followed by Frankie, looking as defiant as ever. Their bid for freedom had, if anything, increased their resentment of captivity. I knew we would have a rough few months ahead of us.

As the capture team drove off, one game ranger shouted over his shoulder, 'See you soon!'

This was no polite goodbye. His meaning was clear. He was saying these animals were bad news. He had no doubt that the herd would break out again and he would be back, this time with bullets, not darts. I felt like making an angry retort but couldn't think of one quickly enough.

Just before nightfall I took a drive down to the boma, parked some distance away and with great caution walked towards the fence. Nana was standing in thick cover with her family behind her, watching my every move. There was absolutely no doubt that sooner or later they were going to make another break for it.

Then in a flash came the answer. I decided there and then that contrary to all advice, I would go and live with the herd. I knew the experts would throw up their hands in horror as we had been repeatedly instructed that to keep them feral, human contact in the boma must be kept to the barest minimum. But this herd had already had too much human contact of the very worst kind, and their rehabilitation, if such a thing was even possible at all, called for uncommon measures. If I was to be responsible for this last-ditch effort to save their lives, I should do things my way. If I failed, at least I would have done my best.

I would remain outside the boma, of course, but I would stay with them, feed them, talk to them, and, most importantly, be with them day and night.

There was no doubt that unless we tried something different, they would continue trying to break out and would die in the attempt.

I discussed it with Françoise and she agreed that the conventional approach to settling in the animals didn't seem to be working. I asked David if he wanted to come along and was answered by his broad smile. The boma was about three miles away from our house, so we packed the Land Rover with basic supplies. The vehicle would be our home for as long as it took.

I also brought along Max, who was always great company outdoors. He'd matured into a true bush dog. A hushed command from me would see him crouched by my side or on the Land Rover seat, fully alert but as silent as a gecko whenever an animal approached. I knew he would behave around the elephants.

THE FIRST DAY we spent watching from a distance of about thirty yards. Each day we would get closer, but it would be a gradual exercise. Nana and Frankie watched us continuously, rushing up to the fence if they thought we were getting too close.

Night came, swiftly and silently as it does in Africa. There is perhaps half an hour of gloaming and then it is dark. But darkness can be your friend. The wilderness seethes with life as the nocturnal creatures scurry out from holes and trees and crevices, brave in the knowledge that most predators are resting. The sky switches on its full power, untainted by urban electrical static. I never tire of watching the megawatt heavens, picking out the zodiac signs and revelling in the glory of the odd shooting star.

David's whisper woke me. 'Quick. Something's happening at the fence.'

I threw off my blanket and blinked to adjust my eyes to night vision. We crept up to the boma through the bush. I could see nothing. Then an enormous shape morphed in front of me.

It was Nana, about ten yards from the fence. Next to her was Mandla, her baby son.

I strained my eyes, searching for the others. Despite their bulk, elephants are difficult enough to see in dense bush during the day, let alone at night. Then I saw them; they were all standing motionless a little way behind her.

I quickly glanced at my watch: 4.45 a.m. Zulus have a word for this time of the morning—*uvivi*—which means the darkness before the dawn. And it's true. In the Zululand bush, the darkness is most intense just before the first shreds of haze crack the horizon.

Suddenly Nana tensed her enormous frame and flared her ears. She took a step forward.

'Oh shit! Here she goes,' said David, no longer whispering. 'That bloody electric wire had better hold.'

Without thinking I stood and walked towards the fence. Nana was directly ahead, a colossus just a few yards in front.

'Don't do it, Nana,' I said, as calmly as I could. 'Please don't do it, girl.'

She stood motionless but tense like an athlete straining for the starter's gun. Behind her the rest of the herd froze.

'This is your home now,' I continued. 'Please don't do it, girl.'

I felt her eyes boring into me, even though I could barely make out her face in the murk.

'They will kill you all if you break out. This is your home now. You don't have to run any more.'

Still she didn't move, and suddenly the absurdity of the situation struck me. Here I was in thick darkness talking to a wild female elephant with a baby, the most dangerous combination possible, as if we were having a friendly chat.

Absurd or not, I decided to continue. I meant every word and intended for her to get what I was saying. 'You will all die if you go. Stay here. I will be here with you and it's a good place.'

She took another step forward. I could see her tense up again, preparing to go all the way. I was directly in their path, something I was well aware of. The fence cables would hold them for a short while but I would still have only seconds to scramble out of their way and climb a tree, or else be stomped flatter than an envelope. The nearest tree, a big *Acacia robusta* with wicked thorns, was perhaps ten yards to my left. I wondered if I would be fast enough. Possibly not . . . and when had I last climbed a thorn tree?

Then something happened between Nana and me, some infinitesimal spark of recognition, flaring for the briefest of moments.

Then it was gone. Nana nudged Mandla with her trunk, turned and melted into the bush. The rest followed.

David exhaled like a ruptured balloon. 'Bloody hell! I thought she was going to go for it.'

We lit a small fire and brewed coffee. There was not much to say. I was not going to tell David that I thought I had connected for an instant with the matriarch. It would have sounded too crazy. But something had happened. It gave me a sliver of hope.

EACH DAY was the same. As the sun came up, the herd would start endlessly pacing up and down the length of the fence, turning on us and charging if we dared to get too close, halting only at the electric cable. The naked aggression and agitation, the fiercest I have seen from any animal, blazed nonstop whenever we approached the fence. And they would glare ferociously as we backed off and watched from a distance.

As they were in a confined area we had to provide them with extra food. This posed a problem, as whenever we attempted to get close to the fence to throw bales of alfalfa into the enclosure, they ignored the food and erupted in paroxysms of rage.

The only alternative was to arrange bales at opposite sides of the boma and, as I distracted the elephants at one end and they came at me, David—an immensely strong young man—would leap onto the back of the truck and toss more bulky bales over the fence on the other side.

Then they would spot him and turn and charge in his direction. As he backed off I would throw food over from my side. Then they would come at me, and David would continue. They would eat only when we moved well away.

I spent the rest of the day just watching them, trying to pick up some vibe other than rage. It now seemed that Frankie, the second-in-command, was the main aggressor. Nana was fractionally calmer—although by no means settled. Could I get through to her? I didn't know; I just hoped.

But one thing was certain: the elephants always knew David and I were around. I would spend hours walking round the boma, checking the fence and deliberately speaking loudly so they heard my voice. Sometimes I would even sing, which David uncharitably remarked was enough to make even him want to jump straight onto the electric fence. If I ever caught Nana's attention I would look directly at her and focus on positive gentle communication, telling her time and time again that this was her family's new home and that everything she would ever need was here. Most of the time, though, I spent sitting or standing still at a chosen spot near the fence, purposefully ignoring them, just being there doing nothing, saying nothing, showing I was comfortable whether they were close by or not.

Slowly but surely we became an integral part of their lives. They began to 'know' us, but whether that was a good or a bad thing, I wasn't sure.

However, the alarming ritual that took place during *uvivi*, when they seemed most determined to break out, continued. Every morning at precisely 4.45—I could set my watch by it—Nana would line up the herd facing their old home in Mpumalanga. She would then tense up, yards from the fence, and for ten adrenalin-soaked minutes I would stand up to her, pleading for their lives, telling her that this was now their home. The words I used were unimportant as Nana obviously didn't understand English; I just concentrated on keeping the tone as reassuring as I could. It was always touch-and-go, and my relief as she ghosted back into the bush with her family was absolute.

When the sun eventually rose, David and I would retire to the truck, shattered by these tense stand-offs, saturated in sweat even in the early-morning chill. Silently David would start a small fire near the Land Rover and put the coffeepot on.

'Are we going to win?' he once asked over a steaming mug.

'We have to,' I replied, shrugging with despondency. 'Somehow we just have to calm them down.'

The fact was I still didn't know how to do it. All I did know was that the price of failure was unthinkable.

CHAPTER FOUR

David and I had driven up to the main house for a much-needed break and a cold beer. We were chatting on the front lawn when we heard Françoise scream.

She came running towards us.

'What's the matter?' I asked.

'Snake . . . big one! On the stove, in the kitchen.'

'What happened?'

She had been cooking pasta when a rat suddenly jumped out of the air vents above the stove and landed on a pot next to her. A split second later a grey blur streaked down, whipped itself round the bar on top of the stove and sank its toxic fangs into the mesmerised rodent in one lightning hit. Françoise, who had never seen a snake that close before, dropped the spatula and bolted.

I ran to the kitchen to see the snake gliding fast towards me, heading for the lounge. It was a Mozambican spitting cobra, known locally as a *mfezi*. Despite what Françoise had said, it was average size—about four feet long. But *mfezis* have certainly earned their reputation of being second only to mambas as the most dangerous snakes in Africa. A bite is fatal if untreated, although spitting is their main form of defence, and when they do so they unleash copious amounts of venom from virtually any position.

It was heading in Françoise's direction, so I rushed to get a broom to catch it. I have a strict rule that no snake is killed on Thula Thula unless the situation is life-threatening. If they're in the house, we capture and put them back into the bush. I have learned that, with a cobra, this is most easily done by slowly easing a broom towards it as it rears up and then gently pushing the broom along the floor and under the snake until it leans over on top of the bristle head. It's then lifted up, carried outside and allowed to slither off.

Although some neurons in my brain still jump whenever I see a snake— the same atavistic impulses that kept our ancestors in caves alive—I have no problem with them. They are vital for the environment and do immeasurably more good than harm by keeping vermin populations from exploding. Like almost all wild creatures, they will attack only if threatened; they're far happier running away.

I rushed back with a broom but I was too late. Max had already cornered the reptile, now reared to almost a third of its length with its long, thin hood flared, exposing a yellow-pink underbelly scored with black bars. It was a compelling sight, loathsome yet stunning.

'Come here, Max! Leave him, boy.'

But the usually obedient Max didn't listen. Fixated on the *mfezi* he silently circled the upright serpent, which tried to twist round to face him.

'Maxie . . . leave him, boy,' I commanded. If the snake bit him, he could die. The neurotoxic and cytotoxic (nerve and cell-destroying) venom would reach his vital organs far quicker than in a human.

'Max!'

Then Max lunged, biting the *mfezi* behind its head. I heard the crunch as his jaws snapped shut like a bear trap. He bit again and again.

He dropped the snake and came towards me, wagging his tail. The snake was chopped into three distinct pieces, its head still quivering from contracting nerves.

Max looked mighty pleased with himself. I was just relieved—until I saw his eyes. He was blinking furiously. The spitting cobra had lived up to its name and hit bang on target. *Mfezis* are extremely accurate up to about eight feet and actually spray instead of spit. This means a fine mist of highly toxic venom comes at you as a sheet, rather than as a single globule, and it's vital to wear glasses and shut your mouth when threatened by them—especially when you're trying to move them off with a broom.

Françoise quickly got some milk. We bathed Max's eyes and I rushed him to the Land Rover. The nearest vet was twenty miles away in Empangeni, and if we didn't get there soon, Max could go blind. However, the fact that we had managed to clean out most of the poison with milk so soon after the attack augured well.

The vet agreed that the milk had countered the poison, squeezed some paste into the pupils and said Max would be fine.

As we left, he jumped into the car, tail thumping like an overjoyed wind-screen wiper.

'Who the bloody hell do you think you are?' I admonished him. 'Rikki-Tikki-Tavi?'

Indeed, Max had been as quick as Kipling's *Jungle Book* mongoose. Throughout the fight he had never barked, extremely unusual for a dog. His utter silence had been his key asset. Most dogs prance in front of a snake, yapping furiously, giving the reptile an easy target. Instead, Max had slowly padded round it without uttering a sound. The *mfezi* had trouble twisting to face him on the slippery tiled floor, enabling Max to get behind it.

Later that night David and I returned to the elephants. Max, who adopted an almost bored expression whenever I checked his recovering eyes, came with us.

We inspected the boma and cat napped for a few hours in the Land Rover. Then at 4.45 a.m. I heard a slight rustle near the fence. I knew, with dread, it was Nana preparing for her predawn break-out attempt. I walked down, by now knowing exactly where she would be. Once again, Mandla was at her side, the rest of the herd queuing behind.

'Please don't do it, girl,' I said.

She stopped, tense as a spring as she watched me. I carried on speaking, urging her to stay, keeping my voice as low and persuasive as I could. I kept using her name.

Then she suddenly shifted her stance to face me head-on. The furious stare from her mucous-rimmed eyes faded for a moment. Instead there was something else flickering. Not necessarily benign, but not hostile either.

'This is your home now, Nana. It's a good home and I will always be here with you.'

With unhurried dignity, she turned away from the fence, the others breaking rank to let her through and then following closely behind.

After a few yards she stopped and let the others go ahead. She had never done that before—she had always been the first to disappear into the bush. She turned and again looked straight at me.

It was only for a few seconds, but it seemed to go on for ever.

Then she was swallowed up by the darkness.

AS THE WEEKS PROGRESSED, the herd gradually started to settle down. So much so that we were now able to approach the fence at feeding time without being charged. We also got some much-needed sleep.

Living rough in the wilderness is a salve for the soul. Ancient instincts awaken: forgotten skills are relearned, consciousness is sharpened and life thrums at a richer tempo. Initially the abundant wildlife regarded us as unwelcome colonisers. They wanted to know who we were, what we were, and what were we doing on their turf. Wherever we went, hundreds of eyes watched. I had that prickly sensation of being under constant surveillance, and whenever I looked up, a mongoose, wart hog or tawny eagle would be peering from a distance, taking in everything, missing nothing we did.

But soon we too were creatures of the wild. The larger animals got used to us and, sensing we posed no danger, started to move around us freely. The resident impala ram and his harem, normally as skittish as colts, grazed thirty or so paces away as if we were part of the scenery. Zebra and wildebeest came past regularly while kudu and nyala browsed nearby.

It was late spring, and birds of all shapes and sizes, feathered in an explosion of African colours, chirped and sang the stories of their lives to all who would listen, while snakes—including the lethal black mamba—sought shade from the baking sun. My favourite was a beautiful rock python that lived in a group of boulders beside a gully. He was still a youngster, less than five feet long, but watching his olive and tan body rippling over the ground was as special as you could get.

I always kept a firm grip on Max's collar whenever this yard of elastic muscle glided past. Although he had long since learned not to chase most wild animals, Max still had a thing about snakes. Given half a chance he would have been onto the python in a blink.

The Land Rover's two-way radio aerial also made a great scaffold for a one-inch bark spider that imperiously took up residence. Despite her diminutive size, she was an absolute dynamo. Every evening she strung out her web using the aerial as a support, and every morning she gobbled it all up, saving each precious milligram of protein snared in the gossamer threads, only to rebuild it again at dusk. We named her Wilma, and her three-yard-wide web was an engineering marvel, an absolutely formidable supersticky trap that seized any flying insect in a grip of silky steel, including four-inch long-horned beetles, which she would methodically suck the life out of.

At dusk, animals that lived in the sun went off to sleep wherever they felt safest. The landscape emptied, but not for long. It was soon repopulated under the light of the African stars by creatures of the night. Wart hogs gave way to bush pigs with short, stiletto tusks; tawny and martial eagles were replaced by giant eagle owls that scouted the skies on silent wings, swooping down on vondos—plump, oversized bush rats whose sluggish vulnerability is countered only by their prolific breeding capacity. Fiery-necked nightjars with bear-trap mouths customised for snatching insects in mid-flight soaked up the fading heat from the baked ground before soaring into the heavens. Bats, thousands upon thousands, scudded through the air, and bush babies, among the cutest creatures alive with their cuddly little bodies and huge eyes, screeched raucous mating calls from the tree tops.

Hyenas, perhaps the most maligned and misunderstood of all Africa's animals for their unfair reputation of being savage scavengers, but one of my favourites, skulked in the alleys of the dark looking for dinner. *YOOUP YOOUP, YOOOOUP* they called, marking their territory with their manic cackles. Huge doglike footprints the next day sometimes showed that they had come in for a closer look at us. We used the spotlight intermittently to track this seething theatre, only because leaving it on for too long lured swarms of bugs that attacked us in squadrons. It's bad bush practice to keep a light on continuously, as light attracts insects, insects attract frogs, and frogs attract snakes. Our only permanent illumination was the campfire.

One morning we woke to find leopard droppings near the Land Rover. The local male had marked his territory right where we were sleeping, delivering a firm feline message—this was also his space.

LIVING SO CLOSE to the ground, so to speak, also gave me plenty of time to study the herd, and I became fascinated by their individual quirks. Nana, huge and dominant, took her matriarchal duties seriously and, like a fussy housewife, utilised every inch of the boma's confines to the maximum. She marked out the best spots for shade, the best shelter from the wind and—uncannily—knew feeding times to the minute. She also knew exactly when the water hole and mud pond were due to be refilled by us.

Frankie was the herd's self-appointed guardian. She delighted in breaking away from the rest and storming past us at full speed, head held high and glaring fiercely just for the hell of it.

Mandla, Nana's baby boy, was a born clown whose antics kept us endlessly amused. Full of bravado he would regularly mock charge us—just as long as his mum was close by.

Mabula and Marula, Frankie's son and daughter, were always quiet and well behaved, seldom straying far from their mother.

Nandi, Nana's teenage daughter and mirror image, was much more independent and would often wander round exploring on her own.

And then there was Mnumzane, the young bull and son of the previous matriarch who had been demoted from crown prince to pariah after his mother's demise. He was no longer part of the herd's inner circle and spent most of his time alone or on the periphery of the group.

This was the elephant way: herds are fiercely feminised, and once a male approaches puberty he is evicted. This is nature's method of scattering its seed, otherwise all herds would be interbred. But the trauma of young males being ostracised from their families can be heart-wrenching, similar to desperately homesick boys being sent to distant boarding schools. Usually in the wild they meet up with other young evicted males and form loosely knit *askari* bachelor herds under the guidance of a wise old bull.

Unfortunately we didn't have a father figure for Mnumzane, so he was simultaneously going through the agony of losing his mother and sister, as well as being evicted from the only family he knew and loved. Come feeding time, Nana and Frankie would roughly shoulder him away, and he got scraps only after everyone else had had their fill.

We saw he was losing weight, and David made a point of feeding him separately. Mnumzane's lowly status was confirmed one evening when we heard a series of prolonged high-pitched squeals. Denied the use of the Land Rover by Wilma's web-building activities, we sprinted to the other side of the boma to see that Nana and Frankie had the youngster cornered and were shoving him onto the electric fence.

'Look at that,' David panted as we ran up. 'They're using him as a battering ram, trying to force him through to make an opening.'

So they were. Mnumzane, caught between hot wires and a mountain of flesh and tusk, was screaming himself hoarse as electricity jolted through his young body. The more he screamed, the more they pushed.

Eventually, just as we were about to intervene—although I'm not quite sure how—they released him. The poor fellow bolted and ran round the boma at full speed, loudly trumpeting his indignation.

He calmed down and found a quiet spot as far away from the rest of herd as he could. There he stood and sulked, miserable to his core.

This incident showed that Nana and Frankie understood exactly how an electric fence worked. They knew that if they could bulldoze Mnumzane through the live wires, they could break free without getting shocked.

Despite this, to my intense relief, by now the dreaded dawn patrol had stopped. Nana no longer lined up her brood at the northern boundary, threatening a mass break-out, and despite the odds we seemed to have made some sort of progress in the few weeks they had been there. But neither of us expected what happened next.

THE NEXT MORNING, soon after sunrise, I glanced up to see Nana and baby Mandla at the fence right in front of our little camp. This had never happened before. As I stood, she lifted her trunk and looked straight at me. Her ears were down and she was calm. Instinctively I decided to go to her.

I knew from hard experience that elephants prefer slow, deliberate movements, so I ambled across, ostentatiously stopping to pluck a grass stem and pausing to inspect a tree stump—generally taking my time. I needed to let her get used to me coming forward.

Eventually I stopped about three yards from the fence and gazed up at the gigantic form directly in front of me. Then I took a slow step forward. Then another, until I was two paces from the fence.

She did not move, and I felt sheathed in a sense of contentment. Despite standing just a pace from this previously foul-tempered wild animal who until now would have liked nothing better than to kill me, I had never felt safer.

I remained in a bubble of well-being, completely entranced by the magnificent creature towering over me. I noticed for the first time her thick wiry eyelashes, the thousands of wrinkles crisscrossing her skin, and her broken tusk. Her soft eyes pulled me in. Then, almost in slow motion, I saw her gently reach out to me with her trunk. I watched, hypnotised, as if this was the most natural thing in the world.

David's voice echoed in the surreal background. 'Boss.'

Then louder, 'Boss! Boss, what the hell are you doing?'

The urgency in his call broke the spell. Suddenly I realised that if Nana got hold of me it would all be over. I would be yanked through the fence like a rag doll and stomped flat.

I was about to step back, but something made me hold my ground. There it was again, the strange feeling of mesmeric tranquillity.

Once more Nana reached out with her trunk. And then I got it. She wanted me to come closer, and without thinking I moved towards the fence.

Time was motionless as Nana's trunk snaked through the fence, carefully avoiding the electric strands, and reached my body. She gently touched me. I was surprised at the wetness of her trunk tip and how musky her smell was. After a few moments I lifted my hand and felt the top of her colossal trunk, briefly touching the bristly hair fibres.

Too soon the instant was over. She slowly withdrew her trunk. She stood and looked at me for a few moments before turning and making her way back to the herd that had gathered about twenty yards away, watching every move. Interestingly, as she got there, Frankie stepped forward and greeted her, as if to welcome her return to the fold. If I didn't know better I would have said she was giving her a 'well done'. I walked back to the camp.

'What was that about?' asked David.

I was silent for a while, absolutely awestruck. Then the words tumbled out, 'I don't know. But what I do know is, that it's time to let them out.'

'Let them out? From the boma?'

'Yes. Radio Ndonga and tell him to make sure the outer fence is fully powered. We'll let them out into the reserve early tomorrow.'

At 5 a.m. a game guard radioed me from the energiser shed to say that the power was 'off' in the boma. David lifted the gate's hefty horizontal eucalyptus poles off their hinges.

I called out to Nana, who was standing at the fence about fifty yards away, and deliberately walked in and out of the entrance a couple of times to show it was open.

Then David and I went and stood on top of an ant hill at a safe distance from the entrance to get a grandstand view.

For twenty minutes nothing happened. Eventually Nana ambled over to the gate and tested the space with her trunk for some invisible impediment. Satisfied, she moved forward, herd in tow, and then inexplicably stopped halfway through the exit. For some reason she would go no farther.

Ten minutes later she was still standing there motionless. I turned to David. 'What's going on? Why doesn't she go out?'

'It must be the water in front of the gate,' he said. 'The trench we dug for the delivery truck is full of rain and she doesn't like it. I think she won't go through because it's too deep for Mandla.'

Then, for the first time, we witnessed a graphic demonstration of Nana's Herculean strength.

On either side of the gate stood two eight-foot-high, eight-inch-wide eucalyptus poles sunk thirty inches into concrete. Nana inspected these with her trunk, then put her head down and gave a push. The shafts buckled as the concrete foundations popped out of the ground like corks.

David and I stared at each other, stunned. 'My God,' I said, 'we couldn't even have done that with the tractor. And to think that I was letting her touch me!'

The way round the trench was now clear and Nana wasted no more time, hurrying the herd down a game path directly to the river. We watched the thick summer bush swallow them up.

As soon as the herd disappeared, we struck camp. All this entailed was throwing sleeping-bags and a fire-blackened kettle into the back of the Land Rover, but it was symbolic in the sense that we were moving on.

Max was still at the boma gate, watching the woodland that had seemingly gobbled up the elephants. I called him and he looked up askance, as if asking if I wanted him to pursue the animals. If I had said 'Fetch!' I have no doubt he would have bounded into the bush. Size meant nothing to him: he was absolutely without fear and had no concept that a single lift of Nana's foot would have converted him into a pancake.

After dropping David off at the lodge, I drove to the Ovambo guards' cottage to give them an update.

I was about hundred yards away when Ndonga came sprinting up, waving his arms. 'Quick, Mr Anthony. Turn off the motor and keep quiet,' he whispered. 'There's a leopard about forty yards ahead . . . just to the right of us.'

I killed the engine and squinted into the bush, my eyes scouring every inch of the area where he was pointing . . . and saw nothing.

'A leopard out in broad daylight? Can't be.'

Ndonga put a finger to his lips. 'I saw it just two minutes ago as you were driving up. Just keep still . . . it'll come out again. Just watch that big bush over there. That's where it came down.'

The thicket was certainly big enough to hide a leopard. But leopards are primarily nocturnal and it would be highly unusual to see one wandering round at midday.

Then out of the corner of my eye I spotted one of the Ovambos come out from behind the house and nod at Ndonga. He was wiping his hands with a rag, which he quickly stuffed into his pocket when he saw me looking at him.

Ndonga, who had been crouching near the car, stood up.

'Well, I suppose you're right, boss. Your Land Rover would have frightened it off anyway. Pity. It's the first leopard I've seen on Thula.'

I nodded. We knew there were several leopards on the reserve from their tracks, and the markings I'd seen recently by the Land Rover had confirmed it, but they had been vigorously hunted before we took over and as a result were so secretive that few had seen them.

'So what's happening, Mr Anthony?' he asked.

'We've let the herd out. I want all of your guards to go on patrol and track them. Also, check the fences. Make sure the power stays up permanently. And double-check that there are no trees anywhere even remotely close by. I don't want the elephants shorting the wires again.'

'I've already done that. All trees near the fence have been chopped.'

The last time I had heard that was just before the herd had escaped from the boma. I didn't want to risk it again.

'You're sure?'

'Of course.'

'Well . . . OK. See you later.'

I drove off. The recent rains had brushed the bush in colours of green and gold, and the fecund earth throbbed with life. Unfortunately, as beautiful as it looked, this rampant foliage would make the elephants more difficult to track. We needed to know all the time exactly where they were in case they attempted another break-out.

Biyela, our loyal gardener and everybody's friend, ran up to welcome us back as Max and I got out the car, glad to be home. As I walked through the door, Françoise told me that Ngwenya, my security *induna* or foreman, wanted to see me.

He was sitting on a tree stump outside the verandah of the rangers' quarters about thirty yards from our house. This was unusual. He obviously didn't want to be seen approaching me. I walked over.

'*Sawubona*, Ngwenya.' I see you.

'*Yebo*, Mkhulu.'

We spoke for a bit about the unusually wet weather and the elephants. Then he got to the point.

'Mkhulu, we all know strange things are happening.'

'Such as what?'

'Such as the shooting of *nyamazane*'—game—'on Thula Thula.'

I stiffened. I had been so absorbed in the elephants that the poaching problem had been put on a back burner.

'But now I am also hearing strange stories,' Ngwenya continued. 'And the strangest of all is that people are saying that Ndonga is the man who is doing the shooting. The man killing our animals.'

'What?' The blood drained from my face. 'What makes you say such a serious thing?'

Ngwenya shook his head, as if he too couldn't believe it. 'Ndonga shoots the buck, but the skinning is done by the other Ovambos and by Phineas, the gate guard. Then sometimes a truck with ice comes late at night with no lights and fetches it. Or sometimes Ndonga takes the meat to town.'

'How do you know this?'

'It is what the people here are saying. Also, I am told the other Ovambos are unhappy. They complain in the village that they are doing all the hard work and Ndonga gives them no money. He gives them only meat. Not even good meat—they get maybe the head and shins. That's all.'

'How long has this been going on?'

Ngwenya shrugged. 'Since the day you came. But I have found this out only now. That is why I have come to you.'

'Thanks, Ngwenya. Good work.'

'These are dangerous times.' He eased himself off the stump. 'The Ovambos must not know I have spoken to you. *Sale gahle*, Mkhulu.' Stay well.

'*Hamba gahle*, Ngwenya.' Go well.

I sat there, stunned as if I had been smacked on the head. This was a horrific accusation, not just because the poachers had killed so many animals, which was bad enough. But to add insult to injury, if Ngwenya's allegations were true, my own employees were guilty of poaching my animals with my own rifles. The Lee-Enfield .303s that the Ovambos had been issued with belonged to Thula Thula.

'Boss.'

I looked up. David was standing next to me. 'The electrician has arrived.'

I nodded, remembering that we had booked the man to check the fence's electrics thoroughly now that the elephants had been freed. As we got into the Land Rover the radio crackled into life. It was Ndonga. I tensed with anger. My head guard might be innocent and I had to give him the benefit of the doubt, but Ngwenya's story rankled deep.

'We've found the elephants. They're right on the northern boundary.'

'Excellent,' I replied, fighting to keep the fury out of my voice. 'Keep an eye on them and wait for us. We'll be there in about fifteen minutes.'

With the electrician squashed between us, straddling the Land Rover's gear stick, and Max on David's lap, we drove off. It made sense that the herd had emerged at the far border, the direction of their previous home, but nevertheless it was chilling news. Were they still determined to break out, I wondered?

As Ndonga had said, gangs of workers had indeed chopped down all the trees within felling distance of the wires. Narrow vehicle tracks had been hacked out to make a rough road for anti-poaching patrols and maintenance checks along the boundary, so it was relatively simple to keep the animals in sight as we followed from a distance.

Nana was moving down the line, the tip of her trunk just below the top electric strand, sensing the pulse of the surging current. With her clan following, she had walked almost the entire twenty miles of the reserve's perimeter using her natural voltmeter to check if there was any weak link—any section without power in the fence.

By now it was nearly four o'clock. It had taken the animals most of the day to circumnavigate the reserve, and I was relieved to see that despite checking for breaks in the power, Nana was not attempting to make direct contact with the fence.

But just as the herd was completing its tour, we saw a large acacia standing proud right next to the wires that Ndonga's clearing gang had inexplicably missed. It was the only 'danger' tree along the entire border that had not been felled, and it stood out stark as a monument.

'Damnit,' groaned David. Both he and I knew what was going to happen next.

Sure enough, Nana and Frankie stopped, saw the tree and loped over for a closer inspection.

'No, Nana, no!' I shouted as they positioned themselves on either side of the acacia and started shouldering it, testing its resistance. There was no doubt they were going to shove it down, and if we were going to prevent the inevitable break-out we needed to get closer. There was a gate nearby, and we sped out of the reserve and onto an adjacent track, putting us on the opposite side of the fence.

As we arrived, the tree was creaking wildly on its roots and Nana gave a mighty heave. With a rending 'crack' the trunk splintered down onto the barrier, collapsing the poles and snapping the current, causing an almighty short circuit. Forsaking caution I rushed up and snatched at the wires to see if they were still live. As I feared, the fence was dead. And with the herd almost on top of us, we had a real problem.

'No, Nana, don't do it!' I yelled with only a tangle of dead wires and flattened poles between us. My voice was raspy with desperation. 'Don't do it!'

Fortunately, the frenetic clicking and snapping as the wires shorted had spooked her and she took a hasty step backwards. But for how long?

Thank God the electrician was there and, as I pleaded with the agitated animals, he and David got to work. With Nana, Frankie and the youngsters barely ten yards away, they calmly untangled the bird's nest of wires, chopped the tree free, reconnected the cable, straightened the poles and got the power going again.

While all this was happening, I continued speaking directly to Nana as I had in the boma, using her name often and repeating again and again that this was her home.

She looked at me and for at least ten minutes we held eye contact as I kept talking.

Suddenly, as if baffled by what all the fuss was about, she turned and backtracked into the bush. The others followed and we exhaled with relief.

It was only then that I realised I hadn't even considered picking up a rifle in case everything went amiss. My relationship with the herd had certainly changed for the better.

HOWEVER, SOMETHING ELSE caught my attention during the commotion, something more sinister. It was the Ovambos. As the tree had come down, to a man they had bolted like startled rabbits. This was strange, I thought. These much-vaunted rangers were actually petrified of elephants, not quite what you would expect from experienced men of the bush.

Then it flashed. It was as if I was seeing clearly for the first time. A fog had miraculously lifted. Despite their braggadocio, these men were not game rangers at all. They never had been. They were soldiers who could shoot straight, but otherwise knew precious little about conservation. They were now out of their element. I had always wondered why the Ovambos, who were supposed to be top-drawer trackers, had led us the wrong way during the original break-out. Now I knew.

Any remaining niggles of doubt in my mind dissipated. It was suddenly as obvious as the sun beating down on us. The guards were indeed the poachers, just as Ngwenya had said. They were the ones who had been plaguing the reserve for the past year, decimating the buck population. The last thing they wanted was a herd of wild elephants on Thula Thula.

Having no experience with elephants, let alone this unpredictable herd, they realised that with angry jumbos around their poaching racket would be ruined. The reason was simple. Most poaching is done in the dark, and one would have to be a brave—or monumentally foolish—man to trample round in the bush at night with this temperamental herd on the loose. It would be suicide. They desperately needed to engineer another escape so that their lucrative sideline could continue.

Even though the evidence was completely circumstantial, the jigsaw pieces started fitting together. I remembered Bheki telling me how a gun 'spoke' at the boma on the night the elephants first escaped. Could someone have deliberately fired those shots to panic the herd and prompt a frenzied stampede?

This also explained why the fence wires had initially been strung on the wrong side of the boma poles. And of course there was no leopard at the cottage earlier this morning. I would bet that they had been butchering illegally slaughtered animals and my unexpected arrival had almost caught them red-handed—literally. Ndonga had to distract me while they hurriedly hid the evidence. That's why the game guard had come out from the back of the house wiping off his hands: they had been covered with blood.

And what about the tree that had been left standing right at the fence? That was probably the most obvious clue of all. It was far too coincidental not to have been deliberate.

I had been set up. Totally fooled.

However, not only had we been grotesquely betrayed, but—more importantly—the elephants were now in danger. 'David,' I said, pulling him aside. 'I need to talk to you.'

CHAPTER FIVE

There was a stunned silence when I told David my suspicions. He was all for some direct action, but I refused. 'I understand you're pissed off. I feel the same, but we have to do this cleverly. This is our biggest opportunity to smash this damn poaching ring once and for all. They can't know we're onto them.'

David looked at me, unconvinced.

'We've got to pretend everything's OK until we get all the evidence,' I continued. 'Otherwise we'll blow it. At the moment all we've got is hearsay and they will just deny everything.

'We can't let the guards out of sight, even for a minute. We've got to get two of our best rangers up to their house permanently. Get Ngwenya to brief them so they know what's going on. I want them living and working with the Ovambos twenty-four hours a day.'

The next morning we were out early to see what the elephants were doing. After a couple of hours bouncing round in dense bush we found them grazing in the middle of the reserve, about as far from the fence as you could get. Mnumzane was a hundred yards or so from the main group, stripping leaves from a small acacia. We eased forward until we were close enough to see them clearly, and I did a head count. Seven—all there, engulfed by long grass and succulent trees and stuffing their mouths like kids at a birthday party. With nearly double the rainfall of their previous home, which meant double the food yield, Thula Thula truly was a pachyderm paradise.

'They're exploring, and they like what they see,' said David. 'This must be better than anything they've known before.'

PHINEAS WAS THE GATE GUARD who had been used to skin the slaughtered animals. He was a simple, sickly young man, having long been afflicted by AIDS, the scourge of modern Africa. On the streets the slang for AIDS was 'slow puncture', a particularly apt description of how the disease gradually saps one's life, and frail Phineas was no exception. We had moved him from the labour team to far less demanding gate duties to ease his day.

I sent for Phineas and, as is customary in rural Zululand, he came in without knocking. Crouching low, he moved across the room and then sat down without being asked. He averted his eyes and stared at the floor, which is considered good manners.

'*Yehbo*, Phineas,' I greeted him.

'*Sawubona*, Mkhulu,' he replied, without looking up.

Instead of first politely discussing one's health or the weather, again customary in rural Zululand, I went straight for the jugular.

'Phineas, I hear that you have been tricked into skinning animals that the Ovambos have stolen.'

The effect was instant. Phineas glanced around wildly, as if looking for an escape route. Then his sickly pallor turned even more ashen as, his breath labouring out in wheezes, he no doubt cursed his bad luck.

'Come, Phineas,' I said, pressing the obvious advantage of surprise. 'Everybody knows what has happened and I don't want to hand you over to the police. Jail will be a bad place for you. I am offering you the chance to help us.'

'Ndonga promised me money,' he said, his voice quavering. 'Then he did not pay me. I am sorry, Mkhulu.'

He then gave me full details of the poaching ring, exactly how many animals and what species they had shot, as well as times and dates. I was astounded at the scale of the operation. These bastards had slaughtered at least a hundred animals—which translates into several tons of meat, and thousands of dollars of profit.

I now had my first witness. In the meantime my rangers were busy moving into quarters next to the Ovambos, while David was Ndonga's 'new best friend', constantly shadowing him and seriously curtailing any poaching activities. I also started calling Ndonga over the radio at all hours, day and night, asking where the Ovambos were, setting meetings in the bush and making surprise visits to their house.

The tension was starting to tell. Ndonga didn't suspect we knew anything but he was as jumpy as hell, never knowing what was coming next. Whenever the Ovambos went out in a group, my rangers would radio me and we would drive up to them from nowhere, exchanging pleasantries and just hanging out. The confusion on their faces was almost comic. The main thing was that they be given no opportunity to poach.

Oblivious to all this human intrigue, Nana and her family appeared to be settling in well, and I decided to spend a morning watching them, just to see for myself.

After about an hour's drive I found them shading themselves under a sprawling giant fig next to the river. It was still early, but already the mercury had rocketed to almost 100 degrees. I stopped the Land Rover, crept forward and settled down under a leafy marula tree about fifty yards downwind. They stood motionless but for the gentle flapping of their ears, cooling themselves as best they could. Elephant ears are the size of a hefty woman's skirt and act as a natural air conditioner. Behind each massive flap of cartilage is a road map of veins that pumps gallons of blood just beneath the skin, and gentle fanning cools the corpuscles, which in turn lowers the body temperature.

A draught eddied through the saplings and cosseted my back. The wind was edging to the south. When I had arrived I was downwind, but with the subtle shift I now had to move fast.

As I stood I saw the tip of Nana's trunk suddenly angle and swivel towards me, snatching a trace of scent. She then stood back and, lifting her trunk to verify the odour, turned to face in my direction.

Collecting my binoculars and water bottle I climbed into the Land Rover with Max just as she started advancing towards me, the rest of the herd falling in behind her. There was plenty of time to drive off, but I was intrigued by the fact that she was actually heading my way.

I manoeuvred the Land Rover into a good getaway position, steeled my nerves and waited. At the last moment, just yards from me, she changed direction ever so slightly and walked past the vehicle, followed by her family, each member turning to stare as they passed. Frankie, who was bringing up the rear, splayed her ears and gave an aggressive shake of her head towards me.

Then suddenly she swung off the back of the line, trumpeted harshly, and started coming at me, fast as a truck, her ears flared and trunk raised high. I knew instinctively it was a mock charge, and the worst thing to do would be to drive off as this could encourage her, perhaps spark a real charge. I braced myself as she pulled up spectacularly just yards away in a whirlwind of flapping ears, dust and rage. After tossing her head in anger once or twice, she stomped off back to the herd with her tail angrily erect.

I stared after her, transfixed. Even though I had seen it many times, a charging elephant is one of the most awesome physical spectacles in the world. I'll have to be careful with Frankie, I thought, once I had regained my ability to think. She was still too ill-tempered, too eager to vent her fury. Even though Nana was the matriarch, Frankie was far more dangerous.

I followed them for a bit, thorns squeaking and stabbing the Land Rover's paintwork, until the bush became too wild and I turned off on an old overgrown track and set course for home.

DURING THE NEXT FEW DAYS, fresh information about the poachers kept popping up, all of it helpful. The Ovambos, unable to hunt due to our constant surveillance, had taken to slipping out into the village at night and getting rat-faced drunk at the local shebeen (a traditional, usually illegal, tavern). The more they drank the more they talked, and we made sure we always had an informer there. With alcohol-fired machismo, they bragged openly about their exploits. Slowly we were piecing together our case.

'OK, what do we do now?' David asked.

'We go to the police and give them the statements. I have set it up with a lieutenant who's expecting us.'

The next day we drove into Empangeni, met with two senior policemen and recounted the full story, handing over all the affidavits.

'This is an open and shut case,' said one after reading Phineas's statement. 'They're as guilty as hell. We'll be out there later to make the arrests.'

That was exactly what I wanted to hear, and at 5 p.m. on the dot two police vans arrived. David and I led them to the Ovambos' cottage. It was strangely silent, with no one to be seen. Leaving the cars quietly, we split into two groups, heading for the front and back of the building.

We were too late. As we burst into their rooms, all we found were rifles strewn on the floor and cupboard doors flapping open. All their personal possessions were gone. No doubt they saw us coming and instantly hot-footed it. They were now running for dear life through the bush and, without knowing which direction they had taken, there was no way we would catch them before dark.

The police said they would put out a general alert for the fleeing guards, which was all we could do for the moment. 'They are probably halfway to Namibia by now,' one of the police said ruefully.

Back at the house I recounted the drama to Françoise and we strolled outside, watching the blood-red sun ease itself down beyond the sweeping hills. The reserve looked tranquil. Perhaps I was imagining it, but with the guards gone the whole mood had changed—as if some particularly malignant force had been purged.

THULA THULA, AT LAST, was finding its equilibrium. The elephants weren't trying to be serial escapers and the poaching problem was largely solved, although I knew we would never entirely stamp out poaching. On another front, my discussions with the *amakhosi* and the tribes about converting their surrounding cattle land to a game reserve were continuing well. Trying to persuade thousands of Zulus, for whom cattle are an iconic form of wealth, that they should switch the use of their land to wildlife was an ambitious undertaking and fraught with many complications, cultural and otherwise. Patience and persistence were the keys.

So now for the first time I could concentrate on our core mission—running an African game reserve.

It is a tough, rewarding life. Each day starts at dawn and not only are there no weekends, but if you are not careful you can also quickly lose track of the days of the week. Fences have to be checked and fixed daily, roads and tracks must be repaired and wrested back from bush encroachment or you lose them for ever. The never-ending invasion of alien plants needs constant attention—some plants are intruders from other countries, varieties that don't have natural enemies in Africa and are not palatable to wildlife, so their growth is rampant. Then there are game counts and veld assessments, dam inspections and repairs, fire breaks to maintain, anti-poaching patrols, maintaining good relations with neighbouring tribes, and a hundred other things to do. But it is a good, clean life, with just enough danger and adventure to keep you on your toes and enjoying it.

The elephant herd was settling in nicely and staying away from the fences. I spent as much time as I could near them. Despite being out of the boma for only three weeks, they were already stuffing themselves on myriad delicacies and noticeably putting on weight.

It wasn't just the elephants that were adjusting. With the removal of the Ovambo guards, scores of other animals suddenly appeared on the landscape, as if by magic. Wherever I went I saw kudu, nyala, herds of wildebeests and impalas and a host of smaller game scurrying about seemingly without a care in the world. Hyena became more brazen in the evenings, and we even got occasional glimpses of leopard, lynx and serval, the beautiful tawny black-spotted cats of the night, whose pelts are unfortunately still highly prized. The more the creatures lost their fear of poachers, the more of them we encountered, and with mounting jubilation I discovered that we still had healthy populations of almost all of Zululand's indigenous animals. The whole reserve was now truly energised, and us with it.

Immersed in the bush each day with no pressing problems reignited another of my loves: birdwatching. With its diverse habitats, Thula Thula has over 350 identified species of bird and is an absolute haven for 'twitchers', those unusual people obsessed with spending every free moment watching birds.

Plum-coloured starlings, turquoise European rollers that winter with us, the gorgeous bush-shrike, blood-red narina trogons and countless others boasting plumages so flamboyant, the visual feast was unbelievable. Catching sight of a gwala gwala in flight, the only time it flashes its vivid scarlet wing feathers, can send the soul soaring.

ONE MORNING, Françoise joined me on the quad bike, a four-wheeled all-terrain motorbike, while I tracked the herd. As we zoomed off on a dusty track, I marvelled at the profound transformation she had made in adapting to a life in the bush. Her sophisticated upbringing in the buzzing metropolis and boulevard cafés of Paris were light-years removed from the African outbacks of my youth. With her arms tight round my waist we rode through a shallow section of the Nseleni River to a high lookout point to see if we could find the elephants.

The hill had a panoramic view, and we spotted them briefly in thick bush bordering the river below, close to where we had just come through. We must have missed them by fifty yards or so, and it worried me that I hadn't detected them—especially with Françoise riding pillion.

'There they are again,' I pointed, and we watched as the elephants loped into view about a mile away, moving in single file across the deep green flood plain and disappearing back into the riverbed.

'They're moving off. Let's give them a bit of time to cross the river and go after them.'

About ten minutes later we rode back down the hill onto the flood plain and I slowly eased the bike down the cutting into the lazily flowing river, driving through with feet held high to avoid a drenching. Once on the other side, I gunned the motor to scramble up the steep incline and we shot to the top of the river bank.

Absolute disaster! I suddenly became aware of huge grey shapes morphing all around us. Incredibly we had ridden bang into the middle of the herd! The elephants had stopped to graze right at the exit of the river crossing—something I had not anticipated.

Shock shuddered through my body. I suddenly felt minuscule, puny, unprotected on a tiny bike surrounded by edgy five-ton mammals. And, even worse, I had Françoise with me. My throat tightened as my mind raced: how do I get out of this? With a river and steep bank behind and a herd of agitated elephants in front, the options were limited.

What was even more disconcerting was that we had also cut off Marula and Mabula, who were slightly behind us, from their mother Frankie. They panicked and started squealing loudly. And if there was one single thing that could aggravate our already dire predicament even more, it was getting between an aggressive female elephant and her frightened young.

We were in trouble. Deep trouble.

Nana, who was a few yards away on our right, took two menacing steps forward with her trunk held high, and then thankfully stopped and backed off. That was terrifying enough on its own, but the real problem was coming from behind her: Frankie.

I frantically tried to turn the bike and make a bolt for it, but the river bank was too steep, the bike's turning circle too wide. We were trapped.

Trying to sound as unconcerned as possible, I said to Françoise, surprised that my voice was still steady, 'I think we have a problem.' I was absolutely horrified that I had placed her in such mortal danger.

By now Frankie was furiously reversing out of a thicket, trying to swivel and charge us. I drew my 9mm pistol and handed it to Françoise to protect herself if anything happened to me. Basically, it was a peashooter as far as an elephant was concerned, but, as a last resort, a shot might distract Frankie.

I then stood up on the bike to face Frankie, who was now coming directly at us—fast, furious and deadly. I pleaded for this to be a mock charge, desperately looking for signs that she just wanted to scare us away from her young. The key indication of this was if her ears flapped out. But no—with mounting horror I watched her fold her ears back and roll up her trunk to take full impact when she hit. A rolled trunk meant she was going all the way. This was for real, and with that awful realisation my sensations heightened surreally, like in a slow-motion car crash. I heard someone hammering in the far-off village as if it was next door, while high above me I watched an eagle soaring and marvelled at its graceful flight.

On she hurtled, her huge frame blotting out all else. Lifting my hands as high above my head as I could, I started yelling at her, then began screaming at the monstrous sight in a last-ditch attempt to pierce her mist of rage.

Then, just as I thought we were goners, her ears suddenly cracked out and she broke off and unrolled her trunk. But the massive momentum hurled her right up to the bike where she towered directly above us, glaring angrily through tiny eyes. I involuntarily sat down on the bike and looked up at the crinkled underside of Frankie's throat in petrified wonder. She shook her huge head in frustration, showering us in the thick red dust from a recent sand bath, and then backed off a few paces.

Marula and Mabula scampered past her. After making another two or three terrifyingly threatening gestures at us, Frankie turned and followed her son and daughter into the bush, away from us.

I eased stiffly down off the saddle and turned to Françoise. Her eyes were tightly closed and I gently whispered that it was over. It was OK. The two of us sat still, too stunned to do or say anything.

Eventually I found the energy to start the bike and pulled off in the opposite direction to the herd. We drove through the bush, which seemed so still after the charge, as if the birds and trees themselves knew what had happened.

Back home I told the staff about it. 'I can't believe you're still alive,' said David, whistling through his teeth. 'She must have made a conscious decision not to kill you. Why do you think she did that?'

A good question. Elephants rarely break off once they're at full steam and I still couldn't believe that Frankie had actually halted at the last minute. Why had she changed gear, dropping down from a lethal real attack to a mock charge? It was virtually unheard of.

The next day I got on the bike and drove back to the river crossing where we had so nearly lost our lives to try to figure it out. I needed some answers. But try as I might, the crucial moments of the charge were a total blank, as if my mind couldn't grapple with the horror.

So I retraced our route, driving through the same river crossing several times, mentally scrolling over the incident again and again. Slowly the details started fleshing out. I remembered I had been standing on the bike and screaming as she charged. But what was I yelling?

Then in an instant it came flooding back. I was screaming, 'Stop, stop, it's me, it's me!'

That was all. In retrospect it sounds rather ludicrous, but that's exactly what happened. To shout 'It's me!' at a charging elephant, the most aggressive female in a herd protecting her panicked babies, is about as lame as it gets. Yet it stopped her, and I knew then that she had somehow recognised me from the boma. I still believe she had spared our lives because she had witnessed her matriarch's interaction with me the day before I let them out.

Chapter Six

The southern white rhino is very big. Surprisingly big—especially if you are on foot and one steps out of the bush in front of you. It's the second-largest land mammal on earth and can easily weigh three tons. It is prized by poachers for its horns, of which the one just in front of me had a particularly fine pair.

We had just had three rhinos delivered to the reserve, and this female, still doped from the sedative, had groggily wandered away from the other two. This posed a big problem. The elephants were close by and, unknowingly, she was ambling directly towards them. We had to cut her off—and trying to dissuade a mountain of muscle and horn still hungover from travel tranquil-lisers from going in her chosen direction was not something I relished.

'David,' I called into the radio. 'I've found her. Can you bring the Landy across? We're at the south end of the airstrip.'

'Roger, boss,' came the instant reply.

I watched this beautiful creature not fifteen yards away walking unsteadily on short dumpy legs that could usually propel her into an unbelievably fast charge in no time. Clad in a prehistoric suit of armour impervious to almost anything except a bullet, she tottered along, completely unaware of my presence. A magnificent 40-inch horn like a sabre at the tip of her elongated head added gravitas to an already imposing form. This was the stuff poachers dream about.

Max stood by me, transfixed by the beast. Bush-hardened as he was, he was not used to rhino this close, and apart from his twitching nose taking in the scent, he didn't move. I kept a wary eye on the herd browsing upwind, then I heard a soft sound behind me and turned to see Mnumzane coming up the airstrip downwind, testing the air.

Damnit! Of all the bad luck . . . we were too late; he must have caught either my scent or the rhino's and started to walk slowly in our direction.

'David,' I whispered into the radio, 'Mnumzane's right here.'

'So am I, boss,' he replied as the Landy bounced out of the bush onto the airstrip. Giving Mnumzane a wide berth, he pulled up next to me and jumped out, leaving the motor idling.

'Somehow we have to keep Mnumzane and the herd away from her,' I said pointing to the dazed rhino.

'I brought the horse feed you wanted. That should delay him for a while,' he replied.

'Yeah, but the smell might also bring the other elephants over. We're going to have to shield the rhino with the Land Rover, put ourselves between her and any elephant that gets too inquisitive. But first let's try and get Mnumzane out of the way.'

David jumped into the back of the Landy and sliced the first of the large sacks of horse pellets. He placed the open bag at the tailgate and crouched down next to it. 'I hope they like this stuff.'

'We'll soon find out,' I said, getting behind the wheel and driving slowly towards Mnumzane.

David was making light of it, but this was a deadly serious business. Elephants will usually bother rhinos only if they don't get out of their way—which rhinos invariably do. However, our latest addition was still shaking off the effects of sedatives injected to pacify her during the journey to Thula Thula, and thus would not be able to take in her surroundings. If she stumbled into Mnumzane or the herd . . . well, anything could happen.

What we planned to do was to divert Mnumzane's attention from the groggy creature by giving him a taste of the protein-rich pellets and then enticing him as far away as possible by laying a food trail. It was dangerous work, as David would be completely exposed on the open back of the pick-up as he poured the feed out to excited elephants following just yards behind. Mnumzane was only a teenager, but he still weighed about three and a half tons and we had to be very careful.

I cut across in front of the youngster, then reversed back to where he stood confused and a little petulant about the noisy intrusion into his space. David chucked out some feed and I drove off a short distance. To my dismay, he ignored the offering and resumed his meander up the airstrip towards the rhino.

'Reverse again!' shouted David, holding the bag ready to pour. 'But this time get much closer.'

'OK . . . but be bloody careful.'

I gingerly edged the vehicle backwards . . . 'Closer, closer!' David called, keeping a wary watch on the young bull.

Suddenly, not liking what was going on, Mnumzane lifted his head aggressively and turned sharply towards us, ears spread wide.

'Just a little bit more,' said David, ignoring the elephant's blatant warning, and just as I thought we were too close he quickly tipped the bag and I slammed the vehicle into first, easing off with David laying a long trail of feed away from the rhino.

Mnumzane watched us go, relaxing his flared ears and unfurling his trunk to smell the pile of pellets on the ground. He snuffled some into his mouth and a few seconds later he was piling in like a glutton. The ploy had worked.

'That will keep him busy, and we've plenty more chow if the others come across,' said David, hopping off the back and getting into the passenger seat, shoving Max between us.

At the mention of the other elephants, I looked up to where they were grazing about forty yards away. As I did so, Nana's trunk suddenly snaked up. Even though she was upwind, elephants have such a superb sense of smell that they can pick up minute eddies swirling ever so slightly against the prevailing current.

'Here we go,' said David. 'She's smelled something. Either the rhino or the food, and now she's inquisitive. Just pray that she doesn't come this way.'

But of course she did. With the herd following, she started moving towards us, checking the air continuously, sniffing for the source of the scent.

'Damnit!' We now had the herd coming in on one side of the poor rhino and Mnumzane on the other. Even worse, they weren't advancing in single file, which would have been much more manageable. Nana was in the centre, with Frankie, her daughter Marula and first-born son Mabula on the left, while Nana's young son Mandla and stately daughter Nandi spread out on the right.

Straight in front of them, still secreted in the bush, was the woozy rhino, which to my dismay had begun settling down for a rest, making herself even more vulnerable.

'OK,' said David, 'let's do it again, draw them away with the feed.'

He leaped onto the back of the Land Rover and this time cut open two bags and got ready to pour a trail while I reversed in.

The reaction of the herd was interesting. They picked up the scent and cautiously came towards us while David scooped pellets out as fast as possible. Mabula and Marula stopped and started sniffing at the strange fare, but the rest, led by Nana and Frankie, continued on, slowly following the trail left behind the Land Rover.

Then—of all things—the Land Rover stalled and I couldn't restart it. Thankfully the cabin rear window had long since lost its glass and, with Nana almost on top of him, David somehow squeezed his large body through the tiny gap and dived onto Max in the passenger seat in a tangle of limbs.

Then the elephants were on us. We were surrounded.

Fortunately it was the feed the elephants were after, and the two adults yanked the remaining bags off the back and tried standing on them to smash them open. Frankie, frustrated in her attempts to open one bag, grabbed it by the corner with her trunk and flicked it high into the air— thankfully in the opposite direction from the now-sleeping rhino. It sailed above our heads for at least thirty yards and landed with a thud, scattering its contents. Given that the bag weighed 120 pounds and she had grasped it with only the tip of her trunk, the height and distance of the throw was truly awesome.

The elephants loped off after the broken bag, and while they were busy gorging themselves we were able to sneak out to fix the Land Rover. It was a disconnected fuel line, and soon we restarted it. Now knowing that they loved horse feed, I radioed for more and we were able to lay juicy trails, leading the herd far away from our new arrival.

We weren't so lucky with Mnumzane. He had unfinished business with the rhino, and soon lost interest in the scraps of feed on the ground, walking back towards where she lay.

There was nothing left to do but get between them and keep him away as best we could. My heart jumped at the thought, for even at his age he could easily toss our vehicle over if he wanted to. Bull elephants don't like to be forced to do something against their will.

I drove past Mnumzane up to the drowsy rhino and blocked his path, leaving the motor running. He could easily walk round us of course, so the plan was to keep moving in front of him, obstructing him from the rhino and hope he got the message without feeling he had been interfered with. And particularly without provoking a charge.

On he came until he was about ten paces away, and then he stopped and watched us guardedly, assessing the situation with elephantine intelligence. As we predicted, he started making a wide circle round the vehicle. Now came the tricky part, because not only would he be much closer, but he would realise he was being thwarted.

'Hold on,' I said quietly as I gently moved the Landy forward to block him.

Again he stopped, this time less than five yards away, and then he changed tack. I reversed and, as we started moving, his ears flared out and he swung to face us head-on. He had taken up the challenge, and the tension in the Landy ratcheted up as he took an aggressive step towards us, head held high.

'Shit!' said David quietly.

'No! Mnumzane, no!' I called out of the open window, ensuring that my voice conveyed intention rather than anger, or worse still fear. 'No!'

Again he stepped forward, ears belligerently splayed, tail up. This was no game.

'No, Mnumzane! No!' I called again, as I reversed in a tight semicircle to keep him away. 'No!'

Out of the corner of my eye I saw the rhino wake up, stumble to her feet and start moving off, giving us precious space in which to manoeuvre. Relieved, I swung the Landy round until we faced the temperamental elephant head-on with about ten yards separating us.

As we confronted each other he began swinging his front foot, a sure sign that he was going to charge. Without thinking, I dropped the clutch and briefly lurched the Landy at him and, then again, challenging him directly.

'Whoa!' said David, gripping the dashboard. 'Here he comes!'

Then, as we braced for the inevitable charge, he suddenly broke and ran off, trunk held high. I had to press home our advantage and immediately followed him, goading him away until he reached thick bush and disappeared.

'Flippin' hell,' said David, expelling breath with a whoosh. 'That was a close one. I wouldn't try that with an adult bull.'

He was absolutely right. Mnumzane's youth was on our side, but it had worked and the rhino was safe. We posted a ranger with the rhino with instructions to call if any elephants reappeared, and I went off to find Mnumzane and make my peace with him.

FRANKIE'S CHARGE at Françoise and me, terrifying as it was, had in its own strange way strengthened the bond that I had been building with the herd. The fact that the matriarch Nana had not joined in was an impressive break-through. She had launched a few aggressive steps towards us, which is only to be expected of a wild elephant, but then she had almost instantly halted. To me, the fact that she had not overreacted was significant.

Frankie, who had a sinister reputation already, had broken a full-blooded charge as soon as she recognised me—something virtually unheard of in the elephant world.

However, what happened a few months later was even more surprising.

Françoise and I were fast asleep when Bijou's persistent growling woke us. Bijou—'jewel' in French—is Françoise's tiny Maltese poodle, the obligatory accoutrement of almost an entire nation of French women. She was not a watchdog, so when she started growling I realised something serious was going on.

I jumped out of bed, grabbed my shotgun and then heard what the problem was—a heavy scraping on the roof accompanied by soft thuds. Max was sitting at the door, ears cocked, watching me quizzically for instructions.

I pulled on some trousers and then tentatively opened the top half of the stable door leading to the garden, shotgun at the ready.

Whoa! A giant figure suddenly loomed up and I got the fright of my life, hastily stepping back and tripping over Max, then staggering backwards until I slammed into the opposite wall, sprawling in an undignified mess on the floor. I somehow managed to keep the cocked shotgun from hammering into the wall and discharging a shot.

For there, standing in the doorway, casually pulling the grass from our thatched roof, was Nana.

Woken by the commotion, Françoise was sitting up in bed holding Bijou tightly—staring at the apparition in the doorway. Like her, I couldn't believe my eyes. Recovering my composure I got up and walked towards the door and—not really knowing what to do—began talking softly to her.

'Hey, Nana, you scared the hell out of me. What are you doing here, you beautiful girl?'

I will always remember her response. She stretched out her trunk, and I did likewise with my hand as if it was the most natural thing in the world. I stood a little closer, taking care to stay at the edge of her reach so she couldn't grab me, and she moved the tip of her trunk over my T-shirt and then touched me on the head and face. I held my ground, completely entranced by the exhilarating combination of danger and affection. Considering that she couldn't see what she was doing as her eyes were above door level, she was surprisingly gentle.

She then lowered her head and moved forward, almost as if she was trying to come inside, and with that Bijou barked. The spell was broken.

I doubt whether many people have had a ten-foot, five-ton wild elephant trying to squeeze into their room via a narrow door, but, take it from me, it is not a soothing experience.

Bijou and Penny went ballistic, sprinting round the room barking like banshees. Surprised, Nana backed off a few paces and flared her ears.

Alarmed that the dogs were going to be stomped flat, Françoise grabbed Penny and stuffed her into the bottom of a built-in clothes cupboard. She then rushed after Bijou who, assuming the unlikely role as protector of the realm, was now for reasons known only to her having a go at Max, shrieking at him in high-pitched Maltese. I'm convinced that Nana was just too awesome for the tiny poodle to grasp and thus she assumed all the confusion was to be blamed on a bemused Max, who sat patiently ignoring her.

Françoise caught her and, as she was putting the semihysterical pooch into the cupboard, Penny pushed open her door and came back into the fray. She wasn't going to let anything—not even an elephant—get between her and Françoise.

Françoise managed to scramble Penny into her arms again and, as she pushed her back in the cupboard, Bijou bolted out. It was an absolute circus. Eventually we locked all three dogs in the bathroom, and I was able to concentrate on Nana.

With all the commotion she had moved off about ten paces, and it was only then that I saw that the entire herd was with her.

'This is amazing,' I said to Françoise who had joined me at the door. 'This is completely bloody amazing.'

As they moved off to the front of the house I dashed across the lawn to the rangers' quarters to wake David.

He shot up in his bed. 'Poachers again?'

'No. The elephants are here. Come quickly.'

I rushed back to Françoise.

'You'd better wash before you come near me,' she said, pointing at me with feigned revulsion on her face. I looked at her, perplexed, then put my hand on my chest to feel a gooey, sticky mess.

'Your head,' she said, wrinkling her nose. 'It's also all over your head.'

I strode over to the mirror and saw exactly what she meant. I was covered in pachyderm slime. I must have had half a pint of mucous from Nana's trunk spread all over me.

'I'll wash later. David is joining us on the verandah. Let's go and watch.'

I let Max out of the bathroom and the three of us sneaked across the lawn to the rangers' house, keeping a sharp eye out for any stray jumbos, and then went out onto the front verandah. Here, Françoise had a grandstand view of the herd destroying her cherished garden: they pushed over trees, tore apart her favourite bushes and ate every flower they could find. I must say she seemed less entranced by the visit than I was.

David came out and joined us. 'This is unbelievable. They're all here,' he said, eyes straining against the gloom, 'except Mnumzane.'

'No, he's here too. I saw him earlier.'

David found him standing alone in the dark about twenty yards away. 'Poor guy. They tolerate him, but only just. He's got no adult relatives so he's always a johnny-come-lately. I really hope he turns out OK.'

'He's a big boy,' I replied. 'He'll be fine.'

Nana looked up from the garden she was demolishing and, with a bunch of prized shrubs in her mouth, ambled over to us. Max, who had moved a few paces onto the lawn, silently retreated to the relative safety of the verandah and then followed Françoise when I suggested she go inside in case Nana got too close.

We decided to play it safe, and David and I moved back inside the double door and watched her imposing bulk approach. She stopped at the low verandah wall and, for the second time that dark morning, stretched out her trunk to me. She couldn't reach me, so I decided to hang back.

However, I underestimated her persistence—and her strength. Frustrated at my reluctance to come to her, she decided to come to me, trying to squash her vast frame between the two brick pillars that straddled the verandah entrance. This obviously didn't work, and we watched openmouthed as she then gently placed her forehead on the left pillar and gave an exploratory shove.

That certainly got my attention. I remembered what she had done to the gate poles at the boma and had no doubt she would bring the whole verandah roof down if she wanted to. I hastily stepped forward and she stopped shoving and lifted her trunk. Once again she snaked it over the top of my body. It was a good thing I hadn't changed for I received another liberal basting of slime, while the sound of her deep rumbling stomach reverberated through the house, drowning out the thumping of my heart.

Satisfied, she eventually ambled away and joined the rest of the clan as they finished off the few remaining exotic plants in Françoise's now obliterated garden.

Then, suddenly, an eight-week-old kitten of ours slipped past us and, completely oblivious of the herd, walked out onto the lawn. We noticed only after it was too late, and watched in horror—there was nothing we could do to get it back, as it was now among the herd. The elephants got very interested in this tiny thing and all sauntered over for a close inspection. Still the tiny cat didn't react—I think these alien creatures around it were simply too big for it to comprehend, just as they had been for Bijou. Soon it was surrounded, and as the elephants put their trunks out, waving the tips around this tiny curiosity, it would swipe at them with its paw.

Eventually the elephants got tired of it and walked off, leaving the kitten alone on the middle of the lawn.

Except Frankie. She initially walked away, and then, when she was about twenty yards off, she suddenly turned and ran at it. It was a sight I don't think I will ever see again—a five-ton elephant charging a five-ounce cat.

The kitten finally realised something was wrong and skittered back to us just in time.

We stayed up watching until the first hint of light, when Nana moved off with the herd in tow. They were soon eaten up by the dense bush.

I stared after them. A sense of emptiness seeped into my universe.

CHAPTER SEVEN

Each day I made a trip into the bush to spend time with the herd, not only to check on their habits and movements, but also because it was so invigorating being out there with them. Most importantly, I wanted to continue investigating some strange aspects of their communication that intrigued me. I had opened the door to a brave new world and wanted to take advantage of every minute in the bush alone with them.

I was on foot searching for elephants on a hot afternoon when, for a split second, it felt as if the herd was right there, as if I had been daydreaming and walked into them. I quickly gathered myself and looked around, but surprisingly they were nowhere in sight.

A little later it happened again. It was the lightest touch and then it was gone. Again I looked around but there was still no sign of them. Something inexplicable was going on. I was surprised that in all the time I had spent with elephants I had never noticed anything like this before.

So I waited, going back to doing exactly what I had been doing before—just being part of the bush, and not expecting anything to happen. Suddenly I got it again, a strong sense of anticipation that the herd was close by, and with that Nana emerged out of a nearby thicket followed by the others. I was gobsmacked. I had somehow picked up that they were there well before seeing them.

In time I found that this experience also manifested itself in reverse. Sometimes while searching for them I would eventually realise that they were not in the area at all, that they were somewhere else. Not because I couldn't find them, but because the bush felt completely empty of their presence.

After a couple of weeks of practice I started getting the hang of it and, eventually, under the right circumstances, it became easier and easier to find them. Somehow I had become aware that elephants project their presence into an area around them, and that they have control over this, because when they didn't want to be found I could be almost on top of them and pick up nothing at all. A little more experimentation and research and it became clear what was happening. Much like a lion's audible roar, the herd's deep rumblings, although well below human hearing, were permeating the bush for miles around them, and I was somehow picking this up, even though I couldn't hear it. They were letting everything and everyone know where they were in their own elephantine way, in their own language.

One morning, while driving gingerly along a boulder-strewn track, I sensed that the elephants were around and then heard a distinct trumpeting. I stopped and a few minutes later it echoed again, this time considerably closer. Suddenly a breathless Mnumzane lumbered out of the woodland, stopping right in front of the Land Rover, cutting me off and staring intently at me through the windscreen. He had never come that close before.

He was absolutely calm and I sat in the vehicle, my heart beating loudly. Twenty minutes later I was much more relaxed and he was still there, browsing all round the Landy and showing no inclination to leave.

Then the radio squawked into life and he tensed at the guttural invasion of the elemental serenity. It was the office, requesting that I return to base. But as I started pulling off, Mnumzane quickly moved in front of the vehicle and, without malice, deliberately blocked the way. Puzzled, I switched the Land Rover off and he nonchulantly returned to his grazing. However, as soon as I keyed the ignition he again moved into my path, relaxing only when I switched off.

It was clear that he didn't want me to leave. I rolled opened the window. 'Hello, big boy. What's up today?'

He slowly, almost hesitantly, came round to the window, standing a yard or so away, looking down at me with his wise brown eyes. He rolled his head in a leisurely fashion and seemed completely content, emanating easy companionship; I felt as though I was in the presence of an old friend. This was what intrigued me: the emotions that I experienced when I was with them. For it seemed to be their emotions, not mine.

They determined the emotional tone of any encounter. This is exactly what Nana had done to me in the boma. And this is what Mnumzane was doing at this very moment—passing on the sensation of being with an old friend. I recalled too the hostility in the boma when they first arrived. The antipathy reached out across the wires and you could feel it all round the enclosure, whether they were in sight or not.

My attention returned to Mnumzane, and then it dawned that he had chosen me for company over his own kind. I felt absolutely humbled, the hairs on my arm stiff with goose bumps as this colossus towered above me.

He continued feeding, and the nearby trees took a hammering as he moved from one to the next, snapping branches like twigs and stripping the leaves, creating a clear browse line. Every now and again he would lift his massive head and unfurl his trunk at me, sniffing to make sure I was still there. After about another thirty minutes he turned and stepped aside to let the vehicle through.

'Thank you, Mnumzane. See you tomorrow, my friend.'

His tilted his head for a moment and then with that peculiar graceful, swaying gait melted into the bush.

I drove off. When the radio barked with David asking where I was, I didn't answer. I was too awed to speak.

As I SPENT more time with Nana and her charges, they too started coming closer and closer until they were happy grazing near the Land Rover. I was watching them on one occasion when Nana stopped feeding and walked up to the vehicle.

I didn't move. I could sense that she was being friendly so I didn't feel threatened, but I was totally unprepared for what happened next. Infinitely slowly—or so it felt—she stretched her trunk through the window to greet me. It was shockingly intimate and, although she had touched me before both in the boma and when she came up to the house, I believe this was the elephantine equivalent of an affectionate pat. She was letting me know that she was just fine with me being out there with them on their turf.

Even Frankie was becoming more accommodating and would stand quite close to the vehicle with Mabula and Marula. The battle-axe had a soft side, and once even started reaching out with her trunk, but lost her nerve and withdrew as soon as I put my hand up.

Despite the feel-good factor, I never forgot that these were wild elephants, and whenever they came close I manoeuvred the Land Rover continuously to ensure I was never cut off or put in a situation where I felt trapped or uncomfortable.

These encounters gradually became more and more spontaneous, and as the months went by I started getting individual greetings from the rest of the herd. They didn't go as far as putting their trunks in the car as Nana did, but they would come right up and lift them as if waving. What they were doing, of course, was smelling me. I seemed to have been accepted as an honorary member of the group.

But in the process the Land Rover was taking a hell of a beating. Elephants are extremely tactile, always touching, pushing and brushing against each other, and when these hefty jumbos bumped the vehicle, which they did all the time, they left crater-sized dents. They also loved to play with anything that protruded on the vehicle. My wing mirrors were long gone, yanked off as if they were made of paper. Both radio aerials went the same way and I had to have screw-ons fitted, which I could remove before venturing out to meet the herd. The windscreen wipers were stripped off so often that I gave up replacing them, just driving with my head out of the window if it rained.

For some reason they found the texture of metal fascinating and would spend hours feeling it. They loved the heat pinging off the engine, especially if the weather was cold, and would rest their trunks on the hood for long periods. In summer when the hood was searing hot they would lay their trunks down on it and then quickly yank them off, only—inexplicably—to scorch themselves again a few minutes later.

Nana and Frankie, who had both been impregnated before arriving at Thula Thula, were coming to the end of their term and I kept a special eye on them. Elephants have a gestation period of twenty-two months, which meant that, amazingly, they had gone through two dartings and captures, and had been on the run while pregnant without adverse effect.

Every week or two they came up to the house, so we eventually strung an electric wire round Françoise's garden, otherwise they would have trampled it flat and gobbled up the shrubbery again. But even that didn't deter them from visiting: they would stand patiently at the wire until I came down and said hello.

One week I went to Durban on business and on my return was surprised to see all seven elephants outside the house, waiting expectantly as if part of a reception committee. I put it down to coincidence. But it happened again after the next trip, and the next. It soon became obvious that somehow they knew exactly when I was away and when I was coming back.

Then it got . . . well, spooky. I was at the airport in Johannesburg and missed my flight home. Back at Thula Thula, 400 miles away, the herd was on their way up to the house when, as I was later told, they suddenly halted, turned round and retreated into the bush. We later worked out that this happened at exactly the same time as I missed my flight.

The next day they were back at the house as I arrived.

I soon accepted that there was something extremely unusual about all this, something that transcended the limited realm of my understanding. What has been scientifically proven is elephants' incredible communication ability. Elephants transmit infrasound vibrations through unique stomach rumblings that can be received over vast distances. These ultralow frequencies, which cannot be detected by the human ear, oscillate at similar wavelengths to those transmitted by whales, vibrations that some believe quaver across the globe.

But even if those wavelengths vibrate for only hundreds of square miles, it still means elephants are potentially in contact with each other across the African continent. One herd speaks with a neighbouring herd, which in turn connects with another until you have conduits covering their entire habitat.

When scientist Katy Payne, of the Elephant Listening Project at Cornell University, discovered these elephant sound waves it was a startling break-through, one that would change our entire concept of elephant behaviour. There is a concrete link between advanced congenital intelligence and long-distance communication. For example, a frog's communication skills consist solely of primal mating croaks, as its pond constitutes its entire universe. It has no need to expand farther.

But elephants are communicating across vast distances, which shows that these giants of the wilderness are far more developed than we ever believed. They possess a vastly greater intellect than previously thought.

If you doubt this, consider the following: would elephants have evolved such incredible communication abilities just to transmit a series of meaning-less rumbles and grunts? Of course not. Evolution is ruthless: anything not essential to survival withers on the gene-pool vine. Thus it is only reasonable to postulate that elephants are using these advanced long-distance frequen-cies for a specific purpose—to communicate coherently, one to another and herd to herd.

So are they telling each other about what is happening to their world and what we as humans are doing to them? Given their intelligence, there is no doubt in my mind that this is exactly what is happening.

EVEN THOUGH the Ovambos were long gone, poaching continued sporadi-cally and, while we tried our best to stamp it out, losing the odd impala on a game reserve—while galling—was tantamount to shoplifting from a depart-ment store. But then a professional gang targeted us, killing one of our rhinos. It was a southern white rhino female, the one we had distracted Mnumzane from, her gore-congealed snout grotesquely crumpled as both horns had been cleanly severed.

When they returned for a second helping, we went after them, wounding and capturing three of the gang, and turning them over to the police. The battle with poachers is all about bush rumours and reputation. They will always go where pickings are easiest, and the syndicates, many of them employed by the same buyers, all speak to each other. The news of our victory would spread like wildfire and we would be left alone for a while.

After a peaceful few weeks, in which I was able to spend wonderful sessions with the herd, we got the terrible news that Phineas, the gate guard and our prime testifier against the Ovambo guards, had died. A few days later I got more bad news. The Ovambos, who had been tracked down to Durban, had abandoned their jobs in the city and to all intents and purposes disappeared from the face of the earth.

I reported all this to the prosecutor, who looked over the file and said, matter-of-factly, 'I'm sorry, Mr Anthony, but we no longer have a case.' He closed the file and shrugged.

As always with running a game reserve, one problem disappears and another crops up. Our next challenge came with an unexpected visit from our accountant. He had bad news: our money was running out fast. We had not opened the reserve to guests as we were still settling the elephant herd, and so we had been operating on capital with no income coming in.

'You need to increase your bottom line,' he said. 'Unless you do something to start making money, and quickly, there's going to be a problem.'

It wasn't just cash flow. Thanks to a series of interest-rate hikes, our budgets had been thrown into disarray. I scrutinised the numbers from all angles, trying to crunch them this way and that, but to no avail. It seemed as though we had to throw in the towel. The thought of putting Thula Thula on the market made me feel ill.

Then Françoise spoke. 'Let's build the little luxury lodge we've always wanted. We need to attract guests if we want to generate income—and we can't do that without building some accommodation for tourists.'

'No. That means borrowing money at these extortionate rates,' said the accountant. 'That means even more risk.'

He scratched his head, punched a whole lot of figures into his calculator and then looked up at us.

'You know, Françoise may be onto something. Building a small "boutique" guest lodge may sound crazy in the current financial climate, but it actually makes sense. You need to start creating more revenue. And getting guests is one way to do it.'

I stared at the figures gloomily. 'Well, I think the elephants are now settled enough for us to bring in visitors. But we don't have lions yet, and tourists will want to see big cats.'

Françoise looked at me, eyes shimmering with enthusiasm. 'You know what? I will cook to replace the lions. God knows Zululand needs a place with quality food.'

She came from a family of superb cooks and had studied under top French chefs in Paris. Suddenly it all clicked into place.

'You're right,' I said, feeling as though a weight had been yanked off my shoulders. 'A small luxury lodge with a gourmet restaurant would give us an edge. It may just work.' I gave her a hug. 'Let's do it.'

Before we knew it, a beautiful lodge about two miles from our house started to materialise, rustic yet opulent and set in a grove of mature tambotie, marula and acacia trees on the banks of the Nseleni River. The new Thula Thula was being born. By the end of the year, two years after moving there, our boutique lodge was up and running.

There are two types of game-reserve lodges in Africa: those owned by big corporations, and those owned by conservationists who need the lodge so they can earn income to continue their conservation work. We were certainly among the latter. But in any event, Françoise proved to be right, and our lodge, staffed entirely with local Zulus, was soon getting regular bookings. With plenty of hard work and a bit of luck we could be all right.

DAVID LOOKED WORRIED. 'Notice how quiet everything is?' We were sitting on the lawn watching the tree-studded hills of Thula Thula shimmering like a mirage in the early-morning thermals. 'It's the elephants,' he said. 'They've gone to ground . . . we can't find them anywhere. If we hadn't checked the fences, I would've sworn they've broken out.'

'Nah. They're happy here. Those break-out days are gone.'

He shrugged. 'Maybe. But where are they? We're not even seeing signs of them on game drives.'

I pondered this for a while. The herd was now so calm that we had been able to take reserve guests up reasonably close, providing excited nature lovers with excellent photo opportunities.

Then an image of Nana suddenly flashed through my mind, mirroring the last time I had seen her when she had stretched out her trunk into the Landy. Her belly was as swollen as a barrel . . . of course, she must have gone deep into the bush to give birth. As we didn't know the date of conception, we weren't sure exactly when she was due.

I loaded up the Land Rover with a day's supplies and set off, searching as far into the most impenetrable parts of Thula Thula's wilderness as I could get. But there were no fresh signs of them whatsoever. I looked in all the lush feeding areas and their favourite hidey-holes, but again not a trace of them. The largest land mammals had seemingly vanished into thin air.

Well, not quite. Finally, in the early afternoon, I noticed some fresh tracks in an area we call Zulu Graves, a 200-year-old burial ground dating back to the days of King Shaka, founder of the Zulu nation.

'Coooome, Nana!' I called out, singing the words in the timbre they were now used to. 'Coooome, my *babbas* . . .' They always seemed to respond to the Zulu word for 'babies'. In this case, I didn't realise how prophetic my call was.

Suddenly the bush started moving, alive with the unmistakable sound of elephants, and the mixture of thrill, fear and affinity I experienced every time I was in their presence coursed through my veins. I called out again, high on anticipation.

'Coooome, *babbas*.'

Then I saw her. She was standing well off the rough dirt road, watching me but reluctant to advance farther. That's strange, I thought. She normally comes.

She dithered for some time, neither coming forward nor retreating into the bush, almost as if she was uncertain of what to do next. Then I saw why. Standing next to her was a perfectly formed miniature elephant, about two-and-a-half feet high—perhaps a few days old. As I had suspected, she had just given birth. I was looking at the first elephant to be born in our area for over a hundred years.

Not wanting to intrude, I stood there with my heart pounding, wishing I had brought a camera. Then she took a few steps forward, then a few more, and finally started walking slowly towards me with the baby tottering alongside on unsteady feet, its little trunk bobbing like a piece of elastic.

She was still about thirty yards away when suddenly Frankie appeared, ears flared. It was a stark signal for me to back off. I jumped into the Land Rover, reversed to create a safe zone, then switched off and watched.

Gradually the rest of the herd emerged from the bush, eyeing me warily while milling round Nana and the baby.

I watched enthralled as the tactile creatures continually touched and caressed the little one. Even Mnumzane was partially involved, standing at the periphery as close as he was allowed, watching the goings-on.

Then Nana, who had been facing me, started walking up the road. I quickly got in, slammed the vehicle into reverse and edged farther back, acutely aware of the granite bush maxim that you don't go anywhere near an elephant and her baby. But she kept coming, and I figured they wanted to use the road, so I reversed off at right angles into the long grass to allow them to pass well in front of me.

To my absolute surprise, Nana left the road and followed me, with Frankie and the others just a few yards behind. I was no longer in her way, so there was no need for this. They could have just strolled past—this was a conscious decision to come after me, and my heart started thumping over-time. I quickly shoved Max off the front seat onto the floor and threw my jacket over him. 'Stay, boy,' I said as he settled down. 'We have visitors.'

Squinting hard into the sun, I tried to detect any hint of hostility, any edginess that I was intruding in matters maternal. There was none, not even from fierce-tempered and still very pregnant Frankie. All around, the bush breathed peace. It was as if a group decision had been made to come to me.

Nana ambled up to my window and stood towering above the Land Rover, dominating the skyline. Below her was her baby. Incredibly she had brought her newborn to me. I held my breath as her trunk reached into the Land Rover and touched me on the chest, the sandpapery hide somehow as sensitive as silk, then it swivelled back, dropped and touched the little one, a pachyderm introduction. I sat still, stunned by the privilege she was bestowing on me.

'You clever girl,' I said, my voice scratchy. 'What a magnificent baby. I don't know what you call him. But he was born during the first spring showers, so I will call him Mvula.'

Mvula is the Zulu word for rain, synonymous with life for those who live with the land. She seemed to agree and the name stuck.

Then she slowly moved off, leading the herd back the way they had come. Within minutes they'd evaporated into the bush.

Two weeks later they had disappeared again and I made another trek to Zulu Graves. They were there, at exactly the same place and time as before. This time it was Frankie with a perfect new baby. I went through the same backing-off procedure to ensure I didn't invade their space, and eventually she too came to me, herd in tow. However, she didn't stop like Nana had, just doing a cursory walk-past to show off her infant.

'Well done, my beautiful girl,' I said as she slowly came level with the window, maternal pride in full bloom. 'We will call him Ilanga—the sun.'

I shook my head in wonderment. A little over a year ago she had almost killed Françoise and me on the quad bike. Now she was proudly parading her baby. We had travelled a long road together.

That evening they all came up to the house. Frankie's little one had walked nearly four miles through thick bush and she was barely a week old. This time Frankie stood in front of the others right at the wire facing me.

'Hello, girl. Your baby is so beautiful! Really!'

Frankie stood caressing her calf. All the while she was looking directly at me. This was the closest we had come to linking directly with each other.

These almost inconceivable experiences had a sequel several years later when my first grandson was born and the herd came up to the house. I took baby Ethan in my arms and went as near to the patiently waiting elephants as his worried mother would allow. They were only a few yards away. Their trunks went straight up and they all edged closer, intensely focused on the little bundle in my arms, smelling the air to get the scent and rumbling their stomachs excitedly.

I was repaying the compliment to them, introducing them, trusting them with my baby as they had with theirs.

CHAPTER EIGHT

A few days after Ilanga's birth a message arrived from the principal chief in the area saying he wanted to see me, and I drove out to his kraal—homestead—in the country. As was customary, I called out my name and waited at the rustic gate next to the cattle enclosure to be invited in.

Nkosi (Chief) Nkanyiso Biyela was the essential cog in the Royal Zulu project to involve tribes in conservation, and he and I had become good friends. Descended from Zulu royalty, he conducted himself as an aristocrat and, with his beard, handsome wide features and regal pose, looked remarkably like King Goodwill Zwelethini, the reigning monarch of the 10 million-strong Zulu people, to whom he was related.

I was then shown to the *isishayamteto*, the large thatched hut reserved for important matters. Some freshly brewed Zulu beer was placed on the floor, and the *Nkosi*'s aide brought it to me for a sip straight from the traditional calabash. Zulu beer is a wholesome, low-alcohol drink brewed from maize meal and sorghum. While the yeasty ripeness smells like cheesy feet and is guaranteed to turn up a tourist's nose, it's a taste I acquired years ago and this was a particularly good brew. I asked the *Nkosi* to pass my compliments to his wife, the brewmaster.

'Thank you for coming,' he smiled, accentuating the wrinkles on his good-humoured face. 'I want you to attend the tribal court and speak about our game-reserve project. My people must hear directly from you on the matter.'

We left the hut and walked across to the courtroom where the *Nkosi* held council and tried cases once a week.

There were perhaps a hundred people squashed inside the hall, many in traditional clothes, with others standing outside. I was shown to a chair in the front row while the chief went to the podium.

He introduced me and I stood to speak.

The project was sensitive, principally because it involved both actual and potential cattle land. I had already spent the better part of two years holding meetings and workshops throughout the area, explaining the workings of conservation and outlining the benefits that ecotourism would bring to communities in this desperately deprived area.

It was a tough task. Over the past month I had been taking tribal leaders into the Umfolozi reserve and was shocked to discover that most of them had never seen a zebra or giraffe—or much of the other indigenous wildlife so iconic of the continent. This was Africa, their birthright. They lived on the borders of an internationally acclaimed game reserve, yet as a direct result of apartheid they had never been inside. Historically they considered game reserves to be white concepts, mere excuses to seize their land. They had absolutely no idea what conservation was about, or even why the reserve was there. Worst of all, a large chunk of it was traditional tribal territory that had been unilaterally annexed, and this resentment had festered over the generations. It was historically their land and it had been wrested from them with no consultation whatsoever. No wonder they were at best ambivalent about what they perceived to be the white man's concept of conservation.

Looking at the sea of faces before me in the room, I talked about the huge potential the Royal Zulu project promised in improving their lives. I spoke of job opportunities, skills training, wealth creation and education—all which would spring from the project. I appealed to them all to support the project, not only for themselves, but for the sake of their children—and, most importantly, for the sake of the earth, the mother of us all.

But old habits die hard; old resentments burn long. As soon as I finished speaking, cattle owners who coveted the land for their herds sprang to their feet, giving impassioned speeches about the Zulu heritage of keeping cattle. It was all about tradition, and the conservative cattle owners did not like the idea of change. In rural Zululand cattle are a primary form of currency, and they didn't want the status quo to alter, whatever the reasons or benefits.

'How will you pay your *lobola*, your dowry, if there are no cattle? We will have no wives!' one thundered to sustained applause.

'And what about sacrificing cows to the ancestors? Are we now going to use bush pigs?' shouted another to derisive laughter.

The discussion went on in the same vein for the next couple of hours until the *Nkosi* finally put up his hand to end it. Despite obvious opposition, I was not displeased with the outcome of the meeting. I had achieved an important goal. Everybody now knew I had been invited by the *Nkosi* and that he would not have brought me if he was against the project.

But if I was aware of that, so were the cattle owners. The significance of the *Nkosi*'s summons would not be lost on them, and I sensed clashes ahead.

THAT NIGHT, David told me he was resigning to go to England. He had met an attractive young British guest at the lodge, whom I noticed had kept extending her stay.

'It's just "khaki fever", David,' I teased, referring to the well-known attraction uniformed rangers hold for some female guests. 'When you get to England, whatever you do don't take off your uniform or it will all be over.'

Nevertheless he left and it was a massive blow to us. He was an integral part of Thula Thula and had been my right-hand man and friend for so long it was like losing a son. He loved the bush so much—I just couldn't imagine him in rainy England.

The lodge had just opened, and David had been a tremendous help to Françoise in getting it up and running, but she took it with her customary good humour. 'I know guests sometimes steal a towel or soap,' she said, 'but this one stole our ranger.'

Sadly we had to move on, and she advertised in various wildlife publications for a new reserve manager. The first applicant phoned from Cape Town.

'I'd like to come up for the interview but the flight's expensive,' said the caller. 'So if I come all that way and spend all that money, I must get the job.'

This was not the conventional method of impressing potential employers; in fact, it bordered on impertinence. I was about to tell him to take a running jump when I paused for a moment . . . perhaps Brendan Whittington Jones, a name more suited to a firm of august lawyers than a game ranger, could afford a touch of 'unusualness'. He certainly had impressive credentials on paper. But how could I decide on his merits—or, as his phone call suggested, otherwise—without first seeing him? This really intrigued me. All my life, I have been attracted by unusual approaches.

'Do you play sport?' I asked, the question coming out of nowhere.

'Yes. Hockey.'

I mulled this over for a second or two.

'You can start as soon as you get here.'

My father was an international hockey player and, for whatever reason, he always said it was a sport that attracted the right sort of people. I decided to follow his advice.

Brendan arrived a few days later with a battered suitcase containing his sum total of worldly goods. He was an athletically built young man with a shock of strawberry-blond hair, a slow smile and a deliciously sardonic sense of humour. He would need it to sustain him at Thula Thula.

He had a degree in zoology and wildlife management with a major in entomology, and he loved insects with an almost mystic passion. However, he also loved other animals, and his bright attitude and innate sense of fairness quickly won over Françoise and the staff.

It wasn't long before he had adopted an epileptic young wart hog that he called Napoleon. The grandly named hog had been abandoned as an infant by his mother, and we had found him wandering aimlessly on the reserve, lost and alone and easy prey for any passing leopard or hyena. The poor creature, we found out later, sometimes had seizures, which is probably why it had been dumped by its mother. However, Napoleon soon regarded Brendan as his surrogate mother and even joined him in his bed at night. Max also took to Brendan immediately and tried to emulate Napoleon by slipping out of our room one night and getting into the new ranger's bed.

Going into Brendan's room the next morning was an experience. Once you had cut through the fog of sweaty bush clothes, Max's jowly head emerged from the blankets, followed by the quizzical Napoleon, then, a little later, a bleary-eyed Brendan.

Soon after Brendan had settled in I received a surprise call from David. He had just landed in Johannesburg.

'It didn't go well in England, boss. I've just got back to Johannesburg.

I'm stuck in a traffic jam and I hate it. Can I have my job back?'

'But I've just employed someone else.'

'I don't care. You don't have to pay me, I'm coming anyway. I'll be there tonight,' he said, putting down the phone before I could reply.

The summer rains had fallen in torrents over Zululand and the Ntambanana River had burst its banks, cutting off Thula Thula from Empangeni. The roads were quagmires and virtually impassable. David's father drove him as far as he could, to where the Ntambanana was in full spate and completely swamping the concrete bridge. No problem for David: he somehow forged the raging river in the dark on foot and then hiked a sodden twelve miles until he reached Thula Thula.

He arrived sopping wet and covered in mud but ecstatically happy to be back in the bush. Brendan took one look at this drenched, muscular apparition and then shook his head, laughing.

'OK. I'm handling the scientific side and will concentrate on the environmental studies—which you really need to get done. He could have his old job back.'

They complemented each other extremely well and in time they became the closest of friends, so much so that the staff nicknamed them 'Bravid the clone ranger'.

LATE WINTER, with its mantle of copper, chocolate and straw, had cloaked the land. The bush had shed its dense summer foliage and game viewing had soared magnificently for the increasing number of guests who were discovering Thula Thula.

'We must put in burns this year,' I said to David and Brendan. 'We have to open up some of the thicker areas.'

All game reserves burn sections of the land in late winter, primarily because the act-of-God fires that have raged through the countryside since time immemorial are nowadays always extinguished as soon as they take hold. A wilderness needs fire for a variety of reasons, not least to regenerate itself. Dead growth is burned off and the land is reborn as green shoots take root among the fertile ashes.

We always burned our lands late in winter, as all smaller life forms were hibernating and thus safe underground. Burns are done in selected blocks, usually defined by roads and rivers, which act as natural firebreaks. They are called controlled burns, which is a misnomer, for I've yet to see a fire that could safely be labelled 'controlled'. Fires have an inconvenient habit of jumping breaks, and wind shifts can switch their direction in an eye-blink.

Malicious fires—arson, in other words—are even worse because by the time you reach them they are already at inferno stage.

David and Brendan nodded at my instruction. 'When do you want to burn?' asked Brendan, eyeing the skies. It was vital to pick the weather just right, with a mild wind blowing in the direction you want your fire to run.

'Let's select the areas, and if the wind is right do it the day after tomorrow.'

Within hours, the decision was wrested from our hands.

'Fire!' shouted David into the radio with binoculars fixed on the highest hill on the reserve. 'Fire behind Johnny's Lookout! Code Red! Code Red!'

Even with the naked eye I could see the first wisps of smoke streaking crazily into the sky.

Every able-bodied man on the reserve responds immediately to a Code Red: rangers, guards and work teams instantly stop what they are doing and rush to the main house as fast as they can. Those close by sprint; those far off leap into the nearest truck.

Within minutes we had about fifteen men assembled, and David and Brendan gave a quick briefing and organised them into teams. They clambered onto the vehicles, grabbing as many bottles of drinking water as they could carry. It was going to be a hard, thirsty day.

David was in the first truck and braked briefly to pick me up. 'This was started on purpose,' he said as I got in. 'Three men were seen running away. I've sent Bheki and Ngwenya to the other side of the reserve to check for poachers in case it's a diversion.'

Arson was a new poaching tactic—or at least new on Thula Thula. One group had cottoned on to the idea that starting a fire on the far side of the reserve would suck up all our manpower and thus they could hunt on the other side at will. It had worked.

It was a mild day, and as we already had plenty of firebreaks set up in preparation for the controlled backburns to arrest the fire, I wasn't overly concerned and expected we should wrap this one up quickly. Our teams split up, with Brendan's group driving half a mile or so in front of the blaze, ready to set the first backburn, where fires are lit across the front of the approaching fire in order to destroy anything flammable in its path. It's called backburning as the fire is set to burn backwards, towards the main fire coming at it.

'OK, everybody is in place,' barked David into the radio. 'Go!'

Brendan's team immediately lit clumps of grass and started dragging the backburn along the edge of the road, spreading it out wide in front of the fast-advancing flames.

We couldn't have timed it worse. Ten minutes later the wind switched and a squall came screaming out of nowhere, sweeping the backburn away from us to join the main fire already flaring rapidly across the veld. Instead of one fire to fight, we now had two. From a routine drill, we were now in big trouble.

Four hot, sooty hours later our water was finished, our backburns were failing, and the flaming monster was ripping through the bush completely out of control. Watching it effortlessly jump block after block I realised with horror that we were now fighting for the life of Thula Thula itself.

All animals understand fire well. Provided they are not trapped, which can cause blind panic, they watch developments carefully and will either cross a river or backtrack behind the blaze and wait on the previously scorched patches where they know they're safe.

This time the fire was a formidable foe, with the intense heat popping burning clods of grass high into the sky. The Zulus call them *izinyoni*, birds' nests, and these sizzling ashes caught in the superheated vortexes were the dreaded harbingers of the main fire, sparking as they blew ahead and settled in tinder grass, starting new burns every few minutes.

Then incredibly the blaze jumped the river as nimbly as a galloping Derby contender. I stared from my vantage point with mounting despair. We weren't going to make it. This was too big even for professional firemen. With the howling gale rendering the backburns totally useless, my men, armed only with buckets, hand pumps and fire beaters, had precious little chance of winning the day.

The inferno then leaped across another break, and the chaotic gusts swirling round the hill ripped into it, driving massive black-orange flames up the slope below me.

I froze, despite the intense heat. There was a crew directly in the blaze's path that would be frazzled in seconds if we didn't get them out. Without a word David sprang into the Land Rover, flicked the headlights on and drove as fast as he could into the smoke and flames. All I could hear was the vehicle's horn blaring as he drove to let the trapped men know where he was. No one could see anything in the billowing soot.

Ten minutes later he broke back through the smoke. There, sitting on the back of the vehicle, was the missing fire crew. Biyela, our gardener, was calmly smoking a cigarette.

As he jumped off the truck I shouted to him: 'Did you get a light for your *bhema* in there?'

He looked at his cigarette. '*Hau!*' he laughed with delight.

We desperately piled onto the Land Rover and David sped off, just yards in front of the flames. There was only one road out of the area, and as long as David kept his foot to the floor, perhaps we could make it.

As we raced for our lives I scoured the bush below us looking for any sign of the elephants. The fire could not have come at a worse time for Nana and Frankie with their two new babies. I was terrified they would be trapped, and as the situation worsened I could think of little else.

The road took us parallel to the advancing fire, which was now a mile wide, flaring and roaring and leaping on our right, drowning us in toxic fumes and swirling tendrils of smouldering ash.

'The elephants came through here!' shouted David above the crackling bellow of the flames. He pointed to the ground. 'Those tracks are as fresh as hell.'

I motioned for David to stop and quickly got out and felt the dung between thumb and forefinger. It was slimy and wet, sure evidence that they were nearby.

'They stopped here!' I shouted back. 'Probably to rest the babies, but more so I think to let Nana assess the situation. I think she is trying to get to Croc Pools.'

I looked back at the barricade of flame and felt my stomach tighten. Trees were being incinerated whole without pause. Nothing in its path could possibly survive.

'God, please make it, Nana,' I said under my breath as I got back into the vehicle.

David gunned the engine and we bounced down the track as fast as we could. We made the top with the flames minutes behind and the men in the back cheered wildly. But I feared their jubilation was premature. The awful reality was that we were still trapped. There was no road out; the towers of flames were rampant on both sides, about to engulf us within minutes, and for the first time I felt panic slithering into my thoughts.

'Where to?' yelled David. 'Hurry or else we've had it!'

Then in a flash I realised what we had to do. Nana had shown the way.

'Croc Pools!' I shouted back. 'If Nana thinks it's safe enough for the herd it'll be safe enough for us.'

Somehow amid the acrid blinding smoke David found the turnoff, and ten bumpy minutes later we rounded the corner at the pools just as Nana was shepherding the last of her charges into deeper water. She and Frankie were standing at the edge of the dam in the shallows with babies Mvula and Ilanga, making sure the others were safe.

Nana looked up at us, and only then did I understand why they were there. It was not just because of the water: the veld around every game-reserve dam is always overgrazed, and consequently there was little fuel for the fire to consume in a thirty-yard radius.

Clever, clever girl, I thought. In our haste even we hadn't thought of Croc Pools, let alone the natural safety barrier.

We drove to the opposite side, manoeuvred the Land Rover into a bare spot as close to the pools as we could, splashed water over it to cool it down and then waded knee-deep into the water. The coolness and relief were exquisite.

There is a good reason why this particular stretch is called Croc Pools, and I looked around hurriedly. There in the reed beds to our left were two huge crocodiles lying still in the shallows, watching through hooded reptilian eyes. Fortunately, because of the drama of the fire, their major concern was survival; the last thing on their minds was lunch. We would be fine where we were. For good measure, though, I reached down and grabbed Max's collar tightly.

AS HADES ITSELF APPROACHED, we watched yellow-billed kites soaring and swooping down on seared insects fleeing the flames, while flocks of glossy starlings darted in and out of the smoke doing the same. Two large monitor lizards came hurtling out of the bush and splashed headlong into the water next to us. Then a herd of zebras came galloping out of the fumes and stopped. The stallion sniffed the air before changing direction and speeding off with his family. They knew exactly where they were going—they would outpace the fire.

The thick smoke poured from the burning bush over us, obliterating the sun, and we stood together in the surreal murk of midday twilight, broken only by the flaming orange and red of the biggest inferno I have ever seen.

Then it was on us, the heat sizzling and hissing across the water. Yet in that intense theatre I became aware of something transcending the din and fury and chaos. I felt Nana's stomach rumblings roll across the water, a dominating, calming presence. There she stood, towering over the dam, shielding the babies with her body and spraying water over herself.

And then the sizzling abyss swept past and the sun broke bleakly through the murk and mayhem. We stared out at the blackened, apocalyptic landscape, gulping air into smoke-seared lungs. We had made it, thanks to Nana. She had saved us all.

Suddenly the radio came alive. 'David, David, David! Come in! Where the hell are you guys? I've got big problems here, I need men fast.'

It was Brendan.

'We're on our way!' yelled David as we scrambled for the Land Rover. 'Hold on for fifteen minutes. We'll be there.'

'The fire's jumped our boundary,' shouted a soot-blackened Brendan as we arrived. He wiped a grimy paw over his bloodshot eyes. 'It's those bloody chromolaena weeds. The farm next to us had hundreds of acres of that alien rubbish growing thick and wild on their land between us and their sugar cane. The fire's right in the middle of the cane now. No doubt they'll blame us for it.' *Chromolaena odorata* is particularly bad in a fire as it has a high oil content, and as each bush takes light it burns in a bright fireball, destroying trees and bushes close by.

The ever-shifting gusts at last switched favourably, and using that to our advantage Brendan got a last-gasp backburn going and I watched, throat in mouth, as his little fires gobbled up the bush in front of the flaring wall, starving the advancing blaze.

Now we were able to respond to the incessant calls for help on the other side of the reserve, where all the remaining staff had gathered in a last-ditch Alamo-style stand to protect the lodge and houses.

Exhausted to our bones, there we confronted another wall of fire. As the inferno thundered over the hill, and just as it seemed the thatched lodge and our homes were about to be atomised, a phalanx of 4x4s loaded with firefighting equipment came revving through the smoke. Every nearby farmer had heeded our emergency calls and now a wall of water confronted the wall of flames. The cavalry had truly arrived.

Thirty minutes later the seemingly unstoppable holocaust had collapsed. It was now just a mopping-up operation. But, in its wake, it had destroyed more than a third of the reserve.

Fortunately the change of wind, which so nearly wiped us out, also brought the first pre-spring showers. That night a torrent of fresh rain sluiced clean the charred black earth.

The next morning, elephant, rhino, zebra, impala and other animals were out on the burned areas, eating fresh ash as they always do after a fire, absorbing the salts and minerals their bodies craved.

Two weeks later the areas that had been so apocalyptically torched were emerald green. Thanks—unwittingly—to the poachers, the bush clearing was done perfectly and we now had thousands of acres of virgin savannah.

None of us, however, forgot that we had almost lost Thula Thula. Or that we had an elephant to thank for our lives.

CHAPTER NINE

Most of my interactions with the herd had been from a Land Rover. This was deliberate, as I wanted them to get used to vehicles. It worked: our guests had great safaris and photo opportunities as Nana and her family acted as wild elephants do, oblivious of the Land Rovers, provided of course the rangers kept a reasonable distance and respected their privacy.

But now I wanted to do it on foot, not only as I planned to introduce walking safaris, but I wanted the herd to get generally acclimatised to humans in the bush, or else labourers and rangers would always be at risk.

Taking Max with me, I set out to find them for my first experiment. The herd was in an open area, grazing and browsing on the plentiful summer offerings. Nearby there were big trees for me to climb, a somewhat crucial consideration if something went wrong and I had to run for it.

Perfect! I pulled over next to a spreading marula and got out, leaving the Landy's door open for hasty access if necessary. It's vastly different communicating with elephants out in the open on foot compared with doing so from vehicles.

Purposely going upwind so they could get my scent, I zigzagged towards the herd, ambling along as if on a Sunday stroll, Max by my side. Everything was going well until I was about thirty yards away and Frankie's trunk swivelled near the ground as she got my scent. I immediately stopped as she peered myopically at Max and me, but after a short while she ignored us and continued feasting. So far so good, and I continued my erratic approach in their general direction.

Just five paces closer and Frankie suddenly lifted her head sharply and aggressively spread her ears.

Whoa! I stopped, but this time she continued glaring at me until I backed off for five or six paces. That seemed to make her happy and she went back to grazing.

I repeated the process several times over the next hour, a few paces in and then out, and always got the same reaction. Studiously ignored, then angrily confronted. That's interesting, I thought, she has created a boundary: outside I am welcome, inside she gets tetchy.

After checking the distance and making sure I could reach the Land Rover at a run if things went awry, I pushed through the imaginary boundary and walked closer in.

That did it! She swung round, took three aggressive steps towards me with trunk held high, and I backed off—pronto.

I then drove to the other side of the spread-out herd, got out and repeated the process with Nana. The same thing happened, except that Nana would let me get much closer than Frankie did, and her reactions were petulant rather than aggressive.

Over the next weeks, through trial and error, I learned that the herd set a very real, albeit invisible, boundary inside of which nothing—well, no human anyway—could enter. By repeating the exercise in the neighbouring Umfolozi reserve I discovered that generally a bull would tolerate closer intrusions than females. The reason was simple—big bulls are very confident of their ability to defend themselves and allow you to get closer. The smaller the elephants, the less confident they are and the wider the space they demand. A mother and newborn baby away from a herd had the widest boundary.

So far so good, but to have walking safaris on Thula Thula I needed a completely settled herd, otherwise the risk was not worth it. More research was needed, so I did my experiment again, but this time with Vusi, a well-built, fleet-footed young ranger who bravely volunteered to be the guinea pig. All he had to do was repeat my earlier procedure of slowly walking round the herd as I watched their reactions. I dropped him off, estimated the herd's safety boundary, told him where it was, and then told him to walk.

Big mistake. Thankfully Vusi hadn't gone too far when Frankie bristled on full alert and the startled ranger legged it back to the Landy quicker than Carl Lewis.

A bit more experimenting with the brave young man and it became clear that as far as the herd was concerned, the boundary with a stranger was much, much wider.

OK, so how could I get the elephants to draw the boundary in? Not only for me, but for anyone walking on the reserve? I started hanging round the edges of the safety periphery, minding my own business until they got used to me being on foot, and then I slowly tried to move a bit closer. The key to this was patience: it took endless hours of just being there. I also found that ignoring them or facing away attracted less attention.

Although tedious, this was an extremely tense procedure, and I was constantly ready to dash off at a hair-trigger's notice.

Eventually I started to despair. I was making zero progress; even Mnumzane would not come closer while he was with the herd—until one day Nana ambled over in my direction to access a small tree she fancied and shrank the no-go boundary by half without even looking up at me. A little later Frankie and the others joined her.

Then it dawned. As far as the herd was concerned, the boundary was not set in stone. They will reset it—but only when they are good and ready. It has to be their decision. You can't do it. Only they can.

From this I also gleaned another important rule in associating with wild elephants, and that is never to approach them directly, but rather put yourself in their vicinity and, if they want to, they will come closer to you.

Then one day Nana and Mvula were a little way from the herd grazing when she slowly started walking in my direction. Good God! Had she decided to come across to me? She had approached me before in my vehicle, which she knew, and at the boma and the house, but on those occasions I was safe. This time, unless I bolted before she got any closer, I would be stuck out in the open without any escape route whatsoever.

She lumbered on in such a friendly way that I steeled myself and decided to stay and see what happened, gambling that the rest of the elephants would stay away.

Closer and closer she came, with Mvula scampering at her heels. I glanced nervously down at Max, who was watching keenly, dead still. He looked back up at me and suddenly wagged his tail. He hadn't sensed anything dangerous. I hoped his judgment was on track, for this was a very big elephant coming at us.

Suddenly some atavistic survival trigger, vehemently at odds with my decision to stand fast, jerked and the compulsion to flee this gargantuan alien shape exploded within me. I could scarcely breathe. It was all I could do to hold my ground. To this day I don't know how I managed not to bolt. But stay I did and then she was there, her huge form towering above me, obliterating the sky.

I think she sensed my trepidation for she purposefully stopped about five yards away and simply started grazing again, oozing tranquillity. When you are standing five yards away from a wild elephant you are acutely aware of every little thing that goes on around you, especially the elephant's emotional state.

Five minutes later she was still there, and I realised we were actually hanging out together. She was slowly moving around grazing, and I relaxed enough to notice that she had the most graceful table manners. Her trunk would search out and deftly encircle a chosen clod of grass, which she would pluck and delicately tap on her knee to dislodge soil from the roots and gently place in the side of her mouth, leaving just the roots protruding. A gentle clamp of the molars and the roots would drift away while she savoured the morsel. I noticed too that she was very fussy about what she ate, and the scent of each plant would be carefully sampled before being devoured.

Her browsing was no less fascinating. She would adroitly remove the leaves from a young acacia, place them in her mouth and then snap off a branch. As soon as she had finished chewing the leaves, the stem would go in one side of her mouth, like a kebab, and a little while later be ejected on the other, stripped white of all bark.

All the while Mvula would peek at Max and me from behind his mother's tree-trunk legs, occasionally stepping out to get a better look. Max sat silently, occasionally moving a few yards to smell where Nana had been standing, but otherwise was just motionless.

I was intensely focused on this magnificent creature standing so close to me. All the while Nana kept glancing across or staring at me. Every now and then she would turn her massive body slightly towards me, or move her ears almost imperceptibly in my direction. Her occasional deep rumblings vibrated through my body.

So this was how she communicated . . . with her eyes, trunk, stomach rumblings, subtle body movements and, of course, her attitude. And then suddenly I got it. She was trying to get through to me—and like an idiot I hadn't been responding at all!

I looked pointedly at her and said 'Thank you'. The alien words echoed across the silent veld. The effect was immediate. She glanced across and held my gaze for several deep seconds, before returning contentedly to her grazing. It was almost as if she was saying, 'Didn't you see me, what took you so long?'

The final piece of the puzzle clicked perfectly into place. While I had been standing there like a robot, she had been prompting me to accept her presence and give some sign that I recognised her. Yet I had been as stiff and rigid as a plank. When I finally acknowledged her, just with a simple 'thank you', she instantly responded.

I had learned something of this before in dealing with some animals, but that 'eureka' moment with Nana really drove it home to me. I had at last grasped that the essence of communicating with any animal, from a pet dog to a wild elephant, is not so much the reach as the acknowledgment. It's the acknowledgment that does it. In the animal kingdom, communication is a two-way flow, just as it is everywhere else. If you are not signalling to them that their communication has arrived with you then there can be no communication. It's as simple as that.

Eye movements are perhaps the most important. A flick of the eye, a look or the tiniest glance may seem like nothing to humans, but in the animal world it's a very big deal indeed. Attitude, facial expressions (believe me, elephants can smile beautifully) and body language can also be significant.

I looked up to see Frankie leading the bunch across. There was no way I was going to risk that sort of interaction with the entire herd. I immediately took my leave, thanking Nana and telling her I would see her again soon, humbled by the experience.

After Nana had deliberately let me 'hang out' with her and Mvula, everything changed. It was now easy being around them, and even Vusi, my guinea-pig ranger, could walk to within a reasonable distance without reaction. A little later I got four rangers to stroll past the herd a few times as if on a game walk and—*voilà*—we had done it. Even Frankie didn't raise an eyebrow.

Nana had obviously taken her decision and communicated it to the rest of the herd. And from that I learned another important lesson. Previously traumatised wild elephants appeared to regain a degree of faith in new humans once the matriarch has established trust with just one new human. But it must be the matriarch. My close relationship with Mnumzane hadn't altered the herd's attitude towards me one iota, despite the fact that they obviously communicate all the time.

Now, thanks to Nana, guests could walk in the wild near these magnificent creatures, an experience to be savoured for a lifetime. Yet barely two years ago Frankie had tried to kill Peter Hartley, the manager of the Umfolozi reserve, while he was tracking them during the break-out.

That put it all in perspective. We were moving along well.

HOWEVER, IT WASN'T just us 'tracking' them. One evening, when the lodge was full and a candlelit dinner was being served on the verandah to animated guests gushing about the day's bush experiences, Nana suddenly appeared on the lawn right in front of the lodge, herd in tow.

Wow, she is a bit close, I thought, watching her movements carefully. And with that the cry went up.

'Elephant, elephant!' shouted two first-timers who, immediately shushed by more seasoned bush lovers, continued pointing excitedly, while others grabbed for cameras as the whole herd came into view between the lodge and the water hole. It was a great game-viewing experience, but the problem, as I quickly realised, was that they were not going to the water hole, they were coming up towards the lodge.

Elephants operate on the steadfast principle that all other life forms must give way to them, and as far as they were concerned foreign tourists at a sit-down dinner round a swimming pool were no different from a troop of baboons at a water hole.

Nana came towards us without breaking step. I waited until I knew that she was definitely not going to stop or alter course, and whispered loudly to the guests. 'Let's go! Go, go!'

This prompted a rush for the cover of the lodge.

But there are always some people who know better. They're always men, usually in a group, and without fail they choose to pick the most ludicrous occasions to 'prove' their manhood. As the guests hurried off to safety, one particular 'big city' group stayed exactly where they were, lounging exaggeratedly over the dining chairs and feigning indifference as the herd drew nearer.

Frankie looked up and flicked her ears at the unmoving group, who, unable to recognise the customary warning, stayed put. Not getting the appropriate response, she then took a few quick steps towards them, ears flared like a cape and trunk held high.

'Bloody hell!' shouted one. 'She's charging!' Chaos erupted and chairs flew everywhere as the 'macho' men blindly ran into each other in a most unedifying every-man-for-himself stampede.

Satisfied that she had got the respect she deserved from this errant group of primates, Frankie dropped her ears and fell back in behind Nana as they all ambled across the lawn up onto the lodge's game-viewing patio. They stood huge and imposingly out of place, surveying their alien surroundings.

The coast was clear, and, attracted by the strange paraphernalia of the fully decorated dining table, they moved over to explore. The investigation of the delicate fare with their heavy trunks led me to believe that whoever coined the phrase 'a bull in a china shop' had never actually seen an elephant in a china shop. Glasses and plates were swept aside by careless trunks and smashed all over the place. Similarly, candles and holders were tossed on the floor and then the tablecloth was violently yanked from below the remaining crockery and cutlery, completing the debacle.

Discovering that some of the mess was in fact edible, they delicately picked up and ate every bread roll and the salad remnants off the floor, walking over glass shards as if they were paper. The table was roughly shoved aside, cracking open as it did so, and I watched in amazement as first one chair then another went airborne. Tiring of the dinner, they focused on the now obvious purpose of their visit—the swimming pool.

That's what they're here for, I thought. They know about the pool. They've been here before, probably late at night.

The swimming pool was their new water hole. All Nana was doing was simply clearing the guests away as she would do to any other animals so they could drink in peace.

She dropped her huge trunk into the pool and sucked gallons of the sparkling clear water up her elongated prehensile nose. Throwing her head back she delivered it messily to her gaping wrinkled mouth and gave the rumbling go-ahead to the others.

And they had an absolute ball. Mvula, Ilanga and Mandla, to the delight of the now peeking guests, cavorted around, slipping on the tiles, while the larger animals drank their fill and bathed themselves in huge squirts and sprays.

All was sort of going well until suddenly Nana picked up my scent. She slowly swung round and lumbered towards where I was standing next to a thatch pole just inside the lodge patio. I held my ground as she lifted the tip of her dripping-wet trunk across to my chest. The show of affection was understandably misinterpreted by several of the hidden guests, who, by now certain of my impending death, bolted silently for the safety of the bathroom.

'Clever girl! You found the cleanest water on the reserve—and managed to scare the hell out of everyone in the process,' I added, with just a touch of discipline in my voice.

I took a step forward and raised my hand to the body of her trunk and caressed her. 'But you really are frightening the guests and you really do need to leave now.'

Nana decided otherwise, and five minutes later she was still standing there peacefully, while in the background Frankie stared and flicked her ears at any guests who so much as moved from their hiding places.

Nana really needed to go; the lodge certainly wasn't the place for her and her family to visit, so I took my leave of her and backed off three or four paces under the thatch, clapping my hands lightly and encouraging her to move off.

Well, she didn't like that at all. Moving forward she leaned her head on the support pole in front of me, and gave a heave. With that the lodge's whole roof shifted and, controlling my urge to shout, I quickly moved forward again and resumed stroking her trunk and speaking soothingly to her. Incredibly, she leaned forward again, this time with more force and, judging by the melancholic groaning of the timber supports, it seemed that the whole structure was on the verge of collapsing.

I instinctively did the only thing I could and, putting both hands high on her trunk, pushed back on her with all my strength, pleading with her not to destroy our livelihood.

And there we stayed, her leaning on the pole and me pushing back on her for an eternal thirty seconds before she stepped back, shook her head at me and walked away, taking a huge dump on the patio to show her disgust.

It was a game, of course. Nana could have collapsed the pole easily, and my puny effort at pushing her off was but a feather in the wind. She was just making a point.

The rest of the herd followed as she walked down onto the lawn and eventually moseyed off back into the bush.

'Now I know you are completely mad!' shouted an astounded and angry Françoise coming out from behind the bar and ignoring the emerging guests. 'What the hell are you doing? Do you want to die? Oh-là-là, you are crazy, *non*? Pushing an elephant!' And with several loud shouts of '*Merde!*' she stormed off to the kitchen to try to resurrect the dinner.

The next morning we put up a single electric strand round the lodge grounds at adult elephant-head height. To keep Nana happy, we also set up a pipe from an underground well to a drinking trough just outside the wire.

The arrangement works well, and even if the wire is down, they never try to come back to the lodge.

NEXT MORNING, Marion Garaï of the Elephant Management and Owners Association phoned. As before, she had unusual news. 'Can you take another elephant? I've got a fourteen-year-old female that desperately needs a home.'

'What's the problem?'

'It's a real shocker. To give the short version, her entire family have been shot or sold and she's completely alone on a big-five reserve.'

Big-five reserves are so named due to their quarry's reputation as the most dangerous animals to hunt—elephant, black rhino, buffalo, leopard and, of course, lion. An elephant may be a big-fiver—in fact, number one on the list—but a juvenile could not survive for long without the protection of its herd if lions are about. No lion would dare attack an adult tusker, but an adolescent would be relatively easy prey for a pride.

Then Marion added fuel to the fire. 'Even worse, she's been sold to a trophy hunter.'

She delivered that snippet almost as an aside, but she knew it would get me going like nothing else. What type of person would shoot a terrified teenage elephant for a tawdry fireside trophy?

I had to consider the implications of introducing a new elephant into the herd. On the credit side, Nana and her clan were settled and I was pretty confident she would accept another young female into her family.

'I'll take her.'

The hunter was upset—he wanted his cash back. Thankfully a donor of Marion's came to the rescue and paid his blood money. A week later the juvenile was on her way to Thula Thula.

David, Brendan and I prepared for another stint in the bush while our new arrival acclimatised. We even parked the Land Rover in the same position as when the original herd was in quarantine, wondering if Wilma, our industrious bark spider, was still around to weave her silky web on the aerial.

The transport truck arrived in midafternoon and backed into the loading trench. We all craned forward for a good look. It was a good thing I didn't blink, for as the door opened the youngster sprinted straight into the thickest part of the boma's bush. And there she hid for the next few days, coming out only in the dead of night to eat the food we were tossing over the fence. Whenever we crept round trying to get closer, she bolted to the far side as soon as she sensed us. I have never witnessed such terror in an animal. There was no doubt she thought we were going to kill her, just as humans had killed the rest of her family.

Using the techniques I had developed with the herd, I started to talk to her gently, walking round singing and whistling, trying to get her used to me as a benevolent presence. But no matter what I did she remained petrified, rooted to the spot in the densest part of the thicket.

For almost a week there was no change in her emotional tone or attitude, so eventually I decided I needed to interrupt the process. Instead of trying to communicate with her, albeit in a roundabout way, I came up to the fence, picked a spot and just stayed there, saying nothing, doing nothing, just studiously ignoring her. Just being there.

Each morning and each afternoon I chose a different spot, always shifting fractionally closer to her hiding place and repeating the procedure.

The third day prompted a reaction—but not quite what I wished. Instead of being soothed, which was the whole idea, she came out of the bush furiously, charging like a whirlwind at me.

Her charge, as ferocious as it seemed, didn't gel. I could sense that this poor creature, a couple of tons of tusk and flesh that could kill me with a single swipe, had the self-confidence of a mouse. She needed to believe in herself, to know she deserved respect and was a master of the wilderness. She needed to believe she had won the encounter. So I decided to back off with some major theatrics. I decided, counterintuitively in an environment where the strongest survive, to let her know that in this instance she was the boss. It wasn't that hard to fake; if there hadn't been a fence I would've been running for real.

She pulled up at the fence in a cloud of dust and stared, dumbfounded—she had probably never seen humans run before. Any charge had probably been followed by the thunderclap of a rifle. She watched, or rather smelled, my retreat and then swivelled and ran back into the thicket with her trunk held high in victory—the first time I had seen her do that. She had seen off an enemy. More importantly, she had turned fear into action, which, for the moment at least, was a huge improvement.

SHE SLOWLY STARTED getting her nerve back and even began coming out into the open during the day, wandering round the boma. Whenever she emerged from the thicket, I tried to ensure I was around, and she watched with beady eyes as I once more started talking to her and singing at random, alternating that with just being there quietly. During these encounters she never uttered a sound, whether she was intrigued, angry or frightened. A trumpeting elephant is bush music. Yet this distraught creature was as silent as the air, even when coming at us at full tilt.

Then one day she charged while we were pushing food over the fence. For the first time her hunger overrode her fear and she wanted to shoo us away. And for the first time she was trumpeting for all her worth. But instead of a clear, clean call she was honking like a strangled goose.

David and I looked at each other. Now we knew why she had been silent. The poor creature had destroyed her vocal cords, screaming herself hoarse for help, calling for her mother and aunts, lost and pitifully alone in the wilderness while lions circled. She really was a special case.

To try and lighten the mood we affectionately named her ET, short for *enfant terrible*—terrible child.

Even though she started tolerating me marginally more, she was still profoundly unhappy. Her fear and loneliness gloomed the entire boma. Sitting round the campfire at night, usually a time for talk, we too could feel it. Often we just crept into our sleeping-bags and lay on our backs, staring at the stars. She had slid hopelessly back into an abyss of abject despair. Then she slipped farther away and began walking endlessly in large figures of eight, oblivious to her surroundings. She was so depressed I feared she might die of a broken heart, so I changed tactics.

I went looking for the herd. They were the only solution.

'Coooome, Nana, coooome, *hahhas*!' I called out once I saw them. Three hundred yards away Nana looked up, trunk reaching into the air. A few calls later she sourced the direction of my voice and they all started ambling through the bush towards me, pushing easily through wicked thorn veld that would rip human skin to shreds. As they advanced I marvelled at this magnificent herd, these beautiful creatures, fat, grey and glowing, and how content they were with their new youngsters.

Now I needed their help. But first I was going to try something in the wilderness I had never done before: get them to follow me.

As they approached I gently footed the accelerator and eased ahead for about fifty yards and Nana stopped, perplexed at why I was moving off. Then I called them and, after milling about for a bit, she came on. As she got near I drove off again; again she stopped, confused.

Again I called 'Coooome, Nana!' willing her forward, calling out, telling her it was important, that I needed her. The words meant nothing, but would she get the emotion, the urgency?

Amazingly she started following, and eventually just kept on coming without me even calling, her family following fractionally behind. Three miles later we were at the boma.

I stopped thirty yards from the fence and Nana came towards me, paused for a moment, and then saw the youngster. She looked back at me, then went to the fence and emitted a long set of stomach rumbles.

ET was as still as a tree, peering at the herd through the dense foliage, lifting her trunk to get their scent. For some moments this continued. Then suddenly, excited as a teenager at a funfair, she came out and ran to where Nana was standing at the fence. These were the first of her own kind she had seen in a year.

Nana lifted her python-thick trunk over the electric fence, reaching out to ET, who responded by raising her own trunk. I watched entranced as Nana touched the troubled youngster, who demurely acknowledged the matriarch's authority. By now the rest of the inquisitive herd had come forward, and Frankie, who was also tall enough to get her trunk over the electric strand, did so as well. There they all stood, their stomachs rumbling and grumbling in elephant talk.

This went on for an animated twenty minutes as scents and smells were exchanged and introductions made. Nana turned and moved off, deliberately walking past the gate where she had originally pushed over the poles to get out. I had no doubt she was showing ET the exit and simultaneously letting me know to open the gate. I had asked for her help and she had taken her decision: 'Let her out!'

But with all the elephants around we could not get anywhere near the gate and could do no more than watch as ET moved along with them on the inside of the boma fence until she reached the far end and could go no farther. She backtracked up and down the fence, desperately trying to find a way to join them and 'honking' in despair. It was heartbreaking to watch.

But would she allow us? No chance. Every time we approached the gate she thundered across, enraged at our presence, as if we were preventing her from joining the others. Eventually she stopped, exhausted by her continuous stampedes, and we were able to move in and quickly remove the horizontal gate poles and electric strands.

Nana, who had been waiting nearby in thick cover watching all this, then came back out of the bush round the other side of the boma with her family following in single file. Deliberately and slowly, she once more walked past the now open gate. ET rushed out of the thicket but again missed the exit and followed them on the inside of the fence until she could go no farther.

This time Nana didn't wait. She kept going towards the river, and just as I thought we would have to close the boma for the night, ET backtracked to the gate and was gone, her trunk twitching just inches off the ground as she chased after the herd's scent in a gaiting run.

We switched off the power to the boma fences and packed up. Half an hour later as we were driving home we saw them moving away across the open savannah. They were still in single file but already the pecking order had been established. ET was second-last, holding the tail of the elephant in front with Mnumzane behind her. He was resting his trunk on her back as they moved along. Comforting her.

Walt Disney himself could not have scripted a better ending.

CHAPTER TEN

Françoise named our new boutique hotel the Elephant Safari Lodge and threw herself into making a success of it. To keep the bush atmosphere she limited accommodation to just eight luxury chalets spread out round a large thatched lodge on the banks of the Nseleni River. Most courageously she refused to bring in professional help, preferring instead to train Zulus from the next-door village for all positions. The Franco–Zulu communication challenges that ensued provided daily entertainment for David, Brendan and me.

'No TV, no newspapers, no cellphones,' she insisted. 'This must be a natural wilderness experience, an antidote to city life.' And it was, complimented by the fine food that she produced and presented with all her inherent flair. I balanced this against the knowledge that if I hadn't met Françoise, the guests would probably be sitting on log stumps round a fire with a sausage on a stick and using a bush toilet.

The lodge changed everything for both of us. It was a long day, starting with the early-morning game drive and ending only when the last guest went to bed. I quickly learned that in today's world, if you want to survive as a conservationist, you had better learn all about wines and how to mix a good Martini.

Some time previously my old friend *Nkosi* Nkanyiso Biyela had died, succeeded by his son Phiwayinkosi Biyela, a good man of iron integrity and a true leader. But the various tribal factions were taking the opportunity to flex their muscles. I had faced down one accusation of gunrunning and harbouring terrorists, but I knew the cattle cabal was still lurking in the background trying to disrupt the Royal Zulu game reserve project. However, being busy with the introduction of ET into the herd, I couldn't give it much thought.

Then my mother phoned from her office in Empangeni, her voice scratchy with worry. The Security Police had contacted her, trying to get hold of me, and the news they gave her was enough to terrify any mum. Police informers had infiltrated the homestead of a powerful local *induna* of an adjoining tribe who controlled an area to the east of Thula Thula, and had learned that assassins had been hired to kill me.

It had to be the cabal. In fact, according to police information, the rogue *induna* had openly said that if I was bumped off, he and his followers would be able to seize the tribal trust land. Even though it legally belonged to five different clans and I was just the coordinator of the project, they believed that without me involved they could then stake their own claim and torpedo the project.

The police even had the names of the assassins, but said they could not act as their information was only hearsay. However, it came from sufficiently reliable sources to be credible, hence the warning.

I know, and love, Zulu culture. It's part of my daily life. But I also know that if a person does not confront a problem instantly, it can balloon out of all proportion. Fierce blood feuds still flourish today for reasons no one remembers. There was no way round it: this threat had to be confronted head-on, and quickly. I had to pay the *induna* an early visit.

A good friend and extremely courageous old man, Obie Mthethwa, deemed it was too dangerous for me to go to the headman's kraal alone and volunteered to accompany me. Obie was a senior councillor to the Mthethwa clan, one of the most powerful Zulu tribes, and well respected in the area. He and I had become good friends over the years, and his presence would be invaluable.

I told Obie the names of the assassins fingered by the police. He knew them by reputation. '*Tsotsis*,' he said spitting on the ground, using the Zulu pejorative for thugs. That afternoon we drove over rutted tracks deep into rural Zululand to the headman's home.

It was a picturesque village with traditional round thatched huts neatly set out on top of a hill. People were finishing their daily chores, herd boys bringing in cattle, mothers calling in children, everyone preparing for the night. The smell of the evening meals wafted across the village.

We were made to wait almost an hour until it was dark before being summoned into the kraal. This was an ominous sign, and I took much comfort from the fact that Obie was with me. Then we were escorted to the *isishayamteto*, the largest thatch and clay hut, traditionally used for important business.

Shadows pulsed on the walls from a single candle flame, which illuminated the room's simple furnishings, a table and a few flimsy wooden chairs. I noticed immediately the *induna* was alone. This was extremely unusual, as advisers or councillors always accompanied him. We had seen some of them outside while we waited.

Where were they now? What was it he didn't want them to hear?

Then, as is Zulu protocol, we began asking about each other's health, the health of immediate families, and the weather. While all this was going on, I manoeuvred the back of my chair against the wall so no one could sneak behind me. I wanted to face whatever danger came at me headfirst.

Eventually the *induna* asked the nature of our visit. Speaking in Zulu, I explained that the police had told me there was a contract out on my life and that the hit men hired to do the killing came from the *induna*'s tribe.

'*Hau!*' he exclaimed. 'It cannot be my people. They hold you in esteem, Mkhulu. You are the man who is going to bring them jobs with the new game reserve. Why would my people want to kill you?'

'I know that is true. But the police say their information is also true. They say it is not all of your people that want to kill me—just a gang of *tsotsis*. They believe that if they kill me, they can grab the land for themselves.' I paused for an instant and stared directly at him. 'But we both know that it is not my land. It belongs to other tribes as well, and killing me will not make it someone else's land.'

Again the headman appeared astonished, and I was starting to wonder if perhaps the police information was off-target. He was either innocent or a virtuoso liar.

At that moment we heard a car pull up outside, followed by the traditional shout of identification. About ten minutes later four men walked in. They had come to report to their *induna*. He told them to sit, and they squatted on the floor on their haunches, keeping their heads lower than their boss's as a token of respect.

As they settled down, Obie grabbed my arm and whispered in English, 'These are the killers—these are the *tsotsis* whose names the police gave us.'

At first they did not recognise Obie and me in the dim light. But as their eyes grew accustomed to the shadows the sudden startled looks on their faces betrayed them.

I was wearing a bulky bush jacket and in my pocket was a cocked 9mm pistol. My hand slid round the butt. I gently thumbed off the safety catch and pointed it through the jacket straight at the closest man's belly.

Obie leaned forward, grabbed my arm hard again and whispered, 'This is very dangerous. We have to get out. Now!'

But there was no way out. I looked directly at the *induna*, hand tight on my gun.

'The police have given me the names of the men out to kill me. Those names are the same as these four men.' I pointed at them with my free hand. 'Does that mean you know what the police are speaking about?'

The contract killers sprang up and started shouting at me. 'You lie—you have no business here!'

I jumped up to face them, keeping a firm grip on the pistol. Obie also stood up, squared his shoulders and glared at the assassins.

'Stop this noise!' he commanded with iron authority. 'This is the *induna*'s house. He must speak—not you. You must show respect.'

The *induna* gestured at us all to sit down.

'Mhkulu, I do not know where you get these stories from. I do not know why the police are lying about me. I do not know anything of what you say. All I know is that there is no killing list with your name on. Anyone who says so is a liar.'

The words were smooth, but there was no doubt his attitude had radically changed. He was now in full retreat, indirectly accusing me of calling him a liar—a heinous slur in Zulu culture.

'Then why is it that these men walk so easily into your house?' I persisted. 'Does this not seem suspicious?'

There was no answer.

'And what's more,' I added, 'the police know I have come to talk to you. My visit here has been fully reported to them and they await our return. If Obie Mthethwa or I do not get back home this night, they will know what happened here. They will find you and you will suffer the full consequences of your actions.'

Again, the *induna* did not reply.

I knew it was unlikely I would be able to shoot my way out, but I certainly would take a couple of these cutthroats with me in the attempt. Perhaps that would also give Obie a chance to make a break for it.

I focused on the candle, just a stride away on the floor. If anything started I planned to kick it over and plunge the room into darkness. The *induna* was also looking at the candle, no doubt harbouring the exact same thoughts. He then looked at me.

We both knew why.

The *induna* broke his stare first. I could see he was now unnerved—particularly as he now believed that the police knew we were at his kraal. He had been completely caught out by the arrival of the assassins and the fact that we knew who they were. All his earlier denials were now obvious lies.

The contract killers looked at their boss, unsure of what to do. The four of them could easily overpower us, but, as experienced gunmen, they could also tell I had a primed pistol underneath my jacket. If they went for their guns, I would get the first shot off, straight at the nearest man. It was now up to their boss what he wanted to do.

The stand-off was tense and silent. Nobody moved.

I finally provided the *induna* with a way out.

'I am not calling you a liar. Maybe the police are, but that is a matter between you and them. All I want is your word of honour that I am in no danger from any man of your tribe—any man who answers to you.'

He quickly agreed, grabbing the escape line with both hands. He gave his assurance that I would not be harmed by any of his people, stressing again that there was no hit list.

That was all I needed. The main aim of the meeting had been achieved. The *induna* would be a fool to go back on his word of honour. He also knew he would be the prime suspect if anything happened to me—whether he was guilty or not.

As a parting shot I said our discussion would also be reported to *Nkosi* at the next council meeting. We then left. When we got in the car, Obie let out a large 'whoosh' of breath. We had just stared death in the face, and I looked at the old man with gratitude and respect. He had the courage of a lion and had put his life on the line for the purest motive of all—friendship.

With that, the cabal was now in full retreat. They knew the police had infiltrated them, that there was an informer in their midst. I also had assurance from one of their leaders that I would not be harmed. It remained to see whether he would keep his word.

I WAS KEEN to see how ET was settling in with her new family, and spent as much time as I could out in the bush near them. However, it didn't take long to experience the consequence of her inclusion. While Nana and Frankie were as content as always with me in the vicinity, ET went ballistic if I came near, especially if I climbed out of the Land Rover.

On the plus side, she may have been mad as a snake at me, but she was absolutely ecstatic with her new family. And to see this previously depressed creature joyously bonding with the other youngsters, pushing, pulling and playing with all the physicality that elephants so enjoy, was simply phenomenal.

Mnumzane was still on the periphery, being shooed off if he got too close, and somewhat bemusedly watching the newcomer being accepted. I reckon I was his best friend—albeit by default—and whenever I drove past he would trumpet and chase after me. I always stopped, and he would then block the road, trapping me for as long as possible as he browsed round the Land Rover. I loved our 'chats' together, but this didn't disguise his loneliness or unease. His newfound relationship with me, however expedient, was not natural and concerned me a little. Elephant bulls are always pushed out of the herd at puberty, and eventually they get over the rejection and join a loose affiliation with other bachelors.

However, we didn't have other bachelors, and to bring in a dominant bull to provide Mnumzane with a father figure was not something KZN Wildlife would consider. New rules set by KZN Wildlife demanded a larger reserve for elephant bulls, and it would have to wait for the Royal Zulu project to come to fruition. Mnumzane was thus stuck in no-man's-land, living partly on his own and partly on the fringes of the herd.

MAX WAS AT THE LODGE dozing on the patio when he sat up sharply, sniffing the air. His nose followed the drift of the unfamiliar scent and quickly found its source. It was a bush pig, a hulking boar making his way rapidly across the lawn towards the lodge.

A bush pig is about two to three feet high, roughly the same size as a wart hog, and to the untrained eye the two are easily confused. But that's where the similarities end. A wart hog has semicircular tusks and frightens easily. A bush pig is feral to its core and should be avoided at all costs in the wild. It's a real fighter, weighing up to 140 pounds, and uses its lower incisor teeth with devastating effect on any creature that underestimates it.

Max didn't know about that. There was an intruder in his territory and the wiry hair on his back sprung up. Characteristically, he did not bark, and at a sprint he cut the boar off, forcing it to confront this unusual threat. I say unusual because even a couple of hungry hyenas will avoid taking on a healthy adult bush pig.

The big boar held his ground, refusing to back off, and Max took up the challenge and began circling, looking for an opening. Then the boar did a little mock charge, and that was that. The fighting genes of Max's terrier forebears kicked in and he smashed into the big pig in a silent, full-blooded charge.

I was at the main house at the time, but fortunately David was nearby. Realising the terrible danger Max was in, he forgot his own safety and ran at them screaming.

Too late. The boar swivelled and rammed his shovel-shaped head under Max's gut, hoisting him high into the air. As Max toppled over, the boar was on him, slashing with dagger-like incisors at his soft underbelly.

Max scrambled up and came at him again, fast and furious, but the boar, using his superior bulk, bowled him over once more, hacking with lethal accuracy as Max rolled, desperately trying to regain his footing.

They parted briefly, the pig standing firm, with Max—his pelt now slick with blood—circling warily, again looking for an opening. Both were completely oblivious to David's yelling.

Once again Max propelled himself forward and after another vicious melee the bush pig, unaccustomed to such determination from an obviously smaller opponent, retreated into the bush.

Seconds later Max proudly trotted back to David, ignoring the fact that his stomach had been gutted and his entrails were hanging out in ropes.

'Max, you're a complete bloody mess,' said David, shocked rigid. He picked the dog up, making sure the slithering intestines followed, and sprinted to the Land Rover. He didn't ease his foot once in the twenty miles to Empangeni, slamming on the brakes only at the surgery. The vet said it was touch-and-go when he began operating.

I visited Max regularly, and a few days later he was back at Thula Thula, tail thumping away. Except for a fence of stitches in his stomach, he looked none the worse for wear.

THE NUMEROUS NYALA grazing literally outside our bedrooms reminded me that we had a surplus of these magnificent antelope on the reserve, and I decided we should sell some to other reserves for breeding purposes. A phone call later and a game-capture specialist was on Thula Thula darting the animals, which we placed in a boma with plenty of fresh water and alfalfa until we had reached the sell-off quota. We would then load them into the customised van and he would deliver them to the buyer.

Brendan was overseeing the capture and radioed to say we had our quota and the van would be leaving the next morning. It had been a long day. I was tired and looking forward to an early night. Thus I was surprised to be woken by a radio call from Brendan at 11 p.m. 'You'd better come down. The most amazing thing has just happened.'

I cursed, pulled on some clothes and drove down to where Brendan and the team were waiting. The first thing I noticed was that the door to the boma was open.

'Where're the nyala? Surely you didn't load at night!'

I turned to the game-capture man, who was standing with his staff staring at the open door. He looked as though he had seen a ghost.

'You're not going to believe what happened,' he said.

'Try me!' My patience was somewhat aggravated by lack of sleep.

'We were sitting by the boma, just chatting,' he said, 'when we heard the elephants come. A couple of minutes later Nana led the herd into the clearing and so we moved right off—some quicker than others.' He grinned, looking at Brendan. 'We thought she had smelled the alfalfa.

'Then the herd stopped, as if on instruction. Nana walked alone to the boma. Just as we thought she would smash through the fence, she stopped at the gate. It wasn't locked because the clasps were folded and were secure enough. She started fiddling with the clasps and got one open, then the other, and then pulled open the door. We couldn't believe it, she actually opened the damn door!'

He looked around as the others nodded.

'Then, instead of going for the alfalfa, she stood back and waited. After a few seconds a nyala came out, then another, and before we knew it they had all found the gap and were gone.

'The weirdest thing is that as the last one fled, Nana just walked off and the others followed. They didn't even go for the alfalfa—a pile of prime chow and they just ignored it.'

It took me a bit of time to digest it, but there was no doubt they were telling the truth. There were elephant tracks all round the boma, and Nana had thoughtfully dumped a steaming pile at the gate as a smoking gun. The lock clasps were also all smothered in trunk slime.

How or why this occurred remains a mystery for some, but it's a mystery only if you grant elephants limited intelligence. Nana, once a prisoner of the boma herself, had decided to let the nyala go free. It is as simple—or complicated, if you like—as that. There can be no other explanation.

Of course, the next day we had to start all over again, capturing fresh nyala, and this time we strung an electric wire round the nyala boma to prevent another rescue mission. To me the trouble was worth it. I had never felt prouder of my elephants.

MISTAKES IN THE BUSH have a nasty habit of being irrevocable. As I have no desire to be a dead hero, I usually err on the side of caution by a healthy margin. Whenever I park the Land Rover near the herd, I always make sure I have a clear escape route. Or when I approach them on foot, I never venture too far from the vehicle.

But this time I was caught unawares. By the time I saw her coming, it was too late. ET was hurtling out of the bush like a missile, and there was no way I could scramble to the safety of my vehicle in time. I was in big trouble and had no option but to defy every instinct and force myself to hold my ground and face the charge.

All of a sudden, Nana, who was about twenty yards off, moved across at surprising speed for her bulk and blocked the charge with the broadside of her body. The youngster stumbled, knocked off course. Clumsily regaining her balance, she meekly swung round and lumbered to the back of the herd while Nana resumed grazing as if nothing had happened.

I stared, barely breathing, pulling body, soul and nerves back together. That was certainly a first for me. In fact I had never heard of it before, a wild elephant blocking the charge of another to protect a human. Nana was radically changing the way I perceived her species. Over the past few weeks I had been wondering how to handle ET's constant aggression, and here Nana was doing it for me, disciplining and teaching her not to hurt me.

Before ET's arrival I had planned to start cutting back on my visits to the herd. My sole purpose was to rehabilitate them in the bush so that they remained truly wild elephants, supremely at peace in their environment. It was crucial that the herd learn to trust a human, but only one, which would stop them from attacking people but still keep them feral. Wild elephants that become accustomed to people generally can be extremely dangerous and unpredictable at times and almost always end up getting shot. For this reason I never interacted with the herd for guests.

My idea was that once the herd was settled I would gradually withdraw until there was no more contact. I believed I was almost there.

But ET was still a major problem. While the herd comfortably tolerated Land Rovers cruising past, ignoring them as they should, ET was doing the exact opposite. She regularly made threatening moves and gestures at the vehicles, which was alarming guests and upsetting the rangers. Wilderness bush walks, a favourite with visitors, had become too dangerous.

Consequently, I needed to spend more time with her. So instead of cutting back contact as planned, I was now forced to increase visits—with some alarming consequences, as I'd just experienced. Through trial and error I had learned several techniques for how to approach an aggressive elephant. One was to ignore it, which always worked wonders as it piqued curiosity and usually prompted a benign acknowledgment of my presence. But that would come later. In ET's case, I decided she needed to be challenged directly. Mind games would probably not work here. I had to confront her head-on.

Obviously I couldn't start on foot. Instead I would approach in the Land Rover, stop in front of her and wait, engine idling. Then as she started charging and got close I would jerk the Landy forward at her once or twice in rapid succession, just a yard or so, but usually that was all that was needed to make her stop and think again. To an elephant this is in effect saying, 'I'm not messing about here; I'm ready to fight—so back off.'

This move always broke her aggression. Then I would lean out of the window and say in a firm but comforting voice, 'ET, if you don't mess with me we can be friends.' I was in effect demonstrating my position of seniority in the herd's hierarchy.

I SWEAR Nana and Frankie knew exactly what I was doing with their unruly adopted child. If not, how do you explain the one instance when ET came at me out of the blue from a thicket, once again catching me on foot without an escape route? On this occasion I hadn't seen her, as I had approached cautiously, thinking she was with the herd in the thick bush ahead when, unusually, she was on her own on the flank.

This time it was Frankie who reacted. She sprinted up alongside the galloping youngster and placed her tusks on ET's rump, forcing her hindquarters sideways and down onto the ground. As ET sprawled in a cloud of dust, Frankie stood over her until ET clambered up in that ungainly way that fallen elephants do and sulked off to join the others. To have Frankie, once the definition of aggression, protect me was little short of phenomenal.

The third full-blooded charge was broken by Nana in a somewhat bizarre way. I was about thirty yards from the herd, just sitting and watching, when ET started stampeding towards me. But to do so she had to run right past Nana, who was grazing a little way ahead. She heard the youngster coming and tilted her head. As ET began building up a head of steam Nana lifted her trunk and held a pose, waiting. When ET drew level she reached out and touched her ever so gently right in the middle of her forehead with the tip of her trunk.

ET stopped dead, as if she had been whacked on the skull with a sledge-hammer. Yet all Nana had done was almost caress her.

I BELIEVED ET was making progress, and that working day after day with her was making a difference. I was wrong: it was effective only when she was actually with the herd.

Two junior rangers and I were following the elephants on foot from a safe distance. ET knew she stood no chance against me with the matriarch and her deputy around, so she decided to become clandestine. She broke away from the herd, surreptitiously moving off to the side as the rest moved on, and waited in ambush. Before I knew it, I heard that awful sound as the bush came alive with snapping branches and she galloped into the clearing, dipping her head in the awesome way that elephants do when they start a charge—her prize at last within grasp without Nana or Frankie to stop her.

I looked at the out-of-reach Land Rover behind me, and shouted at the rangers, 'She's coming! Don't move! It's OK . . . it's OK! Just don't move.'

Running away can all too easily convert a bluff into something lethal, and even though it's possibly the most frightening thing to do, a mock charge must be confronted at all costs.

'No! No!' I yelled at ET as she came on at us. 'No!' I raised my arms above my head screaming at her as she thundered on.

At the last moment she broke off, swinging away at a lumbering gait, trunk high. Then despairingly I watched her turn a wide circle and head back at us. 'She's coming again! Stand still . . . don't move. Don't move!'

But I was talking to myself. The two young rangers, having just wit-nessed their first-ever up-close-and-personal elephant charge, decided that to stand still for another was the most insane notion ever conceived. They disappeared so fast I thought they had been beamed up to the top of the giant fig tree next to us.

That was fine for them, but it left me confronting a charging ET alone. Emboldened after seeing the rangers ignominiously bolting and clambering up the tree—the very scenario I was trying to prevent—she was now more determined to press home her advantage.

The moment I know that a situation with elephants has got hairy is when pandemonium switches into slow motion and the shrieking, mind-numbing fear leaches out of my body and is replaced by a blissful calmness. And so it was this time. I watched abstractly as I screamed at her until she was virtually on top of me. Then at the last moment she went swinging past. I can tell you that she very nearly didn't pull out of that one.

She kept running, joining the herd who were ambling across to see what all the fuss was about. Personally, I thought that Nana could have reacted a little quicker.

I looked up at the two tree-hugging rangers. 'Jeez! That was unbelievable!' shouted one from the top of the tree, giving me a thumbs up. 'I can't believe you made it. I thought you were a goner. Well done.'

Yeah, thanks.

The herd was getting closer. The still-agitated ET was with them, so I hurried over to the Land Rover and drove under the giant fig, deliberately calling Nana and Frankie to me. I smiled coldly at the arboreal rangers who were watching the elephants milling beneath them and gave a return thumbs up. I was going to teach these two runners a bush lesson, all right. By fleeing, they had put all of our lives at risk.

I talked to the elephants for a short while, jokingly chiding Nana for not being there for me and sternly chastising ET for what had happened. Then I drove off, leaving the two rangers to make their own way home.

THE AFTERNOON BREEZE barely stirred the bush. Mnumzane was browsing languidly at the side of the road and I was about ten yards away, hanging around the Land Rover saying whatever came into my mind, both of us content in each other's company. It was one of those days where you just felt like hanging out with friends, basking in the warmth of sunshine and companionship. As usual, I did all the talking and he did all the eating. But something had changed and I couldn't quite put my finger on it.

Max, who by now was used to having Mnumzane around, and in turn was totally ignored by Mnumzane, was under the Landy making a bed for himself, digging a hole to get to the cooler earth just below the surface.

I had come to see Mnumzane because one of the rangers had told me of a huge ruckus among the herd that morning, complete with prolonged trumpeting and screaming that could be heard a mile away. I had just checked on the herd, who were grazing a few miles off, and they seemed fine. Mnumzane too seemed calm . . . but there was something else: his once palpable insecurity seemed to have vanished. He seemed to have a new-found sense of self-assurance.

He walked over to me and I studied this huge bull elephant now standing not ten feet away. There was no doubt that he seemed more confident, more deliberate. Towering as he was almost five feet above me, I needed every ounce of the warmth and reassurance he dished out so liberally when we were together.

He then lifted his trunk towards me. That was extremely unusual. Mnumzane seldom put out his trunk and, if he did, he didn't really like me to touch it. He then turned and moved off into the savannah. That too was different, for I was always first to leave our bush sessions, with Mnumzane invariably trying to block my way by standing in front of the Land Rover.

Later on, as the setting sun cloaked the hills in reds and gold, the elephants visited the water hole just in front of the electric strand at the lodge. This was always a treat for the guests. The herd was drinking and splashing around when Mnumzane emerged imperiously out of the bush, and with head held high he moved swiftly towards the water hole. Now that's strange, I thought. Usually he skulks round the periphery.

Nana looked up and saw him, and—to my intense surprise—with a deep rumbling she moved off, calling the herd away. Too late. Mnumzane, picking up speed, singled out Frankie—the herd's prize fighter—and smashed into her so hard that the blow thundered across the bush, smashing her backwards and very nearly tossing her over. Seeing what had just happened to their champion, the other elephants started scurrying off with indecent haste. I caught my breath as Mnumzane swung to face Nana, ears spread wide, head held high.

She quickly placed herself between the threat and her precious family and then turned and started reversing towards him, which is not just a sign of subservience, but also bracing herself to best absorb the pending meteoric impact. I winced as she took the colossal charge on her flank.

Satisfied that he now had the respect he believed he deserved, Mnumzane eased over to the water and drank alone, as was his right as the new alpha elephant. From now on he would always drink first.

Mnumzane had come of age.

Things changed on the reserve after that. Mnumzane no longer gave way to vehicles—or anything else, for that matter. He would stand in the middle of the road and finish whatever he was doing before moving off in his own sweet time. Any attempt to move him along would result in a warning, which was always heeded. Nobody wanted to be charged by the new big boss of the reserve. Everybody quickly learned bull-elephant etiquette, namely to stay the hell away from him, or else.

CHAPTER ELEVEN

'**B**oss! Boss come in, come in!'
It was David on the two-way radio.
'Standing by. What's up?'

'There's a big mistake here,' said David, using the word 'mistake' in the Zulu context to mean a major problem. 'I'm up from the Kudu River crossing. You better get here quickly. We have another dead rhino.'

'What the hell happened?'

'Come and see for yourself. You're not going to like this at all.'

Puzzled, I picked up my .303, half expecting an encounter with poachers—as had happened after our first dead rhino—and ran for the Land Rover with Max at my heels. What was it that David wouldn't tell me over the radio?

The crossing was about twenty minutes away, and driving along my focus was snapped by Mnumzane loping off across the veld to the left of me. Despite my haste I stopped. Something was wrong; I could sense it from where I was sitting.

I called out, but instead of coming to me he lifted his head, spread his ears and deliberately moved off. Every new elephant reaction intrigues me, and normally I would have trailed him to find out what was going on, but David was sitting on a crisis.

Ten minutes later I reached David. He was squatting on his haunches in the shade of a young umbrella thorn tree, staring sombrely at the ground. I pulled up next to him and got out.

'What happened?' I asked, looking around. 'Where's the rhino?'

He stood up slowly. Then without a word he led the way down an old game path and into a clearing. In the middle lay the grey carcass. It was a female. From the look of it, her death was recent.

Her horns were still intact. That surprised me, for I had expected them to be butchered off, the first thing poachers do. I walked up to the immense, motionless body, looking for bullet wounds. There were none.

I then scrutinised the corpse for signs of disease or other causes of death, while David stood by silently. Except for some nasty fresh gashes on her armour-plated hide, she had been strong and healthy. In fact, even in death she was so imposing that I half expected her suddenly to rise up.

I was so transfixed by the grim scenario that I hadn't taken in my wider surroundings, and as I looked up I was shocked. A tornado could not have done more damage. Bushes were crushed and trees lay sprawled and splintered all over the place. The earth itself had been gouged up, as if a bulldozer had lost its driver and careered round recklessly flattening everything. Nothing made sense; no rhino could cause such havoc. What the hell was going on?

I instinctively looked to the ground for answers. Rhino spoor was everywhere, heavy and mobile in its tread, yet unnatural in its twisting and turning patterns. Then elephant tracks jumped out at me: big, heavy pachyderm spoor, the earth-wrenching footprints of an enraged bull in full cry.

Mnumzane!

'He killed her, boss.' David's words whispered into my thoughts. 'She put up a helluva fight but she was no match for him—never could be.'

I nodded, not wanting to believe it. But the tracks told the story as clearly as if they were on celluloid.

'I once saw an elephant kill a black rhino at a water hole in Namibia,' David continued, almost as if speaking to himself. 'He hammered the rhino so hard it shot back thirty feet and went down and died right there, its ribs smashed in, collapsed over the heart. And then the elephant put his front foot on the body and stood over it rolling it back and forth as if it was a plaything. The power was just unbelievable.'

He stared at the corpse in front of us. 'I know she is a white, and nearly twice the size of a black rhino. But still, she stood no chance.'

A slight flicker in the bush to my left caught my eye. Max had also seen it, and following his gaze through the foliage I caught sight of a camouflaged rhino calf silently watching from a nearby thicket. It was Heidi, the dead animal's two-year-old daughter. A rhino will fight to the death under most circumstances—but with a youngster, that's an absolute given.

'What a mess!' I fumed, my words echoing harshly through the bush. 'What the hell did he do that for? The bloody idiot!'

'We . . . we're not going to shoot him, are we?' said David, and for the first time I realised why he had been so downcast.

Shoot Mnumzane? The words shocked me rigid.

In most South African reserves, aggressive young male elephants, orphaned by earlier culls and reared without sage supervision of adult bulls, have gratuitously killed rhino before. And when they did, retribution by reserve owners was swift and harsh. Rhinos in South Africa are rare and very expensive. Elephants, on the other hand, are more plentiful and comparatively cheap. Past records indicated that elephants that killed rhino before would do so again.

'No,' I said trying to reassure myself. 'We're not going to shoot him. But we really have a bloody big problem on our hands.'

I paused, trying to get my head round it all. 'Let's unpick this slowly. First, Heidi will be fine, she's big enough to survive without a mother and she will herd with the other rhinos.'

'Secondly, we have to retrieve the horns,' interrupted David. 'The word will get out and they're too much of a temptation for poachers. I'll get the men and we'll cut them out, clean them and put them in the safe.'

I nodded. 'Good thinking. I'll phone Wildlife and let them know what happened. They're not going to be too happy with the way she died but I'll speak to them about that as well. The carcass will stay here and there'll be plenty of hyena and vulture activity for guests.'

David started to say something, then paused. 'Boss . . .' again almost whispering, 'you're sure we're not going to shoot Mnumzane?'

The million-dollar question. One I didn't have an answer for, so I decided to wing it. 'I'll go and find him and see what I can do. I need to spend time with him and try to work something out.'

IT WAS AN HOUR and a half before I found him browsing near the Gwala Gwala Dam. I approached slowly, pulled up about thirty-five yards away, got out and leaned on the Land Rover's hood, unsheathing my binoculars. I didn't call him, but he knew full well I was there. Instead he chose to ignore me and continue grazing, which is exactly what I wanted. A swift scan of his body with the binoculars showed the scars of battle.

Congealed blood revealed he had been gored in the chest, and there were deep grazes on his flanks. This had not been a brief encounter: the battle had been fierce and long, probably because he was not used to fighting.

Eventually he finished eating and looked at me.

'Mnumzane!' I called out sharply, focusing on intonation rather than volume. 'Have you any idea of what you have done, you bloody fool?'

I had never used that furious tone with him before. I needed him to understand I was extremely angry about the death of the rhino.

'This is a big problem, for you, for me, and for everyone. What the hell got into you?'

He stood motionless as I berated him, and it was only after I drove off that I saw him move away.

From then on I tracked him daily, staying near him as much as possible, but if he approached I deliberately drove off. I could see that bugged him.

Then I found him near the scene of the crime. I immediately drove to the rotting remains of the rhino still festering on the ground and, making sure I was upwind of the intolerable smell and in a good getaway position, I gently called him.

Obviously pleased to hear my usual genial tone of voice again, he ambled over towards me. I let him keep coming until he was right at the kill, and then leaned out the window and lambasted him in a firm and steady voice, stopping only when he uncharacteristically turned and walked off in the opposite direction.

There are those who will say that all of this is nonsense, that of course elephants don't understand, that I was wasting my time. But I believe Mnumzane got the message. He never hassled a rhino again, let alone killed one. Our relationship returned to normal and he would again emerge for a chat in the bush, like in the old days.

He even, on occasion, came up to the house to say hello, and there was no one more relieved than David.

Shortly after this incident David knocked on my door, looking a little doleful. 'Can I come in, boss?'

'Sure. What's up?'

'My mum and dad are leaving the country. They're going to England. Emigrating.'

You could've knocked me over with a twig. David's family came from pioneer Zululand stock and were well respected throughout the area. This must have been a big decision for them.

David noticed my astonishment and smiled, almost embarrassedly.

'That's not all. I'm going with them.'

This time I nearly did fall over. If I couldn't visualise David's family in England, I could do so even less with him. He was a man of the bush— something of which there is precious short supply in England. The wild was his element.

'You're sure it's not khaki fever again?' I asked smiling, remembering that the last time he had left us was for a pretty English tourist who fancied hunky game rangers. That lasted only a month or so before he came charging back, asking for his old job.

He laughed. 'Not this time. It's been a terribly difficult decision, and as much as I'm going to miss Thula Thula, I have to go with my folks.'

He left later that month. Being David, with his inextinguishable cheerfulness, he soon landed on his feet in Britain and joined the British Army. He was selected for an officer's course at Sandhurst Military Academy and did a tour of combat duty in Afghanistan as an officer—where I believe his outdoor prowess and natural leadership skills helped make him a superb officer.

THERE HADN'T BEEN a snakebite on Thula Thula for nearly sixty years. This is not surprising, for although Thula Thula, like every African game reserve, slithers with serpents of all types and sizes, these intriguing reptiles avoid man for three very good reasons. First, they don't want to get stomped on and will move away long before you get near them; secondly, humans are not their prey; thirdly, they have long since learned that we kill them for no other reason than that they exist.

There is, however, one snake that is a law unto itself.

'We've just lost two zebra,' said John Tinley, the veteran ranger from KZN Wildlife's Fundimvelo reserve next door, who had stopped in for a cup of tea one day. 'Both dead, right next to the water hole, fat and healthy, no sign of disease and not a mark on them.'

He looked at me, waiting for comment, testing me.

'OK, what happened?' I said, taking the game out of it.

'Black mamba,' he replied, blowing on his hot tea. 'Killed both of them. Stone dead.'

'You're sure?' I asked, amazed at what I was hearing. A zebra can weigh 600 pounds. 'Two of them?'

'The spoor doesn't lie. There isn't another snake that leaves marks like that. You may have seen the fire. I burned the bodies. Don't want anybody or anything eating that meat, not even hyena.'

As soon as he was gone I got on the phone, and after a couple of calls I sank back in my chair. He was right, a mamba can easily kill a zebra; in fact, it can kill almost anything—lion, towering kudu bulls . . . even giraffe have been dropped. As for humans, one mamba packs enough venom to kill up to forty adults.

The mamba grows up to fifteen feet long and is as thick as a man's arm. It's also the fastest snake around, sometimes hurtling along with its head three or four feet above the ground. To complete the picture, it's not actually black, more of a metal grey. However, the inside of its mouth is pitch-black, hence its name. The sight of a mamba gliding with its coffin-shaped head raised several feet above a grassy plain is the ultimate game-viewing experience.

'Code Red! Snakebite at the main house!' the rapid-fire call came out of the Landy's radio as Brendan and I were parked out in the bush with the herd, watching Mandla playfully wrestling with the much larger Mabula.

Brendan's reply was cool and calculated, just what was needed to calm the panic. 'Who was bitten, where, and what type of snake?'

'It's the new trainee, Brett. We think it may be a black mamba. We're trying to find it so we can do the identification.'

As the voice trailed off I felt sick to my stomach. Black mamba! Flooring the Land Rover's accelerator I rushed back to the house.

The drive from Thula Thula to the hospital in Empangeni was about forty minutes, way too long in the case of a full-dose mamba bite, which can kill in half that time. Also, we didn't keep mamba serum on the reserve. In fact, nobody keeps it on hand, for the simple reason that it goes rotten after a short time. Sometimes the serum could kill you as surely as a bite.

I pulled into the parking area behind our house in a billow of dust, leaped out and ran over to where the rangers were gathered round a large dead snake, hoping against hope that it wasn't a mamba.

It was.

'Who took Brett to hospital?' I asked.

'Nobody. He wanted to pack a suitcase, but we're going to take him now,' came the absurd reply from another trainee.

'What! Does he know it was a bloody mamba?'

'Yes, but it was only a small bite on the finger.'

'Only on the finger! For Pete's sake—it's a mamba! It doesn't matter where it bit!'

I couldn't believe what I was hearing and yelled at Brett, who had just appeared from his room carrying a suitcase as if he was going on holiday, to hurry. I then took a deep breath: the last thing I wanted to do was panic the kid. 'Brett,' I said quietly. 'Please don't run as it will only increase your heart rate and spread the venom. This is a mamba. OK? Show me the bite.'

He gave me his hand and there on the finger was the fang wound. I exhaled with relief. Just one puncture.

'Did it hook into you?' I asked.

'No. It just struck at me and moved off, but my finger is sore as hell.'

'Are your hands tingling?'

'Yes, strange you should say that. So are my toes.'

Tingling in the extremities are the first symptoms of a mamba bite, a sure sign that venom was in his system.

'That's from the bite. You must go right now. Just slow everything down—your breathing—everything down.'

I then turned to the driver. 'Go like hell,' I hissed, making sure Brett couldn't hear me. He nodded and sped off.

I looked at my watch. Six precious minutes had passed since the bite, and we had no way of knowing how much venom was in his body. If it was anything more than just a scratch we had to accept that he would be dead before they got halfway to town. I put the horrible thought of the phone call I'd have to make to his family out of my mind.

'What happened?' I asked Bheki.

'*Ayish*, that young man doesn't listen. Brett took a broom to the mamba. I told him this snake was too dangerous and that you use the broom only for *mfezi* but he did not listen. I tried to stop him but it was too late and the mamba bit him.'

'Who shot the mamba?'

'I did. It was very angry and moving everywhere.'

Ten minutes later I picked up my cellphone and dialled the driver.

'How's Brett?'

'Sweating and salivating. But he's still coherent and it's not far to the hospital. I'm just about flying at this speed.'

'OK, let us know when the doctor is with him.'

As bad as it sounded, I knew from that rudimentary diagnosis that Brett had a slim chance. He was in for a rough ride, but if the bite had been lethal he would already have started vomiting and losing muscle control, the final fatal symptoms.

Ten minutes later we heard from the driver that they had arrived at the hospital. Brett was rushed into intensive care and stayed there for two days fighting for his life. And it wasn't even a bite, just a fang fractionally nicking a finger.

We have often seen mambas since that incident, all of them just carrying on with their lives, but that bite will go down as our only snake crisis in over half a century. And it's a story the trainees will never forget.

CHAPTER TWELVE

Nana's oldest daughter Nandi's swollen stomach was attracting a lot of finger-pointing. Nandi—which means 'good and nice'—had blossomed into a dignified, confident twenty-two-year-old adult. And she was very pregnant. The father, of course, was Mnumzane, and with Nandi ballooning like a keg we were expecting a big, healthy baby. The whole of Thula Thula was waiting for the good news.

Johnny, a likable new ranger, was first on the scene when it happened. Blond, good-looking in a boyish way, he had recently joined us, and his easy smile made him popular with the staff. He radioed me and, surprisingly, didn't sound that happy. 'We've just found Nandi down near the river but we can't see the baby properly. The herd's gathered round and won't let us anywhere near her. They're acting most peculiarly.'

It was midmorning and the sun was already blistering down, the mercury topping 100 degrees and still soaring as I leaned over and groped for my cap on the Land Rover's floor. Max sat in the passenger seat, head out of the window, tongue lapping at the passing scents.

I found Johnny and Brendan easily enough. Just as Johnny had said, fifty yards away stood the herd, gathered in an unusually tightly knit group. I walked off into the bush, trying to find a spot from where I could get a peek. At last I got a glimpse of the brand-new baby on the ground in the middle.

The fact that it was lying down sent alarms jangling. The infant should already be on its feet. All wildlife in Africa stands, albeit tottering, almost instantly after birth, and for a good reason. A vulnerable baby on the ground is asking for trouble, an easy snack for predators. Even elephants, with their formidable bulk, move away as soon as possible from a birth spot, where the smell of the placenta will attract lurking carnivores.

I started approaching on a slow zigzag path, carefully watching to see how close they would let me come. I got to about twenty yards away when Frankie caught a glimpse of me and rose to her full height, taking two or three menacing steps forward until she recognised who it was and dropped her ears. But she held her position, and from her demeanour I could tell she didn't want me any nearer. Once she was sure I had got the message, she turned back to the baby lying in front of her.

I could now at least see what was going on, and my heart sank. The little one was desperately attempting to stand up. Time and time again it tried, patiently lifted by the trunks of its mother Nandi, its grandmother and matriarch Nana and its aunt Frankie. But, heartbreakingly, each time as it rose halfway up it fell back, only to start trying to get up again.

With absolutely rotten luck the baby was lying in the middle of the only open space among the trees, right out in the blazing sun. To compound matters, it was also off the grass, lying on hot sand.

There was nothing to do but wait, watch and hope, so I sent the rangers off on other duties, got myself a bottle of water from the Land Rover and found a shady spot as close as I could to the elephants. I called out so they all knew I was with them, and Max and I settled in for the duration.

I took out my binoculars and managed to focus in on the baby. It was a girl, and the problem was starkly evident. Her front feet were deformed; they had folded over themselves in the womb, and each time she tried to stand, she was doing so on her ankles.

An hour later her attempts to stand were becoming weaker and less frequent. This did not deter her mother and aunts who, if anything, renewed their efforts with each failure. By worming their trunks under the little body, they lifted the baby up and held her on her feet for minutes at a time, then gently let her down, only for her to crumple to the ground again.

Elephants always find deep shade on hot days and stay there. Their humungous bodies generate a lot of heat, so keeping cool is a priority. Looking up at the sun I cursed. It was firing full-strength, and these poor animals were in its direct blast. Yet none shied off for the shade of the trees, barely twenty yards away. There they stood in the midday solar furnace guarding the baby, even the younger elephants, which were doing little more than watching. Nor did any leave for a long draught of cool water at the river less than half a mile away. Their sail-like ears were flapping overtime, fanning as much air as they could, attempting to regulate their overheated bodies.

It was only then I noticed that the baby was permanently in the shade of its mother's and aunts' shadows. Not just because they happened to be standing round her, but because they were taking conscious care to do so. They took turns to act as an umbrella, slowly shifting their positions to ensure the struggling infant was always out of direct heat.

Three hours later and the baby started to succumb. She didn't want to be moved any more and trumpeted pitifully when family trunks lifted her yet one more time. She was fatigued beyond measure.

Eventually Nana stopped and they all just stood there, waiting with the baby lying motionless in front of them. With the binoculars I could see she was still breathing and fast asleep, but she must be nearing the end. In the late afternoon, when the day cooled fractionally, the elephants started again worming their trunks in tandem underneath the baby, trying to lift her onto her feet. They kept it up until nightfall, failing agonisingly each time.

I drove the Land Rover in closer and beamed the headlights onto the scene to help them. Towards midnight the baby was pitifully weakened and I resigned myself to the fact that not only was she not going to make it, but there was nothing I could do. I called out a goodbye, saying I would be back, then drove back up to the house and went to bed.

WHEN I RETURNED the next morning as dawn broke, incredibly the herd was still there, still trying to get the now almost completely limp body to stand. I couldn't believe it; the dedication of these magnificent creatures was beyond comprehension.

The sun started climbing, and by 10 a.m. I knew we were in for another steamer. And still they continued. But what more could they do? A few minutes later, Nana backed off a few paces for the first time and stood alone, as if assessing the situation. She then turned and walked off without stopping. Her trunk dragged, her shoulders stooped, a portrait of dejection. The decision had been made.

The rest of the herd followed and were soon out of sight on their way to the river to slake their arid gullets. Yet Nandi stayed behind. As the mother, she would be there to the end, protecting her baby from hyenas or other predators. She manoeuvred her crippled daughter in her shadow and stood still, head down, exhausted, resigned to her first-born's fate, but determined to protect the infant to its last breath.

I studied the baby through the binoculars, certain she was now dead. Then, almost imperceptibly, I saw her head move. My heart pounded with excitement. She's still alive, barely, but still alive! And with the herd gone, a crazy plan came into my head.

I sped to the house and loaded a large open container on the back of the Landy, filled it with water, and threw in a bag of fresh-hewn alfalfa. Brendan summoned the rangers.

'OK, guys,' I said, 'this is what's going to happen. I'm going to try and reverse right up to Nandi, give her a sniff of the water and alfalfa, and then slowly move off to try and draw her away from the baby. There's a sharp corner in the road about thirty yards off, and if she follows me there she won't be able to see the baby. That's when I want you guys to sneak in from the other side, get in as fast as possible, load up the baby and then speed off.'

I paused for a moment, scanning their eager faces. 'But if Nandi sees you taking her baby, there won't be enough of you left for me to bury. So if you're not comfortable with this, don't come with me. It's bloody dangerous. I really mean that.'

There wasn't a moment's hesitation. 'We're in,' was the unanimous reply.

I nodded my thanks. 'OK. I've phoned the vet and he's on his way with a drip as the baby will be dangerously dehydrated. I have also put a mattress in the back of the truck for her.'

We quickly drove down, got into position, went over every aspect of the plan once again and then tested our radios. 'We've got only one chance,' I reminded them. I got in the Land Rover and started reversing towards Nandi, calling out to her as I got closer to let her know it was me.

Her first reaction was uncharacteristic. She moved between the baby and the approaching Landy and then charged, trumpeting loudly to scare me away, kicking up a cloud of dust. She had never come at me before so I stopped and, leaning out of my window, started talking to her soothingly. As she walked back, I gently started reversing again, only to prompt another noisy stampede. I kept talking, and the third time I reversed her charge had no steam at all. As she turned away I saw her physically jolt as she got the intoxicating scent of fresh water and food. She stopped and turned.

'Come, *babba*,' I called gently, 'come, beautiful girl, come on. You're hot; you haven't had anything to eat and drink for twenty-four hours. Come to me.'

She paused and then tentatively took a few steps forward, ears straight out, hesitantly checking everything, and then walked up and dipped her trunk into the trough and sucked in a yard of water, which she squirted messily into her mouth, spilling it everywhere in her haste. Then her screaming thirst kicked in and she started drinking insatiably off the back of the vehicle, and I moved forward very, very slowly. Without hesitation she followed, slugging bucketfuls as we moved along. She still hadn't stopped when we were round the corner, out of sight of her baby. I couldn't believe how thirsty she was.

'Go, go, go!' I whispered into the radio. 'I can't see you so neither can she. Let me know as soon as you've done it.'

I continued talking to Nandi, calming her with my voice, keeping her distracted, and then for what it was worth I told her what we were doing. 'Unless I take your baby, she's going to die. You know that and I know that. So when you get back she won't be there, but if we save her, I will bring her back to you. That I promise.'

A few minutes later, a breathless call came through. 'We've got her. She's alive—just—we're moving off.'

Nandi drank every drop of water and then tucked into the alfalfa. When she finished, she looked at me in acknowledgment and walked back to where she had left the baby. I reversed, following her, and watched as she started nosing the ground. With her superb sense of smell she would have immediately caught the scent of the rangers. After sniffing round for a few long minutes, she stopped for a while and turned and slowly moved off in the direction of the herd.

When I arrived back at the house the baby was lying motionless in the shade on the grass and the vet was connecting the second drip bucket into a bulging vein behind her ear.

'She's barely alive and very dehydrated,' he said. 'The next few hours will tell if she makes it.'

I walked off and made a few phone calls, querying what milk substitute a wild orphaned baby elephant would take. We needed the exact mixture, and, having got the formula from Daphne Sheldrick's famous animal orphanage in Kenya, I sent a ranger into town to buy the ingredients as well as some jumbo-sized bottles and the largest teats on the market.

While I did that, Françoise started converting the spare bedroom, right next to ours, into an elephant nursery, scattering straw in bales on the floor and putting down a firm mattress for her to sleep on.

'She'll be comfortable here,' she said with more confidence than I felt. 'We will name her Thula.'

I nodded. It was a good name.

I went back to the baby and inspected her front feet crumpled in on themselves.

'She's huge,' said the vet. 'In fact, too big. That's why her feet were squashed back, folded over in the womb. She was simply too big for the womb and her feet had nowhere further to grow. But the bones aren't broken and the muscles are intact and loose enough to manipulate into the correct position. Hopefully they'll straighten out with some exercise.'

He walked round her. 'Her ears are also worrying me a touch. They've been burned raw by the sun and sand and she may lose the fringes. I'll prescribe some ointment.'

Just then Thula lifted her head quite strongly. A drip is a wonderful thing with wildlife. Sometimes it works so powerfully it's like watching a resurrection, and so it was with Thula, who was suddenly springing back from the dead. Holding the drip we carried her to her new room. She instantly fell asleep on the mattress.

JOHNNY, OUR NEW RANGER, stayed with her and would do so round the clock until she was healed. Orphaned elephant babies need the constant companionship of a surrogate mother, otherwise they rapidly decline, both physically and emotionally. Johnny, who had joined us a only few months back, was going to be just that—a chore he accepted with relish.

The next morning Thula took her first giant-sized bottle from him and drank the lot.

The following day she was much stronger, so Johnny fashioned a canvas sling and hung it from the towering marula tree on the lawn. We gently carried Thula out and she protested vigorously as we slipped the sling under her stomach, lifting her up while Johnny eased her deformed limbs forward. We then lowered her with her feet in the correct position.

Our plan was simple: we had to strengthen her front feet or else she would die. And there she stood, wobbling like a wino at first, but gradually gaining some balance. We repeated this procedure several times between meals, and by evening she was standing steadily with the aid of the sling.

I whistled softly. Perhaps we could save her after all—perhaps I would be able to keep my pledge to the herd. The progress this tough little infant had made in one day alone was inspirational.

The next morning she started taking uncertain steps supported by the sling and by the third day she was walking unaccompanied, albeit slowly with plenty of fall-downs. Yet she never complained. Within a week, although limping badly, this gallant little creature was hobbling round the lawn with Biyela following behind carrying a large golf umbrella to protect her from the sun. She had captured our gardener's heart: from now on it seemed his mission in life was to keep the sun off her frazzled skin.

As the days went on she got stronger, the limp receded and, apart from having some trouble lying down, she was healing beautifully. Although I instructed everyone that she should never be alone, I could have saved my breath. Johnny was always there, and off-duty staff members regularly came up to the house to make a fuss of her. Everyone loved her indomitable spirit, and Thula flourished under this utter devotion from her new family. Even Max, who would fight any creature for no reason other than that it was there, followed her round the lawn on her daily walks, his tail wagging like a feather in a gale.

ONE LATE AFTERNOON, a sunset in paradise, I was walking her through the bush outside the garden, acclimatising her to the longer grasses, thorns and trees that would be her future home, when suddenly I saw the herd appear at the top of the road. They had decided to come to the house for one of their periodic visits.

The timing could not have been worse. I was well outside the electric wire, and to be caught with Thula in the open by her mother could be calamitous. 'Come, Thula! Come, my girl!' I called anxiously, looking over my shoulder, and made for the gate about a hundred yards away as fast as I could urge her. We made it to the gate just and I pushed Thula on to Biyela, and then turned to watch the herd coming up.

They drew level a few minutes later, and Nana's trunk shot up like a periscope, the tip switching until she fixated on where Thula had just ambled out of sight. She turned, her stomach rumbling. Nandi and Frankie joined her, scenting the air, analysing floating molecules Thula had left behind. They were like detectives at a crime scene and eased forward just inches from the electric wire.

I went to Thula's room, made sure she was closed in with Johnny and called a ranger to double-check the fence's current. I then waited, guiltily hoping they would leave. Twenty minutes later they were still there and I felt I could no longer ignore them.

I felt that at least I should let them know their baby was alive. I went to Thula's room, took my shirt off and swabbed it over her body, put it back on and wiped my hands and arms all along her. I then walked back down to the fence and called them.

Nana came over first, and as her trunk swept just above the single electric wire in greeting I stretched my hand out as I usually do. The response was remarkable. The tip of her trunk paused at my hand and for an instant she went rigid. Then her trunk twitched as she sucked in every particle of scent. I offered both hands and she snuffled up my shirt and vacuumed every inch. Nandi the mother and Frankie the aunt stood on either side, trunks snaking as they too got the olfactory messages that Thula was alive and close by.

All the while I talked to them, telling them how we helped Thula cheat death, what was wrong with her feet and why she had to stay with me for a little longer. I told them we all loved her because she was so brave and happy. I told them that they could be proud of their newest little member, who was fighting so gamely for her life.

I have long since lost my self-consciousness at chatting away to elephants like some eccentric. Eventually they read whatever they could from my shirt, and these three magnificent elephants stood there before me like a judicial panel assessing the evidence.

After much deliberation they moved off, and I could tell that they were relaxed and unconcerned. I felt a glow ignite inside me. They trusted me, and I knew I could not let them down.

The weeks passed by and Thula was doing well. Then one morning Johnny called from her room and I went through to find her struggling to get up.

'She can't stand,' he said, pushing and pulling to try and get her on her feet. I climbed in and helped. Eventually, after much squealing and protesting, we had her up; she tottered briefly and then limped outside.

Biyela and his umbrella appeared as if by magic, and as we followed I saw that it took far longer for her to loosen up. So did Biyela, and I watched as he spoke softly into her weakly flapping ears. I then realised she wasn't just stiff in her feet, she was in acute pain—not just the pain she had bravely fought before. Her right hip also seemed to be troubling her. This was serious, and I called the vet.

'Short of doing X-rays, which is impossible, I can't tell you what's wrong,' he said. 'Nothing is broken but she has badly inflamed joints in her front feet and hip, probably caused by the way she walks.'

He then prescribed some anti-inflammatories and instructed us to ease off on long walks.

The next morning it was the same. She couldn't stand up. The same happened the following day. My concern rocketed.

A week later she wouldn't drink. Johnny, unshaven, wild-haired, despondent and soaked in the milk he was trying to coax her to take, summed it up. 'She's just not interested any more.'

I looked at Thula, who was in the corner facing the wall, apathetically swinging her trunk. Three days later a disconsolate Johnny told us she slipped away during the night while he was with her.

Thula's death affected everybody, particularly Françoise. I have never seen her sob so bitterly. We've had lots of animals living with us over the years and we were close to them all, but with Thula it was different. Her cheerful disposition, her refusal to surrender until the last few days, inspired everyone. She had shown us how life could be joyous despite pain, meaningful despite brevity. How life should be lived for the moment.

Her body was taken out into the veld by Johnny to allow nature to take its course.

I later went out alone, found the herd and led them to the carcass. They gathered round. This time I didn't speak; I didn't have to tell them what had happened. For a moment I held my head in my hands; I had let them down. When I looked up, Nana was outside the vehicle's window, her trunk raised in her familiar greeting pose. Next to her was Nandi. They then moved off.

The remnants of Thula's skeleton are still there, and every now and again Nana leads her family past and they stop, sniffing and pushing the bones around with their trunks, in an elephant remembrance ritual.

DEATH IS CYCLICAL, a fact that is witnessed more in the natural order of the wild than anywhere else. Max was now fourteen years old and too old to accompany me into the bush he loved so much. The old warrior, who had survived poachers, snakes and feral pigs double his size, had succumbed to chronic arthritis in his hind legs. As I left him in his basket one morning, he tottered about in a vain attempt to come with me. A year back he would have been in the front seat of the Land Rover. Now he could barely walk.

It's funny how these things happen so quickly. It seemed just yesterday that we were out and about on our adventures. I had been told by Françoise and a few close friends that I had to face up to the fact Max was no longer bulletproof. He was very old and in pain and not going to last much longer, but it was just too dire for me to consider. I countered that with the best veterinary help I could get, but recently he had all but stopped taking food, and sadly I knew his time was coming.

Even so, I was surprised to see Leotti the vet's car parked in the driveway so early in the morning as I got back from a dawn delivery of Cape buffalo. She was sitting next to Max's basket in the lounge. With her was Françoise. She seemed on the verge of tears.

Max tried to get up to greet me and fell over. He tried again. He wouldn't give up.

Leotti, who had treated Max throughout his numerous escapades, including regular *mfezi* fights, looked at me and shook her head.

'Françoise phoned me about this. Lawrence . . . I know you love him but'—
she gestured at my loyal friend—'it would be cruelty for this to carry on.'

She stood up. 'I will be waiting outside.'

As she closed the door, Françoise put her arms round me and squeezed
for a moment. Then she too left.

I sat down next to my beautiful boy, lifted his rugged, spade-shaped head
onto my knee and he looked up, licking my hand as he always did. Even in
his dotage he was still a superb creature.

He and I sat for about ten minutes, just us together. I told him how much
I loved him, how much I had learned from his courage and loyalty, and that
the life in him was eternal. I braced myself and called out to Leotti.

She came in. The syringe was ready, and she administered that loneliest
of all injections as I held him.

I was inconsolable.

Chapter Thirteen

About a month later I woke at 6 a.m. with something shaking my
shoulder. It was Françoise.

'So,' she said in that delightful way the French have of being as
direct as an arrow, 'exactly when are we are going to get married, *mon chéri*?'

I rubbed the sleep out of my eyes. This was serious talk at this time of the
morning and I had to engage my brain quickly.

'Married? We are married. We're married under common law. In fact,
we've been married longer and happier than most people I know. Almost
two decades—a lifetime,' I added with a yawning grin to rob any unin-
tended offence.

'Well, I don't understand this common-law business you always talk
about. You just say that to do me out of a real wedding,' she replied, throwing
a cushion at me with a laugh that didn't fully disguise her intent.

'I know. That's because you turned me down.'

'Turned you down? When, exactly?'

'So you don't remember? That shows just how important it was to you.'

Despite the easy banter, we both knew that the eternal battle of the sexes
was in full cry, and I was thankful when the two-way radio blared at that

moment, giving me a pretext to rush off into the reserve. We'd been together for years and all of a sudden the marriage 'thing' was rearing its head. It wasn't that we weren't happy. Françoise was absolutely fantastic, and we had been crazily in love since the moment we met, but my theory in life is that if things ain't broke, why fix them?

I kissed her as I left. She responded cheerfully . . . and I breathed a sigh of relief. A month later I had to go to England, and while I was away my mother called, asking when I would be returning as she wanted me to meet some government officials that would be visiting Zululand. I gave her the date and she phoned back to say the meeting was confirmed. I let Françoise know and a few days later caught the flight home.

I arrived on a Saturday morning and, after greeting the herd, who came as always to meet me at the fence, walked up to the house.

Françoise went off to prepare the lodge for the VIPs and I dressed in my best khakis— well, OK, the ones with the fewest holes in them. I walked to the front entrance of the lodge, battered bush cap in hand, and peeked inside. It was packed to the rafters. There was a wedding going on. This was nothing unusual, as we often do functions for overseas couples wanting a romantic Zulu wedding in the bush. I turned and walked out, bumping into my mum. I kissed her hello.

'Where are your VIPs? We can't meet them here. There's a wedding going on.'

She nodded, with a strange smile on her face. Something was up.

'Hang on . . . who is getting married? Anyone we know?'

'You are.'

There must be some innate male defence mechanism that kicks in at moments like this. I heard the two words she said, but neither registered.

'OK, well, let's take the government people to the conference centre, out of the way of all this stuff.'

She shook her head, still with that strange smile. There were no government officials. My mum linked her arm through mine and we walked into the thatched lounge. Everyone stood and started clapping.

This was an ambush, a joint operation planned by both Françoise's family and my own. I recognised her best friend from Paris sitting with the Anthonys in pride of place. They must have been in on this for some time: you don't fly out from Europe just like that.

My staff were also dressed in their Sunday best, standing in rows facing the minister at the podium, smiling and clapping. They too had been co-conspirators. The only person surprised was me—although stunned would be a more apt description.

Now, my mother is the dearest person in the world to me. If it was anyone else I would have at least put up an argument. But she had me firmly by the arm, surrendering her grip only when I was at the podium and shaking hands with the minister.

There I stood, smiling and nodding at guests, feeling like an absolute idiot, knowing that they knew I had been utterly outmanoeuvred. I looked down at my shoes, which gleamed back at me. Even they had been shined in a way I had never seen before. I then looked up to see Ngwenya and Bheki in their finery nudging each other and grinning hugely.

For the polygamous Zulus, what was taking place was contrary to their way of life and they were never going to let me live this down. Indeed, my Zulu friends are genuinely mystified that I don't have multiple wives. You white men are so stupid, they would say. Everybody knows one woman is too strong for one man. Two are even worse as they will gang up against you. You must have three, as one will always be fighting with the other two to take the pressure off you.

Chauvinism? Sure, but then every woman I've told this story to has battled to hide a knowing smile. Well, at least for the first proviso.

My train of thought was broken by appreciative murmurs from the crowd as Françoise walked in. I turned as she came up the aisle looking absolutely gorgeous, and as her beautiful eyes fixed on me everything came together and made perfect sense. I was willingly caught up in her magic and totally agreed to the surprise proceedings. It was all just so right.

A ring magically appeared, and when asked if I took this woman to be my wife, a chorus rang to the rafters: 'He does!'

And I did.

We never have loud music at the lodge, but that night the bold rhythms of Africa throbbed across the reserve in celebrations that went on until the early morning.

SOMETHING STRANGE was going on with Mnumzane. It happened out of the blue. A young ranger was on a game drive with two guests, a married couple, when they rounded a sharp corner and unexpectedly ran into him coming in the opposite direction.

He started ambling over. The ranger panicked and reversed too fast, smashing into a tree. They were stuck with Mnumzane coming straight for them. To the frightened ranger's credit he didn't reach for the rifle. Instead he told his passengers to sit tight and make no sound as Mnumzane strode up to the vehicle. I know first-hand that this is one of the most frightening sights imaginable. A six-ton bull literally breathing down your spine is something else all right. Then he lightly bumped the Land Rover, and his tusk actually grazed one of the guests' arms. Somehow the man didn't scream.

Showing great presence of mind, the Zulu tracker jumped off his seat on the front of the vehicle and sneaked round to the other side, surreptitiously helping the guests off the vehicle. They all fled into the bush. Mnumzane fiddled around the Land Rover for a bit without causing any damage, and then moved off. Once they were sure he was gone, they crept out of their hiding places and drove at speed back to the lodge.

After that encounter, Mnumzane started on occasion approaching our open guest game-drive vehicles. But again, the reports I got were that he was never angry, just curious. It was not dangerous, as the rangers would merely drive away as soon as he approached. The bigger problem was that this was totally out of character: he simply was not behaving as an elephant should. Elephants automatically ignore us humans as long as we don't move into their space.

Then I discovered the reason for his sudden interest. Prompted by a few pointed questions, a staff member told me that two of our young rangers had been teasing the bull, driving up and playing 'chicken' with him, daring each other to see who could get nearest then speeding away when he approached. They had seen me with Mnumzane—totally without my knowledge, as my interactions with him were deliberately kept private—and thought that they would also try to get up close. It never occurred to these two idiots that taunting the ultimate alpha male from a game-drive vehicle that normally carried guests on viewing safaris was teaching him a terribly bad habit. Both rangers had resigned before I found this out, and hopefully they have since embarked on careers far removed from wildlife.

The most non-negotiable rule on the reserve was that no one was allowed to have any self-initiated contact with the elephants. Anyone who disobeyed that law would be instantly dismissed. Perhaps my biggest failure was to trust that all my carefully chosen staff had the same ingrained ethics and common sense that David and Brendan had shown.

I had also just bought a brand-new white Land Rover station wagon. The faithful old battered bush-green Landy had now gone round the clock a good few times and had to be retired, her innards due to be cannibalised for other vehicles. It was a sad day for me. The well-weathered seat, the basic dashboard, the worn-smooth gear stick, the bush-smell of the cabin . . . I loved her.

Taking delivery of this spanking new vehicle, I decided to do a test drive in really rough terrain to see if she was as rugged as my old Landy. She performed beautifully off-road, but eventually a tight copse of trees forced me to make an extremely tight 360-degree turn. I had just about completed this when suddenly I felt unaccountably apprehensive.

An instant later Mnumzane towered next to me. He had appeared silently from the shadows as only an elephant can, and was just standing there. I looked up into his eyes and my heart skipped a beat. His pupils were cold as stones and I quickly called out his name, repeatedly greeting him. It took ten chilling seconds before he started relaxing. I completed the turn, talking continuously to him as he gradually settled down and let me go.

I drove off with a heavy heart. Things were not the same any more. Perhaps his aggression had been because he had not recognised the new vehicle. I fervently hoped so. But he shouldn't be approaching any of our vehicles, let alone acting aggressively towards them.

Then in another incident our lodge manager Mabona was driving up to the house when Mnumzane appeared from nowhere and blocked her path. Doing exactly as she had been taught, she cut the engine and sat motionless. Mnumzane moved to the back and leaned on the car, shattering the rear window. The crackling glass surprised him and he backed off, giving Mabona enough time to turn the key and accelerate away.

After this we hacked out a dozen or so outlets on the road to the lodge where vehicles could rapidly reverse and turn if necessary. I also had all encroaching bush on the track cleared so we could see Mnumzane before he got too close. However, my senior rangers remained unhappy. 'He trusts you, but it's very different for the rest of us.' They wouldn't go near him, and all walking safaris were stopped if he was anywhere in the area.

A FEW WEEKS LATER I was taking some VIP visitors on a game drive in my Landy as the sun was setting. We were crawling along at five miles per hour when out of the twilight the herd appeared, crossing the road fifty yards ahead.

It was the first time my two passengers had seen an elephant, let alone a herd, and their excitement attested, as always, to the ancient bewitchment of Africa. I switched off the engine to let them savour the moment, perhaps one they would not experience again.

Then I saw Mnumzane bringing up the rear. I knew he was now in musth, a sexual condition in which a bull elephant's testosterone levels shoot up by an incredible fifty times, and this is when bulls can become dangerously unpredictable, especially when following females as he was doing now. I never dared interact with any bull in musth. It was just too volatile. Anyway, I was with guests, so it was out of the question.

Nana was leading her family towards Croc Pools, and I waited for about five minutes to make sure they were well off the road before I started the Land Rover and again moved forward.

Suddenly the man in the passenger seat started shouting, 'Elephant! Elephant!'

The yell shook me rigid. What was he on about? The elephants were gone. I strained my eyes, searching the headlight-illuminated track in front, unable to see anything.

'Elephant!' he shouted again, pointing to his side window.

It was Mnumzane, barely three yards away in the dark. Prompted by the loud noise, he stepped forward and lowered his massive head right onto the window as if to see what all the shouting was about, and with instant dread I saw his eyes. They were stone cold, and there was malevolence in the air.

Mnumzane then prodded the window with his trunk, testing its resilience. Realising that at any second he was going to shatter through and in the process crush my passenger, I slammed the vehicle into reverse while desperately pleading with the two men to calm down. All I managed to do by reversing was to skid Mnumzane's tusk across the glass, snagging it at the edge of the door with a jarring bang. He lifted his head and trumpeted in rage. With that I knew we were now in grave danger. As far as Mnumzane was concerned, the car had 'attacked' him. In retaliation, he swung in front of us and hammered the bull bar so hard my head smacked the windscreen as we shot forward like crash-test dummies. Then he put his huge head on the bull bar and violently bulldozed us back twenty yards into the bush, stopping only when the rear wheels jammed against a fallen tree.

I opened my window and screamed at him, but it was tantamount to yelling at a tornado in the dark. I watched in horror as he backed off sideways to give himself space to build up speed, then I lost sight of him as he moved out of the headlights. At least the guests had stopped yelling. All three of us were now deathly silent.

There was only one way out. As he set himself up for the charge I revved until the engine was screaming and dropped the clutch, trying to wrench the

Landy out of his way. Too late. He came at us out of nowhere in an enraged charge. The shock of the colossal impact jarred my teeth as he smashed his tusks into the side of the Landy just behind the back door and then heaved us up and over.

Ka-bang! The Landy smashed down, landed on its side, then flipped over onto its roof and into a thicket as he drove on with his relentless attack. Another almighty charge flipped us back onto our side.

My shoulder was on the grass through the broken side window, and the guest in the passenger seat was practically on top of me. My head hurt terribly from the strike on the windscreen as I tried to gather my senses. I wasn't injured, but my biggest concern was that this wasn't over. In fact, our ordeal was in its infancy. Bull elephants have a terrifying reputation for finishing off what they start. To confirm this, just inches away, Mnumzane stomped round the upturned vehicle in a rage.

I had to snap him out of his red mist, and amid all the confusion I somehow remembered that elephants that have been exposed to gunfire sometimes freeze when they hear shots. I also knew that it could go the other way, that the gunfire could prompt a final lethal attack, but I had no choice.

Twisting round, I drew Françoise's tiny .635 pistol from my pocket just as the Landy shuddered with another titanic blow. I pointed at the sky through the broken windscreen and fired . . . again and again and again. I fought the compulsion to fire all eight shots in the magazine. My last-ditch plan was that if he got to us I would shoot the final four slugs into his foot and hope like hell it hurt enough to divert his attention and we could somehow get out and run for our lives.

To my eternal relief he froze. It had worked. As he hesitated I called out to him but I was trembling so much my voice was way off-key. I gulped lungful after lungful of oxygen until everything steadied and tried speaking again. As my voice calmed, he recognised me and his ears dropped, the anger visibly melting from his body.

I then told him it was OK, that it was me, and he had frightened the hell out of me—that he didn't need to be angry any more. Thankfully he recognised my voice and slowly came right up to where I lay on my side in the cab. His feet, practically the size of dustbin lids, were literally inches from my head. All he had to do was lift his foot onto the flimsy cab and that would be it. I aimed my puny gun at his foot and then watched entranced as he pulled out shards of the shattered windscreen, then gently reached in and put his trunk onto my shoulder and head, touching me, smelling me all over.

All the while I talked to him, telling him we were in terrible danger and that he must be careful.

He could not have been more gentle. Eventually he walked off and started browsing on a nearby tree as if nothing had happened.

'The radio, the radio!' whispered one of the guests. 'Call for help!'

Françoise took the call and relayed the bush version of a mayday to get to us fast. Luckily there were rangers on a night-time viewing safari close by who had heard the shots and they were with us in minutes. But whenever they approached, Mnumzane started challenging their vehicle, keeping them away.

Then, as I started to despair, I heard the ranger anxiously calling out on the radio, 'The whole herd is here . . . They're coming straight towards you. Oh my God, they're going to your Landy, what must we do? Over.'

'Nothing,' I replied, relieved. 'Just wait.'

This was good news, not bad as the ranger thought. Leaning forward out of the vehicle I could just see Nana and Frankie, followed by the herd, and I called out to them repeatedly.

But, unusually, they ignored me completely. Without breaking stride, they walked right past us and then, to my astonishment, surrounded Mnumzane, jostling him away from us. He could easily have butted them off—he certainly had the strength—but amazingly he didn't. From my cramped horizontal position on the ground I could hear their stomachs rumbling. I have no idea what the communications were, but moments later Mnumzane left with them.

When they were about fifty yards away the rangers sped up, climbed on top of the Land Rover and pulled us out via the smashed side windows, one by one. Thankfully, incredibly, no one had a scratch.

My brand-new Land Rover was not so fortunate. The bemused insurance company took one look at the wreck and assigned it to the scrapheap. They had never before paid out a claim for an 'elephant incident'.

OUR TRAUMATIC ESCAPE had me going in a dozen different directions trying to figure out what to do. Predictably the 'I told you so' brigade kicked off with a vengeance, with some wildlife experts saying that Mnumzane should be put down immediately; that he was an accident waiting to happen; and that if I didn't do it now, someone was going to get killed.

Once again I rose to his defence and refused to shoot him. Then early one morning I was radioed by a safari-drive ranger to say that he had had a breakdown and had left the Land Rover to go and get parts. When he returned, the vehicle had been smashed off the road and overturned.

Even before I got there, I knew what had happened. Mnumzane's spoor was all over the place. He had found the vehicle and destroyed it, flipping it upside-down and off the road. Despondently I surveyed the damage.

There was no way out. He was completely out of control. If I left it any longer someone was going to die.

I took a slow, lonely drive home and called a friend.

'I need to borrow your .375,' I asked, numbed by the words coming out of my mouth.

'Sure, why?' came the reply.

'Nothing major, thanks. I'll have it back by tomorrow.'

I wanted maximum firepower, so I drove into town and collected the rifle and eight rounds of heavy-duty ammunition. Without telling anyone, I went out onto an adjacent property, marked a tree and fired three shots, sighting the rifle to make sure it was perfectly on target. An hour later I found my big boy grazing peacefully near the river.

At the sound of my car he looked up and came ambling over, pleased to see me as always. Feeling absolutely treacherous, I got out, readied the rifle on the open door and took aim, his familiar features looking completely out of place in the telescopic sight. As he arrived I was still standing there, wracked by emotion, unable to pull the trigger . . . tears flowing freely.

I couldn't do it. I stuffed the rifle in the car as he stood by, warmly radiating greetings in that special way he had. I gathered myself and said goodbye to him for the last time, telling him we would see each other again one day. A few moments later I drove off, leaving him standing there, palpably bewildered by my hasty departure.

The next morning two sharpshooters I had phoned earlier arrived. I was standing outside on the lawn when I heard two distant shots. As the finality of it came crashing home I was seized by a terrible loneliness, both for my beautiful boy and for myself. After years of friendship I had failed. I forced myself to go to where Mnumzane's immense body was lying, the hunters nearby. I was pleased he hadn't fallen badly, lying on his side as if asleep.

'Goodbye, great one,' I said, and got back into the Landy and went to call the herd, to bring them, to let them see what I had done.

What I had had to do.

A COUPLE OF DAYS LATER I was sitting on a termite mound near a grove of acacias, deep in thought, when a Land Rover approached and Vusi, who had been my 'guinea-pig' ranger in initiating walking safaris, got out. A powerfully built man with steely self-assurance whom I had just promoted to senior ranger, he told me he had just driven past Mnumzane's body.

He paused for a moment, looking at me directly. 'There was only one tusk.'

I instantly snapped out of my reverie. 'What do you mean only one! Where's the other?'

'It's gone. Stolen.'

Just then Ngwenya walked up, carrying the single tusk over his shoulder, and lowered it heavily onto the ground.

'There is something that will interest you,' said Vusi, abandoning the topic of the theft. 'Feel here.' He knelt down next to the magnificent piece of ivory, his fingers running lightly over its length. 'There is a bad crack.'

I crouched next to him. I had always known that the tip of Mnumzane's tusk had a slight crack, but as this is fairly common among elephants, I didn't worry much about it.

But then I followed the path of Vusi's fingers with my own and whistled. On closer inspection the crack was much bigger and deeper than I had realised; in fact, the tusk was splayed right open at the end, and the blackened interior was visible. A tusk is just an extended tooth. And, exactly as with a human, a break like that in a living tooth is a magnet for infection and absolute torture, as anyone who has ever had an abscess will attest.

'*Yebo*, Mkhulu,' said Vusi. 'There was a big swelling right at the top of the tusk, deep inside. I cut it open. It was rotten.'

I whistled again, for now everything made perfect sense. Poor Mnumzane had been in so much pain for so long that he just couldn't stand it any more. That's why he became so evil-tempered. And, I suddenly realised, that's exactly why he went berserk and flipped the Land Rover over. When I reversed I jarred his excruciatingly sensitive tusk on the edge of the Landy's window. He must have seen blinding stars in his agony. It took the gunshots from my pistol just to yank him out of it.

I sat down on the lawn and put my head in my hands. All it would have taken was a dart of sedative, a good vet and some antibiotics and we could probably have taken his pain away. And he would still have been with us.

THAT AFTERNOON I received a surprise phone call from *Nkosi* Biyela. We had been in regular contact, but usually through his *izindunas*, or headmen.

'I would like to meet with you,' he said cheerfully. 'I will come to Thula Thula tomorrow afternoon late.'

'I look forward to it,' I replied, heartened by the call. 'And may I make a suggestion? Please bring your wife and stay the night with us at the lodge as our guests.'

'Yes, good idea, thank you. It will give us time to talk about our game-reserve project. I will see you tomorrow then.'

The game reserve, the Royal Zulu, was the main reason I had come to Thula Thula all those years ago. My heart jumped—especially as he had referred to it as 'our project', which was a first since the idea had been presented to his father Nkanyiso Biyela twelve years ago. I had pursued the vision relentlessly, but as so often happens in Africa, the delays and complications at times seemed insurmountable. *Nkosi* Biyela was the key to its success, as he was by far the most powerful chief in the area and controlled the biggest chunk of the land. And he wanted to talk!

The next afternoon he arrived, and we drove through the reserve observing the lush wilderness and robust wildlife and talking about the future.

'Whose land is that?' asked the *Nkosi*, pointing to a stretch of heavy bush just outside our boundary.

'It is yours.'

'Good! Then I would like to join it with you,' he said. Simple as that.

I realised he wanted to continue and held off a reply. He then got out of the Landy and looked around, pointing to the KZN Wildlife reserve that adjoined Thula Thula to the north.

'That I know is Fundimvelo. It was my grandfather's land. They have offered it to me. I will take it back and join with you. We will then do the joint project you have spoken of for the benefit of my people.' Again, simple as that.

'Thank you, *Nkosi*.'

'Now the Ntambanana land, why are they taking so long in releasing it to us?' he asked, referring to the tract of bush and thorn on my western boundary. Ntambanana was originally land excised by the apartheid government from various tribes some decades ago and was now being returned. The Biyelas had the biggest claim over it.

'I do not know, *Nkosi*. It worries me as well.'

'We must start pushing them now,' he said, referring to the local government. And when *Nkosi* Biyela talks about 'pushing', it certainly gets people's attention.

In those few minutes—completely out of the blue—he had described most of the land that made up my dream African game reserve, but not all of it. There was one last piece of the jigsaw, the most important piece:

Mlosheni, an 8,000-acre section that ran north from Ntambanana right up to the White Umfolozi River, the gateway to the world-famous Umfolozi game reserve. Once we had that, we could lower fences with the Umfolozi reserve and have a massive tract of pristine Africa.

'Mlosheni,' I said, then hesitated.

'What of Mlosheni?'

'Mlosheni will join us to the Umfolozi reserve. It is important.'

'Of course! I have spoken with my *izinduna*, it is already agreed,' he said matter-of-factly. 'The animals will migrate as they used to before the apartheid government put up the fences.'

I reached out and we shook hands. I was elated, scarcely able to believe what I was hearing. This project would do more for his people than anything that had ever happened before, and my mind raced, assessing the benefits to wildlife as well. *Nkosi* Biyela would lead a coalition of traditional communities into a brave new world.

The next morning, after a hefty breakfast with the *Nkosi*, during which his enthusiasm for the new project seemed, if anything, even more animated, I switched on the TV news. The looming war against Saddam Hussein in Iraq was being ratcheted up by the hour. It seemed now that an invasion was inevitable. But that morning the news also featured a clip on the Kabul Zoo in Afghanistan, and filling the entire screen was a lion, blind in one eye with a tormented face full of shrapnel. A Taliban soldier had thrown a grenade at him. I knew I had to get to Iraq and make sure the same thing didn't happen to the creatures at the Baghdad Zoo, the biggest menagerie in the Middle East.

EPILOGUE

When I returned from my Iraq rescue mission six months later (you can read about it in my book *Babylon's Ark*), the herd was waiting for me at the gate of the reserve itself. This was an event, as I was told they had been in deep bush for most of the time I was away. Nana and her family followed me to the main house and milled around outside the fence. I got out of the car and spoke to them, my voice croaking with emotion. There were now fourteen of them. The four very latest ones were Mnumzane's progeny—he would live on both spiritually and physically.

As they stood there, sniffing the air, something soared in my heart, and I knew then just how much this herd meant to me. And, even more importantly, the lessons they had individually taught me.

They say you get out of life what you put in, but that is true only if you can understand what it is that you are getting. As Nana and Frankie's trunks snaked out to me over the fence, it dawned that they had given me so much more than I had ever given them. In saving their lives, the repayment I had received from them was immeasurable.

From Nana, the glorious matriarch, I learned how much family means. I learned just how much wise leadership, selfless discipline and tough, unconditional love is the core of the family unit. I learned how important one's own flesh and blood actually are when the dice are loaded against you.

From Frankie, the feisty aunt, I learned that loyalty to one's group is paramount. Frankie would have laid down her life in a blink for her herd. To her, nothing was more important—there was no question about this being a 'greater love'. And the love and respect she received in return for her courage was absolute.

From Nandi, I learned about dignity and how much a real mother cares, how she was prepared to stand over her deformed baby for days without food or water, refusing to surrender until the last breath had been gasped.

From Mandla, I saw how tough it can be for a baby to grow up on the run in a hostile world and how his devoted mother and aunts ensured he made it as best he could.

From Marula and Mabula, Frankie's children, I saw first-hand what good parenting can achieve despite adverse circumstances. These beautiful, well-behaved children would be what we in human terms would call 'good citizens'—something often in short supply in our world. They saw how their mother and aunt treated me and, in return, they accorded me the respect one would give to a distinguished relative. I loved them for that.

From ET I learned forgiveness. I had managed to reach out to her through her heartbreak and distrust, but only because she had let me. She had given birth while I was away and was standing close by looking at me, proudly showing off her baby. I made a special fuss of her.

And, of course, there had been Mnumzane.

I looked at them through the fence, feeling not only the warm peace of being home after six months of mayhem in a war zone, but revelling in the fact that my greater family was now also with me. The rumbling of their stomachs as they gathered at the fence was the most soothing sound I have ever heard. Just as Nana had done to me in the boma eight years ago, I felt surrounded by a sense of extraordinary well-being.

It was now clear that a wise masculine role model was needed in our ever-growing family. With Thula Thula being expanded dramatically into adjoining tribal trust lands as part of the Royal Zulu project, we would be able to import a mature bull to teach the growing number of young males on the reserve the facts of life.

I will have no interaction with the new generations. The whole idea when I initially adopted the herd was to release them directly into the bush. I never planned to have any connection with them. I wanted only to get Nana, the matriarch, to trust one human. Once that was achieved, and she knew her family would no longer be molested, my mission was accomplished.

Today, when I drive past the herd, Nana and Frankie may still approach me. Nandi, Mabula, Marula and Mandla and of course ET also still know me; although they acknowledge my presence and may still come forward behind Nana, they do so with greater reservation.

But the youngsters ignore me as I do them. Totally. I am an outsider. The relationships I had with their grandmothers will never be repeated. They will have no direct contact with humans whatsoever—not with me, nor my rangers. And that's the way it should be.

They are going to grow up just as I wanted my original group to. Wild. If there is one thing I disapprove of it's the unnatural capture and taming of wild animals, whether it's an elephant or a bird.

To me, the only good cage is an empty cage.

lawrence **anthony**

1: Françoise and Lawrence Anthony, with
Bijou, outside their lodge at the Thula Thula
Game Reserve, Zululand, South Africa.
2: Nana, the matriarch of the herd, with her
new baby (Mnumzane's son) following
behind, explores the author with her trunk.

3: Anthony and Mabula eye one another.
4: 'Big boy' Mnumzane arrives for a chat.
Lawrence Anthony is 6ft 3ins tall but only
reaches the elephant's tusks.
5: (background): the herd take a bath in the
Gwala Gwala Dam.

PETER LOVESEY

SKELETON HILL

The ancient city of Bath has witnessed Civil War and conflict, so it's no surprise when part of a skeleton is unearthed on Lansdown Hill during the re-enactment of a battle. But then Peter Diamond, Bath's head of CID, is shown a fresh corpse beside Beckford's Tower close by, and the investigation becomes puzzling.

Even more so when his boss suddenly and inexplicably pulls him off the case . . .

I

Two men lay dead on a battlefield and one said, 'Hey!'

The other stayed silent.

'I'm talking to you with the head wound.'

Now the other one stirred. 'I'm dead,' he said through his teeth, like a ventriloquist. 'We're not supposed to talk.'

'Get real. No one's looking at us. The action is all over there.'

Both were in the Royalist army commanded by Lord Hopton.

The re-enactment of the Civil War battle for Bath had moved closer to the spectators, leaving the so-called dead and dying as background decoration. The setting was spectacular, high on Lansdown, 700 feet above the city and with views across three counties. Unrelieved by even a breath of wind, the July sun belted down, overheating everyone.

The one who had spoken first was on his back on the turf and the other was two yards away, the stage blood on his head wound drying.

'You're new to this, aren't you?'

'My first time.'

'I thought I hadn't seen you before. You're a mess.'

'I came prepared with a bag of blood. You can have some if you like.'

'No, thanks. I'll be up again soon. The reason I'm dead is that I want to cool off. I'm Dave, by the way.'

'Rupert.'

They didn't shake hands, seeing that they were supposed to be slain.

Rupert grinned. 'Should we get up and join in again?'

'You can if you want,' Dave said. 'I'm thirsty. Fancy a can of lager? I got here early and put some by.'

Rupert didn't hesitate. 'Which way?'

'Follow me. Leave your pike. You can pick that up later.' With that, Dave got up and trotted down the hill in the opposite direction to the fighting.

'We look like deserters,' Rupert called from close behind.

'So what? You can bet they had some in those days.'

Their raised voices caught the attention of a couple of women kneeling beside the wounded, but they were camp followers giving comfort to their own, the despised Parliamentarians.

'See that fallen tree? That's where it is.'

There was no question that they were breaking the rules by quitting the battlefield. Rupert had the sense not to mention any more of his anxieties to his new friend. With luck, no one had spotted them except the two women. All the spectators were massed behind ropes a few hundred yards away.

The fallen tree must have been blown down in one of the great storms of recent years. Its exposed root system, stark against the sky, formed a canopy ideal to hide under. They sank down in its shadow.

'Should still be reasonably cool.' Dave burrowed in the earth and took out a can of Heineken. He handed it to Rupert.

Rupert removed the ring-pull and gulped some down. 'This is a lifesaver.'

'Brought you back to life for sure.' Dave raised his can. 'To King Charles.'

Rupert did the same. 'The King, God bless him.'

Even though the lager wasn't chilled it was bliss to drink. Dave explained that on battle days he usually found a spot where he could stow some away. 'In weather like this you've got to look after yourself.'

'I can see I've got a lot to learn,' Rupert said.

'I'm in the cavalry and we smuggle the odd tinny into our saddle holsters, but pikemen can't risk it. You wouldn't get past the bag inspection.'

'What are you doing on foot if you're in the cavalry?'

Dave laughed. 'If you get a boil on your arse as I have, you don't want to think about mounting a horse. Today I'm infantry and grateful for it.'

'And you're serious about joining in again?'

'That's why I'm in it, for the fighting. Aren't you?'

'Well, I'm a historian,' Rupert said. 'They had what they called a lecture day in October and I was invited to give a talk. I thought it would be interesting to come along and get a sense of what it's like to re-enact a battle.'

'And is it anything like?'

Rupert the historian smiled. 'Not if I'm brutally honest. This is put on mainly for the spectacle, so the audience has to have a view. The real point of interest in 1643 was Sir William Waller's brilliant tactics.'

'Waller? He's the enemy.'

'Yes, and in the real battle we outnumbered him by a couple of thousand, yet he moved his army in the night and outflanked us. When our side woke up, the Parliamentarians had the high position along the top of Lansdown. Our Royalist army was on Freezing Hill, that one to the north. When we attacked we had to come down from there and fight our way uphill.'

'But we saw them off.'

'Finally, and at great cost. Not much of that is being shown here. I suppose a battle on a steep hillside wouldn't work as a spectacle.'

'Flat ground is better,' Dave said, looking across the plateau of Lansdown to where the action continued. 'Safer for the horses, too.'

'And the scale is so different,' Rupert said. 'The Royalists had upwards of six thousand men, against about four thousand defending Bath for the Parliamentarians. Today's turnout looks pathetic beside those figures. Hopton lost three hundred in the real battle. I doubt if we started with that many.'

'This is only a minor muster,' Dave said. 'We do have bigger turnouts.'

'According to the accounts, there was so much smoke from the cannon and muskets that they couldn't see more than a few yards ahead.'

'Hell on earth by the sound of it.'

'Most battles were. A far cry from this little show.'

'Stop knocking it. We go to a lot of trouble to get the uniforms right. And all the weapons have to be accurate replicas.'

'Firing blanks and thunderflashes.'

'What do you expect?' Dave said. 'We're putting on a show for the public, and we do the best we can with what we've got.'

'The real thing wasn't very satisfactory anyway. They fought to a standstill and nobody won on the day.'

'Fancy another?' Dave dug his hand into the loose soil again.

A shake of the head from Rupert. 'One was good. That's my limit.'

Dave was groping up to his elbow among the earth and dead leaves, the search increasingly agitated. 'I can't find it. There were six here.' He used both hands. 'Some tosser must have nicked them.'

'One of the enemy?' Rupert said.

'Probably. Bloody Roundheads. I did see one of them about earlier.'

'At least he had the decency to leave the two cans we had.'

'You call that decent?' Dave was still scrabbling in the hole. 'There's something down here, but it isn't a can.' He lifted out an object over a foot in length, narrow and with bulbous ends. 'Only an old bone.'

'Some animal must have buried it,' Rupert said. 'A fox, I expect.'

'Whatever this was, it was bigger than the fox when it was alive.'

Rupert said, 'It's a femur. A thigh bone.'

'But of what?'

'Might be a deer.'

'I've just had a spooky thought,' Dave said. 'It could be human.'

'Up here on Lansdown? How would it get here?'

'This is the spooky part. What if it belonged to one of the soldiers who was killed in the battle?'

There was a moment when nothing was said. The sounds of the fighting were distant now, muffled by a sudden breeze.

It was Rupert who spoke next. 'You could be right. The army would have buried their dead up here before they moved on.'

Dave shook his head. 'Makes you think, doesn't it? Here we are, all dressed up and playing soldiers, and this was a guy who really bought it.'

'That does put a different perspective on the day,' Rupert said.

'I've a gut feeling it is.' Dave placed the bone respectfully between them, as if he didn't wish to handle it any more. 'What shall we do with it?'

Secretly excited by the find, Rupert decided to appear indifferent. 'Put it back, I suggest.'

Dave was a bit of a mind-reader. 'An archaeologist might be interested. They could arrange a dig and find more bones, even some of his armour.'

'Along with your missing beer. Should confuse them.'

Dave shook his head. 'Some bastard had the beer.'

'I wasn't serious.'

'You're right about the bone,' Dave said. 'I vote we leave it here.'

'That's the decent thing,' Rupert said. 'I'm with you, Dave. He's rested here for over three hundred years. We don't have any right to disturb him.'

Dave replaced the bone and covered it.

'RIP, whoever you are,' Dave said.

They slung their empties a respectful distance from the interment and returned to the battle.

AFTER THE FIGHTING was over, the King's Army assembled behind the standard and made a dignified withdrawal from the field, marching to the slow beat of a single drum. This wasn't true to history, but it made an impressive spectacle for the crowd watching from higher up. There was spontaneous applause. The Parliament Army would make a similar exit later.

When they reached the road that runs along the top of Lansdown, the marchers broke step and headed back to the car park at the racecourse where they'd left their transport. While some loaded up and stowed away the weaponry, others attended to the horses or prepared barbecues.

Rupert, new to all this, took his cue from the regulars, assisting where he could before slipping away to his car and changing out of his sweaty battle costume. He was still curious about the femur Dave had unearthed. If it was part of the remains of a Civil War soldier from the original battle, this was an exciting find. There was a good chance of finding more bones—perhaps a complete skeleton—lower down. And, if so, surely there would be metal objects preserved, a breastplate, a helmet or a sword.

How pleasing it would be to bring a group of students to the site and supervise them in a dig. He could visualise himself writing a paper about the discovery, giving a lecture, doing an article for *History Today*.

First he would need to establish that the bone was human in origin. Carbon dating ought to pinpoint its age. The university had the technology, so why not make use of it?

His conscience troubled him a little. He and Dave had talked about putting the dead soldier's femur to rest where they'd found it. To retrieve the bone secretly would be underhand. Dave wouldn't approve, but then who was Dave? Just a simple guy who liked playing soldiers. He wouldn't understand the pursuit of historical truth.

Rupert joined in a barbecue for a while, then slipped away. He crossed the car park and the golf course and made a detour so as to cross the road out of sight of everyone. The light was fading slowly, a glorious summer evening, comfortable for walking. Rupert had studied the map the previous evening to get a full appreciation of the battleground and its all-important contours. Disappointingly, the re-enactment had not followed the original action with any precision. If he ever had any say in the planning, he'd insist on a more authentic approach, but he doubted that he'd play soldiers again.

He entered a field, staying roughly parallel with the road, and crossed two stiles, still well short of the true site of the infantry action: the valley between Lansdown and Freezing Hill where a counterattack by the Royalists had forced Sir William Waller's army to retreat. At the end, the Royalists were in control of Lansdown, but at the cost of the most casualties.

The uprooted tree came into view and Rupert quickened his step.

Nobody was in sight and the light was fading fast. The vast root system was silhouetted like some beached sea creature with tentacles, sinister and monstrous. In its shadow he had difficulty locating the precise place where the bone was buried. He knelt and poked his fingers in to find where the earth was loose. There was a place where both hands sank in easily.

His fingers touched something solid. He pulled the bone from the hole.

Sorry to disturb you again, my friend, he addressed it in his thoughts. He stood up—and froze. A hand was on his shoulder.

'YOU'RE OVERWEIGHT,' the doctor said. 'How do you exercise?'

'I lift the odd pint.'

'It's not funny, Mr Diamond. You could be killing yourself. Your blood pressure's too high. How are your motions? Are you regular?'

'What?'

'Big jobs,' the doctor explained.

Diamond said after a crushing pause, 'Young man, how old are you?'

The doctor twitched. 'My age isn't under discussion.'

'Well, let's discuss big jobs, seeing that you mentioned them. Mine is a big job. I'm in charge of CID in the city of Bath. The Police Authority insist on this annual medical and your not-so-big job is to give me the once-over and declare me fit for work. Correct?'

'Not entirely.'

'Let's get one thing clear. You're not my doctor. I haven't come to you for treatment. I just need your signature on that form.'

'*You* may see it that way.'

'Believe me, I know about forms. I spend a large part of my time filling them in and most of them are pointless. Yes, I'm a few pounds overweight and have been for years. It doesn't stop me doing my job. So, why don't you sign me off and call in the next guy?'

'I can't do that. Unless you take your state of health more seriously, it may not be just your job you lose.'

Diamond picked up his shirt. 'Are you telling me I'm ill?'

'Unfit is a more accurate term. Some sensible eating would be a start. A brisk walk at least once a day. Do you drive to work?'

'I don't have the time to walk.'

'Get up earlier. Do you live alone?'

'These days, yes.'

'Then you won't disturb anyone by setting the alarm.'

'I don't need you to tell me how to run my life.'

'You need somebody, Mr Diamond. That's *my* job.'

'Are you going to sign that certificate?'

'With misgivings.' The doctor picked up his pen.

Diamond should have left it there. Instead, he asked, 'Why didn't they send the doc we've seen for years, about my age, who I sometimes meet in the Crown and Anchor?'

'He died. Heart. He didn't look after himself.'

Difficult to top that. 'Well, at least he had warm hands.'

The doctor looked over the top of his glasses. 'Not any more.'

BACK WITH HIS TEAM, still buttoning his shirt, Diamond said, 'Passed. He's not the quack we usually get. Looks fifteen years old, out to make an impression.'

'He didn't impress you?' Halliwell asked.

'That's putting it mildly. How about you? Have you been in yet?'

'Next but one.' An anxious look crossed Halliwell's features. 'It's just pulse and blood pressure, isn't it?'

'That's what I thought, until he put on the surgical glove.'

'He's kidding,' John Leaman said. 'Can't you see the grin?'

Diamond switched to Leaman. 'So when's yours?'

'I'm excused. They gave me a medical when I did weapons training.'

Diamond rolled his eyes. Typical that Leaman should escape. 'You hold the fort, then. I need some lunch after what I've been through.'

Still nettled by the young doctor, he asked for extra chips with his burger. 'I just passed my medical,' he told Cressida in the canteen. 'While I'm at it, I'll have an extra spoonful of beans.'

'Building up your strength?' she said, smiling.

'It's a good principle. You never know what's round the next corner.'

'Could be a nice young lady, Mr D. If you like, I'll spread the word among the girls that you passed your medical.'

His romantic prospects were fair game. The kitchen girls knew about his friendship with Paloma Kean. What they didn't know was how much he missed his murdered wife, Steph.

He looked for a table, always a tricky decision. If he joined other people, they would be lower ranks and uncomfortable in the presence of a superintendent, but an empty table left him vulnerable to Georgina, the assistant chief constable. Many a burger and chips had been ruined by some sharp questions about the way he was running his department.

A face from the past looked up from a newspaper. A Lord Kitchener moustache flecked with silver. Brown, unforgiving eyes. The man had once been head of CID operations but had been given extended sick leave three or four years ago after receiving a severe head injury.

'John Wigfull. I thought you'd long since left the madhouse.' Diamond placed his tray on the table.

Chief Inspector Wigfull didn't move. There was no handshake. They'd never been that friendly.

'They brought me back as a civilian,' he said. 'I'm the new media relations manager.'

'Are you, indeed?' Diamond popped a chip into his mouth. 'So I can look forward to you keeping the press boys off my back.'

'In the modern police we encourage openness.' Wigfull had always had a talent for making Diamond feel he was one of a dying breed. 'In the past we haven't maximised our use of the media. It's a two-way process. There's potential for information-gathering from the public.'

'Like the old Wanted posters?'

Wigfull looked pained. 'We're in the twenty-first century. My brief is to make the police more approachable.'

'You wouldn't be thinking of giving out my phone number?'

'Not at all, but I may at some point arrange for you to be interviewed by a magazine or newspaper.'

Diamond frowned. 'You can stuff that.'

'Don't look so worried, Peter. You're not even halfway up my list.'

A put-down calculated to injure Diamond's pride, and it succeeded. He lifted the top from the burger and poured on some ketchup. He wished he'd sat with someone else.

'I'm feeding titbits to the media as well,' Wigfull added. 'Human interest stories like the missing Cavalier.' He spoke the last two words in a throwaway tone, as if Diamond should have known all about it.

'What's that—an oil painting?'

'It's what I said—a missing Cavalier. You won't have heard of this because it hasn't come to CID. There's no crime that we know of . . . yet.'

'Go on, then.'

'Two weekends ago they re-enacted the Civil War Battle of Lansdown. The real thing was in 1643 and they had a major muster three hundred and fifty years on, in 1993.'

'A what?'

'A muster is the term they use. It made a colourful spectacle, I'm told. There are societies like the Sealed Knot who take it very seriously.'

'Pathetic,' Diamond said. 'Cut to the chase.'

'As I was trying to tell you, they had another muster this year. One of them fell in the battle and hasn't been heard of since.'

'Killed?'

'If he had been, you'd have heard about it. There would have been a real corpse when the fighting came to an end.'

'You just said he fell in the battle,' Diamond reminded him.

'It's all pretence. They lie down for a while and then join in again. Somehow this one went missing. No one reported it, but two days later his car was found in the racecourse car park. His costume was in the boot.'

'Pity. It spoils your story, doesn't it? You're not looking for a missing person in a big hat with a feather.'

'He was an infantryman. They wore helmets.'

'Doesn't matter, does it, if his stuff was in the car? You say his motor was found, so you must have checked with Swansea for his name.'

'Yes, we know who he is. Rupert Hope, a history lecturer at Bristol University. Parents living in Australia. They haven't heard from him since the incident. Neither have any of his university colleagues,' Wigfull said.

'Another missing person. I expect he'll turn up.'

'But why would he abandon his car?'

'Has anyone tried it, to see if it starts? If the car was giving him trouble, he may have got a lift with someone else.'

'That doesn't explain why he disappeared. He's been gone twelve days.'

'Try this for size, then. After the battle, they all get together for a few drinks. Your Cavalier gets stonkered and one of his mates offers to drive him home, but on the way back to Bristol they have an accident.'

'We'd have heard.'

'Hold on. The driver is killed, but your man gets out and walks away. He's hit his head, lost his memory. Nobody knows there was a passenger.'

'So where is he now?' Wigfull said with scorn.

'In the funny farm. Check for the guy with delusions that he's a Cavalier.'

Wigfull took him seriously, as usual.

THE NEXT MORNING a woman walked into Manvers Street Police Station with three greyhounds and a large bone. 'I've always obeyed the law,' Miss Hibbert told the desk sergeant, 'and I want to know if I can keep this.'

Sergeant Austin, with eighteen years' experience, had seen some shocking things across this desk. He eyed the bone without much interest. 'You want to keep it?'

'For these chaps. They're rescue dogs. Life hasn't given them much in the way of treats.'

'Where did you get the bone, ma'am?'

'Up on Lansdown. I thought I'd better check with you in case it's human.'

'Human? Let's hope not,' Sergeant Austin said, turning the thing over in his hands. Catching sight of the bone again, one of the dogs reared up and tried to take it back.

'Get down, you brute!'

'Who are you calling a brute? There's no need for that,' Miss Hibbert said. 'He's muzzled. He can't bite you. Down, Hector.'

Sergeant Austin rubbed the back of his hand. 'He got me with his claw.'

'You shouldn't have shown him the bone. Has he drawn blood?'

'If you really want to know, he has.'

'Then I'm sorry, and I'm speaking for Hector as well. It wasn't intentional.'

'Let me see, Sergeant.' The speaker was the doctor, on his way to carry out more medicals. 'One of these dogs attacked you? Are you up to date with your tetanus jabs? I have some antitoxin on the premises.'

'It's just a scratch,' the sergeant said. 'I don't need a jab.'

'Sorry, Sergeant, I must insist for your own safety.'

'OK, thanks,' the sergeant said without any gratitude at all.

'And what are you doing with that femur? It looks human to me.'

THE BONE WAS TAKEN UP to the CID office and shown to Peter Diamond. He had no training in forensic anthropology, but if the doctor thought the thing looked human it had to be taken seriously. He went downstairs to speak to Miss Hibbert, who had taken the dogs outside.

'What I'd like to do,' Diamond said, when he'd heard her story, 'is go up to Lansdown with you and see exactly where you found the bone.'

'I just walked all the way into town,' she said. 'That was downhill. If you think I'm tramping all the way up again, you've got another think coming.'

'Are the dogs all right in a car?'

'They're angels . . . if you treat them right.'

With the angels on the back seat, Diamond managed the drive without anything worse than a damp nose prodding the back of his neck.

Lansdown was at its most enchanting under a cloudless sky.

While the superintendent was locking the car, Miss Hibbert released the dogs. They raced away across the open down.

The cool air at this altitude was as good as champagne after the humidity of the city. 'I should come here more often,' Diamond said, filling his lungs. 'Is this their regular walk?'

'Every day, rain or shine.' She led him across a field and down a steep incline towards a fallen oak tree. The fine parts of the root system had long since succumbed to the weather, leaving only the major roots exposed.

'Here?'

'I didn't see precisely where they got it from,' Miss Hibbert said, 'but they were fighting over the bone when I caught up with them.'

On cue, Hector raced in and started burrowing in the soil below the roots. He was joined by the others. The ground looked soft.

'Stop them doing that, will you? This could be a crime scene.'

Miss Hibbert produced a rubber ball. 'Try throwing this down the hill.'

'Me?'

'They like you, I can tell. Besides, men are better at throwing.'

He flung the ball as far down the slope as he could and the dogs chased after it. Gratifying. His cat didn't chase anything except birds and mice. Try throwing a ball for Raffles and you'd end up fetching it yourself.

He paced the area, studying the ground, thinking back to his lunch-time conversation with Wigfull about the missing Cavalier. The re-enactment of the battle must have happened hereabouts. But he couldn't imagine the femur having anything to do with the lost lecturer, Rupert Hope. The stained, off-white appearance suggested it had been in the ground for years.

The dogs returned with the ball and dropped it at Diamond's feet and gazed up at him with confidence. 'You win,' he said, stooping. The ball was damp to the touch. He threw it downhill again.

'I'm not going to get that bone for my dogs to chew on, am I?'

He smiled, admiring her nerve. Staunch women like this, used to standing up for their rights, had his respect. 'Not now we're treating it as human.'

'If I'd been less public-spirited, no one would have known.'

'True, but if it was your leg bone, or mine, we wouldn't want it thrown to the dogs, even charming dogs like Hector, would we?'

She appeared to agree, but was looking thoughtful. 'Do you think there could be more bones under here?'

He put up both hands. 'Don't even think about letting the dogs do any more digging.'

BY THE END of the day the area round the tree was marked off with crime-scene tape and a luckless constable was posted to guard the scene overnight. In the morning, a forensic anthropologist confirmed the femur as human, probably from an adult of average height. In theory, that single bone could reveal its owner's sex, age at death, ethnic origin and how long ago death had occurred.

Diamond returned to Lansdown with two of his team, DC Ingeborg Smith and DI Keith Halliwell, and watched the white-suited crime-scene investigators slowly sift the earth below the upended root system. He told his colleagues about the information an anthropologist could get from a single bone. 'First we want an estimate of the length of time since death. Carbon dating should establish that much.'

'Do you think it's ancient?' Halliwell said.

'It didn't look fresh to me. There was a Civil War battle up here three or four hundred years ago. I expect some bodies were buried in haste.'

'There were Iron Age settlements long before that,' Ingeborg said. 'The bone could be two thousand years old.'

The excavation was slow. After another hour, the man in charge, a cantankerous character called Duckett, reported that they'd reached a level where the earth was more compacted.

'You mean it hasn't been disturbed?' Diamond said.

'I didn't say that. The section we've just cleared was extra loose, as if someone had dug here in the past few weeks.'

'Like Miss Hibbert's dogs?'

'More than that. It's too much for animal activity alone.'

The digging resumed. Twenty minutes later, one of the team in the trench said, 'There's something here.' She had exposed a patch of off-white.

'Another bone?' Diamond said. 'Hook it out and we'll see.'

Duckett glared at him. 'If you don't mind, Superintendent, we'll do this the approved way, leaving everything in situ.'

Soon enough, the outlines of the object were revealed.

'It *is* a bone,' Diamond said.

'A tibia,' Ingeborg said.

Soon some foot bones were unearthed at the lower end of the tibia.

'Can we get someone else clearing at the top end where the skull is?' Diamond asked. The painstaking progress frustrated him.

'We'll do this in our own good time,' Duckett said.

Almost as if to provoke the police, the excavation slowed. Brushes, rather than trowels, were being used. At regular intervals photos were taken.

'What time is it?' Duckett asked eventually.

'Three thirty, just gone,' Diamond said.

'Is it, by Jove? Take a break, people. We've been going two hours.'

The police were forced to watch the CSI team sit down, open their flasks and look at newspapers. 'At this rate, we'll be here all night,' Diamond said to Halliwell.

'I heard that,' Duckett said, looking up from his crossword. 'You don't have to worry. We stop at five. Will you be guarding the site overnight?'

'He's winding you up, Guv,' Halliwell said.

'I think he means it,' Ingeborg said.

Duckett hadn't finished. 'Now that we've located remains, we'll need to put up a tent to screen off the trench.'

'We can do that, me and my officers.'

'No, thanks. Not while we're at work in the trench.'

'But you're not in the trench now.'

'It's a specialised job.'

'What—putting up a bloody tent? Ridiculous.'

'This isn't one of your Boy Scout tents, Officer. This is a metal-framed inflatable job. I can't allow any untrained person to handle it.'

The break came to an end about four. Ingeborg phoned the station to get a man out to guard the site.

'I was expecting answers by now,' Diamond said, pacing the turf. 'All I'm getting is high blood pressure.'

After another twenty minutes there was a clicking sound from the trench. Duckett was snapping his fingers.

Ingeborg said, 'I think he's asking for you.'

'He's asking for something, that's for sure,' Diamond muttered.

He went over. More of the skeleton had been revealed, enough to see that the body had lain on its side in a foetal position.

Diamond stood over the trench. 'You've got something to tell me?'

'You asked about the skull,' Duckett said. 'There isn't one—not where it ought to be, anyway. This would appear to be a headless corpse.'

THAT EVENING, Peter Diamond had a pub meal with Paloma Kean, the one woman he'd been out with since his wife had died six years ago. Their friendship—still more of a friendship than a relationship, although they'd slept together—had carried them both through tough times since. They drew strength from each other. She understood his moods, his brash manner. And he treated Paloma with the warmth that sprang from a shared sense of humour and physical attraction.

They managed to get a candlelit table on the patio at the Hop Pole. With a pint of Barnstormer real ale in front of him and steak pie on order, Diamond was more expansive than usual, telling Paloma about his frustrating day.

'You got out of the office, anyway,' she said, when he'd finished. 'I like Lansdown. The history isn't as obvious as it is here among all the old buildings, but you get a sense of it whichever way you look.'

'The Civil War, you mean?'

'Not just that.'

'Iron Age settlements?'

Her eyes widened. 'You have hidden depths.'

'I was briefed today by Ingeborg, our pet culture vulture.'

'Did she mention Beckford's Tower?'

He'd often driven past the folly towards the city end of the hill, two miles from the crime scene. Today he'd noticed its sunlit octagonal gilt lantern on the skyline. 'He was a weirdo, wasn't he, William Beckford?'

'An extremely rich weirdo,' Paloma said. 'I provided some costume drawings for a TV company doing a documentary on him, so I read the books.' She had amassed a huge collection of archive material on historical costume and built a successful company used by the film and television markets. She told him more about the eccentric Beckford; how he created a mile-long landscaped walk across country to his tower and would set off each day from his home in Lansdown Crescent accompanied by a dwarf servant and four dogs. 'I'll lend you a book.'

'Thanks.' He doubted that he'd do more than dip into it.

The food arrived and for a while eating had priority over conversation. Then Paloma asked, 'What have you got lined up for tomorrow? Another day watching the dig?'

He shook his head. 'Some chance.'

She raised her eyebrows. 'But you said you've got a headless body. That's murder, surely?'

'War injury. My best guess is that the head was blown off by a cannonball in the Civil War. A case for *Time Team*, not me and my lads.'

'Doesn't the coroner get involved?'

'Too true, he does. And when Forensics report to him they're stuck with all the paperwork. I'm not daft. Anyway, I've got other fish to fry.'

'Here's a thought, then,' Paloma said. 'All this talk of Lansdown reminds me that one of my clients offered me a free day at the races any time I want. How would you like a flutter on the horses?'

'He was chatting you up.'

'*She*. A lady owner, in a long-term relationship with a rock star. She has a double annual badge for the Premier Enclosure.'

'You think you can pass me off as the rock star?'

She laughed. 'That *would* be a challenge. No, we go as ourselves. Shall I check the date of the next meeting?'

'Why not?' he said, thinking this was a long-term suggestion.

It turned out that there was an evening of racing at Lansdown the next day. Cynic that he was, he suspected she'd planned this all along.

POLICE WORK has a knack for springing surprises. In the morning Diamond took a call from the forensic anthropologist who had examined the femur.

'You said it was found up at Lansdown?' Dr Peake said.

'Correct. We've found all of him, bar the skull. It's a good bet he was a Civil War victim who failed to duck when a cannonball came his way.'

'Have you evidence for the Civil War connection. Are there any relics?'

'Give us time. We're still digging.'

'Mr Diamond, are you certain that the femur I was sent belonged to the skeleton you're talking about?'

'Put it this way, Doc. It came from the same hole in the ground and the headless soldier is missing a thigh bone. Why?'

'Because the indications are that this bone is comparatively modern. Say within the past twenty-five years.'

Diamond said nothing for several seconds. 'Are you sure?'

'"Sure" isn't a word much favoured in my profession. We prefer "probably" or "maybe". There are too many variables.'

'Did you carbon date it?'

'I hate to disillusion you, but radiocarbon dating isn't of the slightest use for the short periods in forensic medicine. There was no indication that this bone is ancient.'

'We're not talking *ancient*, Doc. A few centuries.'

'Anything over fifty years is classed as ancient in my work.'

'Ouch. You don't have to get personal.'

Peake didn't get the joke. 'These are the terms we use.'

'What are your reasons?'

'For saying the bone is modern? For one thing, the appearance. A modern bone has a smooth, soapy texture. And the density. Bones a hundred years old or more are lighter in weight and tend to crumble.'

'That's observation. Have you done lab tests?'

'Indeed we have. The nitrogen content is a good indicator. It reduces with time. Typically, a bone three hundred and fifty years old contains a percentage of two point five. Your femur came in at four point three.'

'Too much for a dead Cavalier?'

'Way too much. We also ran a fluorescence test. A modern bone will fluoresce under ultraviolet light, but an ancient one fades away to nothing. The femur gave a positive result, not the strongest, but fitting into the time frame I'm suggesting. Approximately twenty-five years or less.'

'I don't know whether to thank you or not. You've made me look a bloody fool, but on the other hand you've given me a mystery to work on. Shall we meet up at Lansdown this afternoon?'

LATER HE WENT looking for John Wigfull and found him studying a computer screen. 'Is this urgent?' Wigfull said. 'I'm at work on a press release.'

'About the missing Cavalier, by any chance?'

'No, that went out yesterday. Peter, if you don't mind, I'm in the middle of something. My time is precious.'

'Mine is as precious as yours, old chum. I'm not here on a social call. How long is it since the re-enactment man disappeared?'

'Over two weeks now. Why—have you heard something?'

'I'm dealing with a buried skeleton found up at Lansdown. I thought he was a Civil War soldier—a real one—but I'm told the bones are modern.'

'Rupert Hope wouldn't be bones already,' Wigfull said.

'I worked that out for myself. This one is without a head.'

'You think he was decapitated? Murdered?'

Diamond rolled his eyes. 'I'm trying to keep the proverbial open mind.'

'A headless corpse. It might make an item for the press.'

'Not yet, we're still digging. Meanwhile I'm interested in your missing Cavalier. Be sure to let me know when he turns up.'

BACK AT THE DIG, the crime-scene team were on another break. An inflatable tent the size of a small barn had been erected over the excavation. Inside, nothing seemed to have changed since Diamond had last seen it.

'It looks the same as it did last night,' Diamond said on emerging from the tent.

'Skeletons do, on the whole,' Duckett said, looking up from his paper.

Diamond contained his annoyance. 'I don't know if this makes any difference at all to your rate of work, but we could be dealing with a recent murder here. I've got an expert coming out. A forensic anthropologist.'

'We heard. That's why we downed tools. He won't want it disturbed any more than it has been already.'

This was probably true. Diamond turned his back and gazed across the landscape, just as Ingeborg's head and shoulders appeared over the brow of the hill. Beside her, at about the level of her bobbing breasts, was a man in a white zipper suit carrying a cardboard box almost as big as himself. 'This is Dr Peake,' Ingeborg told Diamond when she was close enough.

'Lofty,' the small man said. 'Ingeborg kindly gave me a lift here. Let's have a look.' He dropped the box, put on surgical gloves and entered the tent, followed by Diamond and Ingeborg. 'Ah, beautifully presented. Full marks to the diggers. Give me a few minutes with the young lady.'

Diamond had got accustomed to men making a play for the attractive Ingeborg. 'You can have your few minutes with me. I'm the senior investigating officer here.'

Lofty Peake said, 'I was speaking of the deceased.'

'You said "young lady".'

'Look at the pelvis. Obviously female.'

Time for a rapid rethink. Diamond had convinced himself the victim was male ever since he'd linked the death to the Battle of Lansdown.

Lofty Peake was on his knees beside the skeleton, his face close to the bones. 'Has she had her picture taken?'

'The victim? Yes, repeatedly.'

'Soil samples taken? A search made for trace evidence? I think we can lift her, then. I'll find out more in the lab. First impressions suggest she was a young adult, average in height. The chances are that she was killed elsewhere and the head removed to hinder identification, but you have to search the area.' He asked for his cardboard box and started lowering the bones onto tissue paper. 'It goes without saying that the forensic team will collect the soil samples,' he said as he worked. 'We might learn something.'

'Fibres?' Diamond said.

'Hopefully. Clothing deteriorates pretty rapidly in damp, acid soil like this. Cotton won't last longer than a year and a half. Silk and wool are gone in three years. Synthetic fibres such as acrylic may last longer. Leather is fairly durable. The micro-organisms win in the end.'

'If you can estimate how long she's been here, we'll run a check of missing persons for the years in question.'

'In the fullness of time, Superintendent.' Lofty lifted something that had dropped as he raised the pelvis. It was about six inches long. 'Proof positive that she isn't ancient,' Lofty said. 'I think it's a zip fastener.'

THE TWO-YEAR-OLDS cantered down to the start for the main race of the evening and Paloma was looking at the filly she'd backed at 17 to 2. 'My Stylist's moving well,' she said, holding the binoculars to her eyes.

'You've done this before,' Diamond said.

'Mm. I don't know about yours. It's looking nervous.'

He'd been under pressure from Paloma to put his ten pounds on a runner called Lady Policeman at 25 to 1. Instead he'd preferred Best Brew, the 11 to 8 favourite. He knew enough about gambling not to fritter away his money on a name with a chance connection to his life.

The course looked velvet in the evening sun and there was a buzz of expectation about the main race of the meeting.

Down at the start the handlers were having difficulty. Bucking and whinnying, one filly pulled back for the second time.

'I think it's yours,' Paloma said.

'May I borrow the glasses?'

Now he had the magnified view of another attempt to steer Best Brew forward. It reared up, almost unseating the jockey.

The starter gestured at the reluctant horse and appeared to say something. His hand went to the lever.

'I think he's ruled her out,' Diamond said in disbelief.

The gates crashed open and the field—apart from Best Brew—hurtled from the stalls for the five-furlong dash. Diamond handed back the binoculars. 'So much for my ten pounds.'

Eleven runners thundered away to the loop at the far side of the course, urged on by their jockeys and the crowd's roar. Over the public-address system came the measured commentary of the track announcer. 'The early leader is Bluestocking, followed by Lady Be Good and My Stylist.'

'Go, baby!' Paloma said.

'Bluestocking still leads. My Stylist is moving up. Lady Be Good now third . . . Coming to the two-furlong marker, nothing to choose between Bluestocking and My Stylist . . .'

'Go, go, go!' Paloma shouted, and Diamond joined in.

'In the last hundred yards, My Stylist leads. Lady Policeman is finishing fast on the outside . . . Photograph.'

Paloma was making little jumps. 'What was the other horse?'

'Lady Policeman—the one you told me to back. And I didn't listen.'

They threaded their way through to the winner's enclosure, where everyone seemed to have an opinion about which horse had won.

'The result of the Tipping Group Fillies race . . .' The talking everywhere stopped. '. . . first, My Stylist.'

Paloma grabbed Diamond and embraced him. 'She won! She did it!'

Feeling a big debt of gratitude to the horse, they watched her led in by her lady owner, who was in a peacock-blue hat and pink suit.

'Isn't she gorgeous?' Paloma said in a carrying voice.

The owner took it as a personal compliment and beamed at them. It was announced that the presentation of the Tipping Group Trophy would be made by Sir Colin Tipping.

'Local sponsor,' Paloma told Diamond. 'He heads a firm of chartered surveyors. Once owned a horse called Hang-glider that won a classic.'

Well informed, as well as a winner, he thought, wondering where she'd learned so much racing lore.

'And by a happy coincidence,' the announcement continued, 'the winning owner is Sir Colin's daughter, Mrs Davina Temple-Smith.'

The grey-haired and grey-suited Sir Colin duly handed over a sterling silver model of a galloping horse on a black marble plinth.

'Let's collect your winnings,' Diamond said in Paloma's ear.

Two rows of bookies were paying out to the successful punters. Paloma found the right man and collected. Before they moved off, someone shouted, 'Watch out!'

The bookie turned to look and said, 'Flaming hell!'

A scruffy-looking man in jeans and a hooded jacket was ambling across the racecourse, oblivious to the horses being cantered past for the start of the next race. A jockey yelled at him.

'A few beers too many,' Diamond said.

The man was grabbed by one of the course police and dragged over the rail, so close to Diamond and Paloma that they heard him say in a refined drawl, 'Thank you, Officer, I'll be on my way then.'

'What the hell were you up to?' the constable asked.

'Crossing over for a bite to eat. All the food seems to be this side.'

'You must be nuts. What's your name?'

'Noddy.'

'Definitely drunk,' Diamond said.

'He's trouble, that one,' the bookie said. 'He's been here and acting daft since I set up two hours ago. I don't think he paid to get in.'

'Neither did we,' Paloma murmured to Diamond as they moved off.

They found the champagne lawn where the winning owner was treating her friends. They heard someone say, 'I'm so delighted for Davina. She looks every bit the socialite, doesn't she, and she was probably in surgery as usual this morning. She deserves this.'

'*Doctor* Davina, then?' Diamond said to Paloma.

A woman near them shook her head. 'She's a local vet.'

A waitress was moving among them with a tray loaded with filled glasses. When they'd taken theirs, Diamond raised his glass. 'To My Stylist.'

Paloma's eyes were still shining. 'It was luck,' she said.

'When we saw the horses parading you knew what to look for.'

'There are too many variables for anyone to get it wholly right,' she said, confirming his impression that she knew more than she'd said up to now. She was such a different personality from Steph, who'd never concealed anything. He immediately rejected the notion of concealment. Paloma wasn't sneaky. She chose not to air her knowledge unless it was useful. Hidden depths was a better way of putting it.

TWO DAYS LATER the police were alerted to a man trying to break into cars in the small car park behind the stands at Bath racecourse. It wasn't a race day so there weren't many vehicles parked there—just a few belonging to staff.

'Deal with it, will you?' the sergeant on duty radioed to a patrol car. 'A Major Swithin reported it.'

PC Andy Sullivan, the driver, was thankful for the job. He'd been stuck all week with a new 'oppo', Denise Beal, who thought silence was the eighth deadly sin. Even when he had the two-tone siren going she didn't stop.

The sight of Major Swithin did the trick. When they drove up the approach to the racecourse, Denise went silent in midsentence. The major was in the middle of the road waving a shotgun.

Sullivan lowered the window and said, 'I hope you have a certificate for that, sir.'

'Of course.' The major was probably closer to eighty than seventy, a silver-haired man in a Barbour and flat cap. 'Good thing I had it in the car. If you need some support arresting this scum, you can count on me.'

'Right now, I'm counting on you to put the gun on the path. Is it loaded?'

'You can bet your life it is. I know about firearms.'

'Then you know it's illegal to have a loaded shotgun in a public place. Do as I say. Now!'

The major obeyed. 'Anyone would think *I* was the criminal.'

'Thank you, sir. Stand back, please.' Sullivan stepped out of the car, retrieved the gun, opened the breech and removed two cartridges. 'You are Major Swithin, I take it?'

'Who else would I be, looking out for you? I wasn't proposing to shoot you—or the car thief, come to that.'

'What's the gun for, then?'

'In case I spot a fox. The Socialists stopped the hunt from destroying them, so it's down to public-spirited people like me.'

Sullivan returned the gun. 'This man you saw. What was he doing?'

'Trying to steal a car. He was going from vehicle to vehicle trying the doors. A rough-looking herbert, unshaven, shabbily dressed.'

'How long ago was this?'

'Fifteen minutes maximum. My wife has him in her sights.'

'Your *wife*? Is she armed as well?'

'With the field glasses. I left her observing him.'

'You'd better get in the car.'

With the major in the back seat they drove off at speed while he continued to justify his actions. 'These days John Citizen has to pitch in and help with law and order.'

'Up to a point,' said Andy Sullivan as they approached the line-up of cars in front of the turnstiles.

'That's Agnes looking out of the roof of my Land Rover.'

Agnes must have been standing on the seat, for she was very obvious, an elderly woman in a deerstalker peering through binoculars.

The police car drew up beside the ancient Land Rover. Major Swithin was the first out. 'Any sign of the blighter, Agnes?'

The old lady lowered the glasses. 'I spotted him heading for the grandstand end. I think he knows we're onto him.'

'That *is* a possibility,' Sullivan said, exchanging a look with his colleague. She was still tongue-tied. 'We'll take over, then. You stop here, the pair of you. I'll need a witness statement.'

Sullivan headed for the open gates to the left of the turnstiles, followed closely by Denise Beal. Once through the gates they faced the two grandstands along the finishing straight. The whole complex had plenty of places where a fugitive from justice might hide.

'We'll split up,' Sullivan said. 'You check the stands, I'll do the stabling area over there to the right.' The stables were a good 200 yards away.

'What if I find him?'

'Keep him talking till I arrive. That shouldn't be any problem for you.'

Few places are as bleak as a racecourse enclosure on a day of no racing. This was only her second month in the police and, for all Andy Sullivan's confidence, Denise Beal felt uneasy. A pigeon flew from a ledge so close to her face that she felt the rush of air. She gave a squeak of fright. Good thing macho PC Sullivan wasn't there to hear it. Moving on, she came to an industrial-sized rubbish bin, easily large enough for a man to hide inside. She debated whether to lift the lid, then thought better of it and rounded the corner of the Paddock Bar, giving it a wide berth. She was relieved to see no one crouching there. She moved on and down some steps. From here she had a good view of the course: not a living soul.

Then she noticed a movement in the shadows. A man was leaning against the wall with arms folded, showing no reaction to her. He fitted the major's description, rough-looking, unshaven, shabbily dressed. Probably in his mid-forties. Denise looked to see if by some miracle Andy was in sight, but he wasn't.

She stepped up to the man and said, 'Do you mind telling me what you're doing? You're on private property.'

'If you say so.' The voice was educated.

'What's your name?'

'They call me Noddy.' He seemed to be serious.

'Are you local, Noddy?'

'I must be, mustn't I? I'll be on my way, then.'

'Hold on a second.' She stared into the far distance. Still no Andy. 'Were you in the car park just now? Someone like you was seen there.'

'If you say so.' That phrase again. It didn't come across as defiance or evasion. This guy was passive to the point of resignation.

'Have you been drinking, Noddy?'

He shook his head. Denise wondered if he was just some simple-minded guy unable to cope with modern life. She had a strong sense that no one would rush to congratulate her if she handcuffed Noddy and pulled him in. So she did what they'd advised at training school: used her initiative. 'On your way, then. Sharpish. And stay away from cars.'

He nodded three times, then shuffled off—towards the end Andy Sullivan would come from.

'Not there,' Denise said and pointed her thumb behind her, towards the golf course. 'That's your best way out.'

She eventually linked up with Andy Sullivan. He asked if she'd seen anyone and she shook her head. For all her compulsion to make conversation, she respected the old adage that all truths are not to be told.

LOFTY PEAKE phoned Diamond later in the week with his findings. 'Your victim was about five six in height and, leaving some margin for error, I'd say she was aged seventeen to twenty-one. Pity we don't have the skull because you can tell a lot more from that.'

'I doubt if we'll find it now.'

'Incidentally, the head was hacked off with some force.'

Diamond had a brief, vivid image. 'After death?'

'I've no way of telling. She appears to have been healthy. The skeleton was normal in development, with no evidence of earlier fractures.'

'Now the critical question,' Diamond said. 'How long is it since she died? When we last spoke, you said up to twenty-five years.'

'When it comes to telling the age, more bones don't necessarily yield more information. You want a time frame. The answer is—and this can only be an estimate—that the bones have been in the ground for more than ten years. No soft tissue remains and there's some coarsening and discoloration that I would expect from the temperature changes of a series of summers and winters. Yet there are still traces of the candle-wax odour given out by the fat in the bone marrow, so these remains are not all that old.'

'You found the zip under the pelvis. Presumably it was a zip fly from a pair of jeans. All of the fabric had rotted away, I suppose?'

'Completely. Nothing remained in the soil samples and the crime-scene people found nothing else of interest. No coins, jewellery, belt buckle, shoes. Not even the hooks and eyes of a bra.'

Diamond thanked Lofty and went to look for Ingeborg. She was at her desk.

He told her about the time frame. 'We're looking for a young woman aged seventeen to twenty-one who went missing between 1984 and 1999.'

She turned to look at him. 'Nineteen eighty-seven, Guv.'

'That isn't what I said.'

'That was the year of the great storm. October 1987 when so many trees came down. She was buried in the hollow left by a tree's roots.'

She was bright. He wished he'd thought of that. 'But can we be sure that tree came down then?'

She nodded. 'I checked with the Lansdown Society. They're a mix of landowners and wildlife enthusiasts who monitor everything up there.'

'And they knew about that tree?'

'As soon as I asked.'

'So the time frame is twelve years. You're a star. You can become a megastar by checking the missing-persons register for those years.'

'I already have, Guv. I looked at all the local counties, made a list of missing girls under twenty-five, but I'm not confident she's on it.'

'Can you show me?'

Ingeborg worked her computer and four names appeared on the screen.

'So what's the problem with them?'

'Look at the descriptions. The first girl, Margaret Edgar, was five foot eleven and Hayley Walters was only half an inch less. Gaye Brewster had broken her left arm and had it pinned some weeks before she disappeared. That would surely have been noticed by Mr Peake. Olivia Begg was about the height of our victim, but she went in for body piercings and nothing like that was found. She went missing only in 1999, at the margin of our time frame, and even that's in doubt. There was an unconfirmed sighting of her in Thailand two years later. I doubt if she's ours.'

Diamond exhaled, a long, resigned breath. 'I've got to agree with you, Inge. They're not serious candidates.'

'So what else can we do?'

'Ask ourselves questions about the killer. Why choose to bury the body at Lansdown?'

After a moment's reflection she said, 'It's remote. He wouldn't be noticed if he picked his time to dig the grave.'

'True.'

'Where the tree was uprooted the soil would be looser to work with. He'd have a ready-made hole in the ground.'

'He'd still have to transport the body there.'

'You could drive across the field in, say, a four by four.'

'This is looking like someone who knows Lansdown well,' Diamond said. 'Either that, or he got lucky. The body was undiscovered for at least ten years. It was buried deep enough to avoid the interest of foxes and dogs for a long time.'

'It was a dog that found the bone in the end,' Ingeborg said.

'I wonder why, after so long. Miss Hibbert didn't say anything about the dog burrowing. She seemed to suggest he found it near the surface.'

'What are we saying, Guv? Some person was digging there? Why?'

'When I was about eleven we used to make camps in the woods and smoke our fathers' cigarettes. The space under the root system would make a good camp if you dug into it. Do kids still make camps?'

'I expect so—but Lansdown's a long way from habitation.'

His thoughts went back to something John Wigfull had told him. 'A few weeks ago they re-enacted a Civil War battle up there. Grown-ups playing soldiers. If you were defending a stretch of ground and needed to dig in you'd be glad of a position like that.'

'It wasn't the Western Front,' Ingeborg said. 'The Civil War was all about man-to-man fighting, not trenches.'

'You'd need to store your supplies so you'd look for a place like that, partly sheltered. If they unearthed a femur in the heat of battle they're not going to give it much attention. That could be how it came to the surface.'

'Does it matter?'

He didn't answer that. Thanks to John Wigfull, he could air his second-hand knowledge with impunity. 'Most weekends in the summer there's a muster somewhere. The Sealed Knot came to Lansdown this year and they've been before. They had a major muster in 1993, the anniversary.'

'Of the Battle of Lansdown?'

'Three hundred and fifty years on. We're looking for a killer who buried his victim in the hole left by the tree. She's been buried at least ten years. I'm thinking about 1993, right in the middle of our time frame.'

2

Unfortunately, there was no better way of progressing the case of the headless skeleton than to employ the services of the new media relations manager. Wigfull was still behind his computer when Diamond came in.

'Any results?' Diamond asked.

Wigfull didn't look up from the keyboard. 'Early days.'

Diamond picked up a paper from the desk. The *Bath Chronicle*. He'd noticed a Post-it Note marking an inside page. 'Oh, yes. A definite result.'

The picture editor had superimposed Rupert Hope's face on several well-known images. In one he was the Laughing Cavalier of Frans Hals and in another a Van Dyck portrait of Charles I.

'It's not the press release I gave them,' Wigfull said with bitterness.

'They've been creative. The phone will start ringing soon.'

'It already has. A number of people claim to have seen him locally. They seem to expect a reward. It's not a game.'

'It makes good copy. That's what your job is about, isn't it—feeding juicy stories to the media?'

Wigfull twitched in disapproval. 'It's more than that. I'm not just here to get publicity. I'm after results.'

'Which is why I'm here,' Diamond said. 'I told you about my headless skeleton. I know more now and I'm ready to go public.'

'You want me to inform the press?'

'Don't sound so gloomy, John. This is your chance to make the nationals.' He pulled up a chair beside Wigfull. 'A young girl, under twenty-one, buried on Lansdown minus her head. We need to know who she was. Who remembers a girl going missing in the nineties?'

Together, they drafted the press release. When it was done, Diamond returned to the CID office and spoke to Ingeborg. 'The Lansdown Society. You said you'd been in touch with them about the fallen tree.'

She gave a nervous cough. 'That wasn't strictly true, Guv. A friend of mine did some work for them. That's how I heard of them.'

'I was thinking they could be useful to us. I tried looking them up. They don't seem to have a phone number or a web site.'

'I don't think they're a public organisation.'

'How did your friend get to hear of them?'

'Perry's a cartographer. They commission him to make maps of the land use up there. He knew about the tree and it definitely came down in 1987. It would have been removed, only it has some rare lichens on the trunk.'

'Getting back to the Lansdown Society, what's it about?'

'According to Perry, they want to keep the down unspoilt. They monitor everything that goes on.'

'Does much go on?'

'More than you'd think, particularly at weekends. Football, golf, hang-gliding, kites.'

'Sounds harmless enough. They must know all about the Civil War events. I bet that tests their tolerance, muskets and cannon going off and cavalry charging across the sacred turf. How do I get to meet them?'

'I could ask Perry.'

'Do that. Is he, er . . .?'

'Just a friend.'

LANSDOWN IS INDEED a place where much goes on. Sundays and Bank Holiday Mondays through the summer see a large car boot sale in the race-course car park. The setting, with views into Somerset and Wiltshire, is unequalled. But the downside is that it's exposed to the elements.

On this breezy Sunday anything that wasn't weighted down was taking to the air. The various structures used as rain covers or sunshades were under threat from gusts. More than one table collapsed. It wasn't surprising that a visitor in a hooded jacket was able to move through the sale helping himself to food. He'd got some way before one of the traders asked him for payment for a meat pie he'd picked up from her pie stall. He replaced it at once.

'You can't do that,' she told him. 'It's got a bite out of it.'

The man shrugged and moved on.

'Hey!' the woman said. 'That's no good to me. I can't sell it. That's theft.'

He was already some way off.

The pie woman asked the copper-bracelet trader on the next-door stall to take over. 'He's not getting away with it. I'm going after him.' Snatching up the pie, she set off through the crowd and caught up with the man. 'This is your pie, mister. You owe me one pound fifty. Just pay for it and that's the end of the matter.'

'Madam, I can't,' he said in a refined tone. 'I have no money on me.'

'What are you doing here if you've got no money? This is a sale, not a free-for-all.' Her shouting was getting attention and she felt compelled to take action rather than lose face. 'All right,' she said. 'Citizen's arrest. I'm nicking you for theft. Someone call the police. Who's got a phone?'

The man under arrest shook his head. 'Not me.'

'I wasn't asking you.'

Uncertain what to do next, the pie woman grasped the man's arm and led him back towards her van. He came like a lamb.

It was the copper-bracelet trader who reluctantly called the police on her mobile. 'They said to keep him here, dear, and they'll send someone.'

The result of all this was that no trade was done in the next half-hour. The man had his own aroma competing with the appetising smell of the pies.

When two police officers eventually made their way through the crowd, the pie seller explained what had happened. She showed them the pie.

'Do you want to press charges?' PC Andy Sullivan said.

'I want to be paid for my pie, that's all.'

It's the job of uniformed police to defuse a situation whenever possible. Andy Sullivan spoke to the prisoner. 'Why don't you give the lady the money and settle the matter?'

'Because I haven't got any money, Officer.' The man was polite, well-spoken and logical. Not the usual troublemaker.

'What's your name?'

'Noddy.'

PC Denise Beal wished she was a million miles away. She could see her short career in the police coming to a quick end if Noddy recognised her.

Sullivan moved his face closer to the prisoner's. 'If you mess with me, my friend, you'll regret it. Now tell me your name.'

'That's what I'm called. Noddy.'

'He's not right in the head,' the copper-bracelet woman said.

'Hold on,' the pie woman said. 'I've lost half a morning's trade through him. I'm taking him to court.'

'Where do you live?' Sullivan asked the man.

The copper-bracelet woman said, 'Toyland.'

Sullivan told her to be quiet. Then he turned back to the man.

'I'm living up here for the present. Anywhere that's dry on a wet night.'

'So you're homeless?'

The man nodded.

This touched the heart of the copper-bracelet woman. 'Did you hear that? He's homeless. You can't take a homeless man to court.'

'I can and I will,' the pie woman said. 'He's a thief. You can't argue with the evidence.' She held up the pie. But such was the force of her feelings that her thumb and finger met in the middle and the evidence fell in bits on the ground. 'Oh, buggery!'

'I was going to say "crumbs",' the copper-bracelet woman said, giggling. 'Case dismissed, I reckon.'

This was too much for the pie woman. She caught hold of the other trader's scarf and wrestled her to the ground. They rolled over and over in a flurry of bare legs and black underwear, all dignity gone.

'Get them apart,' Andy Sullivan said to Denise.

It took half a minute but at least Denise was in trousers. She'd had recent training in detaining a suspect resisting arrest and she succeeded in getting the pie woman's arm behind her back and forcing it upwards so the other woman could squirm free.

The copper-bracelet woman said, 'I could do her for assault.'

'I don't think that's a good idea,' Sullivan said. He nodded to Denise. 'You can let go of her now.'

The pie woman got up, mouthing obscenities. 'Where's he gone?' she demanded. 'What happened to the thief?'

In all the distraction, the man known as Noddy had gone.

LATE THE SAME EVENING, Diamond took a call from Ingeborg, saying she'd made contact with her friend Perry, the link to the Lansdown Society. Two of the committee, Perry had told her, had a regular Monday-morning round of golf and it might be an opportunity to see them. Major Swithin and Sir Colin Tipping met at ten.

Diamond wrote down the names 'Tipping sponsored a horse race I watched the other evening.'

'I didn't know you followed the horses, Guv.'

'Horse racing or golf, I take it all in my stride. I assume that's the course up at Lansdown. I'll make it a threesome and ruin their morning.'

EARLY ON MONDAY, Diamond looked in at Manvers Street and told Keith Halliwell about the press conference fixed for the afternoon. 'Basically we're going public about the skeleton in the hope it will jog someone's memory. John Wigfull is setting it up, but you may get enquiries during the morning. I'll be at the golf course, so you're in charge.'

Not many cars were parked outside the clubhouse. Rather than go inside, Diamond made his way to the first tee. Even on an August morning, it was cool up here and he wished he'd worn a sweater.

He checked his watch. Two minutes to ten. No sign of the Lansdown Society. Then a whirring sound came from the side of the clubhouse and a golf cart glided across the turf to arrive at the tee precisely on time. One of the two riders was definitely Sir Colin Tipping. The other had more than a hint of military swagger as he stepped off and approached Diamond.

'Is there a problem?'

'Not to my knowledge,' Diamond said. 'Would you be Major Swithin?'

'I would. We have our round booked for now. It's a regular arrangement. Are you a member?'

'Visitor.'

'You know visitors have to produce a handicap certificate?'

Not the friendliest of welcomes, Diamond thought. 'I don't want to play.'

Sir Colin Tipping looked just as distinguished as he had in the winner's enclosure. Today he was in a loose-fitting yellow sweatshirt and check trousers. 'What's this, Reggie?' he said. 'Have you hired a professional to improve your game?' He chuckled at his own humour.

Diamond showed them his warrant card. 'I don't want to hold up your round, gentlemen. All I want is the benefit of your expertise.'

'If that means tips on golf, he's picked the wrong fellows,' Tipping said. He grinned at Diamond. 'Our combined handicap is bigger than the national debt.'

'It's about Lansdown,' Diamond told them. 'I understand you both take a personal interest in this area.'

'Who told you that?' the major asked.

'The reputation of the Lansdown Society is well known.'

'What do you know about the Lansdown Society?'

'He wants to be a member, Reggie,' Tipping said. 'Shall I tell him about the secret initiation ritual with the custard pies?'

Diamond wasn't sure which of these was the more tiresome: the churlish major or the laugh-a-minute knight of the realm.

'We came here to play golf,' the major said. 'Can't this wait?'

'We'll talk as you play your round. Who goes first?'

'I don't care for this at all,' the major said.

'Get on with it, Reggie,' Tipping said. 'Let's make a start, or we'll never get round.'

The major's ball travelled not very far and missed the fairway. 'I might as well give up now,' he muttered. 'No one can play under these conditions.'

'Watch me,' Tipping said. He positioned his ball and struck it twice the distance the major had. 'That puts me in charge of the buggy. Why don't you hop aboard, Superintendent? Reggie doesn't have far to walk.'

Tipping started up and they whirred up the fairway. 'Don't get the wrong impression of Reggie,' he said to Diamond. 'He's a good man. Our society couldn't function without him.'

'What does it do, exactly?'

'We try to make sure that this historic hill is respected. We don't have any official status, but we keep an eye on the multifarious activities people engage in up here—and I know what you're thinking. Who was the lady who said she didn't mind where people made love as long as they didn't do it in the street and frighten the horses? We take much the same view. But if someone tries holding a barbecue, or a motorbike rally, or anything that damages the turf, we tell them politely to find another place.'

'So do you patrol the down looking for offenders?'

'Impossible. We're a small group. We act on tip-offs. We're in touch with the legitimate organisations that use the place and they keep us informed.' He stopped the cart. 'I'll take my second, if you don't mind.'

Diamond watched him take a huge swing and miss the ball completely. His second attempt sent the ball some way along the well-mown surface.

As the cart moved on again, Diamond said above the hum of the motor, 'Did you hear about the skeleton we found?'

'Yes, we knew early on that you people were up to something. This may sound uncaring considering some poor soul died, but your digging could have been a concern. Do you know who the victim was?'

'A young girl, some years back.'

'Why would anyone bury her up here?'

'Possibly because she was killed up here.'

'On Lansdown?'

The cart stopped again. Tipping chose a club and shifted the ball another ten yards. He strode to the ball and struck it again, with more success. 'Par for this hole is four,' he said. 'I take about nine usually if my putting is tidy.'

When they moved off, Diamond asked, 'How long has your society been in existence?'

'We formed in the year they staged the mock battle, the three hundred and fiftieth anniversary. Some of us of like minds were concerned that real damage might be done to the land, with all the cannon and horses and so on. We formed this group to meet the re-enactment people and lay down certain procedures. Afterwards we decided to formalise the society and monitor some of the other activities.'

'Like the horse racing?'

'Are you a racing man?'

'No, but I saw you present the prize to the winning owner last week.'

'My daughter Davina. Wasn't that charming? I sponsor a few flat races during the year but I haven't owned a horse for some time.'

'Hang-glider?'

'That was a great horse. Sad story. Do you know it? He ran his first races here and showed such promise that I sent him to be trained at Lambourn.

Won a big one in Ireland. Everyone was certain he was set for greater things and then he popped a tendon in his near foreleg. Devastating.'

'Was he put down?'

'Lord, no. He was fit to put to stud and I would have been a very rich man as a result. I had a certain Arabian sheikh lined up as the next owner. Then the worst of all things happened. I was asked to parade my horse in front of the crowd one last time at an evening meeting. A lovely tribute. Sadly, it was the last I saw of him. Some evil-minded bastard stole him from his box.'

'What for—a ransom?'

'No. We never heard a word. My theory is that they put him to stud secretly and his progeny are winning races at long odds. All I got was some paltry insurance money.'

'You lost a lot?'

'Getting on for a million.' He stopped the cart beside his ball. 'How far off is the green, would you say?'

'Seventy yards. Maybe seventy-five.'

'One good hit, then.' Tipping took his shot and struck the ball about halfway to the green.

It would have been simpler to walk, but they couldn't leave the buggy on the fairway. 'How many members of the Lansdown Society are there?' Diamond asked when they were in motion again.

'Five now. In the original group there were seven men and one woman, the formidable Augusta White, magistrate.' Tipping halted and hauled himself out of the buggy.

'Is she still in the society?'

'Oh, yes. Splendid woman. Useful to have the law on our side.'

Diamond walked onto the green.

'Take out the pin. I'm going to try a long putt.'

Diamond did so. The ball rolled past and off the green again.

'I'm a little disappointed in you and your Lansdown Society, Sir Colin,' Diamond said, trying a different approach. 'I thought you missed nothing of what goes on up here, yet someone is killed and buried and you don't seem to have any knowledge of it.'

'I'm concerned, naturally, but it's a mystery to me.'

'You were one of the original members?'

'I was, along with Reggie and Mrs White.'

'Aren't you going to take another putt?'

He winked. 'I'm taking it as holed.' He picked up his ball.

There was a shout of 'Fore!' from behind them.

'That's Reggie,' Tipping said.

Another shout. 'Move the bloody buggy. It's blocking my line.'

'As if he ever hits straight,' Tipping said. He returned to the golf cart and moved it off the fairway.

Diamond could see the major hunched over his ball, not all that far from the green. By luck or skill the ball stopped inches from the hole.

'Not bad. Was that your seventh?' Tipping asked his opponent.

'Fifth.' The major held up five fingers.

'Tap it in, then. That hole is halved.'

'You took six?' the major said. He asked Diamond, 'Did he really?'

'I lost count,' Diamond said, not wishing to get involved. 'I was distracting him, anyway. Questions about the buried skeleton. Do you remember anything suspicious going on around the fallen oak tree some years back?'

'"Some years back" is far too vague. Can't you be more precise?'

'All right. After 1987, when the tree came down, and before 1997.'

'What do you mean by suspicious?'

Diamond said, 'A car or van parked near the tree. People digging.'

'No,' the major said. 'I would have noticed.'

'You said Mrs White is the other founder member of the society. There were eight originally. Who were the other five?'

'Two of them are dead,' Tipping said. 'The others moved away. Jamie Fleming went back to Edinburgh. He was our policeman—before your time. George Philpot bought a villa in Italy. Who was the other one?'

'Underhill,' the major said. 'The vicar of St Vincent's.'

'Of course. He was given a new parish in Norfolk.'

'So you had the Church and the police on side as well?' Diamond said, impressed by the power base of this small group.

'Still do. We recruited the next incumbent at St Vincent's, the Reverend Charlie Smart.'

'And who is your policeman?'

'Policewoman. Assistant Chief Constable Georgina Dallymore.'

Diamond's boss. He couldn't believe it.

JOHN WIGFULL'S DAY started well. The desk sergeant said two people were waiting in connection with the missing Cavalier. Strictly it wasn't his job to interview witnesses, but he'd worked in CID for years. Besides, the Cavalier was his pet project. He would meet these people himself.

The first was a woman who'd seen the piece in the *Bath Chronicle* and recognised the missing man as a down-and-out who was stealing food from tables at Sunday's car boot sale at Lansdown. 'I had you lot come out to him after he helped himself to one of my meat pies, but the bobbies let him walk away scot-free. And when I got home and saw last week's paper there the thieving bastard was, all dressed up in a fancy hat.'

'Are you sure we're talking about the same man? He isn't a down-and-out, as you put it. He's a university lecturer.'

'It was him. No question.' Her eyes widened. 'Now you mention it, though, he didn't sound like a dosser. The voice was posh.'

'How was he dressed?'

'In muddy old jeans and one of them hoodie things, and he smelled.'

'Don't you think you might be mistaken?'

Her face reddened. 'Are you calling me a liar?'

He was tempted to answer, 'Yes—and a time-waster, too.' He'd met plenty like her. 'Frankly, madam, we know who the missing man is and he isn't the sort to behave the way you describe.'

'Is that so?' she said in an explosion of outrage. 'I came here out of the goodness of my heart, giving you important information, and you treat me like I'm a liar. You can stuff it.' She marched out.

Wigfull's spirits improved when Mrs Swithin came in: one of those well-bred old ladies you know will keep their emotions in check. 'Is the photo in the paper reliable?' she asked first. 'I'm talking about the face, not the way they dressed him up. Is that really the missing man?'

'Rupert Hope, yes. He's an academic at Bristol University.'

'I have to tell you, then, that he's been behaving out of character, trying to open people's car doors in the racecourse car park. Reggie, my husband—the major—was convinced he was up to no good, so we phoned the police. I possess a powerful pair of binoculars and I had the man in focus for quite ten minutes and saw his face clearly.'

'What was he wearing?'

'A hooded garment and blue denim trousers.'

The same man, apparently. Wigfull's promising morning took a roller-coaster plunge. 'Did the police come?'

'Yes, but the man had left. It was Wednesday of last week and the car park was unusually quiet. We're often up there keeping an eye on things.'

'Did the man actually break into any of the cars?'

'No, I think they were all locked.'

'And did the police catch up with him?'

'As it turned out, no. They returned later and took statements. We had to wait almost an hour. Anyway, we saw the item in the *Chronicle* and agreed it was our duty to get in touch with you.'

'You did the right thing.' Wigfull was thinking as he spoke that he'd done the *wrong* thing in letting the pie woman go. 'We heard of another sighting as well. It begins to look as if our man is behaving erratically.'

'Either that, or he's a Trotskyist. The universities are full of left-wing people trying to change the world.'

The world had moved on a bit since Trotsky, but Wigfull had a rough idea what she meant and he thought Mrs Swithin a dependable witness.

Just to be certain, he returned a couple of overnight phone calls about the Cavalier. More sightings. Rupert Hope must have been wandering about Lansdown for days drawing attention through minor misdemeanours. Probably not as a left-wing protest, but drunk, drugged or unwell.

Why, then, hadn't the officers on patrol picked him up?

He picked up the phone and asked to have the occurrence file checked. It turned out that the same two officers had responded to both calls.

PETER DIAMOND drove back from the golf club thinking dark thoughts about the Lansdown Society. If they monitored everything that happened on the hill they may well have heard or seen something suspicious connected with the burial of the body. And as guardians of the terrain—vigilantes—they might conceivably be suspects. Vigilantes took the law into their own hands. What if they'd found some undesirable flouting their rules and killed her, maybe by accident? They'd have been well placed to find a burial site.

The substantial fly in the ointment was Georgina. Diamond had never shirked a confrontation. Noting that the ACC's Mercedes was parked in her reserved space outside, putting her on the premises, he went up to her eyrie.

'Troubles, Peter?' she said when she saw him.

'Not really, Ma'am. I just want your advice about the Lansdown Society. I was told you're a member.'

'That's right.' Her voice took on a defensive tone.

'Sir Colin Tipping and Major Swithin seem to think it's because you're in the police that you're one of them.'

'I want to make it clear, Peter, that I didn't join in my official capacity. I happen to support the conservation of the countryside. I know why you've raised this. It's the skeleton, isn't it?'

'Right, Ma'am. I was hoping the society might know something.'

'And do they?'

'Not the two gents I saw this morning.'

'They're the most likely to know. When was your victim buried?'

'Some time after 1987, when the tree was blown down.'

'Ah, well.' She spread her hands. 'The society wasn't formed until 1993.'

'Yes, but we have a ten-year time frame.'

'If Colin and Reggie say they can't help, it's no good coming to me.'

Colin and Reggie. He had to be careful here. A conflict of loyalties was looming. 'The other founder member is Mrs White, the magistrate. I might have a word with her—unless you would like to approach her yourself.'

The ACC folded her arms. 'Is this your only line of enquiry? I can't see it being very productive.'

'Forgive me for saying this, but you seem a close-knit society.'

'Perhaps we don't have anything to tell you.'

'It's no easy matter when your victim is dry bones and no one remembers anything.'

'So this *is* your only line of enquiry.'

'I'm speaking to the press this afternoon. We'll see if memories are jogged when the papers get onto the story.'

'That's more like it. Are you taking advice from John Wigfull, our new media relations manager? He's well up on all the latest interview techniques.'

'I'm sure. About Mrs White . . .'

'Well?'

'I'll speak to her myself, Ma'am.'

TO HIS CREDIT, John Wigfull had marshalled most of the local press and some of the nationals as well. Poster-sized photos of the site and the skeleton in its grave formed a backdrop for Diamond's statement. Press kits stuffed with pictures were handed to everyone.

After outlining the facts, Diamond stressed repeatedly that the team were waiting to be contacted by anyone with a memory of anything suspicious going on near the fallen tree ten to twenty years ago.

One TV reporter pressed him to speculate on whether the killer had removed the head to prevent identification.

'We don't know yet how she died. Murder is a possibility, but we can't discount a fatal accident. Whoever buried her didn't want the body discovered. That much is clear.' Long experience had taught him how to steer an interview to a close. 'I've told you all I know. With your help, we'll carry the investigation a stage further.'

Wigfull was fishing for compliments afterwards. 'I thought it went rather well. These events work so much better with good visuals like the posters.'

'Let's see what results we get,' Diamond said.

Ingeborg rushed in, bursting to tell them something.

'Someone phoned in already?' Diamond said. 'That *is* a result.'

Self-congratulation started spreading over Wigfull's features.

'No, Guv,' Ingeborg said. 'This has nothing to do with the press conference. A body has been found. The thing is, it's Lansdown again.'

THE VICTORIAN CEMETERY in the shadow of Beckford's Tower would have made an ideal location for a Gothic horror movie. Weathered obelisks, tablets and carved figures showed above a waist-high crop of brambles, cow parsley and nettles. Only the main pathways had been kept mown and a cluster of policemen and crime-scene investigators could be seen standing beside a trampled section marked with police tape. The main point of interest, a clothed body, lay face down in the narrow space between two graves.

Diamond, with Keith Halliwell in support, found a familiar character directing operations. Duckett looked up and said, 'You again?'

'I was about to say the same thing but the cadaver interests me more,' Diamond said. 'Head wound, then.'

'Nothing gets past you, does it?'

It *was* rather obvious. A gash at the back of the victim's head revealed a strip of dented skull between encrustments of blood —as ugly a wound as Diamond had seen in some time. 'Has the pathologist been by?'

'And gone.'

'How recent was the death?'

'Some hours.'

Diamond leaned over the body looking for other signs of injury.

Duckett spoke again. 'I can tell you what happened. See the beer can over there?' He pointed to a dented Foster's can lying on one of the graves. 'He was stonkered, lost his footing and hit his head.'

'How do you know all that?'

Duckett beckoned with his finger and showed Diamond a small patch of dry blood on the raised edging of the adjacent grave. Some had trickled down the side. 'In my job, you can't afford to miss a thing.'

'So why is the wound at the back of the head?'

'He fell backwards. Drunks often do.'

'He's face down.'

'You don't see it, do you?' Duckett said. 'He falls backwards, bounces his head on the stone and is thrust sideways, ending up like this.'

'It's a vicious-looking injury for a simple fall,' Diamond said.

'That granite edge is really sharp. Feel it.'

Diamond ran his fingers along the angle of the stone. Then he inspected the beer can without touching it. 'There's rust in the angle of the dent. It must have been slung away some time ago.'

Duckett quickly modified his theory. 'Well, he may not have drunk from this particular tin, but there's no denying that he hit his head.'

Deliberately, Diamond crooked his finger just as Duckett had. 'Come and look at this drop of blood you found on the stone.'

Some of the other crime-scene investigators were getting interested. With an impatient sigh, their leader crouched by the grave's edge.

Diamond said, 'What do you make of this?'

A small green blade of grass had adhered to the bloodstain.

Diamond spelled it out. 'If he cut his head on the stone I might expect to find a hair, not a piece of grass.'

'The paths are mown once a week. Of course there are clippings about.'

'Yes, but how did this one get where it is?'

'The wind, I suppose.'

Diamond glanced around the cemetery. Not a leaf was moving.

'Show me, then.' Duckett tried to sound unimpressed.

'Blood trickled from the head wound onto the grass.' Diamond pointed to a dark brown patch beside the victim's head. 'This looks like an attempt to cover up a crime. He was attacked from behind, fell face down and bled heavily. His assailant dipped the weapon in some fresh blood from the grass and let it drip on the edge of the grave to fake an accident.'

'Why would anyone bother to kill a tramp?'

'I can think of several reasons.'

'A blow from behind, you say? What with?'

'Call it a blunt instrument.'

'That old cliché?'

'You'd better make a search for that old cliché.' He couldn't resist adding, 'In your job you can't afford to miss a thing.'

Duckett made a performance of turning his head, surveying the sea of weeds. 'I'd need an army for a job like that. It's going to take days.'

'Better start soon, then. Your scene, my friend.' Diamond turned to Halliwell. 'See if you can raise some help, Keith.'

Halliwell used his mobile.

'Who found the body?' Diamond asked Duckett.

'The man who mows the paths. At about eight this morning.'

Diamond looked at what the corpse was wearing, noting the torn jeans and mud-spattered hooded jacket. 'Any idea who he is?'

'No.'

'Have you been through his pockets?'

'We're not total amateurs. We found sod all. He's a vagrant. Get the smell.'

It was true that the clothes had the smell of the unwashed, but the victim's skin didn't show the deep layer of grime Diamond would have expected. The hands were in a reasonable state. The hair was greasy, but had been cut by a professional at some time.

'OK if I lift the head? I'd like a sight of the face.'

'I suppose,'

Diamond grasped some of the brown hair above the forehead. The nose had bled, but otherwise the features were undamaged. A man of forty or so, he estimated. 'Can someone get a photo?'

The cameraman on the team took several shots before Diamond lowered the head. 'How soon can I get copies?'

'Soon as I finish here.'

Diamond got up. 'I've seen enough. Let me know if you find the weapon.'

The drive down the hill to Manvers Street was mostly silent. The two police officers had reached Broad Street when Diamond said to Halliwell, 'Two suspicious deaths on Lansdown. Is that pure chance, Keith?'

A pause for thought. 'They don't have much in common considering one happened up to twenty years ago. One a burial and the other just left in the open to be discovered. One a young woman—'

'All right, I hear what you're saying.' The stress was showing. 'You know what's on my mind, don't you?'

'Georgina?'

'Spot on. She won't like me running two murder enquiries if they're not connected.'

'We don't know if they're murders yet.'

Diamond grinned. 'That's not bad. I could run with that for a while.'

'Difficult to do, anyway,' Halliwell said. 'Run two murder enquiries.'

'I'd give it a go.'

Within the hour Diamond had a series of crime-scene pictures on his desk and on the computer. They included six close-ups of the dead man's face.

'Come and look at these, Keith. Something is familiar.'

'Do you know him?'

'No, I don't. Never met the guy.'

'Do you want them on a board where we can see them?'

'Good thinking.'

'Shall I set up another incident room?' Halliwell was excited. A much more promising investigation was in prospect.

Diamond hesitated. They already had an adjoining room where information on the skeleton case was being processed. He thought about Georgina's likely reaction to two incident rooms. 'Not yet, Keith.'

'Up at the graveyard you seemed certain he was murdered.'

'I'm inclined now to soft-pedal on that,' Diamond said. 'Make some calls to all the local refuges, the Salvation Army, and so on. See if they can throw any light on this.'

'Are you going to attend the PM?'

A casual enquiry, but both men knew what was behind it. Diamond didn't have the stomach for post-mortems.

'Tomorrow morning, I expect,' Diamond said. 'Although I've got to be here in case of developments. Could you stand in for me, Keith?'

'I was thinking about visiting a refuge for the homeless.'

Diamond frowned, then inspiration dawned. 'Ingeborg can do the refuges.'

'Leaving me free.'

'Free to go to the ball, Cinderella.'

RAFFLES THE CAT, who had taken to sleeping at the end of Diamond's bed, was roused unusually early next morning. To add insult to injury, his wrong-headed owner then went to the garage instead of the shelf where the cat food was stored and started sorting through old newspapers stacked for collection. Ten minutes of leafing through copies of the *Bath Chronicle* brought a result. He'd found the picture feature on the missing Cavalier.

'That's my baby, Raffles,' he said. 'And now we'll celebrate by opening a new tin of chicken in jelly.'

JOHN WIGFULL ARRIVED at his office soon after nine. His moustache twitched in annoyance when he saw Peter Diamond seated on the corner of his desk.

'Something the matter?' Wigfull asked.

'Far from it,' Diamond held up the newspaper. 'The missing Cavalier.' With an air of triumph he produced one of the glossy photos of the dead man and held it beside the pictures in the paper.

Wigfull gave the picture a squint. 'Who's this, then?'

'Come on, John. I know it's early in the day, but you can see it's the same guy as the one in the paper.'

'He doesn't look the same.'

'He's dead, that's why. We found him yesterday in the graveyard up at Beckford's Tower.'

'You think this is Rupert Hope?'

'I'm sure of it. Look at the hairline, the eyebrows, the mouth.'

'I suppose it could be him,' Wigfull said. 'How long has he been dead?'

'Yesterday, or the night before. No longer.'

'What did he die of?'

'I don't want to anticipate the post-mortem, which is happening as we speak, but my money is on the wound at the back of his head. What I need to know from you is where the story came from. Who reported it?'

'The university people. The last anyone saw of him was on the day of the battle re-enactment.'

'So he went missing for two and a half weeks and ended up probably murdered. I'm going to have to find out a lot more about this guy. Did you speak to anyone from the Civil War Society?'

Wigfull shook his head. 'I'm not a detective. However . . .' He turned pink. 'I did speak to a couple of people who responded to the newspaper appeal. One woman said she'd seen him at the car boot sale at Lansdown on Sunday. He helped himself to a meat pie. She described him as a down-and-out but said he had a posh accent. The other witness saw a similar man apparently trying to break into cars.'

'Where?'

'The same place—the racecourse car park—but the Wednesday before.'

'He was acting suspiciously and she didn't report him?'

'She did. Both women did. And there was a quick response from us.'

'Us?'

'Uniform. They seem to have used the softly, softly approach, but that's what they're encouraged to do. These were misdemeanours.'

'They spoke to the guy?'

'At the car boot sale, they did, for sure. The pie woman didn't think much of the way they dealt with him. She wanted him clapped in irons.'

'They must have got his name.'

'Erm . . . ' Wigfull looked shamefaced. 'He said it was Noddy.'

Diamond recalled the evening he'd been at the races with Paloma and seen the drunk almost knocked down by horses cantering to the start.

'Who were they, these cops?'

'I didn't enquire. That didn't seem important at the time.'

'Have you told anyone else?'

'No.'

Diamond put it to him straight. 'Basically, John, you goofed. You're here to deal with the press. These witnesses are under the impression they reported incidents and we, the police, are dealing with them.'

'It was just a missing-person enquiry. I thought CID wouldn't want to be bothered with that.'

'It's murder now.'

'I'll give you their names and addresses.'

THE POST-MORTEM on the body found in Lansdown cemetery had been underway for twenty minutes and already Keith Halliwell was yawning. He'd worked late last evening on the skeleton case.

'Wishing you were elsewhere, Mr Halliwell?' Dr Sealy, the pathologist, asked.

'I'm OK.'

'I know you're OK. I'm asking if you're bored. Because I can promise something of particular interest when we get to it.'

Up to now all that had happened was a slow disrobing of the dead man. As each garment was removed the police photographer took a picture.

'Where exactly are we on identification?' Dr Sealy asked, sipping coffee during another photo interval.

'My guvnor, Mr Diamond, says he knows the name.'

'Your Mr Diamond is a smart cookie. Who is the victim, then?'

'Rupert Hope and he was a history lecturer at Bristol University.'

Dr Sealy peeled the boxer shorts from the body and dropped them into a plastic evidence bag. 'If I were one of Mr Hope's students I wouldn't sit in the front row. He hasn't changed his underwear for some time.'

'He was living rough.'

'A lecturer living rough? And why was that, do you think?'

'I've no idea.'

'Well, let's see if this gives you an idea.' Dr Sealy was standing at the end of the dissection table. 'Step closer, Mr Halliwell, and take a proper look at the head wound.' The dead man's head was propped on a block.

Halliwell wasn't squeamish. He eyed the split flesh and blood-matted hair in a dispassionate way. 'So?'

'You're not really looking, are you?' Sealy pointed with his gloved finger. 'Here, to the right of the laceration, some healing has taken place.'

'After death?' Halliwell saw for himself the remnants of a scab with pink new skin forming a line more than two inches long. 'How can that be?'

'You're looking at a wound that was made when Rupert Hope was still alive. A separate wound, just to the right of the fatal blow inflicted later. What we have, Mr Halliwell, is evidence that this unfortunate man was struck on the back of the skull twice within a few weeks. The first time wasn't fatal. The second plainly was.'

3

A fresh corpse had to be a new priority for Peter Diamond. Another press conference, irksome, but necessary. He'd already asked John Wigfull to set it up for 2.30 p.m., in time to make the evening news and morning papers. The story that Rupert was the missing Cavalier was a gift to headline writers. With luck, some witnesses would get in touch by tomorrow. This new case was going to stretch his resources. Not an insurmountable problem, he thought. He'd ask Georgina to add some manpower.

The assistant chief constable didn't see it his way. 'Peter, it isn't on.'

'What isn't, Ma'am?' he said.

'Another murder enquiry.'

He tilted his head as if he must have misheard. 'It's our job. If two come together we have to cope. Plenty of keen young coppers are out there wasting their time on binge-drinkers and kids nicking sweets. They'd jump at a chance to work on a murder.'

'I'm saying we can't take this on.'

'Where's it going, then? We can't walk away from it.'

'Bristol. The victim came from there.'

'Yes, but the killing was on our patch, not theirs. I called a press conference for this afternoon.'

'Go ahead with it. Tell them this will be conducted from Bristol. Any calls to this station can easily be transferred.'

'What exactly is the problem?' he said, trying to stay reasonable. 'Is it the skeleton? It can go on the back burner while we deal with Rupert Hope.'

'It cannot,' Georgina said. 'You've set up an incident room and spoken to the press. Your people are working on the case.'

'They're on the new case as well. Halliwell is at the post-mortem as we speak. Ingeborg Smith is checking hostels for the homeless.'

'It's not efficient to have the same officers investigating two unconnected murders. I can't justify it to headquarters.'

She had a point there. His brain whirred. 'How about this? I hand the skeleton case to Keith Halliwell. He's got years of experience and he's ready to lead an enquiry. Then I can give all my attention to the Cavalier.'

'And have two incident rooms going simultaneously? Not in my police station. I've made a decision, Peter. This is final.'

Desperation drove him to say, 'What I meant is that it frees me up to go to Bristol and head the enquiry from there.'

She stared at him. His dislike of change was known to everyone in Bath. 'You're willing to relocate to Bristol?'

'It's a short drive when the traffic is light. I'll be getting there early and coming back late.' He could hardly believe he was speaking these words. 'And Halliwell deserves a case of his own.'

She'd gone silent. She was definitely wavering.

He dangled a real tempter. 'You won't see me for at least a week.'

That did it.

'I'll see what can be done. I'll have to speak to colleagues there.' Her eyes rolled upwards. 'They don't know what's about to hit them.'

He left her office wondering if he'd made the right decision. There wasn't time to ponder it for long. The press conference was in twenty minutes.

WHEN HALLIWELL RETURNED from the post-mortem, Ingeborg was outside the press conference with eyes that had just seen a unicorn.

'The boss said the incident room will be in Bristol Central. He's in charge and he's going to be there.'

'That's news to me.'

'It's about resources, he told them. Plus the fact that the dead man spent most of his time in Bristol.'

'Resources? Doesn't sound like the guvnor talking,' Halliwell said.

Diamond emerged, bouncy as ever. 'There you are, Keith, back from the dead. What's the story?'

Halliwell told him about the partly healed wound. 'Dr Sealy says it could well have caused concussion and loss of memory.'

'Which may explain his odd behaviour.' Diamond rubbed his hands. 'This is good, Keith. We must step up our enquiries here in Bath.' He paused before adding, 'When I say "we" I'm not including you, old chum. As from this moment you're heading the skeleton investigation.'

'Get away.'

'Check with Georgina if you like. It's official.' He clapped a hand on Halliwell's shoulder. 'You owe us all a drink.'

'But what about you, Guv?'

'I'll be handling the new case from Bristol. You don't have to cheer. It's only temporary.'

'What about me?' Ingeborg asked. 'Who am I with?'

'For the record, you're with Keith, right? I'm not asking you to come to Bristol. But I need someone here I can rely on, and you may find yourself doing things for me between whiles.'

She frowned. 'Serving two masters?'

'As a first step, find me the two patrol-car officers who met Rupert Hope.'

'Now, you mean?'

'I could be in Bristol tomorrow.'

A REMARK OF GEORGINA'S had stayed with Diamond longer than anything else she'd said. *It's not efficient to have the same officers investigating two unconnected murders.* But were they unconnected?

The two sets of human remains on Lansdown had been found within a couple of miles of each other and had little else to link them. They were separated by about twenty years, by the method of disposal and the sex and age of the victims. Lansdown was the one discernible link. It would not be wise to make too much of that.

And yet . . . the repeated trips up the hill to one crime scene or the other kept reinforcing his hunch that these cases were linked. Maybe the Lansdown Society had a point. Someone needed to keep an eye on things.

Towards the end of the afternoon two nervous-looking constables in uniform were ushered into his office by Ingeborg.

'You're the pair who spoke to the man whose body has been found?'

The male constable was twisting his cap like the steering wheel he would rather have been behind. 'I'm Andy Sullivan, sir, and this is PC Beal.'

'Doesn't she have a name?'

The young woman at Sullivan's side said, 'Denise, sir.' She looked straight out of school, with fine, blonde hair pinned up and pale skin of the kind that obviously coloured at the slightest personal remark.

'You were sent to deal with an incident up at the racecourse, right?'

Andy Sullivan asserted his seniority as spokesman. 'Two incidents on different days. The first was suspicious behaviour, tampering with car doors. We met the complainants, a Major Swithin and his wife, but the suspect had already left when we arrived. He was seen heading for the enclosure area. We conducted a search and unfortunately didn't find him.'

Denise Beal cleared her throat. She'd turned beetroot-red this time. 'Actually, I did find him. Behind one of the grandstands.'

Sullivan swung to face her. 'You didn't tell me.'

'No. I kept it to myself. I, um, thought he was simple.'

'You spoke to the man whose body has been found?' Diamond said.

'I didn't know who he was.'

Sullivan said, 'This is totally new to me.'

She said, 'You were a long way off at the time.'

'You'd gone different ways?' Diamond said.

Sullivan said, 'I was checking the stables.'

'You sent her round the enclosure area while you took a stroll along the racecourse? How long have you been in the police, Denise?'

'Six weeks, sir.'

Diamond gave Sullivan a look. 'So what did you say to the guy?'

'I asked him what he was doing there and who he was. I was trying to keep him talking until Andy arrived. He said he was known as Noddy.'

'Did you ask for a proper name?'

'I tried. He didn't seem to have an answer. That's why I thought he was simple. He was smelly from living rough, not boozing. I asked if he'd just come from the car park and he didn't seem to know.'

'Did you notice anything about his speech?'

'Yes. He had a nice voice. Educated. He didn't act like a villain.'

'All right,' Diamond said, and brought Sullivan back into the discussion. 'The second time you were called to deal with this man was when?'

'Sunday morning, sir. He'd been nicking food at the car boot sale.'

'I know a bit about this,' Diamond said. 'This was the meat pie.'

'The woman said she'd made a citizen's arrest, but I thought we could deal with it on the spot,' Andy Sullivan said. 'I asked him his name and got the same answer.'

'Noddy?'

'He did do a lot of nodding while he was talking to us. I can understand someone calling him that,' Denise piped up.

'Did you think he was taking the piss?' Diamond asked Sullivan.

'It didn't come across like that. He didn't seem to know much about himself. I tried to find out where he lived and didn't get a proper answer.'

Denise confirmed it. 'He said he slept anywhere that was dry.'

'What else did you discover?'

'That was about it, sir. Unfortunately, it got out of hand after that because the pie lady attacked another woman and we had to separate them. When we'd sorted that, the suspect had gone.'

'You must have heard by now that your man Noddy has been identified as Rupert Hope, a university lecturer who has been missing for a couple of weeks. This was the man who was murdered in Lansdown cemetery. He was probably suffering from memory loss. The post-mortem showed he took a heavy blow to the head about two weeks before he was killed.'

'That's awful,' Denise said. 'He was gentle, no threat to anyone. If we'd arrested him, it couldn't have happened.'

'Don't lose sleep over that,' Diamond said. 'You did your job.' He liked what he'd seen of this young woman. She cared more about what had happened to the victim than her own good record. She'd make a better copper than Sullivan.

After they'd left the office he thought more about his own sighting of Rupert Hope on the racecourse and the shambolic, wayward figure he'd cut. He'd misjudged the man. Everyone seemed to have got him wrong. This investigation was more personal now.

KEITH HALLIWELL looked in. 'You don't mind me asking, Guv? As I'm running the skeleton enquiry now, I wonder if you've got any pointers for me.'

'You want some tips?' Diamond said.

Halliwell grinned sheepishly. 'We looked at the missing-persons index and there was no one obvious. I can't see how we can move on until we identify the woman. We know her approximate age and when she died, within a year or two, and that's all. Without the skull we can't use dental records.'

'I doubt if you'll find the skull. The point of the killer removing it is to hinder identification.'

'I was looking for encouragement.'

'OK. Has anything resulted from the press coverage? There are always members of the public who call in.'

'Some have. I'm not optimistic.'

'Have you done a computer search of our own files from the nineties?'

'A lot of case notes are still on paper.'

'Still has to be done,' Diamond said. 'And you'll need to go through the local papers of twenty years ago. A disappearance could have been reported. Look for mentions of Lansdown in particular.' Privately he was relieved it was now someone else's job. 'And there's one other thing.'

'What's that?'

'Have the zip fly we found with the body cleaned up in the lab. They might find something on it. We assumed she was wearing jeans. What sort— cheap or designer? You sometimes get a manufacturer's mark on the tab.'

'Doesn't it have to be shown to the court as we found it?'

'It's been photographed, hasn't it? And the chain of evidence isn't in doubt. We have a right to make a forensic examination.'

'And will it help, knowing which brand of jeans she wore?'

'We don't know yet, do we?'

BEFORE SETTING OUT for Bristol, Diamond had one more interview in mind. He believed there was mileage in the Lansdown Society. Self-appointed busybodies dedicated to keeping the place respectable were allies he needed.

Mrs Augusta White, the magistrate, was easy to contact. 'Yes, of course I know you,' she told him over the phone.

'I need to speak to you today, Mrs White, if you don't mind.'

'If this is really necessary you can meet me in the YMCA fitness centre. Shall we say in three-quarters of an hour? Wear something light.'

'I wasn't aiming to work out.'

'You'd better make a show of it. They don't like men standing about eyeing the women. It's a gym, Mr Diamond.'

The YMCA was no great distance from the police station. On the way he called at a sports shop and picked up a white T-shirt, cheap trainers and a pair of shorts. At the front desk he showed his warrant and the receptionist sent him downstairs to the gym.

He spotted Augusta White's tightly permed silver hair at once. She was pedalling steadily on an exercise bike. He reckoned Mrs White was about half his weight.

'Why don't you step on the treadmill next to me?' she said when he emerged, kitted and ready to go. 'Put it on a setting you can handle.'

He started at an ambling gait he was confident he could tolerate for ten minutes or so, by which time Mrs White would surely be exhausted.

'This is about the Lansdown Society,' he said. 'I've already spoken to Major Swithin and Sir Colin Tipping.'

'Sir Colin told me. I can't think what you're hoping to get from me that you haven't heard from them. They're about as discreet as a chorus line.'

'I reckon you have a better memory than theirs. You formed the society in 1993, I was told, to see that the down wasn't mistreated by the people staging the mock battle up there.'

'Correct. And later we put ourselves on a more permanent footing.'

'Do you happen to remember if anyone was seriously hurt in the battle? You know why I'm asking?'

'I know about the skeleton you found. It's female, isn't it? Women do take part. Sometimes. The less adventurous prefer a support role. They call themselves camp followers.'

'A camp follower could still be hit by a stray cannonball, I expect.'

'I watched the battle,' she said, 'and I'm absolutely certain real cannonballs weren't used.'

'This woman was minus her head.'

'Lord save us, if there had been a serious accident like that, the papers would have been full of it.'

'I know. I'm working on the theory that the death was covered up. She was buried close to the battleground.'

'Surely people would have raised the alarm: family, friends, work mates?'

'Unless she was a loner.'

'Loners don't join in war games, Mr Diamond—certainly not female loners. Most of them join because their boyfriends or husbands are part of it.' She took a hand off the handlebar and raised a finger. 'Ah, I see it now. You want to link it with the killing of the man found in the cemetery. He was one of the battle people, a Cavalier.'

'We can't ignore the possibility.'

'It's far more likely that your skeleton lady had nothing to do with Cavaliers and Roundheads. My guess is that she was the victim of a sex crime . . . How are you doing? Do you want to step off?'

'I'm all right. Is the battle area popular with courting couples?'

'Don't ask me. You're the policeman.'

'Yes, but you people patrol it regularly.'

'"Patrol" is not the way I think of it. We're not vigilantes, you know.'

Speak for yourself, he thought. The major, for one, seemed to think he had a mission to catch anyone who misbehaved. 'The problem with the sex murderer theory,' he said, 'is that he'd need to have a spade with him to bury his victim.'

'Drivers sometimes carry spades routinely in case of snow. Or if they're treasure hunters, or have an allotment. One can think of reasons. Murderers can be resourceful when it comes to covering up their crimes.'

'And I dare say some crimes are committed on Lansdown.'

'Of course.'

'Any habitual offenders up there?'

His calf muscles were aching. He'd need to step off soon.

She laughed. 'You're scraping the barrel now.'

'No. This man Rupert Hope was attacked twice in two weeks. He was living rough. We could be looking for someone with a grudge against him. Maybe someone who gets violent when drunk. As a magistrate you must see a few.'

'Regularly, but not specially linked with Lansdown. If you don't mind me saying so, you've turned rather pink.'

He could feel his face glowing. 'I'm stopping presently. In your rambles over the last couple of weeks did you see Rupert Hope at all?'

'How would I know?' she asked. 'Was his head bandaged?'

'Probably not. How do I switch this thing off?' The controls were a blur. She leaned right across him and touched the screen.

'Thanks for that. It suddenly got difficult.' He stepped off, panting.

Augusta White continued pedalling. 'You don't mind if I continue? I have another mile to go.'

HE'D ARRANGED TO SEE Paloma at her house in Lyncombe that evening. Having driven there, he felt a sharp pain in his back when he tried to rise from the car seat. It was ridiculous, but he couldn't get out. He had to sound the horn.

Paloma came out. With her help he got vertical and limped inside, where he explained about the session at the fitness centre.

'What were you on?' she asked.

'A treadmill,' he said, 'and I was only walking, for pity's sake.'

'You must have moved in a way you wouldn't normally. I can see the pain you're in. You'll probably need to take a couple of days off work.'

'Some chance.' He told her about the Rupert Hope investigation.

'Peter, no one is indispensable.'

'That's exactly my point. They can replace me and I don't want to be replaced. The boss will hand the whole thing over to Bristol CID. I've got to put in an appearance even if I'm on crutches.'

'Crutches wouldn't look good. We have to get you mobile. Ice and heat.'

She spread cushions on the floor and he removed his shirt and trousers and lay face down in his jockey shorts. He was alone for about ten minutes and the ache eased enough for him to think how ridiculous he must look. His relationship with Paloma hadn't reached the stage when anything goes.

She returned and the ice was applied. His intake of breath was like a rocket launch.

Paloma said, 'These are packs of frozen peas. If you were a millionaire footballer you'd have a medic and the spray, but you're not, so you've got me and Captain Birdseye. Is it helping?'

'It's going numb. I don't like to think what the hot part will be.'

'Wet flannels heated in the microwave. Take it from me, you wouldn't get better treatment if you flew first class to America.'

'I'll take your word for that.'

Paloma frequently made business trips to Los Angeles to advise on period-costume designs for films. It was a mystery to Diamond why a high-earning professional was interested in an overweight Bath policeman who travelled in the tourist section.

A flannel was applied and he gave a fair imitation of a peacock screeching.

She said, 'I hope there was a payoff for this. Did you get something out of the session on the treadmill as well as a stiff back?'

'Less than I hoped for. The Lansdown Society members spend a lot of time keeping an eye on things, but they seem to miss all the violence.'

'What's the object of this society?'

'To keep the place peaceful and unspoiled.'

'They're not much good at it if a man was attacked twice and murdered.'

'I'm beginning to think it's more about giving the members a sense of importance. Let's face it, Lansdown has never been all that peaceful. I wouldn't mind betting the Iron Age saw plenty of brutality. Then we know about the Civil War battle. And in the Second World War, fighter planes were taking off from Charmy Down airfield. Bath had its share of the bombing.' He was breathing more freely. 'That feels better after the first shock. I'm grateful.'

Paloma insisted on one more application and he manfully agreed. 'You shouldn't think of driving to Bristol tomorrow,' she said, applying the frozen peas to Diamond's back. 'Can't you switch cases and stop in Bath?'

'Halliwell doesn't have the seniority to lead the Bristol team. I have to get there somehow. A murder investigation can't be put on hold.'

'What's your plan?'

'There are three obvious lines of enquiry: Hope's work at the university and the people there, the battle re-enactment he took part in, and—hardest of all to crack—the possibility that it was a random attack.'

'What about forensic science? Doesn't that trap most murderers now?'

'It's not the easy ride they make out. We always hope for traces of DNA, but if you can't find the weapon and the victim didn't put up a fight, the possibilities reduce sharply.'

'Footmarks?'

'The crime-scene people will do their best to find some. The trouble is that the cemetery is a public place. You get a fair few visitors walking the paths, especially as Beckford's Tower is there, a tourist attraction.'

'Which reminds me,' she said. 'I must get that Beckford book for you.'

'Thanks.' He'd rather hoped she'd forgotten it.

'How are you feeling now? Ready to think about food? I was planning to send for a Chinese.'

'Suits me,' he said, 'so long as you don't make me use chopsticks.'

SHE INSISTED on driving him to Bristol headquarters in the morning. The treatment had eased the back pain but she wanted to be certain he didn't go into spasm after a few miles in heavy traffic. He agreed it wouldn't make a good start to ask his new team to carry him inside.

She drove his car confidently through the notoriously confusing one-way system to Trinity Road, where he was able to get out unaided. His mind had been on what he'd say and he hadn't thought how Paloma was getting back.

'The train,' she said. 'I know my way to Temple Meads.'

He nodded. 'This place confuses me.'

'Don't let it show.'

When Diamond looked in, the day shift had gathered for what was known in the trade as morning prayers, but there was nothing worshipful about it. The duty inspector was reporting on an early-morning drugs bust. He stopped in midsentence and said, 'Can I help you?'

'I expect so,' Diamond said, and introduced himself.

The inspector's manner changed from sniffy to servile. 'Would you like to address the meeting, sir?'

'What I'd really like to address is the porcelain, before I meet the top brass,' Diamond said. 'Which way is it?'

The lower ranks enjoyed that. He was off to a good start.

Twenty minutes later he sat down with his CID team, twelve detectives ranging from a muscleman with a silver earring to a veteran with bifocals. He had to be careful. For all he knew, the owner of the silver earring might be the inspector. He needed an icebreaker. He picked up a set of crime-scene photos and commented that someone had made a useful start.

A slim black guy gave the slightest of nods. 'Septimus Ward, DI, sir.'

'The senior man?'

Septimus nodded a second time. No hint of a smile. It was up to Diamond to win this lot over.

'You're the experts here, being local, so I'm in your hands. How much can you tell me about the victim, Rupert Hope?'

Some looks were exchanged. No one seemed willing to say anything.

He added, 'There was nothing found—mobile, wallet or credit cards. He was a university lecturer, and that's about all we know.'

This was so different from the briefings in Bath. There, Ingeborg or John Leaman would have offered something. He was doing all the talking.

'Does anyone here know any background?' he asked.

Septimus relented a little. 'He was from these parts, went to Clifton College, did his university studies here, took a higher degree at Oxford and then came back as a lecturer. I don't think he has any family left in Bristol.'

At least there was communication. 'The parents are in Australia,' Diamond said. 'I know that much. He lived in a flat in Whiteladies Road.'

'Alone?' another man asked.

'Apparently, yes.'

'No relationships?'

'None we know about. Let's get digging, then, everything we can get on this man: friends, enemies, work habits, nightlife. We'll be looking in particular for anyone with a reason to dislike him. I gather he was friendly and good at his job, so anyone with a grudge should stand out. Septimus . . .'

'Sir.'

'Thanks for that, but "Guv" will do. You can divvy up the duties. We need statements from his landlord and neighbours. Anything of note about visitors in recent weeks, changes to the routine and so on. Another team goes through the flat looking for anything about recent contacts: letters, phones, address book, computer. The third and fourth team do the university, talk to lecturers and students, look in his office or locker, or whatever they have. By tonight I want to know this man better than I know myself.'

'Does this operation have a name, Guv?' Septimus asked.

'You can call it what you like as long as you do a good job.'

'Operation Cavalier?'

'If you like. Cavalier it is.'

'Do you want to be out and about yourself, Guv?'

A loaded question. Talk about respect. He could earn some for himself by leading from the front. He remembered his bad back. 'No, someone has to get this place up and running. And I'll need an office manager.'

Heads turned to the beefy owner of the earring. He said, 'Fair cop. You've got me bang to rights.'

This caused amusement.

'What's your name?' Diamond asked, suspecting he was being set up.

'Chaz . . . Guv.'

After the rest of them had quit the room Diamond asked Chaz his rank and learned that he'd made it to sergeant, indicating that somebody rated him. 'Do you know what this involves, Chaz?'

'Common sense, isn't it? We need staff. Someone to take calls, two or three computer operators to file the statements, an indexer, an action allocator and probably an admin officer as well.'

Encouraging.

In the first hour, Chaz not only conjured up the equipment, the phones and computers, but the civilian staff as well. He saw them as they arrived and told them precisely what their duties were.

'You've done this before,' Diamond said.

'No, Guv. I'm a born organiser.' Chaz simply stated a fact.

Before noon, the first call came in from Rupert Hope's flat. The search team had found an address book and a diary and started up his computer. 'I'll have a patrol car pick up the tower unit and bring it here,' Chaz said. 'Use your time looking through his drawers.'

Steadily a picture of the murdered man was taking shape. He'd been passionate about his subject and an inspiring teacher, regularly taking his students on field trips. History in his eyes wasn't about dead people, it was the key to enlightenment and the hope for a better society.

'Good at his job,' Chaz said with approval.

'So it seems,' Diamond said. 'We could be looking at jealousy as a motive if he was that special.'

'Some other lecturer?'

'Maybe.'

The team at the flat reported that Rupert Hope must have been keen on personal hygiene. The towels were clean and every surface was immaculate. It was evident that he hadn't been back there while he was living rough. He'd been reading about the Civil War and left several bookmarks in pages with references to the Battle of Lansdown. 'This is good,' Diamond said to Chaz, 'but I'd like to find someone he treated badly.'

The computer tower arrived and one of the civilian staff was given the task of extracting everything of possible use. The dossier on the dead man was growing appreciably without yet providing much.

'Did they find the murder weapon?' Chaz asked.

'No. And they've had time to search the entire cemetery now.'

'Do you know what it was?'

'Something heavy and blunt, probably more like a cosh than an axe.'

Diamond told the team when they assembled late in the afternoon that Operation Cavalier had brought a good result. 'Thanks to your efforts we know a whole lot more about this guy. Chaz has drawn up a profile and each of you gets a copy. No obvious leads have emerged, unfortunately.'

While they were leaving he overheard someone say, 'Reading between the lines, he's up shit creek without a paddle.'

DIAMOND LOWERED HIMSELF into the car seat uncomfortably, but once behind the wheel he felt OK. The evening rush was over and he presently found himself on the Keynsham bypass with a chance to think. A sunny evening. He'd call Paloma later and suggest they meet for a drink.

Approaching Saltford, an overtaking motorcyclist appeared alongside him. The bike's blue lights were flashing. He was being pulled over.

He came to a stop in a lay-by and lowered the window.

'Switch off the engine, sir, and step out of the car.'

He turned the key and summoned up a smile. 'Switching off is the easy part. The getting out could be difficult. I've got a stiff back.'

'Should you be in charge of a car in that case?'

'It only flared up today. Look, I'm in the Old Bill myself.' His warrant card was in his back pocket and impossible to reach in his present condition. 'Peter Diamond, Detective Superintendent.'

In a situation such as this, rank is supposed to count for nothing. If he'd committed an offence there ought to be no favours. In reality, most traffic cops are lenient when they find they've stopped one of their own.

This one was an awkward cuss. 'If you were the chief constable I'd still ask you to step out. The law's the same whoever you are.'

Diamond opened the door, put out a leg and felt a strong twinge in his back. He gripped the roof and heaved himself out, emitting a yelp of pain.

'The reason I stopped you is your nearside brake light isn't working.'

'I wasn't aware of that. Thanks, Officer. I'll get a new bulb.' Biting back his fury he added, 'Now, if you'd like to see my warrant card . . .'

'I'd rather see your driving licence.'

He snapped, 'Oh, come on, it's a brake light, not drunk driving.'

'And your tax disc is out of date.'

'Is it?' He turned to see for himself. 'You're right.' He'd been sent a reminder weeks ago. 'I'll renew it on the Internet the minute I get home.'

'The licence, please, sir.'

Diamond produced it and the cop used his radio to check with the Police National Computer. Then, 'I'm reporting you, sir, for driving an untaxed vehicle. You can finish your journey, but don't be so unwise as to use the car again until you get the new disc. And the brake light.'

'YOU CAN BORROW MINE,' Paloma said in the Crown that evening.

'I appreciate the offer,' he said, 'but I'll hop aboard a patrol car.'

'I doubt if you'll hop anywhere in your present state. Let me take you.'

'No. I've thought of a way I can use this to my advantage.'

'What's that?'

'I'll tell you if it works.'

She took a sip of her white wine. 'Are you any nearer to finding who killed this man?'

'We concentrated on the victim today, building up a profile. The problem is that here was a harmless guy who put a lot into his job and didn't make enemies of people. Mind, he wasn't all that popular in the staff room.'

'Did the students like him?'

'Apparently. He made big efforts to bring the history to life for them.'

'And in the process showed up the other lecturers? Was that what made him unpopular? Enough to justify murder?'

'That would be stretching it.'

'Look at it another way, then. Your victim may have been a harmless guy, but he had a knack of annoying people. He seems to have caused an upset at the car boot sale.'

'Nicking stuff because he was hungry.'

'You don't know what else he got up to while he was living rough.'

'I know one thing. He was at the races. Remember the guy who wandered across the course when the runners were going to the start?'

'That was Rupert?' Paloma put her hand to her mouth.

'Has to be. He gave his name as Noddy. I took him to be a drunk.'

'That's awful, Peter. I thought the same as you. How wrong we were.'

He nodded. 'We saw something and we made an assumption, like the people who saw him trying the doors of parked cars. I've been assuming professional jealousy played a part in his death. It could be more basic.'

'Someone who caught him misbehaving up at Lansdown and saw red?'

'Exactly. I must find out more about those days when he was behaving erratically. I'd hoped to get help from the Lansdown Society. They're the resident snoops.'

'They can't be everywhere. You're more likely to hear from someone who happened to be passing by.'

'Walking the dog?' He laughed. 'You're so right. You can have a thousand coppers doing a fingertip search, but nothing beats a dog's nose.'

'You wouldn't have found that skeleton without the dog's help.'

He sighed and shook his head. 'The skeleton isn't my case any more.'

She smiled faintly. 'It still rankles, doesn't it?'

'Slightly.'

They finished their drinks and Diamond said he'd better get home.

Paloma said, 'I suppose it's no use offering you a back massage?'

'I couldn't take it.'

Her face creased in sympathy. 'Are you feeling worse, then?'

'Quite a bit better, thanks to you, but your touch would inflame me.'

'Really, Peter, what you're saying hadn't crossed my mind.'

'It crossed mine, and I'm in no state to make a move, more's the pity.'

'Hurry up and get better, then.'

APPRECIABLY MORE MOBILE next morning, he took the bus into Bath and arrived early at the police station. The desk sergeant was chatting to a MOP—a member of the public. 'Ah,' he said, spotting Diamond, 'here's somebody from CID. Inspector, can you spare five to talk to this gentleman—your name, sir?'

'Dave Barton.' The MOP turned his gaze hopefully on Diamond. 'It's about that skeleton they found on Lansdown,' he said.

'Sorry,' Diamond said raising a hand. 'That's Inspector Halliwell's case.' You'll need to see one of his team.' He let himself through the door behind the desk and started the painful climb up the stairs to Georgina's lair.

'Peter,' she said, as he knocked and entered her office, 'why aren't you in Bristol?'

'That's what I came to tell you about. There's a technical hitch.'

'Have a seat. You're not ill, are you? You don't seem to be moving freely.'

'That's another story. This is something else, something embarrassing. I was booked by a traffic cop on the way home last night. One of my brake lights had gone.'

She flapped her hand dismissively. 'That can happen to anyone.'

'He happened to notice my tax disc was out of date.'

'Oh. Have you applied for a new one?'

'I did when I got home. It takes a couple of days to come through. I'm off the road until I can get it all sorted. What I'm saying is that I won't be going into Bristol today.' Chew on that, Georgina, he thought.

'Ah.' She placed her hands palm down on her desk. 'Have a word with George Pallant. He'll fix up a ride for you.'

George Pallant was the inspector in charge of transport. Diamond had covered this. 'They're doing a vehicle check on the London Road today. You know what that does to manpower. I'll phone Bristol and tell them to manage without me.'

Georgina took an audible breath. 'We can't have that. Where is your car?'

'At home. I came in by bus. I don't intend to spend the day twiddling my thumbs. I can make myself useful to Keith Halliwell.'

'He doesn't need you interfering.' A sound of exasperation came from deep in her throat. She plunged her hand into her pocket. 'Here. Take mine.' She tossed a car key across the desk.

This was a development he hadn't prepared for. 'Your Mercedes? You're lending it to me?'

'I am,' she said with an air of righteousness. 'I have a meeting here tonight of the Crime Prevention Panel and I won't be needing the car until late. Let's have no more shilly-shallying. Get to your duties, Peter.'

He couldn't believe she'd entrusted him with her gleaming silver Merc, a measure of how much she wanted him out of Bath and out of her hair. More than that, she'd outfoxed him. He'd be going to Bristol after all.

DIAMOND DROVE carefully, not only because it was Georgina's car, but because he always did. Somewhere at the back of his mind was also a superstition that bad luck comes in threes. He'd hurt his back and been booked. If a third mishap was coming it had better not involve the Mercedes.

He tried to be more constructive. An action plan for the day was needed. The information-gathering on Rupert Hope couldn't last much longer. Paloma may well have been right: the last days at Lansdown could be the key to the mystery, a spur-of-the-moment killing by someone Hope had upset. Running the investigation from Bristol meant the emphasis was on former contacts and earlier events. Was that all a waste of time?

His thoughts were interrupted by a loud rumbling from the car, which was slowing perceptibly. He braked and put on the hazard lights. A busy dual carriageway wasn't the ideal place to stop.

He guessed what was wrong: a flat tyre. When he eventually—and painfully—hauled himself out, he found he was right. A perfectly good tyre with plenty of tread had run over a nail.

What now? He didn't fancy changing the tyre while his back was still giving twinges. Better phone for assistance.

Fortunately he had his underused mobile with him. Unfortunately it needed charging. He flung the phone on the back seat and went to look for the spare tyre and the jack. Lifting the tyre wasn't easy. He managed to rotate it out of the boot and onto the roadside. At the sixth attempt he fathomed how to assemble the jack. By degrees he succeeded in getting the punctured tyre clear of the ground.

Could have been raining, he told himself to raise morale, while using the wrench to free the first bolt. The raised morale didn't last long as he applied himself to the task. He removed all the bolts and with a supreme effort lifted off the damaged wheel and shoved the spare into place.

Nice work, Diamond, he said to himself. All it needs now is to tighten the five bolts and lower the jack. For a technophobe this isn't a bad effort.

There was one more hitch. The bolts wouldn't tighten properly. He kept turning the wrench but they wouldn't go all the way in.

A voice behind him said, 'In trouble, are we?' It sounded familiar.

He turned and found himself eye to eye with the same traffic cop who'd stopped him the evening before. The sense of surprise was mutual.

'You?' the cop said. 'What's this—your second car?'

'It belongs to the assistant chief constable.'

'Oh, yes?'

He recalled that the cop hadn't inspected his ID last night. Probably thought he was a fantasist.

'Thanks to you, I had to borrow this one and it got a puncture. If you'll lend me a hand tightening these bolts I'll be on the road again.'

The cop tried and didn't succeed and Diamond felt justified.

'Is that the owner's manual on the ground?'

'Well, it's not the works of Shakespeare.'

'Let's have a look.' The cop thumbed through the pages covering advice on changing a tyre. 'You know what? You're trying to put on the spare with the wrong bolts. I wouldn't mind betting there's a different set for use with the spare.' He went to the boot and came back in triumph with a set of bolts in an unopened bag. 'These are at least an inch shorter. You've been driving the bolts into the hub. Wouldn't surprise me if you've done some serious damage. Did you say this car belongs to your boss?'

It took another hour, but eventually a breakdown lorry came out from Georgina's Mercedes dealer in Bath and took the stricken car away. Diamond rode with the driver. 'Any idea what this will cost me?'

'I guess you'll need a new subframe and with it the flange, angular contact and rim lock. With tax you won't get much change out of a grand.'

'Jesus!'

'That's not counting the new tyre. You'll want a new tyre by the looks of the old one.'

He didn't ask the price.

THE GOOD NEWS, he stressed to Georgina when he got back, was that the garage was fixing everything. He would collect the car at five and drive it back to Manvers Street—as good as new.

She listened to his account in a stunned state. He admitted full responsibility and said he'd pay for repairs. He was out of the office and on his way downstairs before her mouth closed.

Fish and a double portion of chips went some way to absorbing his own shock. Now that he'd informed Georgina, he was feeling better about the whole sorry episode. He'd been right about misfortunes coming in threes. He'd had his three now. He could move on with confidence. He'd already called Bristol and asked Septimus Ward to stand in as senior investigating officer for the rest of the day. There was plenty to keep the team busy.

So he left the canteen with a smile. He felt free to pass on his story to Keith Halliwell and anyone else who would be amused by it.

The incident room was buzzing. Civilians he'd not seen before were working computers. A large map of Lansdown was covered in markers he didn't understand. There were photos of the skeleton in its grave and laid out in the lab. On another wall, events were listed on a chart. Halliwell, a phone to his ear, was too busy to listen to stories of Georgina's car.

Ingeborg came in. 'Hi, Guv. I thought you were in Bristol.'

'I was. You seem to be busy. Getting anywhere?'

'Keith thinks so. We had a new witness in this morning. He only just left. I don't know what it was about, but Keith and Leaman took the statement and they seem fired up.'

'I think I met the guy. He was in first thing.'

'I'd better get on,' said Ingeborg. 'I'm doing the map.'

He decided to leave them to it. The story of the Mercedes could wait.

In his office, he tried some cautious movements to see if his back had worsened as a result of the tyre change. He placed a hand on the filing cabinet and tried a gentle plié, like a ballet dancer at the barre.

Behind him came the sound of a throat being cleared. He turned to find Halliwell standing in the doorway. 'Am I interrupting, Guv?'

'Not at all,' he said. 'You should see my Nutcracker.'

Halliwell didn't get it.

Diamond said, 'I looked in at the incident room a short while ago. You were up to your eyes in work.'

'Inge told me you came. Is everything OK? I didn't expect to see you here.'

'Car trouble.'

'Ah. Too bad. But as you're here, I can pass on something of interest. We took a witness statement this morning.'

'Dave Barton?'

'You know already?'

Diamond shook his head. 'I met him briefly.'

'Well, I don't know how much he told you, but you might like to read the statement. He was there when they re-enacted the battle and it seems he teamed up with Rupert Hope.'

'My man?' Diamond's interest quickened.

'They were both in the Royalist Army, as Dave calls it, and they were killed—pretend killed. He offered your man a lager. He'd hidden a six-pack before the battle, buried it at the base of a fallen tree.'

'Our tree?'

'My tree now,' Halliwell was sharp to point out. 'They quit the battlefield for a while and went to look. They found two cans and had a drink and then felt in the hole for the others and they'd gone. Someone must have helped themselves. Dave started burrowing. He didn't find the other tins, but he pulled out a bone that seems to have been the femur—my femur.'

'I thought the dog found that?'

'I'm coming to that.'

'Did they know what it was?'

'They worked out that it was human and they assumed, like us, that it probably belonged to some soldier killed in the real Civil War. They agreed the decent thing was to let him rest in peace, so they buried it again.'

'In the same place?'

'Yes. Then they both went back to the battle and Dave never spoke to Rupert again. He didn't know he was dead until I told him.'

'It's been all over the television.'

'I doubt if he bothers with the box, and he said he doesn't read papers. He's the outdoor type. Likes his riding and his shooting and his beer. Someone told him in the pub last night that a skeleton was found and it was part of a murder investigation and that's why he came forward.'

'Are you sure he knew nothing of Rupert Hope's death?'

'It came as a shock when I told him. He's a good actor if it was put on.'

'What's Dave's job?'

'Blacksmith. He's got the smithy at Bradford on Avon.'

'Got you.' Diamond's thoughts went briefly to blunt instruments. 'I'd better read that statement. This could change everything, Keith.'

After speed-reading Dave-the-blacksmith's statement, Diamond took it upstairs for another session with Georgina.

Her door was open and she was on the phone to her garage, talking about rim locks and flanges, getting their version of the damage.

'Didn't you believe me?' he asked.

'That's not the point, Peter. I wanted to hear it from them. What have you got there? The estimate?'

She couldn't get the damaged Mercedes out of her head.

'No, Ma'am. It's a witness statement taken this morning from a black-smith by the name of Dave Barton.'

'Do you think it's significant?' she said.

'I certainly do,' Diamond replied. 'We've been appealing for witnesses for days without success.'

'He doesn't appear to have seen anything unlawful.'

'With respect, that isn't the point. He and Rupert found the skeleton and, some time after that, Rupert was attacked.'

'What are you suggesting—that this Dave was the assailant?'

'No, it's more basic than that. We thought the leg bone was found by a dog. We didn't know these two guys found it first. What we have now is a definite link between the skeleton and the Cavalier.'

'There's a difference of twenty years between the two deaths.'

There were times when Georgina closed her mind to reason. This would work so much more smoothly if she came to her own decision and believed she had made it independently. To encourage the process, Diamond spaced his words. 'Rupert had the femur in his hands and not long after that he was attacked and later murdered.'

'That isn't in dispute.' She still hadn't cottoned on.

He was forced to spell it out. 'Ma'am, I need an operational decision from you. We can't treat these cases as separate incidents. I'm asking you to centralise both investigations in Bath from one major incident room.' He didn't say who should be in charge. She may have worked that out for herself.

4

Keith Halliwell would be heartbroken. His first chance as SIO snatched away just when he'd got everything up and running.

Diamond was known to be a bruiser who let nothing stand in his way, but Halliwell was the nearest he had to a friend in the team. The news of the decision shouldn't come from anyone else. He went to the incident room and asked Halliwell to drive him to the garage to collect Georgina's car.

'Guv, I wish I could spare the time,' Halliwell said. 'I'm running a murder case and you know what that's like.'

'Sorry, Keith, but I do know what it's like and Leaman can take over for twenty minutes. We need to talk.'

In the car, Diamond went over the logic of drawing the two enquiries into one. Through focusing exclusively on the skeleton case, Halliwell, like Georgina, had missed the significance of Dave Barton's statement.

'As I see it now,' Diamond summed up, 'neither you nor I will get a result working in isolation.'

'You're telling me you're taking over again,' Halliwell said.

'I'm telling you there has to be cooperation.'

'And I have to step aside.'

Diamond saw the look and heard the despair. Fortunately the deal he'd done with Georgina had a sweetener. 'Nothing as daft as that. You were appointed SIO for the skeleton enquiry and that's what you remain.'

'So how will you fit in?'

'Not the way you think. There's going to be a new SIO for the Rupert Hope case, an inspector from Bristol called Septimus Ward.'

'I know Septimus,' Halliwell said. 'Met him on a firearms course. He's OK.'

'Good. He's going to be transferred here with the pick of the Bristol lot. The investigation is under one roof now.'

'Two incident rooms in Manvers Street?'

'Just the one.'

Halliwell shook his head. 'You're joking.'

'I'm afraid that means some rearranging. You'll need to transfer some of the display material to computer.'

'I prefer it where I can see it. Mine is the hard case to crack, going back twenty years. I'm dealing with masses of information.'

'You'll get your share of resources, Keith, I guarantee.'

'So what's your part in this?'

'I'm the CIO.'

'C is for chief? Keeping your distance?'

'Exactly. At one remove from all the action. You and Septimus are the hands-on leaders.' But even as he spoke, he could see the faint smile playing on Halliwell's lips. Both knew it would go against nature for the big man to keep his distance.

They reached the garage and Halliwell asked, 'Do you want me to wait?'

'No need. Wish me luck driving the Merc back to Manvers Street. I've done enough damage for one day.'

SEPTIMUS WARD and three others arrived in the morning and Diamond explained that they'd be heading the Rupert Hope side of what was now a major investigation. 'Presently we'll all drive up to Lansdown,' he told them.

A police minibus had been booked and Diamond—sexist when it suited—had invited Ingeborg along as a morale-booster for the newcomers. She was already telling them animatedly about Bath's nightspots.

He injected a more sombre note. 'You may find this weird,' he told everyone. 'The terrain could be as crucial to this enquiry as the people in the case. What is it about Lansdown that made it suitable for murder? Keep this in mind as we look at the sites.'

The bus was parked in the lay-by closest to the battlefield and the team strolled across the field and down the scarp to the fallen tree. Septimus appeared at Diamond's side, looking earnest, wanting to confide.

'You asked us why Rupert's killer chose Lansdown. Could the Civil War be the reason?'

'Go on. I'm listening.'

'Maybe his killer was another re-enactment freak. I don't know how seriously they take this rivalry between the armies,' Septimus went on. 'Rupert was new to the game. What if he got excited in the heat of battle and did something that wasn't in the script? One of the enemy may have got angry and hunted him down after it was over.'

'Roundhead versus Cavalier?'

'Except it's more basic. One of their lot taking out one of ours.'

Diamond took stock. There was some logic to it. Tribal hostilities accounted for a lot of modern violence. He liked the new man's thinking.

They'd reached the fallen oak. 'The tree blew down in the great gale of 1987,' Diamond told everyone. 'The uprooting of the tree left a large hole and some loose earth where the rain sank in. Some time after, a killer made use of it to bury the body of a young woman, but hacked off the head and disposed of it somewhere else. I can tell you very little about the victim or how she was killed. Under twenty, average height and reasonably healthy so far as you can discover from a bunch of bones. We think she was clothed because we found a zip fly, probably from her jeans.

'Last month, the Battle of Lansdown was re-enacted here and one of the Cavaliers called Dave decided to bury a six-pack of lager at this spot. He says he invited Rupert to join him after they were both supposed to be dead in battle. The two men had never met before.' He turned and pointed. 'They crept away from the fighting up there and found the first two tins but it seemed someone else had helped himself to the other four. Dave was pissed off, as any of us would be. He burrowed up to his elbows in the earth and came up with the femur that belonged to our victim. After some discussion these two decided the bone could very well have belonged to a victim of the real Civil War. They buried it again and rejoined the action on the battlefield. That's the gist of the witness statement we just had in.'

'Is he telling the truth?' one of the newcomers asked.

'I can't be a hundred per cent sure, but if Dave is the killer he's an idiot to come forward.'

'Why now, and not earlier?'

'He doesn't follow the news. Heard someone talking in a pub.'

'I'll buy that,' Septimus said. 'Plenty of people don't look at a paper.'

'But do you see the point?' Diamond said. 'Soon after this, Rupert was cracked on the back of the head and in a matter of days he was hit again and murdered. Two victims linked by this spot where we're standing. This is why we're combining the two enquiries.'

Septimus spoke. 'Could be coincidence. These killings are twenty years apart and don't have much in common. The MO was different in each.'

Keen as this new SIO was, he could have used more tact. Best make light of it, Diamond decided. 'If you're right, I'm wasting my time and yours, but let's take a look at the place where Rupert was found.'

Subdued, they walked back to the bus for the short trip to the graveyard.

The terrain around Beckford's Tower had been transformed from when Diamond was last there. All of that swaying vegetation had been scythed and cleared by the search team. After such an effort it was a pity nothing had been found.

The immediate site was still taped. 'You can see some staining on the ground where his head was,' Diamond told them.

'What was he doing here?' one of the party asked.

'Very likely looking for a place to sleep. He could have slept in the dry in the gateway we just came through.' This thought had come to Diamond when he saw the stone benches in the section behind the façade.

'It doesn't chime with all we've been finding out about the guy. A bright, outgoing lecturer who wants to sleep in a cemetery?'

Ingeborg had heard enough. 'If you'd been cracked on the head so hard you had an open wound in your skull you might behave out of character.'

Diamond nodded. 'All the evidence suggests Rupert was suffering from loss of memory following the first attack.'

'What's the story of the tower?' Septimus asked, looking across the graveyard to its tall Italianate centrepiece.

Ingeborg glanced at Diamond. 'Mind if I explain?'

He gave a shrug. 'Go ahead.' He'd got Paloma's book on Beckford beside his bed at home, still unopened.

'There was this millionaire called William Beckford who lived halfway up the hill in Lansdown Crescent. He had the tower built here in the 1820s and filled it with his treasures, then bought up all the land in between and created his own private walk. It was over a mile and he used to walk up the hill each morning.'

'And ended up in the cemetery?' Septimus said, and got a laugh.

'Dead right,' she said. 'In point of fact it didn't become a cemetery until a few years after his death. When Beckford was alive it was a fabulous garden with shrubs from all over the world.'

'How do you know all this?'

'I was a journalist before I joined the police.'

'An investigative journalist,' Diamond added. 'Gave us a hard time until we stopped all that by recruiting her.'

'Anyway,' Ingeborg went on, 'Beckford's daughter inherited the tower and gave it to the Church of England as a cemetery on condition that her father was re-buried here. He's in that granite tomb behind you.'

Septimus was looking around him. 'I don't see any recent graves. Isn't the cemetery used any more?'

'Not this part,' Ingeborg said. 'It's now owned by the Preservation Trust and left as a wild garden.'

'All done?' Diamond said. 'As you see, the wild garden was cleared. A fingertip search was made for the weapon and nothing was found. I'm not surprised. This is a crafty killer. Some attempt was made to pass off the death as an accident.' He showed them the bloodstain on the adjacent grave and explained about the blade of grass.

Septimus said, 'Did he leave any shoeprints?'

'None we could link to the killing.'

'The crime itself looks more like a mugging than a planned murder. They're often the hardest to solve. Was anything of value taken?'

'He had no wallet or cards when he was found. From the way he behaved at the boot sale he was skint.'

'And we don't know where the first attack took place?'

'Unless you have a theory.'

'Somewhere on this hill, I guess.'

'I'm sure you're right. His car was still in the racecourse car park. His Cavalier costume was inside, so we can be pretty sure he returned with the others after the battle and changed.'

'And got clobbered. What do these toy soldiers do at the end of the day?'

'From what I can make out, they hang out among the camper vans and cars. There's a beer tent.'

'If his car was still there,' Septimus said, 'it seems the first attack came that evening.'

'That's my reading of it,' Diamond said.

'My best bet is still on one of the Roundheads. Could any of their weapons have made the kind of wound he had?'

'Possibly. We're in blunt instrument territory here. But equally it could have been a car tool or a lump of wood. What's that?'

A beeping sound.

'Sorry,' Ingeborg said, taking her phone from her pocket. She took the call and then said, 'It's Keith. There's a breakthrough in the skeleton case.'

CHANGES HAD BEEN MADE in the incident room. More workstations and computers were in place and one of the boards had been cleared. But the big change was in Halliwell. He had the face of a lottery winner. 'Guv, it paid off,' he said, waving a transparent evidence bag. 'Just like you said it might. This came back from the lab this morning.'

Diamond held the bag under a strip light and saw the silver glint of the teeth of the zip. He passed the bag back. He'd never been noted for delicate handling of anything. 'Show me.'

Through the plastic, Halliwell manipulated the tiny tab on the slider to reveal the underside. 'There.'

Diamond squinted at the metal surface. He could just make out a symbol. Maybe as a law-and-order man he was preconditioned, but the figure seemed to him like the upright and crosspiece of a gibbet. 'What is it? A logo?'

'I thought it was just a symbol at first. I've been on it all morning, talking to various experts. It's Cyrillic, their equivalent of a capital G.'

'Cyrillic—the Russian alphabet?'

'Right. If the jeans came from Russia—or one of the old Soviet Union countries—there's a good chance our young lady wasn't from Britain at all.'

'Unless we imported them.'

'We're talking about twenty-odd years ago, Guv. We weren't doing business with Russia. When did the Berlin Wall come down?'

Ingeborg said, 'November 1989. Inside our time span. The boss is right. She could have bought them in Oxford Street.'

'No chance,' Halliwell said, so fired up he wouldn't be persuaded. 'The Berlin Wall came down and the borders were open and East Europeans flooded into the West. She's a young Russian who ended up in Britain and was murdered. It's not surprising she doesn't feature on the missing-persons index.'

'Hold on, Keith,' Diamond said. 'Cheap Russian jeans may well have retailed in our high-street shops in the early nineties. Have you found out where these zips were manufactured?'

'Give me a break, Guv. I only heard about this at ten fifteen this morning. Most of the time I was trying to work out if the logo meant anything.'

'That's the next step, then. There must be a list of Russian manufacturers. As it happens, I know someone with a good knowledge of the fashion industry. She may be able to throw some light.'

'Fine,' Halliwell said without enthusiasm. 'I'll go on the Internet. Let's use every resource we can. We may pin it down to a particular city.'

While this was being aired, Septimus and his colleagues from Bristol had stood in the background, getting their first view of the accommodation and not liking it. 'Couldn't we have a room to ourselves?' Septimus asked.

'That would defeat the whole purpose,' Diamond said. 'If you're in another room you might as well be back in Bristol.'

Leaving them to get over their discontent, Diamond called Paloma and explained about the zip. 'I thought you might have the answer.'

'Off the top of my head, no,' she said, a cool note in her voice.

'I'm sorry. Am I abusing our friendship?'

'It's becoming rather businesslike, that's all. Let me think about this.'

Halliwell was manically tapping a keyboard.

'Any joy?' Diamond asked.

'Not yet. I'm trying various things. You put in "zip fasteners" or "zippers" and you get so many hits it isn't true.'

'Keep your hair on.'

'Oh, God.' Halliwell clapped a hand to his head and swung round. 'I forgot to tell you. The lab said they found a clipping of hair under the tab.'

'A hair? And no one noticed until now?'

'It's small. A few millimetres, that's all. She said it was dark brown or black and rather coarse.'

'Why should one hair survive, when nothing else was found?'

'I suppose if it was tight under the tab it may have been protected. Let's hope they get DNA from it.'

'If it's as small as you say I wouldn't bet your house on it,' Diamond said.

Paloma rang back soon after and asked if he could get to Bennett Street in the next twenty minutes. 'The Assembly Rooms, front entrance.'

'We're only identifying a zip,' he said. 'Couldn't we do it somewhere less formal, like a pub or a tea shop?'

He could hear the sigh down the phone. 'It's where the Fashion Museum is,' she told him.

'You win,' he said. 'See you shortly.'

'WE'RE MEETING MY FRIEND Marcia Martindale,' Paloma said. 'If she doesn't know, nobody in Britain does.'

Disregarding the splendours of the Assembly Rooms, where Jane Austen once took tea, they went down into the basement to the Fashion Research Centre where Marcia was waiting. She was over eighty and wore a black hat with a crimson band and long feather.

'The zip isn't allowed to leave the police station, being evidence,' Diamond said, 'but I made a sketch of the symbol we found under the tab.'

'The puller,' Marcia corrected him. 'We call that the puller. May I see?'

He put the piece of paper in front of her. 'It's from the Cyrillic alphabet, their version of a G.' He enjoyed airing his new linguistic knowledge.

'I know,' Marcia said. 'I read Russian. It's rather unusual to have the trademark on the underside. I presume the fastener is metallic?'

'Yes.'

She placed her hand on a book the size of a dictionary she had ready on the table. 'The history of the zip is worthy of study. Elias Howe, the American who also invented the sewing machine, applied for a patent as early as 1851, but he didn't go into production with it, and we had to wait until 1914 for anything that worked efficiently to be developed. Of course it transformed the world of fashion.'

Diamond didn't need the history lesson, but contained his impatience while Paloma gently asked the old lady if the book had anything on Russian zips of the 1980s.

'I'm sure it does. This is the *Burke's Peerage* of the zip fastener.' She started turning the pages with arthritic fingers. 'Here's the section on manufacturers. We'll just have to work our way through the letter G.'

'Do they show the trademarks as well?' Paloma asked.

'Yes. Give me a moment.'

They watched while Marcia ran her finger slowly down the entries. But unfortunately the *Burke's Peerage* of the zip fastener let her down.

'Could we be mistaken about the symbol?' Diamond asked. 'We took it to be the Cyrillic G, but maybe it represents something else.'

'Ah,' she said, and snapped her fingers. 'You're cleverer than you look. We'll go through H.'

They waited for her to try again. Working right through the alphabet would take the rest of the afternoon and evening.

Then Marcia gave a little murmur of recognition. 'Got it. "Honta." Here's the logo beside it with a note that it appears on the underside of the puller.'

'So it isn't Cyrillic,' Diamond said.

'Oh, it is, but it isn't Russian Cyrillic. It's Ukrainian. They pronounce the symbol a different way, as an H, so it makes sense that it's not listed with the Gs. Listen to this: "Honta was founded in Kiev in 1991, in the new, independent Ukraine."' Marcia was buoyant. 'What you have here is a piece of history. The choice of logo is an expression of independence. It says Ivan Honta was a leader of peasant revolts in eighteenth-century Ukraine; 1991 was of course the year the Ukraine broke free from Russia. "Honta supplied zips for the Ukrainian Brovary Jeans Company in 1991 and 1992, but ceased trading, as did Brovary, early in 1993." So it was a short-lived company. That's rather sad.'

'Sad for them, but good news for me,' Diamond said. 'It narrows the field appreciably. Do we know if Brovary exported to Western Europe? I'm wondering if the jeans could have been bought over here.'

'I doubt it,' Marcia said, 'but we can check.' The misshapen fingers started turning pages again. 'Here we are, Brovary. "Manufactured for the Ukrainian market 1991–3. Exports: n/a." What's that?'

'Not applicable,' Paloma said. 'They didn't export.'

Diamond rubbed his hands. 'Marvellous. Our skeleton is almost certainly Ukrainian. Isn't it amazing how much you can learn from one zip?'

'What now?' Paloma asked.

'We get onto the Ukrainian Embassy in London and see if they have any reports of missing women from that period.'

'What I meant was, do you have time to take Marcia and me to tea?'

Wrong-footed again. Paloma was right. Marcia had saved him hours of research. 'What a nice idea. Just let me call Ingeborg.'

PALOMA HAD ALREADY RESERVED a table in the Pump Room. She'd planned to take Marcia there whether Diamond joined them or not. The old lady showed her appreciation by putting away sandwiches, scones and three fancy pastries. 'Aren't you going to eat your second scone?' she said to Paloma. 'Perhaps Mr Diamond would like it?'

'I'm defeated,' he said.

'In that case . . .' She reached for it.

'More cream?' he said.

'I'd better not,' she said. 'My nephew is taking me for a fish meal tonight. Good thing we don't wear corsets any more. Now *that's* a fascinating topic. Would you like to hear about the history of the corset?'

WHEN DIAMOND EVENTUALLY got back to Manvers Street, Ingeborg had contacted the Ukrainian Embassy. They'd promised to look at their records and call back.

Keith Halliwell looked up as Diamond approached his desk. 'Ukrainian, then? Your friend had the answer.'

'Some of it. We've discovered where the jeans came from and now we need to find out if the woman wearing them came from the same place.'

'They were made for the home market. That's what you told Inge.'

'That's true, but I can think of ways someone from outside the Ukraine could get hold of a pair.'

'OK, we can't be a hundred per cent sure on this, but I reckon there's one thing we can be certain of. This murder couldn't have happened prior to 1991, when the Honta zip company started up. The time frame Lofty Peake gave us was 1984 to 1999. We knocked three years off that by working out when the tree was blown down and now we've knocked off another four. This is where my events chart comes into its own.'

'Yes?' Diamond said, suppressing a yawn.

'Yes. Inge listed every mention of Lansdown in the *Bath Chronicle* from 1987 to 1999. Now we can erase a whole lot of it.'

'She won't thank you.'

The chart had been converted into a computer file that Halliwell now opened on his screen. 'This is 1991.'

January	3	Mist causes early end to football
	8	Sheep worrying by stray dogs
	11	Boot sales to expand
	13	Lansdown Road subsidence causes traffic chaos
	29	RAF Charmy Down reunion

Diamond peered over Halliwell's shoulder and could only marvel at Ingeborg's staying powers. 'Let's cut to the chase and look at 1993.'

'All action, then. Does it go on like this?'

Halliwell took him at his word and brought up February.

'Skip it. I don't need to look at your chart to tell you something of interest that happened in 1993 and that it was the three hundred and fiftieth anniversary of the Battle of Lansdown. July the 5th.'

'Yes, but they did the re-enactment at the beginning of August.'

'Why was that?'

'Not sure. According to the *Chronicle* it all took place without a hitch in nice weather in front of a big crowd.'

'Nice weather, big crowd,' Diamond rolled his eyes. 'Did that actually make the paper?'

'It's a local paper. They did a picture feature.'

Diamond yawned at the thought. 'Another thing about 1993. The Lansdown Society was formed that year. Did Inge find a report of that?'

Halliwell frowned. 'I don't remember seeing it.'

'I'm not surprised. They're a cagey lot. Don't go in for press releases.'

'Are you trying to tell me my events chart is a waste of time?'

Diamond put a hand on Halliwell's shoulder. 'I can be a pain. You're in charge of the skeleton enquiry, Keith. Be your own man and run it your way.'

THE UKRAINIAN EMBASSY phoned the next morning. They were unable to supply information on any of their nationals who may have gone missing in Britain since 1991. Halliwell's mood swung back to almost suicidal. 'We've hit the buffers again,' he told Diamond.

'Bloody diplomats. Is it political, do you think? Don't they want it made public that some of their people disappeared?'

'It could be sheer numbers. You and I know about human trafficking from East Europe. It's huge—an industry.'

'You think trafficking is behind this?'

'It accounts for a lot of missing people, young women in particular. There's also the black economy. East Europeans as a source of cheap labour, working without permits for cash in hand. No one in an embassy is going to have an accurate record of who is here, let alone who is missing.'

Halliwell sighed. 'If we can't go to the embassy for help, we're screwed.'

'No, we're not. There's always someone who knows. We have to get to the right person, that's all.'

He crossed the room to see Septimus, expecting another gripe, and instead got a more positive response. The Bristol team, he learned, had now got all the witness statements onto the computer. They'd found the canteen and liked the all-day breakfast. They might even survive a few days in Bath.

'I'm overjoyed to hear it,' Diamond said, 'but I'm running a murder enquiry, not a holiday camp.'

'Sure,' Septimus said. 'We have an action plan. We need to question the man who was with Rupert when they found the femur.'

'Dave Barton was questioned already. We have a signed statement taken by Keith Halliwell. Are you thinking Barton is a suspect?'

'I've looked at his statement. He claims he buried the beer and offered some to Rupert. Suppose the reverse happened and it was Rupert who hid the beer and quite by chance happened to choose the spot where the girl was buried. Barton was watching. He had a special interest.'

'Why?'

'Because he killed the girl twenty years ago. He's in his forties now. He's old enough.'

The theory intrigued Diamond. 'Murdered her and buried her there?'

'And thought he'd got away with it. A desolate spot on the side of a hill where not many people go. Then the Civil War Society announces it's going to commemorate the battle. The fallen tree is the kind of place where soldiers might dig a latrine or set up camp. Barton gets worried and decides he'd better join the regiment to keep an eye on things.'

'I believe he's been in it some years.'

'OK, he joined a while ago. It's some years since the first murder. Am I still making sense?'

'Enough to keep me interested.'

'Rupert buries the beer, meets Dave and offers him a drink. To Dave's horror, Rupert finds the bone, decides it belonged to a Civil War victim and wants to excavate the site. Dave persuades him to re-bury it, but has his doubts whether Rupert will let it stay buried. He keeps watch and later the same evening he sees Rupert return to the site. He follows him, cracks him over the head and leaves him for dead. But Rupert recovers enough to wander about Lansdown for days in a confused state.'

'Until Dave Barton finds out and finishes him off?' Diamond rubbed his chin thoughtfully. 'Could it be as simple as that?'

'Can I bring him in again?'

'I think you'd better.'

He wasn't entirely sure that the theory held up, but it demonstrated that Septimus was a thinker. Dave Barton was in for a searching examination.

IN HIS OFFICE, Diamond grappled with the problem of the Ukrainian woman. *There's always someone who knows*, he'd said to Halliwell.

The Ukraine was notorious as a source of cheap labour. Young people from the former Soviet bloc had started coming to the West in numbers after the Berlin Wall had come down and temporary work for cash had always been easy to get in Britain. Some illegal immigrants undoubtedly were murdered and weren't heard of again.

He called Ingeborg to the office. 'You know the local scene as well as any of us, Inge. Is there a Ukrainian community in Bath?'

'Not that I've heard of,' she said. 'Possibly in Bristol?'

'In London, too,' he said, speaking from experience of his years in the Met.

'You're trying to find someone who knew the dead woman?' Ingeborg said.

'Yes, when she first came here, she would surely have looked for some of her fellow countrymen?'

'Unless she was trafficked and had no choice,' Ingeborg said.

'When did trafficking first become a problem?' Diamond asked her.

'It started when perestroika came to the old Soviet Union and travel restrictions were eased in the late 1980s.'

'But we know from the zip that she came in the early nineties.'

Ingeborg nodded. 'Yes and by then they were leaving their country in big numbers, women in particular. They couldn't earn much at home and crooks were only too pleased to take advantage of them.'

'So how did she land up in Bristol?'

'On the game? Who knows? You could talk to Septimus.'

'I will,' he said, 'but common sense tells me she came to London first. I'm going to call an old friend from the Met. He may throw some light.'

LOUIS VOSS HAD RETIRED from Fulham CID some time after Diamond left, but still worked in the same nick as a civilian.

'Forgive my ignorance,' Diamond said after they'd exchanged small talk. 'Would you know the part of London where Ukrainians hang out?'

'Holland Park,' Louis said at once. 'Restaurants, clubs, the embassy.'

Diamond explained about the skeleton and the Ukrainian connection. 'I can't think why she ended up in Bath. I'm hoping to tap into her movements before she got here and London seems the best place to start. I want to meet people who know what was happening about 1992.'

'Can you drink seven straight vodkas?'

'Never actually tried.'

'There's always a first time. I'll see what I can set up for you.'

'SEPTIMUS HAS HAD a brilliant thought,' Ingeborg told Diamond. 'He says if there's a link between our skeleton girl and the killing of Rupert Hope it's *got* to be that big muster they had in 1993. It was a huge event, Guv, much bigger than the one they put on in July. Ten thousand turned up to watch. The spectators were all kept behind a rope barrier along the top edge of the field. But the fallen tree is out of sight on a steep slope on the far side.'

He nodded, beginning to see where this was going. 'That's why Dave Barton hid his six-pack there.'

'Let's stay with 1993 for a moment. What Septimus said was that if a fatal incident happened on one of those two days the obvious place to take the body was down the hill out of sight.'

'But no one was seriously hurt. We know that.'

'How do we know?'

'It would have made the news, that's why.'

'Guv, it was a battlefield. Pikemen fighting, cavalry charges. People were pretending to be dead all over the hill. Who's going to notice if one of the bodies really is dead? You could kill a person and get away with it. Before the end of the battle you drag the body out of sight and you can bury it later.'

She had a point. 'Is this Septimus's brilliant idea?' he said.

'I haven't finished. There were women on the battlefield. They dressed the part. Some of them were supposed to be tending the wounded.'

'Camp followers,' he said, recalling what Augusta White had told him.

'That's a pejorative term,' snapped Ingeborg. 'I call them angels of mercy.'

'Call them what you like, Inge. I'm quoting the Sealed Knot. But I see where you're going with this. Our woman may have died in the battle.'

'Yes, and what a blow it would have been to the whole event. A real fatality. Would it be it so surprising if she was dragged out of sight and buried?'

'Now you're stretching it, Inge,' he said. 'Asking me to believe the Knot connived at the illegal disposal of a body to save their reputation.'

'It needn't have been official,' she said. 'Probably wasn't. A couple of people could have moved the corpse unknown to the organisers.'

'You're suggesting she was killed during the battle? How? By accident?'

'One of the soldiers had murder in mind from the beginning.'

'A premeditated killing. A possibility. How many took part in the muster?'

'The paper said two and a half thousand. But not so many are women and there's a better chance of them being remembered, particularly if one was from the Ukraine.'

He'd pushed the victim's nationality to the back of his mind. 'Now there's a thing. What would a Ukrainian woman be doing in an English Civil War re-enactment?'

'Exactly. If she was there, someone will know,' Ingeborg said. 'So Septimus had his brilliant thought. Why don't I enlist in the Sealed Knot and see what I can find out?'

'Crazy. The first thing they'll ask is what your day job is and you're sunk.'

'I can say I'm a journalist, like I was. Or I'll go undercover.' She was not going to be dissuaded.

'What do you hope to achieve, Inge?'

'Finding people who remember 1993, women in particular. If there's anything to be learned about the murder victim, I'll root it out.'

'I'm sure you're capable,' he said. 'But there's a downside, isn't there? Someone murdered Rupert Hope, presumably because he was a threat. You're going down the same route and you'll be in real danger.'

'Guv, if I was a man, you wouldn't hesitate. If I'm going to have a career in CID I have to do it all.'

It was a telling point. Diamond didn't want her in the front line, but he said, 'Actually, Inge, this is more than I'd ask *anyone* to do. But since you volunteered I won't stop you.'

THROUGH THE ONE-WAY GLASS of interview room one, he watched Septimus and one of his Bristol DCs pitching in to Dave Barton. The blacksmith had asked to bring a friend with him and she turned out to be a razor-sharp solicitor, Miss Tower. She was quick to intervene.

'My client answered these questions before, when he was interviewed by Mr Halliwell. You have the signed statement.'

Septimus said, 'My investigation is different: the recent killing of Rupert Hope. I need to explore areas not covered in the previous interview.'

'You just asked about Mr Barton's job,' Miss Tower continued, 'which you know already, and which has no conceivable relevance to either enquiry.'

On the other side of the glass, Diamond said, 'Except we're looking for the murder weapon and a blacksmith's tool kit has to be of interest.'

'All right, Dave. Let's concentrate on the hobby, the Civil War thing,' Septimus said. 'How long have you been doing it?'

Miss Tower was quick to say, 'Not relevant.'

'I want to find out if he'd met Rupert at any of the meetings.'

Dave said, 'No. He was a Bristol guy. They have their own branch.'

'He told you he came from Bristol?'

'I found out since. Said he was a historian. He went on a lot about the real battle. He seemed to know his stuff.'

'Are you well up on history, Dave?'

'Me? No, I don't do it for that. I like the action, the fighting.'

'Careful,' Miss Tower advised him.

'I meant the dressing up and all that,' Dave added.

'You're a pikeman?' Septimus said.

'Not always.'

'For this battle you were. And so was Rupert. What did you do with your pikes when you went for the lager?'

'Left them on the ground. We picked them up later.'

'And you moved down the hill to where you'd hidden the beer? Did anyone see you going?'

'Could have. There were some dead and wounded lying about. And there was a few women looking after Roundheads, giving them water.'

'Were they close enough to have a view of you and Rupert digging out the beer?'

'They'd need twenty-twenty vision.'

'So they wouldn't have spotted you actually finding the bone? That was a strange find, wasn't it?'

Miss Tower said to Dave, 'You don't need to answer that. You're not here to give an opinion.'

But Dave seemed to decide he was on safe ground. 'First I thought it was from some animal. I put it down fast when I guessed it could be human. Nasty. We agreed it was the right thing to do, to bury it again.'

'And you went back to the battle?'

'That's right.'

'Did you see Rupert again?'

'No. I've never seen him since.'

'You like a drink or two, Dave?'

'Irrelevant. Don't answer that,' Miss Tower said.

'I'm sorry,' Septimus said, 'but I have every right to ask. We need to establish if his evidence would hold up under cross-examination.'

'Good for you,' Diamond said on his side of the glass.

Miss Tower said, 'He's not in court. He's cooperating and you appear to be about to cast a slur on his behaviour.'

Septimus said, 'He testified to me that he hid a six-pack of lager in the ground before the battle. He also testified to DI Halliwell that he hadn't heard Rupert Hope was missing because he goes out in the evenings to the pub. Now, Dave, did you drink at all prior to joining in the battle?'

'A couple at lunch. I was stone-cold sober, if that's what you're asking.'

'Can you be more specific? One pint, two, three . . .?'

'How would I remember?' Dave said.

'Gotcha!' Diamond said.

Septimus said, 'You seem to remember your meeting with Rupert in some detail, but you can't remember how many you had at lunch. Are you quite sure you buried six cans of lager before the battle?'

'I told you. You know what a six-pack is?'

'And at that stage were you aware of anyone watching?'

'Definitely. One of the other army came past. Waller's lot, Roundhead, thieving bastard. Cavalry, too—he was on a big white stallion, wasn't he?'

'You think he had the other four cans?'

'I'm certain of it. I've been over it in my mind lots of times. I reckon he had a good laugh, nicking the enemy's beer.'

'He had the decency to leave some.'

'That's what Rupert said. I told him if that was decent, forget it.'

'When you and Rupert parted, were you still friendly?'

'Of course we were. I'd shared my beer with him, hadn't I?'

'Would it have angered you if he'd returned and dug out the bone?'

Dave frowned. 'Why would he do that?'

'He may have thought it was of historical interest.'

'I'd have been slightly narked, after we agreed to let it rest in peace.'

'Did you go back to check?'

'No chance. After it was over, I was in the beer tent.'

'And did you drive home after?'

Miss Tower slammed her hand on the table. 'Don't answer that.'

Dave gave a faint smile. 'You see? I knew I needed my brief with me.'

5

Diamond had been at his lowest point, hunting the murderer of his wife, when he had last seen Louis Voss. His old colleague had managed to trace a crucial contact. Nobody in the Met was better at working the grapevine. Officially Louis was a civilian, managing what he called his team of computer cuties, but the loss of CID status hadn't cramped his style one bit.

This morning he was in the bar of the Fox and Pheasant, off the Fulham Road, when Diamond arrived with Keith Halliwell. They'd come in Diamond's car, now roadworthy again, with Halliwell acting as chauffeur. 'Keith, meet my old friend Louis, the wizard of ops, as he's known.'

'Was,' Louis said. 'I'm just a geek now. What's your part in this, Keith?'

Diamond said, 'He's the main man, the SIO on the case.'

Louis greeted this with a faintly amused look and ordered drinks.

'This hasn't been easy,' he said. 'The Ukrainians are charming people, but if they once suspect you're from immigration, you're as welcome as a bowl of cold borscht. Waves of young people arrived in London in the 1990s. Life at home was so harsh, particularly for women, that a lot of the young got out. Those escapees will be in their thirties and forties now.'

'The woman we're interested in would have been around twenty when she was killed,' Halliwell said. 'We think she could have been trafficked.'

'To Bath? For sex?'

'Bristol, more likely.'

'It wouldn't surprise me. Trafficking of Ukrainian women is a big problem. The numbers must run into thousands.'

'Hundreds of thousands actually,' Halliwell said. 'The Ukrainian Ministry of the Interior reckoned four hundred thousand in the last decade of the twentieth century. That's to all countries, not just Britain.'

Louis exchanged a glance with Diamond.

Diamond said, 'Keith does his research.'

Louis gave a nod. 'OK, but let's remember the majority come here freely and get work permits. What's the background on your missing woman?'

'A Ukrainian zip fly,' Diamond said.

'And a snip of hair,' Halliwell added.

'Teeth?'

'She was headless.'

'You *have* got a problem.' Louis picked up his glass and drank. 'If you're right about the trafficking, she could have been dealt with by her pimp.'

'If that's the case,' Diamond said, 'her killing will have been used as a threat to keep other women in line. So someone may remember her.'

'From twenty years ago?' A belch from Louis testified to his reaction. 'You always were an optimist. There's a new generation of working girls now.'

'But the older ones may have graduated into madams.'

'There he goes again. All right, I've fixed for you to meet two people at opposite ends of the spectrum. Olena is a pillar of the community, been here twenty-five years. She's a kind of church social worker who looks out for vulnerable girls and does her best to link them up with families. Ukrainians are regular churchgoers—Ukrainian Orthodox. The church is in Ealing, no great distance from here. Almost any girl who visited that church in the last quarter of a century has been given the once-over by Olena.'

'Thanks, Louis. You've spent time on this.'

'More than I intended. The second contact is an alcoholic who has never done a day's work since he got here. There's a Ukrainian pub in Addison Road called the Crimea and Andriy gets his glass filled up by passing on the low-life gossip. If any scandal is remembered about your lady, Andriy is the man to ask. Treat him with respect. He has powerful friends.'

'So we know where to find Andriy,' Halliwell said. 'How about Olena?'

'Right now she'll be arranging flowers at the church in Newton Avenue, Ealing. I told her to expect you around twelve thirty.'

SHORT, SLIM, and with the steady gaze of an icon, Olena met them at the church door and said, 'You will come to my flat.'

She was the kind of woman you didn't argue with. 'As you wish.'

The flat was in Meon Road, as close to the church as a loyal parishioner would wish to be. Olena lived on the ground floor. 'I prepared *chorni khleb* and salt for you. It is the custom,' she said. Just inside the door was a tray covered by an embroidered cloth, which she removed to reveal a black loaf and a small bowl of salt. She offered it first to Diamond.

'Break a piece and dip in salt,' she told him.

The bread had a hint of vinegar, but he swallowed it and thanked her.

'No need to speak. You bow your head, so.'

Halliwell received his portion in the approved way, in silence.

'That is good,' Olena said. 'Now we talk in my living room.'

The room was small, with only two chairs at either side of a fireplace, above which the mantelpiece was crowded with photos in metal frames.

'You sit,' Olena said, gesturing to the chairs. 'Both.' She poured something from a jug into three wineglasses. 'Is called *kvas*,' she said as she handed the glasses to her guests. 'Made from black bread and sugar.'

The drink reminded Diamond of cold Ovaltine and he didn't care much for it. 'We came to ask you about a young Ukrainian woman who we think travelled to Bath about twenty years ago and was murdered there. We don't know her name. She would have been about twenty and it's likely she came to London first.'

'Murdered? Why?'

'She must have met bad people, here, or in Bath.'

'With God's help I try to stop girls from meeting such people,' Olena said. 'I would not know.'

'But you may remember a girl who was going to Bath and wasn't heard of again.'

'No, I cannot help. I remember nobody like this.'

'It was a time when people gained the freedom to travel,' Diamond said, unwilling to give up. 'Were you already living here?'

'I am here before then,' she said. 'The church helped me to find work, so I give back. Many who came were young women.'

'Can you remember the names of those you helped?'

'Many. Not all. Some we lost to evil men who take them to be Scots.'

Diamond was mystified. Halliwell said, 'I think you mean escorts.'

'Some write to me still.'

'Even from 1991? We'd like to hear of anyone you're still in touch with from that time in case they remember this woman.'

She took down one of the photo frames. 'This is Viktoriya. She arrive here 1991 to be waitress. The men who offer this job are lying. Soon they force her to sell her body. You understand?'

'What happened? Did she go missing?'

'No. Married to Englishman, living in Barnes.'

'Barnes isn't far from here,' Diamond said.

'Yes. Sometimes she come to see me.'

He glanced at Halliwell. This was promising. 'Where exactly in Barnes?'

Olena wagged her finger. 'She will be frightened. You are secret police.'

'Detectives in plain clothes. Not the same thing at all. We can talk to her without scaring her. In fact, only one of us needs to chat to her.' Diamond smiled in a reassuring way.

Olena shook her head. 'I don't think so.'

Diamond broadened the argument. 'For the sake of the murdered girl and her family. She has a God-given right to be treated properly as well.'

This worked better. They could see the conflict in Olena's eyes. She sighed, a deep, heartfelt sigh. 'You wait here. I get my address book.'

'Are you thinking of dividing forces?' Halliwell said. 'I don't mind going to Barnes if you'd do the booze artist.'

'Sod that. I'm in charge.' When it suits me, he thought.

'What I'm thinking, Guv, is that you could handle another *chorni khleb* welcome, but could you handle the *kvas* as well?'

'You're a devious bastard, Keith.'

Olena returned and handed them a piece of paper with a Barnes address.

A TAXI DELIVERED DIAMOND to the Crimea, an old-style Victorian pub with a field gun as its sign. Inside, blue and green tiles and varnished woodwork made it dark. Plaintive music was being piped through the room.

He approached the only customers, two men on bar stools. They looked about his age and were speaking in a foreign language. He waited for a pause.

'Excuse me. I'm looking for Andriy.'

'In what connection, my friend?' If this was a Ukrainian, he had a better command of English than Olena.

'I was told if I bought him a drink he might help me find someone.'

'That's always possible.' The speaker had a grey baseball cap pulled well down on his forehead, making his pale blue eyes seem a long way off.

'You know him?' Diamond said.

A nod. 'Two double vodkas would be nice.'

As if by arrangement, a bar girl appeared.

'You heard that?' Diamond asked.

She was already filling a glass. 'And for you, sir?'

He pointed to one of the beer handles. 'A half.' He didn't trust himself drinking vodkas. He turned back to the drinkers. 'Which of you is Andriy?'

After some hesitation the second man raised a finger and said nothing. His hunched, comfortable position on the bar counter spoke of many hours of practice. A fine head of black curls sagged between broad shoulders.

'He's your man,' his companion said. 'Knows everyone.'

'Cheers, then,' Diamond said and told them he was from Bath police enquiring into the death of a young woman, apparently Ukrainian, about twenty years ago. 'It's possible she was known here in London.'

'If she was Ukrainian, she probably was,' the man in the baseball cap said. 'What do you say, Andriy?'

Andriy wasn't impressed. 'Hundreds of girls come through London. I don't know where they all end up.'

'This one ended up in another city, dead, probably murdered.'

'So she got in with bad company.'

'Speaking of which,' Diamond said, 'were there any Ukrainian gangs with links to Bath or Bristol twenty years ago?'

Andriy shrugged and looked away.

'He doesn't have an answer,' his companion said.

Yet he was supposed to be a gossip, so why so reticent?

The man with the baseball cap looked at his watch. He said something in Ukrainian to Andriy, then grinned at Diamond and left the pub.

'*Mafioso*,' Andriy said.

'It crossed my mind,' Diamond said. 'Difficult to talk freely with someone like that in attendance.'

Andriy showed him an empty glass. Diamond nodded to the bar girl. She poured another double and then retired to the area behind the bar.

'In the nineties, when your dead woman disappeared,' Andriy said to Diamond, 'there were two big groups bringing women to this country. At that time, the competition was strong. Deadly. Two pimps were killed. One of the women, too.'

Diamond leaned forward, all ears.

'But not your woman,' Andriy said. 'This one was given a funeral at the Ukrainian Church. The year of independence, 1991. The violence made a strong impression and some of the call girls decided to quit. They weren't heard of again. If they had any sense they would have got out of London.'

'Would their pimps have hounded them down? I'm thinking of some vengeful bastard following our woman to Bath and killing her.'

'Depends if she was a danger, I guess,' Andriy said.

'Knew too much? You could be right.' His thoughts were interrupted by a piercing sound from somewhere close. 'What's that?'

'Do you have a phone?' Andriy said.

'Christ, yes.' He took it from his pocket.

Urgency bordering on panic was in Keith Halliwell's voice. 'Guv, I'm in trouble. Can you get here fast?'

Of all the team, Keith would be the last to panic. Diamond sprinted along the street, hailed the first taxi he sighted and gave the address Olena had supplied. 'Put your foot down,' he added.

'Man, you got to be hot for it.' The cabby gave a throaty laugh.

Diamond stepped inside the taxi and, while it rattled through the backstreets, used his mobile to ask Louis to send a response car.

'Say that address again,' Louis said.

'Sixteen Marchant Street, Barnes.'

'We know sixteen Marchant Street. It's a knocking shop.'

Now he understood the cabby's mirth.

The house was part of a shabby Victorian terrace. Broken window boxes spoke of a once-respectable use, but not for some time.

The disrepair wasn't total. A small video camera above the door shifted its angle a fraction. Someone inside had seen him coming.

The door worked on an entry phone. He pressed the control and a woman's voice said, 'Yes?'

'John Smith. May I come in?'

The door buzzed. He pushed it and went inside.

'Upstairs,' called the same voice.

For all she knew, he was a punter and he'd play along with this for as long as it suited. At the top of the stairs, Diamond pushed at a partly open door and found himself in a room furnished with cheap sofas. A blonde, sharp-featured woman in a black trouser suit stood behind one of them.

She repeated the bland 'Yes?' he'd heard over the intercom.

'My first time here,' he said. 'Would you be Viktoriya?'

'I'm Vikki, yes.'

He was assessing the room, trying to decide if heavies were waiting nearby to deal with troublemakers. If Vikki was the madam, she'd need some back-up. 'I'll be straight with you, Vikki. A friend of mine came here an hour or more ago.'

'Who was that?' she said with an ironic smile. 'Another John Smith?'

'He was a police officer. Where is he now?'

'I don't know who you mean,' Vikki said, dropping all pretence of charm. 'No one came here saying he was from the police.'

'He may not have shown you his warrant, but he must have asked you questions about girls who went missing twenty years ago.'

She hesitated. '*That* guy? He left some time back.'

'It won't do,' he said. 'He called me to say he was in trouble.'

Her eyes had turned to the left. He took a step closer and saw the mono-chrome screen she was staring at. He guessed the police had arrived.

'Come on, Vikki,' he said. 'Do you want cops storming through every room in the building?'

Alarmed, she put a hand to her mouth. 'It wasn't my fault,' she said. 'He came asking questions. Anyone could tell he wasn't a punter.'

Then a shot was fired nearby, followed by another, somewhere outside the building. He knew gunfire. It wasn't a firework or a car backfiring.

He started down the stairs just as the front door burst open and two uniformed cops from the Met charged in. They were ready to grab him until he pulled out his warrant card and shouted, 'The garden.'

They carried on past the staircase and through a door at the back into a small kitchen. One cop flung open the door to the garden, which was more of a concreted back yard than anything cultivated: a poor place to hide.

His partner made a leap at the wall and looked over. 'Here!' he yelled and scrambled up and out of sight. The other cop followed.

For a man of Diamond's build, that wall was a major barrier, but he wasn't giving up while Keith was in trouble. He found a wooden fruit box and stepped up, hauled his bulk to the top and toppled over. The two uniformed cops were in hot pursuit of a man who had vaulted over a low fence into a neighbouring garden. A dog started barking.

The second garden was heavily overgrown. Diamond hadn't waded far through the sea of grass when he heard panting. Briefly he thought of the dog and then recognised a human quality in the sound. He found Keith lying on his back, his hand to his chest, blood seeping through his fingers.

KEITH WASN'T SPEAKING. A pink bubble formed between his lips and popped. If his lungs were filling with blood he wouldn't last long.

Diamond took out his mobile and dialled for an ambulance. In all his years in the police, he'd never had one of his team murdered. What could he do? His sense of helplessness was overwhelming. He knew about the so-called grace period from thirty minutes to an hour when the shock to the nervous system means that the victim is, in effect, anaesthetised. When that passes, the pain kicks in and can be fatal.

He looked around him. The house appeared derelict. Really he could expect no help until the paramedics came. The two cops were chasing the man seen running from the scene. So he waited, powerless to act, and the minutes dragged.

At last came the twin notes of the ambulance approaching Marchant Street. The sound got louder and then stopped, followed by doors slamming. A voice came from behind the wall, 'Where are you?'

He stood and shouted back.

A head appeared above the wall. 'All right, mate. Stay cool.'

They slung a stretcher over first, and then two paramedics followed. He stood back to let them assess the injury. It seemed Keith had taken a shot to the diaphragm, just inside the rib cage. While one was taking the pulse the other said to Diamond, 'Why don't you find the best way out of here? We won't want to lug him over that wall.'

As he suspected, the house on this plot was empty, the windows boarded up. But there was a side gate that he forced open. It gave access to the street.

When he got back, the paramedics had transferred Keith to the stretcher. 'You'll have to help me get him to the ambulance,' one said, when Diamond had pointed the way. 'Charlie will drive it round.' So Diamond acted as stretcher-bearer, through the long grass to the gate.

'Shall I come with you?' he asked the paramedics when they'd slid the stretcher inside the ambulance.

'No point, mate. You're better off chasing the tosser who shot him.'

'Which hospital?'

'Charing Cross. What's his name, by the way?'

By the way. As if it was an afterthought.

Diamond told them and one climbed inside with Keith while the other closed the door and then got into the driver's seat and drove off.

The sense of loss was acute.

IN THE NEXT HOUR, Diamond's neglected mobile was much used. He spoke several times to Louis Voss. He got through to Ingeborg in Bath. He also called Sheila Halliwell and broke the news every police wife dreads. She said her brother would drive her to the hospital directly. Then came the inevitable question: 'What was he doing, to get himself shot?'

'We don't fully know yet. Probably pursuing a suspect without knowing he was armed.'

'Weren't you with him, then? I thought he was with you.' She may not have intended it to sound like an accusation, but that was how he took it.

'We split up. He went to interview someone we thought was harmless.'

'Are they ever? I'd better not say any more, Mr Diamond. I don't trust myself to speak. I'll hang up and get on the road.'

More police arrived, organised a crime scene and called out a forensic team. He said as much as he knew to the team leader and then called the hospital. He was told the patient's condition was critical.

Somehow, Diamond had to escape from waiting on events. He phoned Louis at Fulham Road nick. 'Did the two cops locate the guy on the run?'

'They nicked him,' Louis said. 'He's here.'

'Thank God for that. Who is he?'

'He's not saying.'

'Doesn't he have anything on him saying who he is?'

'Peter, if he had, I'd have told you, wouldn't I?'

'Has he asked for a solicitor?'

'How do I get this across to you? He's schtum. We think it may be a language problem. He could be a Ukrainian. Our regular interpreter is on his way back from Manchester. We'll get him in tomorrow morning.'

'Like hell you will. I'll find you an interpreter in the next half-hour.'

He knew of a good interpreter. He stopped a taxi at the end of the street and took a ride to the Crimea pub, asking the driver to wait.

True to form, Andriy was at the bar. He grinned at Diamond, recognising him at once and drained the glass of vodka he was holding. 'We were having a nice conversation and you had to leave suddenly. Was everything all right?'

'It's under control, I think,' Diamond said, 'but I still need your help.'

'Cheers.' Andriy grinned and pushed the empty glass towards the barmaid.

'For this kind of help, you get vodka by the bottle not the glass,' Diamond told him. 'I want you to act as my interpreter.'

'Whatever you want, my friend.' But it took a few minutes to get through to Andriy that he was required to leave the bar and take a taxi ride.

They were driven to Fulham Road nick and went through to the computer room where Louis presided.

'Any more news?' Diamond asked.

'From the hospital?' Louis shook his head.

'This is Andriy.'

'I know all about Andriy,' Louis said. 'I sent you to him in the first place. Is he your interpreter?'

'Fluent in Ukrainian.'

Louis rolled his eyes.

'So where's the prisoner?'

Louis hesitated, then pointed the way downstairs to the cells. 'On consideration,' he said, 'I'd better come with you.'

A dapper man with a pencil-thin moustache, DCI Gledhill, rattled down the stairs in pursuit of them. 'Can I help you, gentlemen?' he asked in a tone that promised more obstruction than help.

Louis explained, stressing Diamond's senior rank in Bath CID.

'This is the Met, not Bath police. We do our own interviewing.'

'I hope I didn't hear right,' Diamond said in a tone that managed to be both subdued and menacing. 'You don't have to tell me about procedures in the Met. I served in this nick for five years. In the Met, of all places, you have to be aware of interforce consultation at every level. I'd hate to think Fulham Road has pulled up the drawbridge and refused interviewing facilities to a senior officer in an emergency.'

'That isn't the case.'

'I'm glad to hear it. Which cell?'

Gledhill sighed, defeated. 'The second on your right.'

Diamond slid aside the cover to the Judas window. The man seated on the bed inside was about forty, sallow, with dark, deep-set eyes. His striped shirt looked expensive and his trousers were tailored, evidently part of a suit. Diamond closed the window. He turned to Gledhill. 'You're welcome to sit in while I interview him. Are we to be allowed an interview room?'

Interview room one was made ready, fresh tapes inserted. 'You can read him his rights, the caution, all that stuff, when he's brought in,' Diamond told Gledhill in a show of altruism. 'Andriy, we'll have you seated opposite us, next to the prisoner, to do your interpreting.'

The custody sergeant brought in the prisoner. Everything about his demeanour suggested he wouldn't cooperate. Gledhill spoke the words for the tape and gave the official caution. Then the focus shifted to Andriy, who appeared as uninterested as the prisoner, probably because he was suffering from alcohol deprivation.

'Andriy,' Diamond said in a sharp tone.

It dawned on Andriy finally that he was supposed to do something to earn his next drink. He turned towards the prisoner. Then he started laughing. 'I know this man. He's no more Ukrainian than you are. He's English and his name is Jim Jenkins.'

'Is this a fact?'

The prisoner looked alarmed to be unmasked.

'*English?* We went to all the trouble and expense of getting an interpreter and it turns out you're English?'

And now Jenkins found his voice. 'I didn't say I was a foreigner.'

Diamond turned to Andriy. 'What can you tell us about him?'

Andriy was looking pensive. 'You hired me to be an interpreter. Two bottles, right? Now you're asking me to be an informer. For informing, the fee goes up. Four bottles.'

DCI Gledhill gave a twitch and said, 'What's this about bottles?'

Diamond said. 'All right, Andriy. Four bottles it is.'

Gledhill was outraged. 'I can't authorise payments off the cuff.'

'The Met pays two million a year to snouts. We're not going to quibble over two extra bottles. Do you want to talk here, Andriy, or in private?'

'Better in private, I think.'

At this, Jenkins decided to wade in. 'That's out of order. You can't let him make up stuff about me without telling me what it is.'

'I'll tell you every bad thing he says, Jenkins,' Diamond said. 'Take him down, Sergeant.'

Protesting loudly, Jenkins was removed.

'Now, Andriy,' Diamond said. 'Give us the dirt on that man.'

'He's a pimp and runs a whorehouse in Marchant Street, Barnes,' Andriy said. 'Before that, for six or seven years, the place was managed by a Ukrainian guy called Sergey. The madam there is Vikki, former call girl, never made trouble. Keeps the house beautiful. Clean bedding and flowers in the rooms. I know all this from friends, not from experience.'

'Go on.'

'Some time last year, Vikki started going out with this Jenkins. Smart, always wore a suit. In July last year, Vikki married him. Overnight, Sergey was called to a meeting with the godfather who owns the house and was told he had to move to a backstreet knocking shop in Fulham. He went.'

'And Jenkins was installed there?'

'An all-Ukrainian house taken over by an Englishman. He is not popular in our community. No one can touch him, because he has the blessing of the high-ups. They don't want to lose Vikki, get me? We think he is using her.'

'That's a dangerous game if he is. Does he carry a gun?'

'He'd be a fool if he didn't.'

'But you say he's untouchable.'

Andriy inclined his head slightly to one side, the Ukrainian equivalent of the Gallic shrug.

Diamond had the picture now, or enough to put the screws on Jenkins. With Gledhill's grudging consent, Andriy was driven back to the Crimea on the understanding that the car would call at an off-licence on the way.

Jenkins was brought back and the questioning started over again.

'What am I charged with?'

'Nothing yet,' Diamond said. 'You're being questioned on suspicion of discharging a firearm with intent to kill. You'd better pray Inspector Halliwell survives the night.'

The pimp's eyes showed alarm. 'I didn't know the man was a cop.'

'You live and learn. Give us your version of what happened.'

A heavy sigh. 'I'm just a businessman. I work for Ukrainians and with Ukrainians. I'm married to a Ukrainian but there's hostility towards me because I'm not one of them. I have to watch my back all the time.'

'Is this why you armed yourself?'

'You bet I did.' He paused as if regretting what he'd said and tried to think of a way of qualifying it. 'By "armed", I mean being on my guard.'

'But you own a handgun?'

'Er, yes.'

'Go on.'

'Today is a bank day. I'm supposed to collect the proceeds, pay the staff and get the surplus to the bank. We deal in cash and it can be a large sum.'

'That I believe,' Gledhill said.

'I was in the office with Vikki getting the money sorted when there was a caller. We have an entry-phone system for the front door, and CCTV. There was something iffy about this guy. He asked for my wife by name. That was suspicious because she looked at the screen and didn't recognise him. I moved into the room next door.'

'Leaving your wife to deal with him?'

'She's experienced. He started talking to Vikki about things that happened twenty years ago. He spoke of some girl who went missing. My wife was trying to be helpful, telling him things, but it seemed to me she was getting herself—and me—in trouble. Bad things happened in the past.'

'You were listening to all this?'

'From the next room. Then the guy let out that the missing girl had been murdered and buried somewhere in the West Country. *Murdered.*'

'Didn't you know about this?' Diamond asked.

'Very little. I heard there were some killings back then, but nobody knows for sure who carried them out, although there are people around today who were minders then and are big wheels now. Stupidly Vikki was rabbiting on about all of this to a total stranger. She spooked me out so much I pulled my gun and stepped into the room.'

'You drew a gun on him?'

'I didn't go in there for conversation. Too much talking had been done already. He took one look at the shooter and was out of there.'

'And you chased him?'

'Down the stairs and into the garden. I wanted to put the frighteners on him. He must have been over the wall like a steeplechaser. That's a high wall and when I dragged myself up he wasn't in sight, but I felt sure he was in that next garden somewhere. The grass was really high. I sat on top of the wall, waiting for him to make a run for it. Finally I saw the grass move and he started to head for the empty house. I shot over his head. But then the stupid sod stopped and turned towards me. I pulled the trigger a second time out of pure tension. He dropped and I realised I'd hit him. I went over to look and I could see he was in a bad way. I was trying to think what to do when the police came over the wall and I panicked and ran off.'

'You're saying you didn't intend to hit him? We're meant to believe that?'

'I've got no experience using guns. You can look at my record.'

'Come on, Jenkins, it's your gun. You admitted that just now.'

'For self-defence. I'm in a dangerous job.'

'You had plenty of time to think about using it. You cold-bloodedly waited for DI Halliwell to show himself and then you loosed off two shots.'

'That's wrong. I want a brief.'

'You're going to need one. And you'd better get praying as well.'

IN THE MORNING Diamond heard that Keith was out of intensive care. A short visit would be permitted. Elated, he took a taxi to the hospital.

In the corridor, his heart sank at the sight of Sheila Halliwell walking towards him. He stopped and turned up his palms in apology.

Sheila offered her face for a token kiss and said, 'He's going to be all right. I'm sorry I was so sharp when you phoned. He told me neither of you could have had any idea he was going to have a gun pulled on him.'

'Is he well enough for me to go in?'

'He must be. He keeps saying there's something he must tell you.'

THE PATIENT was in a side ward, tubed up for a transfusion. He appeared to be sleeping. He had more colour than Diamond had expected.

'We can postpone the funeral by the look of you.'

Keith's eyelids flickered and opened. 'Good to see you, Guv.' His voice was not much more than a whisper. 'I messed up big time.'

'You didn't. You're a hero. Are you sore?'

'Full of morphine. Hard to keep my eyes open.'

'Sheila said you want to tell me something.'

'Yes?' Unfortunately he was starting to drift off. His eyes closed again.

'You got to the house and spoke to Vikki. I know that much.'

Keith opened his eyes briefly. 'She knows, Guv. Vikki knows. You've got to see her.' Then he was gone again.

THIS WOULD NOT BE EASY considering he had Vikki's husband in custody and 16 Marchant Street was a crime scene. Vikki had lost her husband and her livelihood. She wouldn't be in a frame of mind to tell all.

He called at the Crimea as soon as it opened and looked for Andriy, thinking he might know where Vikki lived.

No Andriy.

'I don't understand,' the barmaid said. 'Always he is here when I open.'

He guessed what was amiss. 'Probably sleeping it off.'

His only other contact was Olena. He had to try.

He went first to the church and found her removing used candles from in front of an icon. 'There is nothing I can tell you about Viktoriya,' she said, and contradicted herself by adding, 'She is upset. Distress.'

'Viktoriya is distressed because her husband is at the police station.'

Olena opened a new box of candles and set them out neatly.

'I cannot speak of this in front of St Volodymyr.'

Diamond said, 'Would you light one for my friend, Keith Halliwell, who was shot yesterday? I think St Volodymyr will be sympathetic.'

Olena sighed and walked with him to the main door. On the steps, she said, 'She is at my house. Be gentle, yes?'

Diamond walked the short distance to Meon Road. Vikki came to the door, saw him and slammed it shut. He bent down and talked through the letter-box. 'Vikki, I've come from Olena. Do I have to ask her to leave the church and unlock her own front door?'

After some hesitation, she opened it and glared. The blonde hair was in need of combing and the eyes were red-lidded. She turned her back on him and stepped into the front room.

'Olena doesn't know what goes on in Marchant Street, does she?' Diamond asked.

'She is like a mother to me,' Vikki replied. 'You don't tell your mother things that will trouble her.'

'But she knows your husband is being held for shooting a policeman?'

'She doesn't know it all.'

'Keith is going to pull through. I saw him this morning. He told me you gave him information.'

She shrugged and looked away.

Softly, softly wasn't going to work with Vikki. 'We're holding your husband at present. We have to decide what we should charge him with. Could be illegal possession of a firearm, shooting with intent to kill. He claims that he's inexperienced at using the gun.'

'I've never known him to fire it. We've both been under a lot of pressure.'

'Since he took over from Sergey?'

Her eyes widened at how much he knew. She gave a nod.

He judged that she was as ready to cooperate at this moment as she ever would be. 'I expect Keith asked you about the Ukrainian woman we found buried in Bath?'

She gave an angry sigh. 'We talked about two girls I remember. They were trafficked in 1993. They were in their late teens.'

'Did they work for you?'

She shook her head. 'I was just a call girl. We were all trapped in the game. It was a scary time. The mob was at war for control of this part of London. Pimps were murdered and at least one girl was shot. These two fled. One of them got back to the Ukraine and years later I had a card from her, asking if I knew what happened to Nadia, the other one who escaped.'

'Did you know Nadia personally?'

'Not well. Her plan was to get out of London. After they made a run for it, she took a train from Paddington. That's the last anyone saw of her.'

'Paddington? She headed west. She could have made it to Bath or Bristol. Would they have followed her there and killed her?'

'She wasn't worth the trouble. Girls are just goods. They get replaced.'

Callous words. He could see that in her terms they were accurate. 'Can you describe her for me?'

'About my height. Blue eyes. Straight nose. Very good legs.'

He thought of the femur he'd held in his hand.

'Hair colour?'

'We all changed our hair often. She could have been any colour. It was straight and long. I always thought she was from Cossack stock. She liked watching the racing on TV, just to see the horses. They adore their horses.'

'Do you know her surname?'

'Nadia Berezan.'

'Thanks.' He made a note.

Nadia Berezan, call girl. She was still a long shot, but she was Ukrainian and she'd travelled to the West Country at about the right time. And from what he had learned, no one would have reported her as a missing person.

6

Forced this time to do his own driving, Diamond headed out of London in the slow lane of the M4. For much of the journey he was reflecting on the shooting of Keith, questioning his own motive in sending him to deal with Vikki while taking Andriy for himself. The decision had been taken on nothing more serious than Keith's offer to cope with another *kvas* welcome.

He forced his thoughts to his next skirmish with Georgina. She was certain to hold him responsible for the shooting and she might think an enquiry was required. Diversionary tactics were called for.

At Membury Services he stopped to fill up and let the team know he was returning. Ingeborg took the call. She ought to have been impressed that he was using the mobile but she was completely focused on Keith.

'He's still in the world of the living,' he told her, 'I saw him this morning. And the good news is that we have a name to work with.' He told her about Nadia Berezan. 'Do what you can on that computer of yours to see if there was ever a woman of that name in Bath or Bristol.'

'Wouldn't she have changed her name?' Ingeborg said. 'I would, if I was on the run from the mob.'

'Not so simple as you think, Inge. She'd need proof of identity if she was applying for benefits, as she'd surely need to. A false passport is expensive and takes time to acquire, even if you know where to go for one.'

'I guess.'

'How's it going? The Bristol boys behaving themselves?'

'They're trying to reconstruct Rupert's last few days on Lansdown.'

'And you? Have you successfully infiltrated the Sealed Knot?'

'I don't know about that, Guv. I've started my basic training as a foot soldier. So far it's as exciting as the Girl Guides. Learning how to carry a pike.'

'Where do you meet? I'm tempted to sneak in and have a peek.'

'I'm not telling.'

'By the way,' he threw in casually, 'is Georgina on the premises?'

'She was here at the crack of dawn, extremely uptight about Keith. She'll be over the moon to hear he's recovering so well. I'll tell her as soon as I'm off the phone.'

'I'd rather you didn't. Keep her guessing a bit longer.'

He resumed his sedate drive and eventually left the motorway at Junction 18, south on the A46, the busy route over the rump of the Cotswolds and down into Bath. Only after Dyrham Park he detoured right, onto a road that linked to Lansdown. All the intensity of London and the Ukrainians had left him needing to reacquaint himself with the source of the mystery.

This was a grey, bleak morning and the place names fitted the conditions: to his left was Cold Ashton, on the right was Freezing Hill, ahead were Hanging Hill and Slaughter Lane. He chugged up the steep north scarp of Lansdown and pulled in at the stopping point for the Grenville Monument.

Outside the car, a keen northeasterly chilled the flesh. He wouldn't linger long, just enough to see the view of the vast limestone plateau. In the foreground lay the battlefield where two great armies had clashed, and where, centuries later, 10,000 people had come to watch the first big re-enactment. On the other side, the ground plunged to a wooded area where the skeleton had been buried. Two miles along the road, the top of William Beckford's Tower marked the graveyard where Rupert Hope had been found.

Shivering from the cold, Peter Diamond took a long look at the panorama from the battlefield to the tower. The ground was unremarkable, yet it had endured since the Jurassic period, when a warm, shallow sea covered all of this and deposited the limestone, the source of Bath's prosperity. This ancient hill was the silent witness he couldn't question. He'd hoped that being here would inspire him with a sudden, crystal-clear revelation, but there was none.

GEORGINA'S DOOR was open and she was standing in front of her desk with her arms folded. A portrait of the Queen looked over her right shoulder.

'What on earth happened to result in Keith Halliwell being shot?'

Diamond gave her his version.

'Didn't anyone know it was a house of ill fame?'

A phrase he hadn't heard in many years. Where had she got that?

'We were given the address by a churchwoman. Even if we'd known it was a—er—house of ill fame, I wouldn't have expected anyone to pull a gun on Keith.'

'How is he now? Have you seen him?'

'He's off the critical list.'

'That much I found out myself by phoning the hospital. They seem to think he'll be unable to work for several weeks.'

'I expect so. Good thing we can cover for him.'

Georgina seized on this. 'I don't know how. He was one of your SIOs, a key person in the investigation. How can you possibly replace him?'

'I'll do it myself.'

She took a sharp, audible breath. 'I don't think so, Peter. We agreed you were CIO, an executive role. You shouldn't have gone to London. Your place is here, at headquarters, supervising both arms of the investigation.'

'The trip was arranged through a contact of mine. I had to be there.'

She ignored that. 'From the beginning you wanted to run both inquiries yourself. You managed to get the Rupert Hope case brought back from Bristol on very dubious grounds and shoehorned our Bristol colleagues into the same incident room as the skeleton inquiry. And now you want carte blanche to roll up your sleeves and go to work on the case.'

'Someone has to do it, Ma'am.'

'What about John Leaman?'

'He's needed to take care of all the other stuff that comes up.'

'You've got an answer for everything.'

He nodded and let Georgina have the last word. All in all, he'd come out of it better than he'd expected.

DOWNSTAIRS in the incident room, the team was excited at the possibility that the skeleton had an identity at last. Inge was checking every database she could think of. Others were on the phone trying to prise information from the benefits office, medical practices and women's refuges.

All this energy lifted Diamond's spirits. 'Ukrainians are strong church-goers,' he said. 'She may have gone to one of the churches for help.'

'Which?' Ingeborg said. 'There's no Ukrainian Orthodox church in Bath.'

'She might have looked for a Catholic church.'

DC Paul Gilbert, the rookie in the team, piped up, 'St John's in South Parade, or St Mary's in Julian Road.'

Ingeborg checked her screen. 'He's right. St John's and St Mary's.'

'Worth a go,' Diamond said. 'You're a young woman. Put yourself in her situation. She manages to escape from a vice ring in London. She gets on a train at Paddington and ends up here. Why—what's the attraction?'

'She knew someone. She thought they might help her get a new start.'

'That's more like it.'

'But I've tried looking for Ukrainians in Bath and found nobody.'

'This is where the computer lets you down,' he said. 'Nothing has yet been devised that gets close to word of mouth. We're going to have to get out there and ask people questions.'

'About something that happened twenty-odd years ago?'

'How many Ukrainians have you and I met? I'm sure I'd remember. I have a description from Vikki. Average height. Blue eyes, straight nose, good legs, straight, long hair that could have been any colour.'

'An E-FIT may be better,' Inge said. 'The public respond to visual images.'

'I'll get it organised. Any other reason she might have chosen Bath?'

'She heard about it from one of the punters?'

He snapped his fingers. 'Good thought, Inge. Here's a scenario. The guy lives here and visits London on business. Likes to have sex when he's away from home and gets to know Nadia. She thinks if she can find him he may set her up, but it doesn't play like that. He has a respectable life here. When she traces him, he gets in a panic and kills her.'

'Not bad,' she said. 'Difficult to prove. How would we ever find him?'

A voice said, 'Where's the connection with Operation Cavalier?'

He turned to find Septimus had crossed the room.

'Rupert Hope,' Septimus said, as if memories needed jogging.

Diamond was at his best when a little bluffing was necessary. He hadn't forgotten how important it was to keep both strands of the enquiry linked if possible. 'For businessman read lecturer. Rupert was around in the early nineties, wasn't he?'

'But making regular trips to London?'

'Research. The Imperial War Museum. The British Library.'

Septimus grinned. 'Quick thinking.'

'It's only a theory. How's your side of the investigation going?'

'We've been working on the days between the re-enactment and Hope's death. We traced a few more witnesses who all agreed he was acting strangely. He had no idea who he was, or what to do. He slept rough and wandered about the down until his killer caught up with him.'

'You're assuming both attacks came from the same individual?'

'It's the most likely explanation. Similar injuries.'

'And the attacker didn't leave the weapon lying about. Is the search of the cemetery complete?'

'All done. I think the killer was smart and took the weapon away with him.'

'We're still talking about a blunt instrument, right?'

'Something clean, that left no traces in the head wound. Heavy enough to split the skin and dent the skull, but not to cleave it. Yes, blunt is right.'

THAT EVENING, having found out where Inge was going, Peter Diamond stood in shadow at one end of a disused aircraft hangar watching the clash of pikes as three pairs went through their movements. The ash-wood weapons, sixteen feet in length, looked dangerous, even though the moves were being choreographed by an expert, an officer of the Sealed Knot. Diamond wasn't surprised to see Ingeborg wielding her pike with gusto. Like the others she was wearing casual clothes except for a helmet and leather gauntlet gloves.

'We'll try that again,' the officer said. 'First positions.' They hoisted the cumbersome staves to waist height and rested them on their shoulders.

Engrossed, Diamond failed to notice he was not alone.

'Are you thinking about enlisting?' The voice at his side made him jerk in surprise. The speaker was a woman with a silver ponytail and a black jacket.

'Hasn't crossed my mind,' he said.

'It's good for fitness.' She seemed a fine advert herself, over seventy, he reckoned, yet with the figure of a woman thirty years younger.

He asked, 'Am I in the way here?'

'You're welcome to watch. Is it the young lady who interests you?'

He couldn't get away with anything here. 'Not specially.'

'These days the female recruits insist on doing everything,' she said. 'When I joined more than thirty years ago we delicate creatures didn't think about joining in the fighting. We were angels of mercy, wearing low-cut frocks and leaning over fellows. That's how I met my husband.'

'You've been a member more than thirty years?' This sprightly lady might be a useful witness if she'd been a Sealed Knot member for that long.

Another order was shouted. The soldiers lowered their pikes to the horizontal, pointing to where Diamond and his companion were standing.

'Advancing at point of pike,' she told him. 'It's a fearsome sight in battle.'

'It's pretty scary from here. Are they about to charge us?'

'I don't think so. If you were from Cromwell's lot, you'd be wishing you had your own pikestaff and fifty others with you. Even then, you'd probably not survive. The front men are usually impaled.'

'But you don't injure each other when you put on your mock battles?'

'Thankfully, no. The pikeheads are wood or vulcanised rubber painted silver. Our pikemen fight with points upwards. The officers have to pass a series of safety tests, and that goes for the enemy as well as ourselves.'

'And who are the enemy?'

'The Parliamentarians, of course. We're fighting for the King.'

'And do the Roundheads meet in a hall somewhere and drill separately?'

'They use this place on the nights we're not here.' She gripped his arm. 'Now they're putting the pikes away and they'll do some swordplay. The young lady's done some fencing before. I've watched her. She can take on any of the men.'

He could believe Ingeborg was a fencer.

'I dare say you remember most of the women who've enlisted.'

'Since I joined, certainly.'

'Was there ever one from East Europe? Her name might have been Nadia.'

'Rings no bells with me, dear.'

Ingeborg was clashing swords with a young man who had the swagger of one of the Three Musketeers, but without the skill. A parry, a lunge and Inge whipped the sword out of his hand. It clattered on the concrete, leaving him as hors de combat as Diamond's latest theory.

'If she carries on like this, she'll be picked for single combat,' his companion said. 'That's a massive honour. I'm glad she's joined.'

'She's no angel of mercy, that's for sure.'

She laughed. 'I hope you're not mocking old-timers like me.'

'I'm not. She won't get a husband beating up the guys.'

She turned to look at him 'You're not her father, are you?'

'Lord, no.'

'A Roundhead spy?' She was not giving up.

'I'm a policeman. Peter Diamond, Detective Superintendent.'

She sighed. 'I should have guessed. You're something to do with that dreadful murder of one of our members, the lecturer from Bristol.'

'A detective on the case, yes. I came here hoping to find out more about what goes on. Do you keep a list of former members?'

'I expect so, but it may be restricted information. You'll have to do it the official way and talk to the senior officer.'

'Good advice, ma'am. And is your name restricted information as well?'

She laughed. 'Agnes Swithin.'

'Married to Major Swithin, golfer and member of the Lansdown Society?'

'And one-time handsome Cavalier. Unfortunately the golf took over. I'm sorry to say Reggie prefers the little white ball to good King Charles.'

'So you met Rupert Hope.'

She turned to face him, puzzled. 'Why do you say that?'

'You saw him trying to break into cars. You called out the police.'

Her eyes widened. 'Was that the man who was murdered? I had no idea. Didn't make the connection at all. Why was he doing such a stupid thing?'

'He'd been hit on the head. We think he'd lost his memory.'

'Oh, dear. You've made me feel guilty for reporting him.'

'No need, ma'am. You did the right thing as you saw it.'

At the other end, Ingeborg was fencing with a young man with a better technique. She appeared to be on the retreat when a sudden forward movement drew the opponent's defence and he lowered his sword.

'Good on you, girl!' Agnes Swithin said, clapping.

The instructor wasn't so delighted. 'You could cause damage like that. We're exercising here, not trying out for the Olympics.'

Agnes clicked her tongue. 'He's putting her down because she's a woman.'

'You've obviously fenced with the foil before,' the instructor was saying to Ingeborg. 'Have you used a rapier? You won't get to use one in battle unless you transfer to the cavalry. Can you ride?'

'A bit.'

'You might like to make enquiries.'

At Diamond's side, Agnes took a sharp, accusing breath. 'There speaks an infantry officer. Doesn't want her showing him up. Actually she'd look good on a horse. At least a third of our cavalry are ladies.'

'Really?' After losing one of his team already this week, Diamond wasn't sure he wanted Ingeborg fighting duels on horseback. 'Were you there for the big re-enactment in 1993?'

'This is about the skeleton they dug up on Lansdown, isn't it? Yes, I remember it well and I can assure you I didn't see any foul play. I was too busy with my casualties.'

'Real casualties?'

She flapped her hand. 'A few dents and bruises. Nothing serious.'

'So you didn't spot anyone behaving suspiciously in the battle?'

'I'd remember if I did. If you ask me, the Sealed Knot had nothing to do with that skeleton, whoever it is.'

If that's the truth, he thought, I'm wasting my time here and so is Ingeborg. Soon after, he slipped out of the hangar and drove home.

EARLY THE FOLLOWING MORNING, DC Paul Gilbert called and asked to speak to the boss. There was a rasp of excitement in his voice. 'Guv, I'm at Lower Swainswick with a lady by the name of Mrs Jarvie. She worships at St John's in South Parade. She had Nadia as a house guest for two weeks in 1993.'

Diamond wasn't immune to excitement himself. 'What's the address?'

This was it. The timing was right—1993, nicely inside the time span Lofty Peake had given for the death of the skeleton woman. And it fitted what he'd learned in London about the Ukrainian call girl who'd made her escape to the West Country.

Paul Gilbert's car was outside a cottage almost entirely covered in clematis. The young constable himself came to the door. 'I'd better warn you, Guv. She's elderly—well, very old, in actual fact—and she's also deaf. And I haven't told her what happened to Nadia.'

Gilbert led the way into a back room where the old lady evidently sat by day and slept by night. She was out of bed, dressed in a pink cardigan and blue tracksuit trousers and was seated in a rocking chair with a large white cat on her lap. Two tortoiseshells perched on the windowsill and a sleeping Persian had the eiderdown to itself.

Paul Gilbert hadn't exaggerated. Mrs Jarvie was very old. He introduced Diamond and the only reaction was some adjustment to the hearing aid.

'He wants to ask you about Nadia,' Gilbert shouted.

The old lady opened her eyes and said, 'You don't have to shout.'

'Nadia,' Gilbert shouted again. 'The Ukrainian girl.'

'Are you asking about Nadia again?' she said. 'I told you all about her.'

'You said she was here in 1993. Is that right?'

'I gave her the spare room,' Mrs Jarvie said. 'She wasn't with me very long. She spoke good English.'

'How do you know it was 1993?' Diamond asked. Confirming which year Nadia came to Bath was fundamental to the enquiry.

'I had my eightieth birthday the weekend before she came. I remember giving her a piece of my birthday cake when she arrived.'

'So which year were you born?' Diamond asked, not entirely convinced.

'I'm ninety-six,' Mrs Jarvie said with a sigh. 'If I get to a hundred I get a telegram from the Queen.'

'Yes, but which year?'

'Guv,' Gilbert said, pointing to a framed sampler above the bed with the words: *Bless this house. Julia Mary Jarvie, born 23rd July, 1913.*

The mathematics checked. Diamond thought, Bless this house and bless you too, Julia Mary Jarvie. We've got a date to work to. Would you tell us about Nadia?'

'Who?'

He raised the decibels. 'The Ukrainian.'

'Is it? I hardly ever go out, neither do the cats. They hate getting wet.'

Gilbert stooped close to the old lady's ear and repeated Nadia's name.

'She was a refugee. I took her in as a Christian duty.'

Diamond said to Gilbert, 'Ask her if Nadia said anything about herself.'

This was a complex question for someone who heard about one word in five and didn't always get that right, but this time there was a result.

'She was working in London before she came here, but she didn't like it.'

'Did she talk about her life in the Ukraine?'

She lowered her eyes and stroked the cat. 'It was sad. She grew up in an orphanage and when she got to sixteen a man came and took her away.'

This tallied closely with Vikki's information. Any lingering doubt that they were speaking of the same Nadia could safely be dismissed.

'She had to work for him in London. She didn't tell me what kind of work it was, but I had my own thoughts about that. I don't know how long she was there before she made her way to our church in Bath.'

'But she didn't stay long in Bath.'

'No, she didn't stay,' she said. 'She went off one afternoon and I didn't see her again. Sometimes I wonder if it was the cats that put her off.'

Diamond could sympathise. 'While she was staying with you, did she ever speak of people she knew in Bath?'

'Never.'

'Did she bring anyone back to the house?'

'Men, do you mean?' She shook her head. 'She was no trouble at all. She was never late coming home, except for the day she left altogether.'

'Which day was that?'

'You want to know which day? You're asking for the moon. How would I know one day from another after all these years?'

'It must have been some time after your birthday, on July the 23rd.'

'The beginning of August, then. Or thereabouts.'

'What did you do the night she left?'

'I went to bed at my usual time, thinking she'd soon be coming in. She knew I keep a spare key under the flowerpot beside the front door. In the morning I found her bed hadn't been slept in.'

'Were her things gone?'

'She didn't have any things of her own. She used my towels, my shampoo and soap. Most of her clothes were given by the church.'

'Did you report it? Call the police?'

'It's a pity she didn't find a little job. They say the devil finds work for idle hands. I do hope she didn't go back to her old way of life.'

He had to repeat his question.

'Report it? I thought she might come back. It would have seemed inhospitable if I'd reported her missing. With people like that, who arrive out of the blue, you never know when you're going to lose them again. Would you like to see a picture of her?'

A picture? Would he just?

'There's a wooden box under the bed.' She turned to Gilbert. 'See if you can reach it, young man.'

Gilbert delved underneath and pulled out a dusty rosewood box inlaid with mother-of-pearl. The cat on Mrs Jarvie's lap was forced to move as she opened the box. It was stuffed with letters and photos.

'Here. This was snapped in the garden by my neighbour. That's Nadia with me preparing runner beans for dinner. She had a lovely smile.'

Although the colour print had faded, the focus was sharp enough to provide a clear image. It showed a less decrepit Mrs Jarvie beside a young woman on a garden seat. They had a saucepan between them.

In the picture Nadia appeared untroubled, giving a wide smile to the camera. Her long hair was blonde and long enough to have been drawn back and held in place with combs. He noted that she was wearing the expected jeans and a T-shirt. Her face was a fraction too broad to be conventionally pretty, but the smile caught a moment of happiness that gave life to the image. That photo said more than any E-FIT would have done.

'May we make a copy of this?'

'What are you going to do with it?' the old lady said, frowning. 'I don't want it getting into the newspapers. I'm wearing an apron.'

'We'll cut you out of it. We only want Nadia's head and shoulders.'

'I can't think why.'

He wasn't going to enlighten her at this juncture. They left after replacing the box under the bed, allowing the white cat to reclaim its position.

'Top result, Paul,' Diamond said. He closed a hand over Gilbert's shoulder. 'Now, let's see if the photo jogs some memories.'

He was humming as he returned to the car. Hard facts had emerged at last. He'd found a name for the skeleton victim and confirmed her nationality and her way of life. And now he'd discovered the year and the month Nadia had come to Bath and gone missing. Better still, he could show everyone what this tragic young woman had looked like in life.

He let his thoughts race on from the facts to their interpretation. Nadia had tried to flee from the hell of prostitution at a time when violence had taken over. It looked increasingly as if she had been followed to Bath by some hit man and executed, most likely as a deterrent to any other working girl who had plans to escape. The decapitation seemed to signify a professional killing.

He was forced to admit that the latest developments rather undermined the theory that Nadia's death and Rupert's were connected. If Nadia's was a crime organised by professionals then Rupert's had the hallmarks of a local affair. Georgina might complain when the dust settled, but the world would have moved on.

The first step was to get Nadia's face onto posters, into papers and on television. He'd tell John Wigfull to drop everything he was doing and get the job done fast. After sixteen years was it too much to hope that someone in Bath remembered seeing the girl with her killer?

To his credit, Wigfull didn't demur. He saw the sense in blitzing Bath (Diamond's words) with the picture. It wasn't the highest quality, but fortunately his photographic expert enjoyed a challenge.

Next on the list of priorities was a call to the hospital. Diamond was given the encouraging news that Keith had been allowed out of bed. There was no reason why he shouldn't make a full recovery in a few weeks. Then a call to Louis Voss. 'Weren't you working with the vice squad in 1993?'

'I know what you're going to ask,' Louis said. 'You think Nadia was murdered to order and the order came from London. You want names. Sorry to disappoint, but you're on a loser, matey. I won't say the vice barons are faceless, but they make damned sure you can pin nothing on them.'

'You're saying I should let some hired assassin get away with murder?'

'I'm saying if he was any good at his job you won't find him. More frustrating still, you won't get the guy who hired him.'

'That's as cynical as anything I've heard in the police.'

'Cynical and true. Let me give you something else to chew on. At the time you're speaking of, London was awash with classy foreign girls willing to turn tricks. One little whore making a run for freedom was never worth pursuing to Bath and killing.'

Deep down, Diamond had a strong respect for his old friend's wisdom.

He remembered hearing something similar from Vikki about the girls being replaced. 'If you're right, it means she came to Bath and in a matter of days met someone local who not only murdered her, but removed the head so that we wouldn't identify her.'

'What was it Sherlock Holmes said about the smiling and beautiful countryside and its dreadful record of sin compared to London?'

'HAVE YOU CHECKED your emails today, Guv?' Ingeborg asked, breezing into Diamond's office. 'You're not even switched on.'

'*I'm* switched on. The computer isn't. I'm a detective, not a freak.'

'I think you mean geek. You can access your email from any other computer,' she informed him. 'You could have logged on from London.'

'I had slightly more urgent things to deal with, like Keith being shot and almost killed. What did you want to say to me?'

'That it's high time we heard from the lab about the hair we sent for analysis, the one found under the tab of Nadia's zip.'

She was right. More dramatic events had put the hair to the back of his mind. He wasn't going to let Ingeborg think she'd caught him out. 'The men in white coats always take an age. They phone if there's anything startling. It's academic now, anyway. We're ninety-nine per cent sure who she was.'

'Just thought I'd remind you,' she said. 'Did I catch a glimpse of you when I was at pike drill last night?'

Diamond nodded. 'I told you I might look in. You seem to be handling the weapons all right, but are you picking up information?'

'It's a case of softly, softly, Guv. I want to get their confidence, so I haven't gone in there firing questions at everyone.'

'I met one of the camp followers,' he said.

'Mrs Swithin? Nothing gets past her.'

'I didn't try. I said I'm from CID. Of course, I didn't let on that you're one of my team. Mustn't blow your cover.'

'She mentioned you later. She was a bit freaked that our local unit of the Sealed Knot is under police surveillance. The members don't think Rupert's death has any connection with them.'

'You know who Mrs Swithin is?' he said. 'The wife of Major Swithin, golfer and leading light of the Lansdown Society. The Swithins were the people who reported Rupert trying to break into cars.'

Ingeborg coiled a strand of blonde hair round her finger musingly. 'This is just a thought, Guv. Everyone in the Knot takes the soldiering seriously.

If Rupert was misbehaving, he was letting down the regiment.'

'So he was cracked over the head? Since when has petty theft been a capital offence? The military have other ways of dealing with misconduct.'

Still she seemed reluctant to leave his office. 'I don't know if you heard at the drill. My officer said he thought I might get a place in the cavalry.'

There it was, then, out in the open. Nothing to do with emails. She fancied herself as a cavalry officer.

'Because you can wave a sword realistically? You're bloody good, but—'

'I can ride. I used to have a pony.' Her eagerness was transparent.

Women and horses, he grumbled to himself. 'You're not supposed to be doing this for your own pleasure.'

'I can do my job and enjoy it as well,' she said, still pressing.

'The idea is that you lie low and find out what really happened.'

'I know, Guv, but—'

'Listen, Inge. You don't have the full picture yet. Mrs Jarvie has helped in a major way. We're now certain that Nadia came to Bath shortly after Mrs Jarvie's eightieth birthday on July the 23rd, 1993, and she disappeared shortly after. Let's say two weeks. When do you make that?'

'Early August.'

'Right. Over the weekend of August the 7th and 8th, the Sealed Knot held its major muster, the re-enactment of the Battle of Lansdown.'

'Yikes!'

'This year, Rupert Hope, a new member of the Knot, takes part in another re-enactment and happens to unearth part of Nadia's skeleton.'

'And is murdered.' Ingeborg's eyes ignited like the blue flame of a gas ring.

'It's why I don't want you prancing around on horseback. The best spies keep a low profile.'

IN THE INCIDENT ROOM Diamond gave the team the latest bulletin on Keith Halliwell, then announced that he'd taken over Keith's role as SIO. The whole investigation had a sharper focus now, he said, briefing them on the crucial dates in the summer of 1993. Even the Bristol contingent listened keenly.

'I've handed Nadia's picture to our publicity guru,' he told them. 'We'll plaster the town with it, papers, local TV. There's a good chance someone will remember her.'

'The church?' John Leaman suggested. 'Ask the priest to mention it at Sunday Mass when he's giving his church notices and then have someone ready with a poster and fliers when they all come out.'

'Good thinking, John,' Diamond said. 'Take care of it, would you?'

Septimus spoke. 'What do you hope to get out of this?'

'Now we have a narrower time frame, we're on a similar exercise to the one you've been carrying out for Rupert, reconstructing the days leading up to the murder. Have you made any headway with that?'

'Yes. Altogether we've traced eleven people who remember seeing Rupert. Someone called him Noddy and he accepted it. He seems to have hung about on Lansdown the whole time—twenty-two days, from the day of the mock battle to the morning he was found dead in the churchyard.'

'Living off scraps?' Leaman said.

'Apparently. And until yesterday we were uncertain where he slept. But we found a postman who'd noticed this man early on several mornings near Beckford's Tower. It was enough for us to order another search. We wanted to find if he had a base there, somewhere in the dry.'

'The tower?' Leaman said.

'No, that's got a security system. Valuable items are exhibited there.'

'A burial vault?'

'Are you into horror films?'

There were some sniggers at Leaman's expense.

Diamond said, 'I told you my theory when we first went there. He used the front gate as his bedroom.'

'The *gate*?' Leaman said.

Diamond nodded. 'I suppose you'd call it a gatehouse; a big solid structure facing the street, made by the same guy who built the tower.'

'OK, it's a gatehouse,' Septimus went on. 'Behind is this covered-in part, like a room, with stone seats. Under the seats we found a folded blanket.'

'Where would he have got that?' Leaman said.

'Nicked from somebody's car,' Paul Gilbert said.

'Have you sent it for tests?' Diamond asked.

'You bet. There was a plastic water bottle and some food wrappers. This place is protected from the weather, quiet at night and private. I wouldn't call it comfortable, but it was dry. Someone used it recently, for sure.'

'So he may have been brain-damaged, but he was smart enough to find this,' Ingeborg said.

'If a stone bed in a cemetery on a hill is smart,' Septimus said.

Diamond's thoughts had moved on. 'If the postman noticed him, it's possible his murderer saw him in the area as well. The body was found among the graves—how far from the gateway?'

'Thirty yards, or less.'

'All right. Rupert goes back there one evening and his killer is waiting. The blanket was folded, so he didn't get a chance to lie down. He was attacked on his way. That how you see it, Septimus?'

'Pretty much. Or the killer was waiting in the gateway and Rupert ran off and was caught. It seems to have been an ambush, and it happened late. The pathologist said he was killed overnight. He couldn't say what time.'

'The more I hear about this Rupert, the sorrier I feel for him,' Diamond said. 'For three weeks he was living rough on Lansdown, not even knowing who he was, and no one understood the trouble he was in.'

'Are we still assuming a link between Rupert's killing and Nadia's, in 1993?' Ingeborg asked in her journo mode.

'We are.'

'The Battle of Lansdown?'

'Right on.'

'We don't know for sure if Nadia went to the re-enactment, do we?'

'In the next few days we should find out,' Diamond said. 'We do know that the timing was right.' With that, he drew the meeting to a close.

Alone in his office, he switched on his underused computer. Ingeborg had been right to mention emails. He clicked on the mailbox icon. Masses of unwanted stuff appeared. Scrolling down, looking at the senders, he spotted one from FSS Chepstow. FSS. Forensic Science Service. The subject title was 'Test Report'.

When he read it, he scratched his head and said, 'Oh bugger.'

This required a rethink.

He called Ingeborg in. 'You were right. The lab report came as an email late yesterday. This'll pin your ears back. The hair doesn't belong to Nadia.'

'Her killer?'

'No. It isn't a human hair. It comes from a horse.' He handed across the sheet he'd printed. 'They reckon it was clipped. Horses get trimmed sometimes, don't they?'

She read the report right through. 'Incredible. Can you feature that?'

'There was I thinking we might have got lucky,' he said. 'We end up with a bloody horse.'

'I'm at a loss, Guv.'

'So was I when I first read it. But I've remembered something I was told in London by Vikki. She said she always thought Nadia came from Cossack stock and she justified it by saying she spent a lot of time watching the racing on TV, not for the betting, but for the horses. I don't know a lot about Cossacks except they're fierce warriors and they ride horses. So it's not impossible that when she came here she thought about working with horses.'

'I guess.' She sounded unconvinced.

'If she heard of an upcoming event involving horses she could well have gone there in the hope of getting work as a stable girl.'

'There's some heavy speculation here, Guv. What upcoming event?'

'The re-enactment.'

She took a sharp breath. 'Of course. Plenty of horses there.'

'As you say, it's speculation, but this is the best I can think of. I just wanted you to know I've had a rethink about you joining the cavalry.'

'I can do it?' She gave a scream of excitement and for one alarming moment he thought she was going to skip round his desk and hug him.

DID LANSDOWN ITSELF hold the solution to this mystery? In Diamond's thoughts the great limestone hill loomed larger than any suspect. From inside the bowl of the city it appeared disarmingly scenic but he knew its real character. Up there were places of death, the graveyard and the battle-field. Nadia had been slaughtered and buried on the hill. For three weeks, poor, confused Rupert Hope had roamed the fields and slept in the cemetery until his life had been stopped. This was an unforgiving place.

He'd never set much store on intuition, so why was he nagged by this conviction that the down held another, larger secret?

He told Septimus he was going to drive up to the cemetery for another look. 'Can you tear yourself away from that computer and join me?'

On the way there, Septimus spoke up for his team. 'We haven't just been looking for witnesses. We spent a lot of time on Rupert and his life in Bristol. He comes out of it as the kind of guy nobody could feel threatened by. Popular with students. Not big on socialising. Currently he wasn't in a relationship, though there seem to have been a couple of girlfriends in the past. We checked his bank statements. He spent his money mainly on books, DVDs and theatre visits.'

'You must have checked his computer?'

'The downloaded stuff is heavy on history. The emails are mainly to other historians about research. He kept in touch with his parents.'

They'd reached the cemetery gate. Diamond stopped the car. 'You know, it's possible he was just unlucky.'

They got out and passed through an entrance door to the right of the main gate. 'A gatekeeper could live in here,' Septimus said as he stepped into the section with the stone seats.

'Where did you find the blanket?'

'Under here.' He indicated the seat to their right. 'Deep red, made of some synthetic material. We didn't open it out for fear of losing particle evidence. I'd say it was large and not too clean.'

'He wasn't too clean himself. You think he nicked it from a car?'

'My best suggestion. The fabric was dry, you see. He hadn't found it lying in the open. And he was seen trying car doors.'

'When did you go to the lab?'

'Day before yesterday, when you were in London.'

'What about the other items? You mentioned a water bottle and some food wrappers.'

'We bagged them all up and sent them for examination.'

'Let me know when you get the lab report.' Diamond tried to imagine stretching out on the stone surface. 'Not the most comfortable bed.'

'Cold, too, these late summer nights,' Septimus said.

Diamond stepped outside the gatehouse. 'It can't be more than thirty yards to where the body was found. I'm going to pace it out.'

You wouldn't have known where the body had lain unless you guessed from the state of the ground. The only other indication was on the adjacent grave, a faint blue circle left by Forensics enclosing the suspicious bloodstain. In the next row was a granite sarcophagus a man could easily have crouched behind.

'What's your reading of it, Septimus? Was he chased here, or was the killer waiting?'

'I don't think he was chased. He was hit on the back of the skull. If you're running from someone and they catch you, you turn and defend yourself. I say he walked into a trap and was hit from behind.'

'My feeling, too.'

IN THE INCIDENT ROOM Diamond discovered Ingeborg in seventh heaven. 'I called my drill officer and told him I'd like a transfer to the cavalry and they have a vacancy in Prince Rupert's Lifeguard of Horse. They want me on parade at Farleigh Hungerford on Saturday. Someone pulled out through illness and I have to report for practice tonight. Isn't that neat?'

'Neat, indeed.' He didn't add that she ought to remember why she was doing this. She was a professional and he could rely on her to function as a detective. 'Farleigh Hungerford. There isn't much there, is there?'

She said in a crushing tone, 'Farleigh Castle, Guv. The scene of a major event in the Civil War.'

'And you'll be re-enacting this?'

'I'm not sure. Apparently the castle was taken without bloodshed.'

'Do you have a horse?'

'They're providing one for me. And a uniform. Blue doublet and red sash. I even get to wear the Cavalier hat.'

'I'd like a picture of that.'

He stepped into his office and closed the door. Ingeborg's elation was in sharp contrast to his own mood. His confidence was draining away. He couldn't fault Ingeborg or Septimus or Paul Gilbert. The entire team was among the keenest he'd ever led. Even John Leaman was a beaver with hyperactivity syndrome. And Keith Halliwell had taken a bullet, he was so loyal and brave. How, then, could such an array of talent have failed to produce a single credible suspect? He'd expected by now to have names in the frame and there wasn't one. Not even a motive had emerged.

He had to face the possibility that he'd overplayed the connection between the two murders. It remained speculative. Both bodies had been found on Lansdown, and Rupert had sat beside Nadia's grave and handled her bone before being murdered. But life is full of coincidences.

He feared he'd missed something through trying to link the killings. If he'd investigated Rupert's murder in isolation he might have had stronger suspicions about Dave, who'd come forward long after the original call for witnesses, or Major Swithin, the vigilante who'd called the police to the racecourse, or even the angry woman from the car boot sale. Because these people had no apparent link to Nadia he'd not rated them as serious suspects. In theory, Septimus should have put each of them through the grinder.

Somebody knocked on his door. Didn't they know by now that when it was closed he was not to be interrupted?

Flushed with annoyance, he flung it open. 'What is it?'

Septimus stood there. He took a deep breath. 'The lab just called. They've been examining the blanket I sent in, the one we think was used by Rupert.'

'And . . .?'

'They're saying it's a horse rug.'

'OK, it's not a blanket, it's a horse rug.'

'They removed a number of horse hairs and compared them with the one we'd sent them from the zip fly. They say it comes from the same horse.'

7

Diamond called the lab and asked to speak to the chief scientist. The voice on the line was well used to dealing with awkward policemen. 'Good of you to call back, Mr Diamond. No doubt there's a rational explanation for our findings.' A definite chuckle was audible.

Diamond held himself in check. 'Before I comment, let's clarify what's in your report, shall we?'

'The horse rug your people sent us contains hair clippings genetically identical to the one you submitted previously. We were led to believe that particular clipping had been buried for up to twenty years.'

'Sixteen.'

'Sixteen, then. And we were told this rug had been used recently by a murder victim sleeping rough. There's only one explanation I can think of, and that's that you muddled the clippings in some way.'

'You'd better think again because that's not possible,' Diamond said. 'Your own scientists found the first hair trapped under the tab.'

'Ah, but how many people handled the zip before it reached here?'

'One only, the crime-scene investigator. It was put straight into an evidence bag. We followed correct procedures throughout.' He changed tack. 'What's your basis for saying that the hairs came from the same horse?'

'DNA analysis. Animals have their unique profiles, just the same as humans do. All the top racing thoroughbreds have their DNA on record and it can be analysed from hair samples. We back up every test and I ordered more when this unaccountable result was reported to me. They came back identical to the first batch.'

Diamond felt as if he needed a cigarette, and he'd given up years ago. 'I'd like to speak to my colleagues about this. I'll get back to you later.'

He slammed down the phone and asked Septimus back into the office.

'How could this have happened?' Diamond asked him.

'Not our fault. We bagged up the blanket—sorry, horse rug—where we found it, in the gatehouse, sealed and labelled it and sent it off directly. The zip was already at the lab being cleaned before I came to Bath.'

'Keith Halliwell sent them the zip. He's ultra-careful.' Diamond leaned on his elbows, locked in thought. After some while he said, 'It's not impossible that the horse Nadia came into contact with is still alive. A three-year-old in 1993 could be under twenty now.'

'So Rupert happened to find the rug used for the same horse?' Septimus said on a disbelieving note. 'That's stretching it.'

'No. There could be a logical reason. Rupert the historian had an interest in the Civil War. That's why he joined the Sealed Knot. He must have taken an interest in every aspect of the battle, including the cavalry. I reckon this was some old warhorse that featured in both re-enactments.' Another thought struck him. 'And how about this? The horse is local and kept on Lansdown. I've seen them in fields there. On cold nights they're covered with a rug. By day the rug is going to be stored somewhere. A shed. The place where they keep the fodder. Rupert breaks in and helps himself.'

Septimus digested this and said nothing.

'Something for Ingeborg to check on tonight,' Diamond said. 'She can take an interest in the horses, find out if there's a veteran among them.'

Diamond called the lab again and outlined his new theory.

'Each victim came into contact with the same horse?' the scientist said.

'We're working on the theory that both of them were involved with battle re-enactments on Lansdown.'

'In that case we'll report to you in the usual way. Mind, it would be helpful if you could find the horse.'

'That's next. And it would help me to know more about the rug.'

'It's an under-rug made of soft material to protect the animal from friction from the heavyweight rug. There's a label. The manufacturer was a firm called Phil Drake. Unfortunately it went bust eleven years ago.'

'So if it's at least eleven years old, it's not in the best condition?'

'The original burgundy colour has faded and the fabric is disintegrating, but the deterioration is down to the ageing of the fabric more than use. Materials fade and break down in time, as you know.'

'Apart from the clippings of horse hair, did you find anything else?'

'Why don't you ask outright if we found any human hairs that match Rupert Hope's? Actually, we did. We can say for certain that he came into contact with it.'

Finally, something to be pleased about. Diamond went down to the canteen. To top up his blood sugar he invested in a chocolate-chip muffin. His thoughts were more positive now. By tonight Nadia's picture would be on TV and in the *Bath Chronicle*. If anyone in the city remembered seeing her, the case could be transformed.

Encouraging as all this was, the motive for Nadia's murder still eluded him. He'd rejected the theory that she'd been killed on orders from the London vice ring, but that didn't mean sex was discounted as a motive. Her death had the feel of a spontaneous killing by a stranger—the hardest of all to investigate. An unplanned murder gruesomely covered up on the edge of the battlefield. The best hope was that someone had witnessed something. His thoughts returned to those self-appointed snoops, the Lansdown Society.

He went upstairs for a session with their police representative, Georgina.

'This won't take long, Ma'am.' He closed the door behind him. 'It's about the Lansdown Society. I see you and your fellow members as potential witnesses, invaluable to the enquiry.'

'You seem to have spoken to each of us now,' said Georgina, coolly.

'Actually, no.'

'Come on, Peter. I know for a fact that you questioned Sir Colin Tipping, Major Swithin and Augusta White.'

'There's another.'

'Me?' She clapped a hand to her chest. 'If I noticed anything I'd volunteer it. You wouldn't have to ask.'

'The reverend gentleman.'

'Charlie Smart? He wasn't a member in 1993. He was initiated after me, less than three years ago, when the previous vicar retired. I can't think what he could have witnessed.'

'Rupert Hope in the last hours of his life and possibly his murderer as well. Will I find Charlie Smart at St Stephen's?'

'No, you won't. His parish is up the hill, at St Vincent's on Granville Road, not far from Beckford's Tower. It looks more like a Nissen hut than a church. The vicarage is next door. I'll phone him to see if he's there.'

GEORGINA'S DESCRIPTION of the church hadn't been strictly accurate. St Vincent's was modest in size, but built of brick rather than corrugated iron, and looked inseparable from the office buildings nearby. Diamond could never have identified it until he found a board at the front listing the times of services. The vicarage next door was a similar hutment, fronted by a garden so overgrown that he had to part the foliage to get to the door.

'It's open,' a voice called from within.

Diamond gave the door a push and found himself in the living room greeted by a short, blond man in jeans and a T-shirt with a butterfly motif.

'You must be the myrmidon of the law,' the man said, offering his hand. 'Charlie Smart, incumbent. Would you like a drink?'

'Thank you, but not on duty.'

'Dandelion and burdock cordial won't compromise you,' Charlie Smart said, 'and I speak not only as a man of the cloth but as the one who distilled the same. Try.' He picked up a jug and poured some into two tumblers.

In the cause of good policing, Diamond sipped some and found it marginally easier to swallow than Ukrainian *kvas*. 'Tasty.'

'As a society we impoverish ourselves by ignoring the so-called weeds,' the vicar said. 'Speaking of the humble dandelion, did you know that it's a source of rubber? There's an Asian variety that was cultivated on an enormous scale by the Russians during the war when their supplies of regular rubber were interrupted. It's still grown commercially in the Ukraine.'

Diamond became genuinely interested. 'Have you been there?'

'No. Plants are my thing. Preaching and plants. You'd better stop me if you want to talk about anything else.'

'People, actually, as distinct from plants.'

'Any particular people?'

'Have you noticed anyone hanging about the cemetery recently?'

'You want to know if I spotted the poor fellow who was murdered?'

'Him, or, better still, his killer. We believe the victim was sleeping in the gatehouse for a number of nights before he was killed.'

'Sensible. He'd stay dry there and wouldn't be disturbed. I'm sorry to disappoint you, but I can't remember seeing anything suspicious.'

'As a member of the Lansdown Society, you patrol the down regularly?'

'My rambles arise from my interest in the natural world. Wearing my botanical hat, studying the vegetation, I'd cover the same ground whether I was in the society or not. However, I support its aims.'

'Do you get up to the battleground?'

'Regularly. You're going to ask me about the skeleton and I'm going to disappoint you again. I've lived here only three years.'

'But you know the fallen tree?'

'The old oak? Yes. It's our success story, that tree. The farmer wanted to saw it up and sell the timber, but the Lansdown Society made sure he didn't. There was a rare variety of lichen growing on it, so they got a conservation order, or whatever you get for trees.'

'What's it called?'

'The lichen? To tell you the truth, I don't know. It's no longer there.'

'Could someone have misidentified it?'

Charlie Smart rolled his eyes. 'I can't answer that, not having been here at the time.'

'The others aren't experts like you. None of them are wildlifers. Was the previous vicar a botanist?'

'Arthur Underhill? No, he was a literary man, a Beckford expert, so he was in his element living here. Beckford is still a cult figure. People knock on my door asking the way to the tower. You get the occasional crank who thinks he squirrelled away some of the treasures and masterpieces he stacked in the tower. The auction after his death was a very dubious affair presided over by a crooked auctioneer and his son who absconded soon after.'

'I don't know why Lansdown should give rise to so much crime,' Diamond said. 'It's just one large hill, after all.'

'It's Bath's back room,' Charlie Smart said, 'stuffed with things people want to forget about.'

'WHERE'S INGEBORG?' Diamond asked in the incident room.

Septimus looked up from his computer. 'Somewhere on Lansdown by now, looking for an elderly warhorse. I told her your theory and she got really fired up. She was on the phone to someone in the Sealed Knot, finding out where they stable the horses they use.'

'What's she going to do if she finds the right one?' Leaman asked.

'I expect she'll get a hair sample.'

'To see if it's the same colour?'

'For the DNA,' Diamond said. 'Didn't you know horses have DNA?'

Leaman went quiet.

'Plenty of horses are taken to Lansdown for the race meetings,' Paul Gilbert said. 'Maybe we should make a check up there.'

'Twenty-year-olds, in training?' Diamond said.

Gilbert turned pink. 'I guess not.'

But something was stirring in Diamond's memory. In the quiet of his office, he scrolled through Ingeborg's calendar of events to the few days in the summer of 1993—from Nadia's arrival late in July to the battle re-enactment on August 7th and 8th.

July 24	Rare red kite sighted over Kingswood School
July 31	St Stephen's Church Fete
August 1	Car boot picture said to be Rowlandson print

August 2	Sheep savaged near Upper Langridge. Big cat theory	
August 7	Battle of Lansdown re-enactment	Day 1
August 8	" " " " " "	Day 2

Disappointing. Nothing to link to Nadia except the re-enactment—and that was only because she'd been buried close to where the fighting took place. He scrolled on a little.

August 9	Metal detectorist finds Roman brooch, Charlcombe
August 12	Hang-glider stolen
August 16	Car-boot 'Rowlandson' was forgery

He couldn't imagine Nadia metal detecting or hang-gliding. She'd be trying to get work. Yet he had a sense that the information on the screen mattered to the case. He scrolled back to study the list again.

His phone beeped. Wigfull's voice. 'Just to let you know that your Ukrainian girl is in tonight's *Bath Chronicle*. And the story will be on Points West and HTV News tonight, so the phones should start ringing soon. You'd better not go home early.'

'Nice work, John.' His train of thought had derailed. He took one more look at the screen before stepping into the incident room to see who was willing to do overtime.

A high-profile appeal to the public always brings in responses. Most are made in good faith, even if a high proportion prove to be mistaken. Additionally there are callers who'll have heard about payments to informants. Usually their information is worthless. Finally there are the nuisance callers who make bogus 999 calls.

Diamond went over the procedure with his volunteers, stressing the known facts about Nadia: that she was Ukrainian, under twenty, a Roman Catholic, had lived in London as a prostitute and was in lodgings in Lower Swainswick. She spoke good English, had no family, and she would have been wearing jeans and a T-shirt. 'The trick is that you don't give out any of this. You listen to the information coming in and see if it tallies.'

As if on cue, a call came in, but it was only Ingeborg. 'I've spent the entire afternoon checking on horses, Guv.'

'Any joy?'

'I saw some adorable animals, but none that was old enough. And now I'd better get straight to my evening session with the cavalry.'

'OK. You don't want to be late on parade.'

'God no.'

'One thing, Inge. Don't lose sight of what you're really there for.'

While Diamond had been speaking to her, the first call had come in. Paul Gilbert was taking it. He thanked the caller and rang off. 'Wrong year. They said the Olympics were on in Barcelona. That was 1992.'

'Good thinking,' Diamond said. 'Did you watch it on TV?'

'I was only two at the time.'

'There's a sobering thought. I was working here. Same job, same rank.'

More calls started coming in. One was a definite sighting at Mass at St John's. Nadia had covered her head with a dark scarf, but otherwise she was wearing the T-shirt and jeans.

'Must have borrowed the scarf from Mrs Jarvie,' Diamond said.

After six, when the local news was screened on HTV, a flurry of calls came in, but none proved to be of obvious help. Everyone had memories of young foreign girls asking for directions in Bath. Three would be worth following up, but they appeared to offer little new information. Someone had spoken to a Ukrainian girl at the station on the day she arrived. Two had seen someone like Nadia walking into town from Lower Swainswick.

The evening shift could be left to take any more calls. Diamond thanked the team. 'You never know, someone may call us tomorrow.'

Before leaving, he made a call of his own, to Paloma, inviting her for a drink at the Blathwayt, a pub-restaurant at the top of the hill.

'On Lansdown?' she said. 'Can't you leave your work behind?'

'I'm combining business with pleasure, but the pleasure will be paramount.'

'Smoothie. I don't believe a word.'

HE MADE SURE he arrived early enough to walk through the Blathwayt's several dining areas checking who was there. The bar was doing a brisk trade, but he recognised nobody. Outside was a candlelit section he hadn't seen before and he moved into a seat. He'd ordered the drinks before Paloma drove up.

'I seem to be losing my aura of mystery,' she said after they'd kissed. 'You even know what I want to drink.'

'Is that bad?'

'I'm not going to complain. This is nice, being outside.'

'I don't know if you've been inside lately,' he said. 'It's had a makeover since I was last here. I remember it as dark and seedy.'

'In keeping with its past,' she said. 'Back in the eighteenth century, it was a highwaymen's pub. The road to Bath was perfect for holdups.'

'There's no end to the villainy on this bloody hill. Only this afternoon I was hearing about a firm of bent auctioneers.'

'English and Son. Absolute crooks. How did they come up?'

Diamond told her what he'd learned from Charlie Smart.

'He's right,' Paloma said. 'It's all in the book I lent you. The pair of them disappeared owing a fortune and were never traced and neither were some of William Beckford's treasures. He had one of the finest private art collections in the country, paintings by Raphael and Bellini, Claude and Canaletto. And there were other treasures of gold and silver.'

'A secret hoard?' Diamond thought about it as the possible mainspring for two murders. 'I was coming round to sex as the motive for Nadia's death, but if she happened to have found a stash of valuables, that could have made her a target.'

'Beckford's lost treasures? All the likely places will have been checked long ago.' Paloma took a long sip of her spritzer. 'I saw the picture of Nadia on Points West. Has it jogged any memories?'

'Not enough. I want to know if anyone saw her at the re-enactment.'

She looked doubtful. 'In the cavalry?'

He smiled. 'You're right. I can't believe she was taken on by the Sealed Knot within days of arriving in Bath.'

'It's unpaid, isn't it? They dress up and play soldiers for the fun of the thing. What Nadia needed was a paid job.'

He told her about the lab report on the horse rug. She listened keenly and weighed his theory. 'You think Rupert found a rug belonging to the same horse Nadia came into contact with all those years ago?'

'Sixteen years. It's possible.'

'Theoretically,' she said in a voice already thinking something else. 'You said the rug had deteriorated through age, rather than wear and tear? Isn't it more likely that it hasn't been used in many years and was stored in some outbuilding and found by Rupert?'

He nodded. 'That makes sense, too. We can't dismiss any scenario.' He glanced at some people entering the restaurant, two women and a bearded man tagging on behind, all of them probably in the forty-to-fifty age group. 'That dark woman in the blue suit is familiar.'

'How familiar? An old flame?' Paloma asked.

'No, I don't believe I've ever spoken to her, but I've seen her recently.'

'She's attractive . . . for her age,' Paloma said.

'And the guy with the beard?'

'He's there on sufferance. Staff, probably. She's the boss lady.'

'They don't look dressed for a night out.'

'My guess is that they worked late and she's invited them for a drink.' She clicked her fingers. 'I've seen her, too, and I know where. At the races. She was the woman in the peacock-blue hat we saw getting the prize.'

'Spot on,' he said.

'Davina Tipping, daughter of Sir Colin. He told me she owns her own practice as a vet.'

'And the others work for her, I expect. Davina may be able to advise you on the local horse population. I bet she knows where a lot of them are stabled.'

'I hadn't thought of asking a vet,' he said. He liked the suggestion. 'They're heading for the bar. Let's join them, shall we?'

Paloma gave a resigned smile and followed him. The 'pleasure' part of the outing was over.

Davina and her party had taken their drinks to a table near the open hearth in the centre of the room where a log fire blazed.

'Pardon me for butting in,' Diamond said, 'but you're just the people who can help me. I'm correct, am I not, in saying you're Davina Tipping, the top vet in Bath? I'm Peter Diamond of Bath CID, and this is my friend Paloma Kean. We watched your filly winning the trophy a week or two ago.'

'My Stylist,' Paloma said, trying to soften his none-too-subtle interruption. 'We backed her. These drinks should have been on us.'

'That's generous,' Davina said. 'I started a tab. I haven't paid yet.'

'Peter will see to it,' Paloma said.

There was a strict rule in Bath nick that pub expenses had to be authorised in advance by Georgina. This would come out of his own pocket.

'What sort of help are you wanting?' Davina said. She introduced her companions. Sally and Wilfred worked in the practice.

Diamond said he was involved in a case linked to the re-enactments of the Battle of Lansdown and was trying to get information on a horse that could have taken part in the 1993 event and might still be kept locally.

'It would be getting on a bit,' Paloma added. 'We think about twenty.'

'Twenty isn't unusual,' Davina told them. 'You can get insurance up to twenty-five and some breeds live well into their thirties.'

'I expect they need more treatment as they get older,' Diamond said. 'As a vet, you may know of an elderly horse like this.'

'What colour?'

'Black or dark brown. We've got only a few hairs as evidence. They were found on a burgundy-coloured under-rug made by a firm called Phil Drake.'

'That's going back a bit,' Davina said. 'Where was this rug found?'

'In the entrance gate to Beckford's Tower, being used by a man sleeping rough. Where he found it is a mystery.'

'Out of a stable, I expect,' she said. 'There are more than you might think on Lansdown and I know of two that supply horses for these battle events.'

'I expect this old warhorse would be retired.'

'Not necessarily. A mock battle isn't demanding on agility, a few short gallops, that's all. It doesn't compare with steeplechasing or showjumping.' She spoke with the calm authority that comes with giving expert advice.

'That's helpful,' Diamond said, his ideas moving on. 'Puts a whole new slant on the case. Would you mind giving me the addresses of those stables?'

'Not a problem. I'll write them down.'

Diamond took a pen and notebook from his pocket and handed them to Davina. 'I'll get more drinks.'

It was a cheap round. Sally and Wilfred said they were leaving for home shortly and Davina had promised to meet her father at the golf club.

While waiting to settle his bill, Diamond found himself thinking about Sir Colin Tipping and things he had said that morning at the golf club. Some part of the conversation was niggling at his brain.

'Are you a vet, sir?' the barman asked.

'No.' He was still struggling to remember.

'My mistake. Saw you with the others.'

'No problem. I'm sure you get all sorts up here.'

'The world and his wife, sir.'

Then the connection was made. He realised what he'd missed when scrolling through Ingeborg's calendar of events. Now it was vital that he spoke to Davina's father.

'I don't know if you'll get any sense out of him,' Davina said when he told her what he wanted. 'He'll have sunk a few whiskies by now.'

All the better if the whisky is talking, Diamond thought.

'NOT THE EVENING you expected, was it?' he said to Paloma as they walked to their cars.

'I had my suspicions, if you remember,' she said.

'And you were right.'

She smiled. 'I'm going to leave you with your horsy friends. You'll do better on your own at this stage.'

They embraced and he promised to make it up to her.

In the car, he picked up his mobile. Ingeborg was about to rue the day she had put her own number in the directory. Wherever she was, he reasoned, she should be capable of answering. Her evening training session would be well over.

'Inge? It's me—Diamond.'

'I know, Guv. You're on my display.'

He could hear a background buzz of voices and canned music. 'I was looking at that list of events on Lansdown, the one you compiled for Keith. Do you happen to remember working on July to August 1993, the time we know for certain Nadia was in Bath?'

'Now you're asking. At the time I didn't know 1993 was important. I simply went through the *Bath Chronicle* jotting down anything I found.'

'On one of the days, after the battle, you noted, "Hang-glider stolen".'

'Did I?'

She wasn't usually this vague. He could picture her shrugging at her friends in the bar. 'Are you listening, Inge? What I need to know—and it's important—is if you meant a hang-glider as such, or the racehorse with the same name? At some point— and it could have been 1993—a young stallion called Hang-glider belonging to Sir Colin Tipping was driven away and never seen again—like Shergar.'

'Like what?'

'Never mind.' The kidnapping of Shergar must have happened before she was born. 'A hang-glider or a horse?'

'You've got me there. The missing horse made big news for some days, but I couldn't tell you its name or which year. I can check and call you back.'

'There isn't time. I'll be with Tipping directly.'

'Put it this way, Guv. I can't remember anyone nicking a hang-glider. I'm ninety per cent sure it must be the horse.'

'I'll go with that,' he said.

He had to. Davina was getting into a sports car close by. He followed her the short distance up the road to the front of the clubhouse.

'I can't say what state Fa will be in,' she called as they got out. 'It's my job to collect him so that he isn't breathalysed. Are you coming in?'

'I'd rather see him apart from his friends when he comes out.'

'Give me time to root him out, then.'

The notion of the golf club members being collected like kids after a party amused him, particularly when he saw two other women drive up.

Then a group of four emerged in loud conversation and he saw that Davina had accomplished her mission. The others were Major Swithin and his wife, Agnes. The noise was coming mainly from the major. 'The night is young,' he was saying. 'Where's your spirit of adventure?'

'You've had all the spirit you're getting,' his wife told him.

Agnes steered the major to their Land Rover, leaving Sir Colin and Davina in conversation. Sir Colin looked across the car roofs to where Diamond was waiting.

Diamond went over. 'Just happened to meet Davina in the Blathwayt. There was something I forgot to ask when we spoke before.'

'My daughter's hand in marriage?' Sir Colin said, straight into his music-hall routine. 'So what are your prospects, young man?'

'Fa, that'll do,' Davina said.

'Well, Superintendent, what did you forget to ask?'

'You told me about the horse that went missing.'

'Hang-glider. Don't remind me. I get tearful.'

'Was that in August 1993?'

'You're asking me at this end of the evening? Really, I can't recall.'

Davina said, 'It was 1993, the year you met the Queen at Ascot.'

'You're right. He'd just won the Prince of Wales Stakes. What a win.'

'Tragically his last,' Davina said to Diamond. 'His trainer noticed a slight limp and ultrasound revealed a tendon injury. Fa had to retire him. We were all devastated. Which was when Sheikh Abdul made his offer.'

'May I ask what the offer amounted to?'

'It's on public record,' she said. 'Half a million up-front and fifty per cent of the stud fees. He was expected to cover more than a hundred mares in a season at fifty thou a time. I reckon he was good for five to ten years. Compared to that, the insurance payout was a pittance, under a hundred thou.'

Diamond came to the point. 'The reason I asked about the date is that 1993 appears to have been the year that the young woman whose murder I'm investigating was buried on Lansdown. There was a horse hair found with her skeleton and it's just possible it came from your horse.'

'Good Lord! What makes you think that?'

'I said it's a possibility. Did you employ a girl to groom the horse?'

'Personally, no. You'd have to ask my trainer, Percy McDart, at Lambourn. He looked after all that. He's still in business there.'

'Lambourn? Is that where the horse was stabled?' This was not what he wanted to hear. 'I was thinking Hang-glider was trained locally.'

'Well, you'd be wrong. Any half-decent horse is kept at Lambourn, Highclere or Newmarket.'

'I'll contact McDart. We'd like to check Hang-glider's DNA.'

'How can you do that when he's not been seen since 1993?' Davina asked. 'They didn't keep DNA records then.'

'If anything was kept as a souvenir—let's say a saddle or a rug—we might get hairs or skin particles from it. Do you possess anything like it, Sir Colin?'

Tipping shook his head. 'I collected cheques and trophies, not horse rugs.'

'And did you ever hear from the people who stole the horse?'

'Not a word. They didn't demand a ransom and they couldn't race him. I think I told you my theory—that he was secretly put to stud?'

Davina said, 'I don't believe that one.'

'He'd have produced damned good foals,' her father said. 'Sheikh Abdul thought he was a good investment and so did the blighters who took him.'

'But if the matings were done secretly the foals would have no pedigree.'

'Doesn't matter. When you know something and other people don't, there's money to be made.'

'Not enough,' she said. 'I've never said this to you before, Fa, but I think it was done from personal spite. Someone heard you were about to cash in and chose to bring you down.'

Tipping looked quite shaken. 'I'm not one to make enemies. I've always treated people decently in business and in everyday life.'

'Ask Mr Diamond. Isn't jealousy one of the main motives for crime?'

'It's one to consider, yes,' Diamond said.

INGEBORG WAS WAITING to see Diamond when he arrived next morning, her eyes bright as sword blades.

'It's Saturday, Guv.'

'Even I can work that out,' he said.

'Farleigh Hungerford Castle. I'm wondering if I can leave early.'

'Your performance. Right. What time?'

'Well, as soon as possible. They want us on parade at one p.m.'

'You've had only one rehearsal, haven't you?'

She gave him a pained look. 'Drill, Guv. We call it drill.'

'Before you go, did you find out anything about Rupert last night?'

She shook her head, a fraction too fast for Diamond's liking.

'There's something, isn't there?'

'Our drill instructor was Dave Barton, the man who was with Rupert when they found the femur.'

Diamond paused, taking this in. 'He's a foot soldier, not cavalry. He shouldn't be on a horse.'

'I don't know what he was doing the day of the re-enactment, but he's a cavalry officer, and a good one. I'm not kidding, Guv.'

'He's not the officer type.'

She clicked her tongue in annoyance. 'It's not the real army. You don't have to go through Sandhurst to do the job.'

Fair point, he thought. These people were playing at soldiers.

'He's just your average guy, except he's a top horsemen,' she said. 'Maybe his horse was injured when they had the muster.'

'Did he recognise you as CID?'

'I don't think so. I saw him the day he came in, but we didn't speak.'

He allowed her to leave directly. Much else was on his mind. The previous night's conversation with Sir Colin Tipping had almost persuaded him that the theft of Hang-glider in 1993 was the key to the case. Up to then he'd been assuming Nadia's murder was connected to the re-enactment, that she'd been killed during or shortly after the battle. The discovery that the race meeting took place four days later and a serious crime was committed opened a new possibility. Could she have witnessed the theft of the horse and been killed simply because she was there? They could have bundled her body into a car and driven her a short way up the road and buried her.

Wouldn't it be marvellous if Wigfull's publicity had produced an eye witness who remembered seeing Nadia at the race meeting? He stepped back into the incident room and asked for the latest batch of notes from callers.

A glance through the material was not encouraging. He found the usual mix of guesswork and imprecision. There was another sighting from Sunday Mass in August 1993, but otherwise the result was negative.

He picked up the phone and asked the operator to get a line to the Lambourn trainer, Percy McDart. She called back to say McDart wasn't listed and could Diamond supply the name of the stables he worked for?

A job for Paul Gilbert. Diamond briefed him. 'The *Racing Post* are sure to know. When you reach McDart, make an appointment for later this morning. Say who we are, but not what it's about. I want to see his reaction myself.'

'Will you need directions, Guv?'

'You will. You're doing the driving.'

From across the incident room, Septimus called out, 'Boss, remember the lager that was buried before the battle? We finally caught up with the guy who nicked it.'

Diamond shimmied round the desks to hear more. 'Nice work. Who is he?'

'A Parliamentarian named Bert Pope. He was exercising his horse an hour before the fighting started and he saw a soldier in Royalist red burying a six-pack by the fallen tree. As he tells it, this was one of the enemy, so he thought it fair game to help himself. But seeing as it was a hot day, he left two of the cans. He read about the skeleton being found but he didn't come forward because he couldn't see that the lager had anything to do with it.'

'How did you find him?'

'He shared the drink with some of his friends and told them where it came from. When one of them saw the stuff in the paper, he told Pope he'd better fess up. And he did, eventually.'

'Good. It chimes in nicely with Dave Darton's statement.'

'It doesn't mean Barton is in the clear,' Septimus said at once. His suspicions of the blacksmith had not gone away. 'He was in no hurry to come forward himself.'

'So what's your take on it?' Diamond said.

'It's one of those things you can't prove. He comes across as OK.'

'Inge agrees with you. Barton's her cavalry officer.'

Septimus blinked. 'That didn't come out at the interview.'

'I recall when you asked if he was a pikeman, he said, "not always".'

'Evasive.'

'He's a captain of horse according to Ingeborg.'

'That makes sense now. When I asked him about the cavalryman who saw him burying the lager, he said he'd know the horse if he saw it again.'

Diamond nodded. 'A white stallion.'

'A pale horse.'

'Same thing.'

'You don't get it, do you?' Septimus gave him a gaze burnished with zeal. 'The Book of Revelation. "And I looked, and behold a pale horse: and his name that sat on him was Death."'

FOR MUCH OF THE TRIP along the motorway, those words resonated in Diamond's head. The Bible wasn't often quoted in Bath CID.

Septimus had been consistent in his suspicion of Dave Barton. He'd worked out that ingenious theory that it had been Rupert who had hidden the six-pack, chancing on the very place where Dave (the supposed killer of Nadia) had buried the body all those years before. Dave (the theory went) had been compelled to silence Rupert by murdering him. The interrogation when Dave had brought along his lawyer had been insisted on, and carried out, by Septimus. And now new witness Bert Pope had torpedoed the theory. Dave had been seen in the act of burying the lager. His story was corroborated and Septimus was reduced to quoting doom-laden stuff from the Bible.

Paul Gilbert said suddenly, 'If you don't mind me asking, Guv, I'm not too clear how this racehorse trainer fits in.'

Diamond hadn't briefed the team since his meeting with Tipping. Taking his time, he told Gilbert why it had become necessary to get the trainer's version of what had happened the evening Hang-glider had been stolen.

It wasn't long before they passed Swindon and started looking for their exit. Gilbert had the sat-nav working—just one more gadget Diamond had resolved he didn't need in his own car.

'We're close now,' Gilbert said as he made the fourth prompted turn in under a minute and they started up a lane rutted with mud and cow manure. Sure enough, it opened into a maintained road and in two minutes they were driving towards a complex of stables and outbuildings. Security, Diamond noted, was all around them: CCTV, high walls topped with razor wire, double sets of gates. They had to speak into an entry phone to gain admission.

'They call this a yard?' Gilbert said, marvelling.

'A yard and then some. It's a multimillion-pound business.'

They drew up outside the brick-built admin section. Mr McDart, they learned from a high-heeled receptionist, was at the main stable block.

They found the trainer seated on a bale of hay, short, silver-haired, in a padded waistcoat. His brown eyes assessed them as they approached.

'You must be the long arm of the law.'

'Something like that,' Diamond said, showing his ID.

'Is this another complaint about my horses holding up the traffic?'

'Actually, no. It's about Hang-glider.' Diamond watched for the reaction.

It wasn't panic. Not even concern. Expectation best described it. 'Have you found him after all these years?'

'Unfortunately, no,' Diamond said. 'But we want the facts about his disappearance. It's possible a murder was committed at the same time.'

'Murder? I know nothing about that.' McDart was unfazed.

'But you were there for the races?'

'I was. Hang-glider wasn't. He'd popped a tendon and retired. He was the star, making a final appearance in front of his fans.'

'Trained here?'

'From the beginning. The owner, Sir Colin Tipping, paid a small fortune for him as a yearling. This colt was the real deal from the start.' McDart looked away, remembering, and there was pride in his voice. 'In his short career, he was ahead of everything. He could have done much, much more.' He gave Diamond another gimlet gaze. 'Murder, you said?'

'That's our suspicion. Would you tell us your memories of that day?'

'I drove the horse there myself with my son Charles, who was learning the business in those days, as a stable lad, like I did.'

'Was that safe—driving an injured horse?'

A frown. 'He was three months over the injury. You wouldn't have known there was anything amiss except that he'd have torn it again if he was raced. All we did was walk him in front of the grandstands.'

'You said "we".'

'Charles, actually. I watched from a box in the stands with the owner. It was rather moving. Cheering all the way.'

'So, did your son return the horse to the box?'

'That's right. Locked him in securely and joined some of his friends.'

'Where was the box parked? Among all the others?'

'No. We asked for a spot near the premier enclosure.'

'When did you find out that the horse had been stolen?'

'The end of the evening. Charles came to collect me and we went back to the box. The doors had been forced and Hang-glider wasn't inside.'

'Wasn't there an alarm system?'

'Neutralised. They knew what they were doing. We alerted security and they checked the boxes that hadn't been driven off. He must have been moved to another box and transported that way. By this time it was dark, of course.'

'Did you tell Sir Colin?'

'After he got home. He'd already left. He was shattered when I told him.'

'What I can't understand,' Diamond said, 'is why it didn't become a police matter. To my recollection, CID had nothing to do with it.'

McDart gave a shrug. 'Racing is like that. We have our own security through the British Horseracing Authority.'

'What's your theory about it?'

McDart expelled a long breath. 'Hang-glider was valuable property as a stallion, even though his racing days were over.'

'But it's all about pedigrees, isn't it? Anyone buying a foal wants to know who sired it.'

'Speaking off the record, if I'm sent a foal that can run well, I won't care what sired it. The paperwork can be forged to make it appear right.'

'So could Hang-glider still be alive under some other name?'

'At this distance in time? I very much doubt it.' He paused. 'You still haven't told me who was murdered.'

'A young Ukrainian called Nadia was killed about the same time and buried on Lansdown Hill. She may have been seeking work with horses.'

He shook his head. 'Means nothing to me. I don't employ casuals.'

'I wonder if your son may have met her that evening. Is he about?'

McDart rocked with laughter. 'No.'

'What's the joke?'

'He could have had a good career with me, but he joined your lot.'

Diamond opened his eyes wide. 'The police?'

'Bristol CID. Calls himself Chaz.'

'I'VE WORKED WITH CHAZ,' Diamond told Paul Gilbert on the drive back. 'He's a good copper. I expect he got pissed off being shouted at by his old man.' He reached for his phone. 'Let's see if he's at work this morning.'

The switchboard operator confirmed that Chaz was in and asked if Diamond wished to speak to him.

'Not over the phone,' he said. 'Tell him I'm on my way to see him.'

Up to now, Paul Gilbert had been a model of tolerance, driving at the slow speeds Diamond preferred. Suddenly a manageable trip was being extended into a grand tour. 'To Bristol? Now?'

'Junction 19,' Diamond said. 'I didn't fix a time. You don't have to put your foot down.'

They were on the long stretch between 16 and 17. Gilbert gritted his teeth and said no more about it.

Pleased that so much could be achieved from inside a car, Diamond continued to hold the mobile in his hand. He'd try Ingeborg to see if she'd got to her event in good time. The phone rang a few times and a recorded voice asked him to leave a message.

'Funny,' he said to Gilbert. 'I called Ingeborg and she isn't answering.'

'She's at the jousting, or whatever it's called,' Gilbert said.

'Better not be jousting. I don't want her knocked off the horse.'

'She's more likely to knock the other guy off.'

'I don't know about that. Dave Barton, the blacksmith who found the leg bone, is her commanding officer. Not sure I trust him.' He tried the number again. 'I wonder why she doesn't answer.'

'I expect she's wearing gauntlet gloves,' Gilbert said. 'And she wouldn't want her mobile going off. It's not very Civil War, is it?'

That made sense. Diamond told himself not to fret.

Another mile of green hills went by.

'Which way is Farleigh Hungerford from here?'

'Fifteen to twenty miles from the next exit. Are you worried about her?'

'Not in the least.'

'Barton isn't a serious suspect any more, is he?'

'No. He's in the clear.' Shielding the phone from Gilbert's view, he tried one more time. Still the recorded message.

A disturbing thought was forming. All along, Septimus had clung to his theory that Dave was the killer. The new witness, Bert Pope, the Roundhead, had appeared to confirm Dave's story and prove Septimus wrong.

But had he? Bert Pope had seen 'the soldier in Royalist red' burying the six-pack. They'd assumed the soldier was Dave. It now struck Diamond that he could equally have been Rupert. Septimus could yet be right.

'We'll take the turn to Farleigh,' he told Gilbert. 'And put your foot down.'

Gilbert steered into the fast lane while Diamond, averting his eyes, called Septimus and told him his concerns.

All Septimus could find to say was, 'Oh, man,' several times over.

'So we're on our way to Farleigh Castle,' Diamond told him. 'Put out a call. Get some manpower there. Barton'll be armed with a sword at the very least. If he suspects Inge is police I don't like to think what could happen.' He spotted the sign for Junction 17. 'We're fifteen minutes off.'

This was wildly optimistic, given the amount of slow, heavy traffic. Winding roads, steep hills, tractors crossing: they suffered it all. Mercifully, Bradford on Avon didn't delay them by much. Once they were through the little town the system brought them onto ever narrower lanes.

'We must be close now.' Ahead were flags and the two ruined towers of the castle, strategically positioned above the River Frome. They crossed over two small bridges. Cars were being diverted down a slope into a temporary park in a field.

'We don't have time for that,' Diamond said. 'Put me down here.'

A police patrol car came from the opposite direction with its blue beacon lights flashing. Diamond was already scrambling up a grassy bank into the area below the castle where the crowd had gathered. The hairs on the nape of his neck bristled. Where the display should have been taking place was an ambulance and someone was being stretchered inside.

'What happened?' he asked the first person he met.

'One of them copped it,' he was told. 'Fell off the horse and didn't move.'

He ran on towards the ambulance. An official tried to stop him crossing the rope. 'Police,' he hissed.

The ambulance doors had closed before he got there.

'Who is it?'

'Sorry, mate,' the paramedic told him. 'We've got an emergency.'

He felt a hand on his shoulder. 'Guv, what are you doing here?' It was Ingeborg, unhurt, radiant in her Royalist uniform.

His relief was overwhelming. He would have hugged her if she hadn't been holding the reins of a large black horse. 'I thought that was you in the ambulance,' he said. 'Are you all right?'

'I told you I can look after myself. It's Dave, poor guy.'

'Dave Barton?'

'He came off his horse awkwardly and knocked himself out. The Roundheads were down on numbers, so he was asked to switch sides. Anyone in the crowd will tell you I never even made contact. I swung my sword, he ducked and that was it . . .'

8

It doesn't get much worse than a police officer being questioned about a murder. To avoid the rumour merchants, Diamond had brought Sergeant Chaz McDart out of Bristol Central to one of the few locations where a quiet exchange is possible on a Saturday afternoon: the harbourside. They'd picked a table under the trees in front of the Arnolfini Gallery. This agreeable setting was less secure than an interview room, but with Paul Gilbert's support it was workable. If Chaz tried to make a break for it, the two of them could grab him.

For the moment, their man appeared docile, even allowing that the shaven head and muscled torso suggested he wouldn't come off second best in a fight. When they'd spoken in reception at the police station, he'd said he knew why they were there and they could count on him to cooperate.

Now, over coffee, looking out at the glittering water, he said, 'I'm glad you came for me, really I am. Where do you want me to start?'

'We spoke to your father in Lambourn this morning,' Diamond told him.

'He doesn't know the whole story,' Chaz said in a tone eloquent of a history of family tension. 'He'd have given me a thrashing if I'd told him. I was only a kid at the time, seventeen or thereabouts, son of the boss, serving an apprenticeship. He was tougher on me than on the other lads.'

'What part of the story doesn't he know?' Diamond asked.

'The evening we went to Lansdown Races with Hang-glider. Did he tell you much about that?'

'You and he drove the horsebox there and parked it away from the secure area, somewhere near the Premier Enclosure.'

'Right. And it was my job to parade the horse in front of the grandstands, return him to his box and see that it was properly locked. I did all that. I gave him water and hay and fitted on his travel boots, tail guard and rug. I told all this to the British Horseracing Authority people several times over. I wasn't lying.'

'Economical with the truth?'

Chaz hesitated, then nodded. 'I could have said more and I didn't. All they were interested in was what happened to Hang-glider. It was obvious I wasn't the horse thief, so they didn't question me except for the stuff about the horse. And if they had, it wouldn't have told them anything. A stable lad and a woman. What's wrong with that?'

'This was Nadia?'

Chaz nodded.

Diamond's heart rate quickened. This was what he'd needed—proof that Nadia had been on the racecourse that night in August 1993.

'After I'd settled the horse in its box I had some time on my hands. Dad was in the owners' and trainers' bar with his friends. I went to the marquee. It's a trick known to all the lads. Parties of racegoers get drinking at tables and then hear an announcement about the next race and they're away. Plenty of glasses get left behind more than half full. I picked up some drink or other and looked up and this gorgeous babe was smiling at me.'

'She was already there?'

'Standing alone by another table. She was older than me, in her twenties, wearing jeans and some kind of top. They wouldn't let someone into the Premier Enclosure dressed like that at most courses, but they're not too strict at Lansdown. I introduced myself and she was friendly, standing really close to me. I couldn't believe my luck.'

'Did she give her name?'

'Yes. I could tell she was a foreigner. I asked if Nadia was a Russian name and she said not in her case. She'd been in Bath for a week or two, in lodgings at Swainswick. She'd come to the races because she loved horses.'

'So you told her about Hang-glider?'

'Well, I wanted to impress her, didn't I? I told her about my job and my dad and she said would I mind showing her this famous horse. I took that as a coded way of saying she fancied me and I thought I'd got it made. The horsebox was parked well away from the crowds. I told her it would cost her a kiss to see Hang-glider and she took me into a clinch right away.' He released a sharp breath at the memory. 'I don't know where she learned how to kiss like that.'

Diamond refrained from telling him. 'Did it go any further?'

'I'm coming to that. At this stage she wanted to get inside the horsebox. I unlocked and helped her up. The box was what we called a two-box, with room for a second horse. Hang-glider let her stroke his neck and feed him some titbits. It was obvious she was used to horses. She said she'd give any-thing to work with him and she left me in no doubt what she meant. I stalled a bit and told her he was being sold for stud.'

'What did she say to that?'

'She didn't mind. What she really wanted was a job with horses. Asked me straight out if I could help her get work with my father. I said he liked his stable lads to have the right paperwork and serve an apprenticeship. She didn't let up at all and said she'd sign anything. I was getting jumpy, thinking what my dad would make of this. Then she said something about persuading me and the next thing she was kissing me again. I was really turned on . . . We used the front cab.'

'Locking the box first?'

'You're damn right. My dad would have roasted me if I'd put the horse at risk.' Chaz looked down at the empty coffee cup. 'So I did it with Nadia and it was sensational. The first time I'd gone the whole way. You've got to remember I was just a kid.'

And she was a pro, Diamond thought. 'What happened after?'

'She told me I could have her any way I wanted if I persuaded my dad to give her a job.'

'What did you say to that?'

'I don't remember. My excitement was turning to panic. All I could think about was how to get out of this without Dad finding out.'

The account rang true. Diamond had chastening memories of his own initiation as a teenager. But the empathy went only so far. All the elements for an unpremeditated killing were present: the powerful youth, eager for sex without a thought of what it might cost him, the ex-prostitute desperate for a new start, and the domineering father terrifying the boy.

'How did you deal with it?' he asked, uncertain of what was to come.

'I played for time, telling her I'd try to work it with my dad if she'd come to Lambourn in a week or two. She got a bit stroppy, saying that she needed to meet my father now. Time was going on and I was shit-scared he'd find me with her in the cab. I told her I'd go and talk to him right away. I locked everything up and left her waiting outside. The races were over by then and it was getting dark. People were leaving. Dad was in the bar with a few of his cronies. I wasn't in any hurry to root him out. I was hoping she'd get tired of waiting and simply walk away. A bit unrealistic.'

'Totally, I'd say, knowing her situation. Did you go back to her?'

'No. I hung about for almost another hour and finally Dad came out.'

'Did you tell him about Nadia?'

'No chance. I was hoping she'd have given up and left. If she hadn't, I was counting on Dad to deal with her. He can shoot anyone down in flames. She might have decided she wouldn't want to work for a mean sod like him.'

'I doubt it. What happened next?'

Chaz shrugged. 'Dad and I returned to the horsebox and found it broken into and Hang-glider gone.'

'Was Nadia there?'

He opened both hands. 'Gone. I've never seen her since.'

The gesture was a touch too contrived, Diamond thought. 'Your father said you alerted racecourse security.'

'Yes, it was mayhem. Searches at the exits. People getting angry, wanting to leave. Whoever had done it had got clean away before the search began. They should have contacted the police and made road blocks, but they didn't. The racing world likes to handle its own wrongdoings.'

'Do you think Nadia was in on it?'

He shook his head. 'I've thought about it many times. I was fearful that she'd tricked me. I can't see how.'

'Is it possible the box was broken into while the pair of you were making love in the cab?'

'No. We'd have heard. Besides, I checked that the door was locked.'

'And after? You didn't unlock the box for any reason?'

He shook his head. 'Everything was secure when I left Nadia there. Anyway, the door was forced, which proves it had been locked.'

'You know what really happened—that Nadia was murdered?'

He swallowed hard. 'I do now.'

'When did you find out?'

'Last night when I saw the poster of her. A batch of them was delivered to Bristol Central.'

'Why didn't you get in touch last night?'

He sighed. 'I was shocked. Scared, too. I'd kept this secret—about having sex with her—for all these years. I didn't say anything about it to the security people. I couldn't see how it affected the theft of the horse. Then, last night, this bombshell. I was asking myself if anyone really needed to know. I decided to sleep on it.'

This sounded credible, if reprehensible. 'Didn't it occur to you when the skeleton was found on Lansdown that it might conceivably be Nadia? As a serving police officer, you had a duty to speak out.'

'I know. I should have reported what I knew in case it had a bearing.'

'You worked with me on the Rupert Hope murder—briefly, I know, but you did.'

'It crossed my mind, but I thought of all kinds of reasons why it could be someone else. At the time, I couldn't see any connection, and since then I've been running CID here, covering other cases.'

Diamond wasn't dishing out blame. There was a bigger agenda. 'You heard that a horse rug was found with hairs that matched the single horse hair discovered with the skeleton? Rupert found this rug, an under-rug with the Phil Drake label. Do you recall if Hang-glider had such a rug?'

Chaz looked up. 'He did, yes. It was on his back in the horsebox. I put it on him myself. How the hell could it have turned up after all this time?'

'That was my next question. I need your help, Chaz. What do you think happened that night?'

'It must have happened in that hour after I left Nadia and when I returned with my father. I guess she was killed because she got in the way. They were there to steal a valuable horse and she would have been a witness.'

'Physically, how do you think it was it done?'

'The horse thieves seem to have transferred Hang-glider to a trailer hitched to another vehicle, probably a four by four. There were tyre tracks found by the security team. That way, they would have got on the road before the mass of cars were leaving the racecourse. They could have gone anywhere. Nadia must have been taken with them.'

'She was buried on the battlefield,' Diamond said. 'So the horse was taken elsewhere, sold on to breed on some criminal stud farm, if the owner, Sir Colin Tipping, is right. Did he hold you and your father responsible?'

'He was gutted when Dad told him. He lost a million or more in stud fees. The deal with Sheikh Abdul was all agreed and wasn't signed. There was going to be money on signing and then a percentage of every stud fee the horse earned.'

'Did your father take it out on you?'

'Actually, no. He blamed himself for the lax security. I'd followed his instructions. Of course he knew nothing about Nadia.'

'How long was it before you quit?'

'A matter of months. I was sick of being treated like a fourteen-year-old. I left home, did some part-time jobs and then joined the force. I guess I ought to resign before they sack me.' He was red-eyed.

'I'd wait and see if I were you,' Diamond said.

'WE'LL DRIVE BACK over Lansdown.'

Paul Gilbert took a sharp breath. He'd had a testing day as Diamond's chauffeur. 'Bit out of our way, isn't it?'

This would add at least twenty minutes to the journey, but it was futile to protest. Much as Gilbert was looking forward to getting home for Saturday night, he'd learned that the working day wasn't over.

'Being driven like this has given me a chance to think,' Diamond said. 'We know Rupert found that horse rug somewhere on the hill. I've got a new thought where it might have been.'

Instead of the fast route, they took the old Bath Road and swung along the western side of Hanging Hill to climb the steep ridge where the Royalist Army had once fought its way to the top. Gilbert's little Honda chugged upwards until Lansdown's battlefield came into view.

'Are you thinking of stopping here?' he asked.

'I'll say when.' Diamond was once more preoccupied with a piece of information from the calendar of events Ingeborg had put together. One of the first entries he'd seen scrolling down the screen had not made sense. He hadn't questioned it at the time, because it didn't have any obvious relevance, but he was interested now. The date would have been early in 1991, the year he'd first looked at: Lansdown Road subsidence causes traffic chaos.

Subsidence on Lansdown?

They motored in silence past the racecourse and the golf club. A mile or more ahead, the landlocked lighthouse that was William Beckford's folly appeared on the horizon. The gilded cast-iron columns of the lantern were catching the low sun.

'That's where we stop,' Diamond said.

They approached the tower and parked in the space in front of the gatehouse where poor Rupert Hope had passed his nights.

Diamond spoke again. 'Do you carry a torch?'

'A flashlight, in the boot.'

'Bring it with you.'

Diamond opened the gate and went in. Relieved to find that the flashlight still worked, Gilbert followed.

The stone memorials of the Victorian cemetery appeared theatrical in the orange sunset glow, casting long shadows. Gilbert glanced up at a wind-blown, crumbling angel, its arm pointing heavenwards. This was not a comfortable place to be so late in the day.

Diamond was looking towards the tower. Speaking more to himself than to Gilbert, he started on a barely audible monologue. 'People have been telling me about Beckford from the start. I was even given a book to read. Stupidly I didn't open it. No, that's not quite true. I looked at the pictures. Do you know anything about him?'

Realising he was being spoken to, Gilbert uttered a feeble, 'Not much.'

'He was filthy rich and full of himself. Strutted round Bath in a pea-green tailcoat with his four dogs and a dwarf. Building towers was his thing and this was the last of them. In the 1820s, Beckford buys a house in Lansdown Crescent. Smart address, a hundred metres above the city. Quite a stiff climb. Any idea why he chose to live so high?'

'The air was nicer?'

'You've got it. A dirty great cloud from hundreds of coal fires hung over the city most days. Being Beckford, he also buys a house across the street in Lansdown Place and has a bridge built to link them. Then he builds his tower, a mile up the hill. Not content with that, he buys all the land between his house and here, shuts off the footpaths and makes this private walk. Down the bottom near the house he puts up weird buildings like a mini-mosque and a gateway dressed up as a castle. He steps through the gate with his dwarf and his dogs and heads across country to the plantation.

Come on, I'll show you.' He set off at a brisk pace down the path through the cemetery, with Gilbert a couple of yards behind. Below them, the crimson disc of the sun was directly over Bath.

At a point where the trees permitted a view, he stopped. 'In that book I was telling you about, there's a plan of Beckford's walk and I'm trying to work out where we are. Below us would have been a shrubbery, bushes and plants from all over the world. Lower down was an open quarry that he didn't change because it reminded him of some ruined baths in Rome.'

'The Caracalla Baths, I expect,' Gilbert said. 'Where the Three Tenors did their first big concert.'

'Is that so?' Diamond said. 'You're taking this in, I hope?' He stepped out again, and the Victorian cemetery gave way to rows of more modern graves. 'The walk got fancy again this side of the quarry with more gateways leading you through flower gardens and an orchard.'

He marched purposefully down the slope.

'I don't think we'll get much further,' Gilbert said.

They were blocked by a dense patch of brambles more than head high.

'This wasn't here in Beckford's day,' Diamond said. 'The walk must have gone straight through this. Check the road, will you? See how close we are. Is that Charlcombe on the other side?'

'I'll find out,' Gilbert said, glad of a break. He didn't need to go far to the left to see the lights of a car moving along Lansdown Road. On the other side were offices used by the Admiralty. He also spotted a road opposite.

Returning to Diamond, he reported what he'd seen.

'This is the place, then. Somewhere in this area, Beckford came to a major obstruction in the shape of a lane leading to a farm. To continue the walk he was forced to go underground. So he made a virtue out of necessity and created a seventy-foot grotto. Except this one had to be a tunnel. That's what I hope to find, if it's still here. Where's the flashlight?'

Gilbert switched it on and passed it over.

Diamond swung the beam this way and that, patrolling the margins of the thicket. 'Some time in 1991 there was subsidence along the road and it caused major traffic problems. My hunch is that it happened round here due to Beckford's tunnelling.'

The significance of the grotto wasn't lost on Gilbert. He could see what was coming. He didn't fancy plunging into the brambles.

'I think there's a gap here,' Diamond called. 'I can't get through myself, but you might.'

Resigned, Gilbert joined him and saw where the beam was picking out a space between the long, prickly shoots. 'What am I looking for?'

'I'm not sure. Steps, maybe. Mind you don't fall in.'

More intent on avoiding injury than finding anything, Gilbert edged under a vicious-looking branch. 'Can't see much,' he said.

'There's a way through. There has to be,' Diamond told him. 'Look to your left. Isn't that one?'

Gilbert turned and got his face scratched. Wrestling with brambles in this light was madness. He was about to say so when he noticed something. 'Some of these are bent over. It looks as if someone else has been here.'

'We must be close, then.'

We? Gilbert thought. There's only one of us getting scratched to pieces.

Ducking under an arch of thorns, he felt his foot against a hard edge. 'There may be something here.' Gingerly he pushed his leg forward into a space above a flat, solid surface. 'Steps, I think.'

'I'm coming in with the flashlight,' Diamond said. By attacking the bush like a rugby forward he powered through to Gilbert's side regardless of any discomfort. 'What I'd give for a chain saw.' He located the step for himself. 'Let's get down there.'

Together they forced their way down a short flight of steps and reached an impasse. The light shone on a mass of ivy with branches like cables.

'I think I can see what's in the way,' Diamond said.

Low down, the beam showed what looked like vertical indented bands, largely covered in moss and creepers, but recognisable as corrugated iron. Not only did the light show them the limit of the iron barrier, it revealed a gap wide enough to squeeze through. Gilbert went through and forced the gap wider for Diamond to follow.

'Bloody hell.'

There was no doubt they'd found Beckford's grotto, a tunnel stretching ahead for about twenty feet to where the roof seemed to have collapsed.

'Take care,' Gilbert said.

Diamond wasn't listening. He stumbled inside, picking a way over the debris with the flashlight and intermittently pointing the beam ahead towards a tall structure blocking the way.

Coated in dust, at first it looked like an extension of the rock all around it, but then he saw the gleam of metal and recognised the obstruction for what it was.

A horse trailer.

WITHOUT THE FLASHLIGHT, Paul Gilbert struggled to keep his footing while crossing the rubble. Up ahead, Diamond was squeezing between the trailer and the grotto wall.

'This is what Rupert found,' his voice carried back. 'God knows how. Picking blackberries, maybe.' He reached the back end where the door was. 'A cheap little one-horse trailer, not the transport a top racehorse is used to. Do you have a handkerchief?'

Gilbert edged along the wall and joined him. 'Will tissues do?'

Diamond took what was offered and used it to avoid direct contact with his hand as he pulled open the door and shone the lamp inside.

Neither man spoke. The sight that confronted them demanded an interval of respect.

The remains lay along the left side of the trailer floor, recognisably equine, manifestly long dead. The legs, reduced mostly to bone, were bent under the torso and still covered to the knees in padded travel boots made from some artificial fabric.

Diamond finally said, 'No dignity in death, is there?'

'Is it Hang-glider?'

'Must be.'

'So Rupert took the rug off a dead horse,' Gilbert said.

'Shows how desperate he was. Give me a hand up. I'm going to check the head.' Diamond climbed into the trailer. 'The bridle still fits snugly,' he informed Gilbert. 'Ah—and I see how it was done. The hole is precisely where it should be, front of the skull. They knew what they were doing.'

'Destroying a champion,' Gilbert said. 'That's what they were doing.'

'Don't let it get to you, lad. There's a reason. There must be.' Diamond passed the light beam across the rest of the interior. 'How did they get the trailer here?' They'd slipped into speaking of more than one perpetrator. A set-up as complex as this was too much to have attempted alone.

'You could drive an SUV across the field, no problem,' Gilbert said. 'If the brambles and the barrier weren't in the way, you could reverse the trailer part-way down the stairs, unhitch it and let it roll down. I'm assuming they killed the horse above ground?'

'Seems likely.'

'And after it was done they must have scaled the tunnel opening.'

Diamond clambered down and they made their way out of the tunnel. 'Let's hope we haven't buggered up the crime scene. I'll have to call in Duckett and his layabouts.'

'Do you want to wait for them?' Gilbert said, despairing of his Saturday night out.

'No. I'll borrow your car, if you don't mind. Give me a call when Duckett shows up and I'll send a car to pick you up. Shouldn't take long.' He took out the mobile and phoned Duckett. 'You heard me right the first time. A horse. But there's a definite link to the two murders. Even if you don't start work tonight, you'd better get here and seal the place. Don't be long.'

Buoyed up, he did more phoning. 'I don't care if you have to break your date. Get to Manvers Street fast. There's work to do.'

'Who was that?' Gilbert asked.

'John Leaman, moaning as usual.'

He was less abrasive with Ingeborg and Septimus, but the message was essentially the same. Crunch time had come.

'I'm off now,' Diamond told Gilbert. 'You did a fine job today, lad. Bangers and mash for supper when you get back to the nick.'

'Thanks,' Gilbert said bleakly. 'May I have the flashlight?'

'Sorry, lad. I don't fancy that graveyard in the dark.'

ALL THE KEY MEMBERS of the team were at Manvers Street within twenty minutes of Diamond's return. He updated them fully and set out his plan of arrests and house searches. 'Let's remember we're building a case for the prosecution. We've done the groundwork. We know the perpetrators. They're clever, manipulative and they may yet have more tricks to pull. Now let's nail them.'

He and Septimus drove to a street of detached houses on the side of Lansdown Road. There was a delay before the door opened a few inches on a safety chain and Major Swithin's voice said, 'Yes?'

They were admitted and shown into a large sitting room smelling faintly of cigars. It put Diamond in mind of a club room.

In a cardigan and carpet slippers, the major looked out of sorts. 'What do you want with me?'

'Actually, we want your wife. We'll speak to her alone, if you don't mind.'

'I most certainly do. I object, in fact.'

'In that case, we'll arrest you now and put you in the car outside.'

The major gave a nervous twitch. 'Damn it, I'll fetch her.'

Agnes Swithin came in with a towel round her head. 'I was washing my hair,' she said in an accusing way.

Diamond asked Septimus to speak the words of the caution.

'What on earth . . .?' she said, and was silenced by the officialese.

Diamond took over again. 'We've spoken before about your part in the recent re-enactment of the Battle of Lansdown—'

'I did nothing to be ashamed of.'

'You were an angel of mercy, you told me. You go out on the field of battle and pretend to be dressing wounds and looking after the men?'

'That's what women have done for centuries in warfare.'

'To carry out these duties you need supplies. Which you carry in a bag?'

'A knapsack, or a snapsack, to use the authentic term.'

'And it doesn't get inspected by the officers, so you can carry some modern items as well as rolls of bandage?'

'I suppose that's true.'

'Did you have a mobile phone with you?'

She shrugged. 'Doesn't everyone these days?'

'So the answer is yes. Did you also have your binoculars?'

An impatient sigh. 'I also carried my purse, make-up, comb, glasses, deodorant, camera and certain pills I take for a medical condition.'

'So you confirm you had the binoculars?'

'The re-enactment is a spectacle. One likes to enjoy it. Yes.'

Diamond said. 'After the fighting moved up the field, did you see two of the Cavaliers going the other way, down the slope?'

'Possibly.'

'They stopped by the fallen oak tree, an important landmark to the Lansdown Society because of its rare lichen.'

'I'm not a member of the society.'

'But your husband is. I'm suggesting you watched the two men burrowing in the earth through those strong binoculars of yours, and you decided the Lansdown Society should be informed immediately. Your phone company keeps a record of calls, you know.'

'You've been checking my phone calls? That's outrageous.'

'Mrs Swithin, I suggest you stop this stonewalling and give me the truth. One of those men was beaten over the head and later murdered.'

She'd gone as white as the towel on her head. 'I didn't witness that.'

'Tell me exactly what did happen.'

'As you said, I saw what was going on by the fallen tree and phoned Reggie.'

'Where was he at the time?'

'The golf club.'

'With Sir Colin Tipping?'

'You'll have to ask him.'

Diamond nodded to Septimus, who stepped to the door and jerked it open. Predictably, the major was there, eavesdropping.

'Step inside, Major,' Diamond said, 'and let's hear it from you.'

THE MOON was the only source of light and there wasn't much of that. Paul Gilbert, still on duty in the field below the cemetery, was having doubts. Doubt one: would Duckett bother to come out on a Saturday night to look at a dead horse? Doubt two: would Diamond remember to send a car?

Get a grip, he told himself. Give it an hour and then phone the nick and ask them to send a replacement. It's a job for uniform, not CID. He felt better for that—until he remembered he'd left his phone in the car.

His thoughts turned to the victim, who'd lived up here for a couple of weeks, off his chump. What threat had poor old Rupert Hope presented in his pathetic state? Finishing him off in the graveyard had been a heartless act. This killer had no mercy.

The cool of early evening had turned to shivery cold. What else could you expect on an exposed hill 700 feet above sea level? Rupert had at least found himself a rug and a place to lie down. There was nowhere in this field except the grotto itself, and Gilbert didn't fancy that, but he was starting to understand what had driven Rupert to rob the tomb.

A twig snapped nearby.

He strained to detect a shape or movement.

Then he heard what sounded like short gasps for air.

'Who's that?' he said.

No answer. Only an animal, he tried telling himself. The breathing was too heavy to be a fox. Were there deer on Lansdown? He'd never seen one.

He had nothing to defend himself with. Should have thought of that.

In his heightened state, he started to see shadowy shapes closing in.

'I can hear you,' he said aloud. 'I know you're there.'

A beam of light shone directly into his face. 'Stay absolutely still.' The voice was male, authoritative. 'What are you doing here?'

'My job.' Gilbert managed to add, 'I'm a police officer.'

'You're not dressed like one.'

'I'm CID. Plain clothes. I can show you my ID. Who are you?'

The man with the torch had the advantage and intended to keep it. 'What's a police officer skulking around in the dark for?'

He was cautious. 'I can't say. I'm on duty.' He fished his warrant card from his back pocket. 'See?'

The beam shifted down and Gilbert took his opportunity, grabbed the arm holding the torch, hauled the man towards him, at the same time thrusting out a leg and toppling him over. They both hit the ground and the torch flew out of range. Gilbert clung to the arm and twisted it behind the man's back.

'Who are you?' he demanded.

'A man of God. Charles Smart. I live in the vicarage across the road.'

If this was a try-on, it was a clever one. If not, Gilbert was wrestling with a vicar. 'What are you doing here, then?'

'I saw the light earlier.' This, from a vicar, would have been laughable in other circumstances. 'I came over to see what was going on. Do you mind? The pain in my arm is unspeakable.'

Gilbert let go, made a grab for the torch and shone it on his adversary. The man had wide blue eyes and a shock of blond hair. True to his claim, he was wearing a clerical collar. He propped himself up and massaged the top of his arm, saying, 'That really wasn't necessary.'

'Creeping up on me and shoving a torch in my face wasn't necessary.'

'I'm in the Lansdown Society. I made a solemn promise to keep an eye on things up here. And if you're about to ask me if I witnessed the murder, save your breath. Your superintendent already covered the matter and I couldn't help at all.'

'Did you see the victim roaming around here?'

'No. The first suspicious behaviour I've seen was yours tonight. Lights in the field. A car parked up the road. Very dubious. I dialled 999 straight away. They should be here any minute.'

'Thank God for that,' Gilbert said.

IN THE INCIDENT ROOM, Diamond checked with his team on the results of the house arrests. The suspects were in custody and the evidence had been gathered, labelled and sealed. 'That was the easy part,' he said. 'The real job starts now and I'm not expecting any favours from the suspects. We'll use the interview room with one-way glass, so the rest of you can see how we do. Cavalry Officer Smith, I need you with me for the first one.'

Excitement was written large on Inge's face and no one seemed to mind that she was the first choice, particularly as the suspect was female.

The custody sergeant brought Davina Temple-Smith to the interview room. White-faced and with a sullen stare, she was a different incarnation from the radiant winning owner at the races. She had her own solicitor seated beside her, a woman new to Manvers Street interviews.

After Ingeborg had gone through the preliminaries, Diamond took over.

'We found Hang-glider this afternoon, what's left of him, the neat hole in his skull where he was dispatched with a vet's equipment, the penetrating captive bolt gun. Expertly done, right on the spot, humanely, I don't doubt.'

He might not have said a word for all the reaction he got.

He reached for an evidence bag containing a bolt gun. 'There's no telling if this was the one, but we picked it up from your surgery in case. The question I asked myself was why anyone needed to destroy a marvellous horse worth over a million. The deal with Sheikh Abdul was ready to sign.'

Davina continued to stare ahead.

Diamond gave her the chance to say something that wouldn't incriminate her. 'Your father bought Hang-glider in the yearling sales at Newmarket in October 1990. Remember how much he paid?'

'Two hundred thousand guineas,' she said in an expressionless tone.

'He must have had great faith in the colt.'

'Great judgment,' she said. 'It was a half-brother to a Prix Lupin winner who lost the Irish Derby in a photo. Owning a thoroughbred was my father's life's ambition. He'd raced horses before, but they never had the breeding. Give him credit, he picked a champion.'

'At a cost,' Diamond said.

'Tell me about it.' The bitterness cut through. Was this a factor in her behaviour—father blueing her inheritance on a horse? 'Two hundred thou was just the beginning,' she added. 'A top trainer like McDart doesn't come cheap, and then there were all the extras. Stabling, race fees, transport.'

'Was it funded from his surveying business?'

'No chance. It was his savings, and he took out a loan as well.'

'Good thing it was such a fine racehorse. Did it earn back the money?'

'Hardly,' she said. 'Another season might have made a difference, but it got the injury and that was it.'

'But you insure against accidents.'

'Insurance. That's another expense,' she said. 'It's massive in the case of a racing thoroughbred. They base the premium on the bloodline, the price paid and so on. You're shown a portfolio of options and you have to decide which you can afford.'

'Your father must have bought medical insurance.'

'It covered the cost of treatment, not the loss of income.'

'But all was not lost,' Diamond said. 'Hang-glider's stud value as a classic winner was considerable, and along came Sheikh Abdul with an offer that would make light of all these costs. The agreement was drawn up, but not yet signed by the sheikh. Then this ill-fated farewell to Lansdown was arranged, parading Hang-glider for his admirers to see him one last time.'

'The racegoers knew him,' she said. 'He deserved his tribute.'

'They didn't know he was about to be put down.'

'No one knew.'

'That isn't true, is it, Davina? Where were you that evening?'

'Delivering twin calves at Upper Westwood.'

The answer came pat, as if she'd expected the question. Westwood was the other side of Bath. Difficult to prove or disprove at this distance in time.

'Do you keep some sort of diary or appointment book?'

'For 1993? I threw it out years ago.'

'Yet you remember where you were that evening.'

'Of course. It was a huge, horrible day for our family.'

'Your father lost a fortune. He told me he got a hundred thousand in insurance. It still sounds a lot to me.'

'It didn't cover the outlay,' she pointed out. 'And it was way below the offer he had in writing. He's never owned a horse since.'

'When we question him, as we will shortly, do you seriously expect him to confirm your version of events?'

There was a telling moment of hesitation before Davina said, 'Certainly.'

'Because this isn't only about the killing of the racehorse. We're investigating two murders and we have evidence that incriminates you both.'

'A bolt gun that I bought last year?' she said with contempt.

Her solicitor put a hand on Davina's arm. 'If there's evidence of the sort you're describing, Superintendent, we wish to be informed about it.'

'Forensic tests need to be completed before we can release any details,' Diamond said. 'Meanwhile, we'll have a word with Sir Colin.'

Outside, he said to Ingeborg, 'It's time to talk to the father.'

She said, 'She's got an answer for everything.'

'Up to now.'

DIAMOND ASKED WHERE Septimus was. The DI from Bristol was the obvious choice to have beside him for the second interview. John Leaman said Septimus was using his computer in the incident room.

'Doing what?'

'Checking stuff from way back, he told me.'

'Ah. Should have remembered. A task I set him.'

'Do you want me to fetch him, Guv?'

'He'll come when he's ready.' He looked around the room. Paul Gilbert was in the back row cradling a mug of coffee. 'You made it, then. Did Duckett actually appear?'

Gilbert shook his head. 'There's a lad from uniform guarding the site. Charlie Smart came over to check up on me and I borrowed his phone.'

'You slipped my mind, I have to admit. Have you had supper?'

'Not yet, Guv.'

Diamond took a fiver from his back pocket. 'For you. I meant it, about the bangers and mash. You did well today.' There was an awed silence. Such generosity from the main man was rare.

'Nice to know the front line people are appreciated,' Leaman said. 'The boys in the back room may get a chance to shine some time.'

'All right,' Diamond said. 'It's supper for everyone.'

'Me included?' a voice behind him said. Georgina had come in.

'I thought it was your choir night, Ma'am.'

'I heard there was singing in prospect here.'

'It hasn't begun yet, unfortunately.'

Not long after, Septimus appeared with a piece of paper in his hand.

'Was I right?' Diamond asked him.

A nod. 'It took some finding.'

The two of them took their places in the interview room opposite Sir Colin Tipping, now occupying the seat his daughter had, with an elderly pinstriped Bath solicitor at his side.

'We'll begin with the game of golf,' Diamond said.

Tipping rubbed his hands. 'What a splendid idea.'

'I'm referring to the game you were playing with Major Swithin on July the 17th, the date of the recent battle re-enactment.'

'If you're asking the score, I doubt if I can recall it.'

This would be his defence then, making light of the interview in his jocular style. Better than silence, Diamond thought. 'You'll recall this one because the major took a call from his wife.'

'Wouldn't be the first time. Agnes never lets the fellow off the leash.'

Diamond kept to his brief. 'What Mrs Swithin had seen through her binoculars was two soldiers in Royalist uniform up to their elbows in earth by the fallen oak tree your society has vowed to protect. They unearthed a human bone that they reburied. The major tells me he shared this information with you, as a fellow member of the Lansdown Society.'

'I sometimes think Agnes suspects Reggie of being with some floozy when he's out of her sight. She finds these silly pretexts to call him.'

'Except you didn't treat this as a silly pretext. You completed the round and broke with your usual habit of a drinking session afterwards in the clubhouse. You made some excuse about an appointment and left immediately.'

'Doesn't sound like me. At my age you don't do anything immediately.'

'I spoke to the major at his home this evening.'

'He said I left without having a drink?' He grinned at his solicitor.

'You had reason to be alarmed about what you'd heard. You're going to tell me you got in your car and drove to the battlefield to check the tree, which was supposed to be off limits to the Sealed Knot.'

The solicitor raised a finger. 'Have a care, Superintendent. You know very well you shouldn't put words into my client's mouth.'

'Did I get it wrong?' Diamond said, pretending to be mystified. 'Did he go there for another purpose?'

Tipping looked from one to the other. Suddenly the questioning had turned serious. 'I take a particular interest in that tree. It's host to one of the rarest lichens in Great Britain.'

'It isn't,' Diamond said. 'And I doubt if it ever was.'

Tipping took a surprised breath. 'What's this? A policeman with some knowledge of botany?'

'I'm quoting one of the Lansdown Society. Charlie Smart told me the only lichen on that oak is a common variety found everywhere.'

'Charlie hasn't been with us long. Probably doesn't know where to look.'

'Neither does the British Lichen Society. They have no record of it on Lansdown. Could you be mistaken?'

A climb-down was called for. 'The identification was done years ago by one of our members who passed on. Let's hope the rare lichen didn't hop the twig as well. Why don't we talk about something we know more about?'

Diamond nodded, encouraged by teasing out an admission from the suspect: he'd definitely visited the tree. 'We'll turn to Rupert Hope, then—one of the men Mrs Swithin saw unearthing the bone, a history lecturer. That bone could have been of historical interest if it belonged to a soldier in the real battle. Although Rupert agreed to replace it, he appears to have gone back secretly after everyone left. He thought he'd made a find, you see.'

'That's a stab in the dark, wouldn't you say?'

'Does it matter to you if we get it wrong?' Diamond asked.

'It does if you're accusing me of crimes I didn't commit.'

'I haven't accused you of anything. We know Rupert was attacked that evening because he didn't return to his car. He'd changed out of his battle armour. He was struck on the back of the head with a blunt instrument. It wasn't enough to kill him, but he was left for dead. He wandered Lansdown, suffering memory loss, for over three weeks. Then he was hit again, fatally.'

'Nothing to do with me, old chum.'

'You carry a blunt instrument in your car. In fact, you have a selection of them—your golf clubs.' Diamond turned to Septimus and nodded.

'What on earth . . .?' Tipping said, as the colour rose in his cheeks.

Septimus had stooped down and lifted a bag of golf clubs.

'The nerve of it. Those are mine,' Tipping said.

It was a lightweight bag of the sort golfers without caddies can carry. Septimus unzipped the top. Diamond asked him to count the clubs.

'Thirteen.'

'According to the laws, which I've checked,' Diamond said. 'You're allowed a maximum of fourteen. A dedicated golfer such as yourself won't carry fewer. Where's the missing club, Sir Colin?'

For the first time, he didn't have an answer.

'I expect it's a heavy one,' Diamond said. 'An iron, going by the shape of the injuries to the dead man's skull.'

'Are you accusing my client of murder?' the solicitor asked.

'I'm waiting to hear what he did with the fourteenth club.'

There was still no response from Tipping.

'If you are,' the solicitor said, 'I must insist on an adjournment.'

'Painful as it must be to a golfer to destroy one of his clubs,' Diamond said, 'that seems to have happened here. I don't see how he could have lost it. Rupert survived one crack on the head, but the second did for him. Why the delay? For a few days he was missing. The amnesia had set in. He didn't even remember his own name. The danger for his killer was that Rupert's memory would come back. Worse, he'd taken to sleeping a short distance from Beckford's grotto.'

'Beckford's what?' the solicitor said.

'An underground tunnel that your client knows all about.'

Tipping gripped the desk. All the colour had drained from his face.

'It's a matter of record that Rupert Hope was killed in the cemetery near the tower. He'd found an under-rug last seen strapped to the racehorse

Hang-glider's back. We've done the tests. This afternoon we went into the grotto and found the remains of the horse. Are you listening, Sir Colin?'

A nod. All the fight had gone out of him.

'I've interviewed your daughter and discussed how it was done. Each of you brought your professional skills to the job. In your case, it was knowing the existence of the grotto. You're a chartered surveyor dealing in major civic works. DI Ward, would you take over?'

Septimus was ready. 'In January 1991, a section of the Lansdown Road collapsed near Beckford's Tower, due to subsidence. A survey was commissioned.' He took from his pocket the print-out he'd shown Diamond. 'From the council planning department web site. C. Tipping and Associates carried out the survey. You identified nineteenth-century excavations as the cause; an exploratory dig for the grotto. The tunnel itself was a short way off and you located that as well. Two years later, this knowledge would come in useful. Disposing of a dead racehorse can be a problem.'

'That was your contribution,' Diamond said. 'Davina supplied the veterinary skills, obtained a horse trailer and drove it to the races the night Hang-glider was paraded there. You knew McDart would be in the owners' and trainers' bar until late. You broke in and transferred the horse to the trailer. But there was an unforeseen problem, a young woman waiting by the trailer in the hope of getting a job with McDart. She had to be disposed of. Correct me if I'm wrong. You held her and Davina killed her with the bolt gun and you bundled the body into the Land Rover before driving off with the horse.'

'We insist on an adjournment,' the solicitor said.

'No,' Tipping said. 'Let's nail this now for the bullshit it is.'

'I'm advising you not to say any more.'

'They can't stitch us up like this. There's no motive. Why would I go to all this trouble to destroy my own horse when I was on the brink of the biggest deal of my life? I lost a fortune when that horse was stolen.'

Diamond refused to be sidetracked. 'With the horse in the trailer and the dead woman in the Land Rover you drove to the grotto, right into the field and up to the entrance. Davina used the bolt gun on the horse and you reversed the trailer to the steps and let it roll inside and out of sight. The next night you buried Nadia's body in the hole left by the fallen oak's root system, first removing the victim's head. Why? Because the bolt-hole in the skull would have revealed the form of death and led us to suspect a slaughterman or a vet. I expect your daughter carried out that necessary task and also disposed of the head.'

'You've missed the point,' Tipping said. 'We had no motive.'

'The motive in both cases is the same. These unfortunate people strayed into your danger zone. The only thing you had against them was that they would give you away. With the help of the Lansdown Society you kept watch on the burial site and you were compelled to act when Rupert returned there. He survived one clubbing and had to be given another. I won't pretend it was easy to track you down. Casual killings of strangers are the hardest of all to investigate.'

'Have you finished?' Tipping said. 'You could have saved us a lot of time if you'd addressed the simple fact I raised just now. I had no reason to kill my horse. Quite the reverse. He was going to make me very rich indeed.'

'You're talking about your motive for killing the horse?'

'Yes, Mr Diamond. We're on tenterhooks to hear your theory.'

Diamond locked eyes with him. 'I'm not giving you that satisfaction.'

'So this great hypothesis comes tumbling down.'

'No. It's as safe as any house you ever surveyed. Charge him with murder, Septimus.'

DIAMOND'S OFFER of supper in the canteen was interpreted by all but himself as free drinks in the Sports Bar of the Royal. He had little choice but to join the party and start a tab. Someone bent on mischief—probably John Leaman—got busy on the phone and in the next half-hour familiar faces kept appearing through the door, civilian staff, wives and partners. Paloma arrived and there was a huge cheer when Keith Halliwell, pale, but smiling broadly, walked in with his wife.

Diamond told Paloma, 'This started with an offer of bangers and mash to one deserving case. I'll need to take out an extra mortgage.'

'It's no bad thing to let them feel appreciated,' she said.

'They get that all the time from me.'

For that evening, you might have believed him. There was a moment when the din was hushed and Leaman raised his glass. 'To the guvnor.'

Ingeborg shouted, 'Speech.'

With reluctance Diamond hauled himself upright. 'Apart from thanking you for a job well done, I don't know what to say.'

Georgina said, 'I'll tell you what. We listened through the glass and there isn't any doubt that those two are guilty of murder, but you didn't answer the question about the racehorse. Why did they kill it?'

'For the insurance,' he said. 'It was insured for a hundred grand.'

'But that's a fraction of what was on offer.'

'From the sheikh? Didn't you work that out?'

He took a long look around the room. No one seemed to have got it. 'Even a billionaire sheikh isn't going to buy a horse for stud without proof of fertility. The agreement required an independent guarantee that Hang-glider was up to the job. The trainer's regular vet wasn't eligible, so Tipping asked his daughter's firm to do the necessary and when Davina had the sample tested she discovered to her horror that the sperm count was negative. The horse was sterile. The deal was scuppered and they hadn't insured against infertility. The insurance they had was for illness, foul play or mortality. They were left with a horse that couldn't race and couldn't breed. Between them they decided on the fake kidnapping to activate the foul play option. A hundred grand was better than nothing.'

'Can we prove this?' Georgina asked him.

'Davina destroyed all record of it, as you'd expect. Fortunately, she wasn't the only one with a copy of the report. There aren't many labs in our part of the world that offer equine sperm analysis. The second I checked confirmed a test conducted in July 1993, for Davina's company. The horse wasn't named, but the result was a negative count.'

'And that's rare?'

'Rare enough to make our case, Ma'am.'

Georgina sighed. 'I'm impressed—genuinely impressed.'

John Leaman said, 'You speak for us all, Ma'am. Don't you think our guvnor deserves some recognition?'

She frowned. There were limits. 'What did you have in mind?'

'An honour, Ma'am. As a result of all this, isn't there a new vacancy in the Lansdown Society?'

peter **lovesey**

RD: Your first crime novel, *Wobble to Death* (1969), was written for a competition in *The Times* and had athletics as a background. Why did you choose that unusual subject?

PL: I had already written a factual book on long-distance running. I wasn' t any good at sport, but I was very interested in running and had read a great deal about the history of athletics. When I saw that Macmillan were offering £1,000 for a first crime novel I decided to write one about a Victorian running race and a character called Sergeant Cribb. It won, which was marvellous.

RD: Did you have plans for more books about your Victorian detective?

PL: I had no plans at all. I was teaching in further education at the time and I thought *Wobble to Death* was a one-off. But Lord Hardinge at Macmillans was setting up a crime list and when he handed me the winner's cheque he held onto it for a second or two and said, 'How about the second book?' I had to think frantically about what I could do. Fortunately, my wife, Jax, had read whodunnits and could advise me. I made a number of trips to the old newspaper library at Colindale, where I looked up the background on a variety of different sports. I then worked it all into a series around Cribb.

RD: Had you given up your teaching job by this stage?

PL: I became a full-time writer in 1975 and I was fortunate because soon after that Granada made two television series starring Alan Dobie as Cribb, and Jax and I had scripted seven additional episodes. I was delighted by the casting of Alan, but I found he inhabited the character so powerfully that when I came to think about further storylines all I could see was his face. I'd lost my original character somewhere in the process.

RD: *Skeleton Hill* is the tenth outing of your contemporary detective, Peter Diamond. Was he waiting patiently right behind Sergeant Cribb?

PL: No, he wasn't. I wrote several stand-alone books before introducing Diamond in *The Last Detective* in 1990. I decided to make him a dinosaur character at odds with modern methods and so I surrounded myself with books on modern policing and forensics. The Anthony Award for best novel came my way in the States, and then *The Summons* and *Bloodhounds* won the Crime Writers' Association (CWA) Silver Dagger in successive years—it was a good incentive to continue writing about my crusty Bath detective.

RD: Have television producers ever suggested making a series on Diamond?

PL: Yes, he's been optioned several times, most recently with ITV.

RD: Why did you decide to feature a Civil War re-enactment in *Skeleton Hill*?

PL: The plot demanded that I get to know about the Battle of Lansdown, so I read a couple of books and did some Internet research. Some years ago, we took our children to see a Sealed Knot re-enactment in Bath. The people involved take it very seriously.

RD: What prompted you to focus on the Ukrainian community in London?

PL: I was the 'mystery consultant', checking scripts for a television series called *Rosemary and Thyme* and occasionally put up ideas for plots. One of these involved the Ukrainian community in London, but it was never used. After the series ended I thought, I've done all the research and know a bit about it so I'll use it in my next novel.

RD: Where do you wirite your novels and how do you organise your time?

PL: I have an office in a white-painted 'Vermont style' cabin in our garden in Chichester. It has a pretty little porch and a shingle roof. I always make a detailed plan and I write slowly: about 200 to 500 words a day. I hate drafts so I edit as I go along.

RD: Are there plenty more cases for Diamond to solve?

PL: There are. I'm currently working on a story that is set in the Theatre Royal, Bath. When I was awarded the lifetime achievement CWA Cartier Diamond Dagger in 2000, I hoped that it didn't mean I was expected to hang up my computer and get a set of golf clubs. Thankfully, it didn't, and I have no plans to stop writing books.

Sealed Knot and Civil War

The Sealed Knot Society was formed in 1968 to educate the public, through Civil War re-enactments, on the lasting impact of the 1640s Civil War, when the Royalist forces of Charles I and Oliver Cromwell's Parliamentarians were in bloody conflict. Every aspect of a battle must be authentic: uniforms are made of traditional materials and stitched in the correct way; food is cooked to a genuine 17th-century recipe. The Sealed Knot list forthcoming events, such as the Battle of Lansdown in Bath, as featured in *Skeleton Hill*, on their website. See www.thesealedknot.org.uk/musters.

Grace

Richard Paul Evans

In the winter of 1962, Eric and his younger brother, Joel, help a runaway teenager by hiding her in a den in their snow-filled back garden. The diminutive Grace, swamped by an over-large coat, and with huge, almond-shaped brown eyes, captivates the two boys. But she is vulnerable, and her arrival will change everything—not just the coming Christmas, but Eric's entire life.

One
December 25, 2006

It's Christmas Day. There is Christmas music playing from the radio in the other room—'Santa Claus Is Coming to Town'. It's a little late, I think; Santa's come and gone, as have our children and grandchildren. They've left an impressive mess in their wake, but I don't care. As I get older, I've come to treasure any evidence of family. Snow is falling outside, and all is peaceful and still. In such moments it is possible to believe that the world could still be good.

Something profound happened to me today. It started innocently enough, with a request from my grandchildren to read them *The Little Match Girl*. But by the end of the story, I was crying. Four-year-old Ebony Brooke tried to console me. 'It's OK, Grandpa,' she said. 'It's just a story.'

It's not just a story; there really was a little match girl, and she changed my life in ways I'm still trying to understand. Even the grandchildren sitting before me wouldn't be here if it wasn't for her. As important as she is to me, I've never shared her story. It's finally time that I did.

Who was she? She was my first love. My first kiss. She was a little match girl who could see the future in the flame of a candle. She was a runaway who taught me more about life than anyone has before or since. And when she was gone, my innocence left with her.

There is pain in bringing out these memories. I suppose I don't really know why I feel compelled to write at this time, only that I am. Maybe I want those closest to me to finally know what has driven me for all these years. Or maybe it's just that I still love her and wonder, after all this time, if I can still find grace.

MY STORY BEGINS in October of 1962, about ten days before the world was supposed to end. I think the Cuban Missile Crisis brought us as close as we've ever come as a species to extinction.

My family—me, my parents, and my ten-year-old brother, Joel—had just moved from a palm-treed suburb of Los Angeles to a blighted neighbourhood in south Salt Lake City, just a few blocks from State Street with its nightclubs, bars and pawnshops. My father, a construction worker, had contracted Guillain-Barré syndrome, a serious disorder in which the body's immune system attacks parts of the nervous system. It started with weakness in his legs, and for several months he was paralysed from the neck down; the doctors said that if it got any worse, he'd have to be put on a respirator to breathe. Fortunately, it never progressed that far. The good news, they said, was that he would likely make a full recovery, at least physically. Our financial situation was a different matter.

The first big thing to go was our car, a '61 Chevrolet Impala convertible, which was a pretty fine car even by today's standards. Dad sold the Impala, purchasing in its stead an ugly used utility van from the phone company, which cost him just $200. The van was yellow with wide brown stripes running across its sides. Joel dubbed it 'the Bee', which was appropriate for more than its paint job. The van's motor made a high-pitched humming noise, and it wobbled at high speeds. The back seats had all been removed, and there were no side windows.

Things got worse. My grandmother from Salt Lake City had passed away three years earlier, leaving her home vacant. My mother and her seven siblings had inherited the house and couldn't agree on what to do with it. It was decided that we could live there until they came to a consensus, which, at the current rate, was a little less likely than a nuclear holocaust.

On the day we moved, Joel and I helped Mom load up the Bee. A few neighbours came over to help as well. Dad just shouted orders from his bed. It drove us crazy, but Mom said it made *him* crazy to be so helpless. I guess shouting at us made him feel useful. Fortunately, we didn't have much left to pack.

The Bee pulled out of our driveway, with furniture and luggage tied to the roof. My mother drove the whole way, the passenger seat next to her piled high with boxes. My father sat on a La-Z-Boy reclining armchair in the back of the van, while Joel and I sat on and between boxes and bags, rearranging them as best we could for comfort.

Our new home smelled of mould and looked like it might fall over in a strong wind. What was left of the paint on the exterior was peeling. The interior rooms were covered with wallpaper, most of it water-damaged with long rusted streaks running down the walls. Still, for a couple of boys from the California suburbs, the arrangement wasn't all bad. The house sat on nearly five wooded acres bordered on two sides by a creek that ran high enough to float an inner tube during the summer.

Joel and I spent that summer alone together. Joel loved baseball, so we played a lot of catch, though it bothered me that he was four years younger than me and could pitch a better fastball. I don't remember whose idea it was to build the den. Years later, Joel claimed it was his. Either way, we never could have anticipated the chain of events it set in place.

We had all the materials we needed to build. My grandfather, who died long before I was born, was a pharmacist by trade. He was also a builder, and sheets of weathered plywood were stacked up against the old greenhouse, and warped two-by-fours were piled in the smelly, straw-floored breeze block chicken coop my grandfather had built fifty years earlier.

As far as dens go, ours was pretty big, ten foot by twelve foot, half the size of our bedroom. It had a chipboard floor on which we nailed carpet. The ceiling was about six feet high, though it sagged quite a bit in the middle. One afternoon, Joel and I were taking a lunch break, eating tuna and pickle sandwiches, when Joel said, 'It's going to cave in when it snows.'

'Probably,' I said with my mouth still full.

I studied the sagging ceiling until I saw a solution. After lunch, we dragged a four-by-four beam from the chicken coop, cut six inches off the top with a rusted handsaw, then raised it in the middle of the room to brace the ceiling, pounding it fully upright with a sledgehammer. The pillar was useful in other ways. We put nails in it and used it to hang our torch and the transistor radio I got on my previous birthday.

The fact that the ceiling was low was not a bad thing. We didn't plan to do much standing around, and it was a certain deterrent to adults, though probably not as much as the size of the entry itself. The den's door was only three feet high, which made it necessary to crawl in. Joel pointed out that this would be good in case of an attack, as it would make it easier to defend ourselves. I asked him who he thought might be attacking us. He thought about it a moment, then replied, 'Well, you never know.'

We did our best to furnish the place with the creature comforts of home. For entertainment we had chess, Chinese chequers and Monopoly. We hung artwork: a framed paint-by-numbers landscape, a poster of Superman, and a picture my mother never would have approved of—a pin-up girl Joel came across while we were exploring the garage. The poster was pretty tame by today's standards—a young woman posing in a bright red swimsuit—but for its time, it was considered pretty risqué. For us it was definitely taboo.

Most of our furnishings came from the garage, an A-frame structure with a steeply pitched tar roof and two large wooden doors that opened like a barn. My parents stored some of our belongings in the garage when we first arrived, but with the exception of a brief and unsuccessful hunt for some missing pots and pans, I don't think my mother ever set foot in the place. Probably because it was dark, smelly, and housed more rats than a research laboratory.

To Joel and me, the garage was a wonderland that housed a million things to ignite a boy's imagination. Whenever we needed something, we'd head to the garage, where we'd either find what we were looking for or forget about it in the excitement of a greater discovery. On one of our expeditions, we found a mattress in the rafters above the garage and pushed it down. It looked like generations of mice had made the mattress their home, but they all fled at our arrival (or died in the fall). We swept off the mice droppings and a few dead mice, then dragged it to the den.

There was a water tap inside our den, one of the old hand-lever types. We discovered it after we started building. Since we couldn't move it, we just built round it, later deciding it technically gave our den indoor plumbing.

Even better than plumbing was electricity. Joel found a light socket and an old yellow extension cord, which we ran from the garage. We hung it from the ceiling and attached a light bulb. That night we brought in our sleeping bags and slept there. We stayed up playing Go Fish until two in the morning. When we finally turned out the light, it was darker than a cave, which kind of scared Joel. The next time we slept out, we plugged in a nightlight. It lit the den in an eerie UFO alien green.

One day I was sitting at the kitchen table drawing cartoons when Joel came running inside. 'Hey, come out to the den,' he said excitedly.

I followed him out and crawled through the door to be greeted by the astringent odour of fresh paint.

'What did you do?' I asked.

'I painted.'

'It's *purple*.'

Joel frowned, angry that I hadn't appreciated his surprise and hours of work. 'It's all there was.'

'It looks . . . girly.'

Joel turned red. 'It's all there was.'

THAT SUMMER I worried a lot. I worried that we'd live in that crummy neighbourhood forever, and I worried *a lot* about the approaching school year. I had heard stories about inner-city schools, and I lived in terror of what it would be like to go to one.

I also worried about money, or our lack of it. Every now and then, Joel and I would try to earn some, combing the neighbourhood looking for work. We'd mow lawns and do other odd jobs, but it was a poor neighbourhood, so we never got paid much. Once we helped Mrs Poulsen, a 200-year-old lady who lived at the end of our street, clean out her garage. It took an entire day, leaving us dirty and exhausted. When we'd completed the job, she gave us each fifty cents. I stopped Joel from throwing his quarters at her door after she shut it.

In spite of the wasted day, two good things came from that project. First, we acquired an old fruit dryer. It was a square plywood box with trays that slid inside, which Mrs Poulsen had us carry out to the kerb for garbage pick-up. We dragged the dryer home on the back of our wagon and put it in our den. It actually worked, and we began drying apricots into fruit leather, which, to us, tasted as good as any shop-bought candy.

Second, we spent our day's earnings on milk shakes, which led to my job at McBurger Queen.

McBurger Queen was on State Street about six blocks from our home. The name of the restaurant was my boss's genius. My boss, Mr Dick, believed that by combining the names of the most successful burger joints in America, he would capitalise on thousands of dollars of free advertising and make himself rich. The Queen, as we employees called it, had more items on the menu than a Chinese restaurant. It had sixty different kinds of malted-milk drinks, from grasshopper to caramel cashew (my personal favourite) and almost as many food choices, from fish burgers to soft tacos.

Mr Dick trusted no one. He believed that all his employees were thieves bent on eating his inventory, which was sometimes true but not as true as Mr Dick believed. Once, one of my coworkers saw him in the parking lot across the street spying on us through binoculars. The very week I started working at the place, Mr Dick hauled three of his workers off to take polygraph tests. I don't know if that was legal or not, but in those days, kids our age pretty much went along with everything adults said.

I knew about the tests because Gary, the assistant manager (a forty-year-old guy with chronic, maybe terminal, dandruff), showed me the actual test results from the lie-detector machine with its accompanying graph. The interrogator asked questions like: have you ever stolen money from the till? (No spike on the report.) Have you given away free food? (Small spike.) Do you eat French fries without paying for them? (The spike went off the chart.)

Of course, the shakedown was meant as intimidation for the rest of us, and it worked reasonably well. So, for the most part, we rarely ate on the job, even the mistakes, like when someone ordered a hamburger with no ketchup and we put ketchup on it anyway. At least not without looking over our shoulder a few times before wolfing it down.

IT'S BEEN SAID that parents should give their children roots and wings. That was a perfect description of my parents. Even in a wheelchair, my father was a dreamer with his head in the clouds, and my mother was the roots with both feet planted firmly on terra quaking firma. My mother was always afraid. Afraid we didn't have enough money, afraid her health would give out, afraid something might happen to one of us. When my father got sick, I think for her it was vindication that the gods really were out to get us.

Shortly after our arrival in Utah, my mother got a job working as a cashier at Warshaw's Food and Drug. Her job didn't pay much, but she brought home damaged canned goods and day-olds from the bakery, which helped with the grocery bills.

My mother worked all day, then came home at night, physically and emotionally spent. My father just kind of moped around the house, dreaming up get-rich-quick schemes while he slowly regained the use of his limbs. Joel and I learned that if we spent much time in the house, Dad would think of errands for us, so mostly we just hid out in the den. Then summer ended.

Life at Granite Junior High School was dog-eat-dog. I wasn't big like the jocks or especially smart like the geeks. I had acne and a bad haircut, which, when my dad got partial use of his hands back, was once again administered with his Ronco electric hair trimmer. The hoods, who gathered outside the north doors after school to smoke, took notice of me and made my life even more miserable. They tripped me, knocked books out of my hands, and generally harassed and humiliated me. And I worked at a burger place that paid sixty cents an hour and made you wear a paper cap. That time in my life, nothing was worth remembering; that is, up until the day I found Grace in a Dumpster.

TWO

About ten yards behind the Queen, on the other side of the drive-through lane, were two small structures. One was a sheet-metal storage shed where we kept supplies like napkins, cups, and the five-pound bags of spiced soybean filler we'd mix with the beef to stretch it further; the other was a walk-in freezer. My first night working at the Queen, a coworker named Dean sent me to the freezer for a bag of frozen hash browns and locked me inside for nearly a half hour. I think he only let me out because it got busy and he needed my help.

It was nearly 11 p.m. and the end of my shift when I went out to the shed to restock. With the exception of a streetlight at least fifty yards away, there was no lighting outside, and I was always a bit leery of going out there at night. Gary told me that a few years earlier, one of the evening workers had been mugged by a couple of hoodlums who had been hiding in wait. As usual, I looked around before I stepped out, then slid a rock under the door to prop it open. I quickly ran to the freezer, unlocked the door, retrieved a bag of lard, closed the door, and snapped the padlock shut. I was walking back when I heard something. My heart froze. I looked round but saw no one. Then I heard the sound again. Someone was definitely behind the Dumpster. No. *In* the Dumpster.

I quietly walked backwards towards the Queen, keeping an eye on the Dumpster. Suddenly, a girl popped up; she was as surprised to see me as I was to see her. She was holding a hamburger, which she quickly dropped. She looked familiar. After a moment, she said nervously, 'I dropped something in here. I was just looking for it.'

I realised how I recognised her; she was in my Spanish class. I didn't remember her name; she sat in the back corner of the room and never raised her hand and only spoke when the teacher called on her. I knew she was Dumpster diving, but I didn't want to embarrass her. 'Do you want help finding it?'

'No, I'm OK.'

She pushed herself up and swung her legs over the metal edge so that she was sitting on the flat rim of the Dumpster, then dropped down to the ground. She had short umber hair and beautiful large brown eyes—almond-shaped like my mother's. I remembered seeing her for the first time at school and thinking she was pretty, but then she just kind of faded into the background. She was small, a few inches shorter than me. It was hard to tell what her figure was like, because she wore a coat that was too large for her, but she seemed to be more developed than most of the girls my age. She stooped and lifted her schoolbag, then flung it over her shoulder.

'You're in my Spanish class,' I said.

She looked even more embarrassed. 'Yeah.'

'What's your name again?'

'Grace.'

I was certain I'd never heard it before. 'Grace?'

'Well, the teachers call me Madeline. My full name is Madeline Grace. What's your name?'

'Eric.'

'Oh, yeah,' she said, though I doubt she ever knew it. I could tell she was uncomfortable. I wondered if after I left she would climb back in the Dumpster to look for more food.

'We're just cleaning up. Do you want to come in and get something to eat?'

'That's all right,' she said hesitantly. 'I've got to go.'

'You can have whatever you want. I get the food for free.'

She stood there, caught between hunger and pride, her breath freezing in the air in front of her. Finally, she said, 'OK.'

I led her in the back door past the stoves and stainless-steel food-prep tables, dropping the bag of lard next to the fryer.

Dean, who had locked me in the freezer my first night, was out front mopping the floor.

'Hey, Dean, this is Grace. I'm getting her something to eat.'

'Whatever,' he said without looking up.

Grace stood at the edge of the dining area, just short of the wet tiles. 'I don't want to walk on your floor.'

'Doesn't matter,' Dean said. Dean disliked Mr Dick, and to him any job done less than the boss wanted was a victory of sorts. Then he looked up at Grace, and his expression changed. So did his voice. 'Don't worry about it. Really.' It was obvious that he liked the way she looked. I didn't know why, but his interest in her bothered me.

'What do you want to eat?' I asked.

She looked back at me. 'I don't care. Anything would be nice.'

'We have, like, everything on the planet.'

'What do you like?'

'The pastrami burger, onion rings, baklava, the caramel cashew malt.'

'What's baklava?'

'It's this Greek thing. It has like honey and walnuts, and it's wrapped in . . . uh, paper stuff.'

'Paper?'

'Filo pastry,' Dean said. 'Idiot.'

I blushed a little. 'It's good,' I said.

She smiled. 'Surprise me.'

'The Eric Special coming up.' *Stupid thing to say*, I thought as I walked back to the kitchen. I wondered if she could tell that I never really talked to girls. I remembered that I still had my dopey paper hat on and quickly removed it. In ten minutes, I brought out a tray crowded with everything I had mentioned and a bag of hash browns. Instinctively, I glanced out to the parking lot to make sure Mr Dick wasn't spying on us.

Grace looked over the tray in amazement. 'Wow. You didn't have to get me *everything*.'

'You don't have to eat it all.'

I set the tray down in front of her. She examined each item. 'Is this the . . . bock stuff?'

'Baklava.'

'I'll save that for last,' she said. She peeled back the yellow wax paper from a burger. She took delicate bites at first, each bite growing larger until she was practically wolfing the burger down.

Dean moved next to her, leaning against his mop handle. 'How do you and Eric know each other?'

She answered with a mouth full of burger. 'We have a class together.'

'Cool,' he said. 'So you're what, like sixteen?'

'Fifteen.'

'You look like you're sixteen.' I could tell he wanted to ask her out but wouldn't because I was there. Not out of respect or anything; he just didn't want to be embarrassed in case she said no. Finally he said to me, 'I'm outta here. You can lock up.'

'No problem,' I said.

'Come round again,' he said to Grace. 'It's Dean.'

He walked out of the back door. 'That's Dean,' I said.

'Yeah, I got that.'

'He's kind of a jerk.'

She smiled wryly. 'I got that too.'

The back door shut, and Dean revved his car three or four times more than usual, no doubt trying to impress her.

'Where do you live?' I asked.

'Just west of the school.'

'That's, like, three miles from here. How are you getting home?'

'I'm not going home.' She spun her glass, and drops of condensation gathered on her fingers, which she wiped onto the table. 'I ran away.'

I wasn't sure what to say to that. I remembered that I hadn't seen her in class for a few days. 'How long ago did you leave?'

'Monday.'

'How come you ran away?'

'For kicks.'

Eating out of Dumpsters didn't look like 'kicks' to me. 'What about your parents?'

She took a long drag through her straw. 'They don't care.'

'Really?'

'My stepfather doesn't like me.' She looked down at her watch, an over-sized man's Timex with a flexible wristband. 'It's late. I better go.'

'I need to finish cleaning up,' I said. 'But you should finish eating.'

'OK.'

I WAS AMAZED to see that she finished everything. She threw away her rubbish and stacked her tray with the others, then she walked round to the kitchen, where I was wiping down the counters.

'Thank you. Maybe I'll see you around.'

'Hold on a second.' I filled a large bag with the leftover food we usually threw out and handed it to her. 'You can have that for later.'

She looked in the bag. 'Thanks.'

'Where are you going now?' I asked.

She shrugged. 'I don't know. I guess I'll just walk around for a while.'

'It's supposed to snow again tonight.'

She didn't say anything, just stood there, holding the bag of food. Maybe it was how helpless she looked or how pretty I thought she was, but at that moment, I said the most out-of-character and bravest thing I'd ever said. 'You could come home with me. I live about six blocks from here.'

She actually seemed to consider it. 'Are your parents home?'

'Yeah,' I said, thinking she wouldn't come if they weren't.

She frowned. 'I better not. They might call someone.'

She was right about that. My parents would be on the phone with her parents or the police before she got her coat off. Still, I couldn't let her freeze. Then I had a brilliant idea. 'I know where you can stay. My brother and I built a den outside. It'll be cold, but it's better than nothing.'

'A den?'

'Yeah. It's pretty big. My brother and I slept in there almost every night last summer. It's got a mattress and everything.'

'You sure? No one will see me?'

'It's way out back. You can't see it from the house. I don't think my parents even know it's there. My dad can't walk, and my mother never goes out there. It's the perfect hideout.'

'Why can't your dad walk?'

'He has Guillain-Barré. It's this disease that paralyses you.'

'Wow.'

'Well, they say it's not always permanent. He can walk with crutches now.'

'That's good,' she said.

'So are you coming?'

'Sure.'

We stepped outside and I pulled the door shut, locking it behind us. Light snow had started to fall. I got my bike and pushed it beside me as we started the walk to my home. I wanted to say something clever but had no idea what that might be. Fortunately, Grace was better at conversation than I was.

'So, do you work every night?' she asked.

'No. Usually just three or four times a week.'

'How's the pay?'

'Not good,' I said. 'Almost too small to see with a microscope.'

'Then why do you work there?'

'The cool hats.'

She laughed.

The walk home took us less than ten minutes. As usual, all the lights at my house were off, except in the front room and on the porch. Still the moon was full and reflected brightly off the snow, illuminating the whole place as if the snow crystals held radiance in themselves. I hadn't ever brought anyone home, and I suddenly felt embarrassed by where I lived.

'Thar she blows,' I said. I glanced over at Grace, expecting a look of shock or at least pity, but if she felt either, she hid it well. 'It used to be my grandmother's house. It's kind of a shack.'

'It's not bad.'

She actually sounded sincere, and it made me wonder what kind of a house she lived in. I stopped a few yards from our mailbox. 'We'd better be quiet. Sometimes my mom sits in the front room and reads.'

Grace moved close to me. We passed under the dark canopy of elm that lined our property, pressing along the edge of the driveway towards the garage, the wheels of my bike on the gravel making a lot of noise. I found a dry spot and leaned my bike against the garage wall.

The snow everywhere was about eight inches deep and crusted on top, making it nearly impossible to trudge through quietly. The den was a dark mass in the looming shadow of the garage, its roof covered with nearly a foot of snow. I was suddenly very glad that we'd added the supporting brace from the chicken coop.

I knelt down on one knee and brushed the snow from a chunk of granite we'd placed near the door. Underneath was a rusted key. I unlocked the pad-lock, then pushed the door open and crawled in.

I hadn't been inside the den since the first snowfall; it smelled musty and dank. The carpet was cold and crusted with frost. I felt my way to the post in the centre of the room and stood, fumbling until I found the light and switched it on. It was cold enough inside to see my breath.

Grace crawled in after me, holding the bag of food in front of her. She slowly stood and looked around. 'You built this?'

'Yeah. My brother and me.'

'It's really great.'

'Thanks.'

'It's purple.'

'My brother did it. It's the only colour paint he could find.'

'I like purple,' she said. She glanced at the pin-up poster but said noth-ing. I suddenly felt a little awkward.

'That was my grandfather's,' I said apologetically.

'She's pretty,' Grace said. She looked at the fruit dryer. 'What's that?'

'It's a fruit dryer.'

'Does it work?'

'Yeah.'

She wrapped her arms around herself. 'Maybe we could turn it on.'

'It doesn't make much heat. I'm sorry; it almost feels colder in here than outside,' I said.

'It'll warm up,' she said. 'Eskimos live in igloos. It can't be *that* bad.'

I pointed to the corner. 'That's the mattress. And our sleeping-bags.' I unzipped Joel's sleeping-bag and laid it across mine for extra warmth, but it was cold like everything else. I lit the lamp on the small wooden box we used as a table, and the sweet scent of kerosene filled the room. The sight of the flame at least made it seem warmer.

'That will help,' she said.

'I've got an idea. I'll be right back.'

I crawled out of the den and ran to the house. Fortunately, the back door was unlocked and I tiptoed in. My parents' room was across the hall from the one Joel and I shared, and I could hear my father's heavy snore echoed by my mom's lighter snore. I softly pulled their door shut, then looked through the hall cupboard until I found what I'd come for. When I returned, Grace was in the sleeping-bag with her coat still on. She had found our Etch A Sketch and was drawing. The bag of food was open next to her.

'Look at this,' I said. 'A heat pad.' I plugged it in the opposite side of the extension cord. An amber light glowed on its control box, and within a minute it was toasty warm. 'Try this.'

'This is great.' She looked a little relieved as she put it inside the sleeping bag. 'Have you always lived here?' she asked.

'No, we moved here last May.'

'Do you like it?'

'No.'

'What don't you like about it?'

'Everything. Our first week here, my mom dropped me and Joel off at the cinema. After the show, a gang of kids followed us outside. They wanted to beat us up because we were clean-cut. You know how it is. There's a fight at school almost every day.'

'Where did you used to live?'

'California.'

'I've always wanted to go to California.'

'People were nicer in California. The whole time I was there, there was only one fight at school. And it wasn't so cold there.' I rubbed my nose. 'What about you? You like it here?'

She sighed. 'I wish we'd never come. We moved here from Hawaii.'

Hawaii seemed as exotic as any place I could imagine. 'I've never met anyone from Hawaii. Why'd you move here?'

'My mother got married again. Stan said he had work here, but he doesn't ever work. He just sits around and drinks beer.'

'Think you'll ever go back?'

'I hope so.'

'How's the heat pad?'

'It's really warm.'

'Good,' I said. 'Are you going to school tomorrow?'

'It's Saturday.'

'Oh, yeah, right.' I felt a little stupid. 'Do you want me to bring you something to eat in the morning?'

'That would be nice.'

I pointed to the orange lever of the tap. 'If you're thirsty, it works. Just lift the handle. There's a cup there.' Joel and I had tied a string to the handle of a tin cup and hung it from the tap.

'Groovy. It's like indoor plumbing.'

I smiled. 'Well, I'll go so you can get some sleep.'

'Thanks. Oh, where do you . . .'

I looked at her blankly.

'Go to the bathroom?'

I blushed. 'There's an outhouse on the other side of the chicken hut. It's kinda creepy, but it's better than nothing.'

She nodded. 'OK.'

'All right. Good night.'

I crawled out and shut the door behind me. The snow was falling heavily now. I hoped Grace would be warm enough. At least the den was better than a Dumpster. As I walked back, I couldn't believe a girl was living in my den. I wondered how long she'd stay.

Three

The house was already in motion when I woke the next morning. I could smell bacon frying and hear my mother in the kitchen, talking. I suddenly remembered Grace and felt a strange excitement.

I pulled on a T-shirt and Levis and went out to the kitchen. My mom was at the stove wearing her pink flannel robe. Joel sat at the table eating.

'Good morning,' my mom said cheerfully. 'How do you want your egg?'

'Scrambled. And may I have three eggs this morning?'

'Three?' She turned to look at me, her eyebrows raised.

'I'm just really hungry. Must be a growth spurt or something.'

She began cracking eggs into a bowl. 'It snowed a lot last night.'

I looked out of the window. The storm had dropped more than a foot of snow on the ground. I thought of the den and hoped the roof had held.

'I'm driving Dad to Uncle Norm's this morning. You boys want to go?'

'Yeah, Daddy-o,' Joel said.

Uncle Norm had a two-storey house with a colour television on each floor. Dad and Norm would sit in the two La-Z-Boy chairs and watch football while Aunt Geniel fed us. There was always lots of food: hot dogs, potato salad, and the best baked beans in the world, the kind with brown sugar and strips of bacon laid across the top. While the adults watched football, Joel and I would start up a game of Risk or Monopoly. As far as I was concerned, Uncle Norm's was the only good thing about moving to Utah, so I surprised even myself when I said, 'I'm not sure. I've got a school project, sort of.'

My mother dished the eggs onto a plate. 'Well, make up your mind. We're leaving in fifteen minutes.'

Joel stared at me.

'I've got to tell you something,' I mouthed. I stood up and walked to our bedroom, gesturing for Joel to follow me.

'What's going on?'

I glanced back to be sure our mother wasn't within earshot. 'There's a girl in the den,' I whispered.

He shook his head. 'You wish.'

'Oh, yeah? Come and see.'

We walked back into the kitchen to find our mother gone. As I was scooping the eggs into a bowl, she walked back in. '*What* are you doing?'

'Uh, I thought I'd eat breakfast outside. I miss the den.'

'Eric, it's freezing outside.'

'Please. I won't be long. Then we'll go.'

She shook her head and sighed. 'Just don't leave the bowl out there. And hurry. We need to leave soon.' She walked back out.

I put a piece of buttered toast on top of the eggs, and Joel followed me outside. When we got to the den, I knocked on the door, then pushed it open. It was dark inside, and Little Eva's 'Loco-Motion' was playing on the radio.

'Grace, I brought you some breakfast.' She didn't respond. It was much warmer than it had been the night before. I crawled in and turned on the light. She wasn't there. Joel came in after me.

'She's not here,' I said.

Joel seemed baffled. 'Who is she?'

'A girl I met at the Queen last night. She ran away from home and didn't have anyplace to go. I told her she could stay here.'

Just then, Grace appeared in the doorway. 'Eric . . .' She froze when she saw Joel. Joel stared back at her.

'It's OK,' I said. 'He's my brother. He won't tell anyone.'

She crawled the rest of the way in, then stood. 'I was using the outhouse.'

'How'd you sleep?' I asked.

'Pretty good. It warmed up a lot. The heat pad helped.'

Joel just kept staring at her. Grace put out her hand. 'I'm Grace.'

'I'm Joel. Glad to meet you,' Joel said formally, which coming from a ten-year-old sounded pretty funny.

I handed her the bowl. 'I brought you some breakfast. Scrambled eggs.'

'Thanks. I love eggs on toast.' Grace took the bowl and sat down. She folded the toast and scooped up a clump of the eggs.

Joel asked, 'Where are you from?'

'I live near Granite Junior High.'

'How long are you going to stay here?' Even though I had wondered the same thing, I still wanted to kick him.

'I don't know. A few days . . .' She looked at me. 'If it's OK with you guys.'

'Sure,' I said.

'Groovy. So what are you guys doing today?'

'We're going to my uncle's,' Joel said before I could answer. 'How about you?'

'I don't know. I'll probably go to the library.'

Just then, we heard the strained, quivering honk of the Bee.

'That's Mom,' Joel said.

I said to Joel, 'Tell her I'll be right there.'

After he left, Grace looked at me anxiously. 'You sure he won't tell?'

'He won't tell a soul. You sure you're OK alone?'

She nodded. 'I'm used to being alone.'

'What will you eat?'

'I'll figure something out.'

'I'll bring you some food tonight, just in case.' The horn honked again. 'I gotta go.' I started for the door. 'Wait, I need the bowl.'

Grace dumped the rest of the eggs on the toast. 'There.'

I crawled out. I set the bowl by the back door and ran round the side of the house to the driveway. When I got in the Bee, Joel didn't say a word, but I thought he looked at me with a new sort of respect.

OUR DAY at Uncle Norm's was great as usual. Aunt Geniel was in fine form and laid out a spread of food like none we had ever had at home, even in California. I suppose she knew we didn't have much.

When my mom arrived to pick us up that evening, I asked Aunt Geniel if I could take some food home with us. She usually sent us home with plates of food anyway, but tonight I wanted to be sure. I wondered if Grace was cold and if she had found something to eat. I also worried that she wouldn't be there when we got back.

Aunt Geniel piled two paper platters with cold cuts, cheese, cookies and rolls, and covered it all with Cling Film. While my mother was talking to my aunt, I took the platters out to the van and put them in the back, covering them with one of the cushions we kept back there.

It was dark when we got home. 'You boys go right to bed,' my mom said. 'We've got church in the morning.'

'OK,' Joel said.

'Good night,' I said, and walked out to the kitchen, then ducked through the back door to retrieve the food from the van. I carried it to the den. As I neared, I could see several sets of footprints in the deep snow. I tapped on the wall. 'Grace. It's me.'

I knelt down and opened the door, then shoved the platters through the opening, crawling in after them. Grace was in the corner reading. She immediately set down her book, eyeing the food with great interest.

'I thought you might be hungry,' I said.

'I'm *starving*.'

I set the platters next to her, and she grabbed a roll, took a bite, then tore it open. She stuffed the inside with ham, roast beef and cheese and practically shoved the whole thing in her mouth.

While she ate, I looked around. There was a pile of books next to her. 'You went to the library?'

Swallowing a mouthful of food, she said, 'I got some books.'

I looked at what she'd taken. *The Hobbit. Black Like Me. Catcher in the Rye.*

'Did you like going to your uncle's?'

I nodded. 'Aunt Geniel doesn't have any children, so she spoils us.'

I picked up *The Hobbit*. 'I've read this. It's really good.' I set it back down. 'So what are you doing tomorrow?'

'Nothing. How about you?'

'We have church. But I can get out of it. I was thinking maybe we could do something.' I studied her face for a reaction.

'That would be fun.'

'OK,' I said, trying not to sound too excited. 'It's a date. I mean, it's not a *date*, but we'll do something.'

She smiled. 'See you tomorrow.'

'OK. Bye.'

She waved as I crawled out.

Joel was in the kitchen making himself a glass of Ovaltine when I walked back into the house. 'She still there?'

'Yeah.' I poured myself a glass of milk, measured in a couple of heaped tablespoons of Ovaltine, and began stirring.

My dad called from his room. 'Hey, Eric, what did you do with that food Geniel sent home with us?'

I didn't know what to say.

'You didn't forget it, did you?'

Joel looked at me. Without saying anything, I pointed to the back door.

'Sorry,' I shouted. 'Guess I did.'

My father groaned. 'I wanted another one of those ham sandwiches.'

THAT SUNDAY, I told my mom that I didn't feel like going to church but promised I'd go next week. After my mother left, I went to my parents' door and peeked in; my father was still asleep. I put on my shoes and coat, spooned the porridge my mother had left on the stove into a bowl, and went out to the back garden.

Grace was sitting in the corner of the den eating a cookie. The meat and cheese were gone from the platter, which amazed me since there had been at least five sandwiches' worth. Although she had changed her blouse, she was still in the sleeping-bag, and it was pulled up to her waist. She smiled when she saw me. 'Hi.'

'I brought you some breakfast.'

I gave her the bowl. She set down the cookie and began eating the porridge. It seemed like she was always hungry. Maybe girls just ate a lot.

'How was your night?'

'Good,' she said between mouthfuls. 'It wasn't too cold.'

I sat cross-legged across from her. 'There's supposed to be another big snowstorm this week. Bigger than yesterday's.'

'What day?'

'I'm not sure. I think Wednesday.'

'Figures.'

'Why figures?'

'Wednesday's my birthday.'

'Really? How old will you be?'

'Sixteen.'

This surprised me. We were in the same class, and I was just fourteen.

As if reading my mind, she said, 'People start school later in Hawaii.'

'So what are you getting for your birthday?' I asked. She looked at me with a pained expression. It was a stupid question. 'Sorry.'

'It's OK.' She finished eating the porridge and handed the bowl back to me. After a moment, she said, 'I miss how my birthdays used to be. For breakfast, my mother always made chocolate chip pancakes. Then she would take off early from work, and we'd go somewhere, like the zoo or the park.' A distant look came to her eyes. 'It's been a while. My last birthday, she gave me a cupcake with a candle in it, because Stan was taking her away for the day. I could tell she felt bad about it. Stan plans these "outings" whenever something important in my life comes up. It's his way of showing who's the boss. He's big on who's the boss.'

'I'm sorry,' I said. Again.

She looked at me and forced a smile. 'But I'm here now, so I don't have to worry about that.'

'You must have been really hungry.'

'Because I'm eating so fast?'

'No, because the plate is empty.'

'I put the cheese and meat outside in the snow to keep it cold.'

'Outside? That's not a good idea. There are a lot of animals around here. Rats and raccoons and stuff. Where'd you put it?'

'Just outside the door, around the corner.'

I looked out. The platter was there, but the meat and cheese were gone.

'Looks like they got it. I should get you a bucket or something. You could fill it with snow, like a refrigerator. That's how they used to keep things cold.' I looked at her. 'So I was thinking today we could go exploring.'

'Where?'

'Just out back.'

'Are you sure no one will see me?'

'My dad's still in bed. Mom and Joel won't be home for a few hours.'

'Let's go.' She climbed out of the sleeping-bag and put on her coat. When we were outside, she asked, 'Does your family always go to church?'

'My mom always does. My dad goes sometimes. But most of the time she just takes me and Joel.'

Grace thought about this. 'I wish my family went to church.'

This surprised me. I didn't see her as the churchgoing type.

We crossed the crusted snow of the garden to the south end of the property.

'Did you know it snows in Hawaii?' Grace asked.

'Really?'

'Yeah. Not like this, though. Just at the tops of the volcanoes.'

'I'd like to see a volcano in real life,' I said. 'So how come they start school later in Hawaii?'

'I don't know. They just do.'

We walked up over a small bridge that crossed the creek and connected the street in front of our house to our nextdoor neighbour's place, which was set back at least fifty yards from the end of our dead-end street. The house was dark and looked deserted.

'Who lives there?'

'I don't know. Some old guy. He never comes out.'

The creek below the bridge was a wide path of ice lined on both sides by rows of river willow. 'It's kind of pretty,' she said. 'The way it all froze up like that. Is it safe to walk on?'

'The ice is, like, a foot thick. Joel and I tried to break it with a hammer but we couldn't.'

I walked down the side of the steep bank; I slipped once on the snow but quickly regained my footing. Grace stood at the top of the bank. 'I'm going to fall.'

'I'll help you.' I walked halfway back up and held out my hand. She took it and followed my steps down to the side of the creek. I stepped onto the ice. 'See. It's like concrete.'

She followed after me. 'It feels solid.'

She slipped and I reached out for her. Grace grabbed on to me, laughing. 'It's OK. I'm just clumsy.' She didn't let go of my arm, which I didn't mind.

'Have you ever tried skating on this?' Grace asked.

'I don't know how to skate.'

'I do. It's fun.' She slid across on one leg, the other out behind her, her arms spread wide. 'Look, I'm Sonja Henie.' Suddenly there was a loud crack. 'What was that?' she asked.

'I don't know. Don't move.' Suddenly Grace fell through the ice. The creek was only about four feet deep, but she fell sideways, and her head went underwater.

'Grace!'

She sputtered and flailed about until she grabbed on to the edge of the ice. She leaned up onto it, and it broke, dropping her back in the water. I ran up the side of the bank, holding on to willow branches for support and leaning out over the water.

'Grab my arm!'

She reached over and grabbed me. I pulled her backwards, falling into the bushes with the weight of our motion. Then I pulled her the rest of the way out of the water. She was shivering violently.

I put my arm round her and helped her up the steep, snowy incline. When we were on solid ground, I took off her coat and put mine round her. She seemed disorientated, which I knew wasn't a good thing. I had learned about hypothermia in scouting. They taught us to watch for the 'umbles': stumbles, mumbles, fumbles and grumbles. Grace was stumbling and mumbling. We needed to get inside. My father was home, but it didn't matter; she had to get indoors.

As we neared the house, Grace was shaking so hard I practically had to carry her. I walked as fast as I could with nearly her full weight leaning into me. We finally got to the back porch and I opened the door. I could hear the television; my father must have got up.

'Is your dad home?'

'He won't come out.'

Suddenly my dad yelled, 'Eric!'

'Yeah?' I shouted back.

'Get me a Dr Pepper.'

'Sure. I need to go to the bathroom first.' I turned to Grace. 'C'mon. Hurry.'

We slunk round the corner to the bathroom. I quickly turned the shower on full and steam filled the room. Grace tried to take her clothes off, but her hands were trembling so badly she couldn't do it. I pulled off her coat, then knelt down and untied her shoes. When she had stepped out of them, I pulled her socks down and off. She tried to unbutton her blouse, but she couldn't push the buttons through. She looked at me helplessly. I suppose this would be most teenage boys' ultimate fantasy, but I was terrified.

I reached my hand inside the shower. The water was scalding. I adjusted the knobs until it was warm. 'Get in,' I said.

'My clothes . . .'

'Just get in. You're already wet.'

She stepped inside the shower. The first minute or so she shivered as the hot water soaked through her clothing. Then she seemed to relax.

'I'll be back,' I said.

As I was shutting the bathroom door, my dad called again. 'Eric, where's my Dr Pepper?'

'Coming.'

I got a glass from the cupboard, a bottle opener, and a bottle of the soft drink out of the refrigerator and brought them to him. Even though much of the dexterity had returned to his hands, my dad was still unable to open a bottle. I prised off the cap and poured the liquid into the glass. 'Here you are.'

He stared at me. 'Why are your trousers all wet?'

I looked down. My jeans were soaked. 'I was walking by the creek and kind of fell in.'

'Through the ice? What were you doing by the creek?'

'Walking.'

He just looked at me blankly. 'It sounds like there's water running.'

'Yeah, uh, it's the toilet. . . . You know how it runs sometimes.'

Just then, the Bee pulled into the driveway.

'Looks like Mom came home early,' my father said.

Now I was worried. 'I'm going to take a shower,' I said. 'Mom wouldn't want me to catch a chill.' I hurried back to the bathroom. Grace's clothes were in a pile on the floor outside the shower.

'Are you OK?' I asked.

'Yes.' She sounded normal again.

'We have a problem. My mom just got home.'

She stuck her head out. 'What do we do?'

'Just stay in there. I'll figure something out.'

'I need some clothes.'

'I'll find some.'

Fortunately, my mom saved my clothes after I grew out of them for Joel. I could hear my brother talking to my mother in the hall. When their voices died down, I opened the door a crack and peered out. Joel was just a few yards away.

'Hey,' I called in a loud whisper. 'Get me some of my old clothes from the hand-me-down box.'

'Why?'

'Grace fell in the creek.'

It took a moment for him to make the connection. 'Is she in there? With *you*?'

'Just get the clothes,' I said. 'And don't let Mom see you.'

As if on cue, my mom came round the corner. 'What are you doing?'

'I was just asking Joel to get me some dry clothes. I fell in the creek.'

'Through the ice? What were you doing by the creek?'

'Walking.'

She looked at me with the same blank expression my father had. Then she said, 'Lunch will be ready in half an hour.'

When she was gone, Joel asked, 'What should I get?'

'Just something warm. Not my summer clothes.'

'Does she want underwear too?'

I thought about it. 'I guess.'

I shut and locked the door. A few minutes later, Joel knocked. I cracked open the door; he was holding a stack of clothes.

'Where's Mom right now?'

'She's making lunch.'

'I've got to get Grace out of here.' I thought for a moment. 'I need you to create a diversion.'

Joel smiled and nodded his approval. He had read enough comic books that the idea of creating a diversion clearly pleased him. 'I know. I'll put a dishcloth on one of the stove burners and start a fire in the kitchen. Then, while Mom's trying to put it out, you could sneak Grace out the back.'

I looked at him. 'That's the stupidest thing I've ever heard. Just ask her to help you with your homework.'

'I don't have any homework.'

'Make some up.'

The shower shut off.

'Just give us five minutes. Make sure Mom's in the kitchen. I'll take Grace out through our bedroom window.'

'I can't believe you're in there with a naked girl.'

'Just do it.' I shut and locked the door.

'Could you get me a towel?' Grace whispered.

I took one from the towel rack and, turning my head away, handed it round the corner of the shower. 'Joel got you some clothes.'

'Thanks.'

'I'll just put them on the floor. You can wear them until yours are dry. My parents think I'm showering, so I need to stay in here. I promise I won't look.'

A few minutes later, she stepped out of the shower. 'I'm dressed.' I turned around. She looked better, though it was odd seeing her in my clothes. She looked at herself in the mirror and grinned. 'I've never worn boy's underwear before.'

Joel knocked again on the door. His maths textbook was under his arm.

'Hi, Joel,' Grace said.

'Hi.' He frowned at me. 'I already know how to do all this.'

'It doesn't matter,' I said. 'Go.'

We waited a few more minutes before I again peeked out of the door. I could hear my mother talking. I turned back to Grace. She was wrapping her wet clothes in a towel. 'Let's go.'

Grace followed me around the corner to our bedroom. I locked the door behind us. 'We'll go out of the window.'

'What about my shoes?'

I hadn't thought about that. 'You'll have to wear my snow boots. They're in the kitchen. You better hide in the cupboard while I get them.'

She went inside, crouching beneath a curtain of hanging clothes. I shut the door and walked out to the kitchen, trying my best to look like I wasn't hiding a girl in my bedroom. Joel looked at me quizzically.

My mother looked up. 'I thought you took a shower.'

'I did.'

'And you put the same clothes back on?'

'I mean, I'm about to take a shower.'

I grabbed my boots and hurried past them. Fortunately, my mother's attention had shifted back to helping Joel. When I got back to my room, I locked the door again, then opened the cupboard. Grace was sitting cross-legged on the floor. 'Here.'

She slipped her feet into the boots.

I went to the bedroom window and opened it. I climbed out first, then helped Grace out. We kept to the perimeter of the garden and out of view of the windows of the house. We were panting from the exertion when we finally got back inside the den. Grace climbed inside the sleeping-bag, then lay back.

'How do you feel?' I asked.

'Better,' she said. 'It felt good to shower.'

We were both quiet, and then Grace started laughing.

'What's so funny?'

'Everything,' she said. 'I'm crawling through windows and wearing boys' underwear.' She put her hand on my leg. 'Are you going to school tomorrow?'

'Yeah.'

'I have some things in my locker. Would you mind getting them?'

'Sure. What do you need?'

'Just bring everything. But the most important thing is a red cloth pouch. Whatever you do, don't lose it.'

'A red cloth pouch,' I repeated.

'You'll need my locker combination.' She took a pen and a piece of paper out of her schoolbag and wrote it down. She also wrote 'red cloth pouch' and underlined it three times. 'Here you go.'

I folded the paper and put it in my pocket. 'I better get back inside before my mom finds out I'm gone.' I got down to crawl out.

'Eric, thanks for saving me.'

I looked up at her. She had an expression I'd never seen on a girl's face, at least not one looking at me. I wasn't sure what it meant, but I liked it.

'You're my hero.'

'Any time,' I said.

As I walked back, I realised that I really had saved her. Of course, I wasn't about to win any awards as technically I'd put her in danger to begin with, but when you're a fourteen-year-old boy with acne and a bad haircut, it felt good to be somebody's hero.

Four

I hated being back at school. The day passed at glacial speed, and all day I sat chewing my pencil while my thoughts revolved around Grace.

Spanish was my last class of the day, and for some reason I kept looking back to the corner of the room where Grace usually sat. I felt strangely important being the only one who knew where she was. Mrs Waller was going down the roll when she suddenly looked up. 'Has anyone seen Madeline Webb?'

I looked straight ahead.

'I think she's sick,' a voice said from the back of the room. 'I heard she had pneumonia.'

'Oh.' She made a mark on the attendance sheet, put it back in her desk, and started the class.

As soon as the bell rang, I set out for Grace's locker. I took the folded paper with the locker combination out of my pocket and began turning the dial. It felt a little like I was breaking into a safe. It took me a couple of tries to get the door open.

Inside there was a mirror taped to the door, and several pictures of cheer-leaders cut from magazines taped to the sidewalls. I saw a stack of folded clothes sitting on the bottom of the locker, and it occurred to me that she had been planning her escape for some time. Underneath the clothes was the red cloth pouch. It was nearly as thick as a brick but flexible. I wanted to look inside but didn't. I figured if it was that important, it was best I didn't know.

I collected everything and slammed the locker shut. I looked down at my watch. I was late for the bus. I broke into a run for the north doors, which I usually avoided because the hoods were always hanging around them. Fortunately, they weren't there, but neither was my bus. I could see the last orange bus a hundred yards away from me rounding the corner of the parking lot. I groaned.

'Dang it!' I shouted, which was about as harsh an expletive as I ever used, and started off for home. An hour and a half later, I walked in our front door, my feet soaked and numb from the cold. My father was reading a book. He looked up at me. 'You're late.'

'I missed the bus.' I wiped my feet on the scrap of carpet my mother had put by the front door. 'How are you feeling?'

'Getting better,' he said, which he always said.

I walked out of the living room into the kitchen. Joel was at the table working on a jigsaw puzzle. He looked up at me.

'Where you been?'

'I missed the bus.'

'You walked home?'

'No. I flew.'

He went back to his puzzle. 'Want to help?'

'No. I've got to go to work.' I lowered my voice. 'Have you checked on . . . ?' I tilted my head towards the back door.

'I didn't know I was supposed to.'

'She's probably hungry.'

'It's like having a pet,' Joel said.

I went to the pantry, carefully considering what I could take that my mother wouldn't miss. I grabbed a couple of cans of pork and beans, some Campbell's cream of chicken soup, and a can of string beans. We had an old army cooking pan in the den, and I figured she could heat things over the kerosene lamp. I cut two thick pieces of my mother's homemade bread and put it all in a brown grocery bag along with a can opener, a fork, a spoon, a plate and a bowl. Then I retrieved my schoolbag and went out back. As I neared the den, I could smell something bad. When I opened the door, the smell intensified. The light and the nightlight were off. 'Grace?'

She didn't answer, but I could hear her lightly snoring. I thought it was a little strange that she was napping this late in the afternoon. I set the paper bag inside the door, along with the things from her locker, then rode my bike to work.

MONDAY AT THE QUEEN was the slowest day of the week. I was alone in the back, rolling burritos and stacking them in a plastic container when Dean came in. He jumped up on the counter.

'So, spud, tell me about that girl.'

'What girl?' I rolled another burrito.

'The one you brought by the other night.'

'I didn't bring her.'

'Whatever, you Polack. She was pretty tasty.'

'Yeah, well, she's not your type.'

'Yeah?'

'Yeah. She has taste.'

His eyes narrowed. 'Then why is she hanging out with a loser like you?'

'Lucky, I guess.'

'You're *such* a nerd.'

He went back out front. He didn't say anything else to me for the rest of the shift, but he smacked me in the back of the head on his way out. I had never been happier to hear his car engine rev.

Jackie and I had the late shift. I liked Jackie. She was in my maths class at Granite and was tall, wore braces on her teeth, and had bright red hair. She also played the violin and was on the chess team, which pretty much put her in the same social class as me.

As we closed up, I filled a bag with leftover food. I remembered how Grace had devoured the onion rings, so I put a couple of jumbo-sized orders inside. Jackie saw me stowing the food in my rucksack. 'Mr Dick would purée you if he saw you doing that.'

'I know.'

'Don't worry, I'm not going to tell. I think it's a stupid rule. Mr Dick would rather we throw the food away than take it home. He doesn't respect us.'

'Jackie,' I said. 'We're teenagers. No one respects us.'

'True,' she said sadly.

AFTER JACKIE'S MOM picked her up, I locked the back door and rode home. My legs still ached from my walk from school, and my shoes were still wet. To make it worse, the temperature had dropped into the twenties.

Once I was home, I went straight for the den. The light was still off inside, and the things I had brought from Grace's locker were still untouched by the door. I was suddenly worried.

'Grace?'

Nothing.

'Grace, you OK?' I found the torch and pointed it towards the corner. She was in the sleeping-bag, which was pulled up to her neck. She yawned and rubbed her eyes. 'Yeah,' she said, her voice weak and gravelly. 'What time is it?'

'It's almost eleven.'

'I slept until noon?'

'Noon? It's night.'

She sat bolt upright. 'I slept all day?'

'Yeah.' She didn't look right to me. 'What's wrong?'

'I don't feel well. I threw up.'

Now I understood the smell. I turned on the light. She raised her hand to shield her eyes. 'Are you sick?'

'It's nothing. I'll be fine.'

'Well, you've got to be better by Wednesday for your birthday.'

Her lips rose in a surprised smile. 'You remembered.'

'Of course. It's an important day.'

Her smile spread wider, and again she was looking at me in a way a girl never had. My face felt hot.

'I got the things from your locker. I just put everything there.'

She crawled over and pulled everything out until she found the red pouch. She untied it, then pulled out a large wad of bills. Not just ones; there were tens and even twenties.

I stared at it in wonder. 'What did you do, rob a bank?'

'It's my stepfather's gambling money.'

'You *stole* it?'

She put the money back in the pouch. 'It's not really stealing.'

'How is it not stealing?'

'Look, it's his responsibility to take care of me, right?'

'Yeah.'

'So I'm using this to take care of me, right?' She had a point. She retied the pouch and put it in the sleeping-bag. 'I'm not a thief,' she said angrily, though it sounded more like she was trying to convince herself.

'I'm sorry.'

'It's OK. Thanks for getting my stuff. I hope it wasn't too much trouble.'

I thought of telling her about my walk home in the snow and my frozen feet, but for some reason I just said, 'No trouble.'

I handed her the bag of food. 'And I brought this from work. You don't have to eat it if you're not hungry.'

'I'm always hungry,' she said, which from what I knew of her seemed to be true. She lifted an onion ring and took a big bite out of it. After swallowing, she asked, 'What are you doing tomorrow?'

'Same as today. School and work.'

'That doesn't sound fun.'

'It's not supposed to be.'

'Do you ever play hooky from school?'

I hesitated. 'Sure,' I said coolly. 'Who doesn't?' If I sounded like the liar I was, she didn't seem to notice. The truth was I had won three awards for perfect attendance.

'Great, then let's play hooky tomorrow.'

I was trapped by my own lie. I was proud of my perfect attendance awards. That sounds pathetic, but they were the only awards I'd ever received. Now I felt pressured to throw them aside like yesterday's casserole just because I didn't want to look dumb for some girl. Even worse was my terror of getting caught by a truant officer. I had never actually seen one, but I didn't want to take any chances.

'I can't miss work . . .'

'That's OK,' she said. 'It's just until school's out.'

'What if you're still sick?' I asked hopefully.

'I'll be OK.'

I sighed. 'OK,' I said. 'I better go.' I got down on my knees to crawl out.

'Mañana,' she said.

I walked back to the house with dread in the pit of my stomach. If my parents ever found out I had played hooky, I was dead and buried.

THE NEXT MORNING, I got ready as if I was going to school. Mom made us hot oat cereal for breakfast, and, as usual, Joel put so much raspberry jam in his bowl that his cereal was crimson.

'I'm going to work early,' my mom said. 'We're stock-taking. Want a ride to school, Eric?'

Not once since school started had my mother asked if I wanted a ride. It's like she knew I was up to something. 'Uh, no. Thanks. I'm meeting someone on the bus.'

She looked at me with pleasant surprise. 'You have a new friend?' My mother was always concerned over my lack of friends.

'Yeah.'

'What's his name?'

'Who?'

'Your friend.'

'Oh. Gra . . . ck.'

Her eyebrows rose. 'Grack? That's an odd name. Where's he from?'

'Uh, here.'

'Hmm. Sounds Hungarian. What nationality is he?'

'American,' I said. 'I think.'

'Well.' She looked at the clock. 'You'd better get going. Maybe Grack would like to come over sometime.'

'Yeah. Sure. I'll ask.'

She came over and kissed me. 'Have a good day,' she said, and left.

I grabbed my schoolbag and started walking for the bus stop. My mother drove past me halfway down the street, waving as she went by. As soon as she had turned the corner, I looked back down the street to see if anyone was watching (as if my neighbours suddenly had nothing better to do than to make sure I was going to school). I didn't see anyone, so I turned back. I ducked into our nextdoor neighbour's back garden, then crawled through the hole in the fence and crossed into our garden. I knocked on the den door. 'It's me.'

I crawled inside. Grace watched me enter. 'I wasn't sure if you were going to come or not.'

I dropped my schoolbag on the floor. 'Why?'

'You just seemed a little . . . nervous.'

I was glad she hadn't said 'afraid'. 'Where are we going?' I asked.

'The mall.'

The mall? I thought. The place was probably teeming with truant officers. *We might as well play hooky in front of the school.*

The mall was a forty-minute walk from my house. We probably could have reached it sooner except I insisted we keep to the back roads, which Grace didn't seem to mind.

If there were truant officers at the mall, they didn't see us. This made me wonder if they were just bogeymen that school administrators and parents made up to keep us in line.

We walked, unstopped, into store after store as Grace looked at clothes. For me we made a stop at a bookstore and a model shop. On the way back, we ate lunch at a diner. 'Ain't you a cute couple. You two playin' hooky?' the waitress asked.

'Science Fair,' Grace said.

I ordered a hot dog with relish and a side order of French fries. Grace ordered a bowl of tomato soup with a grilled cheese sandwich. Afterwards, we each ordered apple pie.

When no one was around, Grace asked, 'So, do you like playing hooky?'

'Sure.'

'You were afraid we were going to get caught, weren't you?'

'A little.'

'Me, too. But I was so sick of sitting inside all the time; I had to get out. Sometimes you just have to take chances.' She looked up at a clock on the wall. 'We have about an hour of school left. I've got to pick up some things. Do you mind?'

'No.'

'Good. I'll pay for lunch. You've fed me enough.' Grace brought out the red pouch and paid the bill, then we started back home. On the way, she said, 'I need to go to Warshaw's.'

I felt a wave of panic. 'I can't. My mother works there.'

'Oh. Will you wait for me outside?'

I thought about it. 'OK.'

I sat out on the kerb at the side of the store, watching shoppers come and go and praying my mother didn't come out. Grace was gone for nearly twenty minutes—long enough that I began to fear she'd been captured. I was relieved when she finally emerged. She was pushing a shopping trolley with two large grocery bags. I walked over to meet her. 'Is your mom really thin with brown hair that combs back like this?' She raked her hair back over her ears.

'Yeah.'

'I think she rang up my groceries. She's pretty. You look just like her.'

I suppose that was a compliment, but I was more concerned that Grace had been seen by my mom. 'We better go home,' I said.

I pushed the trolley to the edge of the parking lot, then we both took a bag and started walking. My bag was pretty heavy.

'What did you buy?'

'Food, mostly. I got some bread and shredded wheat and milk; it should last me for a while. I've felt bad that you've had to feed me.'

'I don't mind,' I said.

'You've been really sweet. You're always nice, aren't you?'

Somehow this sounded like an insult. 'Not always. I can be trouble.'

She grinned. 'But you're mostly nice. Do you know how I know? When you first saw me eating food out of the Dumpster, even though we weren't friends then, you pretended that you didn't notice.' She smiled. 'Thank you for that.'

'I just didn't want you to be embarrassed.'

'I wish there were more people like you.'

That was probably the nicest thing anyone had ever said to me. It took us about thirty minutes to get home. We carried the stuff to the den. I packed her milk in the snow while she dragged the rest of the groceries inside. I climbed in after her.

'Want to play cards?' she asked.

We played blackjack and Go Fish for about an hour. She won most of the time, and even when she didn't, I had the feeling she was letting me win. Finally I said, 'Do you know what time it is?'

She looked at her watch. 'It's almost four thirty.'

'I've got to be at work in half an hour.'

'Today was fun,' she said.

'Yeah, it was.'

It had been fun. But I was sure there would be heck to pay.

ON TUESDAYS I worked the early shift, which happily meant I didn't have to close up. Even better, it was payday. I was glad Grace and I had bought food earlier, as it was far too risky to sneak any out today. Mr Dick had come by to drop off our paycheques, which he always did grudgingly, and then he stuck around to make sure we were earning our wages. Just before I left,

I folded my cheque into the front pocket of my trousers. When I got home, I went straight out to the den. Grace was reading.

'So about tomorrow,' I said.

'What's tomorrow?'

I figured she just liked to hear me say it. 'Your birthday . . .'

She smiled. 'Can we play hooky again?'

'I better not. But we'll have a party. What's your favourite kind of cake?'

'Chocolate.'

'Chocolate it is. Anything else you want?'

She shook her head. 'Just cake.'

'It will be fun. I'm going to invite Joel. Is that OK?'

'Yeah. He's cute.'

I felt a pang of jealousy. 'Well, I better get inside before my parents wonder where I am.'

'Good night, Eric.'

'Good night.'

As I crawled out, I was thinking how much I liked the way she spoke my name. I walked along the driveway back to the front of the house and went in through the front door. My mother and father were in the living room, my mother reading a magazine and my father in his La-Z-Boy watching TV.

'Hi, honey,' my mom said.

'Hi.' I sat down on the floor next to her to watch the television. At the commercial break, my mom said, 'How was your day?'

'It was fine,' I said.

'What did you learn at school?'

'Nothing.'

This is the standard reply millions of schoolkids every day give to their parents and one that no parent has ever questioned, even though this was probably one of the few times it was technically true.

'Do you think you could cash my cheque tonight?' I asked my mom.

'It's too late. The bank's closed. I'll have to do it tomorrow on my lunch break. You don't want me to just put it in your savings account?'

'No.'

'How come?'

'I don't know. It's just good to have some cash around.'

'You've been such a good saver; don't get out of the habit.'

I took the cheque out of my pocket and gave it to her. 'I'm gonna go to bed,' I said.

'Do you have homework?'

'Uh, no. Not today.'

I went into the kitchen and made myself a glass of Ovaltine, then headed to my bedroom. The lights were off. As I climbed under the covers, Joel, who was always asleep by eight, asked, 'Where were you today?'

I hesitated. 'School.'

'No, you weren't.'

'Yeah, I was.'

'Liars go to the devil.'

'I'm not lying.'

There was silence, then Joel's voice softened. 'I'm not going to tell anyone.'

I breathed out. 'OK, I played hooky. You satisfied?'

He didn't say anything.

'How'd you know anyway?'

'I waited for you at the bus stop. I wanted to get a milk shake or something.'

'Oh.'

'You spend all your time with that girl.'

The sadness in his voice made me feel bad. 'I'm having a birthday party for her tomorrow. She wants you to come.'

'Really?'

'She said so.'

'I'll think about it.' Neither of us spoke for a minute, then Joel asked, 'Do *you* want me to come?'

'Yeah. Sure.'

'I'll think about it.'

'I'm buying a chocolate cake.'

'OK. I'll think about it.'

Five

In spite of my fears, no one arrested me at school the next day. In fact, it appeared that no one even missed me. Only my English teacher, Mrs Johnson, asked where I was. I said I was sick, which wasn't a complete lie, since I had had a stomachache after lunch (though probably just worry-induced indigestion). Mrs Johnson made a sharp tick in the register as I took my seat and didn't even ask for a note from home. I guess I just looked so squeaky-clean that no one thought I was capable of breaking rules.

My mom went to the bank in her lunch hour and left the money from my paycheque on my bed. When I got home from school, I got the rest of my money from the jar under my bed, then rode my bike about a mile and a half to the nearest hardware store to get Grace's present.

I had decided several days earlier what to get Grace for her birthday. It was the most expensive thing that I had ever bought. The box it came in was way too big to fit in my schoolbag and too bulky to hold under my arm. I had to balance it between my handlebars and straddle it with my legs. It was a miracle I made it home alive.

I stowed the box in the garage, then I walked to Heller's, a small bakery just three blocks from our home, where I bought a small round chocolate layer cake. It was covered with dark fudge frosting, and the woman from the bakery wrote *Happy Birthday* on it in red icing. She asked if I wanted to put a name on it, but I said no.

I brought it home and put the cake in a suitcase in the garage, then I went inside to get Joel. Not only had he decided to attend the party, but he had also drawn Grace a birthday card and put one of his favourite baseball cards inside. I almost said something about girls not liking baseball cards, but for once I did the right thing and just kept my mouth shut. We were about to go out to the den when my mother stopped me.

'Eric, we're about ready to eat. Would you please set the table?'

'Sure. Just give me a minute.'

'No, right now.'

I turned to Joel and whispered, 'Go tell Grace we have to eat first.'

'OK.' He ran off.

I got the dishes and was setting them round the table when my mother said, 'So Mr Berg asked me if you have a girlfriend.' Mr Berg was an assistant manager at Warshaw's and the last person on the planet I would expect to show an interest in my love life. 'He said he saw you outside the store with a young woman.'

My heart froze. I began laying down the knives and forks. 'Must have been someone who looked like me,' I said.

'He said she was pretty.'

'Then it definitely wasn't me.'

My mother said, 'Don't be so hard on yourself. You're a handsome young man, just like your dad. Trust me, someday you'll have to beat the girls off.'

I just wanted this conversation to be over. 'Sure, Mom. So, what's for dinner?'

She smiled at my obvious deflection. 'Meat loaf.'

That night at dinner, my mother recounted the earlier conversation about Mr Berg with my father.

'I don't know why Eric doesn't have a girlfriend,' my dad said as if I wasn't there. 'I had my first crush when I was twelve.' Then, as if this reminded him of something, he said to my mother, 'Hon, let's go to a movie tonight. I've got to get out of here.'

'After I do the dishes.'

'Let the boys do them. There's an eight o'clock showing of *If a Man Answers* at the Avalon.'

My mother looked at her watch. 'We'll have to hurry.'

It wasn't even seven, but since my father walked about as fast as a mummy in the Saturday horror matinée movies, they always gave themselves a lot of time. They left Joel and me sitting at the table—a surprisingly convenient turn of events.

I filled the sink with soapy water while Joel cleared the table. Before they left, my mom came to check on us. 'We'll be back around ten. I expect you to be asleep before we get back.'

'OK,' we said in unison.

She kissed us on our foreheads, then put on her coat. We heard the Bee crank to life and drive away, spitting gravel behind it.

'Hurry,' I said. I rinsed the dishes and put everything on the drying rack. When I was finished, I climbed up on the counter to reach the highest shelf, where the matches were kept. I shoved two matchbooks into my pocket, then started looking for candles but couldn't find any.

Joel remembered that he'd seen some candles in the Christmas ornament box and ran off to get them. He returned with a single long white candle that tapered into a point. 'It's all there is,' he said.

I grabbed a cake knife, utensils and three small plastic plates while Joel retrieved his homemade birthday card. We put on our coats and went out to the garage.

Joel was impressed by the size of my gift. 'What's in the box?'

'You'll see.'

I carried the box, plates, and utensils. Joel carried the cake. Outside the den, I set everything down and shoved the candle halfway into the cake. Then I knocked on the wall. 'We're here.'

'Come in,' Grace sang.

I climbed in, and Joel handed me the cake. I left the big box outside the door. As usual, Grace was wearing her coat. She stared at the cake.

'Happy birthday!' Joel said as he crawled in. He actually crawled right over to Grace and handed her his card. 'I made you this,' he said proudly. It bothered me that he'd got to her first.

She smiled. 'Thanks, Joel.' She looked at his card. He'd drawn a picture of a girl in a box beneath the words *Happy Birthday Grays*.

'That's a picture of you,' he said. 'Your nose isn't really that big. I just don't draw that good.'

'Thank you.' She opened the card. 'Wow, a real Joe DiMaggio card. That's so special.'

'You know who that is?' I asked.

'Of course. This is a very special card.' She turned to Joel. 'Thank you, Joel. I'll always treasure it.' Then she hugged him.

She was just being nice, I told myself. But she looked pretty happy. Joel looked pretty happy too.

'I brought a cake,' I said. I handed it to her. 'It's all chocolate. The frosting and everything. I bought it. Myself.'

'Thank you, Eric.'

'We could only find one candle,' I said.

'Can I light it?' Joel asked.

Joel was really getting on my nerves.

'Sure,' Grace said.

'OK,' I said. I surrendered a matchbook.

It took him about half a dozen matches to get it done. I got more annoyed at each spent match, but Grace just watched happily.

'OK, now that it's *finally* lit,' I said, 'let's sing.'

Joel joined in. 'Happy birthday to you, happy birthday to you, happy birthday dear Grace, happy birthday to you.'

Grace clapped.

'OK,' I said. 'Now make a wish and blow it out.'

Grace turned to me. 'If it's OK with you, I'd like to look at it for a while.'

'Sure. Whatever you want. It's your birthday.'

She stared into the flame for a moment, then said, without looking at either of us, 'I can see things in flames.'

'What do you mean?' I asked. 'What kind of things?'

'I can see the future.'

'Like a fortuneteller?' I asked.

She nodded. 'Uh-huh. What do you want to know?'

I felt a little funny. I remembered seeing something like this once on television. There was a proper way to phrase the question. 'O, seer of the future,' I said, 'what does my future hold?'

Without acknowledging whether or not I'd asked correctly, she looked intently into the candle, seeming to lose herself to the flame's irregular swaying. She looked at me and said, 'Someday you will be someone who is feared.'

I suppose I expected about anything but that. 'You must have the wrong guy,' I said. 'The only thing that fears me is a doughnut.'

'Last summer I saw a grasshopper hop away from him,' Joel said.

'The flame never lies,' she said. 'You *will* be feared.'

'How about me?' Joel said. 'Do me.'

Grace gazed back into the dancing flame. After a full minute, she looked back at Joel. 'You are going to be someone famous. Someday, people will ask for your autograph.'

Joel smiled broadly. 'Really?'

'Famous for what?' I asked, even more annoyed that his fortune was clearly better than mine.

'I don't know,' she said matter-of-factly. 'Joel, I better get your autograph now before I have to pay for it.'

This is absurd, I thought.

'OK,' Joel said. Grace had a pen in her bag, and Joel signed the back of the baseball card. 'I'll give you all the autographs you want.'

'One will be fine, thank you.' She took back the pen, then stowed it with her card in her bag. 'All right. I'm going to blow the candle out now,' she said. 'Here goes nothing.' Even though there was only one candle, it took her two tries.

'Darn it,' Joel said. 'I'm not going to be famous.'

'What I see in the candle isn't a wish,' she said. 'It's what's going to happen.'

All I could see was that Grace was giving way too much attention to my little brother. 'Now it's time for my present,' I said.

'There's more?' she asked.

'Yeah.' I climbed halfway outside the door and pulled in the box. It wasn't wrapped, but I had folded its paper bag round it.

'It's really big,' Joel said proudly.

'It sure is,' Grace said.

'Yeah. I didn't have a chance to wrap it.' I pushed the box her way. 'You take it out.'

She lifted the box from the bag and set it on the ground for all of us to admire. It was a General Electric-brand electric space heater capable of 2,500 BTUs of heating power.

'This is for me?'

'Yeah. That should keep it plenty warm in here.'

'Omigosh!' She was clearly more impressed with my gift than she was with Joel's dumb baseball card. 'You bought that for me?'

'Yeah. Let's try it.' I opened the box and pulled out the heater. It was about two feet wide, two feet high, and the beige colour of surgical cabinets with a chrome mesh face. I set it in the corner, unplugged the nightlight, then plugged in the heater, turning the dial all the way to HIGH. There was the whirring of an internal fan, then the coiled metal filaments began glowing red, followed by a rush of heat. For the first time that winter, the den became comfortably warm.

'That is *awesome*,' Joel said.

Grace said, 'I'm so happy. I'm going to take my coat off!'

Her pleasure pleased me. 'It works good,' I said. Joel and I took off our coats too.

I looked over at her, and she was looking at me with that look again. The one that made me feel funny inside.

'You shouldn't have,' she said, which was what my mother always said to my father on birthdays. 'That must have cost a fortune.'

I nodded. 'Pretty much.'

'I don't know what to say. You are the best man in the whole world.' Tears welled up in her eyes as she smiled at me.

Joel looked back and forth between us. 'Can we eat the cake?'

'Sure,' she said.

I retrieved the cake knife from my coat and cut three large servings. It was an incredibly perfect moment. I had the admiration of a beautiful girl *and* chocolate cake. I had never before had the former, rarely the latter, and never simultaneously.

'Ah,' Grace sighed with pleasure. 'This is *so* delicious.'

Joel had frosting all round his mouth. 'Yeah, this is the best cake ever.'

'There's plenty,' I said, feeling even more magnanimous than before.

'We need milk,' Joel said.

'I have milk,' Grace said. She crawled out and brought back the milk we'd packed in the snow. Grace poured the milk in the tin cup, which we passed round, and then we all had seconds of the cake. Nothing had ever tasted that good to me before.

'Hey,' said Joel. 'What has two humps and lives at the North Pole?'

'I give up,' Grace said.

'A lost camel.'

It wasn't much of a joke, but for three kids high on chocolate cake, it was like the atom bomb of jokes. Grace laughed so hard that milk shot out of her nose, which made us laugh even harder.

This launched a competition as we each tried to better the last joke. We were laughing so hard that we were crying, and Grace kept saying, 'I'm going to wet my pants.' That night, the den was the best and happiest place on the entire planet.

Finally we ran out of jokes, and our laughter faded. 'We better go before Mom and Dad get home,' Joel said. Grace and I just looked at each other. 'Well, I'm going,' he finally said. He crawled out.

'Thanks for coming, Joel,' Grace called after him. 'And for the nice gift.'

'I better go too,' I said.

'Wait.' Grace put her hands on my cheeks. 'Thank you, Eric.' Then she kissed me on the mouth. Not a short peck like one from my mom or Aunt Geniel, but a real kiss that lasted more than ten seconds.

It was the first time that I had ever been romantically kissed. It was even better than the chocolate cake. When we finished kissing, we just looked at each other. I probably looked dizzy. She just looked happy. 'This was the best birthday I've ever had,' she said.

'Me, too,' I said. She laughed and it was soft and sweet like a wind chime. I think she was pleased to have so disorientated me.

'See you tomorrow.'

I got down on all fours to crawl out. 'Bye.'

'Good night.'

Joel was still waiting for me outside the door. When we'd taken a few steps, he asked, 'How much was that thing you got her?'

'Twenty-seven dollars.' I put my hands in my pocket. 'Did you see what she did?'

'What?'

'She kissed me.'

'On the mouth?'

'Yeah.'

'Whoa!'

'Yeah,' I said. 'Whoa.'

He looked down as our boots left deep impressions in the snow. 'Was it worth twenty-seven dollars?'

I smiled. 'Sure was.'

Six

T he following Monday started out badly and deteriorated so rapidly that I really shouldn't have been surprised that the day ended with the threat of total global annihilation.

Between first and second period, the hoods locked me in my locker. I was in there for nearly twenty minutes before a passing janitor let me out.

Then as I went into class, my maths teacher stopped abruptly in the middle of his lecture and told the whole class to turn and look at me. He said that since I had disrupted the entire class with my tardiness, I owed them all an apology and an explanation of why I was late, which, of course, proved to be of great amusement to my fellow students.

Never believe things can't get worse. At lunch I slipped on a slick of water in front of the whole cafeteria. My tray flew up in the air, and I ended up wearing most of my lunch. As was customary at Granite Junior High, everyone applauded. Not only did I get humiliated, but I didn't have anything to eat either.

When I got home from school, my mother was waiting to take Joel and me to the dentist, who discovered three cavities in my molars, which prompted a ten-minute lecture on proper dental hygiene. We got home just in time for me to hop on my bike and ride to work.

WHEN THE UNIVERSE has conspired to create the perfect, crappy day, it is only reasonable that I would be scheduled to work with Dean.

Around ten o'clock, a wino stumbled in, which was a fairly common occurrence. They usually just asked for a glass of water, grabbed a handful of soda crackers, then asked if we had any extra food lying around. Mr Dick had made it very clear that we would be fired if we gave food to 'hobos and other vagabonds'.

This man didn't ask for anything. He was holding a brown bottle and staggering a little. I suppose he just wanted an audience. Dean and I had started closing. I was in the front wiping down the counters while Dean mopped.

'Hey, buddy. You hear the news?' he said, a broad smile revealing gaps where his teeth were missing.

'What news?' Dean asked without looking up.

'This is the end.'

'The end of what?'

'Everything!' He began laughing as he stumbled back out the door.

'Bum,' Dean said.

TWENTY MINUTES LATER, Dean, still mopping, said, 'Hey, doesn't that scuzzbucket out there belong to you?'

I looked out. To my embarrassment, the Bee was in the parking lot. I walked to the door, wondering what it was doing here.

'Better tell your mom to move it. Dick told us to throw away all the rubbish in the parking lot.'

'Shut up,' I said.

My mother had climbed out of the van and was walking towards me. I unlocked the door and opened it, preferring to meet her away from Dean. She wore a grim expression. 'You need to come home.'

'I can't. We're not done yet.'

'It doesn't matter; you need to come home. Now. Have you heard the news?'

I shook my head.

'I'll tell you when we get home. Is there anyone else here?'

'Dean.'

She stepped inside. 'Dean, I'm Eric's mother. I'm taking Eric home with me. You need to go home too.'

Dean just held the mop handle and stared, not sure what to make of her. 'We're not done. We'll get in trouble if we don't finish.'

'Trust me, it doesn't matter. Just get home as soon as you can.'

'What's happening, Mom?'

'Just come.' I followed her out to the Bee. She wasn't crying, but she was close. We put my bike inside the van. On the way home, she said, 'I love you, Eric.' Something about the way she said it frightened me.

When we got home, Joel was still up. Joel was *never* up past 8:30. He was sitting in the living room across from my father. Obviously whatever was happening was really bad. I was even more afraid.

My mother sat down between Joel and me. My dad began talking. 'Tonight, President Kennedy said on the television that the Russians have been sending atom bombs to Cuba. The Navy has been ordered to stop all Russian ships sailing to Cuba. What this means is, there could be a war.'

I looked back and forth between my parents. 'You mean with atom bombs?' I asked.

My dad nodded. 'It looks like it.'

Like all kids of our generation, we knew about atom bombs. In school we watched black-and-white films of mushroom clouds and nuclear winds and pictures of smiling adults walking quickly and in an orderly fashion to fallout shelters. We had been religiously schooled in bomb drills, climbing under atom-bomb-resistant desks with our hands laced securely over the back of our necks. The possibility of a nuclear holocaust was just something we carried around in the back of our minds, like an overdue library book.

'We're going to have a family prayer, then I want you to go to bed,' my dad said.

'Can I sleep with you?' Joel asked my mother.

'Of course.' She looked at me. 'Eric?'

'I'm OK,' I said.

We knelt down and prayed. Afterwards, my mother reminded us to brush our teeth, which, under the circumstances, seemed absurd but, in a way, hopeful. We hugged, then I brushed my teeth and went to my room alone. I turned off the light and crawled into bed, waiting for my parents to go to bed so I could tell Grace. My mother came in and sat on the side of my bed. 'Are you afraid?'

'Yeah, a little.'

She leaned over and kissed me. 'President Kennedy will take care of us,' she said. 'He has children too.'

As soon as my mother left and I heard her door shut, I went to the bedroom window and climbed out. I ran to the den and knocked on the wall. 'Grace.'

She turned on the light as I climbed in. 'What's wrong?'

'It's really bad,' I said. 'President Kennedy said on TV that the Russians have atom bombs in Cuba. There might be a nuclear war.'

She stared at me. 'Is that for real?'

'Yeah. My mom and dad told us, and they looked really scared. Here, you can hear for yourself.' I turned on the radio. At first there was just a blast of static. I ran my finger over the plastic knob until I heard talking. A couple of men sombrely discussed President Kennedy's address. As they spoke, Grace looked more and more afraid. I turned it off. We were both quiet for some time. Finally she said what we were both thinking.

'I don't want to die.'

'Me neither.'

'It's so unfair. We didn't do anything. We're just kids, and we might die because of something we have nothing to do with.'

We were both quiet again, and the only noise came from the heater.

'I don't think we're going to die,' I said. I didn't sound very convincing. I wondered if it had been such a good idea to tell her. Maybe it would be better if none of us knew.

'If we do die tonight,' she said, 'I don't want to be alone.' She looked so frightened and vulnerable. 'Will you hold me?'

I put my arms round her, and she laid her head on my shoulder. After five minutes or so, I turned off the light. The glow of the heater bathed the room in amber radiance. We lay back on her mattress and I held her until she fell asleep.

In the middle of the night, I woke to her talking in her sleep. She was crying, 'Please don't. I don't like that. That hurts.' Tears were streaming down her face.

I gently shook her awake. 'Grace, it's OK. You're dreaming.'

She stopped and opened her eyes and for the longest while just looked at me. Then she snuggled her head into my chest and went back to sleep.

I don't know how long it was that I just looked at her. She was so beautiful. I gently stroked the hair back from her forehead. Then I kissed her and pulled her into me as I fell back asleep.

I WOKE BEFORE Grace did. The dawn light was stealing through the cracks round the den door. It was another half hour before Grace's eyes fluttered and opened. She looked at me, then brushed her hair from her face. 'We're still here,' she said.

'Yep.' Then I realised we were still here. 'What if my mother's looking for me? She'll *kill* me.'

Grace lay her head back on my chest. 'Just tell her the truth.'

'Are you crazy?'

'Not about me. Just tell her you slept in the den because you thought it might be safer. No mother would ever get mad at her kid for that.'

I don't know how Grace knew these things, but I figured she was right. She usually was. I kissed her on the forehead.

Joel was in the bedroom getting dressed when I climbed back in through the window. 'You been out back?'

'Yeah. Are Mom and Dad up?'

'Mom is.'

I walked out to the kitchen. I soon learned that the crisis wasn't over. That morning, Khrushchev had a message for President Kennedy. It was printed in large type in the morning newspaper:

I HOPE THAT THE UNITED STATES GOVERNMENT WILL DISPLAY WISDOM AND RENOUNCE THE ACTIONS PURSUED BY YOU, WHICH MAY LEAD TO CATASTROPHIC CONSEQUENCES FOR WORLD PEACE.

With the fate of humanity lying in the balance, we went to school. Maybe half the kids stayed home; even some of the teachers didn't come. I suppose Joel and I went to school just because we had to do something. My mom still had to work. In fact, the store was even busier than usual, because people were stocking up on staples.

That night, Grace, Joel, and I listened to the radio and played Chinese chequers in the den.

TWO DAYS AFTER Kennedy announced the blockade, two Soviet ships, flanked by a nuclear submarine, had moved within a few miles of the US flotilla. It was a global game of chicken, with the whole world watching and wondering who would turn first.

By that afternoon, no Soviet ships had crossed the blockade, but twenty-three missile sites in Cuba had become fully operational. An American U2 plane was shot down over Cuba and the pilot was killed. Fidel Castro seemed to be the loudest and brashest of the leaders involved in the conflict; not surprising since he held the littlest stick. The Soviets were eerily quiet.

Every time we heard a plane, we looked up and hoped that it had wings.

THE NEXT DAYS passed in a kind of surreal slow motion. Suddenly, everyone was an expert on nuclear armaments. People talked openly and knowledgeably about isotopes, point zero, radioactive fallout, and, in general, death.

America had about nine times as many bombs and missile warheads as the USSR: 27,000 to 3,000—enough bombs to kill the Russians thirty times over. The Soviet Union only had enough nuclear missiles to kill us all just once, which, frankly, wasn't very comforting. The Soviet missiles weren't as accurate as ours, so to compensate for this, they had created bigger bombs like the Czar, a fifty-megaton monster that would swallow entire cities, the largest nuclear weapon ever exploded.

The one thing on everyone's mind was whether this would be their last day alive. I suppose that's not necessarily a bad thing. For once we didn't worry much about the unimportant things—just family, friends, and God. And Grace.

On Friday night I asked Grace if she wanted to go home. Her eyes filled, but she replied, 'No.'

THEY SAY THERE are no atheists in foxholes. On Sunday, six days into the crisis, Americans flocked to churches. While our country was praying, President Kennedy and UN secretary-general U Thant reached an agreement with the Soviets. Khrushchev agreed to dismantle the missiles in Cuba in exchange for a no-invasion agreement and a secret removal of the Jupiter and Thor missiles in Turkey. The news flooded the airwaves, and the world breathed a collective sigh of relief.

People celebrate in different ways. Some people lit firecrackers. Others honked their horns or clanged pans. Up and down our street, there was no sign of life. It's probably the one place on the planet that an atom-bomb blast might have gone unnoticed.

Seven

As intense as the last days had been, it was surprising how quickly everything returned to normal. It was like a near-miss at a road junction; everyone just keeps on driving.

As I was walking to my art lesson, the principal's voice blared over the school's PA system. 'Attention, teachers and students, your attention, please. This is Principal Allen. We have a missing student. If you know anything concerning the whereabouts of Madeline Webb or have seen her in the last two weeks, please report immediately to my office. Thank you.'

Principal Allen's voice echoing down the hallways sent shivers through me. I felt as though I was wearing a T-shirt that said, I KNOW WHERE SHE IS. I avoided any eye contact as I made my way to my next class.

As soon as I got home, I went straight to the den. Grace had been painting watercolour pictures of flowers. I had no idea where she had acquired the painting supplies, but I didn't ask.

'Everyone at school's looking for you,' I blurted out. 'Principal Allen made an announcement.'

'You didn't tell anyone where I was, did you?'

'No.'

'Then what's the problem?'

'What if someone finds out?'

'How will they find out? I'm in a den in a field behind your house.'

'But what if they do?'

'It's no worse than if I go back.'

'But, if they find you . . .'

She looked at me with sudden understanding. 'Are you afraid for me or for you?'

I hesitated. 'Both.'

'Well, you don't have to worry about me. I can handle me.'

The conversation wasn't going the way I had hoped. 'The question is,' I said, failing to conceal my exasperation, 'when are you going back to school?'

She looked at me as if I was stupid. 'Never. If I go back, my parents will find me.'

'But you can't just skip school.'

'Why not?'

I had never questioned this before. 'Kids go to school. It's what they do.'

'Why?'

'To learn things.'

'Why? So we can learn how to make atom bombs and kill ourselves faster?'

'No. So we can improve our lives.'

'Right,' Grace said sardonically. 'My mom graduated from college and it didn't do her any good. In fact, I think school makes you dumber.'

As a three-year recipient of the perfect attendance award, I took offence at this. 'How could learning things make you dumber?' I said. 'That's just stupid.'

'I didn't say "learning"; I said "school". School makes people lazy. They stop thinking things out for themselves and just plug in the facts other people want them to think.'

'Like what?'

'How about what really happened to the Indians?'

I didn't know how to respond, since, frankly, I wasn't actually sure what had happened to them. 'We need school to learn socialising skills.'

'What *socialising skills* has school taught you?'

She had a point. The only social lesson I had learned at Granite was that big dogs eat small dogs, a particularly disturbing lesson when you're a small dog.

'You're just parroting the Establishment,' Grace said. 'They can tell you anything and you'll just believe it.'

'Give me one example,' I said.

'OK. In Christopher Columbus's time, why were people afraid to sail?'

'Everyone knows that,' I said. 'It's because they thought the world was flat.'

'You're sure of that?'

Her saying that made me not so sure. 'Yeah . . .'

'Guess what year the first globe was invented?'

'I have no idea.'

'Fourteen ninety-two. It was the same year Columbus sailed. If they thought the world was flat, why were they making globes?'

'You just made that up.'

She shook her head. 'No, I didn't.'

I couldn't tell if she was making this up or if she really was a lot smarter than me. The latter seemed likely. Either way, I was losing the argument. 'What does Christopher Columbus have to do with you living in my den the rest of your life?'

She looked at me, stunned. 'Fine,' she said between clenched teeth, then began grabbing her things and shoving them in her bag. 'You want me to go? I'll go.'

'I didn't mean that.'

'Yes, you did.'

Even though she was turned from me, I saw her furtively wipe a tear from her cheek. I touched her shoulder. 'Grace . . .'

She pulled away from me. 'Don't touch me.'

'Please, stop.'

'No.'

I grabbed her arm. 'Grace. I never want you to leave. You're the only good thing in my life.'

She stopped, then turned back and looked at me. Her face was streaked with tears. 'You mean that?'

'Yes.'

She brushed her cheeks with the back of her hand. We just sat there looking at each other, then she leaned forward and kissed me for the second time. It made me feel better.

'I better go,' I said. 'I have to go to work.'

'Every time I kiss you, you say you have to go. Should I not kiss you?'

'No.'

'No, I shouldn't kiss you, or no, I shouldn't *not* kiss you?'

I was thoroughly confused. 'You should kiss me.'

'Are you sure?'

'Yeah. I just haven't done a lot of it. I'm probably not very good at it.'

Her eyebrows raised. 'No, you're a pretty good kisser.'

'Really?' I felt myself blushing.

'Really.' She smiled. 'Have you ever had a girlfriend before?'

'I had a crush on a girl last year.'

'What happened?'

'Nothing. I never told her I liked her.'

'You're kind of afraid of girls, aren't you?'

I felt stupid. 'Maybe a little.'

'I think that's sweet.' She took my hand. 'Do you want to be my boyfriend?'

I kept looking at her, waiting for the punch line. 'What exactly does that entail?'

'Well, for one thing, you can't have any other girlfriends.'

Fat chance of that, I thought. 'That's no problem. Anything else?'

'You can kiss me anytime you want.'

'Are you serious?' I asked, barely concealing my excitement.

She laughed. 'Yes.'

I couldn't believe it. I felt like I'd just been given a key to an ice-cream parlour. 'Like, I could kiss you right now?'

'Yes.'

I just stared at her.

'So?' she said. 'Are you going to kiss me?'

'Oh. Yeah.' I slowly moved forwards to put my lips on hers. Even though we'd already kissed twice, up to this point she'd pretty much done the heavy lifting. This was a first for me. I was as awkward as a nurse giving her first injection.

'You're not going to hurt me,' she said.

Our lips touched, and she closed her eyes. It was incredible. It was like Christmas, my birthday, and scones for dinner all rolled into one. When we finally parted, there were big smiles on both of our faces.

'See, you are good at it,' she said.

'Yeah,' I replied, slightly breathless. 'Let's do it again sometime.'

She laughed. 'Sure—that is, unless you still want me to leave.'

'I never want you to leave,' I said. 'You should never leave.'

'Then,' she said coyly, 'I shouldn't go back to school?'

'School makes you dumb,' I said.

She grinned. 'You better go. You have work.'

'Right. I'll see you after.'

She cocked her head. 'Bye, Eric.'

'See ya later.'

For the first time in my life, I was smitten, dashed on the rocks of femininity. I had just been given permission to kiss the most beautiful girl in the world. It was better than winning the lottery.

EVERY HALLOWEEN, my mother made an enormous cauldron of chilli, and a big batch of hot crusty rolls that Joel and I would consume smothered in butter and honey. Those were good times. Part of that tradition was my mother saying, 'Where are you boys putting all that?' and her favourite, 'You must have hollow legs.' We were never quite sure what that meant.

After dinner, my parents retired to the living room for television and candy-bowl duty, while Joel and I dressed up in our Halloween costumes. Oddly enough, Halloween costumes were the one thing we had plenty of. My mother liked to sew, and back when she stayed home, she made us new costumes every year. She even once helped make costumes for a school play I was in. We saved them all.

Joel went as the Lone Ranger complete with mask, bandanna, a cowboy hat with a drawstring, and a cap gun. I went as the devil with a red cape, a long tail and horns. We had a pitchfork too, but even though it looked cool, I wasn't about to lug that round all night.

After we were dressed, we went out back, taking chilli and rolls for Grace, as well as a costume we thought might fit her. She devoured the chilli and rolls as happily as we had. Then she tried on the costume, a clown outfit my mother once wore. It was a little big on her, but no one would notice. That's kind of the point with clown costumes.

She put on a red, foam rubber nose and a bright orange wig, and she lined her mouth with a wide slash of lipstick. She decided to be a sad clown, so she drew tears on her cheek with eyeliner. By the time she'd finished, I couldn't have picked her out of a police line-up.

'You really can't tell who I am?' she asked.

'Nope,' said Joel.

I shook my head. 'Your own mother wouldn't recognise you.'

It was hard to tell with all the make-up, but I think she frowned when I said that.

WE DECIDED THAT we would go for an all-time candy harvest record. With ambitions as high as ours, we'd have to go some distance to find fertile ground—someplace far away from our poor, stingy street. Grace said, 'I know the perfect place. But we'll have to take the bus to get there.'

Joel and I were open to going any place that promised more candy. The bus ride was only fifteen minutes long, and our destination turned out to be as fruitful as Grace promised. It was a crowded suburb of small, tidy homes built close together, just ripe for the picking. There were scores of children out and the streets looked like an elementary school Halloween parade.

The three of us swept the streets with remarkable efficiency. For the first two hours, we rarely even had to say 'trick or treat', as invariably someone would already be at the door dispensing candy to another group of children.

As evening fell, the crowds started to thin, and by ten o'clock, most of the little kids had gone home to bed. We continued to add to our haul, carrying bulging pillowcases over our shoulders like Santa Claus. Although it was a reasonably warm night, relatively speaking, we still had to wear coats over our costumes.

We had worked our way over by my school when Grace led us down a small, dead-end street with pumpkins smashed in the middle of the road. The houses were smaller than the homes on the other streets we'd been to and not as well cared for. A couple of the homes had dilapidated cars parked in front, with flat tyres or wheels missing altogether.

'This doesn't look like a good street,' Joel said. 'Let's go down a different one.'

'I second that,' I said.

Grace continued on as if she hadn't heard us. She walked past several homes, then stopped at the edge of the front lawn of a small bungalow. The home was pretty much the same size and construction as the other houses on the street, but it was in even worse shape. The grass was engulfed by orange-berried firethorn bushes that also spilled over and poked through the front and side chain-link fence. One of the windows was broken and was covered with a sheet of plywood held in place with duct tape. There was a motorcycle and an old red Ford pick-up truck in the driveway as well as another pick-up that was up on blocks.

Grace just stared at the house. The curtains over the picture window were drawn, but a light was on, and I could see the silhouette of a woman moving around inside.

'Do you know who lives here?' I asked.

She turned to me with a peculiar look in her eyes. 'This was my house.'

My heart raced. 'You shouldn't be here.'

She just turned back and looked at the house. 'Would you ring the doorbell? Please.'

I glanced back at the house, then again at her. 'Are you sure?'

'I want to see my mother.'

Joel stood next to me silently, staring at the house. I could tell he was afraid. I suppose I was too. I took a deep breath. 'All right. Come on, Joel.'

We went to the front gate and opened it, then marched up the path. There were no pumpkins or Halloween decorations, but I didn't think the house needed them. It was kind of scary already.

'Trick or treat,' I yelled. Joel said it too, but almost inaudibly.

After another minute, I went to ring the doorbell, but it was covered over by duct tape on which was written *Doesn't work*. I knocked instead. I was glad when no one came and was ready to go, when I heard footsteps. The door opened. A balding man stood in the doorway. He was taller than my dad and had a large belly. He wore a white sweat-stained sleeveless T-shirt, and his trousers were secured by braces. He held an open can of beer.

'Trick or treat,' I said.

He looked me over. 'Well, if it ain't Scratch himself.' He looked at Joel. 'Who are you, Howdy Doody?'

'I'm the Lone Ranger,' Joel said.

He looked back at me. 'Guess that makes you Tonto, sweetie.' He punctuated his remark with a swig from his can. Even if I hadn't already known who he was, I wouldn't have liked him. He looked out across the front lawn where Grace had been. I panicked.

'Are you going to give us candy or not?'

He looked back at me. 'Oh, a smart aleck. Show me a trick first. That's the deal, ain't it? No trick, no candy.'

I heard a woman's voice. 'Quit giving them a hard time, Stan.'

He looked at me. 'You think *you're* the devil?' He laughed. 'Here's a trick for you. Get on all fours and bark like a dog. Go on.'

I turned. 'C'mon, Joel, let's go.'

'Oh, don't like that, huh?'

We walked away.

'What a couple of Marys,' he yelled after us. He laughed, then slammed the door.

'I told you this was a bad street,' Joel said.

When we reached the pavement, Grace was gone.

'Where'd she go?' Joel asked.

'I don't know.' I was sure she'd be waiting for us. When we got near the end of the block, we found her sitting on the kerb behind a rubbish bin. She was sobbing so hard she could hardly catch her breath. I knelt down next to her. 'You OK?'

It was a while before she could speak. 'Let's go home, please.'

I helped her to her feet and we all walked five blocks to a bus stop. 'Was that your stepfather?' I asked.

She didn't answer.

'We didn't like him either.'

Grace didn't say anything else all night. She didn't even want her candy.

Eight

Another Monday at the Queen. I was standing up front at the till when a woman about my mother's age walked in. She had a bouffant hairdo that looked like it was a yard high and pretty eyes that matched her blue topaz necklace. In one hand she held a rolled-up poster.

'May I help you?' I asked.

She said with a slight Southern accent, 'I would like to speak with your manager.'

'Our assistant manager's here,' I said. 'I'll get him.' I walked to the back where Gary was checking receipts. 'Gary, there's a woman up front asking for you.'

'Tell her I'll be just a minute.'

I walked back out. 'He'll be right with you.'

'Thank you.'

The woman slowly paced round the lobby until Gary arrived. From the way he looked at her, it was obvious he liked what he saw.

'Can I help you?'

She recognised his interest, and her voice became honey-sweet. 'I sure hope so. I'm Cindy.' She extended her hand. 'It's a pleasure to meet you.'

Gary reached out, eager to take her hand. 'Pleasure's all mine,' he said, wide-eyed.

'So you're the man in charge here?' She was working him like a rented mule.

'Yes, I am.'

'I'm from the Granite PTA. You've probably already heard that one of our students is missing. Would it be permissible to hang a poster in *your* establishment?'

Gary just stared at her. I could guess at the battle going on in his head between a request from a pretty lady and the grief Mr Dick would give him.

The blue eyes won out. 'Uh, sure, miss. Just put it on that wall above the newspapers.'

'Thank you kindly.'

As she walked to the wall, Gary leaned over to me. 'If Mr Dick asks, I didn't know about this.'

'Sure,' I said. *What a pansy.*

The woman took out a sticky tape dispenser and set it on a table. Then she unrolled the poster. Below a black-and-white image of Grace, it read in thick block letters:

MISSING
MADELINE WEBB
SIXTEEN YEARS OLD
Last seen at Granite Jr High
If you have information regarding her whereabouts,
please contact the police.

It seemed to me an eternity before the woman had the thing hung. When she finally got all four corners taped up, she walked out with Gary's gaze following her every step of the way. After she drove off, he walked out from behind the counter and looked at the poster.

'What school do you go to?' he asked.

'Granite Junior.'

'Do you know that girl?'

'I had a class with her.'

He shook his head. 'Her poor parents must be crazy with worry.'

'Mr Dick will probably go bananas when he sees that,' I said.

'Probably.'

'Maybe I should take it down.'

Maybe it was the lingering memory of those eyes, but to my surprise, Gary chose that moment to grow a backbone. 'No. We should leave it up. It's the right thing to do.'

DEAN CAME INTO work about an hour later. I hoped he wouldn't see the poster, but, of course, it was the first thing he noticed.

'Hey, corndog, you see that poster out there? That girl looks just like the paper shaker you brought in.'

'No, she doesn't.'

'It looks *exactly* like her. What did you do, kidnap her?'

'My friend's name is Grace. Not Madeline.'

This stumped him. 'Well, you have to admit she looks like her.'

'No, I don't,' I said.

'You're such a ditz,' Dean said, and he went to get an overall.

That night I closed up with Jackie. While she was mopping up the back, I went out front and took down the poster. I rolled it up and hid it until Jackie left. Then I put it in my coat and rode home to show Grace.

'I FEEL LIKE a criminal,' Grace said, staring at the poster. 'I wonder who told the PTA.'

'Probably your parents.'

'My mom might. Stan wouldn't. He's glad I'm gone.'

I looked at her. 'What if he's not? I mean, maybe you got him wrong.'

She looked at me, and there was darkness in her eyes. 'No, I didn't get him wrong.'

The next morning, Joel and I were eating our porridge when my father hobbled into the kitchen and sat down at the table. My mother handed him a cup of his special roasted barley stuff, then left the kitchen to get ready for work. Dad poured some milk into his cup and stirred until his drink turned the pale colour of caramel.

Then he casually began sifting through the stack of mail on the table.

When he got to the electric bill, he stared at it almost as intently as Joel had stared at the pin-up poster the first time he saw it. 'Holy cow.'

Joel and I looked over at him.

'Our electric bill went up nearly ten dollars. You boys need to start turning the lights off. You think money grows on trees?'

'No, sir,' I said.

'Joel?'

'No, sir.' Joel turned and glared at me.

My father pushed aside the mail and started reading the paper. After a few minutes, he looked up. 'Here's something for you, Eric. Do you know a girl named Madeline Webb?'

I looked up at him. 'No, sir.'

'Hmm,' he said. 'It says here she goes to Granite Junior. You're in ninth grade, aren't you?'

'Yes, sir.'

'You sure you don't know her? She's in your grade.'

I shrugged.

'Look, here's a picture of the girl.' He turned the paper round to show me. It must have been an old picture of Grace. Her hair was shorter now, and she'd gained some weight.

'Oh, her. She's in one of my classes.'

He turned the paper back round. 'This article says her parents think she's been kidnapped.'

'Why would they think that? I mean, maybe she ran away or something.'

He looked over at me. 'If she ran away, she would have left a note or packed a bag.'

I ate a couple more mouthfuls while my dad moved on to the sports section. 'Tex Clevenger retired from the Yankees. Might as well go out on top. Joel, don't you have his card?'

'Yes, sir.'

When I finished breakfast I asked, 'Could I take that page?'

Without looking up, my father asked, 'Which page?'

'The one with the article about the girl at my school.'

He handed me the local section.

'Excuse me,' I said. I carried my bowl and the newspaper over to the sink. As I rinsed out my bowl, Joel joined me.

'Thanks for getting us in trouble,' he said.

'You don't know it's the heater. Besides, she'd freeze to death without it.'

'Yeah, and now she's in the paper. Someone's going to find her, and we'll be dead.'

'No one's going to find her, and I'm the one who's dead, not you.' I rolled up the paper. 'I'm going to show her the article.'

I said goodbye to my parents, grabbed my schoolbag, and went out of the front door. But once outside, I doubled back and ran to the den. As I opened the door, I could hear music coming from my transistor radio. *'She-e-e-e-e-ry babe-e-e- . . .'*

I crawled inside, a little winded from running. 'Grace.'

She raised her hand. 'Wait, I love this song. It's The Four Seasons.'

I waited for the song to end. *'Come, come, come out tonight . . .'*

When it was over, she turned to me. 'OK, what?'

'You're in the newspaper.' I unfolded the paper and read, "Middle school student missing. Madeline Grace Webb, daughter of Stan and Holly Webb, has been missing since October eleventh.'"

'Let me see.'

I handed her the paper.

After she finished reading the article, she dropped it on the floor. 'I hate that picture of me.'

'There's a lot of people looking for you.'

She did her best Cagney imitation. 'They'll never take me alive . . .'

I picked up the paper. 'I'm glad you think it's funny.'

'Stop worrying so much. Everything will work out.'

'How do you know that?'

'I saw it in the candle.'

I had no rebuttal to that. 'OK, I'm off to school.'

'Say hi to everyone for me.'

I turned back.

'Just kidding.'

As I walked to the bus-stop, all I could think about was how I hoped the candle was right.

'I'M KIND of like Anne Frank,' Grace said as I crawled through the den door when I got home. She was sitting in the corner holding a small, yellow vinyl book with a locking strap.

I nodded as if I understood. 'Does she go to Granite?'

Grace laughed. 'She was a Jewish girl who hid from the Nazis during the Second World War. Didn't you read the book?'

'No.' I had never heard of it.

'They were going to send her family to one of those death camps, so they hid in the back of a building. She kept a diary the whole time. Just like me.'

'You keep a diary?'

'Every day.' She held up the yellow book.

'What do you write in it?'

'Whatever I feel like writing. Things I did. People I talked to. Stuff like that.'

'Am I in there?'

'Of course. You're all over the place.'

'Can I see?'

She looked incredulous. 'No. You don't just show someone your *diary*.'

'Then who do you write it for?'

'Yourself.'

'That's dumb. You already know everything that happened to you. It's like telling yourself a secret.'

'And people can read it after you die.'

'What good is that?'

She frowned. 'Maybe it will give someone hope.'

I guess I was just too selfish to think of that.

As I LOOK BACK, I realise just how much things have changed since those days. America was a different place. More private. Children were considered the property of their parents, and what happened in someone's home was no one's business but theirs—not the school's, not the neighbours', not the church's, and especially not City Hall's.

While we lived at my grandmother's house, there was a family across the creek from us. The Williamses. They had, I think, twelve or thirteen kids.

These kids, singularly and collectively, were meaner than wolverines. It seemed that at least one of them got in a fight at school every day, often with each other. Teachers at Granite used to say, 'Someone needs to discipline those children,' but I don't think that was the problem. Their dad taught Sunday school at our church. His pet sermon was that if you spared the rod, you would spoil the child, as if anyone wanted his advice on child rearing.

I think Mr Williams spoiled his children with the rod or belt or whatever else he could get his hands on when the spirit moved him. The Williams children would come to school with more bruises than a two-week-old banana. I figured their fights at school were just their way of making everyone else look, if not feel, like them.

The only time my father ever beat me was when I was eleven years old, and we were still living in California. One summer, my mother's cousin from Phoenix came to stay with us. She had two of the most obnoxious boys I'd ever met. Our parents were visiting and so they told us to go outside and play. Joel and I took them out to play in the driveway. They shoved and pushed a lot. Then one of them tripped Joel on purpose. Joel hit the concrete and skinned up his knees and palms badly enough to draw blood. Joel was only seven at the time and he started to cry. I was already mad at the boys for tripping Joel, but then they started teasing him for crying. Before I knew it, I punched the older of the boys right in the nose. He let out a yelp as blood ran from both his nostrils.

'You're gonna get it,' his little brother said. 'We're gonna tell.' Then the two of them scurried inside to tattle.

Two minutes later, Mom stormed out of the house. I assumed she would take my side when she heard the whole story. Instead she dragged me by my arm into the house. Once inside, my dad took off his belt, something I'd previously only heard about, and whipped me on the backside five times. I can still remember each stroke. Then my parents made me apologise. I don't remember who I was more mad at, the boys or my parents.

Nine

The next month passed like a dream. Grace and I had settled into a routine, almost like a married couple. With all the publicity, Grace was no longer safe walking outside in daylight. Even the library had posted a 'missing girl' poster on their front door.

The thickness of her red pouch had dwindled, and I had to start bringing her food again. I sneaked food when I could, but I was also spending much of my wages feeding her. I knew Grace felt bad about this. She apologised and thanked me, usually in the same breath. And while she wasn't eating as much as she had when she first came, she still seemed to be gaining weight.

During the day, Grace spent her time reading, listening to the radio, and writing in her journal, but mostly just waiting for me to get home from school or work.

Her routine necessitated a change in my schedule as well. On the nights

I worked, I would come straight home, tell my parents good night (if they were still awake), then slip out of my bedroom window.

We held hands and took long moonlit walks either on our street or in the surrounding neighbourhoods. We talked about things I still think about today. Grace had a wisdom about life that far surpassed mine. On one of those walks, we talked about love.

'Do your parents love each other?' she asked.

'Yeah. I think so. They still fight sometimes, but they always make up.'

She pondered my reply, then asked, 'Have you ever been in love?'

'I don't know,' I said softly. 'How do you really know when you're in love?'

She stopped walking and smiled at me. 'When you don't have to ask.'

ONE EVENING, we walked about a mile to a small park just east of Seventh and Forty-fifth. There was no one there but us. The trees were barren and the ground covered with snow. We sat on a bench, and Grace lay her head in my lap, looking up at the stars.

'What am I going to do?' she asked.

I honestly had no idea. 'Where's your *real* father? Won't he help?'

'I don't know who he is. He was gone before I was born.'

'Do you have any other family?'

'I have an aunt in Denver. But my mom got in a big fight with her.'

'About what?'

'I don't know. My mom just said my aunt's awful, and she'll never talk to her again as long as she lives.'

I ran my fingers through her hair. 'Maybe you'll have to go back,' I said.

She just closed her eyes. I knew she never would.

I DON'T REMEMBER everything. Like most memories, the good times fade while the hard times remain sharply chiselled on the tablets of our hearts. One of those times was the day before Thanksgiving when Grace fell ill.

I had just got home from school and went back to the den to find the light off. The heater was on high, bathing the room in bright orange light. The den felt like a sauna.

'Grace?'

She moaned softly.

I crawled to her side. 'Are you OK?'

'I don't feel well.' Her speech was slurred.

'Are you being sick again?'

She shook her head. 'This is something different.'

I leaned over and felt her forehead with my cheek like my mother always did when I was ill. 'You're really hot.'

'My chest hurts. I think I have pneumonia.'

The word scared me. In California, one of our neighbours died of pneumonia. 'You're going to have to see a doctor.'

'I can't.'

'But pneumonia's *serious*. You could die.'

'He'll just give me pills. Do you have any pills?'

'What kind of pills?'

'Penicillin. Penicillin cures everything.'

'Maybe my dad has some. He has all sorts of pills. I'll go see.'

I ran back to the house and went to my parents' bathroom. Rooting through their medicine chest, I found an amber bottle with penicillin. I pulled off the cap. There were only two pills inside. I was pretty sure she'd need a lot more than that. I took the pills and a damp flannel out to her.

'We only have two pills.' I filled the tin cup with water and helped Grace sit up. She took both pills, then lay back down. I draped the wet facecloth across her forehead. She closed her eyes and fell back to sleep.

THE NEXT DAY was Thanksgiving, and fate dealt us a winning hand. We put on our Sunday best and went to Uncle Norm's. Thanksgiving dinner was to Aunt Geniel what the Sistine Chapel was to Michelangelo. That year we enjoyed an amazing feast. There was spiced roast turkey, giblet brown gravy, mashed potatoes, candied yams, green beans, honey-glazed baby carrots, herbed apple stuffing, cranberry and orange relish, rice pudding and pumpkin pie.

While everyone was eating dessert, I went in the bathroom and looked inside their medicine cabinet; there were two full bottles of penicillin.

The labels on the bottles said to take one pill four times a day for ten days. I did the sum: four times ten was forty pills, minus the two I'd already given her. I needed thirty-eight pills.

I poured the entire contents of one of the bottles into my hand. There were twenty-four pills. I counted the pills from the other bottle. There were only nine. I was five pills short. But Grace wasn't very big, so maybe they'd be enough. I poured them all into one of the bottles and shoved it into my trouser pocket. I returned the other bottle to the cabinet, then decided that I better take the empty bottle as well. I put it in my other pocket, then returned to the table. I hated stealing from Aunt Geniel's house, but I was certain that she would give the pills to me if she knew what they were for.

We didn't leave until around eight, when my mother announced it was getting close to Joel's bedtime. Aunt Geniel loaded us down with enough leftovers that I knew Grace's share wouldn't be missed.

THAT NIGHT I TOOK Grace the pills and two large plates of food. She made a turkey sandwich with cranberry sauce. As good as the food was, she didn't have much of an appetite. She ate a little, then we both lay back together on the mattress. Holding her was my favourite thing in the whole world.

'Do you know what I'm most grateful for this Thanksgiving?' she asked.

I had no idea. 'What?'

'You.'

I smiled. 'I'm grateful for you too.'

We just lay in happy silence. After a few minutes, she rolled over to look at me. 'So I've been thinking. Do you believe there's a hell?'

'Sure. Doesn't everybody?'

'Well, what if this *is* hell, but we just don't know it?'

'That's crazy. Hell is like lakes of fire, and there are devils with horns and pitchforks. There's none of those around here.'

'But what if hell's not really like that?' Grace asked.

'Everyone says it's that way,' I said.

'I don't think Jesus ever talked about fire and brimstone.'

'Then why do they teach us that at church?'

'To scare us.'

'Why would they want to scare us?'

'I don't know. I just don't think God wants us to do good things because we're scared. I think he wants us to do good things because we're good.'

I thought about it. 'You're talking gibberish,' I said.

She sighed. 'Yeah. Maybe I'm just sick.'

BY SATURDAY evening, Grace was feeling a lot better, and her appetite had returned. After my parents went to bed, I raided the refrigerator and brought out a plate of cold tuna casserole. I was amazed at how quickly she devoured the food. When she was done, I asked, 'Do you want more?'

She looked embarrassed but nodded. I went back inside and filled another plate, which she downed nearly as fast. Afterwards, we held hands and went for a short walk up and down my street. When we got back, she said, 'Do you have any rubber bands?'

'A million of them.' I wasn't exaggerating by much. My father had spent years making a rubber-band ball that was now nearly as big as a softball.

'Would you get me a couple?'

'Sure. Now?'

'Please.'

I ran inside the house and returned with a dozen or so elastic bands. She looped one through the buttonhole of her trousers and secured the other end around the button. She sighed. 'These were getting too tight.'

'Maybe you shouldn't eat so much,' I offered.

She looked stricken. 'Maybe *you* shouldn't be so rude.'

I frowned. 'Sorry.'

She sighed. 'I'm sorry too. I'm just upset.'

'About what?'

She looked at me and squinted. 'Nothing. Just a girl thing.'

I nodded without understanding. She might as well be a space alien for all I knew about 'girl things'.

Ten

It was the only Monday night of the month that I'd had off. That night, our family sat round the television set. Joel and I were locked in an intense game of Chinese chequers, oblivious of the television until the newsman said, 'The hunt goes on for a missing Salt Lake girl. Madeline Grace Webb, a student at Granite Junior High, has been missing for more than sixty days. Police suspect foul play and are currently investigating several leads but are asking for your help. There's a $500 reward for any information leading to her whereabouts. You may contact the Salt Lake police directly for further information. In other news . . .'

I looked back at Joel. He was scared. Five hundred dollars was a fortune. Everyone would be looking for her.

'That's the girl from your school,' my father said.

'Yeah,' I replied, stiff with panic.

'Oh, my. They still haven't found her?' my mother said.

'Don't worry, they'll find her,' my dad said. 'Or at least the man who took her. And when they do . . .'

Joel looked at me.

'What do you think they'll do to him?' I asked.

'Who knows? The electric chair's too good for people who steal children. I'd just hate to be him.'

I felt light-headed. 'May I have an Ovaltine?' I asked.

'Sure,' my mom said.

I walked to the kitchen, then slipped out the back door, running to the den. I quickly crawled inside. 'Grace!'

Grace was curled up in the corner reading. 'Hi,' she said happily, setting her book in her lap. She saw the distress on my face. 'What's wrong?'

'You were just on the television.'

'Honest?'

'Well, not you. But they were talking about you. And they showed a picture of you.'

Grace didn't share my excitement. 'So?'

'The man on the news said that you've been kidnapped, and the police are looking all over for you. They put out a five hundred dollar reward.'

'Well, you know I wasn't kidnapped.'

'This is really serious. You were on *television*.'

She lifted her book and started reading again.

'Didn't you hear me? *Television!*'

'I heard you. I just don't care.'

'You don't care? People think you were kidnapped. Or maybe dead. This is *really* serious.'

'It's always been *really* serious.'

'You think this is fun,' I said. 'It's time you did the right thing.'

'And what is that?'

'Not worrying everyone.'

Grace wore a dark, angry expression. 'You still don't know, do you?'

'Know what?'

'Why I ran away.'

I didn't know I'd missed something. 'You said it was for kicks.'

'And you believed me?'

'Why wouldn't I?'

Grace's eyes narrowed. 'You are *so* gullible. You live in this world where you think that deep down inside everyone means well and monsters are make-believe. It's not true. People aren't all good. And there really are monsters.'

I was confused. 'Monsters? You mean like Dracula—'

'No!' She threw her book against the wall. 'You're so stupid.'

Her words stung. 'No, I'm not.'

'Don't you know why I've been throwing up and why I'm getting fatter? It's not because I'm sick or eating too much. It's because I'm pregnant!'

The word stunned me. In those days, 'pregnant' wasn't a word that even adults used casually. 'How can you be . . . ?' I choked on the word. 'You're not even married.'

She groaned. 'That's what I'm talking about. You're so naïve. Don't you even know where babies come from?'

'I know . . .' I suddenly made the connection. 'Who?'

She didn't speak for a few moments, then started to cry. She said, 'My stepfather made me.'

I stared at her in disbelief. 'Your stepfather?'

She was crying so hard I could barely understand her. 'If I'm sent back home, something really bad will happen.'

I felt sick for drawing this out of her. I felt sick for my youth and for my stupidity. And I was aching from all the mean things she had said to me. Half of me wanted to hold her; the other half wanted to run. She continued to sob.

'He's a very bad man. He told me that if I ever told anyone what he did to me, he would hurt me and my mother. He said no one would believe me anyway. And you know what? They won't. They always believe the adults.'

I tried to absorb everything she had told me. Finally I said, 'I believe you.'

'I know you do. But you believe everything everyone tells you. You're just a boy.'

This was the most hurtful of all the things she said. I looked away from her. 'I guess I am. Well, I better go.'

'Eric?'

I couldn't answer her; the lump in my throat was too big. I crawled out of the den without looking back. I heard her calling after me as I walked back to my stupid house, finally sure of exactly who I was. I could pretend all I wanted, but in the end I was still just a stupid, gullible, naïve boy.

MORNING FELL LIKE a sack of concrete. My head ached and I had a sick, tight sensation in my chest akin to panic. All the good feelings I'd had over the last weeks were gone. It was the last day of school before the Christmas break, a half-day, and something I'd looked forward to for weeks. Now I didn't care. I didn't have anything to look forward to. I told myself that I wished she was gone.

I went to the kitchen and made Grace toast with butter and put it and a banana inside a brown paper lunch bag. I walked out without my coat. I didn't knock, just opened the door and tossed the bag inside like I was feeding an animal at the zoo. 'Here.'

Grace had been waiting. She stuck her head out of the den door. 'Eric, can we talk?'

'No.' I turned.

'Please, don't go.'

I walked away.

'I'm sorry I was so mean.' She started to cry. 'Please, Eric. Talk to me.'

I kept walking until I was nearly at the edge of the garden.

She yelled after me, 'OK, I'll leave. You'll never have to see me again.' She stopped, overcome with emotion. 'But I have to say something to you. Please,' she sobbed. 'You're all I have.'

I stopped and turned back. 'What do you want?'

Grace climbed out of the den and scrambled to her feet. It was the first time in more than a month that I'd seen her outside in the daylight. I could see how much her figure had changed.

'I'm the stupid one, not you. I hate myself. I just want to tell you I'm sorry from the bottom of my heart. I'm sorry I said you were just a boy. You're not. You've been brave and kind and good. All you've done is protect me and take care of me, and that makes you more of a man than any man I've ever met.'

I didn't say anything.

'I'm so sorry. I'd rather face my stepfather than hurt you again.'

I stood looking at her, her nose wet, her eyes red and swollen. I exhaled, then spoke in a normal voice, 'Get back inside; someone might see you.'

'I don't care. You're the only one in this world I care about. If I don't have you, I don't care what happens to me anymore.'

I walked back to her. 'Don't say that.'

She shook her head. 'I mean it.' Then she said in a lower voice, 'I cut myself for you.'

'What?'

'I cut myself for you.' She lifted her arm to show me. There was a mass of blood dried to her forearm.

I gasped. 'What happened?'

'I punished myself. I wanted you to see how bad I felt.'

'That was stupid,' I said, crouching down to gather up some snow. 'Let me see that.' I rubbed the snow on her arm. It washed away the dried blood, leaving the fresh, deep cuts in her arm exposed. The wounds made me sick to my stomach. 'Don't ever do that again.'

'Will you forgive me?'

'Yes. Now get back inside.'

'Will you kiss me?'

'Yes.'

She leaned forward, and I met her halfway, pressing my lips against hers. We kissed intensely. Finally I pulled away. 'We'll make plans after school. No one's going to find you.'

'OK. Whatever you say.' She got on her knees to go back inside. 'I love you.'

'I love you, too,' I said.

I walked back to the house. My mother was standing inside the door holding a bottle of maple syrup. She looked at me with a peculiar expression. 'Were you talking to someone out there?'

I walked past her. 'No.'

SCHOOL WAS a waste of time. In English we did a crossword puzzle with Christmas themes, and in maths we used a Pascal triangle to determine the exact number of items accumulated in 'The Twelve Days of Christmas'. (The answer is 364, the only thing I remember from junior high maths.) After class was dismissed, I asked my art teacher, Miss Tioné, about van Gogh. 'Is it true he cut his ear off?'

'Yes.'

'Why did he do that?'

'Well, there are a lot of different theories. Some people think he was drunk. Some say he did it to give to his beloved. Some even think another artist did it. Why do you ask?'

'I just heard that sometimes people might hurt themselves when they feel bad.'

The room was vacant except for the two of us, and she sat down at the desk next to me. 'A few years back, I had a student who had cuts on her arm. The first time I asked her about it, she said she had a mean cat. But after a few weeks, I knew she was doing it to herself. I asked her why. She told me that it was her way of dealing with strong feelings.'

'Strong feelings?'

'Anger. Fear. Sorrow. Rejection.'

'That makes sense,' I said. 'Thank you.'

I noticed her glancing down at my arms. 'Eric, is there something you'd like to talk about?'

I looked at her, and we both knew there was. 'No, ma'am. But thank you.'

She smiled sympathetically. 'You're welcome. Have a nice Christmas.'

'Thanks.' I smiled and walked out of the room.

AFTER SCHOOL, I went straight to the Queen. Halfway through my shift, I raided the first-aid kit. I stole a bottle of iodine and a roll of white medical tape and gauze. When I got home, I took everything to the den. I laid out the tape, then opened the bottle.

'Put your arm out,' I said to Grace.

The cuts—there were six in all—were dark and scabbed, each about three to four inches in length. I poured the entire bottle of antiseptic on her arm. There was alcohol in it, and I thought she might cry out in pain, but she just grimaced. Grace was pretty tough. The iodine stained her forearm a yellowish brown. I wrapped the gauze round her arm and taped it on. We didn't talk about why she had cut herself. I think that would have been more painful than the iodine.

When I finished, she asked, 'What day is it?'

'Tuesday.'

'I mean the date.'

'December eighteenth.'

'It's just a week before Christmas.' She frowned. 'It doesn't feel like Christmas. Except for the snow.'

'That's because you don't have any decorations.' I thought about it. 'I know, we can decorate the den. There are some Christmas lights in the garage. And I know where there's a perfect tree.'

'I've always wanted to cut down a real Christmas tree,' Grace said.

'It's far enough back that no one will see you. We can do it tomorrow.'

She pressed down the gauze, then looked up into my eyes. 'I can't wait.'

JOEL AND I FORAGED through the garage for Christmas decorations. We found two boxes containing three long strings of tinsel, some red frosted glass balls, painted pine cones, a star for the tree, a wreath and three strands of Christmas lights, which we thought we'd probably need to get just one to work.

We also found a sledge and some rope to carry back our tree. We couldn't find the handsaw until Joel remembered that we'd left it in the chicken coop.

We took everything to the den. Grace squealed with delight when she saw what we'd found. We put everything inside, then the three of us started our trek to the back of our property. No one had been out there since the first snowfall, so the snow was undisturbed and high, coming up to our thighs in places. We were all winded by the time we reached the tree.

'It's perfect,' Grace said. 'I know just where to put it.'

It took the three of us half an hour to saw through the trunk. I could have done it faster myself, but everyone wanted a turn. We tied the tree onto the sledge, and the three of us lugged it back to the den.

We had no tree stand, so we just leaned it in the corner in the bucket Grace had been using as a fridge. Grace turned the radio on and found some Christmas music. Then we set about decorating the place. Bing Crosby's 'White Christmas' filled the small room as we encircled the tree with the silver garland, then hung the ornaments.

Grace picked up the wreath. 'I know where this is going,' she said. She hung it right over Betty, which was the name she'd given the pin-up girl on our pin-up poster.

To our surprise, one of the strands of lights actually worked. 'It's a Christmas miracle,' Grace said.

I could never tell if she was joking.

Eleven

That year, Christmas Eve fell on a Monday. The Queen was closed. Not because Mr Dick wanted us to be with our families but because experience had taught him that he'd most likely lose money that day if he stayed open.

I spent the morning Christmas shopping. I followed my mother's suggestion and got Joel a new baseball and some baseball cards. I bought my mother some lilac-scented perfume and a pretty jewellery box, and my father some of his favourite delicacies: a tin of sardines, some smoked sausage and a jar of herring in sour cream.

I had been working on a surprise for Grace for nearly three weeks. I wished that I could spend Christmas Eve with her, but I knew it wasn't possible; we always went carolling as a family. I was more anxious about pulling off Christmas Day, anyway.

Every Christmas Day, our parents led us on an excruciating marathon of visits to just about anyone who claimed to be a relative. Now that we were in Utah, we had a plethora of aunts and uncles to choose from. For my surprise to work, my family would have to go without me. I had a plan to make that happen.

I came home and hid all my presents in the garage. Joel had gone shopping with my mom and dad. I went out back, knocked once on the den, then crawled inside. I had caught Grace off-guard. She was crying.

'What's wrong?'

She wiped her eyes with the back of her hand. 'Nothing.'

I sat down next to her. 'It's got to be something. You can tell me.'

'I'm just emotional. Being pregnant . . .' She didn't finish but burst into tears again. I put my arms round her.

'What is it?'

She suddenly sobbed out, 'I miss my mom.'

I pulled her closer. 'I'm sorry.'

'I . . . I . . .' She kept sobbing. 'I don't understand why she chose him over me.'

I didn't understand either. I just let her cry.

When she began to settle down a little, I said, 'Tell me something.'

'What?'

'What was Christmas in Hawaii like?'

She sniffed. 'Well, it's different.'

'In what way?'

'Santa wears a swimsuit.'

'That's not a pretty image.'

She wiped her eyes. 'He comes on a surfboard. He wears a red aloha shirt.'

'That's groovy. What else?'

'Since they don't have chimneys, he leaves the gifts at the door.'

I wiped her cheeks. 'You need to teach me how to say "Merry Christmas" in Hawaiian.'

'*Mele Kalikimaka.*'

I tried. 'Mel . . . vin Kawa . . . something.'

'It's not that hard. Say what I say. Mele.'

'Mele.'

'Ka.'

'Ka.'

'Liki.'

'Liki.'

'Maka.'

'Maka.'

'Now all together. *Mele Kalikimaka.*'

'Mele . . . what you said.'

She laughed. I was happy to hear it. 'I know what you're doing,' she said.

'You do?'

'Yes. And it's working.'

'Good.'

'I love you,' she said.

I kissed her forehead. 'I wish I could spend tonight with you.'

'Me, too. But I'll be OK.'

'You're sure?'

'Yes.'

'Promise me that you'll only think of good things. I have a big surprise for you tomorrow. So promise.'

'I promise.'

Then we kissed until I heard my family return.

JOEL WAS ALWAYS the first to wake on Christmas morning, though usually at some inhuman hour like 4 a.m. This led to the instigation of the 'sunrise rule', which basically meant no waking our parents before there was discernible sunlight. It was overcast that morning, so Joel got away with fudging it a little.

In our home, Christmas morning was governed by iron-clad tradition. Every year, we started Christmas by gathering in my parents' bedroom to read the second chapter of Luke. I don't know how my mother remembered whose turn it was each year, or even if she really did, but she always seemed to know.

That morning it was my turn to read. For the first time in my life, the words actually meant something to me.

'*And it came to pass in those days, that there went out a decree from Caesar Augustus, that all the world should be taxed . . . And Joseph also went up from Galilee . . . unto the city of David . . . to be taxed with Mary his espoused wife, being great with child. And so it was, that, while they were there, the days were accomplished that she should be delivered. And she brought forth her first-born son, and wrapped him in swaddling clothes, and laid him in a manger, because there was no room for them in the inn.*'

I suppose now I understood a little of what Mary was going through. Grace was with child, and I took her in. The den was like a stable or at least not a whole lot nicer.

'*Glory to God in the highest, and on earth peace, good will towards men.*'

After I read the scripture, my mother led us in a family prayer, then my dad got out his wind-up Brownie movie camera and went out into the living room to wait for us, shouting instructions like a Hollywood film director.

Not surprisingly, there weren't a lot of presents that year, and my parents had strategically spaced them to make it look like more. I noticed that they hadn't bought gifts for each other.

Joel got a new baseball mitt and bat, which was all he really wanted; a navy-blue sweater and grey trousers; and the ball and baseball cards I had bought him.

I got a green argyle sweater and a pair of brown corduroy trousers; two board games, Life and Mouse Trap; and a book about frontier men. Joel got me a large box of Swedish Fish wine gums.

After the last present was opened, my mom and dad went back to bed while Joel and I played with our new treasures. About an hour later, my mom got up to make breakfast. I was setting up the Mouse Trap game in the living room when my mother came in and sat by me.

'I'm sorry there wasn't much this year,' she said.

'I got plenty,' I said, trying to balance the game's small plastic seesaw. 'Besides, that's not what Christmas is about.'

My mother said nothing, and I looked up to see she was looking at me, pride evident in her eyes. 'Eric, I don't know everything that's happening in your life right now. But I know this has been a hard year for you, losing our home, coming to a new school and leaving all your friends behind. But you've grown up so much. I'm so proud of you. Maybe coming to Utah wasn't such a bad thing.'

I smiled. 'Maybe not.'

She smiled back at me. 'Come on, let's have some breakfast.'

MOM ALWAYS MADE special breakfasts on Christmas: cranberry corn muffins from scratch, hash brown potatoes with cheddar cheese, fried eggs and sausages. We looked forwards to the Christmas breakfast table almost as much as the tree.

After breakfast, we all helped my mother clean up. Joel and I put on our new sweaters and slacks while my parents dressed in their Sunday best.

Then I went into the bathroom and put a facecloth under hot water and held it to my forehead until it was hot. I dried my face with a towel and walked to my parents' room.

'Mom.'

She was rubbing cream into her hands. 'Yes, dear?'

'I don't feel well. I think I have a fever.'

She turned and looked at me. 'You do look a little flushed.' She put her cheek against my forehead. 'You're warm.'

'Would you mind too much if I just stayed home and went to bed?'

She frowned. 'Maybe we should stay home with you.'

I hadn't anticipated that response. 'Mom, I'm almost fifteen.'

'I know. But it's Christmas. I just want us to be together.'

'I don't want to ruin your plans. I'll be OK.'

She ran her fingers through my hair. 'OK. Why don't you go lie down, and I'll get you some aspirin.'

I went to my bed. She came in a few minutes later with a glass of water and two aspirin. 'Here you are.'

'Thank you.' I took the pills and handed the glass back to my mother.

'We're going to be going soon. Do you need anything?'

'No. Thank you.'

'If you need anything, you can reach us at Aunt Estelle's or Aunt Gail's a little later. We won't be home until after dark.'

'OK,' I said. 'Have a good time.'

'You get feeling better.' She kissed my forehead. 'You already feel cooler.'

'Must be good aspirin.'

She grinned. 'Merry Christmas.'

'Merry Christmas, Mom.'

Five minutes later, Joel walked into the room. He was angry. 'You faker! Now I have to go alone.'

'Sorry.'

'No, you're not. You just want to be with *her*.'

'We have special plans.'

'But what about me?' His face screwed up like he was going to cry and he stomped out.

As soon as the Bee pulled out of the driveway, I got out of bed and went to my parents' bedroom. I opened one of my mother's drawers and took out one of her silk scarves. Then I set about getting ready for my surprise. It was more than an hour later when I went to get Grace.

'JUST A MINUTE,' Grace said as she came out. She held two small packages in her hand.

'What's that?'

'I have surprises, too.'

When we got to the house, I pulled the scarf from my pocket. 'Before you go in, I need to blindfold you.'

'How exciting.'

I rolled the scarf up and tied it around her eyes, then took her by the arm, opened the door, and led her through the kitchen into our dining room. I took the things she carried and set them on the table.

'Just a minute. Don't go anywhere.'

'It smells like coconuts,' she said. 'What are you doing?'

I turned on the stereo in the living room. The bright strum of a ukulele filled the room.

'Hawaiian music,' she said.

While she stood there, blindfolded, I kissed her. I didn't think her smile could have grown larger but it did. 'That's a nice surprise.'

'That wasn't my surprise. Just an opportunity.' I untied the scarf.

She rubbed her eyes, then looked around the room.

'Mele Kalikimaka,' I said. 'Welcome to Hawaii.' I had clipped pictures of Hawaii (as well as a few places that I thought looked like Hawaii, like Fiji and Formosa) from my mom's National Geographic magazines and hung them on the walls of the kitchen. I had decorated the table with a thatched bamboo runner, and on the table there were two candles placed in coconut shells.

'Candles,' Grace said.

'Well, they were supposed to be tiki torches, but I couldn't find any.'

She laughed. 'Good thing. Try explaining to your parents how you burned down their house holding a luau for a runaway girl.'

I smiled. 'Before we eat, we need to dress the part.' I lifted a small box from the table. 'For you.'

'Really?' She lifted the lid, and her face lit up. She pulled out the cloth inside.

'It's a Hawaiian muumuu.'

She let it unfold. 'Oh, it's beautiful. Should I put it on now?'

I nodded. 'You remember where the bathroom is?'

'I do,' she said.

'But first.' I handed her another box. She excitedly lifted the lid. Inside there was a bright red flower. 'That's for your hair.'

She was positively beaming. 'I'll be right back.'

She walked down the hall to the bathroom. When the door shut, I went to my room and put on a bright red Hawaiian shirt and a plastic lei. Then I went back to the dining room. When she walked in, I just stared. She had never looked more beautiful. Her eyes sparkled, and the soft fabric of her dress hung gracefully on her body. She was glowing. I was tongue-tied.

'Look at you,' she said. 'You look so cute.'

'I'd much rather look at you.'

'Thank you,' she said coyly. 'I like the flower. I thought it was plastic, but it's real.'

'I know. They look fake. It's called an anthurium. But I'm sure you already knew that.'

She just smiled at me.

'I have a lei for you too, but it really is plastic.' As I draped the lei round her neck, she kissed me.

Then she whispered, '*Mele Kalikimaka* to you too.'

I pulled out her chair, and she sat down. 'I made us a Hawaiian luau feast. At least the best I could do in Utah. I'll be back.'

I went to the kitchen and brought back our first course: a bowl of pineapple chunks in heavy syrup and two virgin piña coladas with little paper umbrellas. She clapped with delight.

'There's a Polynesian woman at Heller's. She told me what to make.'

Over the next hour, I brought out ham and white rice, rice noodles and yams.

As we were finishing the last course, she said, 'I can't believe you really made all this.'

'Pretty much. Except what's next.'

'What's next?'

'Glad you asked.' I went to the kitchen and brought back a pineapple upside-down cake. 'Dessert.'

I set it down at the table and cut two pieces, serving hers first. Then I sat down, watching her expectantly. She took a small bite.

'How is it?'

'It's delicious.'

'Do they eat that in Hawaii?'

She picked up a piece of the cake and held it to my mouth. 'You try it.'

I took a bite. 'That is good.'

'Told you.'

For a moment we just looked at each other. The earlier excitement had evolved into pleasant peace. Then I said, 'Remember that night when I asked you how you really know when you are in love?'

'Yes.'

'I understand.'

Grace's eyes began to well up with tears. She came over and sat on my lap, laying her head on my shoulder. She began to cry softly. I gently rubbed her back. 'It's OK.'

'This is the best day of my life. You're the answer to all my prayers.' She leaned back from me and wiped her eyes.

'Oh, our candles are going out,' I said. The smoke from a dying candle snaked up towards the ceiling.

She turned back and looked at the remaining candle. 'Before it goes out, what do you want to know more than anything?'

I didn't answer her for a long time. Then my smile vanished.

When she saw me frown, her smile disappeared as well. 'What is it?'

I looked down, afraid to say what I was thinking. 'Nothing.'

'No, what is it?'

I took a deep breath. 'I want to know how this ends.'

She breathed out slowly, then she turned and stared into the flame. It felt like for ever before she spoke. 'My stepfather is gone.'

'Where?'

'Somewhere he can't hurt anyone ever again.'

I waited for more, but she didn't offer anything. 'Where are you?'

She didn't answer.

'Do you see Hawaii?'

She stared into the flame, and I saw a trace of sadness in her eyes. Suddenly she looked back at me, as if the flame had released her. 'I see Hawaii all around me,' she said. She kissed me. Then she said, 'Let's dance.' She took my hands and pulled me up.

The song playing was slow, a Hawaiian lullaby. She draped her arms round my neck, resting her head on my shoulder. I put my arms round her waist, savouring the warmth of her body next to mine. We gently rocked back and forth. It was the greatest moment of my life. Suddenly she leaned back. 'I haven't been completely honest with you.'

'About what?'

'Promise me you won't be angry.'

'You couldn't say anything that would make me angry.'

'OK.' She closed her eyes tightly, then touched her forehead to mine. 'I've never been to Hawaii.'

'What?'

'I'm from Cheyenne, Wyoming.'

We stopped swaying. 'Wyoming?'

'Hawaii was just someplace I've always wanted to be, the way some people think of heaven. After Stan . . .' She paused with the hurt that name carried. 'It was a place I would go in my mind when he was . . . hurting me.' She looked at me. 'Hawaii was my dream. And you gave it to me.' A tear fell down her cheek.

'It's OK,' I said. 'I don't care where you're from. I'm just glad you're here.' I tried to pull her back into me, but she stopped me.

'There's something else I have to tell you.' She looked down for a moment, then back into my eyes. She brushed a strand of hair from her face. 'I called my aunt.'

'The one who hates you?'

'She doesn't hate me. She was really nice. I found out what really happened between her and my mom. Before my mother got married, my aunt told her that she didn't like Stan and that she shouldn't marry him. My mother got really upset and told her she never wanted to talk to her again.

'Then my mother told Stan, and he called and screamed at her and told her if he ever saw her or if she called the house, she'd regret it. She was actually worried about us. Especially me. When I told her that I'd run away, she said she wasn't surprised. She asked me to come and live with her.'

'In Denver?'

Grace nodded.

'Did you tell her *everything*?'

'I told her about the baby.'

'What did she say?'

'She didn't ask who the father was. I wasn't ready to tell her yet. But she said it was good that I called and that she'd help me. She wanted me to come right away.'

'When was this?'

'Last Friday. I told her that I couldn't leave before Christmas.'

'Why not?'

She looked at me, puzzled that I didn't know. 'Because of you. I don't want to leave you.'

Now my eyes filled with tears. It was a few moments before I could speak. 'This is good news, right?' I said, trying to sound happy.

'Yes. It is.'

'When are you leaving?'

'Friday.' She suddenly smiled. 'You should come with me.'

'I can't.'

'I know it's impossible. I just . . .' She paused. 'I can't imagine being without you. You're the best friend I've ever had. You're the best thing that's ever happened to me.'

She fell back into me, and I pulled my arms tightly round her again. We gently swayed through three or four more songs until the vinyl record began skipping. I went and put the needle back at the beginning of the record. When I returned, she was sitting down.

'I have presents for you, too.'

I sat down. She handed me two gifts. One was a small box wrapped in shiny red paper. The other was a piece of parchment rolled up in a scroll and tied with a yellow ribbon. 'They're not as good as yours.'

'I'll be the judge of that.' I unwrapped the first package; it was a small blue velvet jeweller's box. I opened the lid; inside was an ornate silver locket.

'It's not for you to wear,' she said. 'It's for you to hold. Open it.'

I unclasped the locket. On one side, beneath a small glass pane, was a picture of Grace. On the other side, also beneath glass, was a strand of her hair.

'I thought this way, no matter what happens, you could always have some of me near you.'

No matter what happens. Something about the way she said this frightened me. She handed me the scrolled-up parchment.

I gently unrolled it. It was a poem written in her graceful handwriting. I read it aloud.

I WOULD
by Grace Webb

If only I could shine in your life as you have in mine, I would.
If only I could love you as deeply as you have loved me, I would.
If only I could heal your heart as you have healed mine, I would.
If only I could give you the hope that you've given me, I would.
If only I could stay with you for ever, I would.

We kissed, and I held her until it was dark outside. Then I called my Aunt Gail's house and asked to speak to my mother. She asked how I was feeling and if I had made myself something to eat. She said they would be home in about an hour. Grace helped me clear up. After we finished, we went back out to the den and held each other and talked until we heard the Bee pull into the driveway. I suppose that was one good thing about the Bee; you could hear it coming a block away. I went back inside and climbed into my bed. My mother came in to check on me.

'Your eyes are red,' she said.

'I know. But I'll be OK.'

Joel didn't say anything to me. It was just as well. Grace was leaving in a few days. I didn't know how to begin to think about my life without her.

It was the best and worst night of my entire life.

Twelve

Predictably, work was boring on the Thursday after Christmas, but it was not without some pleasure: Dean quit. I bought myself an Orange Crush to celebrate. At eleven o'clock sharp, I locked the back door, hopped on my bike and pedalled home.

As I rounded the corner at the top of my street, I heard a strange noise: a loud chirp followed by a blast of static. It wasn't until I was two houses away from my home that I discovered the source; there was a black-and-white patrol car parked in my driveway. I wanted to turn around, but I didn't; I didn't know what to do. As I rode to the garage to put my bike away, I wondered if I should tell Grace.

Instead, I walked through the back door hoping the police were parked out front for any reason other than the one I feared. Maybe they'd found out I had played hooky from school.

'I'm home,' I said as I entered. I headed straight for the darkened corridor that led to my bedroom.

'Eric,' my mother called from the living room.

I stopped. My heart was pounding so hard I could hear it.

'Come here, please.'

My father sat in his La-Z-Boy, and my mother sat next to him in a chair she'd pulled in from the kitchen. Two police officers sat across from them on the couch. Everyone was looking at me.

One of the officers was young and tall with yellow hair, the other older, balding, rotund, and as short as my mother. Their guns and holsters looked remarkably out of place in our living room. My father looked angry, and my mother just looked tense.

'Yes?' I tried to keep my voice from cracking.

The older officer spoke first. 'Eric, I'm Officer Steele of the Salt Lake County Sheriff's Office, and this is Officer Buttars. Do you know this young woman?' He lifted a copy of the poster of Grace I had seen at the Queen and a dozen other places.

My throat suddenly felt impossibly dry. I swallowed.

'Eric,' my father prodded. 'Answer them.'

'Sure. Everyone does. She's the girl from my school.'

'Do you know where she is?'

'No.' I looked past them to a family portrait on the wall.

'We've been told by a witness that you've been seen with her,' the young policeman said.

'Who told you that?' I asked.

'That's not important.'

How was that not important? 'I don't know where she is,' I said.

'Have you seen her in the last week?' he asked.

I shouted, 'I said I don't know!'

My explosion caught everyone off-guard, including myself. No one spoke for a moment. Then Officer Steele said, 'Young man, this is a very serious matter. Taking someone against their will is kidnapping. It's a crime that carries a long prison term.'

'I didn't kidnap her.'

'Eric,' my mother said. 'Where is Madeline?'

I glanced between them, feeling completely transparent. I was bad at this. I could tell that they knew that I knew. Dread grew heavy in my stomach like a cannonball. 'Can I go now?'

'Eric,' my mother repeated firmly, 'do you know where Madeline Webb is?'

After a few moments, I took a deep breath, then slowly exhaled. 'I can't tell you.'

'Can't, or won't?' the young policeman said.

My mother said gently, 'Eric. If you know where she is, you need to tell us.'

'I can't.'

Officer Steele started, 'Young man, if—'

My mother interrupted him. Her voice was still calm. 'Why can't you tell us, Eric?'

'They'll hurt her.'

'Who will?' she asked.

'I can't tell you.'

Officer Steele looked at his partner, then at me. 'Son, we've met Madeline's parents many times. I'm sure they would never let anyone hurt her. They are as concerned as any loving parents would be if their daughter was missing.'

I glared at him. *Was he really that stupid?*

The young policeman joined in. 'Son, you're harbouring a fugitive. Do the right thing here and tell us where she is.'

I looked at the floor for what seemed like ten minutes. I could hear the clock in the kitchen ticking.

'Eric!' my father shouted. I jumped. But still I said nothing. I don't know how long we were there. I felt like a fugitive myself, held up in a house surrounded by the police. *Give yourself up. There's no way out of this, Eric.* My brain ached.

'Tell us where she is, son,' Officer Steele said gently.

I took a deep breath, then slowly let it out. 'She's in the den.'

Officer Steele turned to my mother. 'What did he say?'

My mother looked at me sympathetically. 'The boys built a den in the back garden,' she said.

Both the policemen were immediately on their feet, no doubt excited at the prospect of being the heroes who found the missing girl and brought her home. To me they were the enemy, as stupid as all adults seemed to be those days. And my parents had been complicit, abetting the enemy.

'Take us to her,' the young policeman said.

IN TIMES OF HIGH stress, I've found that my mind fixates on the trivial. I suppose it's a defence mechanism. Suddenly all I could see was the guy's feet. They seemed impossibly large, like frogman flippers. I just stared at them until my thoughts were broken by the sound of my dad clearing his throat.

I looked at him. He had the grey look of disappointment in his eyes, but I honestly didn't care. His disappointment in me couldn't be a fraction of mine in him. For the first time in my life, I measured my thoughts against his with equal value. No, *more* so. My actions came from love and duty. His came from ignorance. I suppose it was at that moment I became a man.

Officer Steele walked to my side, grabbing the back of my arm. 'Let's go.'

'I need my boots.' I walked to the kitchen to get them. I considered making a run to the den to tell Grace, but Officer Steele followed me. I picked them up and returned to the front room. I sat on the floor slowly putting them on, but I could only delay so much.

We went out of the front door, then turned back down the driveway, trudging through the snow. I felt as if my feet were carrying me against my will.

Even the moon betrayed Grace that night. It was bright and naked, only slightly blistered by thin, black clouds. It turned the snow-packed ground luminescent. It sickened me that Grace had no idea what was coming.

Then I grabbed on to a thought as frantically as a drowning man grabbing a life belt. Maybe *she did know* we were coming. Maybe she had, like me, heard the police radio. Of course she had. I heard it all the way down the street. *Or maybe she had seen it all in the candle.*

We stopped a few yards in front of the den.

'This it?' Officer Steele asked.

I didn't answer. It was a stupid question.

He walked over as if inspecting Joel's and my work. He pointed at the door. 'Is this the only door?'

I nodded.

The officer put his hand on the front of our structure and leaned in close. He knocked sharply on the door and said, 'Madeline, it's Officer Steele of the Salt Lake County Sheriff's Office.'

We all stood there staring at the door. There was no sound.

'Madeline, we're not going to hurt you. We're here to make sure you're all right.'

Nothing stirred. The policeman got down on one knee and pushed the door open. It was as dark as a cave inside.

'She probably left,' I said angrily. 'She probably knew you were coming.'

He looked at me. 'How would she know that?'

'She just knows things.'

'Get me a torch,' Officer Steele said to his partner.

Officer Buttars left, the sound of his flipper feet clomping through the thick snow as loud as if he were stomping bags of potato crisps. I could feel my mother's gaze on me, but I didn't look at her. I didn't look at anyone. My eyes were fixed on the little door, fearing that Grace would suddenly appear. As the minutes passed, I started to feel some hope that maybe she had run away.

IT SEEMED AN ETERNITY before the younger policeman returned carrying a long silver torch. He handed it to Officer Steele, who pushed open the door, panning inside with the light until he fixed on one point. Then he looked back at his partner and nodded.

My heart stopped. I could only imagine Grace curled up in the corner, shaking and frightened. I wanted to run and tackle him and yell for Grace to run. But I didn't. I just stood as frozen by guilt as by fear.

'Are you Madeline Webb?' he asked. I couldn't hear Grace say anything, but from the officer's body language, I knew that Grace had responded. 'Let's go, Madeline. It's time to go home.'

Only then did I hear Grace's soft voice. I don't know what she said, but the sound of it sent chills through me. More than anything I wanted to run. The Bible talks of a sinner feeling shame so great that he wishes for a mountain to fall on him. At that moment, I wished for that mountain. Or one of Khrushchev's missiles.

The officer stood back from the door. And then I saw her, her hands in the snow, her head crowning at the entrance. She pushed herself up. She had nothing with her but her coat.

'Are you OK?' Officer Steele asked. She nodded slightly. She didn't look at me. I didn't know what I would do if she did. 'Have you been kept here against your will?'

'No.'

'You're not going to try to run away from us, are you?' the young police-man asked. 'We don't want to handcuff you.'

'Don't touch her,' I said.

Only then did she look at me, and I saw in her eyes that she was no longer mine to protect. I had lost the right to speak for her.

Officer Steele put his hand on her shoulder and gently pushed her forward. She walked ahead of us, flanked by the policemen. My parents walked behind me. When we got to the driveway, the young officer opened the back door of the patrol car, and Grace got in.

She didn't even look at me.

MY PARENTS AND I stood there at the edge of our driveway. I had never felt more alone in my life. I felt estranged even from myself, brimming with self-hate. In the darkness beneath the trees, the policemen were no longer people; like Grace, they had turned to shadow, like shades in the land of the dead, on the banks of the river Styx.

The patrol car's engine roared to life, then its headlights blinked on, momentarily blinding us. The car pulled out of our driveway, crunching and spinning on the icy gravel.

I just stood there. After all we'd been through, just like that she was gone.

My dad said, 'Let's go to bed, Eric. We'll talk in the morning.'

Then my mom said, 'You did the right thing.'

At that moment, I saw that my parents were as capable of stupidity and evil as anyone who has ever walked this planet. They were as capable of evil as me.

I walked into the house without a word. I kicked the boots from my feet and trudged off to my bedroom. The room was dark; as usual, Joel had gone to bed hours earlier. I took off my clothes, then climbed under the covers. The prospect of sleeping seemed ridiculous. I felt sick to my stomach. I wished I could vomit the whole night away.

I suddenly became aware of Joel's breathing. I don't know why, but the sound filled me with rage. After a minute, Joel said softly, 'Did they take her?'

For a moment, I couldn't speak. All the rage and fear and anger twisted my mind into a horrible, tight knot. Then I exploded, throwing back my covers and glaring wild-eyed at my little brother.

'You told them! You said you'd never tell and you did!'

Even in the dark I could see his eyes, wide and frightened. 'No, I didn't. I didn't tell *anyone*.'

'You're a liar!' I hissed. 'And she's going to get hurt. Do you *know* what her stepfather will do to her? And it's all your fault.'

His voice cracked. 'I didn't tell anyone, Eric. I promise.'

Deep in my heart, I knew he was telling the truth, but my heart wasn't in control. 'I'm never going to talk to you again. Never. I hate you.'

My words fell off into silence. I could hear Joel softly crying beneath his covers, whimpering over and over, 'I didn't do it.'

I had committed my second act of treason of the night.

I DON'T KNOW what time it was when I woke the next morning, but no one was home. I looked over to Joel's bed. It was made. I just lay back in my bed looking at the ceiling, following its cracks with my eyes, trying to distract myself from what I felt. My heart ached in a way I had never felt before. Grace was gone. I had cut off my brother, and I had unmasked my parents as the sinners they were. I had never felt so alone in all my life. It was the first time in my life that I truly wanted to die.

What seemed unbelievable to me was that Grace was still out there. Was there a chance that she would be OK? Maybe the police were telling the truth, and her parents really wanted to take care of her. Right, and Kennedy and Khrushchev were playing croquet together.

Even if she wasn't hurt, I had betrayed her. It was no use trying to believe that everything was OK. It wasn't. And it never would be again.

WEDNESDAY MORNING after New Year's Eve came like the flu. My thoughts about seeing Grace at school couldn't have been more divided. Half of me couldn't wait to see her. The other half was terrified. I wondered what she would do.

I looked for Grace in the corridors. At lunch I walked round the lunch-room, then I walked to her locker. I didn't see her. At least, I thought, I would see her in Spanish.

I got to class early, and waited outside the classroom until the bell rang. As I walked into the room, I glanced towards her desk; it was empty. Then I sat down in my seat, glancing every few seconds at the door. Only after the tardy bell rang did I believe that she wasn't coming.

It made sense that she wasn't there. After being away from home that long, her parents probably wouldn't let her out of their sight. Then again, they might have discovered that she was pregnant. In those days, unwed mothers sometimes just disappeared, whisked off to other cities so as not to shame their family. Part of me was relieved that she hadn't come, but it was equally matched by disappointment. I missed her. Even her hating me wouldn't change that.

I don't remember hearing anything in class, but my mental absence seemed to pass unnoticed. The final bell rang, and, like everyone else, I began gathering my books when Mrs Waller tapped a ruler against the blackboard to get our attention. 'Class, please stay in your seats for just a moment. I need your attention.'

The class quietened.

'As you know, one of our classmates, Madeline Webb, had been missing. We heard today that she passed away during the holidays. For those of you who were close to her, I'm very sorry.'

The class rose around me and flowed past my desk. I sat there unable to move. Suddenly the tears started to come. I covered my eyes and put my head down on my desk and began to shake. I don't know how long I sat that way before I felt a hand on my shoulder.

'I'm so sorry, Eric.' Mrs Waller stood next to my desk.

When I could speak, I asked, 'What happened?'

She hesitated. 'I can't tell you.'

I looked at her, my eyes wet, dark and direct. 'It was her stepfather, wasn't it?'

She didn't answer me.

'I'm going to kill him.'

'He's in jail, Eric.'

I began to sob. She stood there with her hand on my back with no idea what to say.

I PURPOSELY MISSED the bus. I walked home, glad for the pain and cold. I now understood why Grace had cut herself. I wanted to cut out my heart.

For the first time since I started school in Utah, my mother was home when I got there. From the way she looked at me, I knew that she knew about Grace. I walked past her without speaking. I went to my bedroom and slammed the door. I hated her for knowing what had happened.

She followed me and stood outside my door. 'Eric.'

I wasn't about to give her the satisfaction of needing her sympathy. 'What do you want?'

'Did you hear . . .'

'Did I hear what?'

She paused. 'Did you hear about Madeline?'

'What about it?' I said.

'I'm sorry,' she said, and walked away.

FOR THE NEXT two days, I didn't speak to anyone in the house. I could see the pain my silence caused them, and it made me glad. Whether it was misery looking for company or the pursuit of vengeance, I don't know. It was probably a little of both.

Every time my mother tried to speak to me, I walked away from her. Disrespect wasn't tolerated in our home, but this time neither of my parents challenged me. Maybe they realised what they'd done and felt the guilt I thought they deserved. Or maybe they instinctively sensed just how close I was to the edge. I *was* close. There was something new inside me. Something that felt strong. It had no heart, no reason, and, most exquisitely, no fear. It was hate. It welcomed a confrontation. It hoped for one.

I had decided to run away. I had already packed what I needed and decided to leave the night of Grace's funeral. I had a pretty good idea of what running away would entail. I had taken care of a runaway. I could take care of myself. Even if I couldn't, it didn't matter. If I had learned one thing from all this, it was clarity. I knew who the enemy was. And I knew I would do anything to punish them, including hurt myself.

FRIDAY night, my mother came to my room. I was alone, as Joel had slept with my parents every night since I'd turned on him. The light was off, and I was in my bed, though a thousand hours from sleeping. She knocked once, then stepped inside, staying close to the doorway.

'Eric, can we talk?' she asked softly.

I didn't answer but rolled to my side. I could hear her swallow. She just stood there, a shadow, wondering what to do. Finally she said, 'Madeline's funeral is tomorrow at noon. We'll all be going. I hope you come with us.'

I didn't answer. She sighed. 'Good night.'

She shut the door.

I shouted after her, 'Her name isn't Madeline!'

THE NEXT DAY, I slept until eleven, showered, and got dressed. I stayed in my room until it was time to go, then I walked out and got in the van before anyone else did. No one spoke to me.

The funeral was held at a small church near Grace's home. Before the service, they had an open-coffin viewing. I climbed out of the van and walked inside, apart from my parents. I followed the signs to a small room.

I wasn't prepared for what I saw, but I don't know how I could have been. There was Grace in a wooden coffin. The inside was lined with pink satin. She looked like she was sleeping. My heart felt as if it was being torn apart.

A short, stout woman with black hair stood next to the coffin. She looked frail and her eyes were puffy. I knew who she was and I immediately hated her. I hated her for her weakness and her betrayal of her own daughter. *Now* she stood by her side. I wanted to shout at her, *Hypocrite! Why weren't you at her side when she needed you?*

My parents stood in line and walked up to the coffin. Joel held my mother's hand. He was crying. My parents paid their condolences to Grace's mother, which only made me angrier. They deserved each other. A party of traitors.

I kept my distance, standing at the side of the room, torn between my hate and unspeakable sorrow. I wanted to wake her and run away with her, but Grace wasn't there. Grace was life and spirit, and there was none of that here. It was just a body in a box. Grace had gone somewhere else. I wished I could have gone with her.

Sometime later, the minister said they would be closing the coffin, and if anyone wanted to give the deceased their last regards, now was the time. A few people walked to the coffin and kissed Grace. Then her mother fell on her, crying, 'My baby. My darling baby.'

Everyone in the room watched, moved by the emotional outburst. Many of them started to cry as well. A man in a suit comforted her. I just stood there, watching the drama unfold like bad theatre.

I didn't sit by my family for the service. I sat alone staring at the back of a pew while people who didn't really know anything about Grace talked about her as if they suddenly cared.

As we were leaving the funeral, I felt a hand touch my shoulder. I turned round. It was Grace's mother.

'Are you Eric?'

I just glared at her.

'You're Eric. I know you are. I just wanted you to know . . .' She began to cry. I stared at her, unwilling to offer sympathy. Her voice pitched. 'My baby wanted you. When the ambulance came for her, she asked for you. Your name was the last thing she said.'

I just looked at her as she wiped her eyes with a crumpled tissue.

'Thank you for being there for her.'

'If I was there for her, we wouldn't be here,' I said. I turned and walked away.

GOD HAD FLOODED Noah's world, so why couldn't he have cleansed the earth again? I knew enough theology to remember that a baptism by water is followed by a baptism by fire. Fire seemed appropriate. That coward Khrushchev had missed his calling.

My parents, Joel and I walked into the house without a word. I was done with my family. I had enough money to make it to Denver to see Grace's aunt. And then who knew. The truth is, I didn't care where I went. I spent far less time thinking about where I was going than what I was leaving.

My mother followed me to my room. 'Eric.' She tried to put her arms round me, but I pulled away.

'Stay away from me.'

'Eric. You have to talk about this.'

'I don't talk to murderers.'

'Murderers?'

'You killed her. You and Dad and Joel and her pathetic, worthless mother and those stupid, idiotic policemen who just couldn't wait to be heroes. I told you they would hurt her, and you made me tell them. You killed Grace! You all killed Grace. I hate you. I hate all of you. You should have died, not her.'

My mother was stunned, but her gaze was still full of compassion. 'No, Eric. We didn't kill her.'

'You and the police and Joel . . . you all killed her.'

'Eric, her stepfather killed her.'

Then I fell against the wall, sobbing uncontrollably. 'No,' I said. 'I killed her. I told you where she was. She'd still be alive if it wasn't for me.'

My mother put her hands on my shoulders and turned me towards her. Tears were running down her face. Her voice was strong but loving. 'Eric, listen to me. We didn't kill her. You didn't kill her. A very bad, very sick man killed her, not you. You tried to protect her. But you're only fourteen. It was too big for you. You did the best you could. You loved her, and she loved you.'

'She'll never forgive me,' I said. 'She shouldn't forgive me.' My knees buckled and I fell to the ground.

My mother crouched down, holding me. 'Eric, sometimes horrible, unspeakable things happen in life. What happened was wrong. But it's not your fault.'

I looked at my mother, my face twisted in anguish. 'I miss her so much, Mom. I want to die. I want to die.'

My mother was crying as hard as I was. She stroked my forehead. 'I know you loved her, sweetheart.'

'I can't stand the pain. What do I do?'

She pulled my head in next to her cheek. 'You just keep on living, Eric. And you hope.'

'Hope for what?'

'For grace.'

IT SNOWED on Saturday night. Outside my window, the winter wind had rippled the snow like sand dunes, piling drifts in crusted peaks.

I put on my tennis shoes and climbed of out my window onto the crystalline blanket. The snow slid up my trousers and bit my legs.

For the first time since Grace left, I returned to the den. Our footprints

from that night were gone, evidence covered over at a crime scene.
Everything was white.

The den didn't look the same to me. It was the same feeling I had at the
funeral service staring across the room at Grace's body. She was gone. The
den was just a corpse.

I kicked at the snow by the door and prised it open.

I crawled in and turned on the light. There was frost on the walls, and the
Christmas tree was still there, the water in its bucket frozen hard. Grace's
things were there, just as she had left them. On top of the sleeping-bag was
her yellow diary.

I held it for a moment before I opened it and began to read what she'd
written. She had recorded all that she'd been through, the horror and the joy.
My emotions rose and fell with each page. The happiness she felt that her
mother had found someone and her disappointment when she saw the real
side of the man. She wrote of the first time Stan had molested her. And the
day she realised she was pregnant.

I suppose the diary was a prayer of sorts, written only for God's eyes. On
nearly every page, she wrote of her hopes of finding someone to help her.
Someone to love her—that is, up until the day she met me. As I read each
page, I realised what my role had been in her life and how much I meant to
her. The last thing she wrote was this: *He is the only thing on this earth
I believe in. Eric is my Hawaii.*

I stared at those words. Then I closed the book and held it near my chest,
and I curled up in a foetal position. I had been there for a long time when
I heard something outside. I looked over to the door. Joel was there, looking
at me. He was afraid of me, but he was there, just like he always had been.

'Hi,' I said. I sat up, my back pressed against the wall.

He crawled the rest of the way in and sat down next to me, his knees
touching mine. We sat without words, both of us looking down at our feet.
'It's cold,' he said.

I took a deep breath. 'I'm sorry I got mad at you. I know it wasn't your
fault.'

'It's OK.'

'No, it's not. You're my best friend.'

Joel's eyes welled up. 'I've missed you.'

I put my arm round him. 'I've missed you too, buddy.'

'I really liked her,' he said.

Then I began to cry. 'I know. So did I.'

Epilogue

Christmas tales have always been about redemption. I suppose that's what Christmas is all about. My whole life I have hoped for redemption. Redemption and grace. I don't deserve it, but I still hope.

My father fully recovered from the Guillain-Barré. By the next summer, he was walking without crutches. We moved from that dump of a neighbourhood and built a home in the Cottonwood area, a nice suburb of Holladay. Not long after, my aunts and uncles sold the old house to developers, who bulldozed it, along with the den, to put up cheap apartments. I was glad to know it was all gone.

Years passed. My father was diagnosed with testicular cancer. He died on July 4th, 1976, the day America celebrated its bicentennial. My mother is still alive. She resides in Southern California in a town house about a mile from Joel. She never remarried.

JOEL AND I NEVER spent a summer together like that again. By the next summer, I was into cars and girls and all that comes with growing up. But Joel did all right for himself. Turns out he was better at baseball than any of us knew. He made the varsity baseball team his sophomore year of high school—the first time a sophomore had ever done that. He wore his letterman jacket and had a thousand friends and even more girlfriends. Unlike me, Joel managed to be cool.

He made All State in baseball his junior year and, by his senior year, word of his talent had spread wide enough that he was hounded by scouts from every major college. Joel returned to California, attending UCLA on a full scholarship. He played in the Pioneer Leagues for two years, then played second base for the Mets for another six before his knees gave out. He has a baseball card with his face on it. Imagine that, my little brother on a baseball card. Just like DiMaggio.

Today he has a beautiful wife, four children, two grandchildren, and a 10,000-square-foot house with a swimming pool surrounded by potted kumquat trees. He owns a Honda dealership in Simi Valley. We talk on the phone every Sunday night. I miss him.

Hard things, if they don't kill you, make you grow. Sometimes they even make you lose your fear. I never backed down again. A week after the funeral, one of the hoods bullied me. It took two teachers to pull me off him. He and his friends never bothered me again.

I became a serious student with good enough grades to get into Stanford Law School. After graduation, I returned to Utah and at the age of twenty-nine, I was made assistant prosecutor at the Utah Attorney General's Office. At thirty-four, I was appointed the youngest prosecutor in the state's history. I have spent my life hunting down and prosecuting people like Grace's step-father. I carry Grace's locket into every trial. I've earned a reputation as a fierce courtroom combatant who takes every case personally. What Grace saw in the candle is true of me. I am feared.

A reporter once asked me what drove me. I looked down for a moment, then softly replied, 'Grace.' She wrote it down, but she didn't understand. I wouldn't have explained anyway.

I don't know what happened to Grace's mother; all I know is that she moved out of Utah. A part of me hopes she's in Hawaii. Grace would have liked that.

Stan is still alive, or he was the last time I checked. He got out of prison after seventeen years for 'good behaviour'. I've seen him. I paid him a visit after his release to a halfway house. I needed to know for myself that he wasn't still a threat. I also wanted to let him know that I was, and that I was watching him. My visit wasn't necessary. He was a broken shell of a man, nothing but a shadow and a stain.

I don't know if he paid his debt—that's up to God to decide—but he took something beautiful from this earth. He took something that no one could ever give back.

TODAY I CONTINUE my crusade. I have testified about child abuse before state lawmakers more times than I can remember. I am grateful that the world finally has the courage to open its eyes. My wife asks me when we can retire, but I tell her I'll die in the saddle. With my last breath, I'll continue to fight for these children. There are other Graces out there.

WHEN I WAS a ten-year-old boy sitting in Sunday school, my teacher asked what we would have done if we had been at Calvary. Would we deny Jesus like Peter had? Or carry Jesus' cross? As one who had read more than his fair share of comic books, I said I would take a machine gun and mow down all the Roman soldiers who were crucifying Jesus. My teacher nodded understandingly, then asked, 'Then who would save us?'

I was never able to answer this. The whole thing seemed a colossal miscarriage of justice, but I guess that's the point. But this has always been God's way, wringing good from evil. In some ways, this is also true of Grace's life.

I loved Grace; time has only confirmed this to me. But life goes on and so must we. At the age of twenty-three, I was married to Brooke Christine Mitchell. Four years later, we tried to have a child. We learned that neither of us could. Brooke cried for nearly two weeks.

But, as so often happens in life, from our hurts come our greatest blessings. Brooke and I made a decision that changed many lives: we adopted the first of our eight children, each of them taken from an environment of abuse or neglect. With each child we saved, a cycle has been broken. We now have more than a dozen grandchildren who know only security, peace and a parent's love. What Grace planted in me will save generations from neglect and abuse. I do not take credit for this, but I do take hope in it.

I believe there is a life after this one. I hope it is a place of second chances, a place where all things are made whole. That, to me, would be heaven. If there is such a place, I'd like to see Grace there. I'd like to see her without worry or pain. I'd like to sit with her and hear her sweet voice, feel her soft lips against mine, and laugh until milk shoots from our noses. I hope to look with her into the flame of a candle and hear all about where she's been and where the world is going. Most of all, I hope to tell her how much I love her still. I don't deserve it, but I hope.

Maybe someday, through God's grace, I will.

richard paul **evans**

Richard Paul Evans is the award-winning author of eleven *New York Times* best sellers and five children's books, but there is a lot more to this former advertising executive besides his publishing success. He is a man with a purpose.

It all began in 1993 when he wrote and self-published twenty copies of *The Christmas Box*, a gentle story about grief and the life-affirming significance of Christmas, mainly to express his love for his two daughters in a timeless way, and also to show his empathy with his mother's sorrow at losing a child. He gave the copies to relatives and friends as Christmas presents. What he didn't anticipate was that they would be touched so deeply that the book would be passed on ... and on. Soon, so many people had read and been moved to tears by it that local bookstores were calling his home with orders. With this evidence of its power over hearts and minds, Evans was able to agree a deal with a major American publisher and the novel shot to the top of the best-seller lists.

The public's enthusiasm for that first book prompted Evans to write further, similarly life-affirming stories—*The Sunflower*, *The Perfect Day*, *The Last Promise* among them—as well as several children's books and a nonfiction work called *The Five Lessons A Millionaire Taught Me About Life and Wealth*.

Grace is especially close to his heart, though, in one special respect. 'In some ways, this is the most autobiographical of my novels,' he reveals. 'When I was eight years old, my father lost his job and we moved from our beautiful home in California to a rat-infested place in a poor neighbourhood like the one I describe.'

The author confesses that there were challenges in writing from the perspective of a fourteen-year-old. 'It was a little tricky as Eric, the main character, was frightfully naive and I had to be careful not to allow him knowledge he wasn't ready for. But I guess I haven't lost the inner child.'

Interestingly, Evans says he and his wife initially found success frightening. 'Keri and I were nervous about what the money might do to our children. And we were very happy with our middle-class lifestyle.' So, the couple decided to give back some of the rewards and, in the spring of 1997, they founded The Christmas Box International, an organisation devoted to building shelters and providing help for abused and neglected children. The first projects were on the American mainland, but Evans is now involved in developing two shelters for impoverished children in Peru. In total, more than 16,000 young people have been housed in places paid for by the fund.

'The statistics are appalling,' he explains, 'but I believe we can help them break the cycle of poverty and abuse and live productive, happy lives. The material achievements of *The Christmas Box* will never convey its true success, though: the lives it has changed . . . the mothers and father who suddenly understand the pricelessness of their children's fleeting childhood.'

His desire to share a message of hope didn't end with the books and the charitable work. A visit to his website, www.richardpaulevans.com, reveals an extraordinary section devoted to 'Angel Statues'. The first one was introduced in the pages of *The Christmas Box*, when a woman mourns the loss of her child at the base of an angel monument. The story is mostly fiction: the angel monument once existed but is thought to have been destroyed. The new statue was commissioned by Evans, in response to reports that grieving parents were seeking out the angel as a place to grieve and heal. So, in 1994, on December 6—the date the child in the novel dies—a stone monument with a sculpted angel was dedicated in Evans's home town of Salt Lake City, Utah. Floral tributes from grieving parents are regularly sent to adorn it, along with notes of love. Since that day, a further twenty-five 'angels of hope' have been cast and are in place in memorial gardens throughout America. It's a remarkable development from a simple act of giving a few copies of a little story to friends at Christmas, with the hope of bringing joy and comfort.

OUR LITTLE ANGEL